I0824512

LAWLESS

LAWLESS

David Bell

ISBN 978-93-83868-33-9

This is a work of fiction. Names, characters, places and incidents are used fictitiously. Any resemblance to actual events, locales or persons living or dead is entirely coincidental.

Permission from the Master and Fellows of University College Oxford for the reproduction of the image from University College Ms 165 is gratefully acknowledged

Typeset in Adobe Garamond Pro

First published in 2017

1 3 5 7 9 8 6 4 2

British Library Cataloguing in Publication Data
A catalogue record for this book is available from the British Library.

Publisher: Suman Chakraborty

Quintus
An Imprint of ROMAN Books
London | Kolkata
www.quintus-books.co.uk | www.quintus-books.co.in

Printed and bound worldwide by LSI

For Betsy,
my life-long inspiration

FRANCE 1941

THE SISTERS

Séverine Chevalier heard the sound of aircraft engines when she went out to lock the gate of the sheep pen for the night. Airplanes were heard going over from time to time. The rumour was that they were the English on their way to bomb Italy but they were always high up, out of sight, almost soundless, so no one really knew. This was different: a rough faltering noise that seemed to be coming from somewhere low down and not far away to the east. She pulled her shawl up over her face against the snow flurries as she listened, trying to make out whether the sound was getting nearer or not but then it faded away and all she could hear was the wind blowing hard enough to make her stagger and almost drop her lantern. She slammed home the bolt of the gate, the metal icy to her touch, and stumbled back to the house, calling the dog to follow her. Wherever it was now it had nothing to do with her. There was no point in bothering her sister Thérèse about it.

***

Rear gunner in a Mark V Whitley heavy bomber was the coldest and loneliest job in the world. Lawless had long ago given up telling that to people to impress them but he still believed it and this flight was the loneliest and coldest of the twenty three he had survived so far. From Topcliffe in Yorkshire where the squadron was based, to somewhere—Hawkinge or Manston, he wasn't sure——in Kent for refuelling, then 600 miles to Turin to bomb the Fiat works and back again, a round trip lasting twelve cramped, noisy freezing hours. Only this time it looked like not being a round trip.

When the bombs were released the Whitley had jumped up a hundred feet and straight into a hail of shrapnel from a shell-burst it would have avoided a few seconds earlier. There was a deafening clattering noise and the whole plane shook like a huge wet dog. Something struck his thigh. His turret lost all power, leaving his four Brownings about as effective against a night fighter as wagging a finger at it. His earphones went dead. He shouted again and again into the mike but there was no answering crackle. He felt the aircraft bank and turn and eventually settle on a new course that he assumed was away from the target. The shaking soon lessened to a rough vibration he knew meant the engines had lost synchronisation. There was a light but definite pressure on his back: she was flying nose down, gradually losing height. God, he thought, could she stay high enough to get over the Alps? There was another loud crack followed by a tearing noise and something dark flew over his turret. A gale shrieked past him from behind. A part of the fuselage, how big he could not tell, had been ripped away. Still, she kept flying. The Whitley was slow and could be wayward but she was tough, so they were told, and it was true. He knew. He'd seen the state some were in after getting back from Cologne and Bremen. It dawned on him that there was nothing he could now do. His guns were useless and even if he saw a night fighter lining up for an attack he could give no warning to the pilot Sherwood to corkscrew. He couldn't get out of the turret, jammed as it was at half-traverse to starboard. The vibration was increasing again but she was still flying. He leaned back against his parachute and tried not to doze off. That was a sure way to get frostbite. He must keep turning his head and looking for night fighters even if there was nothing he could do about them because that would help keep him awake. He unbuckled his straps to give his arms and legs more freedom. That was the moment when he discovered that his right leg would not move.

***

Séverine pressed her back on the inside of the door to close it firmly, dropped the bar in place, turned down the wick and hung the lantern on its hook. The dog had already trotted over to slump down beside the hearth. Thérèse was stirring a large iron pot hanging over the log fire. A thick candle shed light feebly on a table set with two bowls, beakers, a ladle, spoons and a board with half a round loaf of bread on it. The rest of the room was in deep shadow. Séverine stamped her feet and shook the snow from her shawl, her breath coming in clouds of fine mist.

'What kept you so long?' said Thérèse, her eyes not moving from the steaming pot.

'Nothing.'

'Must have been something for you to stay out in that.'

'Nothing, I tell you. It's this lantern. It needs cleaning. I couldn't see.'

'I cleaned it this morning. I told you. And I trimmed the wick and put more oil in.'

'Is the soup ready yet?'

At the word soup the dog lifted up its big shaggy head and sniffed.

'Soon. Watch this a minute while I get the oil.'

Thérèse went to a wall cupboard near the window and took out a stone bottle. She paused to pull back the thick curtain a little and looked outside. The feeble light from the room showed snow drifting down in big white shreds that swirled in gusts of wind. Séverine saw her sister peering hard and heard her say something.

'Close the shutter. You're letting draughts in. What are you looking at?'

'I don't know. There was something, like a light flashing. It's gone now.'

'You're imagining it. How could you see anything in this snow?'

'It just cleared for a second. I'm sure I saw something.'

Séverine began sawing slices from the loaf. She held out a piece and the dog padded across, sniffed at the bread, took it delicately from her fingers and swallowed it in one gulp. When no more seemed to be forthcoming, it settled back in its place by the fire with a groan and watched every move made by the sisters as they ate their soup.

'Is there anything else for her?'

'She can have soup if there's any left and bread to soak in it, if there's any of that left, with a drop of oil. There might be some cheese rinds.'

'She needs more than that if she's to work,' said Séverine.

'So do we, so if it clears tomorrow you must go out with the gun.'

'You take it. I have to see to that ewe. Where's the cheese?'

Thérèse placed a thick black disc and a dark green wine bottle on the table. Séverine poured red wine into the two beakers and picked up the cheese.

'Might need the axe to get into this, or Grandpapa's sabre.'

'It's all we've got. When Spring comes round we might get some pélardon if we're lucky.'

While the dog slurped up its soup and chewed the cheese rind the two sisters drew chairs up to the fire and held their hands out to its warmth. They sat in silence for a long time dozing, eyes closed, opening them only when a log slipped and sparks sprang up the chimney.

'Do you remember Mama giving us a teaspoonful of cognac mixed in our milk at Christmas? To welcome the Child, and we mustn't tell Papa?' said Thérèse dreamily.

'Mm, I remember us having roasted goose at New Year and Papa slicing it with Grandpapa's sabre. I can taste it now. Haven't had goose for years.'

'We might not have any goose but we haven't any Germans here, either.'

'They're just biding their time, you wait and see. What is there to stop them?'

Thérèse broke the silence that followed this remark, saying,

'I sometimes think why go to bed when I could just sit here in front of the fire with Caramelle lying across my feet to keep them warm?'

The dog's tail swept the floor briefly at the sound of her name.

'We can't afford the wood,' said Séverine. 'Time for bed. Did you put the bricks in?'

Thérèse answered in the way she did almost every night,

'Naturally. You go. I'll clear up here and let her out for a minute.'

By the time the sounds of Séverine moving about upstairs had ceased, Thérèse had done as had she said and opened the door to let the dog back in but instead of bounding past her back into the warmth, Caramelle was standing in the courtyard, head up, sniffing the air. The snow had stopped. Thérèse called but the dog ignored her and began to bark. There must be a fox about, thought Thérèse, or a sanglier. She half turned, intending to get the shotgun but the dog stopped barking and brushed past her into the house. Well, if there had been something out there, it had gone now. Thérèse closed and barred the door. She went upstairs followed by Caramelle. As she was falling asleep with the warm dog lying beside her, her mind went back to that flash of light through the snow. Séverine was right: she must have imagined it.

***

Stuck in the cramped turret, seventy feet from the nose of the Whitley, Lawless had no idea of the effects of the shell burst there. The only man left alive was the pilot, Sherwood, and he was battling desperately to maintain height and course while pinned to his seat by a gale that swept through the shattered windshield. With no navigator and no instruments to guide him he had banked steeply and swung the Whitley onto what he hoped was a reciprocal course away from the target. He prayed for a sight of the Pole Star, which he could use to set a roughly north-westerly course but at 15000 feet he was still flying through thick cloud. There was nothing to do but fly on, keep her up as best he could, and hope that he would see the Alps soon, he estimated in about half an hour. At least his wristwatch was still working. If he didn't see the peaks, well, there was no point in worrying about that yet.

Lawless sat in a world of darkness with almost no sense of movement. Only the wavering sound of the engines and the gale at his back proved the Whitley was still flying and heading somewhere, *away from Italy* he fervently hoped. He was very cold and his leg had begun to ache.

The Whitley flew over the Alps in cloud cover so dense that Sherwood never saw the mountains but soon afterwards the sky began to clear. His watch indicated he had been flying for ninety minutes since he had turned the aircraft round. The starboard engine was now running rough and his pilot's instinct told him he was losing altitude. The controls were soggy in his straining hands. She was icing up, wing leading edges, perhaps props too. Better a crash landing in France than Italy, he thought. Or a bail-out; no, he couldn't do that. Three of the crew were dead, he knew, but that left Lawless. He might still be alive. Then again, he might not be. If he bailed out and the plane went in, who would ever know? The cloud thinned away and in the feeble moonlight that followed he began to see some features of the land below. He realised that meant he was lower than he had hoped but whatever he tried, nothing seemed to lift the Whitley out of her steady descent. Given the time now, he should be seeing a large river, the Saône, below. He must have flown over the Swiss lake while still in cloud.

Looking down on the port side, Lawless saw a river silvered by moonlight flowing across a plain that grew wider into the distance. Leaning over to his right, he caught a glimpse of snow-topped hills ahead. He tried to remember a map of France and the briefing they had been given but his mind would not focus. The ache in his leg had become a throbbing pain. Then it came to him: the river below could only be the Rhône and the plain was the one that widened towards the Camargue marshes near the Mediterranean. They were hopelessly off course.

The Pole star: oh God, it was 90 degrees or more on the starboard side. Sherwood jammed his foot hard on the rudder bar. There was no answering pressure. The controls had gone. The Whitley continued on course as if she was now in full control. The starboard engine started missing then racing, then missing again. If ever there was a time to bail out it was now but he could not bring himself to leave her—and Lawless. He would get her down. She was close to the snow-covered hills and dropping rapidly. There was a peak ahead on the port side but she would miss that and he could see some wide level areas beyond it. Please God make the snow deep enough to soften the landing. He knew her stalling speed was very low: he had once held her up at under 80 knots. All of that would help. He could get her down. One worry nagged at him: the wing tanks must still be nearly half-full and there were another 130 gallons of fuel in the fuselage tank. The starboard engine backfired, flamed, backfired again. Sherwood watched the prop start windmilling then seize and felt the Whitley lurch and fall away to starboard. That did it. She couldn't fly on one engine.

Lawless was roused from torpor by the staggering movements of the plane. He heard the engine noise drop and felt his turret rise and tilt as the Whitley headed down and banked more steeply. The engine noise rose again and the vibrations grew enough to shake him like dice in a cup. He knew Sherwood was forcing the remaining engine at full power, trying the only thing he had left to stop her spinning straight into the ground. He saw flames streaking from the stalled starboard engine. Fuel was still reaching the hot metal. Any minute now the wing tank would catch and blow up.

Sherwood kept his hands firmly on the useless controls, leaned back in his straps and knowing he had done everything he could, felt completely calm. Cliffs, strange pillars of rock, a few trees standing clear of the snow rushed towards and below him like a film running too fast. He cut power to the port engine and the Whitley sank quickly, staying level. Good girl, he said out loud, just before she struck the ground.

Unconscious after his head hit the Perspex panel of the turret, Lawless never felt the tail section of the Whitley slew round violently and break off, throwing him clear, or saw the wing tank explode and the two sections of the plane rush through the snow drifts like mad blazing sleighs down the long slope towards the gorge, teeter on the edge and then plunge hundreds of feet down, breaking up into flaming shreds as they struck the rocky walls and finally disappeared into the trees and the river below.

***

Death was freezing blackness and moaning, hissing sounds and pain all over. He dared not open his eyes, terrified of what he might see. He put out a hand. It sank into something that he could not feel but it was soft. He stretched out his other hand and the softness was cool and somehow gentle. Pain burned in his leg and throbbed in his head. Idiotically he laughed at the image of himself, arms spread wide, crucified. He opened his eyes and looked up into a clear black sky and the bright, blotched face of the winter moon. The snow was so soft, like a feather bed. It was warm round his hand, the one with no glove. He thought of the freezing cell of the Whitley's turret and shuddered. He wanted nothing but to sleep forever in this luxuriantly soft warmth of snow watched over by the moon.

A stronger gust of wind lifted flakes from a drift and blew them across his face. He raised his hand to brush them away and found he could hardly feel his skin. Frostbite. Get up. Get moving. Find shelter. He turned over and struggled to his knees in the snow, weeping with the effort. When he tried to stand, his leg collapsed under him with scalding pain. Again he got to his knees and tried to push himself up with his hands. The pain made him almost faint. More snowflakes whipped up from the drifts seemed to dance in front of him as if taunting his helplessness. He felt an icy snake beginning to uncoil inside him and looked around desperately for somewhere to hide from it. Through his tears he saw a dark shape sticking up above the snow. It had to be the Whitley or at least what was left of it. He tried shouting Sherwood's name but his voice was a hoarse whisper blown away by the wind. He began crawling forwards on his belly, scrabbling and clawing in the snow with his freezing hands. Something seemed to be hanging onto him, pulling him back so that no matter how painfully he kept dragging himself towards the dark shape, panting and weeping, the thing seemed to get no closer. He cursed it and struck out towards it in futile rage. His fist hit something hard and rough, hard as rock. The shock cleared his mind for an instant. Whatever it was, it was shelter against the wind. He rubbed the half-frozen tears from his eyes and in the moonlight saw a low outcrop with a darker patch at the base. He put his hand to this and it went inside the rock. A cave: somehow he dragged himself inside and pulled in the half-opened parachute that had trailed behind him through the snow. With the last of his strength he began to pile the shrouds of silk over himself. They were so heavy. He began to weep again. He was too weak, too tired. He gave up trying and slumped against the rock, letting his head hang down on his chest and surrendered to the darkness.

***

Thérèse Chevalier was enjoying herself. Séverine hardly ever gave her the chance to go out with the dog and the gun. The wind had dropped and the air was clear and cold as ice. The sun had just risen above the rocky eastern ramparts of the Causse and Thérèse felt so free for once that she began to run over the hard snow that sparkled in its light. Caramelle capered around her barking, came too close and tripped her so that she fell and slid over the frozen crust of snow to end in a drift where she lay laughing helplessly while the dog stood over her, lathering her face with its tongue. She pushed Caramelle away and lay back with her eyes closed as she used to do as a child, willing the sun to warm the tip of her nose. When she opened her eyes again, the dog was gone.

She must have seen a rabbit, thought Thérèse, or a hare. A hare would be better: they were bigger, though harder to catch. She got to her knees and picked up the shotgun. It had been Grandpapa's gun, a single-barrel Verney-Carron, a gentleman's gun Papa said. She remembered his saying that as he held it up and sighted along the barrel. Look at the chasing, he said to her. When she saw the picture of a dog with a bird in its mouth she asked if it was their dog and he had laughed. She always knew afterwards that Papa was a gentleman too because he had a gentleman's gun. Léopold had it for a while after Papa, and Fabrice after him. She felt in her pocket for the cartridges. Séverine had given her only three, all they could spare, she had said, so Caramelle would have to be very clever this morning.

Thérèse slowly raised her head above the drift and saw Caramelle lying motionless on the snow about sixty metres away staring at a hare that sat no more than twenty metres from her. One eye on the dog and the other on where to run, thought Thérèse. Closer, bring him closer, Caramelle, and send him left like you do the sheep. She slid down behind the drift, carefully slipped in a cartridge and closed the gun as quietly as she could. She pushed up the barrel first a centimetre at a time and followed it with her head, looked, then levelled the gun. Neither animal had moved. She gave one long low whistle. The hare's ears went up. Caramelle shuffled forward a metre to her right. The hare stayed still. Thérèse whistled again. Caramelle shuffled forward again and still the hare did not move. Thérèse gave a short sharp whistle, Caramelle rose to her feet and the hare bounded away to Thérèse's right. She fired and caught him in mid-leap, flinging him to the ground. Caramelle swaggered back towards Thérèse with the prize in her mouth and her long bushy tail furiously brushing the snow. He was three kilos or more and quite dead. Thérèse tied him head down to her belt as she had seen Papa do, then with Caramelle running ahead set off to see if there were any more.

At midday she gave up the hunt. It was almost three kilometres back to the house, most of it uphill and harder going because the snow was softer now. She whistled to recall the dog and heard a faint answering bark coming from some way off in the direction of the gorge. She whistled again and again but Caramelle merely kept up her barking. Perhaps she had found something else, a dead cerf or a sanglier that had slipped and fallen from the pillars of ice-covered rock. It was worth a look in case other hunters, or the foxes or vultures, found it first. As she drew nearer the sound of the barking, Thérèse came across long furrows scraped in the snow only partly filled in with the night's fresh falls that set her wondering who might have brought a cart up here at that time of year. She remembered there was a shepherd's stone hut nearby. Caramelle's barking seemed to be coming from that direction.

The dog was pulling and worrying at something in the snow near the hut. Thérèse started to run, the gun bouncing on her back and the hare swinging at her side. It was a long swathe of white cloth and by the sheen of it seemed to be silk. Thérèse was more frightened than astounded. Was it a smuggler's secret store and was the owner watching, ready to shoot? Policemen and soldiers had been seen at the chateau above the gorge, it was said. But silk: she had never seen as much in one piece before: if it was silk. She bent to feel it. There was more, piled up inside the hut. And there was something else in there, partly covered with the silk, a man with his back against the wall and his head down on his chest. She put another cartridge in the gun and called the dog to her.

Séverine would tell her it was nothing to do with them; keep quiet, do nothing and you won't get into any trouble. But what about all that silk? That was worth something. She felt suddenly ashamed of herself. Before things had got so bad a thought like that would never have entered her head. Perhaps he was ill, or lost, needed help. She knelt down in front of the opening. There was dried blood on his face. He looked dead. She poked him gingerly with the end of the gun barrel and he slowly fell over onto his side. He must be dead. And then he began to groan.

***

'Why should we do anything about it?' snapped Séverine. 'We don't know who he is or where he comes from. If we get involved, it will only bring trouble and we have enough of that already without having dead men here.' She was cold and tired after struggling with the ewe, trying to splint and bind its broken leg.

'But I told you, he isn't dead. I heard him groaning.'

'What does it matter? He soon will be in this cold. Let someone else find him and tell the Mairie. Then it's their business and we won't be bothered.'

'I wrapped the silk all round him,' said Thérèse. 'That should keep him alive long enough for us to get him if we go now.'

'No. It'll be dark soon and the snow's soft now, you said so yourself. How could we carry him all the way here? That hut must be more than three kilometres away.'

'On the sled. A man doesn't weigh as much as a load of firewood.'

'We would be seen. There are hunters about. Then there'd be trouble.'

"I might have been seen already, and Caramelle. Then if somebody finds him covered in all that silk and my footprints and Caramelle's in the snow all round the shepherd's hut, they'll know I'd been there and the Mairie would hear about it anyway.'

'Are you sure it was silk?'

'No doubt about it, as white and fine as Mama's wedding dress. Listen, you sit by the fire to get warm and I'll make civet with the hare. There's enough wine and I'm sure there are some juniper berries at the back of the cupboard.'

'Civet will take hours.'

"Have some wine. Rest there. By the time we've had supper the moon will be up and the snow will be hard as ice. It won't take as long to get there and as I did this morning.'

'I can't sit about doing nothing. I must take another look at that ewe. After that I might consider a glass of wine.'

'Bring back a few potatoes, if you can find any,' called Thérèse as Séverine opened the door.

***

When Lawless awoke, he was lying on his side in what seemed to him to be a dim white mist. His head still ached and one of his legs was quite numb. He tried to concentrate, to remember. Noise, pain, cold, such cold, a river, snow, all flashed through his memory.

When had he heard that dog barking? Where was he? There was something soft, like a pillow, under his throbbing head. Had he put it there? How? And something hard was bruising his thigh. It took him an age and great pain to lever himself up to a sitting position and find the Webley revolver he had been lying on. It was against regulations but he always took it with him on a raid. He remembered the infantryman who had sold it to him for a pound in the pub at Topcliffe telling him the beaches at Dunkirk were covered in them, all thrown away by officers. For some reason, the memory cleared his head. Now he knew. He'd crawled into this cave out of the cold; was it last night or last week? The Whitley, she must be outside somewhere. Sherwood had brought her down, he remembered that; then there was a huge rending noise and that was where his memory stopped. He must have dragged his parachute in with him because here he was wrapped up in it; that white mist he'd seen, *and thank God he had* or he would have frozen to death, for sure. Now what? He couldn't move with one duff leg and anyway it was getting dark outside. Another night in the cave, then, and see what tomorrow might bring. He broke open the Webley and counted the cartridges by feel, one by one: six. He snapped the revolver shut and put it handy, by his side. He suddenly felt very hungry. He had a vague memory of some chocolate in one of his uniform pockets. Trying to find it, he kept getting his hands tangled in the parachute. He was too tired to go on. Sleep first and try again later.

***

The bright moon lit their way and the snow surface was so hard they were able to sit on the sled and coast down some of the slopes with Caramelle bounding along at the side. It was the same sled, light but strong, made by Chapelon, Michel, joiner of St Chely la Bastide, with upright handles at the back for pushing and steering, that they had sat on, wrapped in warm rugs and held safe by Papa, while the boys threw snowballs at them as they raced along. Thérèse reached for Séverine's arm, wanting to share the memory with her, but intent on steering the sled past rocky outcrops Séverine shrugged her hand away.

When they reached the shepherd's hut they found Caramelle whining and fussing round the doorway. Séverine lit the lantern they had brought and holding it before her bent low to put her head inside the entrance. In the dim light she saw the barrel of a pistol pointing straight at her face and hastily fell back, dropping the lantern as she did. She grabbed Thérèse by the arm and dragged her away from the hut.

'He has a pistol,' she hissed. 'He pointed it at me.'

'He's alive, then,' said Thérèse.

'Of course he's alive, idiot; how could he aim a pistol at me if he weren't alive? Come on, I'm not going to wait here to get shot. I told you we shouldn't have come.'

'Wait. Caramelle must have scared him. Is he French?'

'How do I know? He's sitting there up to his neck in heaps of cloth. He didn't say anything: just pointed the gun at me.'

'Something has happened here,' said Thérèse. 'Look at all the ruts in the snow and those things lying over there, and there, near that rock. What are they?'

'I don't care. We're going.' Séverine turned to call Caramelle.

'Wait. I'm going to look. Light the lantern again.'

Thérèse was soon back carrying what looked at first like a bundle of rods and lengths of rope. In moonlight everything looks black or grey. The feeble light of the lantern revealed that she had found some thin metal pipes and electrical cables with frayed ends.

'There's a machine gun lying in the snow over there,' she said and lots of bits of metal sheet all twisted and burned. I know it's a machine gun because Fabrice once showed me a picture of one, different from this one but I'm sure it's the same sort of gun. Did you hear me? What are you thinking about?'

'The aeroplane.' Séverine almost whispered the word.

'What aeroplane? What are you talking about?'

'Last night, when I went out to lock up the sheep. I heard an aeroplane not far off, heard its engines in the sky not far away.'

'You never told me.'

'The noise went away. I didn't think it mattered.'

'Well, now you know it did. I saw a flash of light in the sky just after, remember? That must have been it crashing and burning.'

'He's a flyer. The man in there with the gun, he's a flyer from that aeroplane. All that silk, it's his parachute.'

'He must need help. How can we get him out if he has a gun?'

Séverine was thinking. 'Listen. He must have heard us talking so he can't be French or he wouldn't have pointed the pistol at me.'

'Maybe he's wounded and can't talk. Or, my God, maybe he's German.'

'The Germans don't come flying over here, not yet anyway. But the English do, you must have heard that as well as me. He's English, he has to be.'

'We have to help him.'

'Do we? The English didn't help us much against the Germans, did they? They soon ran away and left us, left Fabrice, if you remember, when the Germans got serious. Then they went and blew up our ships at Mers el Kebir last year, remember that as well?'

'They're still fighting the Germans. That's why he comes to be here and you don't like what's going on in France now. I know, you've said it often enough.'

Séverine looked across at the hut again. 'All right, all right. We can't stand out here arguing all night, freezing to death. I'm only interested in that silk and if we want that we'll have to take him as well, I suppose.'

Thérèse had lived with her sister long enough to know when Séverine was being only half-serious. 'What about the gun?' she said quietly.

'Get the wine bottle from the sled. Let's see if he would like a drink.'

***

Lawless heard more sounds outside and, with a great effort, using both hands lifted and levelled the Webley. The same soft light he had seen before shone again in the cave entrance. He felt he must be dreaming when he saw a hand appear out of the darkness holding what seemed to be a bottle. He started to laugh but was overcome by spasms of harsh dry coughing that made the pistol drop from his hands and would not stop. Half delirious from thirst, he vaguely sensed something, someone, near him. He tried to lift the Webley but it was gone and so was his strength. Someone's fingers found his mouth and forced it open. Something hard grated against his teeth and he tried to cry out in pain but a liquid like cold acid filled his mouth and ran down his throat. He vomited it out but more poured in and reached his stomach where it turned into fire.

'Snow!' shouted Séverine, 'give me some snow and fill up the bottle with snow. The wine is too strong for him. He'll choke.'

She melted some of the handful of snow in her own mouth and forcing back his head let the slushy liquid dribble from her mouth into his. He coughed and struggled feebly but she held him tight and did it again. Thérèse squeezed into the hut beside them and handed Séverine the bottle. For another hour they took turns to hold Lawless and drip the cool watery wine into his mouth until at last his choking and retching stopped and he could keep some of it down. He stopped rolling his head from side to side and although his tongue still hung from his mouth his eyes began to focus on them, moving from one to the other. His leather helmet had slipped from his head revealing a deep gash in his brow that ran up into hair that was thickly crusted with dried blood. Séverine made a mouth when she saw this and looked at Thérèse, shaking her head. The wound needed stitches. He licked his dry lips and tried to speak but no sound came out. Thérèse put the bottle carefully to his mouth again but his head dropped and he slumped unconscious against her.

'We must take him back to the house as quick as we can,' snapped Séverine, 'or he'll die for sure. Come on now, turn him round, and pull him out, headfirst. Leave the silk under him, he'll slip out easier on that.'

As soon as they began to move him, Lawless started groaning and rolling his head around.

'He's hurt somewhere else,' cried Thérèse. 'Wait while I look.'

'We haven't time,' shouted Séverine. 'It won't make any difference. Get him onto the sled and back to the house. We can strip him and look at him there.'

'Strip him?'

Séverine ignored the question and started pulling Lawless again by the shoulders. 'Bring the sled close,' she shouted.

He was too heavy for them to lift him bodily and they had to heave and drag him onto the sled while all the time he groaned and flailed about with his arms. They quickly gathered up the silk parachute, piled it on top of him and tied the bundle to the sled as tightly as they could. They waited a few moments to get their breath back then Thérèse took hold of the handles at the rear and Séverine picked up the end of the hauling rope, tied it in a loop round her waist and began to pull. The Webley was left where it had fallen on the floor of the hut, hidden in the darkness.

Where the ground was level or sloped down into one of the shallow valleys that seamed the Causse the going was easy because the snow was so hard but when it came to hauling their load uphill that was another matter. As they struggled upwards and began to tire, the hardness of the snow worked against them and more and more often they slid back half the distance they had striven so hard climb. At the bottom of the next upward slope Séverine called a halt.

'Three kilometres of this will kill us all,' she gasped. 'We're doing it all wrong.' She gulped more of the freezing air into her lungs. 'We must follow the dog. We can't see sheep paths for the snow but she'll find them. They run across cross the slopes.' Thérèse could only nod; speaking was too much of an effort.

'Caramelle! Here now! Good girl!' The dog came up quickly and sat down on the snow in front of Séverine, head up, tongue out, alert. Séverine ruffled the shaggy hair and said quietly, 'Home now. Home, Caramelle.' The dog immediately set off on a line angling across the slope and Séverine gave the long low whistle that the dog knew meant go slowly.

It was a little easier but it was still painfully slow. Thérèse found herself counting each step and each breath, striving to make fifty paces before calling for a rest, then finding forty was all she could do, then thirty. The bulky form of Séverine was always ahead of her. She was never the first to stop. Thérèse would have started to hate her sister if she hadn't been so tired. Séverine was having similar thoughts. *My God, why did I ever agree to this* was the phrase that started going through her brain until it got shorter as she trudged on until without her realising, she was gasping *My God, My God* as a refrain to each step she took. Caramelle plodded on, occasionally stopping and turning her head as she had been taught to see if there was something different she should do.

Next time she does that, I'll tie a rope round her and she can pull as well. The thought was so ludicrous that Séverine started to laugh at herself, the laughter of near-exhaustion. Thérèse really did hate her at that moment and collapsed weeping on the snow. Séverine's laughter turned into coughing, then sobbing and the two of them lay near each other on the bleak hillside still tied to the sled and knowing they were beaten.

Caramelle was puzzled and crept back to go from one to the other, feverishly licking their faces. Thérèse pushed her away and the dog lost her footing and slid away down the slope on her back, wailing in alarm like a baby. The sight was so absurd that both women burst into laughter, with the tension broken and their exhaustion eased. Caramelle slipped and scrabbled her way back up to the sled and sat down behind it, panting heavily, ears down and looking foolish.

'Caramelle, the poor Caramelle! Good girl! Home now, home Caramelle!'

Reassured, the dog set off again, picking her way across the hillside and the sisters began their hauling and pushing once more. After only another twenty metres of climbing they reached level ground and could see a dim light in the distance that they knew was the lantern they had left burning in the window of the house.

***

The warmth inside the kitchen was like the breath of heaven to Thérèse. Caramelle slipped past her and went straight to the fireside where she lay down to lick her paws. Séverine came in with her hands in her armpits and stamped her boots on the stone floor.

'Make the fire up and boil some water while I fetch blankets. We'll have to keep him down here for now.' Séverine clumped away upstairs. Thérèse put more logs on the glowing embers, filled the kettle and hung it from its hook over the fire. She picked up the pile of blankets flung down from the top of the stairs and laid them in front of the fireplace. As she opened the door Séverine joined her and they stepped outside back into the cold. One look at the sled told them that it would not get through the doorway.

'Undo the ropes. We'll have to drag him in on the silk.'

Lawless made no sound when they pulled him off the sled nor while they got him to the fireside and onto the blankets. The dog stood up and sniffed the still bundle curiously.

'All right, Caramelle, now you know what it is. Off you go,' said Thérèse.

'Help me get his things off,' said Séverine. 'Boots first. Put his watch on the table.'

The heavy fur-lined leather boots had kept his feet dry but as Thérèse pulled off the right one Lawless jerked up and gave a sharp cry of pain before instantly fallen back unconscious again. Gasping and straining as they turned, pulled and lifted, they stripped off leather fur-lined jacket and trousers, sweaters, blue uniform jacket and trousers, flannel shirt, two flannel vests and long flannel under trousers until Lawless lay pale and naked in the firelight.

'Stop staring and bring the lantern. I need to have a good look at him. That's better.'

Thérèse drew her breath in sharply and pointed. 'Look at his leg.'

Lawless's right leg was very swollen and dark with bruising. A jagged sliver of metal stuck out from a blood-rimmed puncture in the outside of his thigh. Séverine leaned over and looked closely, feeling the end of the metal with finger and thumb. She sat back, biting her lip.

'That's the worst thing,' she said, 'that and the cut on his head. We'll have to get this out and sew up his head and do it now before he wakes up again.'

'Doctor, he needs a doctor,' whispered Thérèse.

'Doctor? Listen to yourself! Vaudet lives in Florac. That's fifteen kilometres away. He couldn't get here for days, even if we wanted him and we don't. I've sewn up enough cuts in sheep's legs and so have you. We have to do this or he'll die. It's his only chance. You know that.'

'I know, I know, but this is, he's a . . .'

'He's a man. I can see that. He's a man and he needs mending if he's going to be any use to us. Bring the hot water and some clean rags, oh, and the pincers from the tool chest.'

'What do you mean, "any use to us"?'

'Never mind. Bring the things.'

Luckily, the metal splinter had not penetrated to the bone and came out easily with the pincers. Blood ran freely from the wound but Séverine had thought of this and tightened the cord that she had put round the top of Lawless's thigh as a tourniquet while ThérèseThérèse poured a few drops of their precious cognac onto the puncture and padded and bandaged it with strips torn from an old linen sheet.

'I know we're both tired but we have to deal with his head before he comes round again,' said Séverine. 'I'll get the workbasket. You can do this one while I hold him still.'

Thérèse surprised herself. Fighting back her revulsion, she managed the first stitch with trembling fingers and after felt calmer so that the rest was easier as she went on. When it was finished, she looked at the sewed-up wound with the end double-knot and felt the slightest touch of pride.

'Darned as well as a pair of socks,' said Séverine with a tired smile.

'I'm nearly dead,' said Thérèse. 'I have to go to bed.'

'Can't do that,' said Séverine. 'We have to stay with him down here. You can have the side by the fire and I'll take the other.'

'You mean?'

'Yes. We have to sleep with him, to keep him warm. Don't be shy. He can't do anything to us even if we wanted him to.' She laughed. 'He may never even remember.'

***

Lawless was still sleeping when Thérèse got up quietly in the morning to rekindle the fire and put some water on to make coffee or what passed for coffee these days. Caramelle stood by the door waiting to be let out. The dawn was clear and cold. Perhaps the sun would shine today. She heard Séverine moving about in the sheep pen and wondered idly whether she had decided to let the flock out into the yard for exercise while the pen was cleaned out. The flock was their livelihood; seventy breeding Caussenarde de Garrigues ewes and all carrying lambs this year, thank God. She would cook navarin of lamb in the Spring, Mama's recipe: if the hay they had worked so hard in September to scythe and carry and store in the loft above the sheep pen lasted. The winter had come so early this year with so much snow and such biting winds that the sheep had to be brought in before time and even then some had been lost, buried in drifts or fallen from cliffs. It would soon be New Year. If only there could be a thaw to thin the snow cover, it sometimes happened, and the sheep could be let out, guarded by Caramelle, to paw down and find some moss and frozen grass. She heard the water in the kettle begin to boil and turned towards the fireplace. The man on the floor had his eyes open and as she looked, he turned his head towards her. The effort seemed too much for him and his eyes closed again.

Thérèse stood over the sleeping man, looking down at his face. *He looks so young, much younger than Fabrice in the photograph. I could almost be his mother. Séverine certainly could.* She knew now that he was an English flyer. The blue uniform jacket they had taken off him the night before had three chevrons on the sleeve and over the breast pocket a badge in the shape of a bird's wing with the letters AG. It was not a French uniform and Fabrice had told her the Germans wore grey uniforms. And he was a *blond roux.* He had to be an Englishman: only the English had hair like that. She was intrigued to know what this Englishman's name was. When he woke up they would have to call him something. They had seen some papers in his pockets when they undressed him but Séverine had said leave them to the morning when there was more light to see. Thérèse looked at the untidy pile of clothes on the table. She had to look. She couldn't resist it. She felt inside the pocket.

The door banged and Séverine stamped in.

'It's no good. They'll have to stay inside. It's too cold. Where's that coffee? What are you doing there?'

'Nothing, just tidying up.'

'I know what you're doing. Coffee first, then we'll look. My fingers are blue. I could stir the coffee with them and never feel it.'

'He woke up while you were out. He looked at me but I don't think he could see me.'

'He was awake in the night, not for long. I'd loosened that tourniquet and I wanted to see if he was still bleeding. He must have felt me touching him and he tried to speak but all he could do was whisper and cough.'

'What did he say?'

'I don't know. English words, I think. I couldn't understand.'

'Is he going to die?'

'We'll have to wait and see. Do what we can, then wait and see. Do I have to make the coffee myself?'

The drink had a character all its own. Thérèse made it from a mixture of a pinch or two of their precious dwindling store of real coffee, dried dandelion leaves and some powdered roasted barley. A spoonful of honey tempered the bitterness. They had grown used to it and at least it was hot. They each bent over a steaming bowlful, dipping their bread in to soften it and looking forward to the fig jam and cheese that would follow.

'What about the ewe?'

'She'll survive. I've had to part her from the others because she can't get to the hay in time with that bound-up leg. It's worth it. She's bigger in the belly than the others so she may be carrying two.'

Thérèse finished her coffee and turned to look at Lawless.

'Do you think he knows anything about farming?' she said.

'He hasn't got the right sort of hands.'

'They're under the blankets. How can you tell?'

'Last night he put his arm across me and touched my face. His hand was very soft. That was when he was trying to speak. He must have been dreaming.'

Thérèse pretended to be shocked. In fact, she felt a little bit jealous which surprised her.

'Dreaming of you, sister?'

'Hmph! Where are those papers you were fiddling with?'

They emptied all the pockets in Lawless's clothes and strewed the contents on the table. There was some money, a few silver coins with a man's head on one side and three crumpled red banknotes with the number 10, a folded handkerchief, a photograph of a woman sitting on a chair and a man standing beside her with his hand on her shoulder, a packet of cigarettes with a picture of a sailor on the front, a cigarette lighter that smelled of petrol, a little notebook that they set aside to look through later, and best of all, a whole bar of chocolate, broken in the packet and part-melted, but real chocolate, something they had not seen for at least a year.

'There's not very much,' said Séverine.

'Fabrice said soldiers aren't allowed to take anything that would be useful to the enemy when they go to a battle. Do you think he'd mind if we had some of his chocolate?'

'He ought to let us have it all since we saved his life,' said Séverine firmly. One piece now, save the rest for later.'

Caramelle deserves a piece,' said Thérèse. 'She helped.'

The dog approached, sniffing inquisitively, swallowed the proffered titbit and retired to the fireplace, licking her lips again and again.

Séverine picked up the stained and creased notebook and looked at the front cover. *Royal Air Force,* she read. That was clear enough. Below in capital letters were the words AIRMAN'S PAY BOOK of which she understood only the first word. There were nine dotted lines below this, all with just letters, or numbers some of which she guessed were dates but of what she could not understand. Against the top dotted line was the word *Surname* and against the one below, *Christian names,* obviously family name and first names. So, the airman's name was LAWLESS, P.M.

'Lawless,' she said triumphantly out loud. 'His name is Lawless, P.M.'

'Let me see,' said Thérèse, taking the notebook from her. She slowly looked over the front cover, repeating what Séverine had said and then opened the book. 'There's more inside,' she said. 'Look: *family name Lawless* and under that, *first names Philippe Martyn.* And here, on this line, *Date of Birth, 22 December 1921.* His age is twenty years old, Séverine. He is only a boy.'

Séverine was not listening. She was kneeling by the pile of blankets on the floor and looking closely into the face of the unconscious man. 'We must wake him up,' she said. 'I don't like the way he just goes on sleeping. It means he's not trying to stay alive. The cut on his head seems all right but he feels a bit hot. I want to see what that leg looks like.'

'Perhaps he's just very, very tired after all he's gone through. He hasn't eaten anything for a long time and he had only that melted snow to drink last night.'

'Then he must have something more, even if it's only some coffee with honey, or is there any sauce left from the civet? We could try to get some of that down him.'

'Not much; I gave most of it to Caramelle with the rest of the bread and some chestnuts.'

'Bring what's left and warm it up.'

While Thérèse was heating the gravy over the fire, Séverine drew back the blankets to look at Lawless's leg. The bruising had faded somewhat and there was only a small bloodstain on the bandage.

'Help me get him to sit up. I'll hold him while you prop him up with the bolster and the blankets.'

After much pulling and pushing, Lawless was at last sitting with his back against a pile of bedding, nodding and swaying but with his eyes half-open. Séverine knelt beside him and took his chin in one hand to steady his head and parted his cracked lips with the other.

'Just water for now,' said Séverine. 'The sauce may be too rich for him at first. Use a spoon.'

For about an hour they took turns to feed him the water, little by little until he was drinking almost greedily and the colour began to show in his pale cheeks. After that he was able to take sips of the warm gravy from a cup as Thérèse held his head in the crook of her arm. After half a cupful he was clearly very tired again and she let him settle back against the blankets. He looked at her mistily and for a moment she thought he gave a faint smile. Then he fell asleep.

As the daylight was beginning to fade in mid-afternoon, Séverine came into the room with a pile of logs and dropped one while was stacking them at the fireside. She turned to see if the noise had disturbed Lawless. He was looking straight ahead with eyes wide open and perfectly steady.

'Name, rank and number,' he recited in a faint but clear voice.

She had no idea what he was saying.

'Name, Lawless, Philippe Martyn; rank, Sergeant Air Gunner; number four one nine six four four.'

She knelt down in front of him and brought her face close to his.

'Loveless Philippe Martin, 'she said. 'Can you hear me?'

'Lawless, not Loveless. Rank, Sergeant Air Gunner; number, four one nine six four four.'

At least he can hear me, she thought, *but he's speaking English and I'm speaking French and neither of us knows what the other's saying.* She felt like laughing but she had a sudden idea. *He's a soldier: maybe he will obey a command.* Looking him straight in the eye she barked,

'Lawless! I command you to drink this!'

She put the cup to his lips and he drained the contents without protest. Thérèse came in at that moment.

'Look at that! He's taken it all. How did you do that, Séverine? You spoke in French. He's going to be all right now, isn't he?'

'Never mind how I did it. Yes, he's going to live. And now we have to decide what to do with him.'

***

Food and warmth and perhaps the realisation that he was safe for the time being must have brought Lawless out of the trance that made him repeat the military instructions that had puzzled Séverine at first. He was able to eat a little of the stew of potatoes, turnips and chestnuts that was offered him for supper, using the spoon himself and nodding and smiling his thanks. He wondered whether he should reveal that he understood perfectly everything the two women said both to themselves and to him because he had been warned before every raid that were he to be captured he should keep such information to himself until he was sure it would do no harm; and that applied to Vichy France as much as it did to Germany or Italy. He decided to wait until he could at least walk again. He felt a bit of a fraud because they had clearly rescued him and were looking after him very kindly, sharing what food they had with him. Best of all, the terrible pain had gone from his leg. It felt sore but at least he could move it again and they must have seen to that. The woman he knew from what he had heard was called Thérèse poured something into a beaker for him from a large jug. The taste was between sweet and sour, rather familiar. He drank more. Cider: it was cider, not wine. It felt warm in his stomach.

It was embarrassing at first but they had to clean him up, he knew that. Thérèse held a basin for him and looked away while he peed in it. That took some time. The other woman, the older one, he now realised, took away some soiled knickers he didn't know they had put on him and washed his backside with a rough cloth, dried him and slapped him on the buttock as if he were a lad just out of the bath with his mother getting him ready for bed. And bed it was to be. They seized him, pulled a long nightgown over his head and lowered him onto the pile of blankets and pulled one up to his chin. Thérèse cleared away the things on the table and the other woman made up the fire. The dog wandered over to the bed and began to lick his face. Without thinking what he was doing he said,

'Laisse-moi tranquille, toutou, on va dormir.'

Both women turned to stare at him. Lawless felt his cheeks beginning to burn. The older woman smiled tightly.

'So, Mister Englishman, now we know you can speak to our dog. In the morning you may care to talk to us.'

Lawlees started to say something but they were not listening. The lamp was turned down and they both got under the blankets with him, one on each side.

'Dormez bien,' he said weakly but his only answer was a snore from one side and a faint giggle from the other.

***

Lawless woke up before it was light to find the two women still asleep beside him. His thoughts began to wander as they often did in early morning darkness whether he was in his cot on the base or striving to keep from freezing in his turret in the Whitley. The Whitley, well she was gone for sure; he felt a tinge of regret and told himself he was stupid. After all, here he was, warm, safe from flak and night fighters and in bed with two women. He grinned in the darkness. He'd never done that before, although he remembered Verrill, the Navigator and Second Pilot, telling them in vivid detail of his experiences with two girls in Darlington. Jack Verrill: dead now, he supposed. Well, no more raids for him and no more for me, at least for a bit, he thought. His next thought was a worrying one: instructions were that if he were shot down and survived uninjured it was his duty to try to escape capture. But hold on, he *was* injured, so he needn't consider that, at least not yet. Twenty-three raids, or was it twenty-four, and still alive. He was lucky. The others weren't, not this time: Sherwood, Verrill, Sanderson, Forbes. All gone. Must have, or they'd have been found and brought here like him, wouldn't they? Oh God! His mother: he hadn't thought of her until now. There would have been a knock on the door and the policeman outside with that look on his face and his mother would put her hand to her mouth because she knew he must be dead before the policeman said a word. And his Dad, in the classroom with all the boys looking on and the Headmaster coming in and speaking quietly into his ear. They would cling to the hope that he was only missing but the hope would get fainter and fainter because no one knew where he was. He didn't know where he was either. Somewhere east of the Rhône, he was sure of that, and in upland country, it had to be because of the cold and the depth of snow, but France was a big country. He must ask the women. What an idiot he was to let on like that that he spoke French, and to a bloody dog! No, not really, because it was important to find out exactly where he was and how could he ask except in French because they didn't speak any English. Or did they? Never mind that: he must find out because, because, and here that worrying thought came again, his duty was to try to escape. When he was fit again. Leave it at that. He tried to clear his mind of all thoughts but he needed a pee. Oh God, he couldn't go himself. He'd have to ask them to bring the basin and help him kneel. Last time the young one had to hold his dick for him. He squirmed at the memory. A man should be able to hold his own dick. He began to shake with inner laughter at the thought. I can, he thought, I feel a lot better. I can hold my own dick; I know I can. His laughter burst out in a spluttering snort. Séverine stirred, muttered something and turned over, causing her head to come to rest on his shoulder. Christ, now what? He needed a pee, now, and his dick was beginning to stiffen that bit as it did when his bladder was full. Hoping she wouldn't get the wrong idea, he tried to shift away from under Séverine's head and only succeeded in pushing his other shoulder into Thérèse's back. She promptly sat up and turned towards him. It was getting lighter now and he could make out her face above him. Nothing for it, he thought.

'Faire pipi,' he whispered.

Without a word she got up and fetched the basin. He was able to push aside the bedding but could not sit up by himself. She put her arms around his shoulders and pulled him towards her and he found himself sitting upright with something supporting him from behind. There was no time to find out what that was; he needed the basin quickly. After some frantic fumbling he found he could handle himself this time. Having finished, he leaned back with a sigh only to find the firm back support was still there. Only then did he realise it was Séverine's arm.

***

Séverine put her empty coffee bowl down and looked down at Lawless.

'Today, Englishman, you are going to walk. But first we will talk and you will tell us who you are and other things about yourself. Drink your coffee.'

It was a curious drink and would take some getting used to but Lawless had to admit he felt better after it went down. Back in the Mess in Topcliffe they would be having bacon and fried bread and tea with condensed milk to sweeten it. He wondered if anybody was still thinking of him and Sherwood and the others, or were they now just names that had been rubbed of the duties list. He'd seen that done a few times.

'Help me up, please. I think I can sit at the table,' he said, surprised to find his voice was getting stronger.

They seated him in a heavy chair of dark wood with padded arms and a rush seat and sat opposite him with their hands in their laps, unsmiling, waiting for him to begin. It was a bright morning outside and the kitchen was light enough for him to see them clearly for the first time. They were both what his father would have called very handsome women, meaning not especially beautiful but noticeable, with large dark eyes, long straight noses and clear skin, in their case lightly tanned and with reddened cheeks, from much time spent out in the open, he supposed. One had hair that was almost black and the other's was very dark red. Both wore it bound up at the back but he could see it was thick and long. He wondered how long it would be when they let it down. They were obviously sisters but the one with the reddish hair whose name he knew was Thérèse was a little taller and slimmer and had faint lines at the side of her mouth. She was the one whose face softened from time to time when she looked at him. Her sister's had yet to do so. She was the elder, he guessed, and acted that way. There was more strength in her eyes and movement in her face when she spoke. She had a wide mouth with beautifully curved lips. He reckoned she was the one who decided most things in this house. He was no good at ages but he guessed this one was thirty-five or so and Thérèse two or three years younger.

'Ladies,' he said, 'you saved my life. If I thank you a thousand times it is not enough. I regret trying to deceive you and from now on I will speak only French to you, unless you want me to teach you a little English.' There was no answering smile to his so he went on. 'I suppose you have been looking at my things,' he said, glancing towards the pile at the end of the table, 'because you know my name.' He paused to catch his breath. He was not quite as strong as he had thought.

'You are an English flyer and your name is Loveless, Philippe Martyn and . . .'

'Lawless. Law-less, not Loveless, that means something very different. I am Philippe Martyn Lawless.' He liked the sound of 'Philippe' pronounced in the French way, 'Pheeleep' and resolved to keep it that way.

'Your English language is not easy to speak.'

'It is not as beautiful as your French language.'

The older woman looked at him sharply but he gave her what he hoped seemed an honest smile and her expression eventually softened. *Careful with the flattery*, he decided, although he really believed what he had just said.

'Pretty words, Philippe Martyn Law-less; how is it that you speak French so well?' said Séverine.

'Madame, first, will you tell me your own name? I have heard you call Madame your sister, Thérèse.'

'Mams'elle, both: we are not married. Why do you wish to know?'

'It is normal, Mams'elle,' said Lawless simply.

'Séverine Geneviève Duchesne Chevalier. I present my sister Thérèse Angeline Duchesne Chevalier.'

Lawless bowed his head briefly to each in turn. 'Enchanted,' he murmured, noting the brief glance flashed between them. *Wasn't that a Huguenot family name in there as well as Chevalier? Perhaps not a noble family, but gentry at least, at some time anyway, though now fallen on hard times.*

'Well, Monsieur?'

'Philippe, Mams'elle; it is more friendly.'

She ignored that and sat waiting, eyebrows raised, for him to continue.

'My father is a schoolmaster. He teaches French. We have spoken French to each other as long as I can remember. I am, that is, I was, a student of French at the University.'

'You were, you said?'

'Yes, for one year at Oxford and then I was called up for military service.'

'As a flyer, what is the word, pilot?

'No, that is what I wanted. I did fly small aeroplanes at Oxford.'

'But not now?'

'No. They said there was more need for gunners. You have seen my uniform, with the badge: a wing with AG on it? It means Air Gunner. I am a Sergeant Air Gunner.'

Thérèse spoke for the first time, looking at Séverine.

'Sergeant: like Fabrice.'

'Mams'elle?'

'It is nothing,' said Séverine. 'We have found one of your guns.'

'I found it,' said Thérèse, 'not far from where we found you. It is a machine gun.'

'You know it is a machine gun? Is it here, in the house?'

Séverine broke in. 'Of course not: we left it in the snow. We have no interest in such a thing.'

Not you perhaps, but plenty of others might. My Webley! She hasn't mentioned that. 'I understand. Was there anything else?'

'Many pieces of metal, burned, and broken cables.'

'No sign of the others, my . . .'

'Only you. I am sorry.'

'After the winter, when the snow has melted, perhaps then they may be found,' said Thérèse.

'Mams'elle, I must leave here before then.'

Séverine's eyes flared. She dismissed the absurd idea with a wave of her hand. 'Leave? Where would you go? You cannot walk. You have no strength. You cannot leave.'

'Mams'elle herself said I would walk today . . .'

'Do not mock me, Sergeant Englishman!'

'It is my duty to return to England if I can and rejoin my Squadron,' said Lawless, immediately feeling he must have sounded pompous and not a little ridiculous, given the state he was in. He had to accept that for the time being he was completely reliant on these two women.

'Duty, you say. There is too much duty in this world and too many that die because of it. It is impossible for you to leave. I will not permit it.'

Lawless saw that there was no point in arguing with her in this mood but he was puzzled by her vehemence. Perhaps she was just like that, accustomed to getting her own way. Or could it be that there was a reward for turning in fugitive RAF crew like him? In that case why had they not done so already? Obvious: look outside. How could anyone get to the nearest gendarme, wherever he might be, or him get here in this snow? And yet, and *yet*, some nuance in her tone, something he could not identify, made him feel there was another reason. Simple human kindness: she did not look that kind of woman. Now the sister . . . he looked from one to the other. He had to admit he was helpless and unarmed: there was nothing for it but to give in, for now, get better and see what happened then. He smiled at them and raised his arms.

'I surrender. Is there any more coffee?'

The tension eased. Thérèse smiled back at him. Séverine's frown faded to a firm if slightly wary look.

'That is good. I accept. First I will examine your leg and Thérèse the wound on your head. After that you will have coffee. And after that you will walk, yes?'

Lawless smiled to himself. *I accept*: surely a little joke answering his own? And *Thérèse*, not *my sister*: that was better. 'Yes,' he said. I will walk. I promise not to run away.'

He remained seated while they examined him. They were thorough but deft and careful not to hurt him. The wound on his thigh was still very sore to the touch but a healthy scab was beginning to form and there was no sign of infection. He felt Thérèse's fingers in his hair but she did not touch the cut. Séverine put new bandaging on his thigh and tied it in place with a neat knot. She pulled the long nightshirt down to his ankles and stood up. He looked from one to the other.

'Will I live?'

'Perhaps: we have treated many animals and often they live.'

'I thank you. No doctor could have done better.'

'It is necessary. We have work for you. Thérèse?'

'After one week I will remove the sutures.'

'Ah, good. I will look for Grandpapa's canes while you make a little coffee.'

'A moment, Mams'elle,' said Lawless. 'I have something for you. Please pass me my things.' Thérèse brought the small pile of his pockets' contents and put them on the table before him. He picked up the remains of the chocolate bar and offered it to Séverine.

'Please accept this as a payment of the doctor's bill. I have nothing else to offer. No, wait; there is something else. My parachute: you must have it, too. It is silk. Surely you ladies will have a use for that?'

The look on both faces was enough for him to know he had granted a wish they would never have stooped to express. Caramelle was not left out. Lawless ensured that a fragment of the chocolate went her way.

It was more a case of shuffling one foot forward then dragging the other up to it, than walking. At first each of them had to hold an arm round his waist to steady him as he put his weight on the two ebony-handled walking-sticks but eventually he was able to stand shakily on his own. Séverine made him walk six faltering paces across the room, rest, turn and retrace the six paces back. His face grew red with the effort and sweat ran off his brow but she made him do it again before allowing him to sink into the chair.

'Pff,' she said, 'you are stronger already. Soon you will be able to go upstairs. No, no, no, do not go to sleep in that chair. Thérèse, help me to lie him down here. Now,

Sergeant, you sleep and when you wake, you will walk again before you have any dinner. Do you understand?'

Lawless could give only a feeble nod of assent before his eyes closed and his head fell back onto the bolster. As he was drifting off, he heard the two sisters talking. Her voice was very faint, as if coming from a great distance but Thérèse seemed to be asking Séverine what she meant when she said to him 'we have work for you.'

***

'I mean that he can be of help to us, of course not yet but when he is strong again. There is much that a man can do. God knows, it is hard here, just the two of us, working all day, summer and winter, trying to keep this place going. Think what life was like when our men were here. The flock was three times as big and we had a herd, horses for work and riding and Anne-Marie to do the washing and cleaning and Gaston to work with the sheep after he came back from the war. Mama grew flowers in her garden, you had time for your piano and Fabrice even had his pony. What do we have now?'

Thérèse had tears in her eyes. 'I remember I had a new straw hat with a blue ribbon for my birthday and we all went in the cart to Castelbouc for a picnic. It was so hot that day. I was seven.'

'Do you remember Papa's Three Days of Celebration?'

'Oh, yes: in July, the Fourteenth and the Twelfth and in September the First.'

'Bastille, Dreyfus and the death of Louis Fourteenth: all days to celebrate liberty. Papa said all the family must drink a toast: we were given wine with water.'

'Dear Papa and Mama: all so long ago.'

'Not Mama. She left us only last year.'

'Don't.'

'We have to remember all of these things and who we are.'

'I know, I know; I do remember but we are only two women, Séverine, you said that and are we to be like Mama and live and work here until we die?'

'I will never leave La Commanderie. It is ours. It has always been ours.'

'And after we have gone, what then?'

'Now is not the time to think of that. Now is the time to think of now. Listen, I have told you. We are no more only two women. There is a man here now, not a man of this family but I have seen him looking about this room and looking at us and he looks with respect in his eyes. He recognises what we are. That is useful to us.'

'He is too weak even to help himself and when he is better he will go. He has said as much.'

'Not before he has paid what he surely considers his debt to us for rescuing him and making him better. We will use that to persuade him to stay and work long enough for us to prepare ourselves.'

'Prepare ourselves for what?'

'Whatever comes: another winter, more restrictions, more taxes, how can one be sure when we are in the midst of a war?'

'Do you honestly believe he will stay long enough to be of any real help? You yourself said he knows nothing about farming.'

'I have been thinking about that. He knows nothing about the Causses. He does not even know he is in the Causses. He knows no one and he has nothing. How can he get away from here without our help? He would surely be taken by the gendarmes within a day of leaving this house. This will be our bargain with him: we will help him escape when he has done for us what we need of him and not before. Now, no more questions. We must wake the Sergeant Lawless. He is a soldier and trained to obey orders: walk first and then dinner. You see?'

***

'Once more: one, two, three, four, five, six. Satisfactory. That's enough for today. You may have your watch back and sit at the table, Sergeant Lawless.'

'Philippe, if you please.'

'It is too soon for that. There is much about you that as yet we do not know.'

Lawless had to stop himself shaking his head in disbelief. Apparently spending nights together in the same bed and experiencing other intimacies at their hands did not break enough ice to permit the use of first names. It was like some Victorian novel where received formalities obscured the real and earthier side of life. However, this family clearly had its codes and he had to admit a sneaking admiration for them. Putting on a straight face he replied,

'You have only to ask, Mams'elle. I will answer any question, unless, of course, it is about information that would be useful to the enemy.'

'Are you a Protestant?'

He was ready for that one. 'Non-practising, Mams'elle.

He could tell from the momentary inclination of Séverine's head as she cast a glance across to her sister that that was the right answer. The next question was also not a surprise.

'Are you to the Left or to the Right?'

He smiled at her. 'I am a student, Mams'elle. What do you expect?'

'I expect an answer and you are not a student or you would not be here, Sergeant.'

'In my head I am a gunner but in my heart I am still a student. When this war is finished I will return to my books but until it is finished, for me there is no Left or Right. Besides, I have no vote.'

'Hm, you are too young,' said Séverine.

He closed his eyes, trying to forget but thoughts of Sherwood, always losing his pipe, and Verrill, always talking of girls, and many more would not go away.

'I do not feel young any more, Mams'elle.'

'But you are only twenty; do not be so sad,' said Thérèse. She picked up the photograph and looked at it. 'These are your parents, no? Have you a brother or sisters?'

'I am an only child, Mams'elle.'

'They will be wondering where is their son. It is sad for them not to know what we know: that you are here and alive.'

'It is the War, Mams'elle.'

'Ah yes, the War,' said Séverine bleakly. 'We know about wars.' She had picked up his pay book and was looking through it. She pointed to writing low down on the second page. 'It is here, the name of your father, "Herbert Lawless"? And I see the word "address":

that is where he lives and you also? Where is that?'

'It is a small town called Kendal in the north of England. It has a river and there are mountains around it, and beautiful lakes nearby . . .' It was too much. He fell silent.

'You are tired,' said Séverine not unkindly, 'so you must eat. Tonight we have dumplings.'

'Boulettes? My mother makes dumplings with leeks.'

'Here we have dried crêpes and girolles.'

'I will tell you a secret, ladies: the English have a great fear of mushrooms that are not white.'

'You are all mad. I have heard it said and now I know.'

'I do not speak of myself, Mams'elle Séverine. My father taught me to enjoy the food of France, and even persuaded my mother.'

Séverine took the photograph from Thérèse and studied it closely. She seemed not to have noticed his use of her first name.

'Of course, I see now that your father is an intelligent man. Your mother, what is her name?'

'Louisa; she is a piano teacher.'

'But that is very good,' exclaimed Thérèse. 'My piano is in the salon. And do you play?'

'My mother taught me, Mams'elle Thérèse. If there is music I can play a little.'

'I have music but my piano is possibly not in good condition. I have not played it since Mama . . .'

Séverine raised a hand. 'The dumplings, sister, and the sauce: they will spoil if we do not eat now.'

The dumplings were served covered in thick dark gravy flavoured with garlic and thyme. They had a slightly sweet taste that went well with the tang of the dried mushrooms. He declared that they were delicious and was told that they were made with chestnut flour. A small slice of cheese was offered and from the flavour he guessed it was made from sheep's milk.

'My uncle has many sheep. He is what in England we call a hill-farmer. His farm is in the mountains not far from my town.'

From the amused glance that Thérèse cast her sister and Séverine's pursed lips Lawless saw that this conversational remark had hit some sort of mark. He waited for a few moments and when nothing was said, went on.

'He does not make cheese, as you do here. It is not the custom. The sheep are for wool and for meat.' That worked.

'Hm. That is how many sheep?'

'When I last worked for him in my last school holiday, about two hundred but because of the war he now has many more, perhaps three hundred.'

'You say you worked for your uncle, the hill farmer. What did you do?'

'Everything; as shepherd sometimes with the dogs, helping at lambing time, dipping, winter feeding, shearing. I was not very good at shearing. Your dog here is a sheep dog but a different breed from ours.'

'Caramelle? Yes, we have sheep,' said Thérèse.

'Yes, I hear them when the door is opened. I know the smell of sheep.'

Séverine rubbed her hands together and stood up. 'I am cold sitting here,' she said.

Bring the honey and some cinnamon, sister. A little mulled wine will help us all sleep warmer tonight.'

'And with it, a cigarette, perhaps,' said Lawless. 'Is it permitted to smoke in here?' The packet was passed to him and opening it he found that ten remained. Both sisters declined his offer but watched intently as he flicked open the cigarette lighter and lit up. The coughing fit that followed ended only after he had swallowed the beaker of water that Thérèse poured for him.

'Too soon, Sergeant,' said Séverine, pursing her lips in mock seriousness. 'Perhaps someone so young should not smoke. I think we must stay one more night with you here, simply to be sure you are all right, and tomorrow there will be other arrangements.'

***

After dinner the following night Lawless watched Thérèse use tongs to take two large bricks from the fireplace where they had been warming and wrap them in pieces of blanket. 'For our beds,' she said to him with a smile as she went to the staircase. 'You will have the fire to yourself tonight.'

He missed their presence that night. He remembered telling Séverine he did not feel young anymore but alone in the darkened room with the fire burning low and all the bad memories rising up to haunt him, he did feel young again, very young; as young as when the nightmares sent him stumbling to his mother's bed crying to be taken in. He shivered violently and not from cold.

It was only a momentary weakness. He knew it was the shock and the exhaustion that followed shock and the strangeness, the not knowing where he was or what would happen to him, the feeling of near helplessness that made him afraid. *For Christ's sake, get a grip!* He struggled to his feet. It was easier than he expected. *It must be all that marching exercise: just like square-bashing, with Corporal Séverine barking the orders.* He heard himself laughing at the thought. *Lovely mouth, though: far too nice for bellowing by the left, wait for it, quick march!* He took two or three tentative steps towards the fireplace, thinking he might put another log on the fire. *Fire, so nice and warm: it kept them bloody warm down there in the streets of Bremen that night we dropped the incendiaries, didn't it?* He only thought of those things afterwards, never at the time. *Don't think now!* Something cool and moist pushed at his hand. *What the . . . the dog, of course: Caramelle, well she was that sort of colour.*

'You've a cold wet nose, Caramelle,' he said, ruffling the long hair on the dog's head. 'You're in better shape than me. What are you like with the sheep, eh? Are you good? Do as you're told? Left, right, stay, come on.' He said the English words and softly sounded the whistled commands that he had learned to use with Nell and Kitty, mother and daughter, his uncle's collies, on the fells above Windermere. Caramelle made a gurgling noise in her throat and whisked the floor with her tail. 'Good girl, heard that, did you? Right, I know what you'd like.' He made his way to the table and fumbled among the things there. He found the chocolate.

'Six pieces left, Caramelle: one for you, one for me and two bits each for the ladies: how's that, now?'

There was a warm brick in his bed too. How could he have missed that being put there? He felt snug in the blankets with his feet on the wrapped-up brick. As a child he had always become drowsy watching the glow of a fire and it was the same now. The flicker of the embers was, what was the word, alluring.

In his dream Séverine was holding a bowl to his lips but her face was turned away. It was too hot to drink but she didn't seem to hear when he protested. Thérèse appeared and took the bowl from her hands and bent over it to cool it with her breath but it fell to floor and broke. She smiled at him and went away, beckoning him to follow. He could hear a piano playing but Séverine wanted him to lie down and keep warm. He could feel the warmth of her body beside him again and he felt he could sleep now.

The dog made little yelping and growling sounds in its sleep though not loud enough to waken the man she lay beside.

***

In the days that followed, life for Lawless fell into a simple routine. Breakfast was always the same, the household coffee with thick slices of dark bread to dip in, and always at the same time, not long after dawn. There was more of the same bread at midday but with rough red wine, cheese and on occasion stewed sweet shallots. Between these two meals and during the afternoon the women had too much work to get through to spend any time with him. He looked forward to dinner when the house was warmer and there was time to talk but otherwise he had to occupy himself. Sometimes he felt like a prisoner, pacing from one side of the room to the other and back again, and again. As he grew steadier on his feet he began to introduce variations: he would take a few dance steps, foxtrot or two step, turn and reverse with an imaginary waltz partner, stand on one leg, then the other, attempt a quick march in one direction and walk backwards in the other. His legs grew stronger and after five days of exercising he no longer limped and could run on the spot. He considered setting up an obstacle course, a chair here, the low table there, a pile of logs as the first jump, and the blankets folded and laid out for a water jump but thought better of it and attempted juggling with three balls of wool he found in a drawer. As often as not, he ended these sessions feeling a little foolish and hoping no one had seen him.

He spent what seemed like hours looking out of the window, not that there was much to see: the snow-covered courtyard, the grey stone barns with their stone-slabbed roofs and heavy wooden doors, occasionally the muffled-up figure of one of the women trudging from one building to another, carrying a bale of hay or pushing a long-handled wooden wheelbarrow loaded with roots. Séverine told him the ewes needed a lot of attention and she had to spend much of her time cleaning out and inspecting them for foot rot and worm. He was intrigued to discover that she used the same herbal treatment as some old shepherds at home said they remembered: carrots with the leaves on or if that didn't work, a drench made from boiling tansy. He said he would help but she looked him up and down and said not yet. He wasn't sure what Thérèse did when she wasn't preparing the meals or bringing in the firewood and taking out the ashes. He sometimes heard footsteps in the rooms above and sounds that seemed like furniture being moved about. He supposed lots of cleaning had to be done. One morning when she came down the staircase, as he thought, to prepare lunch, he asked what she had been doing.

'Getting things ready.'

'Ready for what?'

'Ready for you,' she smiled. 'My sister says you are cluttering up the dining room. The salon is not for sleeping so you must move upstairs. You will be quite warm there. The chimney goes up through your bedroom.'

'And I will have my own brick?' he asked putting on the voice of a plaintive child.

'Naturally, but you must carry it up yourself.'

'I can carry all three. I am getting better and I feel much stronger. I want to do something to help.'

'We shall see.'

'If I don't do something soon I will get crazy. I think I could go outside now, perhaps help with the sheep or fetch the firewood.'

'First, I want you to sit down here, in this chair and I will take the sutures out from your head. It is time. The wound is clean and sound.'

'Has a week gone by?'

'Ten days. It was necessary to be sure.'

'Ten days?'

Lawless started adding up in his head: *ten days, add two more that meant, what was the date of the raid? Seventh, no, eighth of December, so today is . . .*

'It is my birthday in two days' time, the twenty second of December.'

Thérèse's face lit up with a smile. 'But that is very good! There must be a celebration. And after two more days it will be Christmas. Sit still, please.'

She leaned over him narrowing her eyes in concentration. She had a small pair of silver scissors with long slender blades in one hand. He felt her carefully parting his hair with the other and tensed, waiting for the first snip of the thread that might carry a sting of pain. She dropped her hands and stepped back.

'It is no good. It is too dark here for me to see properly. Go to the window where the light is better. I will bring the chair.'

He stood up and carried the chair across the room himself, thinking that it was the first time he had done something that might qualify as work, or help, since he found himself in this house. She stood over him again and started to work with the scissors, very slowly and carefully. He felt a snippet of thread being drawn from his scalp and winced. She felt his movement but did not stop. His face was very close to her breast. He had only to lower his head the smallest amount and he would touch it. He could see the individual stitches in the heavy woollen coat she wore and how the rows curved and swelled to the shape of her body. He could feel her warmth on his face and smell the scent coming from her: wood smoke blending with lavender and her own strange sweet musk.

She stepped back and looked at him. 'It is finished. You will have a soldier's scar.'

He looked up at her, saw the laughter lines at the sides of her mouth and how large and dark her eyes were and then at her hands holding the scissors and the snippets of dark thread and saw how roughened with work they were but how long and slender were her fingers.

'Thank you,' he said quietly. 'Were they your mother's scissors?'

She gave a little smile and nodded, then turned her face away from him.

***

Lawless bit into the wizened but surprisingly sweet apple he had been offered as dessert at lunch. 'Have you any books?' he said.

The sisters exchanged glances but stayed silent.

'Well, if you won't let me work, at least you can let me read. Have you any Proust or Gide?'

They stared at him.

' Balzac? No? Zola?'

'Oh yes, Zola,' said Séverine,' we have the letter of Zola. Our father kept it in a place of honour in his library.'

'The *letter*, you mean you have a copy of the newspaper, L'Aurore, was it not, with Zola's letter, "J'accuse" on the first page?'

'The same,' said Thérèse. 'Every year Papa made us listen while he read the names of the accused and learn the last words by heart.'

Lawless was astonished by the strong emotion in her voice. He had thought her gentle, docile even.

'Every year, twelfth July, every year,' said Séverine.

'Why twelfth July every year: what were the words?'

'On that day in 1906 Captain Dreyfus was found innocent and regained his place in the Army of France.'

'And the words, what were the words he made you learn?'

' "I have but one passion: to cast light, in the name of humanity which has suffered so much and is entitled to happiness."'

'Ladies,' said Lawless, 'why did your father do this?'

Séverine looked at him for a long time before she answered. She seemed surprised that he should ask such a thing.

'Because our father was a brave and honourable soldier. Some would say too brave because it cost him his career. But I would not say that.' She sat back, regarding him with what he took to be a faintly pitying look. 'I see you are finding difficulty in understanding. Very well: you asked if we have any books. I will give you one of my father's books and when you have read it you may understand why our father, and our family always have tried to live by those words, whatever the cost.'

Clutching his brick taken hot from the hearth and wrapped in a sheet under one arm Lawless followed the two sisters upstairs to be shown the room where he was to sleep. In the dim light of the lantern held by Séverine he could just make out several doors on each side of a wide corridor extending into darkness in both directions from the landing. Séverine held the lantern high, allowing him a glimpse of a high ceiling with ornate mouldings, striped wallpaper with moulded skirting boards at the base and a second staircase rising on a turn from the first. Lawless was only now beginning to get an idea of how big and solid the house was. Even though shadows half-filled it when they entered, he could see that his room was at least twenty feet square. Séverine placed the lantern on a round table by the side of a carved stone fireplace set in a chimneybreast that rose some twelve feet to the moulded ceiling. Thérèse lit thick yellow candles set in heavy brass candlesticks with rounded carrying handles on the mantelpiece. Long maroon curtains with thick white pull cords were drawn across a window in the wall to the right of the door. Opposite the door was a large bed covered with a tasselled white bedspread. To one side was a wardrobe with carved double doors and on the other a tallboy carved with the same rose pattern. All this furniture was of polished wood showing the burrs of walnut.

In front of the window was a washstand with bowl, pitcher and soap dish. The walls were papered in dark green with pale gold stripes.

Lawless looked slowly round the room, taken aback by its sombre richness.

'Whose is the portrait?' he asked pointing to the gilded frame on the wall above the bed. A tall man stood in front of a clump of trees. He wore knee britches and a long frogged jacket and carried a gun in the crook of his arm. At his feet were two shaggy-haired hunting dogs. He had a strong face with a long straight nose and looked confidently out at the viewers. His hair was drawn back from his head and tied in a pigtail.

'An ancestor,' said Séverine.

'A Chevalier?' asked Lawless.

'Of course. Do not stand there with the brick warming your arm. It is for the bed.' She walked across and rolled back the coverlet and sheets.

Thérèse said, 'There are some clothes for you in the wardrobe.'

'Yes, use them,' said Séverine, 'yours are in great need of washing, or throwing away though not, of course, your uniform. We will leave you now. Do not burn the candles too long. They are difficult to find these days.'

'Goodnight, ladies,' said Lawless, giving them a slight bow as they left the room taking the lantern with them.

The light was now too dim for him to see much detail but he still noticed a small book with scuffed leather covers on the table by the fireplace and took down one of the candlesticks for a better look. The title page inside was covered in antique print. With some difficulty he read the first few lines.

MEMOIRS
OF THE
Wars of the Cevennes,
UNDER
Col. Cavallier
In Defenfe of the
Proteftants Perfecuted in that *Country*

He decided to leave reading any further to the morning. He put on the thick fine wool nightshirt he found folded under the bolster and got into bed. Despite the brick he shivered for some time under the sheets before be began to feel drowsy. Only then did it dawn on him that the title of the book was in English.

***

Séverine and Thérèse had almost finished breakfast when Lawless came down the next morning with the book in his hand.

'I am sorry to be late, oh, and I have forgotten the brick.'

'No matter,' said Thérèse, 'later will be convenient. You slept well?'

'Like a log: the bed is very comfortable and the room,' he paused, seeking the right words, 'the room is fit for a prince.'

'No prince will ever sleep in that room!' exclaimed Séverine, glaring at him.

'I apologise,' said Lawless hastily. 'It is just an expression in my language. It was meant as a compliment. I am so grateful, er, and for the clothes, very good and, er, very warm, too,' he added weakly.

'Hm. You are a tall man but thin. Stand, please.'

Lawless got to his feet and stood awkwardly, feeling rather like a boy told to stand up in class by one of the masters.

'On you the suit hangs loosely. What do you think, sister?'

'Perhaps a little but it looks well with the colour of his hair.'

'And the shirt?'

'Perhaps not quite the correct size but it's the best one can do.'

It was time to stop their little game.

'Set me to work, ladies, and I will soon fill it out.'

Thérèse laughed and Séverine almost smiled, Lawless thought.

'Work? Can you lift a ewe yet?'

'Not a ewe, perhaps, but I can lift a coffee bowl and certainly some bread.'

There, she certainly smiled at that, for a second anyway. She actually poured the coffee for him herself, the first time she had deigned to do that, he noted. He took a sip of the scalding liquid, closed his eyes and raised his face towards the ceiling.

'Sublime,' he breathed. 'More delicious than the finest champagne.'

'Stop, enough,' said Séverine brusquely though her eyes actually shone, Lawless could see. 'We have work to do and so have you, Sergeant.'

'And what work is that, Mams'elle Chevalier?' he said, emphasising each syllable of her name.

She pointed to the book at his elbow.

'Ah, of course. I will read it during the day. It is a very old book, published in 1726, a real treasure. I think from the state of the leather it has been much handled, I mean, often read.'

They both nodded, without speaking.

'But not by you two ladies because it is written in English, is that not so?' Neither said anything so he went on. 'You told me that your family has always tried to live by beliefs that this book would help me understand but how do you know what it says when you cannot understand the words?'

'Our grandfather said this book contained truths that all should know about our history so he had a translation made for the family. When his time came our father used to read parts of it to his children. We were very young but I still remember him reading aloud. How his eyes flashed! Thérèse, you remember, don't you?'

'Papa I remember, but now not so many of the words.'

'Perhaps you can read them again,' said Lawless. 'Where is the translation? I should like to see it, if I may.'

'Alas, it is lost, like so many things,' said Séverine.

'Then I can make a new one. At last there is something I can do for you. It is my kind of work.'

'Your work is death, Sergeant.'

He opened his mouth to protest but found nothing to say. Her words were true. He had carried Death with him on the raid and Death had brought him back to this remote old house in this cold land. It had spared him, *why him*, when it had taken all the others? He stared at Séverine with troubled eyes. She saw his torment and although she could not pity she did understand. Such a boy: light-hearted one instant, in despair the next and not yet twenty years old until tomorrow.

'Read the book, Sergeant. It will help you understand.'

***

When Thérèse came in at noon to prepare the lunch she found Lawless sitting at the fireside, absorbed in the book. He watched as she put plates and beakers on the table and took bread from the box. The bulky winter clothes she wore could not hide how gracefully she moved. He could tell she was aware of his look but she paid him no attention.

'Someone, perhaps your father, has written his thoughts on some of the pages.'

'Would you please put more wood on the fire before my sister comes in?'

'On one page where the King is mentioned he has written a very offensive word, one that might have cost his life in those days.'

'Mama used to say that sometimes he could not contain his anger. Do you like walnuts?'

'He uses the same word against the name of the Pope, Clement the Eleventh. Yes, I do like walnuts.'

'Please crack them for me: use this hammer and the block of wood. What is the word?'

'I cannot repeat it to a lady but here it is, page two hundred and seventeen, if you would like to know.'

'You are mischievous, Sergeant. I know nothing about popes.'

'On page one hundred and seventy two, he has written the word "hélas!" against something the Queen of England promised to do but did not. I can show you.'

'You are too strong with the hammer. Do not crush the nuts in with the shells. Séverine will be displeased.'

'"Séverine": your sister is well named. Does she not like me?'

Before Thérèse could answer, the door opened and Séverine came in stamping the snow off her boots. That done she stood with her back to fire. And looked across at the others.

'Hm, warm for once; walnuts with cheese? Very good. We must have red wine, not cider.'

Although he had not quite finished reading through it, Lawless was keen to talk about the book, but Séverine would have none of it until everything was cleared away and they could sit for a few moments in the warmth of the fire while the dog ate her food before being allowed out again.

'Colonel Cavallier, who wrote this book, Mams'elle; the name is similar to yours. Was he of the family, an ancestor?'

'No one can be certain but it is unlikely because although a fine soldier he was a man of common birth, apprenticed at first to a baker.'

'So the portrait in the room where I am sleeping is not of this man?'

'Of course not. It is the grandfather of our grandfather, Colonel Gaspard Duchesne Chevalier.'

'There is a map, Mams'elle, here let me show you.' Lawless carefully unfolded the map, anxious not to crack the brittle paper. 'As it says here, this is "A Map of the *Lower*

Languedoc or the Cevennes". Colonel Cavallier says it describes the places mentioned in the book. I know of "Monpelier" and Nimes and Anduze but please show me where we are on this map.'

'We are not on this map. The house lies about here.' Séverine pointed off the western border of the map. 'Here you have Mende, there you have Anduze,' she said, pointing to the north and then to the east of her first indication. 'There are mistakes and many places are not on this map.'

'Then we are not in the Cevennes where Colonel Cavallier fought his wars. The Cevennes lies to the east.'

'No, no, we are in the Cevennes but here is the Causses.'

'Of course, of course, now I know: the Grands Causses. I forget the names.'

'We are here in the Causse Méjean; there to the north, is the Sauveterre and there to the south, the Causse Noir,' said Séverine, pointing roughly off the bottom edge of the map.

'So, the Colonel did not fight battles in these parts.'

'He did not but many of those who followed him came from the communes of the Causse Méjean because they had the same faith and craving for liberty.'

'As you said, Mams'elle, I begin to understand and I know now more or less where I am. You say we are not on this map but what is the name of your village?'

'Once there was a village but it is no more. It was destroyed. Only the house was strong enough to survive. It is La Commanderie. Do you know what that means?'

Lawless looked at her. Of course, it was all beginning to make sense: the proud manner, the portrait, the faded but handsome furnishings, the very name, Duschene *Chevalier*.

'It means that this house was once a command post, a fortress, of the Templars, after them of the Knights Hospitallers and somehow, after they were gone, it came into the possession of your family and, wait, yes, that is why your name is Chevalier.'

Séverine stood up and struggled into her heavy coat. 'The ewes will not wait,' she said. 'Caramelle, come.' She drew her shawl over her head and tied the ends under her neck. As she went out Lawless called after her that he would have finished the book before dinner but she showed no sign of hearing him.

Lawless turned to Thérèse. 'What I said, Mams'elle, it is true, isn't it?'

Thérèse piled the plates and dishes on a tray and walked towards the kitchen.

'It is true,' she said 'and do not worry, she likes you well enough.'

***

Séverine was in an unusually good humour at supper. She announced that it looked as if at least ten of the ewes were carrying more than one lamb and that all were free of worm. She complimented Thérèse on the food, a thick rich stew of vegetables, chestnuts and pieces of bacon seasoned with herbs and a dish of pears glazed with honey and baked in the oven. Even the weather had pleased her because the sun had shone all day. After the table had been cleared and they had all pulled chairs closer to the fire, she turned to Lawless and said,

'I will take one of your English cigarettes, Sergeant, if you have not smoked all of them.'

'With pleasure, Mams'elle,' he said, thinking she was full of surprises tonight and wondering what might be coming next. He watched fascinated as she drew deeply on the cigarette and lifting up her head, expertly blew a thin plume of smoke towards the ceiling.

'Well now, Sergeant, I am listening.'

'Is it possible that you like English cigarettes, Mams'elle?'

She dismissed that with a wave of the hand.

'The book, Sergeant, the book.'

'Ah yes, the book you cannot read but whose story you know very well because it is your story too. The King's Minister called Jean Cavallier—he was not Colonel then—an obstinate Huguenot. I think you are the same.'

'We are, and we are not. We are because we have kept the same belief, in liberty as Cavallier and we fight for what is ours, and we are not because unlike him we have no need of the religion.'

'You must know, Mams'elle, that it is only a matter of time before your liberty and your land will be taken from you. Already half of France is occupied.'

'Then we shall fight.'

'Chevallier would expect no less but his book tells you how hard the work will be.'

'We are accustomed to hard work, is that not so, Thérèse?'

'Mams'elle, you told me that my work was death. Yours will be the same as mine and that of Cavallier.'

Only the whispering of the flames rising from the burning logs broke the silence that followed Lawless's last words. But he was now asking himself, could he really have been talking like that, like some ham actor in a cheap melodrama? They would have laughed and jeered at him on the base and told him to apply for a job as a war correspondent. He felt a slight itch of embarrassment. The book wasn't written in that way. It was a soldier's straightforward narrative of the increasingly desperate struggle of people, 'Proteftants perfecuted' as the book described them, determined to maintain their freedom of belief against the overwhelming force of official repression, a struggle that ended in betrayal and defeat. Should he say to these two women that history was repeating itself, only this time France itself was showing the 'last dying efforts of a once brave and free nation' as Cavallier wrote at the beginning of his story? Of course not: they knew it well enough.

'Let me read you some of the things he did. I like this man. He was frightened of no one, not even the King; told him to his face that he could never change his religion and become a Catholic. Here it is, in Book Four.'

Lawless found the pages and read the passage, translating into French for them. From the distant look on Séverine's face he thought perhaps she was hearing echoes of her father's voice saying the same words, how long ago of course he did not know. He turned to another page and laughed.

'Look here on page two hundred and thirty six, he steals the Marshal's wine, that's Marshal Montrevel who never seemed to be able to catch him, and sends him a note saying he'll drink to the health of the Marshal's mistress. If you want to know about her, she's mentioned further back, carrying on an affair with the Marshal while her husband was in Paris. Now, this is something you should know: he tells us on page one hundred and fifty seven how the rebels got the name Camizars. It was because they had two shirts so that one could always be washed and clean to wear, although why, he doesn't say. The most men he ever had were about two thousand and the regiments hunting for him had ten times as many. They never had enough money or weapons and supplies and had to rely on stripping the enemy dead after a battle. Here, at the end of Book One he says how they made their own gunpowder and used lead taken from the windows of priests' houses to make bullets. They did have doctors to help, two surgeons who set up hospitals in some caves only the Camizars knew about. How they kept going for so long, I cannot understand. The country must have been devastated.'

'Mama said it was never the same afterwards. Many people could no longer find a living here and left France altogether,' said Thérèse in a low voice.

'We did not leave,' said Séverine. 'We were outcasts in our own land but we stayed and we rebuilt our lives and we waited.'

'For what, Mams'elle?' said Lawless, struck by her steely tone. 'What did you wait for?'

'For the tyranny to poison itself with its own vileness as all tyrannies must do. And in the time of our grandfather's father, it finally did and we won our liberty.'

And what has it done for you in the end, thought Lawless, all that suffering and courage and sacrifice, where has it got you? Two women slaving away in this desolate place, living on memories and looking forward to what?

'Shall I read you some more? There's the meeting with Marshal Villars whom the King sent to finish off the war. Cavallier goes through all the demands he made and which ones were agreed and which were refused.'

'No more now, Sergeant. The end is too sad. Cavallier was betrayed. They were all betrayed.'

'Some of his men thought Cavallier had betrayed them: it's here, page two hundred and eighty. Rolland, one of the other leaders . . .'

'Cavallier wanted the war to end. The people had suffered enough.'

'Did you know Cavallier fled France and went to England?'

'And you have come to France, Sergeant, and to the same place where Cavallier fought.'

'Two young men of the same age and tomorrow is the Sergeant's birthday,' said Thérèse.

The other two looked at her in surprise. She smiled back at them innocently. Lawless felt himself relax. Clearly there would be no more talk of suffering and betrayal tonight. Thérèse had seen to that. It was time to change the subject.

'Good Lord, so it is!' he said with somewhat forced enthusiasm. 'Perhaps we can play the piano, have a sing-song. I know some French songs.'

'I will make a cake,' said Thérèse, 'only a small one. There is not much sugar to spare. What else can we do to celebrate?'

'I can think of one thing,' said Séverine. 'It will be a good day for the Sergeant to go outside and show us how well he can shoot.'

What is she up to, Lawless wondered. And another thing, what was she driving at when she was going on about not leaving and staying and fighting for what is ours. Did she mean France or did she mean this place, La Commanderie?

Lawless had just put the warm brick into his bed and was taking another look at the portrait before preparing for bed when there was a knock on his door and Séverine stepped into the room.

'You are interested in my ancestor? '

Lawless nodded.

'He was killed by the English.'

Lawless blinked. Had she come in especially to tell him that? All he could stammer in response was 'Where?'

'In America, at the battle of Fort Duquesne in 1758.'

Lawless looked at her sharply. 'Wait, wait a moment. "Duquesne"; his name was, er . . .'

'Colonel Gaspard Duschene Chevalier.'

'"Duquesne", "Duchesne": they are the same.'

'Yes, but if you are thinking that the fort was named for him, you are mistaken. It was named for the Governor-General of New France whose name was Du Quesne.'

'Both of them Huguenots.'

'My ancestor, yes. Du Quesne, no: his father renounced the faith to keep his place in the King's navy. So my ancestor was killed no doubt by another Protestant while defending a fort named for the son of an apostate with the same name. It is a strange world, Sergeant, is it not?'

'Why are you telling me this, Mams'elle?'

'I think it is important that you should now know something of the history of our family.'

'I see. Thank you. What else do you think I should know?'

'There is much more but for now, only this. When you said La Commanderie was a command post, a fortress of the Hospitallers, you were right only in part. Yes, it was a possession of the Knights but more like a large farm on their estate, fortified of course, because of the dangers of those times, but a place where sheep were bred and crops grown, as they are now. The important place, La Commanderie for the whole estate where everything was decided was La Couvertoirade.'

'Where was that?'

'It is still there, the village of La Couvertoirade with its walls and towers still strong, fifty kilometres south of here in the Causse de Larzac.'

'I should like to see it one day and more of this house, if I am allowed. Am I right in thinking that your family has always been farmers?'

'Farmers and soldiers.'

'But how did this man, your ancestor, come to be a colonel in the King's army when he was a Huguenot, whereas his father had to change his faith to remain in the King's navy?'

'Different kings, different times, Sergeant: good soldiers were needed in America at that time whatever their faith.'

'I don't think I can be a very good soldier. Look at me, hiding away here when I should be trying to get back to England. I am disobeying orders. A good soldier does not do that.'

'All in good time, Sergeant. You are not ready for that journey yet. You speak the language but not as a Frenchman speaks it and with your hair and such blue eyes you certainly do not look like a Frenchman. If your plans are to succeed you must learn to be a Frenchman and the only way you will do that is to live like a Frenchman here, with us, until you are ready. My sister and I will help you.'

Lawless looked at her uncertainly at first but the more he thought about it, the more he could see the sense in what she was saying. It was worth a try. He would have plenty of time to think up explanations as to why it took so long for him to get back, if he got back. She was waiting for his reply.

'Mams'elle, of course you are right. I will do as you say but tell me, what can I do in return for all your help?'

'I do not find it easy to say this, but La Commanderie has need of a man and you told me you have worked with sheep. I will need to see how much you do know but there are other things that you can do for us as well once you are strong again.'

'What things? I can chop and carry wood and I am good with machines. There is the translation as well. I will need pen and paper for that.'

'All of those are helpful but if we are to make a French farmer of you there is much more to do: lambing when the time comes, and sowing and planting, shepherd's work and haymaking. Can you handle a scythe?'

'Wait, did you say haymaking? In England we do that in the summer. That's a long time off.'

'In the Causses we make hay several times during the year. It depends upon the rain. Sergeant, be patient: it will take time to turn you into a good enough Frenchman to convince anyone who might be suspicious of a man who turns up in their village asking the way. Now, it is late and we all must sleep. Think about what I have said. It is the best way. We do not want anyone else to know who you really are unless they need to know, now do we? Goodnight and sleep well; remember tomorrow will be a busy day.'

He was still trying to sort through all the implications of what she had said when he realised she had opened the door.

'Ah, yes, yes, of course, goodnight Mams'elle, Séverine, I . . .'

He heard her say something as the door closed behind her. He thought it was his name, Philippe. Perhaps Thérèse had been outside and she was speaking to her.

DASHING WHITE SERGEANT

Thérèse watched him standing at the table, tilting up his face and sniffing.

'I used only coffee today,' she said, 'for your birthday. Happy birthday, Philippe,' she added shyly.

'In the morning it is the best perfume in the world. Thank you, Mams'elle.'

Without thinking what he was doing he leaned over and kissed her lightly on both cheeks.

'Thank you, Mams'elle, I mean, Thérèse; like your other name you are an angel.'

At the same moment the door was flung open and in stamped Séverine followed closely by Caramelle.

'What's going on here?'

Lawless strode over to her, seized her hands in his and gave her the same peck on each cheek.

'Politeness, Mams'elle, politeness, French style, that is all. It is my birthday so I am allowed to embrace all the ladies. If I am to become a Frenchman, I must act like one.'

'You are an imbecile,' she said, but she was smiling as she spoke.

'Fools are happy, Mams'elle. Shall we dance?'

He lowered his hands to her waist and twirled her round twice, singing Happy Birthday to Me, Happy Birthday to me as they spun. Caramelle scampered across and capered around them, barking.

'Stop, stop!' she cried. 'You're making me giddy. Down, Caramelle! This is mad; we'll all end on the floor!' Her eyes were shining now, he saw.

'No, no, the smell of coffee has driven me mad! We must all dance on my birthday. Thérèse, join in, come on.'

He held out his hand and she came across and linked hands with him on one side and Séverine on the other.

'Now, we go this way, diddle um tum tiddle iddle um tum tum, now turn and go the other way, lift your knees up high, diddle um tum teedle eedle um tee tum; now we all weave round each other in a line like this, and then we polka, Thérèse you and me first . . . lovely, lovely . . . and now Séverine, how graceful, Mams'elle . . . and now you two together and then we start all over again in a line, up and down, diddle um tum tiddle iddle um tum tum . . . and you can shriek hee oy! Any time you like. Now again, let's get it right this time.'

He drove them until they begged to stop and bent over panting and laughing at the same time, again and again. Caramelle went from one to the other licking their perspiring faces.

'Caramelle, now you: up we go, diddle um tum tiddle idle . . .' Caramelle squirmed to get away and hide in a corner.

'It's called The Dashing White Sergeant and that's what I am today.'

'It is true then.'

'What's that?'

'You English are all mad. It's only seven o'clock in the morning and here you are making us dance about like maniacs.'

'We are all mad and we are proud of it!'

'My head is spinning,' moaned Séverine. 'I must sit down. Hm, is that real coffee? And what's this, apricot jam?'

'Real coffee and apricot jam, yes. It's Philippe's birthday!'

'Oh, so it's "Philippe" now is it? Very well, Happy Birthday, Sergeant Philippe.' She raised her coffee bowl in a mock toast.

'Philippe, only Philippe, please, Thérèse. I hereby renounce my rank of Sergeant in His Majesty's Royal Air Force until, until . . .'

He saw their faces on him, not smiling now, knowing what he was about to say.

'. . . until Caramelle tells me to take it up again, how's that?'

'Or until you do something wrong and have to be told,' said Séverine.

'That is only fair.'

'Well, then, Sergeant, you should know that in this part of France we exchange three kisses on the cheek, not two.'

'I am crushed with shame at my lack of correct manners. Allow me to put matters right.'

'Ah no. You must wait. You must be punished for your mistake. After we have the cake, perhaps, this evening, we may allow it.'

'Then I will truly have my cake and eat it. How do you say that in French? Isn't it something about having the butter?'

'And keeping the money that paid for it,' said Séverine.

'And the smile of the girl who made it,' added Thérèse. 'Don't forget that.'

Everyone spread apricot jam on their slices of bread and dipped them in their coffee. Lawless chewed away happily and drained his bowl. He stood up.

' I'm going to show you another one. It's called the Gay Gordons. Now, this is how you do it.'

'No more now, please. We are going out in a few minutes. Save your strength for walking.'

'It's much better with music. The piano, of course, may we use the piano? I will teach Thérèse the music and we will take turns to play while the other two dance. It will make you so warm you won't need the hot bricks afterwards, I can tell you.'

'Listen to me. Put this coat on and these boots. They should be big enough. Don't forget the gloves and the hat. It's cold outside.'

'Where are we going?'

'Hunting. Near the place where we found you, if it's not too far for you.'

My Webley, thought Lawless, *perhaps I can find my Webley.*

'It's my birthday, ladies; I am ready to go anywhere.'

***

His eyes had grown accustomed to the dimmer light in the house and the bright sun and sparkling snow dazzled him at first. He pulled the brim of the soft felt hat over his brow and squinted. The cold air seared his throat and made his cheeks smart but it was fresh and clean and gave him a new feeling of freedom and excitement. He had never seen the place from the outside before and everything about it was big, the high dark stone walls with their shuttered windows on all sides of a vast square courtyard, space enough for a parade ground, but not today with its heaped-up ridges of grubby snow, shovelled aside to make paths across to the round-arched doorways of outbuildings. The doors and windows of the living quarters faced south and these walls were bathed in sunlight. In the centre of the wing opposite was a wide arched gateway through which he could see snow-covered fields outside. Lawless turned away from the brightness and looked up. Rising two stories higher than the rest of the roofline was a square stone tower with a battlemented top and narrow lancet windows, a lookout and refuge if ever he had seen one. Séverine had been right; this place was fortified, sure enough. He breathed in deeply and caught the smell of a farm, stone, water, manure, the musky scent of animals; outside were fields, hills and snow and at his feet was a shaggy sheepdog with its pink tongue hanging out. He felt almost at home.

The two sisters were wearing sheepskin coats, knee-length leather boots and shawls wrapped over their heads. Séverine had a shotgun slung on her shoulder and a cartridge belt around her waist. Thérèse carried a large canvas game bag with its strap across her breast.

'We have about five hours to catch our dinner,' announced Séverine. Are you two ready?'

'By the left, quick march,' Lawless barked.

It was hardly quick and certainly not a march. For one thing the snow surface was very slippery and it took him time to realise that the only way to cope was to stamp his boots through the crust like the women were doing. That required quite an effort and it was not long before he knew he was not as fit as he had thought but after a while he found some rhythm and managed not to fall too far behind. He could now see that the house stood on the broad level top of a long ridge that from the sun's position he judged to be running roughly north-west—south-east, giving it a clear view in all directions. Before him the ground sloped gently downwards towards a line of distant woods and beyond as far as he could see other similar ridges were aligned like great waves spreading over a wide ocean. Here and there, the slope of the ridges was broken by rocky scarps and isolated pillars of contorted pale stone that projected above the surface of the snow, looking like ruined towers and monuments. He stamped on after the two figures ahead of him, following in their footsteps as they traversed the slope back and forwards as it descended towards flatter ground that led towards the dark line of the woods. The women were standing near an outcrop of rock where the slope levelled out when he caught up with them. They were speaking in low voices.

'It was near here that I shot the hare the other day,' said Thérèse.

'It was a doe so there may be a drove of them,' said Séverine. 'Send Caramelle out. Come,' she said to Lawless, 'follow the dog and be very quiet.'

The lower ground had more outcrops and rock pillars and clumps of bushes and trees that interrupted their view and the dog had long ago disappeared in its hunt, though her tracks were clear in the softer snow. The three humans plodded on following Caramelle's trail with Séverine in the lead and Lawless fetching up the rear. Séverine kept crouching behind outcrops when she could not easily see ahead to take a careful look before going on and Lawless was beginning to think the slow hunt would last all day when she suddenly held up her hand and beckoned them to close up and kneel down beside her.

'Over there,' she whispered, pointing to the right, 'Caramelle lying down. Over there,' pointing left, 'two partridge together under the tree, twenty metres. Philippe, take the gun. Cartridge: take it. Get up very slowly, gun first.'

All seemed good. With his height he could level the gun over the outcrop from a kneeling position. He had them in his sights, two plump red-legged birds idly scratching at the ground under a tree where the ground was free of snow. Sitting target: one shot should easily get both. His slowly squeezed the trigger. Click. Nothing happened. Damn, safety catch! He pressed it to off. It was very stiff. The birds must have heard the noise because they took off, clumsily whirring in opposite directions. He stood up and fired when they were forty metres away and higher than the tree. One seemed to lurch but kept going, the other got clean away.

Séverine scrambled to her feet. She was furious. 'Shit! Missed! At that range! We won't see another all day. You fly up there and throw your bombs out anywhere and you have no idea who you kill and when you're given a gun to do something useful, you can't even remember how to use it! Shit! Now what do we do?'

Lawless was surprised with himself. In the face of this incensed outburst he felt completely calm and moreover, he wasn't going to stand for it.

'Listen, no, listen to me. Never shout at a man carrying a gun. You don't know what he might do. I know I hit one of them, the one that went over there. If you'd only calm down and take a look you'd see that the dog's already gone to search for it. Come on, let's see if she's found anything. Don't just stand there swearing, it's undignified. Come on; I'm asking nicely.' He walked off in the direction he had pointed, still carrying the gun.

Séverine stood open-mouthed. No one ever spoke to her like that. She looked at Thérèse and began to say something but her sister merely shrugged and walked off following Lawless. Séverine watched them go. Her heart was thumping wildly. It was stupid: why had she shouted and sworn like that? What was it about this boy that had made her behave in such a way? If it had been anyone else she'd have given them a withering look and taken the gun off of them. She took a deep breath and the icy air in her lungs seemed to help her calm down. 'Calm down': that was what he had said. She laughed out loud. Obey orders: after all he was the Sergeant. She set off to find out whether he was right.

She caught up with them among some trees just as Lawless was taking the partridge out of Caramelle's mouth. He saw her coming and held it out towards her. There was a smile on his face, not triumphant, she noticed, only pleased—like Fabrice when he'd done something right.

'I should have told you,' he said. 'I just couldn't bring myself to shoot a sitting bird.'

There was nothing to say to that. She gave him a wry smile and a very French toss of the head. Not that it mattered, but he took it to be some sort of apology.

'Where is Thérèse?'

He looked round. 'She was here a minute ago. Listen. Is that her calling?'

'Come on. She's found something.'

Thérèse was standing on the other side of the clump of trees, looking down at the snow. Caramelle bounded towards her and began running about excitedly, sniffing at the ground.

'What do you think?'

Séverine looked carefully at the marks in the snow. 'Sangliers, two or three, maybe more.' She turned to Lawless.

'Yes, I know,' he said, 'wild boar. We don't have them in England.'

'We are in luck,' said Séverine. 'These tracks are very new.'

'Over there,' said Thérèse, pointing. 'I think Caramelle's found their droppings.'

The dog was sniffing at a pile of black glistening sausages about two inches long in a little hollow in the snow.

'A big one,' said Sèverine, 'and they've been digging around here, look.' She pointed to churned-up patches in the snow where soil and stones had been gouged out and scattered over the surface.

'How do they manage that,' said Lawless, ' with the ground frozen solid?'

'Under deep snow it's not so hard and they have very hard snouts and big tusks,' said Thérèse.

Sèverine was crouching beside the pile of droppings. She had taken off a glove and was poking at them with her finger.

'Cold but soft,' she said, 'not frozen. They can't be far away. This is our chance. We must find them. Caramelle! Seek! Good dog, seek!'

'Aren't they dangerous?'

'Not when we have a soldier with us especially one who can hit a flying bird, eh? Here take these: you need the heavier shot for sangliers. We must go. Follow the dog's tracks. She'll make a special noise if she spots them.'

Lawless saw the glint in her eye and caught the controlled excitement in her voice. Thérèse looked very calm. He began to feel twinges of the guilty fascination of the hunt, a bit like that first raid he went on, part dread part cruel intent. He slipped a cartridge into the breech of the gun and set the safety catch. The two sisters set off as hard as they could go, following where the dog had gone. Lawless was soon lagging behind. He saw them disappear into another clump of trees but as he got closer they came running out again and dashed towards him waving frantically for him to stay where he was. He heard the dog giving high-pitched yelping barks and lifted the gun to the ready.

'She's found them,' panted Séverine. 'She'll try to drive them out here but they could turn and go anywhere. So be ready.'

'Where are you going?'

'Over there; Thérèse has gone to the other side. If they see us, they'll turn back this way because the dog will be behind them. Can you hear her?'

He nodded. Caramelle's barks were getting more and more excited.

'They're coming closer. I'd better be off. When you hear one of us start to yell, get ready because they'll be coming out and very quickly. And don't forget the safety catch this time.'

He watched as the two women took up their positions on the edges of the wood and waited for the yelling to start. Silence fell. What was happening? He quickly broke the gun open and checked the cartridge, snapped it shut and shifted the safety catch off and on again. He was ready. Nothing happened. Had they all somehow crept away and escaped? Why had the dog stopped barking? His nerves began to tingle.

Everything came at once: crashing noises from inside the wood, the women starting to shout, the screaming yelps of the dog and a mass of stocky grey-black shapes rushing out of the trees and heading towards him, scattering as they ran. He levelled the gun at the leading shape and fired when it was thirty yards away. The boar was thrown to one side with the impact of the slugs and slithered to rest in front of him, splattering the snow with its blood. The others hurtled past on either side, oblivious of him in their panic to escape. No, not all of them! He heard shrieks from where Séverine had been and whirled round to see her running after Caramelle in the direction of Thérèse who was scrambling towards the shelter of the trees with one of the largest of the boars following her. Slipping and floundering Lawless ran as fast as he could towards them at the same time fumbling in his pocket for cartridges. He had to stop to load the gun when he was about forty yards away. It was a long snatched shot but the boar was nearly on her, not caring about the yelps of the dog or the screaming woman. He was lucky: he had an angle on the shoulder. He fired and hit it in the middle of its massive neck. Perhaps the impact added to the boar's onward rush because it kept going and cannoned into the back of Thérèse sending her sprawling. Lawless saw the animal trying to get to its feet and ran up swinging the gun by the barrel like a club to beat it off as Caramelle snarled and savaged its rear. There was no need. The boar was lifeless when he got there and Thérèse tottered to her feet wiping the slush from her face. He dropped the gun and clasped his arms round her and felt her trembling with shock. Séverine came up and he pulled her into the embrace and all three stood panting with their heads down as Caramelle slunk round them whining and licking at their legs.

When his heart stopped racing, Lawless lifted his head and stood up straight. He looked into their upturned faces.

'Is it always like that?' he said.

Séverine bent down and seized the big boar's bristly ears, trying to lift the head.

'They have both bled out; that's lucky. Your aim was good. This one must be eighty kilos, the other one nearer fifty: that's enough meat for us until the Spring. The problem is . . .'

'Don't forget the partridge,' said Lawless.

'. . . The problem is,' went on Séverine, 'how do we get them back to the house? I know what you're going to say.'

'The sled,' said Thérèse.

'Of course; we must go for it now. Philippe, stay here with the gun. Here are the rest of the cartridges. Do not waste any.'

'I can help, he said. Why should I stay here while you do all the work?'

'Because you are still not strong enough for all the walking and pulling and in any case someone must protect our kill and for that you need the gun. There are hungry foxes in these parts.'

'What about the other boars, the ones that ran away? Won't they be a danger to you?'

'They were all young ones, too timid. They will not come near us again. Now, no more talking: it will soon be midday and if we are to get all this and you back before dark, we must go now.'

'I suppose you will ride the sled down those slopes,' said Lawless. 'I really would like that.'

'You are impossible! Come on, sister, before he makes any more jokes.'

Caramelle seemed in a quandary. She followed the women for a few paces, then turned back towards Lawless and stood, shifting on her paws, looking up at him.

'Don't apologise,' he said to her. 'Off you go; you know who the boss is.'

'How long before you're back?' he called after them.

'Two hours, at least: be patient.'

Well, he couldn't stand around here that long, getting cold. He decided to drag the big boar up to the place where the first one was. That would help warm him up a bit. It was no easy job dragging nearly two hundredweight of dead pig through the snow but he finally managed it and sat down on the body to rest. It was still warm. This one didn't have tusks; the smaller one did. That meant he'd shot one female and one male. Were they mother and son? He hoped not. He looked down at the two animals he had killed. He ran his hand along the rough spiky backs and fingered the gristly snouts. A few minutes ago they'd been rushing about scared, angry perhaps, but alive. He tried but he couldn't stop the bad thoughts coming. Was it like that down there when people heard the siren and ran for shelter and then the bombs came down, the bombs his plane had carried, and ended their lives, and their children's lives, leaving their bodies lying bleeding in the snow? He felt cold again and stood up stamping his feet. Look, he needn't do any more of that, not for a while anyway. These women wanted him to stay here and why shouldn't he, for a bit, until things were better? It would be a help for them. After all, they'd saved his life, hadn't they? He owed them something for that. Maybe the war would be over by then? It would never end. There was nothing but bad news. Stop it. Get up. Do something, anything, to stop the bad thoughts.

He shouldered the gun and started off along a rough path which went through the trees where the wild boars had been hiding. On the other side of the wood the ground continued sloping down towards the line of trees he had seen from a long way further back. It was much closer now. He wondered if there was a river down there and thought he might just have time for a look before the sisters came back with their sled. It shouldn't take long, not long enough for any foxes to turn up and take a few mouthfuls of his pigs; not that he'd begrudge them a bite or two. He grinned to himself: after all, no decent chap could shoot a fox, could he? He set off again.

It was like remembering, or rather half-remembering, things from a bad dream. He'd had this picture in his mind of a cave he crawled into but no, there it was, a snow-covered stone hut with walls only three feet high and a rickety roof of thick stone slabs. There was a low doorway with a lintel above but no door. There had been fresh snow falls but he could see where the older layers had been trampled on and churned up. Those were the marks he had made as he pulled himself inside and wrapped the parachute round himself. He struggled to remember: the women had looked in, or was it the dog first? He shuddered at the memory of the picture of the white ghostly face in the doorway, but that had been Séverine's face, hadn't it? And he had pointed the Webley at her. His Webley! It must still be in there. He crawled in through the low entrance and scrabbled around in the mess of old leaves and dried grass and dirt that covered the floor until his fingers felt the ice-cold metal of the barrel. It gave him immense relief: somehow it made him feel safe. He backed out of the hut and stood up. He broke open the revolver and counted the rounds in the cylinder: six, all there and dry as a bone. He had an almost irresistible urge to fire a shot in the air, to celebrate, to let them know he had a real weapon, not just some old shotgun. Wait: a real weapon? Thérèse had said she had found a machine gun. That was his gun, too. Where was it? He slipped the Webley into one of his coat's deep pockets and started searching, kicking into drifts and lifting up fallen branches: all to no avail, the snow had buried everything. He would have to come again and bring Thérèse with him to show him where she had seen it. He suddenly felt cold again. He ought to be getting back to the place where he had left the dead boars. The women might be there already. Just one more thing: all these deep furrows now almost filled with snow, this had to be where the Whitley came down. Where was it now? He kicked another drift and his toe hit something hard. Frantically he dug into the snow and felt metal, sheet metal. He swept the snow aside with his hands and found a jagged plate of steel and under it something softer. Oh God, please don't let it be what I think it is. Looking the other way he reached further in, gripped the softness and pulled. It was an unopened parachute. He wiped the snow from the charred cover. The owner's name scrawled in indelible ink was just visible: JB Verrill. He got to his feet and staggered away from the nightmare, broke into a stumbling run and never stopped until he reached the remembered clump of trees where the women had just arrived with the sled.

'Where have you been?' said Séverine. 'What's happened? You look as if you've seen a ghost.'

'I . . . I . . .' he stammered. 'I—I went for a walk. I'm so glad to see you. I thought I was lost.'

'Well, it looks as if you've found your way back so you can give a hand loading the sled, the bigger one first.'

One Christmastime when he was a little boy long before the war he'd been allowed for the first time to go out with his father and uncle and the other men to haul the big ash log back to the farmhouse where it was to burn in the open fireplace on Christmas Day. He told his mother proudly how much he'd helped and showed her how red his hands were from tugging on the rope. In fact, the men had soon lifted him onto the log and let him ride. He remembered waving a stick and telling them to Gee-Up.

While they were resting half way up one of the slopes he told the women about it. Were those tears in her eyes, or was it the cold, when Thérèse said what a lovely memory to have.

'You started early,' said Séverine, 'and you were the load again, the last time we used this sled.'

By the time they reached the house Lawless felt he was on his last legs but there was one more job to do before they could get back into the warmth of the kitchen. The sled had to be dragged across the courtyard into one of the stables where the boars were to be stored overnight. Thérèse put a match to a lantern that was hanging from a beam. When he saw the row of big hook eyes in one of the cross beams Lawless knew what was coming. Without a word he took the four smaller hooks tied to ropes that Séverine brought from a bench and pushed the sharp ends through the skin behind the thick Achilles tendons of each boar. He climbed onto a trestle and shoved the other end of the ropes through hook eyes in the beam. With him hauling on one rope and the two women on the other, each boar was lifted well clear of the floor.

'Another thing I learned on my uncle's farm,' he said when all was done and they were locking the door of the stable. 'We're not all that different, are we?'

'In some ways, no,' said Séverine, 'in others . . .' She left the words hanging.

'There was some talk of cake, I think,' said Lawless brightly once they were in the kitchen. 'I'm sure we have like minds about that.'

'Make up the fire,' said Thérèse. 'Supper will not be long. The cake will be for dessert, so you must wait a little longer.'

'Roasted partridge?' said Lawless hopefully.

'Not tonight: it has to hang for a few days.'

'I can hardly wait. When that's gone will it be roasted boar every day until the Spring?'

'Not at all; the butcher will give us other things for some of it and Madame Janquet makes very good charcuterie, hams and dry sausages'

'Where are these people? You've not mentioned them before. Are they neighbours?'

'The butcher is Jean-Pierre Bec and Madame Janquet is the wife of Jérôme Janquet who is owner of the café in St Chely la Bastide,' said Séverine.

'A café? Wonderful! I would love to go to a café for coffee or an aperitif, smoke a Gauloise. When can we go?'

'We think it best if no one knows about you, for the present. For some people in the commune an English flier is an enemy who should be handed over to the gendarmerie.'

Thérèse nodded. 'You are safer here, with us, Philippe,' she said.

'My sister is right. You remember what I told you the other night: that you will have to become a Frenchman in the way you look, and talk and walk and dress? If you can do that, then the people might accept you. It would help if word gets round that you are working for us. What do you think, sister?

'His hair: it's so fair. That would give him away.'

'Hm, he's very pale as well but plenty of work outside should darken his cheeks and he mustn't shave, only clip his beard short. Perhaps we could dye his hair.'

'He has blue eyes as well. Wait a minute: if anybody asks, why don't we say he's from the North and escaped? Fabrice once told me there were two fair-haired men from near Amiens in his battery. I think he said the corporal even called them *les Anglais.*'

'Coming from there, they probably had English fathers as well, if I know anything about soldiers.'

'And it would explain his accent. He ought not to talk exactly like a Cévenol, should he?'

'Thérèse! Sister, what a mind you have: full of deception! He must do as you say.'

'Excuse me, I am here,' said Lawless. 'Can I have a word?'

He had the feeling they were faintly surprised to find him standing behind them.

'Philippe, of course, yes?'

'I'm not sure whether I'm like one of your sheep being prepared for a show or being given a part in a Feydeau farce.'

That brought puzzled looks from both of them.

'You know: a farce? Where everyone pretends to be some one else and nothing is what it seems? No? Oh well, it doesn't matter.'

'Philippe, this is no farce. We are thinking of ways to make sure you are not arrested,' said Séverine in what Lawless now recognised as her reproving voice.

'Sorry, sorry, please carry on, I'm listening.'

She turned back to Thérèse. 'Now, as I was saying . . .'

Lawless put up his hand. 'Can I just say one other thing? Yes? Well, looking and dressing and talking and all that, like a Frenchman won't be enough, will it?'

Again, the puzzled looks came over their faces. 'Explain,' said Séverine sharply.

'You know the most distinctive thing about a Frenchman? Smell. You can't mistake it. It's the Gauloises. I shall need Gauloises now that we've smoked all my cigarettes.'

This time the looks he received were the pitying kind.

'If you really want to be helpful, bring some more firewood from the stable. There's a wheelbarrow inside the door. And don't bring any damp stuff. Lantern! Don't forget the lantern.'

When Lawless had gone out Thérèse started peeling potatoes.

'What are you making?'

'I tried to think of something special for his birthday but we don't have very much that's ready so it's going to be salt fish with beans and potatoes. The beans have been steeping in water all night. You can drain them for me.'

'Sounds all right. He'll be hungry enough to eat anything after today.'

'You were rather hard on him out there.'

'He needs to grow up, don't you think?'

'He did give you a very grown-up answer when you blew up at him and don't forget we've got a partridge and two wild boars because of him. We've never had such good hunting as that.'

'Well, there you are then. It worked, didn't it?'

Thérèse put down the knife and turned to look at Séverine.

'He is only twenty, a lot younger than Fabrice when he left for the Front. Have you forgotten that? And he has already been on twenty something bombing raids when he could have been killed on any one, and he's a long way from home. I like him and I know you do, never mind how you treat him sometimes. He's funny and he wants to play the piano with me, and you want him to stay, to help us out you say, and I like that but if he is going to stay we have to make him feel like one of the family. There isn't any one else.'

Her words came out in a rush and she finished rather breathless, her cheeks flushed. Séverine took her by the hands and kissed her lightly on both cheeks.

'My dear sister, that is exactly what I want him to be, one of the family.'

Thérèse stared at her uncomprehendingly. 'I didn't say that.'

'I know. I did: one *of* the family. What better way is there of making him stay?'

'I don't understand. How could he be one *of* the family? He's already said he'll stay for a time but you know he feels he must try to get back to England.'

'And we will help him do that as best we can but first he must do for us what we have done for him.'

'What do you mean by that?'

'We saved his life: we both heard him say that. In return he must save ours, save the life of this family.'

'I am completely confused. How can he "save the life of this family", as you put it?'

'Thérèse, think! Look at us! We are two unmarried women who will soon be old maids. Where are the men we might have married? Jacques Letreille, Maurice Duchamp, Louis perhaps; I'm sorry, I didn't mean to upset you. Come here. Thérèse, they're all gone, you know that. There's no one left. The family ends with us. Do you want that to happen? Do you want La Commanderie to end up as an empty ruin after all it's meant to all of us and all our ancestors? It doesn't have to come to that. Lawless can prevent it.'

'How?'

'By marrying you.'

'My God! Let me go! What are you saying?'

'Sister, your own words: there isn't anyone else.'

'You know I didn't mean it that way!'

'I know you didn't but if you think about it it's still true.'

'I won't listen to you. You twist everything I say.'

'Tressie, listen, please. You're right; I do like him. Do you think I would be talking like this if I didn't? But he's more like you. I've seen you together and you come alive when he talks to you. I can't remember the last time you played your piano but when he said he could play, your eyes lit up and I could see you wanted to play with him and, remember, he wants to teach you some dance music.'

'I know, that would be nice, but . . .'

'Shh! I think he's coming back. We'll talk again another time. I have to take one last look at the ewes and lock up. How long will supper be?'

'An hour; don't be too long or it will spoil.'

'We'll have a glass of *vin doux* as a toast and some more with your cake; what do you think?'

'Is there any left?'

'Must be a few half-bottles somewhere in the cellar. I'll take a look.'

As Lawless came in with a big basket of logs, he almost collided with Séverine in the doorway.

'Talk to Thérèse,' she hissed to him as she went out. 'Ask her if she needs any help.'

He put the log basket by the fireplace and asked Thérèse if he could do anything. Without looking at him, she shook her head.

'Clear sky tonight,' he said. 'There's a full moon.'

She was pouring water into a pan for the beans and seemed not to have heard.

'"Bomber's moon", some idiots used to call it; ground crew, civilians, not us.'

She walked past him to put the pan on the fire next to the one already there without saying anything.

'Bomber's moon: bright enough for you to see all your way to the target. Bright enough to let every night fighter and flak gunner see you all the way there and back as well.'

She only glanced at him on her way back to the table.

There was a bomber's moon that time when they were over Bremen and Harper's Whitley was hit. It was only a hundred feet away and the starboard engine caught fire and then the wing tank. In a few seconds the entire wing was ablaze and the glare seemed to light up the whole sky around them. Forbes, the flight engineer, was shouting on the intercom, *Christ, we're lit up like a fucking Christmas tree! Blow up you bugger, you're done for anyway, go down or they'll get us all!* He hated himself because he had been thinking the same.

'Philippe, what's wrong?'

She was looking at him in alarm. He shook his head. Had he said those things out loud?

'Nothing, nothing; I'm all right. I was wondering about you. You were so quiet. Is it something I've done?'

'No, no, my mind was on something else, then you started talking but I could hardly hear you. What was it about?'

'Oh, something; it doesn't matter now. Take no notice. Can I help?'

'Bring the big pan, the one we hang over the fire.'

'Hm, looks like fish. Is it?'

'Salt fish; we always keep some. It doesn't go bad.'

'Nothing would go bad if you kept it outside in this sort of weather. Is it always as cold as this in the winter?'

'It's colder this year than the last but we can have sun and some quite warm days in January and the spring and summer are lovely, hot and dry. Too dry sometimes.'

'I've been thinking about the boars. I know what you have to do next. I've seen it done many times at my uncle's farm. Have you any really sharp big knives?'

'You will have to ask Séverine.'

'Séverine seems to decide most things, doesn't she?' he said, smiling.

Thérèse was about to retort that she had persuaded Séverine that he should be brought here, but thought better of it and simply shook her head and looked away.

'Not always. You can help me drain the beans and the potatoes.'

Clouds of steam rose up as boiling water poured into the sink. Lawless looked down at her. She felt his gaze and turned her head away. He bent down and spoke softly.

'It was you, wasn't it? You found me in that hut and went to get Séverine to help you drag me up here. You were the one who saved me. I can tell.'

'Bring them over to the table. They have to dry before I put them in the hot oil. No, we both did it.'

'But you found me.'

'Caramelle found you! I saw her pulling at your parachute and went to look.'

The dog lifted up her head at the sound of her name. Lawless looked down and made her an elaborate bow.

'Caramelle, I owe you my life. You must dine with me tonight.'

Thérèse could not help laughing. He was impossible. How could he be so clownish one moment and so tormented the next?

'Philippe, spread the embers; the fire must not be too hot for this.'

He watched as she poured oil into the big pan and hung it from the hook under the mantle stone. She added sliced onions, followed by garlic and told him to keep an eye on the pan and stir it to prevent burning while she cut the parboiled potatoes into thick slices.

'Smells good,' he said.

'Let me see. Good, now I put in the fish. There. We cook this quickly and when it starts to brown we put in the beans and then the potatoes and some thyme. It won't be long now. You can sit there and watch it. What are you looking at?'

'You. The firelight makes your face glow gold.'

Thierry had once said that to her, only then it had been the sunlight on her face.

The door opened and Séverine came in with a bottle in her hand.

'Why are you two staring at each other? I could smell cooking from across the courtyard. Is it ready? I'm starving. Here's the *vin doux* and this one is *rosé*, for the fish. Now where are those glasses?'

Where was he on his last birthday? It was too long ago to remember, twenty-two raids ago, that long. What a way to remember dates: by the raid he'd been on. Think. Thirsk: The Cross Keys, that was it. Sherwood and Verrill and Forbes were there. Sanderson joined the crew later; that was after Metcalfe bought it two nights later when the night fighter caught them heading home from Stuttgart. Verrill sometimes swapped places with Metcalfe in the front turret. He said it was good for his eyes to stare out into the darkness instead of down at maps and tables in bad light. The truth was he liked to fire the Browning at something. He had his chance that night and Lawless heard him shouting he'd scared the night fighter off and he'd opened up himself by reflex when he heard Verrill firing again but the night fighter must have got in a burst because Metcalfe had his chest blown open by a twenty millimetre. Poor bugger: should have stayed where he was. They'd gone to the Cross Keys in Sherwood's car. Who would get that, now that Sherwood didn't need it any more? Metcalfe hadn't gone with them to Thirsk; said he didn't drink but wished him happy birthday all the same.

'Philippe, happy birthday.'

Happy birthday? God, he was so pissed that time. They'd put whisky in his beer when he wasn't looking, the sods. What a hangover he'd had! He was still being sick when they took off the next night to drop leaflets somewhere, he couldn't remember where. What a happy birthday that was.

'Philippe, Philippe! Happy birthday!'

They were holding up little glasses full of pale brown wine and clinking the one that somehow had been put in his hand. He clinked their glasses and smiled at their bright faces. 'Joyous', the French said: it was more than just 'happy.'

'Do you like it?' asked Séverine.

'What? Oh, the wine, the *vin doux*. Yes, it reminds me, it reminds me, God, not Metcalfe, reminds me of sherry, but sweeter, nicer.'

'Sherry? We never drink sherry.'

'I'm sorry, of course you don't. This is much better. It must be very special. Thank you. You are very kind.'

'How does it feel to be twenty?'

'Hungry.'

***

Lawless felt spoiled and he liked the feeling. His stomach was full of delicious fish and apple cake and in his hand was a second glass of *vin doux*. The fire was warm and the dog was sleeping across his feet. He felt like staying as he was forever. He felt like dozing off.

The sound of a piano roused him. He was alone in front of the fire which had burned low. He pushed the sleepy dog off his feet and stood up to put another log on the embers and listened intently. The music seemed to be coming from the other side of a door to one side of the staircase that he had never noticed before. Pushing it open he found himself at the end of a long silent corridor lit by a single candle in a brass holder on the wall. A faint streak of light shone at the bottom of a door opposite. As he opened the door the music started again inside the room.

Thérèse was seated at a parlour grand piano in the centre of the room with her back to him. A tall candelabra with three candles cast light on the keyboard. She was playing a piece that he knew, a work his mother played when she was in a certain mood. Séverine sat in the shadows in a high-backed wooden chair, listening. She lifted her finger in a sign that he should stay silent. Beginning slowly and simply then moving into a quicker more nervous passage, the piece ended as it had begun, with delicate, wistful notes. Lawless waited for the echoes to die away then clapped softly. Thérèse turned on the piano stool and frowned at him.

'I play so badly. The piano is out of tune.'

'A Bechstein! You have a Bechstein.'

'It was Papa's wedding present to Mama. This is her music.'

'May I see? Hah, Fauré D flat nocturne. I thought so. My mother played this sometimes. She said the first few bars were like a walk in the moonlight.'

'Play for us.'

'I can't sight-read well enough. I would need to practise for a long time and then I wouldn't be as good as you. I've only seen a Bechstein once before, in the College chapel, but only the Organ Scholars were allowed to play it.'

'Your French is very good,' said Séverine. 'To know the word for sight-read is very good. What are these Organ Scholars and this College chapel you talk about?'

'Oxford. That was my world and French was my work. Until I changed it, of course.'

'You changed it?'

'You told me my work was death, Séverine.'

'You can change again and become a farmer, here.'

'And play a Bechstein again,' said Thérèse. 'Play something you know for us. Sit down.'

'You'll regret it,' said Lawless sitting down and feeling the keys. 'I'm so out of practice. The only things I've been playing are silly songs in pubs.'

'What is he talking about now, this man? Do you know, my sister?'

Lawless ran his hands up and down the keyboard in a sequence of chords, started the opening bars of the Moonlight Sonata and began to make mistakes, shifted to some Bach and lost the fingering and stopped.

'God, that's awful. I'm so out of practice.' He started to get up.

'No, no, go on,' cried Thérèse. 'Play an English song.'

His mind went blank. He could play 'Run rabbit, run rabbit' like he did in the Cross Keys with the crew bawling the words and banging their glasses on the piano top but that would sound stupid here after the Fauré; same for 'Blue birds over the white cliffs of Dover'. Think. For some reason his mind went back to school: what about this one?

The two sisters listened to the slow rather yearning little melody and at the end clapped enthusiastically.

'Do you know the words?'

He nodded and played again singing both verses of the old song, seeing so clearly in his mind the music room at school and the class of boys with their song sheets.

'It sounds beautiful but sad, I think,' said Thérèse. 'What does it say?

'It's a love song by an English poet. I don't know who composed the music. It's called "Drink to me only with thine eyes". It won't sound so good in French because I won't be able to make it rhyme.'

It sounded dreadfully dull and halting to him and he couldn't remember the French for 'wreath' and 'withered'.

'I told you it wouldn't sound so good. If I had more time I could do better.'

'It sounded beautiful when you sang. You have a good voice. And now I think we know what it means.'

'Tell me if I'm wrong,' said Séverine, 'but it sounds as if he lives in hope yet I wonder if his love is being returned.'

'There is often some uncertainty about that,' said Thérèse as if to no one in particular, although Séverine cast her questioning glance.

'How about something more cheerful? I said I would teach you another dance.'

'Please, It's too late.'

'Just this one. It's very lively. It will rouse us up and then we can all go to our beds warm and happy. Now, the tune goes like this. It's called the Gay Gordons,' he shouted above the music. 'Now, one more time, try to remember, and then I'll show you how we dance it.'

'No, no no, not me; dance with Thérèse.'

'All right. Now, Thérèse, we stand side by side, I put my arm behind your back, like this, and hold your right hand up. Yes, like that. Now we step forward, come on, one, two, three, four, don't turn: we go backwards, keep hold of my hand, one, two, three, four, very good. Now forwards again, and back again, and stop: I lift your hand high and you turn and turn as we step about. Very good and now we dance, polka steps. Whee! Away we go.'

Thérèse was a natural dancer and soon caught the rhythm and the step sequence. They pranced up and down the room several more times while Lawless de-dummed the simple lively tune.

'Now, Séverine, I insist, you join us and we dance in a line. No, no, you must. You've seen what to do. It's a Scottish dance. The French and the Scots have always been allies. Never mind, you'll soon learn. Right, me in the middle, you on either side, arms behind backs, yes, like that. Ready? De dum de diddle de dum de dum . . . Séverine! You're very good!'

He would go on all night unless something stopped him, she thought. And so would Thérèse, by the look of her: eyes shining, lips parted in excitement, laughing in pure delight as she spun beneath his raised hand. How could they keep on like that at the end of such a day? She had been reluctant to join in at first but the gaiety of the tune and the insistent step of the dance were so infectious that she could not resist and soon she was dancing as wildly as the others and laughing just as uncontrollably when they missed a step or fluffed a turn.

At one point he had slipped away from them to sit at the piano and pound out the music while she and Thérèse took up the dance together and he called the steps and emitted sharp high-pitched yells during the twirling. But now she knew she had had enough. She could not stagger another step and fell back into one of the big high-backed chairs by the fireplace. She watched the others as they began the polka and saw Lawless slow the step, change it, draw Thérèse closer and begin a slow waltz. She had always envied Thérèse her lightness and sureness when she danced. This boy was tall. Were all tall men good dancers? Papa was tall, and he danced so proudly with Mama. The boy looked absurdly young and, was it the light, or did Thérèse really look like a girl tonight? Such young faces, some in her memory, others in the room tonight.

'Séverine?'

She looked up.

'Thérèse is going to play. Shall we dance now?'

Tiredness could wait. Everything else could wait. For a little while she would be young again.

'I have had a wonderful birthday,' said Lawless. 'Two weeks ago we had never met. You have been so kind.'

'I am sorry we had no birthday present for you,' said Thérèse.

'Well, there was something you promised me this morning.'

'What was that?'

He kissed her lightly on the cheek.

'That; thank you. Now, Mams'elle, may I snatch the same gift from you.'

'No: a birthday present must be given, not taken,' said Séverine, and reaching up kissed him instead. 'I am very tired. Would you please bring up the bricks for us?'

'He's a very good dancer, don't you think?' said Thérèse when Lawless was downstairs.

'Have you changed your mind?'

'Changed? You mean . . .?'

'He plays very well, too. You could play duets.'

'I'll . . .'

'You'll think about it, I know. Tressie, you loved it tonight, didn't you?'

'I think you did too.'

'Of course I did, but you, for you it was different. I could tell.'

'I don't know . . .'

'He's coming back. Oh, in the morning early I am going into St Chely to see Bec and Madame Janquet about the boars. I want Bec to take them away tomorrow. Ah, thank you, Philippe. How warm they are. Goodnight you two.'

ST. CHELY LA BASTIDE

'Good morning, Mademoiselle Chevalier; how can I help you?'

'You can send Jeannot with the cart to La Commanderie this morning, Jean-Pierre. I have two fine boars for you. They are hanging in the stable. Both are bled out. I hope you are well, Jean-Pierre, Madame Bec. Now I must hurry and see Madame Janquet about the charcuterie. Oh yes, I need a shoulder of mutton for Christmas. Jeannot can bring it with him. I expect the usual terms for the boars, Jean-Pierre. Goodbye to you.' Séverine threw these last few words over her shoulder as she left the butcher's shop.

'Never changes, does she?' said Jean-Pierre Bec to his wife. He shook his head. 'I don't know how they keep that place going. Jeannot!' he called, and a boy of about fourteen poked his head round the door. 'Get the cart ready to go up to Mams'elle Chevalier's. There's a couple of boars to bring down. Go on, then! You haven't got all day. She'll be back here expecting a lift soon enough. Never changes: didn't even tell me how much they weighed.'

The café in St Chely la Bastide could have been mistaken by a stranger for the front parlour of the owner's house except for the split chestnut-fronted bar with the zinc top that Jérôme Janquet had made himself and sited opposite the door so that he could see all that moved into, out of, or past his observation post. Coffee was brought on demand from the kitchen where Madame Janquet seemed to spend most of her time. Behind the bar were crates of beer in clip-top bottles and on the zinc counter that was continually wiped by Jérôme Janquet stood litre bottles of red and white *vin de pays*, and *Pastis*. The lower of two shelves on the wall behind the bar held glasses and the upper a collection of dusty flasks of various liqueurs and digestifs and a sole bottle of *Gaston de Lagrange* cognac. The furniture consisted of a couple of low tables used mainly by card players, a sofa and matching armchairs covered in cracked and sagging leather and two or three wooden stools. The constant presence of tobacco smoke had rendered the walls and ceiling a uniform mellow brown colour. The Café de la Place had an air of warm and dingy comfort that held little appeal for Séverine Chevalier but it was the centre of the village and the place where things could be found out and other things could be arranged, if the questions were asked in the right way and by the right people, because Jérôme Janquet was also the mayor of the commune of St Chely la Bastide. He came forward to greet Séverine and shook her by the hand. He was a solid-looking man in his late-forties, with short black hair, deep-set eyes and a habitually serious expression. He walked with a pronounced limp but was never seen to carry a stick.

'Good morning, Mademoiselle Chevalier. This is a pleasure. How are you, and your sister, Mademoiselle Thérèse?'

'We are well, thank you, Jérôme.'

'And what brings you here on such a cold day, may I ask, Mademoiselle? The road from La Commanderie cannot be easy with all the snow we've had.'

'Bec is butchering two boars we shot yesterday. I should like Madame Janquet to prepare her excellent charcuterie for me, perhaps more ham than last time. Bec will let her know when the meat is ready.'

'Of course, Mademoiselle Chevalier, I will tell my wife your requirements immediately. Two boars, you say.'

'One of them eighty kilos and the other fifty.'

'Very welcome these days, Mademoiselle. So reassuring to have such a supply at hand for the rest of the winter.'

'Madame Janquet will, of course, reserve an adequate portion of the meat for her own purposes, as usual.'

'That is most kind, Mademoiselle Chevalier. I had no idea you were so skilled with a hunting rifle. Did you have far to carry them? The snow: for two ladies like yourself and Mademoiselle Thérèse, moving such a weight cannot have been easy.'

'If you have a sled and know how and where to pull, it can be done.'

'Of course; nevertheless, I admire the feat. Would you care for something, something warming, perhaps, dare I say, in celebration?'

'Why, thank you, Jérôme. I think I have a moment. As it happens, Mr Mayor, there is another matter I should like to mention to you. Coffee would be welcome.'

Jérôme Janquet had not missed the use of his official title. The fleeting wariness of his look was quickly replaced by a professional smile.

'I will have my wife prepare a fresh pot.' He waved his arm indicating the absence of anyone else in the café. 'Shall we speak about the matter here?'

As soon as the jug of coffee was placed on the table before her Séverine could tell from the scent that it was real. Jérôme Janquet filled the single cup and she sipped it gratefully. She made a mental note to bring up the subject of coffee when next she spoke with Madame Janquet who, apart from her preparation of charcuterie, also kept the only small grocery shop in the village. Jérôme Janquet waited patiently for her to reveal what she had come to say. He knew a great deal about the family Chevalier and its history and had a certain admiration for both. He was a Communist and respected protest when it was directed against the correct targets. One of these targets was the present government of Unoccupied France and another logically was anything German. For some time now the feeling had been growing in him that Séverine Chevalier was of a like mind. This feeling was based on nothing she had said on the few occasions when they met but rather on the depth of exasperation she showed when he had observed her reading yet another new restriction or requirement that the administration imposed as announced in the frequent ordinances that had to be displayed on the notice board at the Mairie. If his feeling proved to be well founded, certain other conversations might follow. Her first words told him that she would take some time in coming to the point. He smiled encouragingly but was on his guard.

'Jérôme,' she said quietly, 'you have a radio and we do not. What is the latest news?'

Uncharacteristically, he decided to take a risk.

'Better than for some time, Mademoiselle Chevalier: the Red Army has driven the Germans back from Moscow.'

'When was this?'

'It was announced on the fifth of December. And, Mademoiselle, two days later the Japanese attacked the American Fleet and America has entered the War.'

'Can you be sure of this?'

He took another, more serious risk.

'When I can, I listen to the English radio broadcasts. So, I am sure.'

She re-filled her cup and stared into it as if searching for something. When at last she looked up he could see from her expression that she had come to some sort of a decision.

'You know what this means, Jérôme?'

'Yes, Mademoiselle Chevalier; it means that Germany has lost the War.'

'And where does that leave France which has, whose so-called Government has, made a despicable pact with the enemy?'

He now thought he knew where this woman stood on this dangerous ground. It was worth taking one more risk to be sure.

'With a chance, Mademoiselle Chevalier, with a faint but real chance: if we go about things intelligently.'

She drank her coffee.

'That is always the best way, Mr Mayor.'

That subject was now closed for the time being, he saw. He waited patiently for what was coming next.

'Mr Mayor, what I am going to tell you is not to be made known to anyone else until the right time comes. Have I your assurance on that?'

Given what had just passed between them Jérôme Janquet had no alternative. He nodded.

'My sister is thinking of getting married.'

It was the last thing he would have expected her to say and hoped his astonishment did not show. He coughed, making excuses while he collected his thoughts and switched on an interested smile.

'The person, the man, concerned is not from these parts.'

'There is a procedure. Papers of identification are needed. It takes a little time, not necessarily long.'

'I am aware of that. They are available. When you see them you will realise they are not of the usual kind but I am sure you will decide that they are valid. I cannot say any more at the present except that there is some connection with the matters we were discussing earlier.'

'I see. I shall, of course, act as the law requires but be assured I will do whatever I can to meet your wishes, and Mademoiselle Thérèse's too, of course. May I say that it is happy news?'

'You may. I think we understand each other, Jérôme, do we not? Thank you for the excellent coffee. My regards to Madame Janquet and now I must leave. Jeannot Bec will be waiting to take me back to La Commanderie.'

'Goodbye, Mademoiselle Chevalier. I will wait to hear from you. Oh, before you go, does Mademoiselle Thérèse have a date in mind? I only ask because notice of a marriage has to be made known not less than ten days before the planned date and there is also a residence requirement of forty days.'

'Not as yet: you understand it takes time to get everything arranged properly. You will be the first to know once it has been decided. Goodbye, Jérôme, Mr Mayor.' She might have added, *we will have much more to talk about, you and I,* but of course that went without saying.

On the cold and bumpy ride back to La Commanderie Séverine had plenty of time to think over what had been said between herself and Jérôme Janquet and what had been implied but left unspoken. She had no misgivings about the commitments she had made. It was necessary that the two were made together. Now they had to be fulfilled. She watched the mule treading its way carefully through the snow-covered ruts and remembered the time when La Commanderie had had its own teams of horses and the men to work them. People said mules were stubborn. She preferred to think of them simply as determined.

***

'Where's Séverine this morning? Is she sleeping in after our late night and all that dancing?'

'She's gone to St Chely about the boars,' said Thérèse, pouring the coffee. She was up long before us.'

'What's this about the boars?'

'The butcher in St Chely will cut them up for us in return for some of the meat.'

'I could have done that. I've seen it done many times on my uncle's farm.'

'It's the butcher's job. He has all the right equipment. It's the way things are done here. Everyone helps everyone else.'

'It's something I could have done to help.'

'You might be needed to load them on the mule cart if it's Jeannot who comes for them.' As soon as the words were out of her mouth, Thérèse wished she hadn't said them.

'Jeannot?'

'Jeannot Bec. He's the butcher's son. He's only fourteen.'

'I'll give him a hand. Is there anything else I can do this morning? What about chopping some wood? I'd like to get on with the translation this afternoon. I've got to an interesting bit, where they attack the Abbot's house at Pont de Montvert, page thirty four or five, I think. They all had a hand in killing him but some of them were caught and hanged later. That's really when the uprising became serious.'

'There's one thing you could do: clear out the ash. I hate doing that. The fine stuff gets up my nose.'

'But Thérèse, you sneeze so prettily.'

'You're impossible. Do as you're told.'

'I am a good soldier: I always do as I'm told. But sometimes I do what I want.'

'You talk too much. There's the shovel. Don't make a mess.'

'I'll do it and I'll chop as much wood as you want but I want something in return.'

Without warning, her heart gave a little jolt. 'And what is that?'

'To play duets before supper, or afterwards if you prefer.'

'Oh. What would you like to play?'

'Let's see what music you have.'

'I haven't time to look now. With Séverine in St Chely I have to see to the ewes as well as make the lunch.'

'I'll get rid of the ash. I've seen the heap where it goes. Then I'll come and help you. Just show me what to do.'

He dipped the last piece of bread in his coffee, sucked and swallowed it and noisily drained the bowl. Thérèse watched him in amusement. It all looked so natural, so familiar. He was starting to act like a Frenchman and a Cévenol at that.

Lawless stood in the doorway watching Thérèse as she bent over one of the ewes, examining its hooves. She had left off her usual head shawl and her long hair was hanging down, veiling her face and spreading over the ewe's head, its dark glossiness vivid against the cream-coloured fleece. His eyes were drawn to the curve of her hips where her skirt stretched tight He felt his breathing quicken. She must have sensed he was behind her and twisted round to look up at him, tossing her hair back as she did so. It was as if someone else had taken over his body and made it step towards her. The ewe she was holding struggled free and burrowed into the rest of the flock. As one, they stared in Lawless's direction and then began to back away and jostle each other in alarm. Thérèse got to her feet, took him by the arm and pulled him out of the pen with her.

'You frightened them. They're not used to you yet. Wait a few minutes and we'll separate one or two and start again. You have to talk to them so that they get used to you and your voice.'

'I'm sorry. I don't know what I was doing.'

'It doesn't matter. They're beginning to quieten down. I was in too much of a hurry. We should have given them some hay first. Here, you take some but go slowly. And talk: you have a nice soft voice.'

Women do things differently, he thought. He remembered the farm in Westmorland. The men were careful not to harm the sheep but not over-gentle with them. As for talking to them: he'd have been laughed at. It seemed to work with these, however. He got the same blank stare from fifty pairs of eyes when he started but they quite soon became less nervous and allowed him to move among them stroking their backs. Perhaps it was the tufts of hay he held out; it seemed more likely than the words of 'Mary had a little lamb' he was chanting softly over an over again, in French he suddenly realised.

'What are you singing?'

'Oh, that: it's a nursery rhyme,' he said, feeling rather foolish.

'It seems to have worked. We can see to them now. Come over here. I'll show you with this one what we do.'

Thérèse bent over the ewe and lifted a foreleg so that he could see the hoof.

'You see? Clean and dry. Now, you look at the other hooves.'

'I've done this before,' he said, checking the other three hooves in turn. 'We usually hold them like this.' He straddled the ewe, facing to its rear and repeated his examination of the hooves.

'Try doing that in a skirt,' she laughed. 'Now, tail, ears, eyes.'

With two of them going through the flock, the work was quickly done. At the end of it he was wondering if her back was aching like his. He leaned backwards, arching his back, then bent forwards, dangling his arms to the floor.

'You're stiff,' she said. 'Here, I'll rub your back. Do this every morning and you'll soon get used to it.'

'I'll happily do it if you promise to do that.'

'You're impossible. There, is that better?'

'Not yet, please carry on.'

'I don't believe you. Take that pitchfork and bring some fresh straw.'

He had to climb a ladder to reach the bales of straw stacked on a platform above the pen.

'Not too much,' she called. 'It has to last the winter.'

He lifted two sizeable sheaves with the pitchfork and threw them down. There was a shriek from below. Looking over the edge of the platform he saw she was covered in straw. He began to laugh as she clawed the stalks from her hair and glared furiously up at him.

'Thérèse, I'm sorry, I'm sorry! Let me help.' He scrambled down the ladder and went across to her.

'Get away! Imbecile! Why don't you look?'

'I am looking. It's very funny. No, don't. Careful with that pitchfork! Look here, here, take this bundle and throw it over me. No? Well, I will. Look. We're the same: both of us covered in straw. We ought to be laughing at each other.' He took hold of her hands. 'Come on, laugh.'

She was still furious but her eyes were beginning to sparkle. He reached down and gently pulled two or three stalks of straw from her hair. She shook her head and most of the rest fell away.

'There now,' he said. 'Almost all gone. What you need is a brush for the rest.' He pretended to look about. 'There must be one lying around here somewhere.'

She burst out laughing and pummelled his chest with her fists.

'You're really impossible! I don't believe you have ever worked in a farm.'

'I tell you I have, my uncle's farm, in Westmorland.'

'Vestmorland? What country is that?'

'Not *V*estmorland. Come here. Push your lips out like this as if you were saying OO, then say OO-EH stmorland. Now close your eyes and you do it.'

She looked suspiciously at him for a moment then did as he said. He bent down and pressed his lips to hers. She opened her eyes and looked up into his, paused, and slowly drew away.

'I can hear a cart coming,' she said. 'It must be Séverine and Jeannot. Stay here. I'll go out to talk to them. It's best if he doesn't see you.'

The cart rolled through the archway and came to a stop in the courtyard. Séverine climbed down, clutching a bulky canvas bag. Jeannot Bec jumped down after her and stood holding the mule's head. He was a wiry boy with an expressionless face and mop of black hair. Thérèse took Séverine to one side.

'Philippe is in with the ewes.'

Séverine thought for a moment. 'I'll tell Jeannot to draw the cart up to the stable and then go with you into the house. Give him some bread and cheese to eat. While he's having that Philippe and I can load the boars into the cart. Make sure he doesn't look out of the window. How did you get all that straw on you?'

'Don't look at me like that. It's not what you think.'

Eighty kilos, Lawless was thinking, that's a decent weight for a man. He took the front end of the bigger boar, where most of the weight was and heaved it upright to get his arms round the chest. They could only just span it. Séverine seized the back legs and together they staggered outside to the cart.

'It's stiffened up,' he gasped.

'Easier—to lift—like—that,' she wheezed.

He managed to shove the boar's head onto the edge of the cart and stoop with his shoulders under the massive chest to heave it upwards as Séverine lifted the legs. The half-rigid black mass rolled onto its side, one small eye fixed sightlessly on the sky. Eighty kilos, twelve and a half stone: he'd weighed about that at his first medical. At his last, two days before the raid in fact, the doc told him he'd lost over a stone in two months and he ought to eat more. Both of them knew it wasn't for lack of eating. Still breathing hard, he looked at Séverine.

'Do the other one now? Before it gets dark?'

He got a wry smile for that and followed her into the stable. The second one was easier: fifty kilos, near a hundredweight: a lot of meat altogether. The smaller boar joined the other on the cart, all four of its legs sticking rigidly upwards.

'Wait in the stable until the boy's gone,' she said. 'He won't be too long.'

'He's bound to wonder how you managed to get two boars onto the cart all by yourself.'

'We thought of that. Thérèse will be out any minute. She will have told him she's coming to help me.'

'Even so, two women lifting a weight like that: it takes some believing.'

'Seeing is believing and we don't want anyone to see you yet. How did you get that straw all over you? Don't tell me you covered yourself with it.'

'It's not what you think, I . . .'

'She's coming: stay in the stable out of sight. He may look out of the window.'

***

Dinner that night was onion soup, peppery and thick with soaked bread and grated cheese heaped on top. While they were eating the baked apples that followed, Séverine said she had important news.

'Jérôme Janquet told me that the Russians have beaten the German army in front of Moscow.'

Lawless looked up startled and bit his lip. 'How stupid of me! I knew that! We heard it on the BBC a day or so before we took off on our last raid. It must have gone clean out of my head after we crashed and I was unconscious.'

'So it is true. Jérôme Janquet said he had heard it on the English radio himself.'

'Yes, yes, it must be true, but,' Lawless looked at the two women, 'don't forget, the Germans are so strong. They will try again. Can the Russians stop them a second time?'

'So, you don't know the other news as well?'

Lawless and Thérèse spoke at the same time. 'What other news?'

'The Americans have joined the War.'

'The Americans? Against Germany? Why? When?'

'Jérôme Janquet says it was two days after the Russian victory. He heard the news on your same BBC. The Japanese attacked the American ships and the Americans declared war against Japan.'

'Two days after, you say? When was that?'

'The seventh of December.'

'My God, that happened and I never knew! I was flying in the raid on Turin.'

'What does it all mean?' Thérèse was bewildered, frightened even, not knowing what to think.

Lawless put up his hand to interrupt her and almost shouted at Séverine.

'Have the Americans joined in against Germany?'

'Jérôme Janquet did not know but he said it means that the Germans have now lost the War.'

'We must find out. Why did he not say?'

'I think because his radio does not always work. Perhaps the bad weather or something else stops it. I don't know but he did seem very certain and I believe he is right.'

'What about us?' said Thérèse. 'Will the Americans fight us now, like the English?'

'The English are not fighting against France.'

'They did at Mers el Kebir,' said Séverine.

'That was Vichy.'

'We are in Vichy. Have you forgotten?'

'What I mean is, oh, I don't know what I mean. This news changes all sorts of things. I must think what I ought to do.'

'Philippe, listen. I will tell you what you should do: for yourself, for us and for the War. You remember how we talked about you turning yourself into a Frenchman as your best way of avoiding being captured? Yes? You have to stick to that. You've made a start: Thérèse has been telling me, and I can see for myself but there are many more things you have to learn and it will take time, so it's important that you stay here so that we can help you. And I will be honest with you: it will help us. I've seen how you go about things and Thérèse has too: she's told me how well you handled the sheep. Think of the other things you've done here. There's Cavallier's book that you're translating for us. You must not give that up. Isn't it like being a student again? And the dances you've taught us, and the piano: Thérèse is playing again because of you. How long is it, just over two weeks since we found you? And here you are sitting at our table, looking as if you really belong here. Oh, I forgot: you said something about Gauloises. Well, I bought some in St Chely this morning. Have one, here you are, and look like a real Frenchman.' She handed over the blue packet and laughed.

Lawless took the proffered packet and pressed it thoughtfully, staring at the trademark winged helmet sign. She certainly had a way of putting things. She hadn't said it but if it hadn't been for these two, he would be dead now. When they'd first talked about him learning to be a Frenchman it was a bit of a joke but the more you thought about it, it did make a lot of sense. He tried to picture himself in heavy boots, rough trousers and thick jacket with a fisherman's cap on his head and a Gauloise stuck in the corner of his mouth and grinned at the thought. He had to admit he did like being here. It was warm, Thérèse was a good cook and he could get back to the things he liked: books and music. He was even beginning to get on with Séverine. She was a tough one but there was something about her. He remembered how she livened up in the dancing and what a real woman's body she had. And Thérèse had too. She'd looked quite beautiful when she turned her face up to him while she was handling the ewe. And there was that kiss. Verrill would have called this a very cushy number. Why not make the most of it? After all, it was one way of living a bit longer. He took a Gauloise from the packet and lit it with his lighter. He'd forgotten how strong they were. It made him cough.

'Hm, you'll have to get used to them before you try the café in St Chely,' said Séverine shaking her finger at him in mock reproof.

He smiled at her, squasheded the cigarette between his fingers and drew on it again. It was easier this time and looked more French. A thought struck him, a guilty thought. Staying here, not trying to escape: wasn't that like being a deserter? Wait: hadn't she talked about doing something for the War? What did she mean by that?

'If I stayed here, helping on the farm and doing what you say, how would that be helping with the War? I'm a gunner. I ought to be up there with another crew.'

'I was coming to that. Can I have one of those?'

He held out the packet of Gauloises and snapped his lighter for the cigarette that she drew out. Thérèse shook her head when he offered her the packet. Séverine leaned back in her chair and eyed him speculatively through the haze of blue smoke she exhaled. He got the impression that she was trying to decide whether to reveal something important, or not.

'When we came back with the sled for the boars, you said you'd been for a walk. Where did you go? Were you looking for something?'

'I don't know. I can't really remember.'

'I think you can. We told you about the machine gun that Thérèse found. I think you were looking for that. I remember your gloves were soaking. I think you had been searching for it in the snow.'

He shifted in his chair, looked down and shrugged his shoulders. 'All right, yes, I was searching. I came across the hut where you must have found me and I started to remember things. The snow was all hummocky. I could tell the ground must have been all furrowed and churned up and then covered again by more snow so I knew, I just *knew* that was where my plane must have come down. But I didn't find the gun. I found something else that proved I was right. I found, I found Verrill's parachute. It had his name on it, so I know it was . . . I know it was his . . . I know. Jack Verrill, he was one of my crew . . . he was, I . . . you would have liked him. I couldn't find him, only his fucking parachute, that's all, not a sign of him.'

He stopped and tried to wipe the tears from his eyes with one hand while the Gauloise smouldered between the fingers of the other. Thérèse watched his face tighten with the strained, haunted look she had come to know. She took the cigarette from his fingers and put her hand over his.

'Philippe.'

'Leave him. Philippe! Listen to me. Give him his cigarette back, Thérèse. Philippe, take it.'

Lawless looked at her blankly, then down at the cigarette between his fingers.

'Smoke it. Like me. Do it!'

Séverine blew smoke into his face. Mechanically he raised the Gauloise to his lips and drew on it deeply, then exhaled the smoke in a long sigh.

'This Verrill, did he smoke?'

'Jack Verrill? Yes, like a chimney.' His voice was coming back. He gave a short laugh. 'He wouldn't have liked these, though.'

'Too strong for him, eh? Not like you. Was he a gunner?'

'Navigator. Sometimes nose gunner.'

'Nose gunner? What does that mean?'

'At the front, where you can see most.'

'Was he the one who dropped the bombs, not you?'

'We *all* dropped the bombs, don't you understand? We were the crew. I have to find the others.'

'We will find them, Philippe. That is what I was going to tell you. Jérôme Janquet is the mayor of this commune. He is a Communist which will get him into trouble one day because it means he is an enemy of our authorities, our so-called Government that has betrayed France and abolished our liberty. Did you know that? Liberty, Equality, Brotherhood, won through the loss of so much blood in the Revolution, all have been thrown away and we are now instructed by the Marshal, Pétain,' she spat out the name, 'that we have Work, Family and Fatherland instead. We have been sent back to the time of Jean Cavallier. Everything won by him and since his time has been stolen from us. I will not have it. Jérôme Janquet will not have it. There are some others, not many yet, who may think like us. This was one of the things that I was talking about with him this morning. He knows about you. I said something about you but not what you are. When he does know, he will treat you as an ally and will help you to escape, you can be sure of that.'

Lawless was silent. She spoke with such quiet intensity about things he had never really thought about very much. The War for him was simple: he just obeyed orders, got in a plane that was flown by somebody else, to a target decided on by somebody he never met, kept watch for night fighters, fired his guns when needed, watched where the bombs fell, came back to base, if he was lucky, slept, woke up and did the same the next night, or the night after that. He never thought about Liberty or Equality as applying to him and being so important. They were just there. Now he was beginning to see how much it really meant for these people here, in a France that was beginning to go the German way. Now the mayor knew about him. Could he be trusted, as Séverine seemed to be saying? There was so much to take in.

'How can I be sure?' Lawless said, warily.

'Because you will help him in what he has decided he must do.'

'I will? How?'

'You are a soldier so you know about weapons. In time we will need them and not only that, but how to use them. That is how you will help.'

'I have no weapons, no, wait a minute, you're thinking about the machine gun, aren't you? My God, you're serious. You're thinking about a rebellion, an armed rebellion: just like Cavallier.'

She looked back at him straight-faced and slowly nodded her head. 'Exactly. We must be prepared for it to come to that.'

Lawless turned to Thérèse. She looked as shocked and surprised as he was feeling.

'Did you know about this?'

She shook her head and said nothing.

'But Tressie knows where we can look for the gun, don't you, Tressie?'

'Séverine, listen. You don't know what you're talking about. This is an air-cooled point three oh three belt-fed Browning machine gun made for use in a Nash and Thomson four-gun powered turret in a bomber. It's not the kind of gun you can carry around and set up to fire on the ground. In any case, where could you get the ammunition?'

'There is a blacksmith, Henri Vabrette, with his forge at Castignac. It's in the same commune not far from St Chely. He can make anything you want in metal and you said you were good with machinery. You could make it work.'

'Even if I could, you haven't any ammunition. A Browning uses a lot, about a thousand rounds a minute.'

'Your bomber must have been full of bullets. If you promise to work on the gun and let Jérôme Janquet have it, I promise you he will search for your bomber and the bullets.'

She leaned towards him and gripped his hand tightly.

'And, Philippe, we will search for your friends at the same time. It will have to be when most of the snow has gone, you understand, but we will look until we find them. Caramelle will help.'

What could he say? She was so determined even if she had no idea of what she was asking to be done. But there was no way round it: he couldn't find the others without their help and he could never forgive himself if he didn't at least try. It was a crazy idea but there was nothing for it but to accept.

'You are absolutely mad, you know.'

'Only the English are mad,' she smiled, knowing he had given in. 'But you are right, I am mad: mad with shame for what has been done to us by other Frenchmen.'

'What else were you talking to Jérôme Janquet about?' said Thérèse.

'Oh, it will keep until tomorrow,' said Séverine. She yawned and rubbed her eyes. 'I'm tired. It's been a long day. I'm going to bed. Don't stay up too late, you two. It's Christmas Eve tomorrow. I can taste that shoulder of mutton already. Goodnight.'

'I'll have to learn how to play La Marseillaise and sing a few verses.'

'Then be very careful, my friend, because the Marshal has selected the parts that may still be sung and if you sing any of the other verses you will end up in gaol. Goodnight.'

Thérèse and Lawless sat looking at each other across the table listening to creak of the stairs as Séverine made her way up to bed.

'How long has she been thinking about this?'

'I don't know, Philippe. She doesn't tell me everything. Perhaps since we had the news that Fabrice was not coming back, or when the Armistice was announced, I don't know.'

'Fabrice?'

'My, our, youngest brother.'

'What happened?'

'All we know is that his regiment was in the fighting near Lille in May 1940. He was a gunner, not like you, but with big guns. The Germans were too strong. He was with some others who got away as far as Dunkerque. He was wounded and captured there and they sent him to a prison camp in Germany.'

Tears began to roll down her cheeks. She clenched her hands together and bowed her head onto the table and sobbed.

'Thérèse, don't say any more.'

He started to get up, thinking to comfort her but she raised her head and put up her hands to stop him.

'No, I want to tell you. A letter came in Spring this year, April, I think. I remember it was a warm day and there were red flowers in the fields, the ones we call Easter flowers. It had a French stamp but we don't know who had sent it; there was no signature. Perhaps whoever sent it thought it was too dangerous to put his name on it. All it said was "Fabrice Duchesne Chevalier, Sergeant 106th Artillery Regiment, died of wounds". No date, but at the bottom of the page was the word "sorry".'

'Thérèse . . .'

'Mama just stood there with the letter in her hands, saying nothing. She hardly ever spoke again; never played her piano again. When she . . . when she died . . . I went into her room in the morning and I thought she was still asleep . . . the letter was on her bed next to her hand.'

'Thérèse, I'm so sorry. To lose your brother and then your mother so soon afterwards is terrible. I don't know how you can bear it.'

'We can't forget them. Just as you can't forget your friends.'

A door opened on the landing above and there was the sound of feet padding towards the top of the stairs. Séverine called down.

'Philippe, are you still there? You did say the turret had four guns, didn't you?'

'Real coffee! How did you come by that?'

'Madame Janquet keeps the grocery in St Chely. How she gets it, I don't know and it's best not to ask. I hinted that she might take a little extra boar meat, off the loin, for herself and the packet just appeared.'

'Did you keep it, the packet? I love the smell of new-ground coffee when you first open the packet.'

'Ask Thérèse; she'll have put it away in the cupboard somewhere. You puzzle me. We were always told at school that the English drink only tea.'

'Not the English who have been to France and sat in the cafés.'

'And when did you do that?'

'On holidays with my parents, once to Britanny, and once to Rouen when I was quite young and three days in Paris with my father for a birthday present when I was sixteen. If it hadn't been for the War, I'd have spent a whole year in France somewhere as part of my studies.'

'Well here you are in France because of the War.'

'Do you know, I hadn't thought of it like that.'

She's very chatty this morning, he thought, almost affable and the breakfast was rather special: real coffee and fried eggs. She must be pleased with him because of last night when he'd more or less agreed to do something about the gun. It looked as if he'd be staying for quite a while if they had to wait for the snow to go before they could search for it. Them, not it: she wanted all four. He'd laughed about that and asked her if she wanted to set up a whole battery. She'd looked him straight in the eye and said yes, why not? Not a smile on her face, deadly serious.

'Where's Thérèse? The coffee's getting cold.'

'Gone for the potatoes and onions we're having with tonight's dinner. She keeps them in the stable where it's cool. The onions are very good, Cevenol onions, very sweet, just the thing to have stewed with the roast mutton.'

'Will she be long? I could take her some coffee. It must be cold out there.'

'Don't worry. She'll soon be back.'

'Last night she told me about Fabrice.'

For an instant Séverine looked as if a stab of recurrent unbearable pain had pierced her. The look went as suddenly as it had come, leaving tiredness and sadness lining her face.

'Little Fabrice. He was born when she was only two years old. The two youngest; they were inseparable. People used to think they were twins. Mama found her in his cot one morning with her arms round him. She said she thought he was cold so she wanted to make him warm again. When he was older he taught her how to swim. She was frightened of the water until he went in with her.'

'Séverine, I'm sorry. I seem to keep saying things that make both of you sad.'

'It's not your fault. You can't make us any sadder than we already are.'

'What can I do?'

'Philippe, if you really mean that, you can give Thérèse back some of the happiness which she lost when she lost Fabrice. You like her, don't you? Tell me the truth.'

'Of course I like her. She's fun. She was a bit cross with me in the sheep pen yesterday but not for long. She started laughing.'

'She hadn't laughed in a year, until you came here.'

'I'm glad I'm doing some good.'

'Are you really? She wasn't laughing when I got back. What else happened in the sheep pen? You both had had straw in your hair.'

'That was before I . . .'

'Before you what?'

'Before I kissed her.'

'You kissed her?'

'It was silly. She couldn't pronounce the word Westmorland, that's where I come from in England, so I told her how to shape her lips so she that she could, and when she did, she looked so pretty that I just, well, I just kissed her. I couldn't help it. I'm sorry. Have I done something terrible?'

'She doesn't seem to think so. She was so happy this morning before you got up, giggling about how you were singing to the sheep and then going on about what a special Christmas Eve dinner she was going to cook for us with more of the *vin doux* because you like it and, oh, all sorts of other things. Then, when she heard you stirring she turned rather quiet and said she must go and get things from the stable.'

'So she does think I shouldn't have done it. Oh God. She went so quiet and looked at me without smiling. Then before I could do anything about it, you arrived on the cart with that boy.'

'No, Philippe, you're wrong. I think she was quiet because she felt herself falling in love with you.'

Lawless was stunned: by Séverine's words and a sudden blinding realisation that he felt the same about Thérèse. The looks, the jokes and laughter, the thrill of the dancing and the piano playing when he was close to her and touching her, the desire that rose in him when he saw or thought of the shape of her body and felt the closeness of her breast when she drew the sutures from his brow, the sheer pleasure he felt just talking to her, listening to the soft goodnights she whispered. In a flash it was all so obvious: he was recklessly in love with Thérèse.

'Say something.'

He didn't know what to say, just stared at her speechless, staggered by what she had said but more by what he now felt. She was wrong, she must be; they hardly knew each other: did that matter? He was wrong; he was flirting, that's all, no, be honest, he would have taken her in his arms if that bloody sheep hadn't distracted her. She was lovely. He did want her; remember that night when the three of them shared the bed and she helped him to . . . no don't think of that now. Can't *not* think of it now. Can't think at all. He shivered violently. Shock. The night fighter was suddenly there, metres away before he saw it, a flash of moonlight on its windshield, and the shock froze him and he couldn't fire and it did and the tracers swirled away and missed and it was gone and still he couldn't move a finger. Shock, like now but not like now. Now it was amazement, amazement at what he now knew and felt and wanted.

'Philippe, be careful. Don't say it to me. Say it to Thérèse. Go now.'

He didn't think to close the door. Cold air seeped into the room. It was minutes before she noticed and got up to drop the latch. She stood for a while at the window, looking out into the courtyard. It was a fine and sunny day. There might be time for a walk with Caramelle after lunch. She sat down again at the table and poured a little more coffee into her cup. It was still quite warm.

'Papa, what have I done?' she said out loud. 'What have I done? What else could I do?'

***

It was some time before they came back. She heard them outside laughing about something and they came in hand in hand.

Séverine was still sitting at the table, cup in hand. She looked up and frowned at them.

'Such a noise! What have you two been up to? Have you been dancing again? What's all the excitement about?'

Thérèse rushed across to the table, pulled Séverine to her feet and kissed her again and again.

'Séverine, Philippe has told me he loves me and we're going to be married!'

'Let me go! Married? What are you talking about? You can't marry him: he's a, he's an Englishman!'

Thérèse drew back. The excitement slowly faded from her face. She turned to look at Lawless, then back, bewildered, at her sister.

'Séverine, please, it's Philippe. Please.'

Séverine put her arms round Thérèse and held her tightly, kissing her hair.

'Tressie, my darling Tressie, I'm sorry: just my silly, silly joke. It's wonderful. Of course you're going to be married.' She whispered in her ear. 'Even if he is an Englishman!'

'Everybody seems to be having a good laugh,' said Lawless from the doorway. 'Can anyone join in?'

'Come here so that I can embrace my future brother-in law; then you may join in.'

'Celebrate, we must celebrate. I'm so happy. Are you happy, Philippe? Séverine, are you happy for us?'

'Yes, I am happy for you; more than I can say.'

'*Vin doux*: can we have some *vin doux* to celebrate?'

'As much as you like; I'll go for it.'

'Wait, wait,' Thérèse cried, 'I've forgotten, I mean I've left, when Philippe said to me, they went clean out of my head. I've left the potatoes and the onions in the storehouse; I must get them, so wait, please, here for me.' She rushed out, slamming the door behind her.

'See what you have done to her?'

'I love her. I didn't know it until you told me but I know it now.'

'Philippe, look at me. You are very young. You are a long way from your home and family and the people you know. The War has done bad things to you: I can see that. No, listen. Are you sure you are not just being grateful to her for saving your life and looking after you? Please think.'

'Séverine, I am grateful, to both of you and that's why I said I would stay and help and I won't go back on that. But it's different with Thérèse. I love her and I want to make her happy.'

'You say that now but you will go, one day. I know you will because of what you are, a soldier. You will have to go back.'

"If I do, it won't be until I have done everything I have promised you and Thérèse. And I will come back when it's over. I promise you that.'

'I wonder if you know what you're doing.'

'Séverine, please don't spoil it for us. We're going to live and work together here, all three of us, and make La Commanderie come alive again. You said I couldn't make you sadder than you already are; do you remember saying that? If you give us your blessing—that sounds old-fashioned but you know what I mean—you can be happier, much happier than you are.'

She had to admit he was right in some ways. He had brought some much-needed cheer to the house with his music and the dancing and that boyish eagerness to do everything. And as he got stronger and started to work, things should be so much easier with the farm. The winter was so exhausting and although Spring might bring warmth and new grass it also meant much more hard work. So why was she feeling like this, uncertain, not a little guilty? That was unlike her, she knew. After all, this was what she wanted, what she had been working for and now that she had told Jérôme Janquet, there was no going back. The plan was working so why did she feel these qualms?

'Séverine?'

'I can't stop you, even if I wanted to, and I don't, so don't look like that. It's just that suddenly everything has changed and nothing will ever be the same again. It must be easy for someone as young as you, falling in love, wanting to get married. You . . . *know so little about life and the pain and loss and fears it brings . . .'*

Horrified, she stopped from blurting that out just in time. How could she have forgotten how near death he was when they found him, how near death he must have been every time that bomber took to the air, how many like him that he had known were now broken, burned and lost?

'Séverine, what's the matter? Why are you shivering? Are you all right?'

'What? Yes, yes, it's nothing. Come here. People from these parts say the warmer the embrace, the tighter the bond. There: we are together. Oh, here she is, with the onions and the potatoes, just like a good wife getting things ready for her husband.'

'And sister,' said Lawless.

'Now it's my turn to ask what are you two up to, embracing like that? Have you been talking about me?'

'Only wondering what was keeping you. Hey, you haven't forgotten it's Christmas Eve, have you? When will dinner be ready? We must sing carols and...'

'Dance,' said Thérèse. 'We must dance.'

'I was going to say, tell ghost stories but dancing is a better idea, yes, much better.'

First, we must drink,' said Séverine. 'Fill the glasses, Philippe; that is the man's duty. More than that: to the brim. Now, touch glasses, stop looking at her like that, Philippe, or you'll spill your wine and we haven't got all that much left. Health and happiness to us all: drink up. Mm, very good. Fill my glass again, Philippe. No, only mine this time.'

Lawless filled her glass with the sweet dark wine. She raised it to him and to Thérèse in turn, and said quietly,

'Whatever it means and for what it's worth, you have my blessing.'

***

'Would you like more mutton?'

' Thérèse, sorceress of the kitchen, I couldn't eat another scrap,' said Lawless, rubbing his stomach and pretending to groan. 'But I could find room for a little more of that wine.'

'The English: always saying simple things in a complicated way.'

'Séverine, it's our way of persuading others to give us what we want. Is that the bottle?'

He rubbed the dusty label with his thumb. 'Chateau Lyn . . . can't read the rest, it's too faded, 1920, I think, 1920! It's older than me!'

'It's the last one.'

'In that case we must drink it very slowly, so that it stays long in our stomachs and longer in our memories.'

'Philippe, can we be serious for a moment?'

'I am serious. Wine is a serious matter and a wine as special as this is a very serious matter.'

'Not as serious as this: your wedding. Arrangements must be made; a date has to be decided.'

'It can't come too soon for me. What about you, Thérèse, my love?'

She was silent: it was the first time he had said that to her in front of Séverine. It made her feel strange but somehow important. She found her voice again.

'Yes, soon, I don't want to wait.'

'You have to wait a little, Tressie, not too long but there are laws.'

'What laws? Will the priest tell us about them?'

'We have no dealings with priests in this family, Philippe. The mayor of St Chely is responsible for all the marriages in the commune. That is the law.'

'It's true, Philippe. We have to be married by the mayor.'

'Jérôme Janquet, I remember his name. You saw him the other day, Séverine. He told you the news about the War.'

'Yes, but that was before I knew anything about you two getting married. If you like, I could go to see him again to tell him about it and find out what you have to do.'

'Isn't it simpler if we just go ourselves?'

'It isn't simple, Philippe. He knows nothing about you and certainly not that you are an English soldier. It needs very a careful explanation but I think that when he is assured that his agreement to perform the marriage will be the way of acquiring one of your guns, he will do as we, you, want.'

'Hm, I see what you mean, but . . .'

'Let Séverine go, Philippe,' said Thérèse. 'She knows him and you don't.'

'All right, it makes sense but we will have to see him pretty soon. We can't just turn up on his doorstep and say, "Please Mr Mayor, will you marry us, Séverine says it's all right." And don't forget we haven't got the gun yet, anyway. I couldn't find it the other day.'

'Don't worry; we know it's there somewhere under the snow. Thérèse and Caramelle will find it. That's agreed then? I'll go the day after tomorrow.'

'Agreed. Séverine, have you any idea how long it takes? I'm getting older every day, you know.'

'You're impossible,' she said laughing. 'You look younger every day to me. It must be because Thérèse is feeding you so well.'

'You are absolutely right. Thèrèse, my love, what's for dinner tomorrow?'

'Partridge; the one you shot.'

'And the day after that?'

'Cold mutton, if there's any left.'

'And the day . . .'

'Give him some more wine, or kiss him, or I will, just to shut him up!'

When the laughter died away and Thérèse was standing behind Lawless with her arms round his shoulders and her head resting on his, he announced that it was now time to sing carols and after that they would dance to cheer themselves up again because carols always made you feel a bit sad.

Especially when you're far from home, Thérèse thought; but this is his home now.

***

'I always had a stocking at Christmas.'

'One stocking? Didn't you have any others?'

'Yes, lots, of course, but I mean a Christmas stocking, full of little presents like nuts and chocolate and oranges and crayons. You find it hanging on the end of your bed when you wake up on Christmas morning and when you're little you believe Father Christmas came down the chimney and left it for you while you were asleep.'

'We used to leave our shoes in front of the fireplace.'

'You can get more in a stocking.'

'Philippe, just like a boy! Always greedy.'

'When I was twelve I got my first grown-up bike for Christmas.'

'There are some stored away in one of the stables, I think. We haven't used them for years. They'll need mending.'

'A bike would be very handy when the snow has gone. I could go to the café on it and we could go for rides and have picnics.'

'I love picnics. Our favourite place was in the woods near Castelbouc. I can show you in the summer.'

'Bananas and tomato sandwiches and tea in a flask, that's what we always had.'

'What else did you do at Christmas? We played games.'

'Opened more presents, went to the church while my Mother cooked Christmas dinner, went for a walk in the afternoon, to walk off all that food, my father said, listened to the King's speech on the radio, played in my room while they slept in their chairs and had cold chicken for supper and sang some carols round the piano while my mother played. Not very exciting, really. Every other year we went to my uncle's farm for Christmas Day. I liked that because I could play with my cousins: Annie's the same age as me and Colin, he was two years older. He was really good at cricket.' *Until he was shot down over Dunkirk.*

'I'm sorry, Philippe, I didn't hear what you said; your voice went quiet. Something about Dunkerque?'

'No, no, "cricket": Colin was good at cricket. It's a game we play in England.'

Séverine came down the stairs, saw them holding hands and said, 'If you have nothing better to do than talk, why don't you take Caramelle and go looking for that gun? I'll see to lunch. Take the shotgun in case you see anything.'

'We'll take the sled,' said Lawless.

'Is it so heavy you need the sled?'

'Heavy enough: we may find some ammunition as well. Where do you keep the shovels?'

***

'This what I really wanted the sled for,' said Lawless. 'Sit behind me and hold on tight. I'll give us a push with the shovel. Come on, Caramelle. We're off!'

On the last downhill slope before the level ground that stretched all the way to the line of woods, the sled slewed sideways and they were thrown off into the snow. Caramelle rushed up to them barking in excitement, wanting to play.

'Shit. Last time something like that happened to me was when Sherwood brought us down on half an undercarriage. I must be lucky: that's three crash landings that I've come through. Didn't have you on the other two, though. Come here.'

'Philippe, stop, you're covered in snow.'

'So are you, does it matter?'

It didn't matter and he was able at last to kiss her as much as he, and she, seemed to want.

'Too many clothes on,' he said. 'I can only see your face.'

'You're impossible. Pull me up. Stop that. Your nose is freezing.'

'Kiss it warm again, then. Yes, like that. I love you, Thérèse. I love you so much I can't understand why the snow isn't melting under my feet. I can't wait to see you without those clothes on, without any clothes on.'

'We have to wait, Philippe, please. I do love you but I have to get to know you more.'

He looked down into her face and sighed as theatrically as he could.

'Then I shall be but your troubadour, yearning hopelessly for you beneath your window, waiting for the moment when your silken kerchief flutters down and I will know at last that you will yield. I may have fallen asleep by then. Don't say it, I know: I am impossible.'

She was shaking with laughter.

'Or should I say until Jérôme Janquet declares us man and wife? Then may I seize you and prove my love?'

'You should and you can. But now, Sergeant, pick up the shovel and the shotgun and let us go.'

'Heartless woman! La Belle Dame sans merci. How can you be so, so, practical?'

'Someone has to be. We can leave the sled. It's not far from here.'

Here's the place again, he thought, and waited for the bad feelings to come. But they didn't, so, no good wasting time, he started to dig into one of the snowdrifts.

'Not there, Philippe: over here. Dig, Caramelle, dig. Seek girl, seek.'

After two or three thrusts where the dog had been industriously digging, the shovel struck metal. They both scraped and swept the snow away and uncovered a large piece of thin metal sheet with a thick broken rod attached.

'Piece of the port tail fin,' said Lawless. 'That's part of the boom joining it to the fuselage just behind my turret.'

She had no idea what he was talking about but it struck her that he was very composed and not at all the shaking, haunted figure she had seen staggering out of the trees when she had come with the sled to this place that other time. He was muttering to himself now, oblivious of her as he dug deeper in the snow.

'Spent rounds chute side plate; belt roller; Perspex; it must be around here somewhere.'

'Philippe, it's here; I've found it.'

'You have? Be careful. Let me do it.'

It was the Browning, no mistaking the black cooling sleeve with its slots and the flared muzzle. About half of its metre-long length was now sticking out of the snow where Thérèse had been digging. He cleared more of the snow away.

'Yes, look, there's part of a belt still in the feedway; maybe, let's see, thirty, forty rounds.'

He was like a boy, going on about his new bicycle, how shiny it was and what good gears it had. She was half-pleased, half-scared of him. The gun looked black and ugly with that gaping snout.

'Wait, lift the lock, safety on, belt comes out, there. We can pull it out now. Can you hold that? Now then, here she comes.'

She held the heavy braid of ice-cold sharp-pointed bullets dangling from her hands as she watched him heave the gun from the snow and, holding it in both hands sweep it in an arc, aimed towards the slope where they were kissing only a few minutes before.

'Philippe, please put it down. It's dreadful. Take these things, please.'

The intense hard look left his face and he smiled at her apologetically.

'I'm sorry, sweetheart. I didn't mean to frighten you. These things, well, I've been living with four of these for so long, I dream of them sometimes and, God, sometimes they don't work when I need them to, in my dreams.'

He put the gun down in the snow and dropped the belt of cartridges beside it.

'Philippe, don't look like that. I know you said if we found it you would let Jérôme Janquet have it. I know you have to do it. Let's just put it on the sled and go away from here.'

'There's just one other thing I want to see and then we can go back. It's over there. Hold my hand.'

He led her to the shepherd's shelter. Caramelle followed them snuffling here and there in the snow.

'I'll go inside first and then you.'

'Why do you want to go in there?'

'Because it's the place where I first met you.'

'All right, but we mustn't stay long.'

'Now then, isn't that nice? All cosy and out of the wind.'

'It smells in the summer.'

'Don't spoil my dream. How do you know anyway?'

'Fabrice and I used to hide from Séverine in here. Well, we thought we did but she knew all the time.'

'It's a bit tumbledown. Does anyone still use it?'

'Well, yes: we do, I do, in the summer sometimes when the sheep are out here grazing and it's a warm night. It's lovely then. You can hear the night birds and look out at the stars.'

'Do you know what I'll do? I'll put the roof stones back in place and stop up the holes that are in the walls and make a door and clean it all out so that it will be fresh and comfortable and then we can come here and sleep together on warm nights in the summer. We could make a fire and cook things and have some nice wine and . . .'

'Yes, and what?'

'And be together and make love and sleep and sleep until the skylarks wake us up in the morning.'

'Philippe, skylarks sing in the afternoon.'

'That's even better. I won't want to get up if you're next to me.'

After a while, she giggled and said,

'Do you know the first thing I did when I saw you?'

'Fell instantly in love with me.'

'No, silly: I poked you in the ribs with the shotgun.'

'Quite right; any farmer would do the same to a trespasser. Was the safety catch on?'

'I think so. I don't know. I'd been looking at all that silk from your parachute.'

'What did I do?'

'Fell over and started groaning.'

She started to giggle again.

'That's not very nice, giggling at me because I was moaning and groaning.'

'Oh I'm not. I was thinking about what you did to Séverine when she looked in here and saw you.'

'Tell me. I can't remember.'

'She said you pointed a pistol at her. Have you still got it?'

'I don't remember anything about that. What are you going to do with it, the silk?'

'I'm not telling you. It's a secret. You'll find out one day. Caramelle! Stop it. Get out. You're all wet!'

'She heard you talking about the parachute and she thinks it's hers because she found it first. You ought to make her a coat.'

'I think she's found something. She's gone over near those trees.'

'Could be a partridge, or a hare, or Christ, another wild boar, and I've left the shotgun where we found the Browning.'

'No, it's not that. She's not making the sort of sound she makes when she can see game.'

'Wait here. I'll go and take a look.'

He hadn't noticed before; hadn't been to look over there, of course. Some of the tree trunks were charred and there were scorched and broken branches strewn around, sticking up from the snow. The dog was digging and snorting and then she thrust her nose into the hole. The tanks must have burst when she hit and sprayed blazing fuel over these trees, but where was she now? There should be more than a few bits of metal lying about. He walked to the far edge of the clump of trees, following the furrows in the snow. It was a clear day and he could see the land sloping gently down towards another long line of trees that curved away on both sides into the distance. Beyond that, a long way off, were what looked like cliffs topped by level ground with patches of green, most likely woodland, he thought.

'Thérèse! Can you come over here?'

Before she reached him he had buried the ammunition box Caramelle had uncovered under the snow again and was looking into the distance, with one hand raised to his brow to give shade from the sun that was now nearing its highest for a winter's day.

'What's over there, between those trees and the cliffs on the other side?'

'It's the gorge,' she said. 'With the river at the bottom: it's really deep there. And over there's Castelbouc, on this side, where I told you we used to go for picnics. Papa knew an old man who rowed us across the river in his boat if we wanted to go over.'

Her voice was faint in his ears. The furrows ran in that direction. The Whitley, she must be down there in the gorge, what was left of her; and of them.

'What did you say?'

'I said it's time we were going. Séverine will be cross if we're late for lunch. We've found what we came for, haven't we?'

'Yes,' he said. 'We've found what we came for. Race you back to the sled?'

***

'Séverine, that was a very good omelette. Where do you get the eggs? The hens can't be laying at this time of year.'

'We put them down in water glass in autumn and they last all winter.'

'Philippe,' said Thérèse, 'can we not have that thing in the house?'

He had left the Browning and its cartridge belt by the kitchen door when they had come in. He could tell Séverine had been pleased when she saw the gun although she had asked if that was all the ammunition they had found. He had kept quiet about the full box under the snow.

'I need to check it to see if it's in working order—don't worry, I'm not going to fire it—and clean and oil it properly; but I suppose I could do that on a bench in one of the stables.'

'It has to be kept well hidden, and the others, when they're found,' said Séverine. 'I'll show you a place in the small stable. When I see Jérôme Janquet tomorrow, I'll wait for the right moment to let him know about it and I think that should make his mind up for him.'

'He will ask questions,' said Thérèse. 'He's not a stupid man.'

'No, he is not: he will soon see that we have something to offer that he has no chance of getting anywhere else. Now, Philippe, the mayor will want to see proof of who you are and where you were born: he will want to know other things, but these are the most important.'

'Oh God, I don't have anything like that. I have a passport and a birth certificate but they're at home. We're not allowed to take things like that with us when we go on a raid. I don't know what I can show him; I'm sorry. Thérèse, I'm really sorry.'

'Wait. What about that little book that we found in your uniform pocket when we brought you to the house? We tried to read what was in it but all we could understand was your name. Where is it?'

'It said when he was born as well.'

'Thérèse, you're right! Philippe where is it?'

'In my room; won't be a tick.' He jumped from his chair and rushed upstairs.

'Not much wrong with him now by the look of it,' said Séverine. 'Do you think he's ever done any ploughing?'

Lawless leapt down the last few steps and nearly fell over Caramelle as he bounded across to the table.

'Here,' he gasped. 'It's my Pay Book. I shouldn't have had this with me either. I don't know why I did this time. Let's have a look. It's all here:
"Surname", "Christian names", "Service number", "Rank", "Date of Reporting for Duty". Then, here on the inside, it gives name again; date of birth again; what I was before I joined the RAF, "Student"; "Married or Single": look, Thérèse, I'm single—aren't you pleased? There's my signature; and down there that's my father's name and address as the "person to be informed of casualties".'

'Philippe, what's wrong? Why have you stopped? There's a lot more written down.'

'Thérèse, I haven't thought about them, my mother and my father, for days now. I feel awful. What must they be feeling? They don't know whether I'm alive or dead. What can I do?'

All his enthusiasm and eagerness had disappeared. He stared helplessly at her. She put her arms round him and whispered just sounds, not words to him.

'Philippe, listen. Somebody in your RAF must have told them something. What would it be? Philippe: did you hear me?'

"Missing",' he said dully. 'They'll have been told I am missing.'

'Missing is not dead so they will still have hope. We can let them know you are alive. I will ask Jérôme Janquet how we can do it.'

'We received a letter about Fabrice, Philippe,' said Thérèse. She looked at Séverine. 'I told him about it.'

'You told me it said he was dead.'

'But you are not and you are safe here. That's what we will say.'

'Listen to her, Philippe. She is right. We can do it. Now, cheer up. What else does your book say?'

He rubbed his eyes with his hands, ran his fingers up through his hair and looked doubtfully at Séverine.

'You promise to do that?'

She nodded. 'What else does it say?'

'This,' he said, pointing, 'is the signature and rank of the officer who verified the entries in the book and that is the date he did it.'

'Good; I hope that will be enough to convince the mayor.'

'Tell him this book is an official document of the Royal Air Force and is accepted anywhere in England: Post Office, shops, railway stations, anywhere, as proof of identity. Look, maybe these numbers and signatures will convince him: these are payments made to me by the Royal Air Force, with the officers' signatures and dates. Ask the mayor if he thinks the *Royal* Air Force would pay me a penny if I were not the person this book says I am.'

'Now now, Philippe, don't think of using that tone with Mr Mayor. That's for me to do, if I have to. Is there anything else useful in the book: what does it say on that page?'

Lawless read the first few words under the heading ALL RANKS and began to laugh.

'God, I'd forgotten about this bit. Listen, it says, "REMEMBER—never discuss military, naval, or air matters in public or with any stranger, no matter to what nationality he or she may belong. The enemy wants information about you, your unit, your destination. He will do his utmost to discover it . . ." no need to read the rest. I'm already guilty. No I'm not. You're not the enemy—I know you're in Vichy but you're against it—and you aren't strangers, so that's all right. What else would you like to know?'

'I think that's enough for one day,' said Séverine. 'I have things to do in the sheep pen.'

'And I must prepare the partridge for tonight. Then I have work to do in my room.'

'What work? I was hoping . . .'

'Secret. You could do the washing up.'

Half an hour later, he dried his hands and called upstairs.

'Done it!'

There was no reply, so Lawless found his coat, picked up the Browning and the belt and went out to work on them in the small stable.

The gun was in such a good condition that he could think that only its mounting and even his entire turret must have disintegrated when the Whitley hit the ground and he was somehow flung out. There were a couple of dents in the cooling jacket but they wouldn't affect the firing. He pushed the tab on the end of the belt into the feedway, felt it catch on the holding pawl, pulled back the cocking handle of the gun and released it. The first round clicked smoothly into place in front of the bolt. He pulled and released the cocking handle a second time allowing the round to slip into the chamber. Not a single hitch: the gun was ready for firing. What it needed was a stand, preferably a tripod. A good blacksmith ought to be able to manage that. It would be heavy. Two men would be needed to work it and perhaps a third to carry the ammunition boxes.

There was a slight noise and when he looked round he found Séverine standing behind him. Her eyes were fixed on the gun lying on the worktable.

'How long have you been there watching me?'

'It works, doesn't it?'

'Yes, it works. Wait there while I take out the belt.'

'I've brought you the oil we always use on our guns. Is it suitable?'

'It hardly needs any. These are always serviced and tested before we take off and it's not been damaged in any way, except for a couple of dents, there, can you see? They don't matter. All it needs is a wipe with an oily rag from time to time and it is to be kept free of dust and dirt.'

'There's a pit under the floor here with a trapdoor. It's perfectly dry down there. It can be kept in a box and no one will find it. Can I see what it feels like?'

'You? Are you sure?'

'I want to know all about it, how it works, what it can do: everything.'

'Séverine, be serious: this isn't a shotgun. It's a very dangerous, noisy battlefield weapon. It takes weeks, maybe months of practice to get used to this gun and we have very little ammunition.'

'I can learn. You can get to know how a gun works without firing it, can't you?'

'Yes, maybe, but you have no idea what it's really like until you've used it in action.'

'If you won't show me, Henri Vabrette will. Remember, the blacksmith I told you about? He was in an infantry regiment so he must know about guns like this.'

'All right, if you say so.'

Lawless drew out the belt, checked there was no round in the chamber and replaced the gun on the table.

'There you are. See what you think.'

He could see she found it heavier than she had expected but she was determined not to let him think she could not cope with it. She stood with her feet apart holding the gun in the crooks of her arms. The expression on her face made him feel uneasy. The skin on his back prickled.

'You take it, Philippe. Show me how to hold it.'

'It needs a stand, a tripod. You can't possibly fire it holding it like this,' he said, swinging the barrel round. 'It's too heavy and it shakes like mad.'

He put the gun down on the table and turned to speak. She thrust herself against him, pulled down his head and kissed him quickly and fiercely enough to bring the taste of blood. Just as quickly, she drew away, turned and walked towards the stable door. Stupid images flickered through his mind as he watched her: Jack Verrill laughing, Caramelle gnawing on a bone, the partridge staggering in the air. Then she was gone. He put his hand to his mouth and stared at the smear of blood on his fingertips. He waited to see if she would come back without any idea of what he would do if she did. He ought to put the gun out of sight but she hadn't shown him where the pit was. The stable floor was covered in old straw. He found an old tattered blanket and wrapped the gun and ammunition belt in it and hid the bundle behind some bales of hay in a corner of the stable. When he went back into the kitchen, Séverine was making up the fire and Thérèse was laying the table. There was a delicious smell of roasting meat. She gave him a little kiss on the cheek.

'Pour us some wine, Philippe. Dinner will be ready soon. I know it's early but we want to have plenty of time to play and sing some carols before bed.'

'I've found that box for the gun,' said Séverine. 'It's upstairs in a cupboard. I'll bring it down in the morning and let you have it before I go.'

A single roasted partridge doesn't go very far between three people but hanging for nearly three days had turned it tender and ripe and Thérèse had grilled it over the embers, basting it with thyme-flavoured oil and honey and catching the juices to make a gravy with red wine and juniper berries. They ate their helpings shred by shred to make them last and soaked their bread in the gravy, eating it with potatoes and shallots. Lawless was given one of the legs and sucked it slowly, closing his eyes in pleasure. Because it was Christmas Day and there was no partridge for her, Caramelle was treated to some of the leftover mutton and the shoulder blade to gnaw. When the partridge carcass had been thoroughly picked clean, Lawless inspected it and said,

'Where's the wishbone? We must pull the wishbone and make a wish. There it is. That one, like a tuning fork, isn't it?'

'Séverine, we haven't done it since we were little. Do you remember? Mama didn't like us to do it. She said it was improper; I don't know why, do you?'

'I think I know,' said Lawless, smiling mischievously. 'But I mustn't say in front of ladies.'

Séverine smiled back at him. 'You're being impossible again. I know exactly what you're talking about.'

'Tell me, tell me,' pleaded Thérèse, pulling Lawless's arm.

'He will tell you after you're married, won't you Philippe?'

'Oh please, Philippe.'

'No, my love, no: your sister is quite right. It must be a secret until that day.'

'You're very cruel to me, making fun of me like that.'

'You two should pull it,' said Séverine. You are the ones getting married so you have the most to wish for. Put it near the fire to dry. It has to break properly for the wish come true.'

When it came to it, Thérèse said she didn't think it was a good idea to sing carols because it would only make them sad by thinking of the times they used to sing them with people who were not with them any more but Lawless persuaded her that one would be all right so they sang 'Silent Night', first in French and then in English. In the silence that always follows, when he should have been thinking of carols round the piano at home, he wasn't. He was in the Cross Keys at Thirsk, two nights after his birthday and still so hung over his fingers couldn't find the right notes on the piano. A navigator from the other flight whose name he never knew played the same carol and there was the same silence afterwards until Verrill shouted, 'Play something cheerful, for Christ's sake,' and the navigator set to with 'Roll me over in the clover' . . .

'Come on, this will cheer us all up,' said Lawless. 'Ladies, take your partners,' and he began to play 'The Entertainer'. 'It's a rag but you can dance a polka to it. Surely you know how to dance a polka.'

It was nearly midnight when Séverine came back into the room where Lawless and Thérèse were trying to play a duet and laughing over their mistakes. She handed the partridge's wishbone to Lawless.

'Time to pull,' she said. 'It's dry enough now; should break easily.'

'Little fingers. Little fingers.'

They hooked their little fingers round the ends of the bone. The gap was so small their fingers were touching. There was a tiny snapping noise and the top of the bone flew out of sight, leaving each of them clasping an equal length of a side.

'I've never seen that before,' exclaimed Lawless. 'I suppose we each get a wish this time. What do you think, Séverine?'

'Men usually win,' she said. 'It's because most of them cheat. Next time we have one, Philippe, you must pull it with me. Then we'll see.'

Back in his room, he tried to concentrate on the translation. He had been covering a few pages most nights before he went to bed. Page 89: the King was told of the insurrection and sent ten thousand men commanded by Marshal de Montrevel to crush it. Why had Séverine done that? He ran his tongue across the inside of his lips; there was a small swelling where she'd pressed them hard against his teeth. This part was quite easy: Cavallier's men running rings round the soldiers. Then there was a disaster at Usez, page 100. Lawless turned to the map: there it was, in capital letters, USEZ with a little diagram of a church and a road marked going south, crossing the River Gardon and on to Nîmes. He knew it was spelled Uzès now. Nîmes: he turned back five pages. Outside Nîmes was where Cavallier had beaten General Broglio and even wounded him. Then Usez: how his luck changed. After Usez they had to hide away in the mountains and live in caves. He remembered telling Thérèse and Séverine about that bit. He couldn't ignore what she had done in the stable. It came out of the blue. He must ask her why. Why was he thinking about Jack Verrill? His parachute, of course: he'd meant to look for that but thinking of Thérèse had taken his mind of it. He felt worn out. One more page and it was the end of Book One.

He turned the handle of his bedroom door, stuck his head out into the dark corridor and listened. The house was as quiet as the College chapel. Why did he think of that? He trod slowly along the corridor, wordlessly thanking whoever had thought of laying carpet there. He paused outside Séverine's room and carefully pressed his ear to the door and turned the handle halfway. Should he? There was a faint sound of breathing. He grinned to himself and padded on until he reached Thérèse's door. His heart began to beat so hard he was sure that she would hear it. He tapped softly on the door. Nothing. Again, louder. Still no sound from inside. He tried the handle. The door was locked. He knew well enough what she had said. *We have to wait, Philippe, please. I love you . . .* Jack Verrill said they never really meant it. Well, he was wrong. Back in his own room the bed was warm. She had put the hot brick in for him without his knowing. I love her, he said to himself, I really do, especially after the way she looked at me when I whispered to her about pulling wishbones.

'There's no need to look at me like that,' said Séverine. 'I only wanted to thank you for keeping your promise about the gun; no more than that.'

Lawless wondered if he would ever understand her. Did she always mean exactly what she said? The sight of guns did strange things to people. Thérèse wasn't the least bit worried about using a shotgun but the Browning scared her. But Séverine: he couldn't forget that look on her face when she saw it on the bench in the stable. She was fascinated by it. She *wanted* to use it. Did that have something to do with the kiss? He wasn't so sure now about his promise to get the gun working and hand it over. When he was on the gunnery course he'd became friendly with one of the sergeant instructors. In the pub one night after a few pints the sergeant told him he'd be all right, he'd pass the course because to him these guns were tools, see? But some of the other buggers, if it were up to him they wouldn't be allowed anywhere near a gun, any gun, because they really liked them and wanted to fire them, not at targets, at *people*, see? Lawless asked him wasn't that what they were being trained to do and the sergeant poked him in the chest and said yes, mate, but you don't have to love doing it, do you?

'Why don't I come with you to St Chely?'

'I think it's best if the mayor meets you here first. There are other things to talk about as well as the wedding and it's more private here.'

'So why are you going?'

'To prepare the ground, Philippe. You know farmers: they always take care to prepare the ground. I shall need your book, if you permit it. Thank you, it will be safe in my satchel. And now I must go. You will find the box for the gun at the end of the passage upstairs. Oh, by the way, how is the translation going?'

'I've just started on Book Two. I read over a few pages to get the sense before I start translating. Cavallier describes how he sets about recruiting more men. You might be interested to read that part.'

'I can hear Thérèse getting up. You could make coffee for her and yourself if you feel like being helpful. I'll have mine with the mayor.'

When she had gone, Lawless made up the fire and set the kettle to boil. He found the coffee mixture in a jar in the cupboard and the packet of real coffee next to it. He put three heaped spoonfuls from the packet into the blue pitcher. Why not, he thought; after all it is Boxing Day. Let the water go off the boil, his mother always said. He filled the pitcher and breathed in the heady scent of fresh coffee. He grinned to himself: if that doesn't fetch her down, nothing will. Boxing Day, he thought. What do the French do on Boxing Day?

They sipped their coffee, looking at each other over the rims of their bowls.

'Séverine left a few minutes ago. She said I should make coffee for you.'

'And you used the real coffee.'

'Yes, because it's for you and because it's Boxing Day today.'

'What is it, this "Berkseeng Day"?'

'I love the way you say it but it's "Boxing", not "Berkseeng". It's the day after Christmas and it's a holiday in England.'

'For the Catholics it is a saint's day.'

'Listen, Séverine is away and we can do what we want until she gets back. I have an idea.'

'Philippe!'

'No, no: listen. In Westmorland on Boxing Day people like farmers go foxhunting. Why don't we take the shotgun and go hunting?'

'For foxes, why?'

'No, sweetheart: for partridges or hares or rabbits, anything we can eat, not foxes. Unless you like eating them.'

'After I have finished with the sheep, perhaps.'

'Show me the place in the stable where Séverine told me to hide the gun in its box, then I'll help you with the sheep and then we'll go: all right?'

'Good morning, Mademoiselle Chevalier. How are you? I've been expecting you. Some coffee?'

'Thank you, Jérôme and a little cognac, if you please. It is a cold day.'

All during the walk from La Commanderie to the village she had been rehearsing what she was going to say, so why was she now feeling these doubts? It was ridiculous. There was no going back now. Jérôme was coming back with the tray. Think; think carefully. She drank the cognac first and then took a sip of the coffee which was poured for her. It was so good. Her mind was now quite made up.

'Mr Mayor, after you have heard what I am about to tell you, you may well think it necessary to pay a visit to La Commanderie to see things for yourself.'

Jérôme Janquet remained silent, looking at her with a polite but non-committal expression on his face. Séverine took Lawless's Pay Book from her satchel and placed it on the table in front of him.

Jérôme Janquet looked down at the little buff-coloured booklet for a few moments before picking it up and opening it.

'I do not understand, Mademoiselle.'

'Because it is in English?'

'No, Mademoiselle Chevalier; when I got this at Maricourt in '16,' he said, tapping his thigh, 'I was taken to an English field hospital where the surgeon saved my leg. I think a French doctor would have taken it off. So, you see, I understand enough English to know what this may be. What I do not understand is where you found it and why you now show it to me and not send it to the Gendarmerie in Florac.'

'It was given to me by the man who owns it: the man whom my sister intends to marry.'

'"Royal Air Force": he is an Englishman. May I ask where he is and what he is doing here?'

'Do you not know that an English aeroplane crashed on the Causse nearly three weeks ago?'

'There was talk of aircraft noise and lights in the sky one night but as you know, the snow was so deep and the reports so vague that our citizens were reluctant to carry out a search and with more important matters to deal with I think they have now put this to the back of their minds.'

'I am glad to hear of it but what I can tell you, Mr Mayor, is that my sister was out hunting for hares and found the aeroplane, or, I should say, parts of it, and one survivor of the crash. He was wounded and we took him in and cared for him. Now his wounds are healing and he is back to health. He is this moment at La Commanderie and this is his book. I should also say that he has given me permission to show it to you.'

'I see now why you said the man Mademoiselle Thérèse was thinking of marrying was "not from these parts" but I did not expect to be told he was an English soldier. He surely must know that it is his duty to try to rejoin his regiment, yet you say he and your sister wish to be married and, forgive me for saying this, Mademoiselle, but after meeting barely three weeks ago?'

'Jérôme, the answer to your last question is simple: they have fallen in love and the reason they wish to marry as soon as possible is *because* he knows it is his duty to try to return to his squadron and with our help he intends to do that. As an old soldier yourself, you must know that these things can happen.'

'"With our help", you say. Please explain.'

'It would be better for you to come to La Commanderie to meet him and hear whatever he has to say. He speaks our language very well. However, he does not speak it like a Frenchman and he does not look and behave like a Frenchman. It is our plan to change that and so give him a better chance to escape. Marriage at the Mairie and time spent working at La Commanderie and, when it seems the right time, coming more and more into St Chely, being seen in your café, getting to know people in the village: all these things will help him fit in and become less conspicuous.'

Jérôme Janquet sat back in his chair, shaking his head slowly from side to side, regarding her with amused admiration.

'I have to admit, Mademoiselle Chevalier, that you are quite ingenious and very persuasive, but we are talking of an Englishman here in Vichy France where our rulers are hostile to Englishmen. There are difficulties.'

'I do not have to remind you, Mr Mayor, that we are not at war with England and as far as I know there is no law even under our present rulers that forbids a French citizen to marry a foreigner who has committed no crime. Is that not so?'

'That is correct.'

'Now tell me, what documents are required and what other conditions are there?'

'Proof of identity, age and domicile is required as well as certification that neither person is already married. Oh, and in the case of a foreigner, that the marriage will be recognised in his or her own country. Does this man have a passport and birth certificate?'

'Of course he does not. A soldier does not carry such things with him into battle. But you have before you proof of all that is required by the law. You may read it for yourself or the owner will explain to you when you come to La Commanderie.'

'I am not sure, Mademoiselle Chevalier, I . . .'

'Mister Mayor, look here: this book is a signed document recording regular payments made to a man serving his country in the Royal Air Force. Is there any document more official than that? Here you have his name, number, rank, and date when he became a soldier. And here, look, on this page, his names again, his date of birth, his address in England and his father's name, even his religion. This is his own signature and that is the signature of the officer of the Royal Air Force who endorsed this document. Yes, and here, it says that he is single which means he is not married. You have everything you need in this book.'

'All that may be so but I am still not sure. I will have to think about this.'

'What else is needed? Tell me.'

'If the man does not belong to this commune he must have been living here for at least forty days and . . .'

'His machine crashed close to La Commanderie on the eighth of December. You could ask when those lights in the sky were seen. Today is the twenty-sixth of December so he has been resident for nineteen days. Let me think. Yes, on the fifteenth of January it will be forty days.'

'Sixteenth of January, Mademoiselle Chevalier.'

'The sixteenth then: we must observe the law. What else is there?'

'Notice of the marriage must be posted ten days before the date arranged.'

'The sixth of January; that is not far off.'

'Mademoiselle Chevalier, please wait a moment. This is something that must not be rushed. You understand my position: the authorities are suspicious of me and will seize any opportunity to have me dismissed. To be absolutely sure that I am following the law precisely I must record this man, what is his name, ah yes, Philippe Martyn Lawless, this man's arrival in the commune from the date that you first informed me of your sister's intention to marry him.'

'That means the first of February at the earliest. My sister will be very disappointed to hear that.'

'I am truly sorry.'

'Can you see no way of bringing the date forward?'

'That is my decision.'

'I see. In that case I think you should consider coming to La Commanderie to see my sister and Sergeant Lawless and speak to them yourself. It would not be wise to have it known that you gave consent to a marriage without having verified that it is the couple's wish, and especially that the man, an English soldier here in Vichy France as you said, and whose book you have before you, does, in fact, exist. Would it, Mr Mayor?'

Jérôme Janquet had always admired the Chevaliers as much for their shrewdness as for their resistance to authority and had to admit to himself ruefully that the woman sitting in front of him lacked none of her family's legendary guile and determination. Her face was all innocence but her words held some threat he could not ignore. He would have to comply but he could not help feeling that there was more to this visit than he had been told.

'It would be a pleasure to visit La Commanderie again, Mademoiselle Chevalier. It is too long since I was last there.'

'Tomorrow, shall we say? I hope you will have lunch with us. Yes? That is settled then. Now, Jérôme, please tell me how is Madame Janquet? We are so looking forward to some of her excellent charcuterie.'

'A hare and a partridge, Thérèse: we're going to live like kings! Good old Caramelle.'

'Poor things; I think they must have been too cold to get away quickly enough.'

'One on a branch and one sitting on the ground. I know it's not very sporting but no one's looking. My watch says it's not yet midday. I'd like to go as far as the gorge this time if you think we have enough time.'

She looked up into the clear cold blue sky; turned her head to see if there were any clouds gathering in the west. The horizon was a faint pink layer that was merging with the blue above. How smooth the skin on her throat was. Her chin had a minute dimple he had not noticed before. He longed to feel it with his tongue.

'If we hurry,' she said.

He seized her arm and started to run, pulling her after him, pretended to stumble, fell, and rolled over and over away from her down the slope. When she reached him he was lying on his back, perfectly still with the dog anxiously licking his face.

'Christ,' he said, 'I won't do that again in a hurry. I banged my bad leg. You ought to lick that, Caramelle, that's the part that hurts.'

As she bent down to take his hand he leaped up and put his arms round her and kissed her on her neck and then her chin.

'Philippe, you frightened me.'

'Not as much as you frighten me, my love. Love is very frightening.'

'If you like, I'll hold you until you stop being frightened.'

He started to make a joke about it, but smiled instead and said please and she did and she was right.

When they came close to the edge of the gorge she said they were near one of the steepest parts and they must be careful because the snow might be too soft. There were stories that avalanches had carried sheep and even people unconscious down into the river where they drowned in the freezing water. In places there was a sheer drop of hundreds of feet with sparse trees clinging to rock walls that were bearded with immense icicles. Far below he could see the river twisting like a grey snake writhing to escape from a trap. He felt her hand on his arm.

'Come away, Philippe; it's too dangerous. I'm worried about Caramelle.'

'There are some trees knocked over on those ledges down there, all in a line going down. Do you see?'

'Big stones fall off the cliffs and knock trees over.'

'In the spring perhaps, but not in the winter when everything is frozen solid. I know that from the hills at home. Let's walk back from the edge: I want to take a look for something.'

She could see their footprints in the snow leading away up the slope. What she had not noticed on the way down was that they had been walking along a sort of sunken road in the snow. Lawless saw it too and pointed.

'That's it! That's where she slid down the slope after she hit, then she went over the edge just about here, knocking down the trees and ending up in the river. If we look, we'll find her down there.'

'We can't look now, Philippe, the snow . . .'

'I know, I know, sweetheart. I have to wait: I know that. But when I can, when the snow's gone, I'm going to look for them. You know I have to, don't you?'

'Yes, I know, Philippe. I will help you.'

'How long will it be? When does the thaw start?'

'After we are married. Can you wait that long?'

'Thérèse, sweetheart, I'm such a fool. I'm so sorry, thinking only of myself again. Of course I can wait for that. But I can't wait to marry you. Come here.'

While they were taking a rest near the shepherd's shelter she said,

'When we get back home Séverine should be able to tell us when the wedding can be.'

'Well, come on then, I can't wait for that either.'

'Look, Philippe, near the tree, sticking up out of the snow, Caramelle, something . . .'

He was off running before she finished what she was saying. He came back swinging the parachute pack by one of its straps.

'Jack Verrill's,' he said. 'Lots more silk for you and Séverine.'

'Well, that's what he said: not before the first of February'

'But that's absurd! Why is he being so difficult?'

'He says he cannot accept the date I gave him for when your machine crashed, Philippe, because there is no proof of it.'

'Does he not believe you?' said Thérèse.

'I think he does but he has to be very careful in case the authorities find him guilty of infringing the law and I have to sympathise with him: they will seize on anything to dismiss a mayor who they think is a Communist. He is coming here tomorrow to see the two of you. Be tactful with him. We do not want to lose this man. We need his help.'

'If only it could have been earlier. February seems so far away.'

'Tressie, don't upset yourself. I haven't finished with Jérôme Janquet yet.'

'You said we need him,' said Lawless. 'If we play our cards right, he may realise that he needs us just as much.'

'Precisely. We must all play our parts. Thérèse, do you think the mayor likes civet?'

***

Jérôme Janquet leaned back in his chair and looked round the room.

'You may not remember the last time I was in this room, Mesdemoiselles; you were too young, but I do. First of August 1914. Your father, the Captain, invited every man in the commune who had received his orders to report for duty to take a last meal here in this room and drink to the victory of France. The next day we marched all the way to the railway station at Cassagnas with mules and the Captain's horses carrying our gear.'

'Cassagnas,' said Lawless. 'Cavallier's men hid out there and made gunpowder and kept their stores in the caves; page hundred and five, I think.'

'What is he saying, Mademoiselle?'

'Sergeant Lawless is translating the book of Jean Cavallier into French for us, Jérôme.'

'Seeing the book was like coming upon a treasure, Mr Mayor. I feel honoured to be allowed to translate it,' said Lawless, hoping he wasn't laying it on a bit too thick.

'Hm, I am impressed, Sir.'

'I remember that day,' said Séverine, 'because I helped to serve the wine and beer and I spilled some on the carpet. Mama was cross.'

'And I remember too,' said Thérèse. 'At least, I think I do. I remember waving at some soldiers.'

'Not so many of us came back.'

'And here we are again,' said Séverine, 'and so are they.'

It was Jérôme Janquet who broke the long reflective silence that followed Séverine's bitter words.

'Mademoiselle Thérèse I congratulate you on your delicious civet. It is my favourite.'

He turned to Lawless with a grin on his face.

'It is different from your English food, yes?'

'In England we call it jugged hare, Mr Mayor. We try to make it but fall miserably short of this quality,' replied Lawless, hoping this time he didn't sound obsequious.

'A man is very fortunate when his wife is a fine cook.'

'And even more so when she is beautiful too,' said Lawless gallantly, and truthfully this time.

Séverine got up from the table. 'We need more wine,' she said, 'and I must see what Jeannot is getting up to. I left him in the kitchen eating like a starved dog so I expect he's waiting for another helping by now. Excuse me. Thérèse, will you come with me for the cheese?'

'Jeannot Bec is shaping up to be a very useful lad,' said Jérôme Janquet after the women had gone out. 'Have you come across him?'

'Apart from yourself, Mr Mayor and the ladies of this house, I know no one else in the commune, but I hope my ignorance will not last much longer.'

'All in good time, Sergeant. I myself never rose above private first class, a poilu: do you know the word?'

'I do, Mr Mayor. My father spoke of them.'

'Your father? He served in France? Was he a front line soldier?'

'In a way: he was a stretcher-bearer in the King's Regiment.'

'King's Regiment, you say: did he ever speak of Maricourt?'

'I don't think so. He never said very much about the War.'

'I understand. Now I must ask you some other questions. I have seen your Royal Air Force pay book but that does not tell me your squadron nor how you came here.'

'I think you must know that I am not able to give you that information. What I can tell you is that I am on active service and that my aircraft crashed near this house. I am the only survivor. I can take you to the place where it crashed if you wish but I can show you now my parachute and that of one of my crew. I think they will prove the truth of what I am saying.'

'When did you crash?'

'Mademoiselle Chevalier tells me it was the eighth of December but I knew nothing of what happened for some days. I would not doubt her word.'

'And now you wish to marry Mademoiselle Thérèse. You have not known her very long.'

'How long after meeting your wife did you ask her to marry you, Mr Mayor: a week?'

Jérôme Janquet gave Lawless a very suspicious look.

'Who told you that?'

'No one, Sir; it was pure guesswork,' said Lawless and laughed.

Séverine came back in to the room, followed by Thérèse carrying a plate of cheese.

'What's all the laughter about?'

'He's just told me he wants to smell like a Frenchman!'

'And he said it can't be any worse than an Englishman!'

'Pf! Men,' said Séverine. 'Why don't I call in Jeannot then you can all three act like boys together?'

'He's impossible,' said Thérèse, although it was not clear which man she had meant.

'I apologise, Mademoiselle Chevalier. I like this Englishman and I believe what he says. But,' and Jérôme Janquet turned serious, 'but, as I said to you there are difficulties.'

'Before you go into those again, Jérôme, I think you should come with the Sergeant and me to see something we found in the snow. The cheese can wait for a few minutes. Thérèse, see that Jeannot does not disturb us.'

Once inside the stable, Lawless heaved the heavy box onto the bench and stood back.

'What is this, Mademoiselle?'

'Open it, Sergeant. Let Mr Mayor see what we have here.'

Lawless lifted the Browning from the box and placed it on the bench. A shaft of sunlight from the doorway made the oiled black metal gleam softly. Jérôme Janquet's eyes widened in astonishment. Still staring at the gun, he said in a low voice,

'Where did you get this?'

'It is from the Sergeant's aeroplane. He is one of the gunners.'

'But you said you said your machine crashed. Does this still work?'

Lawless took the length of ammunition belt from the box and without a word slotted the end into the feeder, worked the cocking handle twice, laid the weapon down and stood back.

'Loaded and ready to fire.'

He could see the mayor's eyes scanning the belt. He was an old soldier, all right. He was counting the rounds.

'Forty rounds: in case you're thinking that's not very many, it shouldn't be difficult to find plenty more when the snow melts. We carried two thousand rounds for the rear turret. I could tell you the range and the rate of fire but I think a soldier first class will have a good idea of those.'

Jérôme Janquet looked from one to the other.

'I could report this to the gendarmerie and have you both arrested.'

'You could,' said Séverine, 'but you will not. The gun would be confiscated and your chance would be lost. And you would remain under suspicion.'

'My "chance": what chance is that?'

'Let us stop playing games, Jérôme. We both know what you are planning and so does the sergeant here because I have told him. Like me you detest our so-called government for what it has done to France in submitting to the invaders and you are seeking ways of opposing it and if possible getting rid of it. That can only be done by force and you do not have anything like the power you need either to cause them any real harm or to persuade enough others to join you in your campaign. We are talking of small beginnings. This weapon will add strength to your efforts.'

'There were four of these guns in my turret,' said Lawless. 'With your help, we should be able to find the other three. Think of that.'

Jérôme Janquet's gaze shifted along the triangle from Lawless to Séverine, to the gun and back again. They watched him weighing the risk in trusting them, could almost hear him thinking, *How much do they know? Who else knows about this find?*

'We had none of these in 1914, then we got two just before Maricourt: two for the whole battalion.'

'Even two must have made a difference,' said Lawless.

'This gun is for use in an aircraft. It can't be used on the ground.'

'All it lacks is a stand, a tripod would be best, and a fitting to allow it to swivel. A good blacksmith could make what it needs.'

'The smith at Castignac, Vabrette: he could do it,' said Séverine.

'You know about Vabrette?'

Only that he's . . . wait; is he one of your men, Jérôme?'

'I don't know what you mean.'

'Jérôme, do you want this weapon or not? If you do, you have to trust us.'

'Mademoiselle Chevalier, I trust you. We are only a few at present and all we have done so far is spread rumours and stick up notices attacking the authorities. It's like a flea biting an elephant. What we need are guns to shoot it.'

'And explosives to blow it to bits,' said Lawless.

'How do we get such things? Were there any bombs left in your machine as well, Sergeant?'

'No. We left those elsewhere. You could make explosives. Chevallier did that. Or you could steal them. He did that as well. Find a chemist to help you, or a quarryman who thinks the same way as you do.'

'He is full of ideas, isn't he, Mademoiselle?'

'He can also train you to use this weapon, Jérôme, and those who join in with you.'

'Very well, I accept your help. But listen carefully. As I said, there are not many of us yet and finding the right people is a very slow and risky business. You know my political beliefs. I want nothing to do with people like those loud-mouthed idiots who spend all their time in the smart cafés in Antibes talking about revolt and never doing anything about it. We have other ideas. We keep quiet, we organise, we plan and when we are ready we will strike. And when we do, the people will know about it and will follow us.'

Here's a man who means what he says, thought Lawless. He had never met a real communist before. Séverine had the same steely resolve. He could see her as a machine gunner. He could not see her as a communist. She had too independent a mind for that.

'We have an understanding, I think, Jérôme. If you wish to turn it into an agreement, there is just one thing you can do for us.'

'I am listening, Mademoiselle Chevalier.'

'Advance the date of my sister's wedding and think of what you are being offered before you speak.'

'Something the sergeant said earlier has given me an idea. For a man on active service, there could be a concession for such an urgent request. I think we could bring forward the date by two weeks.'

'To the sixteenth of January: what do you think, Philippe?'

'If Thérèse agrees, so will I.'

'I think we are finished here for the time being,' said Séverine. 'Shall we go back for the cheese?'

Glancing through the kitchen window Jeannot Bec caught a glimpse of the mayor and Mademoiselle Chevalier walking back across the courtyard followed by a tall fair-haired man he had not seen before. The man was limping but not as much as the mayor.

'Philippe has some good news for you, Thérèse.'

'Darling, the mayor says that we can be married on the sixteenth after all. Isn't that marvellous?'

'Oh yes, marvellous; the sixteenth, but . . .'

'But what? Is something wrong?'

'No, no, it's wonderful, only,'

'There is something, tell me.'

'No, it's nothing. I'm just flustered, that's all. There's so much to do.'

'Well, let's start with another glass of wine, to celebrate,' said Séverine.

'To Mademoiselle and Monsieur,' said Jérôme Janquet, raising his glass. 'The notice will be posted on the sixth.'

'Some cheese, Mr Mayor?' said Thérèse. 'It is not pelardon but it goes well with this wine.'

'Thank you. You know, of course, Mademoiselle Thérèse, that you need two witnesses at the ceremony.'

'I should like one to be Jean-Pierre Bec. He is a good friend. As for another . . .'

'You said you know Henri Vabrette, the blacksmith.'

'Yes, I did; he has done work for us in the past.'

'As it happens he will be in St Chely on the sixteenth to do a little job for me. I am sure he would be glad to stand too. If you approve, I will let him know as soon as the notice is posted.'

'A good choice, Mr Mayor,' said Séverine. 'Don't you think so, Philippe?'

'You won't believe this,' said Lawless, 'but there is a place in Scotland called Gretna Green, where they say you could be married in the blacksmith's forge without anybody else's permission. All you needed were two witnesses. It sounds like a very good idea to me. I should like to meet this smith, Mr Vabrettte.'

After the mayor had left in Bec's cart with Jeannot holding the reins, Thérèse said she had some sewing to do and went up to her room. Séverine was nowhere to be seen so Lawless returned to his translating.

Cavallier was having a hard time, losing some good men and hearing worrying news of strong reinforcements joining Marshal Montrevel's forces. Returning south after a successful action at Vagnas in the Ardèche, his troop was ambushed and he had to shoot his way out. An old woman in the village of Bouquet hid him in her house and warded his pursuers off by telling them she had the fever.

Lawless sat back, trying to picture what it was like living on the run, never staying in the same place for more than a night, gathering a troop together and setting an ambush, sometimes successful, sometimes surprised by confrontation with a bigger force than expected and having to get out fast. Hit and run; know the country and where to hide; have the people on your side against a hated enemy; surprise, always surprise, strike hard and disappear: Cavallier knew it all and Marshall Montrevel seemed to have no way of dealing with such a wily guerrilla fighter.

Then, right at the end of Book Three, Cavallier got smallpox.

He was tired with concentrating hard on old-fashioned print that in places was so faded as to be almost invisible. Lawless rubbed his eyes and closed the book. He looked at his watch: almost six. It was dark outside. The house was quiet. He wondered if Thérèse was still at her sewing. Strange how she had reacted when she heard about the earlier date for the wedding. Was it nerves? He had to admit he felt a bit nervous himself. What would they say at home if they knew what was going on here? And, wait a minute: to get married you had to have permission given by your commanding officer. He almost laughed out loud at the thought: fat chance of that. But was there a way of letting them know? Not the Wingco: his parents. What about this man Janquet? Could he see a way of getting a message to England? Séverine had said something about it. The thought seized him. He should have asked Séverine about it long ago. Come on, there wasn't any 'long ago': he had only been here three weeks. Not very long to know a woman before you asked her to marry you, Janquet had said. And a woman who was older than he was, he knew. Was *that* why she had seemed uncertain earlier? Stop being stupid: they loved each other and that was all that mattered. He heard a door open and voices out in the corridor. The door closed again and silence returned.

'Much more sewing to do?'

'Quite a lot. I'm having trouble fitting the sleeves. I keep making mistakes. I want to take your measurements.'

'Whatever for?'

'Don't pretend. Philippe gave you the other parachute so I'm going to make one for you as well.'

'I don't need a silk nightgown.'

'It will be a present from me and Philippe. You can't refuse that. There's a lot of Mama's silk thread in her workbox. I can embroider the breast for you.'

'Grumpy old me again. Tressie, thank you. Of course I won't refuse such a present. I have one for you. Mama gave me her veil because I'm the elder daughter, she said. But I'm never likely to need it, so it's yours.'

'Séverine, you can't.'

'I can and don't argue. You can give it back if I ever find some old moneybags and drag him off to the Mairie.'

'There is something I have to tell you but promise not to be cross.'

'I knew there must be something when you seemed a bit hesitant about the date.'

'That's just it: the date. It took me by surprise but I couldn't explain in front of the men.'

'You mean . . .'

'Yes, it's my time of the month. What can I do?'

'Tressie, put that tape down and come here. I'm not cross with you. I understand, I really do. I still have them, earlier in the month than you. If you like, I will deal with it, no, you don't have to be embarrassed. I know what to say. Now, what date shall we say?'

'A week later; the twenty third. I will be all right then.'

'Leave it to me. Soup should be enough for supper, don't you think? We had such a big lunch.'

Jeannot Bec told his father that while he had been eating his lunch in the kitchen at La Commanderie, he had looked out of the window and seen a strange man go into one of the stables with Mademoiselle Chevalier and Mr Janquet. He was a tall young man with reddish hair.

'You sure Mr Mayor was with them?' Jeannot nodded. 'Well, you keep your mouth shut, understand? You don't say a word to anybody else.' Jeannot nodded again.

***

'It's very simple,' said Séverine. 'Tell him, Tressie.'

They were sitting over breakfast and Lawless had asked what happened at a French wedding in the Mairie.

'I think I can remember from when Jeanette and Victor were married at the Mairie in Florac.'

'Jeanette was at school with us and Victor Dumanoir was an advocate in Montpellier. That's where they live now,' said Séverine to Lawless.

'You sit together in front of the Mayor who has his sash on.'

'I'm thinking of wearing my uniform, but it's dirty.'

'Look in the wardrobe. I've cleaned it,' said Thérèse. 'Now, listen: we stand up in front of the Mayor,'

'Who has his sash on.'

'Be quiet. I'm telling you. And the witnesses sit on either side of us, or behind us.'

'Vabrette the blacksmith and who's the other? Yes, Bec: he must be Jeannot's father. Is he?'

'Will you listen! Then the Mayor reads out all your details like who you are and where you're from and other things I can't remember but yours are all in your book and we have my certificates. Then he asks us.'

'You've forgotten something.'

'What?'

'The Mayor reads out the sections about marriage from the Civil Code.'

'Yes, I know that. Then the Mayor asks me if I want to marry you and asks you if you want to marry me.'

'And what do we say to him?'

'What do you mean? We say yes. You do want to, don't you?'

'Of course I do. I'll shout it. YES. Mmmmm.'

'Leave all that for afterwards,' said Séverine. 'She's trying to speak. Go on, Tressie.'

'I'm sorry. I'm listening. Then what?'

'Well, that's it.'

'That's it? Is that all?'

'Yes, except we both have to sign the legal paper and the witnesses sign as well.'

'Then we're married: well and truly married?'

'"Well and truly": I like those words, Philippe. "Well and truly".'

'Don't forget the Family Book, Tressie.'

'Oh yes, the Family Book: the Mayor gives us our Family Book.'

'What is that?'

'We have one,' said Séverine. 'I can show it to you. It was given to Papa and Mama at their wedding in 1895. It has the date of birth of their children, Tressie and me and our brothers, so it is a record of what happens in the family. When you are married you will have your own new one for your family.'

'We have nothing like that in England,' said Lawless, 'but some families write dates in a family Bible: births, marriages and deaths. My uncle, the sheep farmer I told you about, he has one. I've seen it. The dates go back nearly two hundred years. The last name in it is my cousin, Colin.'

'When he was born?'

'Yes, and the date when he died.'

Thérèse said, 'In our book the last name is Mama's. I wrote it.'

'I wish I could have met your mother. Have you a photograph of her?'

'Papa had her portrait painted soon after they were married. It's in her bedroom.'

'I think you two should move into that room after you are married,' said Séverine. She glanced at Lawless. 'Then you can see what Mama looked like when she was young.'

'But Séverine, do you mean it? Do you think we should? It was Mama's and Papa's room. All their things are still there.'

'Of course you should. It's time it was used again. It's the right room for a wife and her husband. Your rooms are both too small. Why don't you start getting it ready? Philippe can help me with the ewes while you take a look.'

Thérèse was already half way up the stairs. 'I'll wash the curtains first,' she called down to them.

Séverine watched her go. 'She's so happy, Philippe; just like a little girl again. You won't do anything to change that, will you?'

'Only the War could do that.'

'What do you mean?'

'It could stop me getting back home one day. It's already done it once and I'm glad of it because that's why I am here. Another time it might be different.'

'War: it never seems to go away. Even when the shooting stops it's still there like distant thunder in the mountains, waiting to come back.'

'Aren't we both trying to stop it?'

'By fighting? Isn't that the irony? To stop war we have to make war.'

They looked at each other in silence. Maybe I was wrong about her and the Browning, Lawless was thinking. When she knew how, she would certainly use it, no doubt about that, but would she like doing it? After what she had just said and how she looked while saying it, he wasn't so sure now.

Thérèse has no idea what this boy has done and plans to do again, and doesn't want to know, thought Séverine, looking into the young blue eyes. *All she wants is to be happy with her lover, her husband. If only I were like her.*

'Philippe, there's something I have to tell you and then we'll go and see to the sheep. The wedding will have to be a week later, on the twentythird, not the sixteenth. Thérèse was too shy to bring it up in front of two men.'

'I don't understand.'

'You will. It's a woman's matter. That's all there is to it.'

'Couldn't she have told me?'

'Philippe, you have so much to learn. Now, come on: it's a good day and time we got the ewes outside for a few hours. I need you to help.'

'Isn't that a bit risky? They could wander off.'

'You're forgetting Caramelle: you, of all people!'

FRANCE 1942

RESISTANCE

The days were becoming noticeably longer; he was sure of it, but what was the date? He had no diary and there was no calendar in the house; no wireless and no telephone, either. Neither of the women seemed to care. If there was something that had to be done on a particular date, they just seemed to know when it came round. He would have asked but Séverine had gone into St Chely, why, he was not sure, and Thérèse had shut herself away in her room saying she didn't want to be disturbed. He started totting up the days since the mayor's visit: that had been on the day after Boxing Day. The ewes had been let out the day after: having seen her at work with the flock he was sure that Caramelle could have been among the prize-winners in the sheep dog trials at Rydal Show. New Year's Eve: what a night that had been. They all drank too much of that *vin doux*. He'd gone on and on about New Year's Eve at home: eating frumity and first-footing and home-made wine and singing D'ye Ken John Peel until they told him he was a pagan and please shut up and dance instead. He must have passed out but not before Séverine had given him another of those fierce kisses when Thérèse wasn't looking, or maybe she had been, because he woke up in the morning lying in front of the fireplace in the kitchen. Someone had thrown an old blanket over him and Caramelle had snuggled up close. The ewes had been let out again on New Year's Day in spite of his terrible hangover, and the day after as well because the spell of fine warmer weather had continued. The day after that Jeannot had come to the house with a parcel of sausages and ham sent by Madame Janquet while he was upstairs working on the pages describing how Marshal Montrevel was enjoying the favours of his mistress at Alez instead of enduring the hardships of campaigning against the Camisards, or Camizars, as Chevallier now called his men. Then the weather had changed again, bringing two days of gales that kept every animal and human inside, in his case in one of the barns chopping and sawing endless piles of logs. Adding up, Lawless decided it must be the sixth of January: sixteen days since the winter solstice, the shortest day of the year. The days *were* getting longer and there were only three more to the date when the mayor would pin up the notice of marriage. Lawless was determined to be in St Chely when he did.

Lunch was hard goat's cheese, bread and rough red wine that Séverine had brought back from St Chely. The bread was fawn-coloured and had a sweetish, smoky taste.

'Chestnut flour,' said Séverine, seeing the puzzled look on Lawless's face as he chewed, 'made from chestnuts smoked over wood from the same tree. Do you like it?'

'I'm so hungry from all the chopping and sawing and reading about Chevallier's people starving in the winter that I could eat the wood as well as the nuts. Yes, I like it: it takes the edge of this wine.'

'You can have cider if you prefer.'

'No, thank you; this is fine.' What I'd really like, he thought, is a pint of Tadcaster bitter. 'Do you ever have beer?'

'Not for a long time. The men used to drink it at harvest time. Papa had a barrel for them. Jérôme Janquet keeps beer in his café.'

'That reminds me: I think it's time I went to St Chely, don't you? I wouldn't be surprised if our friend the mayor has let one or two of his people know about me by now and in any case my name's going to be with Thérèse's on his notice board so why not show my face? What do you think, my love?'

'I would like to go. It's been so long since I was in St Chely, or anywhere else,' said Thérèse.

'Then we'll go together and watch the mayor put up the notice and go to the café afterwards and buy some more Gaulois and celebrate.'

'We'll all go,' said Séverine laughing, 'and if we celebrate too much Jeannot can bring us back in the cart.'

'That warm spell saw off quite a lot of the snow. If it doesn't snow again, perhaps we could go on the bikes. Where are they? I ought to see if they need any repairs. I'd welcome a change from chopping wood: that's not doing any good for my piano playing, is it darling?'

'He gave up on the Fauré last night, Séverine, because he said he was playing too many wrong notes but he wasn't. 'He's just too fussy, aren't you?' Thérèse kissed him lightly on the cheek and got up from the table. 'I have to prepare the cassoulet for dinner then I must get on with my sewing. I need to measure you again, Séverine.'

'I'll come up later. Before you go, one of the things I asked Jérôme Janquet this morning was whether there is a way for Philippe to get a message back to England without the authorities finding out that he is here. He says there is. It takes a while but he will arrange for it to be done.'

'That's wonderful. Can we let him have it when we go on the thirteenth? My god! I forgot: did you tell him about the change in date?'

'Of course, I did. It wouldn't have mattered anyway. The notice would have been posted a week earlier than necessary, that's all.'

'It would have mattered to us,' said Thérèse. 'We want to be there when it goes up.'

'I'll show you where the bicycles are, Philippe. I hope the tyres are all right because they're like gold these days.'

There were two sturdy Peugeot boneshakers with curved step-through frames and full chain guards for women and a sporty model with dropped handlebars and cable brakes for a man. Someone had greased and oiled all three and even used saddle soap on the leather before hanging them on long brackets and covering them with a tarpaulin. Apart from the tyres being flat they were all in fair condition. There was even a pump clipped onto the seat tube of one of the women's machines.

'A clean-up, a bit oil and some wind in the tyres and they'll fly like birds, Sèverine.'

'Fabrice put them away before he left at the end of his last leave. He said they should keep until the end of the war.'

'How old was he, Séverine?'

'Thirty one but we still don't know the date he died.'

'Thérèse told me you had a letter about him.'

'With his name and regiment and "died of wounds": that's all it said.'

'And "sorry" at the end,' Thérèse said.

'Yes, "sorry"; not very much, is it?'

'It means a friend sent it, or at least someone who knew him and he told them your address.'

'I suppose that's something, yes; thank you Philippe.' She kissed him on the cheek. 'You may not be able to put much more in the message Jérôme Janquet says he can send for you.'

'It will be enough to tell my mother I'm still alive. I can't bear to think what she's been feeling since I went missing.'

'Courage, as we say, Philippe. Now, Jérôme told me other things. Vabrette will come here to look at the gun and if he can do what you say is needed he will take it away in his own cart. That will be much safer than our carrying it down to St Chely and handing it over there. If anyone gets too nosey we can say that he's come to do some work up here. Bec knows about you but not about the gun. He is a good man who would never talk, but for now the fewer people who know what we have here, the better.'

'Did the mayor say if anybody in the village knows about the crash?'

'He's not sure. He thinks Bec suspects something happened that night. If he does, it must be Jeannot who told him. That boy roams all over the place and he may have spotted something.'

'We ought to find out. How about me talking to him?'

'It may come to that but we don't want to frighten him off. He's going to be useful to us later on.'

'All right. Anything else?'

'Jérôme has had meetings with other Party activists in Le Pont de Montvert and Balsiège, that's on the railway line south of Mende so it's an important place. With Vabrette at Castignac as well it means a network is building up and it will get bigger in time.'

'Are all of them communists?'

'Does that matter? Nobody hates Vichy more than the communists.'

'Hate isn't enough. It can cloud judgment.'

'Wise words from young lips: have you read that in Cavallier's book?'

'As a matter of fact, yes; not in so many words perhaps but I don't think it was hate that kept him doing so well for so long. Knowing when and how to strike, when to lie low and how to make best use of his weapons: those were Cavallier's skills. Janquet's men need the same.'

'You're right, of course, I know. It will be the same kind of war.'

'Has Janquet heard anything else on his radio?'

'Yes; I was going to tell you. Some Americans troops have arrived in England and many more are on their way. And he has heard that another English aeroplane crashed on the same night as yours somewhere in the mountains of the High Alps.'

'They could have been on the same raid as us, maybe even from my squadron. Did he say what kind it was and if any of the crew were found?'

'I'm sorry. I've told you all he knows.'

'Séverine, I wonder if you know what you're getting into. You say it will be the same kind of war as Cavallier's. Then be prepared for the same kind of terrible losses and hardships he and his people suffered. They were hunted, betrayed, tortured and executed; their wives and children were shot and burned in their villages and their comrades sent to the galleys. The King's armies crushed them like a vice; their land was left desolate and the freedom they fought for and thought they had been promised took nearly another hundred years and a revolution before it was theirs. Are you ready for that?'

'Philippe, I could just say, "yes, I am; I am ready for that" but you are a student as well as a soldier so you need to learn. You are English which is why you don't understand: you have never been invaded, defeated and occupied. You have never known real revolution—I know what you are going to say but your republic lasted only a few years before you allowed the son of the tyrant you had executed to return to rule you. How can you understand what we feel and what we are ready to do? Our revolution was not the bloody disaster you English seem to think it was: it was liberation after centuries of tyrrany. The tyrants did come back but only for a while and only because England and the others with kings wanted them back. But we got rid of them again and we shall do the same to this latest disease that infects France. Liberty, Philippe: there is no more precious gift. It is worth any sacrifice.'

'I don't know what to say.'

'You do not have to say anything. All you have to do is help us as long as you can.'

'You know I will.'

'Yes, I know. Oops, I forgot: Thérèse wants to take my measurements again.'

Lawless was feeling a desperate need to lighten the mood.

'What is she making for you; something for the wedding, something silky?'

'Mind your own business. Don't you know it's improper to ask a lady about such things?'

***

Lawless gulped down the last of the coffee and stood up.

'Time to go? You look gorgeous. What about me?'

'I wouldn't say gorgeous but you do look very smart in that suit only I wish you were wearing your uniform coat because the blue matches your eyes.'

'Yours are dark pools of mystery that drown me with pleasure.'

'You're impossible. Hm, there's a little nick on your cheek.'

Lawless pretended to shudder with fright. 'That razor: when you brought it close to my throat I thought I was about to die.'

'That beard had to come off. You looked peculiar. It was bristly and nearly red but your hair is fair and wavy. Any woman would love to have it.'

'Is there a barber in St Chely? I'll have it all cut off and give it to you for a wig. You can wear it at our wedding. It will be my wedding present to you. I have nothing else to give. I will be Samson to your Delilah.'

'Stop it. I'm trying to wipe this spot of blood from your cheek.'

'You have hidden talents. Where did you learn to use a cut-throat razor?'

'From Mama. She used to shave Grandpapa when he came to live with us after the War—the other War—and became too old to do it himself. Mama said I should learn for when I had a husband but until now the only man I shaved was Fabrice and then not very often because he said I brushed the soap up his nose.' Thérèse giggled. 'I did sometimes because he deserved it for being cheeky.'

'It has someone's initials engraved on it. Let me see: A G D C.'

'Aristide Gaspard Duchesne Chevalier: Papa. There is another like it in the case. Bend you head down and stand still.'

She looked so serious and beautiful with the tip of her tongue showing between her lips that he could not resist kissing her.

'Thérèse, I love you. This is the day, well, the first day we let other people know about us. Then it's only ten days more to the twenty third and I will wear my uniform for you then.'

'We'd better be going,' said Séverine, coming into the room. 'Our mayor will be up early today and we can't use the bicycles in this snow. It's an hour's walk to St Chely.'

'What about the house?'

'Caramelle will stay here. She won't let anyone come too close.'

When they set out, Lawless behaved at first like a boy let out of school, throwing snowballs and kicking at the drifts, sending sprays of glittering powder flying at Séverine. Thérèse was infected by his silly mood and ran after him flailing him with her shopping bag and trying to stuff handfuls of snow down his neck. Struggling to get away from her he fell backwards, dragging her down, clasping her in his arms and rolling over and over until she was almost weeping with laughter. Séverine watched them holding each other so close, rubbing their noses together and thinking again, why can't I be like her? She turned her back on them and trudged down the long slope away from the house, stamping her feet in the snow. Half way down, she heard shouts from behind her and turned to see a huge ball of snow ballooning in size as it rolled towards her. She stood looking up at them waving their arms and shouting her name and as the snow boulder was almost upon her. She heard Thérèse scream in alarm and saw Lawless start to run. It almost touched her as it swept past giving out a tearing creaking noise as it gobbled up the snow and seconds later Lawless was at her side, closely followed by Thérèse.

'My god, Séverine, why didn't you jump? It could have killed you.'

'Look before you leap: do the English say that? I was looking.'

'Séverine, you terrified me. Philippe, we shouldn't have done that. It was stupid.'

Lawless seemed not to hear her. Shaking his head slowly and looking at Séverine he said,

'I must say you're a cool one. If that's really what you were doing.'

'Look: it's made a road for us picking up all that snow. Come on. They won't wait for us at the Mairie.'

The sun was at their backs. Still not very high it aimed long tapering shadows of them far across a white plateau that seemed as vast as the Russian steppe to Lawless's imagination.

'You can see St Chely now: down there.'

Thin pale blue stalks of smoke rose up as straight and solid as stone pillars in the cold still air from a round cluster of pale grey houses that seemed to huddle together for warmth and safety like a flock of sheep. The village lay near the end of a wide dry valley that plunged over the edge of the deep winding gorge that separated one stretch of causse from the next.

'I can see a square tower; looks as if the top's falling down at one corner, and a church steeple and some bits of wall with houses built into them.'

'The wall used to go all the way round long ago. One of the old gateways is still there on the other side.'

'The snow never lies deep in this valley,' said Séverine. 'It's very sheltered. That's the line of the road, further down where the tops of walls are showing. Once we reach that we'll soon get there.'

She hurried them along a narrow curving alleyway where the cobbles had been swept clear of snow. There was a sweet smell of woodsmoke and sounds were coming from almost all the grey stone houses but the shutters were still closed. They passed under a couple of arches spanning the street whose sole purpose seemed to be to hold the opposing houses apart and suddenly they found themselves in the village square. In the centre of the side opposite was a solid two-storey building with the word 'MAIRIE' in faded white letters on the lintel over a panelled door. Attached to the Mairie was an ordinary looking house with one large window at street level bearing the painted title 'Café de la Place'. As they were crossing the empty square, the door of the Mairie opened, and out stepped Jérôme Janquet carrying a sheet of paper in one hand and a hammer in the other. Lawless wondered why he looked tight-lipped until coming closer he saw that the mayor was holding four black metal tacks between his teeth. They watched in silence while the paper was nailed firmly in place on the notice board fixed to the Mairie wall.

'I'm sorry your banns has to share space with stupid notices from the Prefecture about not showing lights after dark and fines for selling on the black market. I usually take them down after a day or so and say the wind blew them away but it might be better if your notice were not too conspicuous.'

Holding Thérèse by the hand, Lawless read the notice out loud, in English slowly word by word.

Notice of Marriage

To be celebrated in the Mairie of *Saint Chely la Bastide*

BETWEEN Monsieur *Lawless Philippe Martyn* Profession *Soldier* Domicile *Kendal*

Residence *La Commanderie*

AND Mademoiselle *Chevalier Thérèse Angéline Duchesne* Profession *Farmer* Domicile *St Chely la Bastide*

Residence *La Commanderie*

POSTED *Saturday 13 January*

YEAR *1942* at *10 hours*

BY US *Janquet Jérôme Marcel*

MAYOR of the commune of *Saint Chely la Bastide*

Under the last line was what looked like the Mairie's official stamp in smudged black ink and an illegible signature.

'I hope I've got that right'.

'Is everything satisfactory?' said Jérôme Janquet.

'The only thing is I'm an airman, not a soldier.'

'If you fight on the ground, as you will be doing, you're a soldier,' said Séverine. 'So it doesn't really matter.'

Thérèse squeezed Lawless's hand as she read the plain white announcement. There was shy excitement in her voice when she spoke.

'Nothing like this has happened in our family since Mama and Papa were married.'

'But they were not married here, Mademoiselle Chevalier?'

'No. Mama's family lived in La Couvertoirade but there was a big party here when Papa brought her home. Mama told me it lasted three days.'

'La Couvertoirade?' Lawless frowned at Séverine. 'You didn't say your mother came from there when you told me about it. So, were the families connected?'

'By blood only distantly. They believed in the same things and they fought together. Usually on the same side,' she added with a smile.

'What would they think of me?'

'They would have taken a lot longer to make up their minds. Don't forget, some of them fought against the English and died doing it.'

'In America, yes, you told me that. But it was a long time ago.'

'It goes back further than that. The English came here many times with their archers burning and thieving . . .'

'Séverine, stop! I don't want to hear any more about history today. I want us all to be happy. Philippe and I are going to be married.'

'Thérèse, sweetheart, you're right. Let's celebrate. Come on, Séverine, we're on the same side now. Mr Mayor, will you do us the honour of opening your café?'

'It will be a pleasure, Sergeant, and I have some good news to tell you inside. Mesdemoiselles, after you, if you please.'

Séverine's good humour returned, after a cup of Madame Janquet's strong real coffee and bread brought hot from the bakery by Jeannot Bec.

'Excellent, the apricot jam, Jérôme: my compliments to Madame Janquet. Now, cognac.'

'I have it ready, Mademoiselle. Jeannot, we may have need of you later. Finish your bread and go tell your father.'

Séverine got to her feet and raised her glass of cognac.

'A toast: to my dear sister Thérèse and her fiancé Philippe. Chance brought them together and now through them the family Chevalier will live on. All happiness to them.'

Lawless sensed he was expected to reply. He raised his finger to Jérôme Jaquet who responded by refilling the glasses, not forgetting his own.

'I thank you, Mr Mayor, for taking a risk over me. I thank both these ladies for saving my life. I thank you, Séverine, for doing so much for me, including things I do not yet know about, I suspect. I thank you, Thérèse, for your love and I promise you mine. I thank the family Chevalier for allowing me to become one of them. To you all.'

After the glasses were drained he shook hands with the mayor and embraced the two women. Séverine's cheeks felt hot: the brandy perhaps.

'He speaks well, this man. He has good manners.'

'For an Englishman, yes, Jérôme.'

He lowered his voice. 'Vabrette is here.'

'Is he? Where?'

'In the Mairie. We should talk.'

'Not my sister. I will ask her to collect the shopping. That should give us enough time.'

Henri Vabrette was not big and muscular as Lawless had expected. He found himself shaking hands with a neatly dressed wiry man of medium height with greying hair cut short. The only things big about him were his hands which were huge and heavily veined. He had a cheerful face and bright eyes that appraised Lawless shrewdly while his massive hand crushed Lawless's until it hurt.

'Says his father was a stretcher bearer who knew the poilus.'

'Did he carry you out?'

'The lad doesn't know but I bet he was at Maricourt because his regiment attacked alongside ours that day.'

'He speaks French,' said Lawless. 'All you have to do is ask him.'

'What is it you want?'

Séverine cut in. 'We want you to take a look at a piece of machinery at La Commanderie and tell us if you can make it work properly.'

'I have seen it,' said Jérôme Janquet, 'and I think you could do something with it. The sergeant here can tell you more.'

Vabrette gave each of them a look with his shrewd eyes.

'Well, if Jeannot's taking you all back in Jean-Pierre's cart, why don't I come with you and see what you've got? Always a pleasure to help you, Mademoiselle Chevalier.'

As they were leaving the Mairie, Vabrette poked Lawless in the ribs with an iron-hard finger. 'I'm told you have another job for me here on the twenty third. Is that right?'

'That's right. You don't have to do anything. Just be there. And stay afterwards if you feel thirsty.'

'Blacksmiths are always thirsty, my friend. It goes with the job.'

'In that case I think we should go back to the café. What do you say, Séverine? I need some cigarettes anyway.'

The room in the Mairie had been almost as cold as the square outside but the café had a fuggy warmth. Settling back in one of the shabby armchairs Lawless looked round the room, squinting through the haze of Gauloise smoke which was adding another layer to the nicotine-coated walls. Vabrette and Séverine were talking in low voices, occasionally glancing in his direction. Jérôme Janquet was behind his zinc-topped bar arranging glasses and cups on a battered tin tray. The long walk through the snow, rather a lot of brandy and the rough comfort of the sagging armchair were making it difficult for Lawless to stay awake. He felt a twinge of guilt: he ought to be excited. After all, outside was a notice telling anyone who cared to look that he was getting married in ten days time. And not in Holy Trinity church in Kendal but in a drab cold room of the Mairie of a rundown village in one of the remotest parts of France. It was hard to take it all in. But what was it Verrill had said? *Don't think about tomorrow; take what's on offer today.*

'Coffee, you said, Sergeant.'

He picked up the sheet of paper the mayor had placed on the table next to his cup and read:

Sergeant Philippe Lavless 419644

'I want you to write in English that you are alive and well, then put a little signature.'

Lawless took the pencil offered and did as he was told and corrected the spelling of his name.

'Now write some words your father will know must be from you.'

Lawless thought for a moment then wrote *D'ye ken John Peel.*

'This will be sent to England. I have your father's address. No, don't ask how it is done. It is better you do not know. It will take some time to get there.'

'Is there a chance I will get a reply?'

'I cannot say. It might be dangerous but let us see.'

Lawless started to thank the mayor when Jeannot Bec's face appeared round the door.

'Mams'elle Chevalier is outside. She says it is time to go.'

The cart was standing in front of the Mairie. Thérèse was sitting on a wooden bench at the rear with her bulging shopping bag on her knees. Lawless swung himself up into the cart beside her while Séverine and Vabrette settled on the driver's bench next to Jeannot who promptly raised his whip.

'Stop a moment,' said Lawless. 'Is that the Memorial, there on the Mairie wall? The names . . .'

He jumped down to take a closer look. On the wall of the Mairie , to the right of the door, its top level with the lintel was a white stone plaque, marble, he thought, with words and names carved and picked out in black inside black outlined rectangles. At the top were the words:

SAINT CHELY LA BASTIDE
SOUVENIR A NOS MORTS POUR LA FRANCE
1914—1918

Arranged symmetrically below were two rectangles filled with names. So many names, he thought; always so many names for such small places.

ANGLARS LOUIS
ANGLARS GÉRARD
BERGER PIERRE
BOULAINE HENRI
CHEVALIER ARISTIDE
CHEVALIER LÉOPOLD
CHEVALIER PASCAL
DARGILLAN JEAN
FABRÉGAN BERNARD
FONTAINE CHRISTOPHE
FONTAINE CLÉMENT

GUERQUET JULES
GUERQUET FRÉDÉRIC
LUGNAC HERVÉ
MARTIN ÉTIENNE
PUECH JEAN-MARC
PUECH JEAN-PIERRE
SOUBEYRAN LUCIEN
SOUBEYRAN PASCAL
TOLLAINCOURT ÉDOUARD
VABRETTE MICHEL

Three Chevaliers, father and two sons. Lawless turned to speak but Séverine and Thérèse had their faces turned away. Only Vabrette was looking at him and jerking his head to tell Lawless to take his seat again.

He took Thérèse's hand in one of his and put his other arm around her shoulders. She was silent until they were in sight of the house and then she said simply.

'We never look but I'm glad you read their names. They marched away one hot summer day and never came back.'

Henri Vabrette spent a long time looking at the Browning, even walking round the bench to see it from all angles before he picked it up and weighed it in his hands

'Hm. Ten kilos.'

'It needs a stand, a tripod with a swivel.'

'I could do it but that would double the weight, more when you give it a new stock and it will need one if you intend to fire it lying down: too heavy for one man. What you want is a bipod. I can make one with a sleeve round the barrel just in front of the cooling vents. Loosen a couple of nuts and off it comes for carrying.'

'Let's try it and see how it works. How do you know about these things?'

'Corporal, 153rd. Sat behind a Hotchkiss a few times. Is this the only one you have?'

'My turret had four. This is the only one we've found so far.'

'Ammunition?'

'What you see and a box with two hundred and fifty rounds.'

'Is that all? I'd say that was twenty seconds firing. Am I right?

'Near enough but there is more.'

'We need a lot more, especially if we find the other three guns.'

'Four more: there was one in the nose.'

'Five guns! That's a battery. My whole batallion had only two Hotchkiss in 1916.'

'We carried two thousand rounds for the rear turret guns and another thousand for the nose gunner but we don't know where the boxes are, or the guns, for that matter. The whole lot may have been destroyed in the wreck.'

'Well, we'll just have to see when the snow's gone. It won't be easy because Jérôme wants as few people to know about this as possible. We'll have to set Jeannot on to it.'

'Jeannot? He's only a boy.'

'He knows the woods and the gorge better than anybody. He just about lives there when his father lets him, and sometimes even when he doesn't. And he knows how to keep his mouth shut. Look, I have to be going. What about this gun?'

'Come back for it in a few days time,' said Séverine. 'Drop the word in the café that you're finishing off the job you've been to look at today. How long will it take to do what you said?'

'A day, two perhaps.'

'Good. Bring it back with you when you come to be witness on the twenty third.'

'Not long now then, eh, Sergeant? Soon be a married man.'

'A glass of something before you go?'

'Now you're talking. Thank you kindly, Mademoiselle Chevalier.'

As they were walking across to the house Lawless said:

'That name on the Memorial . . .'

'My twin brother,' said Vabrette.

'Isn't there a word missing?'

'What do you mean?'

'Enfants: 'Souvenir à nos *enfants* morts pour la France'?'

'D'ye know, I'd never thought of that. You are sharp, aren't you? Maybe there just wasn't enough room.'

***

'That was very good, don't you think, sweetheart? I love this piece.' Lawless played a few bars from the second page of the nocturne.

'E natural: you always play E sharp in that chord. Look, C sharp-E *natural*-A.'

'I love your hands. You play much better than I do.'

'Only because you're out of practice.'

'I'd forgotten how to play this kind of thing until I met you. Just about all I was doing was bang out tunes for people to sing when we went to the pubs. Now and again, not very often, if it went quiet I'd play some Chopin, not this nocturne, and they'd listen for a while then the landlord would shout *stop it, play something cheerful* and the noise would start up again.'

'You're saying things I don't understand, Philippe. What is this *pub* and what is a *landlord*?'

'Sorry: *landlord*? You say patron. We would say Jérôme Janquet is the *landlord* if his café was a *pub*. A pub is like a café; well, not really. It's not open all day long and nobody drinks coffee there, usually only beer. Yes, and the beer's different and you can play darts and there's nearly always a piano. Do you understand now?'

'No, but it sounds very, very, er, cheerful.'

'It can be.' *Though not that night after Harper's crew didn't turn up because they were cinders scattered all over Bremen.* Listen, if you want to know what a pub is like, you'll have to go to one. Would you like that?'

'Go to England? How? What about the house and the sheep and . . .'

'No, sweetheart, not now. After. . . ' He stopped.

'After the War, you mean.'

'Yes, after the War: Séverine can take care of things here.'

'I try to think what England is like. I would love to see where you live.'

'We could all go if Séverine found someone to look after the farm for a little while.'

'I don't think she would ever go, Philippe. She's not like me. She hasn't got you.'

'No, she hasn't got me and I sometimes wonder if she wants me here at all. If it weren't for my gun Vabrette took away the other day and what I can do on the farm . . .'

'Philippe, stop it. You still haven't got to know her properly yet. She really wants you to be here because she likes you and you like the farm and the sheep. She has a funny sense of humour. Even I can't be sure sometimes whether she's serious or joking. But you've persuaded her to do things that she hasn't done for years, like the dancing. She loves that. I've watched her with you. She enjoys it. She gets really excited.'

'All right, at least she seems to. She certainly learns quickly. There are times when I think she's more the leader than I am.'

'Well, it's not bad for a man to feel that sometimes.'

'Now, I really must kiss you for that remark. Don't you realise I'll soon be your lord and master? Like Cavallier: did you know he wrote that whatever he commanded his people to do was obeyed and his will among them was a law?'

'Well, well: an English milord. You never told me. One kiss only, milord and very courtly, if you please. And let me remind you, Cavallier wasn't married to me.'

'One kiss here and then can I stay with you tonight?'

'Why tonight when we're going to be married in two more days?'

'Because waiting is so painful. I count the minutes. I don't know what to do. Two days sounds like two years.'

'I'm sorry. I love you but we must wait. You will understand when I tell you. Do you believe me?'

'Oh God, when you look like that I believe anything you say.'

'One kiss then, perhaps two, but no more until . . .'

'I'll never stop then, you see. Hey, let me look at your finger. What have you done to it?'

'Pricked it with a needle, that's all.'

'Haven't you finished all that sewing yet?'

'Séverine's is done and I'll give it to her tomorrow morning. Mine needs a little more embroidery but it should be ready the day after.'

'It's a wedding dress, isn't it?'

'Wait and see.'

'Wait? I'm always waiting.'

***

'It's warmer today, don't you think? H'm, what's that lovely smell?'

Thérèse was stirring the heavy iron pot that hung over the fire. She looked up when she heard Lawless come in.

'Finished out there?'

'Séverine's having a look at one of the ewes she thinks has worm. I couldn't see anything. Is this soup? I thought you never had soup for lunch in France, or have I said that before?'

'Chestnut and mushroom; and herbs, of course. It's not really soup.'

'Because it's got lumps in. Can I give it a stir?'

'No. You always lick the spoon. Wash your hands. You smell of sheep.'

'I'm a French shepherd. *Of course* I smell of sheep.'

'Not in this kitchen. Do as you're told.'

'The icicles hanging over the barn doors are melting. Maybe Séverine's heart is melting as well. She's certainly in a better mood today. What can have caused that, I wonder?'

'I gave her the gown I made from the parachute silk.'

'To wear when she's a bridesmaid tomorrow?'

"Demoiselle d'honneur',' Thérèse said, repeating his words. 'Oh, Philippe, wouldn't it be wonderful if we could have had a wedding like Mama and Papa? Mama had four bridesmaids.' Lawless saw little tears in her eyes. 'No, it's not a bridesmaid's dress: it's a night gown, so you won't see Séverine wearing it. I made two; one for her and one for me. Mine has different embroidery and I'm not going to tell you any more about it. You'll have to wait and see. No, go away: wash your hands and cut some bread when you come back down.'

Lawless found his uniform blouse, cleaned and newly pressed, lying on his bed. He pulled off the heavy woollen jumper he had been told once belonged to Fabrice and put the blouse on. He was surprised to find it a much tighter fit. All that work in the sheep pen and chopping and sawing wood, he supposed. He looked at himself in the long mirror: no tie, no cap. What a mess; improperly dressed on parade. And he badly needed a haircut. Thérèse had said she would do that for him. He had to admit he looked better in Fabrice's suit but he was damned well going to wear uniform at his wedding. That's what you did.

He went to the window and looked down into the courtyard. Séverine was making her way across, Caramelle at her heels. Always that purposeful look about her, thought Lawless. Never casual, never does anything on impulse. But then he wondered, not for the first time, about that fierce kiss in the stable. Without warning, she looked up at his window. Involuntarily he raised his hand to wave and she stopped, kept looking and tilted her head on one side as if asking a question. He turned his wave into a mock salute and saw her laugh and continued on her way towards the house.

'How's the work on the translation going, Philippe?' said Séverine. 'Are you near the end?'

They were drinking coffee after lunch, the herbal variety, Lawless noticed, hoping there might be some of the real stuff again, at least after the wedding.

'There's about twenty pages of Book Four left to do. It's the saddest part of the story because there was just a chance the Camisards could have won.'

'How was that?'

'Well, the King was in trouble. He had wars in Spain, Italy and Germany to fight and needed more men so he took some regiments away from the Cevennes which should have left Cavallier stronger.'

'Is that when Marshal Villars was sent here?'

'Yes; you knew that did you? Montrevel was pretty useless and the King got rid of him. Villars was his best general, a real professional. Cavallier had lost nearly half his men in a big battle at Caverac and all his stores and ammunition. That was really the end. Villars sent a message saying the King wanted the war to end and suggested a meeting to talk about terms and they did meet, in the garden of the Franciscan monastery outside Nîmes. How Cavallier could have agreed to meet in a place like that, I can't imagine. That's as far as I've reached. I haven't translated the rest yet but I have looked through it. Cavallier listed all sorts of demands he was told would be sent to the King but he was never sure if they were. I expect you know what happened after that.'

'The usual things in a tyranny: deception, betrayal, brutality. It's happening again, here, now, in France and it will get worse.'

'There's a saying in English that things have to get worse before they get better.'

'Well for us, I mean the Camisards, it was a very long time before things got better. When was that? Do you know your French history?'

'1789: French Revolution. Declaration of the Rights of Man,' Lawless said, feeling rather pleased with himself.

'No.'

'No? Let me think. Proclamation of the Republic, 1792, er, September 1792.'

'No.'

'No? But that ensured freedom of religion which was what the Camisards wanted most of all.'

'Twenty first of January 1793, when the tyrant king was executed. Only then was the account settled.'

'Tomorrow is my wedding day,' said Thérèse, 'and I can't bear any more of this. Let's talk about something else.'

'You're right, sweetheart. For us, things are going to get better very soon before they get better still. Is there any more coffee?'

***

Lawless put down his pencil and sat back looking at the pile of papers, so untidy and ordinary beside the vital little leather-bound book. It was finished. He would have to go through the every page carefully, checking and amending but now he had other things to do. He would miss it though; the searching for the right word, the attempts to listen to Cavallier's voice, catch his mood, see the man, feel the fear and the excitement of the times. When did he realise he had failed? Was it when his comrade Roland refused to accept the peace terms and fought on after Cavallier had left France? Roland refused all inducements to lay down his arms and died fighting when they cornered him in the end. Cavallier got away. Did he ever return to France? Lawless didn't know. He felt suddenly very cold and lonely. The sun had gone down. It must be five o' clock or later. He had to find Thérèse, feel her warmth.

He met Séverine in the corridor.

'I thought of something you will need tomorrow. I'll show you in your room. The light is better there.'

Lawless opened the door for her.

'Close the door. Light the candle. They look their best in candlelight.'

She opened the small box made of red leather that she was carrying and held it out for him to see. Lying side by side on a square of dark velvet were two rings. Their gold gleamed richly in the light of the candle.

'Mama's and Papa's wedding rings. He left his with her when he went off to the War. This one you can give to Thérèse tomorrow and this one she will give to you.'

'Séverine, I should have thought . . . you are so kind. I don't know how to thank you. They look beautiful.'

'We'd better see if they fit. Here, put this one on my finger. It's the same size as Tressie's.'

He had never touched her hand before. It felt warm and firm as he held it and slowly pressed the ring down her third finger.

'Good. It feels right. Now, give me your hand. It fits, just. Hold your hand to the light, next to mine. See how they shine. What do you think?'

'Thérèse will love them. I love them. They must be very precious to you.'

'When you leave, when you go back to England, as you must, they will stay here. When you return perhaps you will bring your own ring to give.'

He felt a lump in his throat, whether it was the sudden thought of England again or the thought of leaving here, he didn't know. Perhaps it was both. Without thinking, he bent down and kissed her on the brow and when she raised her face to him, on the lips.

'I will; if I'm spared, I will. I promise.'

'Let's put them back in the box,' she said quietly. 'I'll give it to you tomorrow.'

After she left, he sat for a long time in the candlelight, wishing he knew what he felt about what had just happened, or rather which of his many confused feelings he should trust. He had started off in search of comfort from Thérèse and had ended by kissing her sister and he could not deceive himself it was simply in gratitude for her thoughtfulness. Thoughtfulness, or was it purpose? He didn't know. Not for the first time he felt he knew nothing about women. He envied men like Jack Verrill who seemed to get women into bed with a snap of his fingers, or so he said. At Oxford he'd kissed quite a few girls and gone rather a long way with a botany student after too many gins at a party but he'd slept with only one woman and she was at least as old as Séverine, certainly older than Thérèse, he realised with something of a shock.

'Slept' was hardly the right word. *Congratulations on your Distinction, Philip*, the note from his French Language tutor at Granville had said. *Do come and have a glass of sherry to celebrate, 6pm, Friday.* After his second glass she had led him into her bedroom and without a word taken down his trousers and pants, leaving him to remove his socks and shoes by himself while she lay on the large soft bed. She raised her skirt revealing that she wore nothing beneath. He stood looking down at her parted thighs with his heart thumping furiously in his chest. *Don't be shy, Philippe, I can see you're ready.* He needed her expert guidance at first and then it was all right, vigorously all right, in fact, if not lasting very long. Afterwards he felt like dozing beside her but she got up and smiled at him. *Well, that was very nice Philip. I think the only Distinction in the Prelim this year deserved something else besides sherry. Now, if you're quick, you'll be just in time for Hall Dinner.*

As he cycled back to College he was exultant. *I've been seduced and I've lost my virginity!* He whistled *Auprès de Ma Blonde* as he put his bike away. 'I know where you've been,' his fellow linguist Charteris said. 'I was with her just after lunch. She told me she wanted to commiserate with me for failing Paper One.' In the middle of the summer term that followed he received his call-up papers ordering him to report for duty at RAF Padgate on 1 August 1940. He never saw Charteris again.

The sound of the piano playing in the room below filtered through the tangle of his thoughts. They could have a few moments to themselves before supper if he hurried. He had the strangest feeling as he went down the stairs, a sort of nervous trembling inside him, an impatience for something to happen but not knowing quite what it was. He could see it showed from the puzzled look in Thérèse's eyes when she turned from the keys as he came into the room.

'Are you all right? Has something happened?'

'No, no, nothing. I was working very hard to finish the translation, and then I drifted off day-dreaming and woke up with a start.'

She smiled at him and held out her hand. 'What were you dreaming about? Tomorrow?'

'Among other things. I can hardly believe it's nearly time.'

'You sound a little bit nervous.'

'I am. Aren't you? Do you think everybody is? Maybe that's why men go out drinking with their friends the night before they get married: to soothe their nerves.'

'Is that what you would like to do?'

'No chance of that. I mean, no, of course not. I want to be with you.'

'Well, I am here.'

She stood up and held out her arms. He took her hands, drew her close and put his arms round her. She felt warm and soft against him. He pressed his lips into the hollow where her neck met her shoulder and felt her shiver and let her head fall back. Images of thighs parted for him and Séverine's kisses quickened his breathing and the nervous trembling came on again. He tried to force the pictures away but they wouldn't go and he let them stay. He felt himself harden against her and lifted her blouse and pressed his face between the soft full breasts inside her sheer silk vest and breathed in the scent of her. With one hand he traced the swell of her stomach, then downwards and felt her hand take his and press it into the warm depth. His thigh muscles tensed and in a panic he felt the unwanted spasm growing and taking hold, and although he fought against it he couldn't stop the hot pulsing flow that left him gasping and shuddering in her arms until long after it was spent.

He couldn't speak, couldn't look at her as he drowned in a misery of frustration and humiliation. What must she think? What would she do? All the pressing and pestering he'd done and then just when it seemed about to happen, he couldn't hold himself back long enough to perform. He would have wept if he hadn't felt so angry with himself.

'Philippe. Philippe, look at me.'

'I can't,' he eventually managed to mumble. 'I'm so stupid, useless. I'm ashamed. Can't do anything.'

'Lift your head. Look at me, Philippe. Listen, no *listen*. I know this can happen to a man. I had brothers. Fabrice and I, we had no secrets from each another. He told me what happened to him when the schoolteacher first touched him. Fabrice said it was a rush of love. It was the same with you. Don't be ashamed. I should have stopped you. I told you we must wait; that was because it was my woman's time of the month. You tried so hard to wait and I love you for that. There are things I must do but soon we can love each other in the way we both want.'

He managed a weak smile. He didn't know what to say and what came out was silly but it made her laugh.

'I suppose you've seen a ram do the same sometimes.'

'Sometimes: a young one when he's too eager and it all goes to waste.'

He had to laugh at that. She was so understanding, accepting, so full of common sense. She was bloody marvellous. He felt like kissing her all over again but there were sounds outside that meant Séverine was downstairs and, no doubt, wanting supper and would soon be interrupting them. He squeezed Thérèse's hands hard and gave her a shamefaced smile.

'I'd better go and change.'

A FRENCH WEDDING

There was a bottle of very good red wine to go with the roast partridge for supper and Lawless guessed that some had been used in stewing the sweet pears they ate as dessert. Séverine had also produced a litre bottle of *vin doux* which they had started as aperitifs and were now finishing off as nightcaps in front of the fire. She was in a very good mood, joking that the wine would fortify them for the ordeal to come and announcing that the evening sky had been pink in the west so tomorrow would be a fine day.

'We're doing this all wrong,' said Lawless.

Thérèse looked shocked. 'What do you mean?'

'Well, a bridegroom shouldn't see his bride on the night before the wedding, but here I am looking at her. Or, is it not on the morning before the wedding until she comes up the aisle? Oh, I don't know. In any case she's not going to walk up an aisle, is she? Perhaps I should close my eyes now and not look at her until we're at the Mairie. There, where is she? It's all gone dark.'

'Does anyone know what this man is talking about?' said Séverine, laughing. 'Give me your glasses. There's still a little left in the pitcher.'

'He's impossible,' said Thérèse.

'Philippe. Imbecile, open your eyes. Listen, Tressie says you have finished the translation. When can we see it?'

'I need to go through it all first, making sure I've got the spellings and grammar right. It's a sort of proof-reading.'

'"Proof-reading": very good to know that in French. What do you think of the book, now that you've read it all?'

'It has a sad ending but it's funny and serious and interesting and terrible at times. And I think it's a sort of textbook. You'll see what I mean, Séverine, when you read it.'

'Tell us one of the funny parts,' said Thérèse.

'Is there anything left in the pitcher? Thank you. Well, I told you the story about Cavallier stealing Marshal Montrevel's wine. It seems he might also have stolen his mistress as well.'

'How marvellous! Where does he say that?'

'He doesn't write about it himself. I got it from one of those notes pencilled in the margin I told you about. It says there was a strong rumour that she asked to see Cavallier and he visited her to pay his respects.'

'He may have started off paying his respects but I think he wouldn't have left it at that.'

'Séverine! How can you have such suspicions about our hero?'

'Could have been one of the reasons why he left France in such a hurry,' said Lawless.

'That's enough from the two of you. All that wine is making me very sleepy. I think we should all go to bed now.'

'Might as well,' said Séverine. It's a long busy day tomorrow and the wine's finished anyway. Kisses all round. Goodnight you two. I'll let Caramelle out for a bit and then lock up.'

He couldn't find the matches to light his candle. He couldn't find the bloody candle, anyway, and only found the bed when his shin banged into it. He stood by it, swaying in the blackness. She must have put something else in that *vin doux*. It was bloody potent. He giggled to himself as he hauled off his clothes, dropping them on the floor where he stood. Potent. That's a laugh. Better luck next time. He fell back on the bed, scrabbling to pull the quilt over himself. He started humming the song his crew routinely chanted as they took off, 'I don't want to join the Airforce, I don't want to go to war . . .' but was asleep before he could finish the first line.

It wasn't a dream. Something softly heavy really was resting on his thighs. He tried to sit up in bed but hands pushed him back and a warm body pressed down on his. Lips found his mouth and a tongue probed inside. When she sat back, straddling him again, he reached up to touch her face and felt his fingertips run over threads of embroidery and down the sheer silk of her shift.

'Tressie, Love . . .'

'Sh, sh. She'll hear us.'

She raised herself from him and he heard the whisper of silk being lifted from skin and sliding to the floor. She took the hardness in her hand and guided it inside.

'Tressie.'

'Don't speak.'

The feel and the smell and the taste of her and the little sighs and whimpers and the sharp cry she made as she shifted on him were all the more exciting in the darkness, too exciting.

'Tressie, now, please, before . . .' he whispered urgently.

How long they lay silent together in the crumpled sheets, their sweat sticky on each other's skin, he did not know but when he woke it was still dark and she was gone, leaving the musky smell of their lovemaking filling the air.

***

'How's your head? Made of wood?'

'It's been worse. I went for a walk to try to clear it. Is the coffee ready?'

'Help yourself. The bread's in the box. Be quick about it. We mustn't be late at the Mairie. Hm, you don't look too bad in that uniform but you'll need a coat as well. It's fine but it's chilly outside.'

'Where's Thérèse?'

'Upstairs. Still doing her hair I expect. A bride must look her best.'

'Yours is different this morning. It really suits you, drawn back in a bun like that.'

She gave him one of her quizzical looks but he could tell she was pleased.

'I'll go and see how she's getting on.'

Perhaps the herbal coffee had cleared his head. He was certainly feeling better than when he first woke up. It had taken quite an effort to wash and hold the razor steady. He'd had to sit on the edge of the bed for a few minutes before he could face putting on his uniform. Bending down to lace up the shoes Thérèse had found for him was something that he didn't want to remember. What a night! That awful mess he made of himself losing his load and how sweet and wonderful she had been. And all that wine and then, Christ, what followed later! He would never have believed his shy Thérèse could have made love with such, what was the word, abandon: so different from his one other clinical time with the Granville don. He was still feeling a bit drained, literally, he thought ruefully. Why had she come to him last night after putting him off for so long when they were going to be married the very next day? He shook his head. It was baffling.

Coming down the stairs she looked fresh and beautiful and serene, yes, serene, without the slightest sign of the wildness of a few hours ago.

'Do I look all right? I've changed the way I do my hair just for today. You're shaking your head. Don't you like it?'

'Yes, I do. I love the colour. It looks wonderful. It's because I can't believe how beautiful you look; shaking my head, I mean, that's why. You're not tired, are you? It's quite a way to walk.'

'Tired? No, why should I be tired? It's my wedding day.'

Before he could think of anything else to say that wasn't completely fatuous Séverine appeared at the top of the stairway carrying a suitcase.

'There's work for you to do, Philippe, carrying this to St Chely. Don't look like that. It's not very heavy and you can put straps through these loops and carry it on your back.'

'Can I ask what's inside?'

'Our clothes and shoes for the wedding. You don't think we're going to keep these things on for the ceremony, do you? There's room for those shoes you're wearing as well. Put the boots on. And don't worry; Vabrette will be bringing us back in his cart. I don't have to tell you why.'

They were waiting at the door for him when he came down the stairs with the case on his shoulder.

'Sorry, I nearly forgot my pay book. Has one of you taken my sheets? There's only the blanket left on my bed.'

'Men,' Séverine sighed. 'You've forgotten. You're moving into the big bedroom tonight.'

***

Although he had a smile of welcome on his face Jérôme Janquet almost hustled them through the door of the Mairie, glancing back over his shoulder as if wanting to avoid too many people seeing what was going on.

'I see that our witnesses are not present, Mr Mayor.'

'They are waiting in the café for my call, Mademoiselle Séverine.'

'While you are doing that my sister and I should like a little time to ourselves. You have somewhere suitable where we may change?'

Jérôme Janquet thought for a moment and then said,

'I have a small office where I deal with confidential business. You are welcome to use that. Please follow me.'

'Bring the suitcase, Philippe and then wait for us here.'

Having done as he was told, Lawless returned to the cold and empty meeting room where he presumed the ceremony was to take place. It had a high ceiling and lancet windows with leaded glass that had not been cleaned for a very long time. He wondered if before the Revolution it might have been a church or some sort of chapel. At one end was a table covered in green baize and some wooden chairs. On the wall above were two crossed tricolour flags, rather faded, he noticed. A large-scale map of the commune hung in the centre of another wall. Lawless could just make out the date in faded type in one corner: 1908. Several areas on the map were outlined in red ink; properties, he assumed from the names included. He searched for and eventually found the words *Chevalier La Commanderie* inside one of the red-outlined boxes. It was the largest on the map. On the wall opposite was an uneven row of sepia photographs in black wooden frames. Most were of village scenes and people that he judged from their clothes to date from about the same time as the map. At one end of the row was a portrait photograph of an elderly soldier wearing a simple tunic with two medals and some stars and on his head a kepi with lots of braid. He had a big white moustache swept up at the ends, chubby cheeks and piercing eyes. The caption at the bottom read *Joseph Jacques Césaire Joffre, Maréchal de France.* At the other end of the row was a less faded rectangle where another photograph had obviously once hung. There was nothing else to see except a square of threadbare blue carpet in the middle of the floor.

Lawless was studying the map again when the outside door opened and Jérôme Janquet came in followed by Vabrette and another man, all three in the well-brushed dark suits that were probably their best clothes. Vabrette gave Lawless a mock salute, wrung his hand and jerking his head towards the map grinned and said,

'Looking over the new property, eh, Sergeant?'

'Always best to know what you're getting into, my friend.'

The other man took his hand briefly, gave him a nod and muttered,

'Bec, Jean-Pierre.'

'Lawless, Philippe. I thank you for being here. And for your excellent mutton that we have enjoyed.'

'It is I who thank you. I have a request, Sergeant. My wife would like to attend. It is fitting that a married woman is present, she says.'

'She is most welcome.'

'And my son, Jeannot. I don't know why but he has asked.'

'He has been helpful and I should like to meet him.'

Bec nodded his thanks and went outside.

'That was well done, Sergeant,' said Jérôme Janquet quietly. ' Ah, here are Madame Bec and Jeannot. I think all who are coming are now here. Do you have that little book with you, Sergeant? Thank you.'

Over the mayor's shoulder Lawless saw Thérèse and Sèverine coming back into the room and felt his heart give a sudden leap. But for their hair colour they looked so alike in their ankle-length dark blue skirts and fitted jackets, except that Thérèse had her hair piled high with a long lace veil draped over and trailing back down to her waist. She looked at him in way that he had not seen before, composed, unsmiling yet radiant with offering. He sensed a kind of power in her and in Séverine at her side and wondered if this was what comes from a long lineage of possession and authority. From their silence he could tell the others felt it too. He started towards her, reaching for her hand but stopped at Séverine's slight shake of the head.

'Ladies and gentlemen, as everyone is present we will begin,' said Jérôme Janquet, now wearing his mayoral tricolour sash over one shoulder, its blue band nearest his neck.

'Mademoiselle, Sergeant, please stand before me; no, Sergeant, you on her right side. Mademoiselle Sèverine, you may stand a little behind your sister; the witnesses and others further back. Now, as required by law and in my position as Mayor of the Commune of St Chely La Bastide I will read to you from Articles 74, 75 and 165 of the Civil Code of the Republic.'

After adjusting his reading glasses and clearing his throat, the mayor read slowly from a sheet of paper:

"Spouses mutually owe each other fidelity, support and assistance. The husband is head of the family. The spouses together assure the material and moral direction of the family. They provide for the upbringing of the children and prepare for their future. If the matrimonial agreement does not regulate the contribution of the spouses to the expenses of the marriage, they contribute to them in proportion to their respective abilities. The spouses are bound to a community of life."

There was a long pause while Jérôme Janquet replaced his spectacles in their case and folded and put the sheet of paper in his pocket. Lawless glanced across at Thérèse who was looking straight ahead. Her lips were slightly open. He though she might have put on a little lipstick.

'The banns of marriage have been published for the required amount of time and I can assure the witnesses here present that all necessary documents have been provided by both persons and that they give the correct information. However, if anyone here has information that, if proved correct, would mean that this marriage should not take place, speak now. Very well, we will proceed.

Mademoiselle Thérèse Angeline Duschene Chevalier, do you take Sergeant Philippe Martyn Lawless as your husband?'

'Yes.'

Sergeant Philippe Martyn Lawless, do you take Mademoiselle Thérèse Angeline Duschene Chevalier as your wife?'

'Yes.'

'I pronounce you husband and wife.'

In the silence that followed Lawless kept staring straight ahead at the mayor until he realised that the raised eyebrows and sideways glance meant something was expected of him. Of course!

He turned to find Thérèse looking back at him through the veil that she had quietly slipped over her face. Very gently he lifted the lace and kissed her on the lips. She gave a deep sigh and smiled at him. Someone started to clap and the others joined in, except Séverine who poked Lawless in the back and slipped the little leather box into his hand.

Jérôme Janquet saw this happen and when Lawless turned to speak to him was smiling back with his hands spread out in understanding.

Tears filled Thérèse's eyes when she saw the rings and ran down her cheeks as Lawless lifted one from the box, put it first to his lips and then slipped it over her finger. She was still for so long that Lawless began to wonder if she could bring herself to do the same for him. But she took the second ring, her father's, put it to her lips and pushed it down his finger, not easily because her own fingers were trembling so much. There was more clapping after that especially when Thérèse held up her hand to show the ring. When everyone had finished shaking hands and embracing each other, Jérôme Janquet called for silence.

'Our friends now have the pleasant duty of signing the marriage register and after that I can give them their Family Book. Please come to my office, witnesses too and Mademoiselle Chevalier, of course.'

The stuffy little office was hardly big enough to take them all and they had to sign the register standing up. Lawless had never seen Thérèse writing before. She signed first, all her names, in a neat sloping hand as if she were writing in her exercise book with lines to help. The tip of her tongue was just showing as she wrote. Lawless wanted to touch it with his. The mayor blotted the ink with a sheet of well-used pink blotting paper. Lawless signed, thinking his scrawl compared badly with Thérèse's clear script. The Family Book was handed to him with some solemnity by Jérôme Janquet who said it was his responsibility as head of the family to guard it carefully as the record of important events in the marriage notified to the Mairie such as, and here he smiled, the birth of children. It was a small booklet bound in grey card. Lawless glanced over the cover:

Prefecture du Departement de La Lozère
Ville de St Chely la Bastide
Livret de Famille

and below, a statement of more or less what the mayor had just told him, except it also mentioned recording any deaths.

'You doubtless have read there, Sergeant, that the Book is given free of charge.'

'That is most generous, Mr Mayor because as it happens, I had only a little English money with me when I arrived in France.'

That brought a snort of laughter from Vabrette and faint smiles from the others. Séverine took charge.

'If you agree, I think we should all now go next door, to the café. We have something to celebrate: the first marriage in the Chevalier family for 47 years.'

Lawless was looking at Thérèse: no music, no long white dress, no bridesmaids, no flowers, no slow walk up the aisle with her father. What was she thinking? Was this brief transaction enough? He whispered in her ear.

'Are you happy?' and saw in her eyes that she was.

'Oh yes, I have you.'

'Get the muzzle off that bottle, Sergeant,' called Vabrette. 'That's your first duty. The others come later but we won't go into them now.'

Lawless loosened the wire cage on the big fat-bellied bottle and began to ease the cork out with his thumbs, turning towards Vabrette as he did so.

'Take cover, Corporal. That's an order.'

The pop of the cork and the spurt of white spume that almost reached the smith caused everyone to laugh and some applaud. With hands still trembling, Lawless slopped the champagne into the glasses. Jérôme Janquet raised his glass high.

'To the Family Chevalier with its new member.'

'And more to follow,' said Vabrette in a loud whisper.

'Jeannot hasn't got a glass. Mr Bec?'

Jean-Pierre Bec looked at his wife for approval.

'Good. Here you are, Jeannot. You may never get to taste this again. Damn. All right, lick your fingers; don't waste any.'

The wine was working. Everyone was now talking at the same time, getting louder and louder. Lawless found it hard to follow, but most of the talk seemed to be about old times and other weddings. He went round re-filling glasses. More bottles, different this time, appeared from somewhere along with plates of sliced meats and paté and fresh bread and a cake with a ring of plaited straw on the top. Full mouths did nothing to stop the chatter.

Bec touched Lawless on the arm.

'Jeannot says he has something for you, Sergeant.'

The boy was standing apart from the group, his wine glass still almost full. Lawless went across and shook his other hand.

'Jeannot, don't you like it?'

A quick shake of the head. 'Did you taste it?' A slight nod. 'That's all right then. You joined in the toast. Shall I take that?' Another nod. 'Your father says you have something for me. Is it a present? That would be very kind.'

'Not a present, Sir, but something.'

His voice was very quiet. Lawless sensed the boy did not want the others to know.

'Don't worry. Nobody's taking any notice. What is it?'

Lawless took the small bundle that Jeannot pulled from his coat pocket and turned his back to the others before undoing the wrapping.

'My god,' he whispered. 'Do you know what this is?' Jeannot shook his head.

It was what was left of an oxygen mask, a new type they'd been issued for testing on that last raid. The rubber of the face piece had all but melted, but the aluminium disc where the microphone had fitted was intact as were the metal buckles and snap fasteners that had fixed the now charred webbing straps and leather tabs to the missing helmet. There were even some twisted bits of the ribbed oxygen hose sticking to them. Whose was it? Anybody's, Perhaps his own.

'Where did you get this?'

'In the gorge, Sir, half way up, hanging in a tree. There's a shepherds' hut on the top near there.'

'Was there anything else?'

Jeannot nodded but before he could say anything Séverine up to them.

'What are you two talking about?'

'Er, Jeannot was saying he doesn't like the wine. Is there some sirop for him? Jeannot, go and have something to eat.'

'Did I see him give you something?'

'A sort of present. I'll show you later. Thérèse looks happy, don't you think? Is it time to cut the cake? Do you think I'm capable of doing that? I've drunk rather a lot.'

'I'm sure you are, Philippe. I know very well what you're capable of now. Wine doesn't stop you. You should be with the others. We'll have coffee and cognac with the cake and after that I think it will be time to go. Vabrette says he has to get back home before dark.'

'Vabrette? Oh, yes. I'd forgotten. Has he brought it?'

'In his cart: and remember, not a word to Thérèse about it, not today, anyway.'

***

'Waiting's over.'

'No more waiting.'

'Are you sure she won't mind?'

'Who?'

'Your mother: the portrait. She'll be looking down on us.'

'You haven't noticed, have you? I took it down. It's in my old bedroom now.'

'Ah, you're right. I hadn't noticed. I only had eyes for you.'

There were big logs burning in the fire basket and the room was warm.

They stood holding each other in the glowing hive of light made by the fire and the candles on the mantelpiece and kissed for a long time, and then again for a longer time.

'Now, I take off your veil and you take off my tie.'

'Then I take off your tunic and you take off my jacket.'

'Now your blouse. Too many buttons.'

'Now your shirt. Just as many.'

'Now this thing: raise your arms. I've forgotten the word for it.'

'Tricot de corps.'

'Thérèse, don't move. I must kiss these. And hold them.'

'My turn. More buttons down the front. And your belt. There. Lucky you're so slim. They fall down easily. Philippe! What can this be?'

'Soon to be revealed. Now, where are your buttons? Ah, at the back. I love this colour against your skin.'

'You can't pull it down if you keep kissing me there. No, don't stop just yet.'

'You're all soft and rosy in the firelight. Turn around. You have such a lovely back. It curves down, then there's a little hollow here and then it rises here and here . . .'

'My turn again. This won't take long. There, fling them away. Oh yes, yes, that part's soft and rosy in the firelight as well. The rest isn't, soft I mean. And as for these.'

'Don't stop, but don't squeeze too hard. I love the feel of your hand there and the feel of the silk. And the sound of it as it slides down, like that. Here we are, Adam and Eve, in the firelight. You are lovely and you have shadowy parts I've never seen before.'

'Adam and Eve, with shoes and stockings on. You take yours off. I'll do mine.'

'Please walk over there; now back here. Stay in the firelight. I've been watching them move under your dress for weeks and now I want to see them moving just as they are.'

'You wicked man. Of course, I knew what you were up to.'

'Of course you did. That's why you blushed.'

'I never did!'

'You're blushing now.'

'I am not. I'm rosy in the firelight. You said so yourself. Now, where is my nightgown?'

'You're not going to cover yourself up again, are you? Please don't. I'm not. Look.'

'Philippe! It's pointing at me! You'll have to wait just a little bit longer. I made this especially for tonight, from the silk you gave me. It took me hours to embroider the flowers. Wait till you see.'

'All right. Then will you take it off again?'

'No. You will.'

The nightgown was ankle-length, with a high neckline tied with a loop of silk ribbon and full sleeves down to her wrists and shimmering pink where the firelight touched. Her dark red hair let down, hung to her shoulders with two thick strands falling over her breast. Lawless was speechless. She looked as enticing and vulnerable as a young girl. But with the fire behind her, the heavy silk was translucent.

'Don't stand there. Come and see.'

'I can see you, through the silk.'

'I know, but I mean see the flowers I embroidered. They're red roses, red for love.'

He looked at the roses and moved his fingers over them because they were beautiful, but more so because they lay over her softness. He hadn't been able see them the night before, but he remembered the rows of stitches, though not the loops and twirls of silk he was touching now. He loosened the silk bow at her throat and looked downwards through the parting of her breasts and down to the roundness and shadow below.

'Beautiful,' he said and kissed her. 'I love you, Tressie.'

'I love you, Philippe. You can take it off now.'

The sound of silk rustling over her skin again.

'We're both rosy in the firelight now. I want to stay here.'

'Our bed is over there.'

'I can pile all those big pillows here by the fire. It's dark over there and I want to see.'

'Don't be long.'

Kneeling beside her, looking down and feeling the urgency, he was suddenly serious.

'Tressie, love, last night, I must ask . . .'

'Sh, don't say anything. Last night is past. I want to think only of tonight.'

'But, Tressie . . .'

'Come here, down on me.'

'I don't care if she hears us now.'

'Don't talk.'

Once in the night he woke to the sound of her weeping but it must have been a dream because her cheeks were not wet and she opened her arms for him again.

***

'Come back to bed. It's the middle of the night.'

She turned and smiled down at him. She had put on a dark red woollen cloak and was brushing down her hair. She had drawn back the curtains and the room was bright.

'The sun was up hours ago. I thought you would like some coffee. Here. In bed.'

'Real coffee? Here? In bed? With you? How could I say no?'

'You did last night, in your sleep, but when I woke you all you would say was yes.'

' And you said yes. I remember. Twice. I'll say it again. Yes, I would like some coffee as well.'

'Before I do that, I want you to tell me what you promised you would after we were married.'

'What was . . .? Oh, yes, pulling the wishbone until it breaks.'

'Well, tell me.'

'After last night, I think you can use your imagination.'

Thérèse could smell coffee as she came down the stairs. Séverine had a fresh jugful and beakers ready on the table.

'I heard you stirring and decided to give you a treat. I've done all that's needed outside. It's a fine day. You should go for a walk. Take the gun.'

Thérèse put her arms round her sister.

'Séverine, thank you. You've been so kind. It won't be any different, you know.'

'It will. It has to be.'

'But we'll be together here, you and me and Philippe. It will be good.'

'Yes, it will be good sometimes, sometimes not, but that's how it always is. I do know one thing.'

'What's that?'

'We have a chance now, the family.'

Thérèse looked at her hand. 'The rings, Sevvy, Mama's and Papa's: they were meant for you.'

'They might have been but you have your man so they belong to you. Now then, no tears. He'll wonder what's been going on.'

Thérèse smiled at her. 'He's probably gone to sleep again.'

Séverine arched an eyebrow. 'Men. Don't tell me he's been overdoing it. How do you feel?'

'Sore.'

They stared at each other and burst out laughing.

'There you are, then. We have a chance, the family, just as I said.'

'I've been trying to understand what you meant by that.'

'A child, Tressie, that's what I mean. You're not too old to have a child. Mama was only one year younger than you are when Fabrice was born.'

'But a child, now, when everything is so awful; the war . . .'

'Think how Mama would have loved it, to have a grandchild.'

'Mama; do you really thinks so, Sevvy?'

'I think she felt it would never happen after she, after we, lost Fabrice.'

'Poor Mama: she'll never know.'

'It breaks my heart as well, Tressie, but listen: we will tell him all about his Grandmama and Grandpapa and his brave uncles and show him their pictures so he will know what they were like even if they could never know him.'

'Or her, Sevvy, a little girl, think of that.'

'Of course and I'll be an aunt to either.'

'Aunt Séverine: it sounds good. "Aunt Séverine", hm.'

'Listen, take this upstairs before it gets cold and wake him up. If he was listening to what the Mayor said, he may think he's head of the family now but that doesn't mean he can stay in bed all day. We all need some breakfast.'

Lawless came slowly down the staircase with the jug in one hand and two beakers clasped in the other. He was wearing a loosely belted dressing gown that Thérèse must have found for him. At the bottom of the stairs he tried to lift his hand to his mouth to hide a huge yawn, forgetting that he was holding the jug. Coffee dregs splashed over him and his attempts to wipe them off with his wrist only made things worse.

'I'll take those. You'd better sit down. And tighten that belt. You're hardly decent.'

He looked at her across the table with an embarrassed smile.

'Er, sorry about that. These things sometimes happen to me.'

'Is Tressie coming down?'

'I think so. She said she had some washing to do first. I heard water splashing. I was just thinking . . .'

'And not looking what you were doing.'

'Guilty, but what I was thinking was what a nice word sister-in-law is in French. As well as a beautiful wife I have a beautiful sister now.'

'You're wheedling again.'

'Pomading you? Another lovely word. Yes I am, a bit. But it's true: you both are.'

'Everything must seem beautiful the day after you get married.'

'Séverine, why didn't you . . .? I'm sorry. I shouldn't ask. Please forget what I said.'

'It doesn't matter. Once I . . . Thérèse knows. There were reasons.'

She fell silent, looking at him, speculatively, he thought, as if she might be wondering whether she had said too much or not enough. Again he was wrong about her. What she did say took him by surprise.

'What was it that Jeannot gave you? You said you would show me later.'

'I will, but not just yet. I know you want us to look at the gun together and see what Vabrette's managed to do, but keep Thérèse out of it, so let's find some time this afternoon. She wants to go for a walk. How about while she's preparing supper? Oh, she's coming down.' He raised his voice. 'I think you two were dancing beautifully last night. You never told me you knew how to waltz.'

'We used to watch Mama and Papa when we were small.'

'And Pascal used to play for them,' said Thérèse, coming down the stairs.

'Pascal?'

'Our eldest brother. Mama said he would have gone to the Conservatoire but the Army took him instead.'

Same as me, Lawless was thinking but he knew he mustn't say it.

'Coffee's good this morning and the bread, it's really fresh. Everything's good, even the weather.'

'I was telling Thérèse: why don't you go for a walk and take the gun? Give Caramelle a run.'

'Good idea. Come on, Thérèse. Drink up. Bring your bread with you. Let's go now while the sun's still bright; back to the shepherds' shelter where I first met you.'

'This must be where we came the other day. You can just see where we were walking.'

'Only just; there's much less snow now.'

'Has the thaw started? You said it would after we were married.'

'Yes, for today, anyway. There's been a change of wind and that's good. It won't be long now before the ewes start lambing. With luck all the snow should be gone from here by then. Look, has she found something?'

Caramelle was sniffng about near the line of trees marking the edge of the gorge.

With Thérèse following, Lawless moved cautiously, holding the gun ready in case the dog started a hare or a bird. The branches of the big oaks and chestnuts that had been draped with snow when they were last there were now bare and Lawless could see well down the steep slope, though not as far as the river where the trees were thickest.

'I'm going down to take a look. Hold the gun.'

'Philippe, it's dangerous. I don't want you to go.'

'No, listen, Tressie: I'll be very careful. The snow's almost gone and you can see where to go now.'

'Wait a few more days and it will all be gone. We can come back then. Why risk it now?'

'All right, I'll tell you why. Yesterday, in the café, Jeannot gave me something he'd found hanging from a tree in the gorge and I think it must have been down there somewhere. It was part of an oxygen mask, the sort we wear when we fly and it must have belonged to one of my crew. It could even be mine because I didn't have one with me when you found me. And that means maybe not far from here there are other things I need to look for.'

'I understand, but not now, Philippe. Wait only a day or two and bring Jeannot with you when you go searching. I'll come too.'

'Sweetheart, I won't be long and I won't go far down but if I don't have a look now, I won't be able to sleep until I do.'

'In that case I'm coming with you.'

'No, no, it's . . .'

'If I can't stop you, it's only fair that you can't stop me. Besides, I know these parts better than you do.'

He was holding her hand to help her onto the jutting-out rock he was standing on when she pointed down the slope.

'There, look, that chestnut tree on the ledge.'

A big branch had been wrenched off one of the trees leaving a gaping splintered wound.

'Something big and heavy has done that. It could have been one of the engines: they weigh about three quarters of a ton. I'm going down to see.'

Caramelle was already there and burrowing into the snow-spattered leaf pile when they reached the ledge.

'Look at this, stuck deep in where the branch broke off. It's a piece of a pipe which feeds oil into the engine, so I was right. My god, it must have hit with a hell of a force to break that off and stab it into the wood.'

'Caramelle has dug up a few pieces of metal and what looks like a box.'

'Where? Let me see.'

There was a deep dent in the lid but the contents wouldn't have suffered any damage: 500 rounds now, not counting the belt. He kicked sodden leaves and snow over the box to conceal it from Thérèse. She was looking past him down the steep slope.

'Can you hear it: the river? It's a lovely sound, running water. It means the thaw has started.'

Thérèse: her face was alive with excitement. What was he doing, dragging her down here in the mud and slush, searching for things he didn't want her to see? Married yesterday: he should be in the warm with her, in bed, making love. Forget all this, for now.

Think of her.

'Distant music, water music: it's lovely. But not warm enough to swim in. Back to the shelter. Come on, Caramelle, what have you got there? Drop it, no, drop it, oh, all right, have it if you want.'

The dog dodged his hand and backed away. She was lying on the lip of the gorge and had chewed and swallowed most of the strip of flying jacket leather she had found near the ammunition box long before the man and woman reached her.

Lying in her arms in the cramped little shelter, he felt safe. No one knew they were there. This place had saved him from the cold and she had told him how she used to hide away in it and sleep there in the summer when she was a girl. It was their place. He started to tell her this but realised she was asleep. He tried to stop himself because he knew what would happen, but his mind went back to the night when he crawled through the blizzard into this little heap of grey stones. The others never had the chance. Why was he the only one to be saved? The others were out there down in that gorge somewhere, he was sure of that now. Finding that second ammunition box proved it. And the dog: he suddenly realised what it was she had in her mouth: leather and from a flying jacket. Whoever was wearing it when the Whitley went in couldn't be far away. The thaw had started. Tressie had said so. They ought to start searching before the foxes found them. Or wolves? Were there any wolves in the Causses? Must get out.

'Tressie . . .'

She was looking at him.

'How long have you been awake?'

'Only a moment. I thought I heard you talking.'

'Oh. Can we go now?'

'I thought you liked it here.'

'I do, but, well, it's warmer in bed at home. No need to keep your clothes on there. And Séverine told us to look out for a rabbit or something. Where's the gun?'

'Where you left it: outside. Listen. Caramelle must have seen something. She's making that special noise.'

It was a big hare, sitting not more than twenty metres way and its eyes were closed as if it were dozing in the late afternoon sun. Lawless reached for the gun, thinking that surely the hare would catch the sound and be off before he could even take aim. But it dozed on. He felt for the trigger. A sitting target: couldn't miss. Thérèse waited for the shot. And waited. Squeeze the trigger. Couldn't miss. Couldn't. Lawless lowered the gun.

'Let him live.'

'So, you've come back empty-handed?'

'Not exactly, but I'll tell you about that later,' said Lawless.

'He had a big buck hare in his sights.'

'And missed?'

'No, I couldn't bring myself to shoot him. He was asleep, dreaming of all the work ahead of him: all those lovely does he has to please.'

'You're impossible. And now we have no civet to look forward to.'

Thérèse was laughing. 'There's some mutton left over and Philippe has been telling me how to make something he calls Shepherd's Pie. It sounds very nice.'

'I suppose it will have to do. While she's doing that can you give me a hand with one of the ewes, *handsome brother*?'

A joke, he thought. *She only makes jokes when she's being serious. Is it the gun, or something else?*

'You were right. That smith certainly knows what he's doing,' Lawless said admiringly.

Standing on the work bench with its muzzle tilted upwards, the Browning gave him the impression of a hunting dog made to sit back on its haunches, but sniffing the air and ready to leap into action at the word of command. Vabrette had made a tapered sleeve that fitted smoothly over the barrel with a wing nut for tightening. A swivel joint formed from a steel rod inside a welded-on tube connected the barrel sleeve to the legs of the bipod. Completing the job was the promised new stock that was made of polished wood and looked as if it had come from a shotgun.

'Show me how it works now.'

'You?'

'Of course me. How do you expect me to use it if I haven't been shown how?'

'I thought . . .'

'You thought some man would have to be the gunner. Well, I am not just going to carry the bread and sausage and look on. Show me how.'

'All right but let me think a minute. I'm used to firing four of these things altogether from a turret. This is different. Actually firing it is fairly simple, once you know the sequence and I've shown you that although you'll have to practise until you can do it blindfold but it's getting it into position to fire that matters with this.'

Lawless was trying to think back to his basic training when he had learned rudimentary rifle drill and one afternoon had been allowed to handle a light machine gun, a Bren—that had a bipod—though not to fire it.

'Right, well there are two ways you can site this gun. Say you're in a ditch or a trench deep enough to stand or kneel in. I'll kneel in front of the bench to show you. You place the bipod like this, make sure it's steady and press the butt into your shoulder like this and then you're ready to load. The other way is like this. Lie down on the floor next to me. Right, now you lift the butt just a bit and press it into your shoulder, use this sight to aim and away you go. The other thing to remember is that with the swivel joint you can swing the gun from side to side and fire at a wide spread target. Here, you try it. It's all right: it's not loaded. That comes later.'

Although he was aware that she had been watching and listening intently while he showed her, he was surprised at how quickly and deftly she handled the gun herself.

'You're a quick learner, Séverine. If I didn't know different, I'd say you've done this before.'

She eyed him sideways across her hunched shoulder.

'Perhaps you're a good teacher.'

'We should practise every day.'

'We?'

'Yes. The gun needs a team of two at least, three would be better: one to fire, one to feed the belt in and one to bring up the ammunition. Let's try with two. You be the gunner. Lie down again, legs wider apart. Lift the butt. Press firmly or it will bruise your shoulder, and hold the handle. I lie here like this, lifting the belts from the box, passing them into the feedway, that slot on the side of the breech. I'll show you how it works. You aim and press up on the trigger. Short bursts, five or six rounds, are best. That's very good. Now, change places and you feed in the belt. You have to know how to do everything.'

He rolled away to let her take his place and clambered over her to lie behind the gun, very conscious of his thighs touching the swell of her buttocks as he did so.

'You all right? Lift the belt. Feed the tab in. Now me, watch: cocking handle, pull, release. Round in chamber. Cocking handle, pull, release. Trigger: rat-a-tat. Keep the belt feeding in. You have to learn all this and more. From now on when you're working the gun, don't have your hair down like that. Tie it up. You don't want to get it tangled in the belt or the feedway.'

'I will. You sounded quite excited. When can we do it again, properly?'

'Properly?'

'Properly: fire the gun, I mean. Is there enough ammunition for practising?'

'I'll let you into a secret. Thérèse doesn't know.'

'What secret? What doesn't Thérèse know?'

'We have 500 rounds in two boxes. Caramelle dug one up near the shepherd's shelter and I found another today near a tree in the gorge. I buried both of them before Tressie could see anything. She knows we have the gun, of course, although she doesn't know it's ready for use now and she knows it may be used one day but she doesn't want to think about it. She hates the whole idea. It frightens her. We must keep her out of all this.'

'We shall. It was never my intention that she should become involved. She has other important things to do. This is my business. And yours, if you keep to your word.'

'Don't worry about that. I'll do what I said. What do you mean, "she has other important things to do"?'

'If you can't see that, I don't know how to tell you. You are married to her, remember.'

'I will look after her, never fear.'

'Philippe, that's a soldier's promise, and a soldier has no control over his life. My god, Tressie and I should know that well enough. No, don't look like that. I know you mean what you say. I know you will do everything you can. So will I. After all, she is precious to me as well, especially now. Let's get up. This floor is too damp to lie on for long.'

He took her hand and helped her to her feet. She took his face between her hands and kissed him on both cheeks. He sensed her hesitating in the embrace and for a moment thought there might be another of those fierce kisses on the lips but her eyes searched his and she said,

'And so are you.'

In the doorway, she stopped and laughed.

'Precious, I mean, not damp.'

He was searching for an answering quip when she added,

'There's something else. While you were out, Jeannot turned up with a message from Jérôme Janquet. In a few days I have to go away for a while, not long: to meet some people. I'll have things to tell you when I come back. You'll be all right, you two, together, won't you? Jeannot will come up now and again to help. He'll be very useful if the lambing starts while I'm away. I expect you and he will have quite a lot to talk about, and do, perhaps. Now, tell me, what is this thing you call Shepherd's Pie?'

'Words cannot describe it. Only great music can do it justice.'

'Shepherd's Pie, Shepherd's Pie; why have you all gone, why, oh why?'

'Philippe, you look very silly, dancing about like that with no clothes on.'

'What can you mean, "silly"?'

'Well, you're, er, wagging.' She was shaking with laughter.

He looked down. 'I do believe you're right. What can I do to stop it?'

'Come to bed. I have an idea.'

Shortly afterwards he said, 'When I'm first here, there, inside you, I don't want to move. I just want to be there, here, feeling you holding me tightly, all round, slippery, all warm. But I can't, I can't, can you feel that? I can't and I don't want to stay still any more.'

'Don't,' she gasped. 'Don't stay still. Don't.'

The first time he woke up the room was in candlelight and she was standing at the window wearing her nightgown.

'What are you doing?'

'Something woke me, a sound perhaps. I thought there might be something outside. I got up to look.'

'Did Caramelle bark?'

'No; that's strange. She didn't.'

'You look so beautiful in the candlelight with your hair down like that.'

'Come and look. There's a big moon.'

'A honeymoon?'

'If you like. It's pale, a little bit like lavender honey, not dark like garrigue honey. Come and see.'

'I will if you take off that gown so I can see you in the moonlight.'

'If you do it, you'll be able to see the moon as well.'

He stood behind her, holding her as close as a cloak, his hands under her breasts lifting them a little. She leaned her head on one side letting her hair hang down past his hands.

'I can see you and taste you and feel you and smell you and hear you,' he said. 'I can hear your heart beating; or is it mine?'

'The moonlight; you wanted to see me in the moonlight. Can you see what you want to see?'

'Moonlight takes away all the colours. It leaves only silver and grey and black. But it makes some wonderful shadows, like here and under here and there. Is it true that if a woman wants to make love she loosens her hair?'

She turned round and pressed her head against his chest. He put his arms round her back and shoulders. He thought that he could feel his own warmth lingering on her skin.

'I've never thought about it. You were in the barn a long time with Séverine. What were you doing? Was it that awful gun?'

'She wants me to show her how to use it now that Vabrette's finished his work on it.'

'And that's what you were doing?'

This wasn't the right time to tell her about those kisses. He would tell her, one day. Perhaps.

'Yes, there's a lot to learn. I thought you'd rather not talk about this.'

'But you haven't many bullets for it, have you? Or did you find some more today?'

'Tressie, sweetheart, like I said, I thought you wanted to keep out of this but I'll tell you. Yes, I did find a box today and there's another one near the shelter that Caramelle dug up the time we first went back there. Now you know all there is to know. I'm sorry: I thought you'd rather not know.'

'Philippe, my love, I don't want you to keep anything from me. You are right: I don't want to be part of it. Sevvie has told me not even to think of being part of it. But I do need to know what is going on. If I didn't I would make up all sorts of things in my head and that would be much worse.'

'From now on I will tell you everything I am told. I promise. Is that all right?' But he hadn't told her everything, had he? He hadn't told her that Séverine was going away for a while. It was best left to Séverine to tell her, wasn't it?

'Yes, that is what I want.'

'Now can we go back to bed? I think you're getting cold in this moonlight.'

'Is that the reason?'

'Partly.'

The second time he woke up, the candle had burned out but the room was dim with dawn light. She was awake: still, or only just woken up, he was not sure. Her nightgown was where it had been left, on the floor near the window.

'Are you still cold?'

'Ooh yes,' she said, 'freezing.'

***

'Why are you dressed like that?'

'Sit down, Tressie. I've made the coffee. Have some while I tell you.'

'I'll call Philippe.'

'No, don't do that. I'll be gone before he gets up. Jeannot is waiting outside.'

'Gone? Jeannot? What are you talking about?'

'I had a message from Jérôme Janquet a few days ago: the day you went out for that walk with Philippe. I'm going away for a little while, not long, so don't worry. It's to meet some people, make some arrangements. I can't tell you any more than that, who they are or where I'll be. In fact I don't know myself yet. It's best you don't know but you can guess what it's about.'

'It's about that gun, isn't it?'

'Yes, but not only that. Has Philippe been saying anything to you?'

'No; well yes. I made him tell me that day when you were with him in the barn all that time. He said he was showing you how to use the gun and I know you've been doing the same every day since then. He didn't say anything about your going away. Why do you want to do this, Sevvie? It frightens me.'

'Please don't cry, Tressie. Listen, I'll tell you why. If Papa or Pascal or Léopold were here, don't you think they would be doing the same thing as me?'

'But they were soldiers. They had to obey orders; that's what Papa said. And it was a long time ago.'

'And what about Fabrice, our darling youngest brother? That was not a long time ago. Remember what he had said? He said he was going to avenge his father and brothers if he could. I don't have any orders. There's no general to give me orders. But I know what I have to do. I have to do what Fabrice said: for all of them and for France. And now I can do it.'

'Why do you say "now" you can do it?'

'Because, my darling little sister, you have your man and the family is now safe with you.'

'Sevvie, please don't go.'

'Don't worry. I'll be back soon. We'll all be together again for lambing time. Oh, yes, and Jeannot is going to come up to help while I'm away. Now, I can't keep him waiting any longer. Where's my valise? Come here.'

Thérèse clung to her so long in the embrace that Séverine had to lift her arms free as gently as she could. Looking back from the door she gave one final smile that Thérèse's eyes were too blurred with tears to see.

When the sound of the cart's wheels had faded away, the house was very quiet. Thérèse sat at the kitchen table and poured coffee into her cup. Caramelle sidled up and flopped down beside her. She hadn't realised how cold her feet had been until the dog's shaggy head covered them. They all go away. Séverine said she would never leave, but now she had too. Would she come back? She said she would but even if she did, she really had left because something else besides La Commanderie was now important to her. Why was that? Was it because Philippe had come and so she felt free to go? Or felt she ought to go now that they were married? But she had wanted that to happen. Was it because she wanted to keep him in the house with the two of them? Did she have feelings for Philippe? That wouldn't be surprising: he was young and very attractive and there was no one else. Sometimes she felt something in the air between them: when they were dancing together, or arguing; sometimes when Séverine was being sharp with him, as she could be, and he teased her, something he was very good at. She would never admit this, but deep down, she wouldn't really care if there were some flirting or even more between the two of them. She wasn't jealous and that sort of thing was natural, wasn't it? It wasn't sharing, more like understanding and being unselfish. Was she being immoral, thinking like that? She didn't feel ashamed or uneasy; so no, she wasn't being immoral. There: she felt better. She lifted the cup to her lips and made a face. The coffee was cold.

''Morning again, sweetheart. Did I hear cartwheels outside?'

Lawless was coming down the stairs wearing the dressing gown that she had given him. He looked so young with his tangled fair hair. She felt a sudden urge to rush him back up to the bedroom and do all the things they had done the night before again, and again and was glad that she knew she could and there was no one in the house but them to know.

'Tell you in a minute. I'll just make some fresh coffee.'

***

'Have some honey. It's garrigue, the sort you like. Philippe, Séverine has gone away for while. Did she say anything to you about it?'

Glad that his mouth was full of bread and honey, Lawless mumbled:

'Might have said something. Can't remember.'

'You'd remember that, surely.'

'Oh, that's really nice. Is there any more? I don't know. I was concentrating on showing her all the things she needs to know about the gun and she was asking lots of questions.'

'Well, you know now. She said she won't be away long. You know what this means?'

'Tell me,' he said evasively.

'It means we have the place to ourselves until she comes back. It's our house. We can do what we want. Once we've done the work, that is. What would you like to do?'

'Make love to you on that rug in front of the fire.'

'Philippe! Do you ever think of anything else?'

'Yes: the hay loft and an open field in summer when the grass is high and full of cornflowers and . . .'

'You're impossible. Do you know what I would like? I'd like us to play the piano together again. We haven't played anything since we were married.'

'Not on the piano, I admit, but think of all the other games we have played. Sorry, I'm sorry: being silly again. Yes, let's play now.'

'Ewes first. Some are very near their time. We may be in for some sleepless nights. Séverine said Jeannot would come to give a hand.'

'Jeannot? Oh yes, I seem to remember her saying something about Jeannot.'

'You can never tell with Jeannot. He comes and goes without having to be told. He could be back later today.'

'He's been here once already?'

'He came for Séverine. I wouldn't be surprised if he took a look at the ewes while he was waiting for her to get ready. Are you ready?'

Thérèse lifted her skirt and straddled one of the ewes with its head between her legs while she carefully felt and prodded its belly.

'She's looking a bit miserable. Do you think she's all right?'

'It's her first time and she has two. She's rather small and she's in some sort of pain. We shall have to watch her closely.'

'Keep hold while I have a feel. Hm, there, one of them may not be lying right. Let her go now. The others look peaceful enough.'

'For now, but if this one starts early and gets into difficulties it can upset some of the other younger ones.'

'I'll stay if you like.'

'No: we'll let Caramelle watch them while we play. She will soon let us know if anything starts.'

'What a dog! You must trust her a lot.'

'Don't forget, my husband, that she found you and let us know.'

Husband. It sounded strange. He wanted to get used to it.

'What shall we play?'

'Tell you what: I'll close my eyes and pull something out of this pile and hope I'm good enough to play it. I know you will be. Now then, not this: too heavy; this one, damn, dropped it. This one: not too many pages. Now, what is it? Look, Tressie, it's a manuscript. *Trois Gymnopédies*, Erik Satie. I've never heard of him. Looks interesting, though.'

'I didn't know that was in with the others.'

'Someone has copied this out by hand; very nicely too. Look.'

'I know.'

'And there's something written on the first page, very faint, in pencil. I can hardly read it.'

'*Thérèse, de Thierry juillet 1925.*'

'There's something else, very faint.'

'*Lent et Triste.*'

"Slow and sad". *To Thérèse from Thierry July 1925. Slow and sad.* How mysterious. Thierry: is he someone you know? Tressie, what's wrong? Here, let me.'

He gently wiped the tears from her cheeks with his fingers.

'I'm sorry. Something's upset you. I'll put this one back. We'll play something else.'

'No. I want us to play it and then I'll tell you. I used to know this very well so if you like I'll play it through first and then we'll try it together.'

It was a short suite with three movements, hardly six or seven minutes in all. She paused twice for a few breaths between the movements. It was so simple and yet so deep, delicate and seductive, sweet and innocent and yes, sad. Sometimes the notes came like children tiptoeing, sometimes see-sawing, or swooping slowly up and down on swings. It was haunting and melancholic and like echoes of sighs from a long time ago. It was long after the last notes had faded away that he felt able to speak.

'I've never heard anything like it before.'

'Thierry said it was like the music of lost love.'

Until that moment the music had held him but now he felt the first prickle of jealousy.

'Tell me about him, Thierry.'

'Are you sure? You are, I can tell. Séverine says men always have to ask even when they don't want to know. You don't have to be jealous, my darling. Thierry was never my lover. You are the only lover that I have ever had. Thierry was our cousin. His father is our uncle Alexandre, Papa's elder brother. The family lives in La Couvertoirade. You remember? Thierry was the only son so he would have inherited the estate in time. Everyone thought he and Séverine would be married one day. He was always coming here and we would go there and they were always together. They let me play sometimes but I was much younger and I was always with Fabrice. He loved our piano and when I was older we used to play duets. I was only learning then but he was very kind and said I would play in concert one day. We had lovely times, such lovely times. Then, like all the men, he went away to the War. That was in 1917, the year after Léopold was killed at Verdun.'

'Sweetheart, stop now. You look so upset. Never mind any more. Let's play Satie instead.'

'No, no, I want to tell you. You ought to know because this music has something to do with it. Thierry came back from the war. He had a wound in his leg but he said it was healed and he was all right. Sevvy was fifteen then, still too young to be married. In any case the Army didn't let Thierry go. They sent him to Algeria, into the desert. He was there for nearly two years and when he came back he was different, much quieter. He used to come often, to help, because, you know this, there was only Fabrice and us and the farm needed a lot of looking after. But sometimes he would go missing and you would find him standing out in the field just staring into the distance. Séverine said he didn't talk to her as much as he used to and he would never say anything about the War, or what he did in Algeria. We still had horses then and he would go riding, always with Fabrice, not with us. Fabrice told me Thierry used to gallop on ahead, up and up as high as he could go and always away from the road and when Fabrice caught up Thierry would sometimes look at him as if he didn't know who he was.'

'I've seen the War change people, Tressie; they turn in on themselves; sometimes wonder where they are or even who they are.'

She seemed not to have heard him.

'The one thing that didn't change was that he still loved to play our piano. Sevvy never learned, so he would play with me, or Fabrice. Mama said he was very good, not as good as Pascal, but very good. I loved to hear him play. He was always coming up with new pieces. Mama thought that he didn't stick close enough to the classics. She would tell him and he would straightaway sit down and play a Bach partita, nearly perfectly, and she would sniff and say why didn't he always play like that. And we would all laugh. I was much better by then, almost as good as he was, so we played lots of duets and even gave little concerts for the others.

'We were all waiting to be told he and Sevvy were going to be married, waiting for the date to be fixed. Mama said she had a ring for Sevvy to wear: this ring. We waited and waited. Sevvy was getting thinner and thinner and we didn't know what was going on. Then one night she came into my bedroom and I could see she had been crying, something she never did. I was silly enough to ask her why she was crying when she ought to be happy because she was going to be married and when would it be. She said she didn't know because Thierry hadn't asked her. I can still remember her voice when she said that. It was cold and hopeless.

'Then, all of a sudden everything was different. I don't know what happened. Maybe Thierry's father said something to him, I don't know, said something about the family or Sevvy said something, or maybe Thierry just decided he had to do what everybody expected of him. I don't know. But the wedding day was fixed and we were all told it would be in July 1925. We wondered why it was so far ahead but someone told us that it was because Thierry had been given an important commission by the Army and had to go away for a year to carry it out. I wonder how true that was. Fabrice said he had decided himself to go away and live by himself like a hermit in the desert to sort out what he really wanted to do with his life.'

'But he did come back?'

'Yes, he did come back and he seemed better, happier. Sevvy and Mama started spending nearly all their time planning the wedding. Everyone from La Couvertoirade was going to be there and relatives from all over were invited. I was going to be one of the bridesmaids. Mama was so thrilled. Thierry came over every week and stayed sometimes in Fabrice's room. We played a lot of music.'

She stopped talking and played the opening bars of the Satie. Lawless waited for her to go on, half-suspecting what was coming but not daring to speak.

'He was here the day before the wedding with some friends. There was a marquee in the courtyard and we had a long lunch there. It was a very hot day. All of us were cooling ourselves with fans. After lunch most people went off to their rooms to rest. I knew the piano room was always cool even on a hot day and I went there to play. I didn't feel sleepy.

'I was trying to play some Chopin and making all sorts of mistakes when I heard the door open and Thierry came in. He was carrying some sheets of music. He said, ''No, not like that: I'll show you how to play it,' and he sat down next to me. But he didn't play. He embraced me and kissed me on my lips. I was frightened. I nearly screamed. I said he mustn't, mustn't do that. He was being married to Sevvy next day. I began to cry. Look, I'm crying again now. I was only eighteen, Philippe. I didn't understand.

'He didn't say anything at first. Then he gave a big smile and said he was a bit in love with me because I was so pretty, but not like that. He'd come because he thought I would like Satie and he put it on the stand and started to play this music, Philippe, the Second Gymnopédie. It's marked "slow and sad". He played only that one. I was in a trance. I hardly noticed when he stood up. That sad sweet music was still filling my head.

Then he told me he had written out the music himself as a present for me and Fabrice, but he had put only his name and mine on the first page of the score. He said he hoped I would learn to play it and remember him. I didn't move and he didn't touch me again. He went to the door and just before he went out he said he could never marry Séverine because it was Fabrice that he loved but I must never tell. He put his finger to his lips and went.'

'My god! What happened?'

'We never saw him again. He just went away, Philippe. Everyone was there the next day for the wedding but he never came. Everything was cancelled. There was a terrible scandal. La Couvertoirade blamed us. How could they do that? We have never spoken to each other since that day. I was the only one who knew why he did what he did but I was too terrified to tell and he'd made me promise not to. I was only eighteen, Philippe. Sevvy was amazing. We all thought she would go mad but she was just, well, calm. Perhaps that's why La Couvertoirade blamed us: because of her. They thought she must have been cold towards him. I know she wasn't. She loved him. He knew that too. I have kept the real secret all my life until now. You are the only one I have told, Philippe. You won't say anything, will you?'

'Of course not. Tressie, it explains something she said to me not long ago. I started to ask her why she never married and she said there once was someone and you knew. You don't think our getting married has brought all that bad time back again for her, do you?'

'No. She wanted us to be married. I know that.'

'Could she have suspected anything between Thierry and Fabrice?'

'She never said. I don't know. Sometimes she just seems to know things without being told, so perhaps she might have. The sad thing is that I'm not sure if it would have mattered all that much to her. She would have married Thierry because she loved him and because of the family.'

'The *family*?'

'Keeping the family alive means everything to her. Don't you see that?'

'I'm beginning to do so. Tressie, is that enough, or do you still want to play?'

'Yes: you and me together: all three pieces. You play the left hand. You'll love those chords that sweep up from the low single notes.'

In the barn with the sheep Jeannot heard the faint sound of the piano. It meant little to him. Mademoiselle, no, Madame, Chevalier played a lot these days, had done ever since the Sergeant had turned up. When they had finished playing he would have to fetch them because the ewe was in trouble and he and Caramelle needed help with her.

MIREILLE

Lawless didn't want to wake her. She'd been up most of the night with the lamb that couldn't feed. He knew what it was like: it had been with him the night before. Three nights now, he thought. It won't live. But she was determined it would. He left her sleeping and headed for the kitchen to make coffee.

Someone was sitting hunched over the table with his back to the staircase. Jeannot, he thought. How did he get in? Never mind, there was a smell of coffee. Jeannot must have made it. He seemed to know where everything was.

'Morning, Jeannot; any left for me?' Not speaking. 'Anything wrong? Is it the lamb?'

He sat down on the other side of the table. Jeannot didn't raise his head. This must be serious. Lawless leaned across the table and lifted Jeannot's chin with his finger. Big dark frightened eyes stared at him. He took his hand away hurriedly and sat back in his chair.

'Now, who are you?'

The girl kept staring at him, saying nothing. She seemed if anything to shrink further into herself.

'I won't hurt you. I live here. What's your name?'

'Good morning, Philippe. This is Miriam but we are going to call her Mireille. She has come to stay with us.'

Séverine had entered the room without his hearing her. She did that sometimes. She put two cups of coffee on the table.

'Now you're up, I'll bring another cup. Talk to her. She won't answer but that doesn't matter: she hears what you say. She needs to get to know all of us.'

'Hello, Miriam, I mean, Mireille. My name is Philippe. I come from England. Do you know where that is?'

No reply. She looked at him, frozen face, expressionless. Pretty, though: clear skin, pointed chin, very dark wavy hair and big eyes with fear deep down in them.

'Drink your coffee, Mireille. You look cold. Do you feel cold? I can make the fire up, if you like. Want to help me do it?'

Séverine came back with a cup in her hand and sat down beside the girl. She put a spoonful of honey in Mireille's coffee and stirred. Lawless watched the girl's eyes follow the spoon stirring.

'There you are. It's nicer when it's sweet. It's honey from our bees. Taste it.'

The girl glanced at Séverine but made no move to take the cup.

'Oh, Philippe, I forgot. There's something I want you to see in the salon. Leave your coffee there. It won't take a minute.'

She closed the salon door behind her and gestured to Lawless to take one of the armchairs.

'What is it?'

'Nothing really: I wanted to leave her by herself to see if she would take a drink. I think she's had nothing for the past two or three days and I've not had a word out of her. If she does drink that coffee it will be a start.'

'I'm completely in the dark. Who is she? Where's she from? She looks absolutely petrified.'

'She is, and when I tell you the story, you'll see why. With your hair and eyes she may take you for a German. I don't know much about her or where she comes from, but I do know what she is and that's why she's here.'

'Does Tressie know?'

'Not yet. Jeannot does. He brought us up from St Chely early this morning.'

'I'm baffled. You'll have to explain. Why does she have her own name but you want us to call her by another? Wait a minute, *Miriam:* that's a . . .'

'Jewish name: that's right. That's why we have to call her something else, something very French, a good Causse name.'

'She doesn't look very . . .'

'Jewish? Why should she? She is French: French parents, French grandparents, French brother.'

'Brother? Is he here as well?'

'No. It's safer if he's somewhere else.'

'You'll have to explain.'

'I will: later, when Tressie comes down. Now, let's go back and see if she's drunk that coffee. I made it with some of the real kind I brought back with me, so I hope she liked it.'

When they went back to the kitchen they found Thérèse sitting next to the girl with her arm round her shoulder and the empty coffee cup in front of her.

'Tressie, I was going to bring you some coffee in bed.'

'I heard voices and thought Séverine must be back so I came down and look who I found here. I've been talking to her but she won't answer. But she did drink the coffee.'

'This is Mireille. Mireille, this is my sister Thérèse. Now you know everyone in the house. Mireille is going to live here with us.'

'And this is Caramelle,' said Lawless. 'She lives here as well. Come and say hello to Mireille, Caramelle. Come, here.'

The dog padded across the floor and pushed her nose into Mireille's hand. The girl gave a little startled jump and then gingerly lowered her hand and stroked the shaggy head.

'I think Mireille would like some more coffee and some bread, maybe with some honey on it. She must be very hungry.'

'I'll see to it,' said Séverine.

With the plate piled high with slices of bread and honey in front of her and the coffee cup steaming beside it, Mireille still made no move to eat.

'We'll leave you with Caramelle for a minute or two, Mireille,' said Séverine. 'We have one or two jobs to do outside.'

It was a mild enough morning for them to stand talking in the courtyard. Séverine looked up, sniffed the air, squinting her eyes against the light.

'Soon be spring,' she said. 'I can smell it.' She yawned. 'I've been up all night, travelling. I need some sleep. What have you two been up to?'

'We're waiting for you to tell us,' said Lawless. 'Who is she?'

'All right, I'll tell you. Her real name is Miriam Renard but from now on she will be Mireille Chevalier, yes, Chevalier. If anyone finds out about her and gets nosey we can say she is a niece from La Couvertoirade.'

'You said Jeannot brought you up here, so he must know who she is.'

'He does and so do his parents and the mayor as well but they won't tell: they're all part of this.'

'Part of what?'

'Saving her life. Listen, Philippe, Tressie knows this but you don't. Our malicious so-called Government has always been against the Jews and after the humiliation of June 1940 and the Boche breathing down their necks things have been going from bad to worse.'

'A lot of Jewish families escaped from Germany and came to the south because they thought they would be protected here.'

'Tressie's right but then look what happened to them. The Government passed the Statutes on Jews, one in 1940 and another in June last year. Jews have been dismissed from their posts in Government service and more and more find it impossible to carry on their professions because of all the restrictions. Now they are beginning to lose their properties as well. It won't be long before they start being rounded up and put in prison. The law already allows the Prefect to order that for Jews who weren't born in France. There are rumours that the camps are being built and that's why Mireille has come to stay with us.'

'What about her parents?'

'Frightened for themselves and terrified for their children. They know what happened in Germany and they fear the same will happen here. All the signs are that they are right. And the awful thing is that it's our own rulers who have started doing the Boche's dirty work for them.'

'What will they do?'

'Mireille's father is a doctor. He's not even allowed to bandage a cut finger now. Her mother was a music teacher with classes at two lycées. She was dismissed last month. What they're going to live on, I don't know.'

'I ought to go back in and see how she is.'

'All right Tressie; we won't be long.'

'Couldn't they leave the country, go to Spain or England, the parents I mean, and send for the children later?'

'In these times and with this Government? Impossible. Besides, their families have been French for generations. Everything they have, or rather had, is here. Now they feel their children have at least a chance of safety with some of us they will stay put, keep close to the other Jewish families, help each other out and just hope for the best.'

'You said that when the time comes I would be helped to escape back to England: why not the same for Mireille, or her parents?'

'Philippe, you are not a Jew.'

'All right, I get the point. The girl looks frightened to death. Wouldn't it be better if she were with her brother, at least? Where is he?'

'I don't know. In a village in the Velay by now, I think. To be on the safe side we decided to keep details as secret as possible. We all know something but nobody knows everything.'

'I take it from that I'm not allowed to know who "we" are?'

'Not everyone: you know some of us.'

'And I am one of them?'

'You have to be: for our sake and for your own good. Listen: let's go back inside. I'm worn out. I must get some sleep and so should Mireille.'

The bread and honey had disappeared and the coffee cup was empty. From the way in which she kept licking her lips it seemed as if Caramelle had shared in the meal.

'She still won't talk,' Thérèse said, 'but she keeps stroking Caramelle, so she has made one friend at least.'

'She must sleep and so must I. She can stay with me in my room until she gets used to the place. I have an idea where she can go after that. Will you help me make up a bed for her?'

'I've had an idea. Before we do that let me take her to see the lambs. We won't be long.'

'All right. Philippe can help me instead.'

Séverine's room was large but sparsely furnished: a wide bed, with the silk nightgown Thérèse had made for her lying across its dark blue coverlet, a bedside table with brass candle holder, a writing desk and straight-backed chair in front of the window, no pictures on the walls but a large gilt-framed mirror above the mantelpiece, no wardrobe but a door in the wall opposite of the fireplace opening, Lawless presumed, into a dressing room. Séverine drew the long curtains back further, letting the morning light flood in.

'Nice room: I've never been in here before.'

'You tried to come in one night. I heard you turning the handle.'

'Did I? I'm sorry. It was dark. I was trying to find my room.'

'You had just come out of it. I heard you.'

'Sorry, sorry. Shouldn't have done that. Look, can we talk about something else?'

'Yes, while we get Mireille's bed ready. It's in my dressing room dismantled and wrapped in sheets. It needs two of us to put it together.'

The parts of the bed fitted together with thick threaded wooden dowels. It had a headboard with a carving of a rabbit. Séverine spread a plump feather mattress over the horsehair filled base and took sheets and pillows from a cupboard.

'I think she might like to sleep in here, but I'll keep the door open at night to begin with.'

'That's the first time I've seen screws like those for holding a bed together. It's very solid. I like the rabbit.'

'Papa had this bed made for me when I was ten and Tressie went into a sulk until she got one as well. Of course she doesn't need it now she has you but it may come in useful later.'

Lawless went over to the window and drew the curtains back a little.

'They're coming back to the house.'

'Better go down now. You've been long enough in another woman's bedroom, my lad.'

'I'm lost. Where does this door open, into another room?'

'No: onto the landing. From there it's only a step to the top staircase and then up to the tower.'

'That's another place I haven't seen yet.'

'No time now. Look, did you see the nightgown Tressie made for me from your parachute? Remind you of anything?'

'On your bed? Yes, I did. Yes, it's like the one she made for herself but hers has embroidered flowers. For some reason I had thought it had simple lines, like yours, but no, it turned out to have roses. Very pretty.'

As they were walking the short distance along the corridor, Lawless put his hand on her shoulder. She stopped and looked up at him, expectantly, he thought.

'Séverine, Sevvie, I think what you're doing is amazingly brave.'

'It is you who are the brave one.'

'No, no: it's different for me. A few hours of being scared stiff and then back home, if I'm lucky. And if I'm not, it's all over very quickly. The danger for you will never go away. You're taking a terrible risk hiding Mireille, on top of the other things I know you're getting involved with.'

'Philippe, have you forgotten when we spoke of Papa and Captain Dreyfus? It's the same thing all over again and we must act.'

'By helping the Jews?'

'You know the history of this family well enough now. Not only Jews: anyone hunted by the oppressors.'

In that case we ought to get on searching for the rest of that ammunition and the other guns, he thought.

'When will Jeannot be back?'

'Perhaps tomorrow. Now, what's going on down there? Why is that lamb in here?'

'Mireille wants to keep it with her,' explained Thérèse. 'She may as well because the mother won't feed it. Something has made her find her tongue at last: she's given it a name: Rachel. I think it might be her mother's name.'

'It's Hebrew for sheep, so it's a very good name to give,' Lawless said.

His memory suddenly flashed with the picture of Mr Johnson, the Sunday School teacher, telling them about Rachel who was the wife of Jacob. There was something else about Rachel that Mr Johnson hadn't mentioned but that he had found out himself: some funny business between her and her sister and Jacob but maddeningly he couldn't put his finger on it now.

'Well if it helps her to talk, and she can help it to live, I'll allow it, but only until it can walk properly and then it goes back with the others. And she has to do all the clearing up after it.'

'Have you got a Bible in the house?'

'A Bible? What do you want with a Bible?'

'Nothing really: just interest.'

'We have one somewhere. I haven't seen it for ages. Do you know where it is, Tressie? No? We'll have a look for it when there's time.'

'No hurry,' Lawless said. 'It can wait.'

***

The warmer weather and blue skies continued. Séverine began to wonder whether it might be the start of one of those rare years of legend when after a very hard winter the sun came out in early March and lasted until October. The snow disappeared except for some patches in the bottom of deep gullies and on the peaks of the higher hills. Worried that rain might become scarcer than usual in the summer months, Thérèse checked the depth of water in the cisterns under the courtyard that collected rainwater channelled from the roofs, and felt a little more reassured. One morning Lawless burst into the kitchen while Séverine and Thérèse were getting breakfast ready for all of them.

'You know that depression, that sort of big basin on the slope down towards the gorge? It's all green! Green with grass! I've just been watching Jeannot standing in a circle of grass.'

'Couldn't have come at a better time. It should be ready for the ewes after the lambing.'

'Why there? There's nothing like so much grass round about.'

'You find them all over the Causses. There are underground caves everywhere and the rain washes soil down into the cracks and holes that lead down into them, so the ground sinks and in time it fills up with soil and you have a fertile patch, sometimes very big, like that one. We grow oats and barley on it after the sheep have eaten enough of the new grass. The people call them cloups. Fabrice once told me that in Larousse they were called dolines.'

'Where's Mireille?'

'With Rachel in the barn. She still has to feed it in the fenced off part but it's better for it to be where it can hear and smell the other sheep. The mother still won't have anything to do with it, of course.'

'I think Mireille and the lamb saved each other,' said Thérèse.

'When I looked in on them before I came for breakfast I saw a couple of the ewes had wandered off by themselves. You know what that means?'

'They will be dropping lambs before night fall, those two. It's starting.'

'Jeannot must have seen it. He told me he was staying tonight.'

'Go give him a call, Philippe, and fetch Mireille in while you're about it. We might as well have a good breakfast. It could be the last peaceful meal that we get before the fun starts.'

'Have you ever seen a lamb born, Mireille?'

The girl stared back at Lawless with wide-open startled eyes.

'You can today.'

The words raised some eyebrows: Jeannot rarely spoke in company.

'When you two have finished you can go back to the barn and see what's going on,' Séverine said. 'And, Jeannot, make sure those two ewes have plenty of water handy. Then if everything is all right, take Mireille and show her the other barns and stables so she starts getting to know the place. And see if you can make her say something.'

Just as she was going out, Mireille turned and made a made a little sign with her hand to Caramelle. The dog immediately heaved herself up from her place near the fire and trotted out after the girl.

'Hm, I wonder whose dog that is now.'

'And did you also notice Mireille didn't think twice about going off with Jeannot? How old do you think she is, Tressie?'

'I asked her but she wouldn't say. I'd guess about fourteen.'

'I left her to go to bed herself and dress herself this morning,' Séverine said but I did get a little glimpse. I'd say fourteen as well, maybe near fifteen.'

'Same sort of age as Jeannot. They might become good friends. If they ever get round to saying anything to each other, that is.'

'Philippe, not everyone wants to talk as much as you do.'

Late in the afternoon Jeannot came rushing into the kitchen to say they were needed in the barn, quickly.

They found Mireille in the lambing pen putting a bucket of water in front of a ewe that had licked her lamb clean and now seemed desperately thirsty. The lamb was struggling to get up and find its mother.

'Look at her,' Séverine said, 'never seen anything like this before and there she is helping without any fuss. She's going to be very useful. What is it, Jeannot?'

'Another one.'

'Fetch Mireille. She needs to see.'

It was another normal birth: front legs first, hooves pointing down and then the slime covered head with the ears plastered flat, eyes closed, resting on the hooves.

They watched the ewe's body convulse as she pushed and pushed again until the soft white bundle suddenly slid free, the cord breaking as it settled into the straw.

'Mireille, here, take the cloth and wipe his head clean,' Séverine said. 'Go on, she won't hurt you. She ought to be licking him but she's tired. Yes, good, a bit more. Shit, he's not breathing. Stick the straw in his nose. Make him sneeze. Well done. He'll be fine now.'

Jeannot picked up the lamb and put it in front of the ewe where she could see it and sniff it. They all waited in suspense until she began to lick.

'Now watch him, Mireille,' Lawless said. 'In a minute or two he'll try to get up and find his mother because all he wants to do now is suck. If he can't find the place, you'll have to find it for him. Look, I'll show you where.'

Jeannot offered a can of dark liquid to Lawless.

'Oh, yes, I forgot: the iodine. No, you do it.'

Jeannot lifted the squirming lamb with one hand and dipped the end of the short strip of cord hanging from its belly into the iodine.

'What about the other lamb?'

'Already done.'

'That should liven him up. It stings a bit. Yes! There he goes.'

***

Why was Verrill trying to get into the turret? Stupid bugger: he ought to know there wasn't any room. The night fighter was closing in again. He could see the stabs of flame from its exhausts. Any second now it would open fire and Verrill was getting in his way so he couldn't level up the guns. Get out you silly fucker! He tried to shove him away.

'Philippe, stop it. What are you doing? Are you awake?'

'What? Who? Look out! He's coming in again! Dive left, left!'

'Philippe, wake up. It's me, Thérèse. Are you all right?'

'Thérèse? Oh, god. Yes, no, I mean yes. I'm all right. I was dreaming.'

'You were trying to push me out of bed.'

'Sorry, sorry. All right now.'

'You're sweating.'

'Just give me a minute. Is there a towel anywhere?'

'Wait there. I'll get one.'

She made him get up and strip off his nightshirt. He was shivering though not with cold. She rubbed him all over with the rough towel and found him a clean dry shirt.

'Back into bed now. I'll make you warm.'

He tried and she tried but it was no use. The night fighter's guns kept flashing in his eyes. So she held him in her arms and talked to him as she used to do to Fabrice when he was frightened and crept into her bed, and gradually he came back to her and then it was all right.

'What time is it?'

'Four o' clock, or it was when I came upstairs.'

'You've been up all night again.'

'Well you were up the night before and the one before that, with Sevvie. You remember that little ewe, the last one? The lamb was on its side, a big one and she's so small.'

'You should have got me up. What happened?'

'I tried to turn it but I couldn't push my hand in far enough to get a hold.'

'So what happened? Is she dead?'

'No. Mireille did it. She has beautiful small hands. I told her what to do and she managed it while I held the lantern. I wouldn't have believed it. She was so calm. Then Jeannot appeared and took over.'

'Jeannot? What did he do?'

'She had two. He eased out the twin. Luckily it was in the normal position because she was too exhausted to push, so Jeannot did it while we watched. He's still there. Mireille didn't want to leave but I brought her in and helped her to wash and took her up to bed. She was tired out. Sevvie was just getting up. She has gone to help Jeannot.'

'And they're all alive, mother and two lambs?'

'All alive, yes. The mother may not have enough milk for both so we could have two more to add to the other three that need feeding.'

'And you have Mireille who's perfect for the job. She loves it.'

'And Jeannot who doesn't seem to want to go home but he will have to, now that the lambing is all over.'

He'll be back, Lawless thought, as soon as he can get away: and not too soon for me.

'It's done, Philippe: eighty lambs and we didn't lose a single ewe.'

'I'll bring you breakfast in bed, to celebrate.'

'Let's celebrate first and then you can bring me breakfast in bed.'

'Aren't you too tired?'

'Tiredness has nothing to do with it.'

'Jeannot,' Séverine said, 'if you've had enough to eat I think it's time you were going home. Your mother must be thinking you've got lost. You have been such a help. We could not have done without you.'

'You're a trooper, Jeannot,' said Lawless. 'Don't leave it too long before we see you again.'

'Another look.'

"Another look"? Oh, all right. Don't be long. Hm, I think Mireille wants to go with you.'

'I have something for you before you go, Jeannot,' Thérèse called after them.

When Jeannot had set off for home with the walnut cake Thérèse had made for him safely stowed away in his satchel, the others went back to the barn for another look.

'If this good weather lasts we should be able to let most of them out on the grass in a couple of days.'

'It's my guess that Jeannot will be back here just about then,' said Thérèse with a nod towards Mireille who was closely watching the twin lambs snuggled up close to the ewe.

The girl turned to look at them.

'Was I born like that?'

Lawless was first to get over the surprise at hearing her speak for the first time.

'I've never seen a baby born, but yes, I think something like that. Except you weren't covered in wool.'

Thérèse clapped her hands and embraced Mireille.

'I think that's worth celebrating, what do you think, Sevvie?'

'Certainly. *Vin doux*: perhaps with a little water. No water? Very well.'

'There's a job for you, Philippe.' You can help Jeannot.'

'Is he here? What job?'

'Sort out the lambs, rams from ewes and mark them. Jeannot knows where the marker is. Once that's done, we can turn them out.'

Jeannot had already started when Lawless came into the barn: five or six lambs had dabs of blue dye on their backs. It was quicker with the two of them, one to hold the squirming bleating lamb, lift its tail and feel between the back legs for a scrotum and give a nod to the other to use the brush or a shake of the head to leave it alone. Half way through the flock they took a rest, swapped jobs and had finished in less than two hours.

'How many, Jeannot?'

'Thirty five.'

He must have kept count, Lawless realised. He totted up the number of blue splashes. It wasn't as easy as he'd thought it would be. The lambs were now a few days old and some of them were quite adventurous and kept wandering about.

'I make it thirty six.'

'Thirty five.'

'You sure? We don't want to miss one little ram and find out later we've got a lot of happy ladies earlier than we want.'

Jeannot grinned and shook his head. 'Thirty five.'

'I'll believe you. On your head be it. Thirty five with bollocks. When do we deal with them?'

'Mams'elle Séverine will say.'

'Of course, but the sooner the better, don't you think? Now, while we're on our own I want to ask you something else. When can we, you and I, take a look down in the gorge? You know what I'm talking about, don't you?'

'Yes. Mr Janquet said you would ask.'

'Mr Janquet has an interest in this but with his leg he can't come with us. When do you think?'

'Tomorrow.'

'When, where?'

'Dawn, at the shepherd's shelter. Caramelle must come.'

'Jeannot, I think you deserve some coffee.'

It was chilly before dawn and he was glad of the thick sweater that Thérèse had given him. He had pretended to be asleep when she got into bed tired after a long night in the barn and she was soon breathing softly enough for him to know he could get up quietly and dress. He put a note on her bedside table saying he had taken the gun and gone out with Jeannot and Caramelle and would be home before lunch. He hadn't said where they were going but she was bound to guess. He set off at a run with Caramelle leaping along beside him. The short grass was crisp with hoarfrost that would melt into dew once the sun was up. In the misty dove-grey light the only sounds were his footsteps and the panting of his breath. He had a momentary great feeling of freedom, something he hadn't felt for so long that it shocked him, released him, made him laugh out loud. Caramelle's head turned towards him at the sound and then she dashed on ahead. She seemed to know where to go.

Jeannot came stooping out of the shelter as Lawless approached. Without a word he turned and headed towards the dark smudge that was the line of trees on the edge of the gorge. He waited there for Lawless to catch up before he started climbing down. He was as nimble as a goat, sliding like a skier down leaf-covered slopes and leaping from one ledge to another in the rocky parts. Lawless felt like a clodhopper, trying to follow where Jeannot led, but slipping, tripping and once barging into a big chestnut tree so hard his teeth rattled. Jeannot waited until Lawless got back on his feet then pointed at the tree. A branch had been torn off and pieces of metal were stuck in the trunk.

'I've seen this before. Did you come down this way?'

'No. Up from the river.'

'So you've found other things down there?'

Jeannot nodded.

'Show me.'

The first thing they came across was one of the Merlin engines, jammed between two big trees with the three prop blades bent back and twisted pipes and rods hanging from it like entrails from a gutted beast. Lawless gave it only a passing glance and signed for Jeannot to carry on.

When Lawless caught up with the boy again, Jeannot was standing beside a large section of the port wing that had come to rest on a rock platform above a crag. There was a faint smell of petrol in the air. He looked enquiringly at Lawless.

'There's a tank in the wing that may still have petrol in it. Could be useful to somebody one day but not to us now. No time to hang about: keep your eyes open for metal boxes or guns. You know what they look like.' *And bodies, he thought, especially bodies though God knows what they'll look like now.*

The nose section had sheared off aft of the navigator's table and smashed into a big oak tree crushing the front turret back onto the pilot's cabin like a concertina. Lawless gestured to Jeannot to stand back while he clambered over a pile of metal and shattered perspex to look inside the crumpled mass.

The shapeless pile of leather strips and dark cloth drooped over the twisted steering column had to be Sherwood because sticking out of the pile was a gloveless claw-like shiny brown hand which still clasped the throttle controls. Mixed up with the jumble of metal and Perspex that had been the front turret was a Browning twisted out of shape and another heap of leather and some splintered bones: Sanderson.

Lawless began shaking so much he had to hold on to the windshield frame to prevent himself from falling. His chest felt tight. He could hardly breathe. It shouldn't be like this. Their bodies should be neatly laid out on the ground, arms folded over chests, caps over the hands. He thought he might take off Sherwood's watch. Keep it for his mother. He reached towards the brown claw but couldn't bring himself to touch it. There was a smell. He hadn't noticed that before. He drew back sharply and fell into the soft rotting leaves and was sick.

When he felt able to get up again Jeannot was standing just in front of him. That hand helping him must have been Jeannot's. He wiped his face with a rag from his pocket but couldn't get the taste of sick out of his mouth, no matter how much he spat. He looked at Jeannot through bleary eyes. The boy held something out to him, something a bit muddy but blue. It was a service cap, a Flying Officer's: Sherwood's.

'Caramelle found it. And this box.'

It was an effort to have to look. He forced himself to take the cap. The front turret Browning might be useless but at least they now had another 250 rounds of ammunition. He could think of no other way of carrying Sherwood's cap than wearing it. Perhaps Sherwood wouldn't have minded the self-awarded promotion: he had, no, used to have, the right sort of gallows humour. If he ever got back to England he would give the cap to Sherwood's parents. Then he thought, did Sherwood have a wife? Were his parents still alive?

'You've seen this before, haven't you?'

Jeannot nodded.

'Is there much more, down there?'

Jeannot nodded again.

'Bodies, like these?'

Jeannot made a face. 'There was a fire.'

'Show me.'

They reached one of the steepest parts of the gorge, a sheer drop of a hundred feet or so. Jeannot hesitated as Lawless looked over the edge.

'Christ, I can see it! There's been a hell of a fire! The trees are all burned. That's the part of the wing and the rest of the fuselage: they've burned as well. The wing and body tanks must have exploded. If only we'd brought a rope. I could do this if we had a rope. I do a lot of rock-climbing in the mountains at home. There might be a way over there.'

Jeannot wagged a finger and shook his head.

'This way for us. Caramelle will find her own way.'

They clambered down a narrow twisting pathway that judging from the heaps of droppings on ledges was used by wild goats. Caramelle was waiting for them at the bottom. There were only a few yards to go.

The fire had done its job well. The intense heat had reduced scores of trees to short blackened stumps and even set the aluminium skin of the wing and fuselage sections ablaze. All that was left were twisted and blackened metal frames and piles of ash. Lawless walked among the wreckage, kicking at the ash and feeling helpless and hopeless.

'It's no use, Jeannot. There's nothing here to see. Everything's gone up in smoke and my turret with it as well. Let's go back.'

'There is one more piece.'

'Where?'

'In the river.'

There wasn't much of it left. It must have broken up as it rolled or slid all the way down that bloody cliff and been scattered all over the place but at least it hadn't burned. The perspex cover was gone along with the entire port side gun mounting. The turret base was half submerged in a shallow pool and yes, there, depressed at minimum angle on its mounting, was the remaining Browning, twin to the one in the barn. Lawless splashed across the boulders and pools to reach it. Not a scratch on the barrel or anywhere else. How crazy was that? They spent half an hour searching among the boulders and in the pools for belts, ammunition boxes or any sign of the rest of the crew and found nothing.

Lawless sat on the riverbank with his head in his hands, tingling with exhaustion and trying not to think of the climb back up the cliffs. He looked at his watch: they had been out only four hours. Three hours to lunch. He'd said they would be home by then.

'We can't carry the gun with us, Jeannot. In any case I haven't any tools to dismantle it. We'll have to think of something else. Better be heading back. We can pick up the ammunition box on the way. That's something at least.'

'We can walk to St Chely in one hour, perhaps a little more. There is a road all the way on the other side of the river.'

'Why go there?'

'My father will let us take the mule cart to La Commanderie.'

'Jeannot, I feel better already. If we hurry we can have coffee and cognac with Mr Jérôme Janquet and it shouldn't cost us anything once he knows what we've found.'

'What Caramelle has found.'

'As you say. How deep is this water? Go on: you go first.'

Jérôme Janquet gazed up at the yellowed ceiling of his café and tapped rhythmically on the tabletop with his fingertip; in four-four time, Lawless noted as he sipped his second cognac.

'This will take some time to organise. We must have the right people.'

'Vabrette: We can't do without him.'

'Vabrette, yes: I will send word. And two more men to help with the search and carrying: perhaps your father, Jeannot. I will speak to him. You two, of course, and one more; let me think. Yes, Valentin, Serge Valentin, the schoolmaster: he is a young man and one of us now.'

'How long, Mr Mayor?'

'I cannot say, Sergeant: as soon as I can arrange for them all to be available at the same time. I will send you word.'

'Concerning the other matter, my comrades . . .'

'There we shall have to be very discreet but be assured, Sergeant, once we have recovered them we shall treat them with the dignity they deserve. For the time being it would be unwise to lay them to rest in the village cemetery. When the War is over it will be for others to decide but as for now we will find a place for you to approve.'

'Thank you. I think we have found only two of my crew. The two others we may never find. The fire, you understand.'

'Perhaps some of the ash that you mentioned may serve as memory of them in this case?'

Could that be all that was left of Jack Verrill and Ernie Forbes? Twenty-four raids: he'd been with Jack on every one. Jack: a bit of a cynic but he certainly enjoyed life. While it lasted. You always knew when Jack was around: that voice, that laugh. 'Come on, Lawly, stop going through your French verbs, or should I say your French letters, and get 'em in. It's your round, you stingy bugger.' Red hair, red face, big hands, good for a goalkeeper. And now what? You couldn't tell the difference between what was left of him from what was left of the Whitley.

'Sergeant?'

'What? Ah, yes, Mr Janquet?'

'I see you are affected, Sergeant. I understand. Leave this matter with me. Is there anything else I can do for you?'

'Is there, I mean, have you had any reply to my message?'

'Nothing so far but do not despair. It is early days yet . . .'

'Is there any news; about the War, I mean?'

'Some good: the Red Army has been advancing. Most of the rest is bad. Your navy has lost some of its big ships. That is all I know.'

'I have a little good news for you. A certain young person has proved to be very useful in the lambing.'

The faintest of smiles flickered briefly across Jérôme Janquet's face and was quickly gone. He nodded approvingly but said nothing.

***

'Tell Jeannot to come in. I expect he's hungry. He always is.'

'He's had to go back. His father has jobs for him. He'll be here again tomorrow.'

Séverine sniffed, and peered closely at Lawless.

'Have you been drinking?'

'Coffee.'

'That's not coffee I can smell.'

'Oh yes, and a couple of cognacs, only little ones: at the café.'

'You left word that you'd gone out with Jeannot and taken Caramelle and the gun with you, so we thought you'd come back with some rabbits or birds for the kitchen: nothing about slinking off to the café and drinking. Then we found out you hadn't taken the gun after all.'

'You're right. I haven't any rabbits or partridges for you but I do have this big bag of lovely sausages from Madame Bec and we may not have taken a Verney-Carron but we did come back with a Browning.'

'Hmph! Call the others in for lunch. It's bread and cheese and onions. The sausages will do for tonight.'

'I have other things to tell you.'

'While you were away we decided to take the sheep out this afternoon to the pasture that Tressie told you about; not for long, no more than an hour, but the exercise and the taste of a bit of new grass will be good for them and the lambs will have a chance to play. We will all have to be there to make sure they don't stray. Caramelle is very good but she can't be everywhere at once. There'll be a chance for us to talk then without the others knowing.'

'Watch that old ewe, the one with the bell. Once we put her on the track to the cloup she'll lead them all there. She knows her way. The lambs will stay close to their mothers. If any act silly Caramelle will chase them back.'

'Isn't it rather far for the lambs?'

'If any get too tired we can carry them and they can sleep while their mothers graze.'

By the time they reached the cloup all four of them were carrying lambs, Lawless one under each arm. There was hardly any need to watch the sheep: the fresh grass was all they had in mind. Thérèse and Miriam sat with sleeping lambs on their laps while Lawless walked slowly round the flock with Séverine.

'Now at least you know where they are, Philippe.

'It was terrible, Séverine: my friends, seeing them like that. Sherwood, such a bloody good pilot, always got us back and there he was squashed like a bloody fly on a windshield.'

'Philippe, listen to me.'

'Jack and Ernie, nothing left but ash, nothing but ash, Séverine. And look at me, large as life. Why them and not me: what's so special about me?' He grabbed her by the shoulders and shook her as tears streamed down his face.

She slapped him hard across the cheek.

'You are special because you are alive! Being dead they can do nothing! Alive you have so much you can do and I will make sure you do it. Now shut up and raise your hands high. Raise them high or I'll hit you again! Now I slap your palm and you slap mine. Again, the other hand. Harder. Again. Dance, yes move your feet and dance and stop whining about how guilty you feel.'

'What are they doing?'

Thérèse looked to where Miriam was pointing.

'Philippe must be showing my sister one of his English dances. He made us dance some of them not long after he came here.'

'He made you dance?'

'Yes, when he gets an idea into his head, there's no stopping him.'

'He told me he came from England but how?'

'His aeroplane crashed on the Causse in the middle of winter and he was hurt. We found him and brought him to the house. He was worried about his friends but there was nothing we could do then. He found out only today that all of them are dead. It's made him very sad.'

'But he was dancing.'

'Perhaps Séverine persuaded him. It can help.'

'Jeannot told me he was a English soldier.'

'Did Jeannot tell you anything else?'

'Only that you are married: but I knew you were because you sleep together in the same room.'

Thérèse laughed. 'Yes, he is my husband. Do you like him?'

'Yes, I like him. He's very nice but he looks so sad sometimes.'

'He misses his friends.'

'If he is a soldier, will he have to go away, to the War?'

'Oh dear, I don't want to think about it. Yes, he may have to go.'

'I want him to stay. Can we make him stay?'

'I wish we could, Miriam, I wish we could. Soldiers are not their own masters. He may have to go one day.'

'But he will come back, won't he?'

'Yes, he will come back, I'm sure of that. You will see him again.'

'They've stopped dancing now.'

'I'm all right now, I tell you.'

'So now we have two guns and how much ammunition did you say?

'Seven hundred and fifty rounds.'

'That's a lot.'

'Not as much as it sounds. One gun can get through that in less than a minute.'

'Short bursts, Sergeant: that's what you kept telling me.'

'And I hope you remember. When it all starts to happen your finger can get frozen onto the trigger.'

'You said this second gun is as good as the first one that Vabrette worked on.'

'You could fire it now. All Vabrette has to do is take it off the mounting and make the bipod for it.'

'I have to see Jérôme Janquet again the day after tomorrow. I will press him to get everything done before the people start thinking of going fishing in the river again.'

'It can't come too soon for me. Now I know where they are I can't wait to see them properly looked after. I keep thinking about foxes. Are there any wolves in these hills?'

'No wolves, Philippe, not for many years now but I have the same feeling as you. When a place has been found for your friends, you should be there alone, without us, to see them buried. It's best if not too many know about this.'

'I'll come with you to see Janquet.'

'Not this time, Philippe. There are some people I have to meet. I may have to go with them.'

'Go away again: how long for?'

'I don't know. There are more and more things to do, people to see, plans to discuss, supplies to arrange, more children to rescue.'

'It's going to keep on happening, I can see.'

'I'm afraid so and for longer and longer, I expect. I'm relying on you to look after things here. It's asking a lot, but you did say you would do what you could to help.'

'I remember, but it won't be easy, just Thérèse and me.'

'There's Miriam now.'

'Yes, but for how long?'

'Until the end of the War, Philippe. Where else would she go until then?'

DR VAUDET

It was a good place to bury them, a little glade high enough above the river for it to be in no danger from floods. Late afternoon sunlight was filtering through the branches of oaks and chestnuts, catching the green tips of new leaves. There was one grave for all four. Lawless had said since they died together they should lie together. Vabrette and Bec had tamped the ground flat with their shovels. In a few weeks time the grass would have grown again and there would be no sign of what lay under it. A low cairn of granite boulders carried up from the riverbed by Lawless and the schoolmaster Valentin was the only marker and when the lichen grew on that it would hardly be noticed by anyone who happened to come by. Only the five men and one boy standing looking at it would remember where it was and what it meant. Lawless had thought of hiding a bottle with some sort of message in it inside the cairn but in the end decided against. The simple reason was that he couldn't put into words what he felt should be said. Jérôme Janquet told them a record of what they had done would be entered in a confidential file in the Mairie. Lawless placed the last stone on the top of the cairn. They all stood round in silence, a little awkwardly, each man wondering what to do next. Lawless heard wood pigeons calling high up in the trees nearby. Vabrette and Bec, the only ones wearing caps, took them off. Jérôme Janquet cleared his throat. Lawless realised they were waiting for him to say or do something. His mind was blank. What could you say? All he wanted now was for the thing to be over. The words came blurting out.

'Rest in peace, lads.'

'Rest in peace'? There was no rest, no peace: only War.

Vabrette came across and handed him the shotgun Séverine had put in the cart beside him when he drove off with Jeannot.

'We've no trumpet, Sergeant, so fire a salute for 'em. Nobody will take any notice of a shotgun blast in the woods.'

There was only one cartridge for the Verney-Carron. No more were needed because there was only one grave.

With the Browning and the ammunition boxes hidden under some sacks in Bec's mule cart it was time to go. Lawless said he would walk back to the village by himself.

'We'll wait in the café for you, Sergeant,' said Vabrette. 'You'll need a few drinks after your walk. It's the only way.'

Lawless watched them go, three men in the cart and Jeannot and the schoolteacher walking behind. When they were out of sight he went back to the river and spent a long time washing his hands. He couldn't think of anything else to do but after a while the cold clean water began to make him feel better, so it was time to go.

***

'Are you sure?'

'No but I am feeling a bit funny.'

'Funny? What do you mean, "funny"?'

'Tired; but I'm never tired, you know me. And tender.'

'Well you can expect that. I remember your telling me you were sore.'

'There's no need to grin like that. I don't mean there, and in any case that's gone now. I mean here and here.'

Thérèse gingerly touched her breasts.

'He's not squeezing you too hard, is he? Or biting?'

'Sevvy, shut up. If you're going to say things like that, I won't tell you any more. In any case, no he isn't. And I'm late.'

'I'm sorry. "Late", did you say? How much late?'

'Only two or three days. I am sometimes.'

'It sounds to me as if you could be right. Have you told him yet?'

'No. I want to be sure before I say anything.'

'The only way to be sure is to see the doctor. We must go to see Vaudet in Florac.'

'"We"?'

'Yes, I will go with you. I've been thinking of seeing him myself. My veins have been giving me trouble again, worse than before.' Séverine lifted her skirt and rubbed her shin.

'I'd like Philippe to be there as well but how could we all go? It's too far to walk.'

'We might have used the bicycles now that Philippe's mended them but I think there could be a better way: Jérôme Janquet. He has a car.'

'I know he has a car but he hasn't any petrol for it.'

'He has some now. He gets an allowance for his duties as Mayor. And—don't interrupt—I know he has to go to Florac soon because he asked me to go with him. I can't tell you why. He can take us all.'

'I haven't been in a car since before the War.'

'Don't be so mournful, Tressie. If you're right, it's wonderful news. A baby in La Commanderie: think of it! Tressie, what's the matter?'

'I'm frightened, Sevvie. I know you'll tell me I shouldn't be but I am.'

'You're wrong, Tressie. I wouldn't tell you anything of the kind. I know how you feel, believe me.'

'I think that I can hear Philippe outside. The men should be here soon. I'd better get some coffee and breakfast ready for them.'

'It's a job for men, Sergeant, though I've known one or two ladies who quite liked doing it. Worried me a bit, they did.' Vabrette laughed and winked at him. 'Feel like giving a hand?'

'Can't wait, Corporal.'

'Better get cracking then. Jean-Pierre?'

The butcher nodded and got to his feet.

Vabrette had everything planned and told Lawless as they were walking across the courtyard.

'This is how we'll do it, Sergeant. Jeannot brings 'em into the stall one by one. I hold em, you know the way, and Jean-Pierre does the slice and squeeze part. It's pretty quick.'

'And what do I do?'

'You're the MO. You have the iodine and the sponge. It stings and they squeal. That won't worry you, will it?'

'I've heard worse.'

Metcalfe shrieked like a stuck pig. He must have had his mike on send when the twenty millimetre hit him. Sitting in the turret you couldn't see him but Christ, you could hear him.

'You all right, Sergeant?'

'Fine; it's a bit nippy out here after the kitchen.'

In the kitchen Jérôme Janquet sipped his coffee and thought for a moment.

'Yes, I can take you to Florac. In fact it would be very convenient.

Certain people want to take a look at the Sergeant, not meet him, you understand, not yet, but see what he looks like so they could recognise him again.'

'Are you always so cautious?'

'Always, Mademoiselle Chevalier, and I require you to be the same. We are still building our network here in the Cevennes and learning from the mistakes of others. The idea is to be unnoticed. Now the Sergeant is a military man and military men are trained to look the part, walk upright, keep to regular patterns of behaviour, even to write things down, compose reports. Such things do not escape the notice of a trained policeman.'

'I understand what you are saying. My father and brothers were certainly as you describe but I have observed this young man closely, very closely, I assure you and he is different, perhaps because he is so young, perhaps because he is, as he keeps telling us, an airman, not a soldier.'

'We shall see but let us not forget he is also English, a rarity in these parts.'

'But one becoming more French by the day in the way he looks and speaks and even smokes his Gauloises.'

'There I have to agree with you, Mademoiselle Chevalier,' said Jerome Janquet grudgingly. 'He is learning. But we shall see.'

'The noise seems to have died down. They must have finished out there and put the lambs back with the ewes. Shall we join them? My sister will soon be starting to make lunch in here.'

The three men were standing outside the barn smoking cigarettes. A bucket of water stained red with lamb's blood they had washed from their hands stood near the door. Jeannot was nowhere to be seen. Séverine approached Bec.

'All went well?'

'Well enough, Mams'elle. Two'll need watching: bled more than the others. You always get some. We used a bit of string to tie 'em up. That needs taking off tomorrow. Jeannot knows which ones.'

'Good, good. We shall put them all out on the grass again tomorrow and hope they start fattening up quickly. You should be seeing quite a few of them again before too long, Jean-Pierre.'

'Close the door, Jean-Pierre,'said Jérôme Janquet. 'Long meetings are not safe meetings, so I will be brief. Sergeant, Henri here and Serge Valentin removed the other gun from the wreckage of your aircraft and Henri has now finished working on it.'

'And it's in even better shape than the first,' said the smith.

'Where is it?'

'Tucked away where nobody will ever find it, don't worry.'

'But you have no ammunition for it,' said Lawless.

'I was coming to that,' said Jérôme Janquet. 'Jeannot found another box in the river. It was almost covered by gravel. Only Jeannot's sharp eyes could have spotted it. Henri has that as well.'

'So what happens now? I know you and Henri and Monsieur Bec have seen action but the schoolmaster hasn't. He told me he was excused from military service because of his lungs. So I'm the only one here who has ever fired this particular type of gun. You'll learn quick enough but you should at least practise the drill and fire a few rounds.'

'I am ready now,' said Séverine.

Jérôme Janquet held up his hand like a gendarme halting traffic.

'All in good time. Let us not be hasty. What we must first practise is how to work together in a real situation. What I am going to propose will not need machine guns. If my plan works, we shall repeat it when the opportunity arises and after that we may move to more serious targets where the guns will be necessary.'

He paused and looked round the group, fixing his gaze on each face in turn.

'Before I go on I want to make one thing clear and I want the agreement of all of you on this: I am the commander of this cell, this peloton, if you prefer, and my orders are to be obeyed. Is that agreed? Very well. Now, my plan for our first action is this. We need to be more mobile than we are at present. We can take time to reach our target but we must get away as quickly as possible. I propose to use my car to do this. It can carry four, five at a pinch, and also whatever we choose to take from the target.'

'Guns, ammunition?' asked Vabrette.

'If possible, but other things too as I hope our first target will provide.'

'Don't keep us in suspense, Jérôme,' said Séverine. 'What is this first target?'

'Petrol in the lorry that supplies the Gendarmerie in Florac.'

'Petrol? Why do we need petrol more than guns?'

'My allowance is too small for our purposes as well as its official use. We need to build up stocks if we are to use my car for our activities. We may have to travel long distances sometimes to avoid suspicion or detection.'

'And petrol is also very useful for making firebombs.'

'Exactly, Sergeant. They are being used in attacks almost every day now in the Occupied Zone.'

'Good, I understand now but what is your plan for seizing this petrol?'

'I know the route that the lorry takes for its deliveries and I know there is a delivery each week. What I do not know yet is the day and the time that the lorry leaves the depot but I hope to find out when we go to Florac, Mademoiselle Chevalier. Our next meeting will be after I have that information. Agreed? Thank you. One last thing: say nothing of what we have been discussing today to anyone. In fact try your best to forget it. Is that clear?'

'What about Valentin?' said Lawless.

'He will be told if I decide he is to take part.'

'I think it is time for lunch,' said Séverine.

'A moment, Sergeant,' said Jérôme Janquet as the others were leaving the barn. He took a sheet of paper from his pocket and handed it to Lawless.

Yes I ken John Peel and Ruby too were the only words on the paper but he recognised his father's handwriting.

'Now you both know. There was an envelope but I thought it safer to destroy that. There can be no more messages between you, at least for the time being.'

'No matter; at least my mother now knows I am alive.'

'What will your father do now?'

'Let my uncle know, I think; probably not many other people.'

'Your commanding officer?'

'Yes, he may well do that. He may see it as his duty.'

'You realise that if your father does that it means that you also will be expected to do your duty and make every effort to escape back to England?'

'Of course, but I have made commitments to you and I will honour them first.'

'From what Mademoiselle Chevalier has told me, your only commitment was to make your guns available to us and to give some instruction in their use.'

'You know it cannot stop at that.'

***

'Are you all right, sweetheart? You don't look very well.'

'It's the car journey. I'm not used to cars.'

'Séverine, you look a bit pale as well. In fact you both looked under the weather even before we started. That road, so many twists and bumps and the Mayor isn't the best of drivers. I hope you aren't sick on the way back.'

'Stop fussing, Philippe. Open the door and let's go in. It isn't locked. Dr Vaudet will be expecting us and we're very late.'

A middle-aged frizzy-haired woman wearing a white apron greeted them rather sourly and asked their names. On hearing who they were she turned more deferential, forced a thin smile onto her face, asked them to be seated and disappeared along a dimly-lit corridor in the direction of what Lawless took to be the doctor's consulting room.

'You can leave us now, Philippe. The café is in the square with the fountain on the opposite side to the Mairie. Don't forget, order a glass of wine or beer and sit by the window . . .'

'Yes, I know, I know, Sevvie: pick up the newspaper, light a cigarette and wait for Jérôme. I don't know why I can't stay here, Thérèse. You haven't told me what's wrong with you.'

'She can't do that until the doctor has told her, can she now?'

'We'll come and join you as soon as we can, Philippe. I promise.'

Thérèse kissed him as she said this, making him even more concerned.

'Think of it as a sort of test, Philippe: first time out on your own in a strange town. Don't forget the Gauloise. Have you got some matches? You must not use that lighter, you know. And keep your cap on.'

Lawless hunched his shoulders as he walked along the narrow cobbled street with its high shabby-fronted houses to where it joined a wider main thoroughfare shaded by an avenue of tall plane trees in full fresh green leaf. Women with shopping bags and one or two men with dogs at their heels passed him by without a glance. An ancient Citroen with a monstrous gasbag on its roof wheezed along the road struggling to overtake a horse drawing a creaking cart loaded with hay. He fought off the urge to follow the smell of freshly baked bread to the bakery that had to be nearby. He came to the end of the avenue and looked up at the wooded cliffs to the west. He could just see the spire-topped towers of a chateau and much higher, on the crest of the cliffs, pillars of pink-stained rock set like massive totem poles overlooking the town. Florac was tucked tightly in where the valley narrowed between the ramparts of two causses, the Méjean to the west he knew; the name of the other, to the east, he didn't know yet. Thérèse had told him that Florac was loved by rivers. They all wanted to meet there, four at least, she said. One of them, the smallest by the look of it, was there, not far ahead of him, running down from the direction of the cliffs and cascading from one wide pool to another over low weed-draped stone weirs. He stood for a few moments looking over the parapet of a bridge that arched over one of the pools and saw slim grey trout idling near the weeds in the clear still water. It was all so beautiful and peaceful and, yes, ordinary, like the river at home, except for the derelict old building held up by rusty girders overlooking the other bank of the stream. But even that was somehow a fitting part of the scene.

A voice interrupted his thoughts.

'Monsieur, if you please.'

'Sorry, excuse me.'

He stepped into the roadway to let the wheelchair pass by.

The arched bridge: cross it, turn right, fifty metres and he should come to the square with the fountain and the Mairie and the café opposite.

It was yet another Café de la Place. He remembered going into two in Paris and another in Rouen. It became a joke between him and his father: where would the next one be? He was the only customer. The man behind the bar was reading a newspaper. He didn't look up until Philippe had sat himself down at the table in the window and was rummaging in his pocket for cigarettes and matches.

'Morning.'

''Morning. Red, please. Mind if I take a look?' Lawless pointed at the newspaper and struck a match for his cigarette.

'Looking for something in particular?' the barman said, putting a glass of red wine and the heavily thumbed newspaper on the table.

'No; passing the time. Mate of mine should have been here by now. He's always late.'

'Mm. What's your mate's name? I might know him.'

'Here, did you see this? "Big fire in Mende", it says. I was there only day before yesterday! What did you say?'

'Doesn't matter,' the barman said and went back to his stool behind the bar.

Lawless tried the wine. It was surprisingly good; good enough to make him think he might well have another.

Dr Vaudet took off his spectacles and let them hang from their gold chain onto the waistcoat of his dark suit. He was a dapper little man with bright humorous eyes and greying hair combed back from a boney forehead. He beamed at the two sisters.

'Mesdemoiselles Chevalier, what a pleasure it is to see you again! How long has it been? Let me see. Oh, yes, oh dear, forgive me! Of course, your dear mother, poor lady.'

'Almost two years, Dr Vaudet. You were most kind.'

'Can it be so long? A sad, sad time. There was little I could do. Ah, yes, ah, yes.'

He looked down at the floor, shaking his head slowly from side to side as if wondering whether there had been anything else that he might have done. After a moment or two he looked up at them and the smile was back on his face.

'But here you are, here you are. How can I be of service to you two ladies?'

'It is a delicate matter. My sister was married near the end of January . . .'

Dr Vaudet turned to Thérèse.

'And is something troubling you, Mademoiselle, ah, stupid of me! Of course, of course, *Madame* Chevalier . . .'

'Madame *Lawless* Chevalier.'

'*Lawless*? Unusual name, yes. But there we are. My very good wishes to you, *Madame.* How happy your dear mother would have been, yes. "Delicate matter", hm, married some weeks ago; yes, I think I understand. Please to come into my consulting room: with Mademoiselle Chevalier too, if you wish. I find most ladies are more comfortable with a chaperone present on such occasions.'

Séverine listened to the sounds coming from behind the curtain at the far end of the consulting room: clothing rustling, glass clinking on metal, the questioning murmur of Vaudet's voice and Thérèse's soft, hesitant replies, silence, water flowing into a bowl, paper being crumpled up and falling into a basket, the sudden swish and rattle of the curtain being drawn back. Then the sight of Dr Vaudet putting his jacket back on and of Thérèse smoothing her hair and brushing her hands down her skirt. The doctor looked across at Séverine. He seemed rather pleased with something.

'Shall I say this to both of you or leave Madame to tell Mademoiselle?'

'Please, to both of us together.'

'Well then, I am happy to say that you, Madame, are pregnant and in very good health.'

'Oh, Tressie, what wonderful news.'

Thérèse's lips were trembling as she tried and failed to speak but her smile and her tears said enough.

'Madame, if I may break in, I calculate from what you have told me that your child should be born in the first week of November give or take a day or so. Now, let me see, I should like to see you again in a month's time, and immediately should you have any pain. Allow me to say this: you are not the youngest of mothers though not the oldest, but we must take care. You have enough help at home? You have Mademoiselle your sister, of course, but anyone else?'

'My husband, doctor.'

'Hm. I mean women, sensible women.'

'There is Madame Bec in the village and a young woman of our acquaintance.'

'Very well, very well. Now, ladies, if you will wait outside for a few moments I will write down certain things for Madame to know and to do. There is no need for any medicines: you are a strong and healthy woman, Madame. My congratulations to you.'

'You go, Thérèse. I want to have a word with Dr Vaudet myself, about my legs, you remember. No need for you to stay with me. Philippe may be on his way back.'

'Hm. There is little wrong with your legs that I can see, Mademoiselle. You might, I suppose, consider wearing elasticated stockings, if any can be found, that is.'

'Draw the curtain, Dr Vaudet. There is something else I have to ask you that I do not want my sister to worry about it.'

In the sunlit square some children were playing a game, treading slowly around the base of the fountain, first one way then the other and chanting some sort of song until they all suddenly stopped and started pointing: evidently someone was out. The fountain was dry and dusty, and in need of repair. On the side of the square opposite the café was a tall building with crossed tricolours above one of the arches in its frontal arcade: the Mairie. Lawless watched Jérôme Janquet come out of the very same archway and head towards the café.

'Sorry I'm late. I'll have the same as my friend,' he said to the barman.

'The red's not bad. Is that why you come here?'

'It's nearest the Mairie. I have to come from time to time. Official business, you understand.' He drained his glass. 'And the red is good, as you say.' He turned and signalled to the barman.

'I was watching those kids outside, playing their game round the fountain. They go one way, then turn about and go the other then one of them stops in the wrong place and he's out.'

'I'm not sure what point your trying to make.'

'Only that we might find we're doing something like that ourselves one day.'

'Hm. I hope not. May I take a look?'

Lawless pushed the newspaper across the table. Jérôme Janquet lifted and turned it as if wanting to get more light on it from the window but at the same time obscuring the barman's view of them.

'I have the information,' he muttered and then raising his voice went on. 'Did you see this about the fire in Mende?'

'Yes, the warehouse: nobody hurt, it says. Have another?'

'Thank you, no. It's time I was going. People to see.'

'Me too; I'll come part of the way with you.'

Jérôme Janquet put coins on the bar, said goodbye to the barman and followed Lawless out into the square. They made a show of shaking hands and went off in opposite directions and met again on the bridge from where Lawless had watched the trout in the pool below.

'Keep walking. You shouldn't have dawdled when you were here before. Somebody could have thought you were a stranger to the place.'

'Right, I'll remember that. How did you know?'

'Man in the wheelchair.'

'How was I in the café?'

'Better. You didn't notice but we walked past the window a couple of times watching you.'

'I must have missed you but I did spot the big man with the moustache who was squinting sideways as he went by. Who is he?'

'Hm. That's good. Don't ask.'

'All right. Are you going to tell me what you found out?'

'The next petrol delivery is on the sixteenth of this month, a Monday. The lorry leaves the depot in Mende at seven in the morning and normally reaches Florac some time after eight. There are several places on the way where we could wait for it. I will talk to Henri about that. He knows the road better than I do.'

'Any guards?'

'No; only the driver and his mate. They are not expecting any trouble. They will be waiting for you at the doctor's by now. I'll see you in half an hour from now at the same place I left you.'

Before Lawless could say anything else his hand was grasped briefly and Jérôme Janquet walked off across the bridge.

Lawless could think of nothing else. He kept turning round to look at Thérèse and smile or laugh and reach for her hand until Jérôme Janquet stopped the car and told him to change seats with Séverine in the back so that he could concentrate on his driving. Thérèse lay with her head on his chest and his arm about her and slept for the rest of the journey to St Chely.

'Can't you take us as far as the house? My wife isn't in any condition to walk all that way.'

'I can't risk it with the road in the state it's in. It needs a lot of work after the winter. I will get some men onto it as soon as I can. Then we'll see.'

'Philippe, don't fuss. There's nothing wrong with me. Anyway, it's a lovely day and I'm so happy I want to walk, and dance as well and you're not going to stop me, is he, Sevvie?'

'Nor me. We all need some fresh air after sitting so long in that smelly old car.'

'Well, let's have a drink to celebrate before we set off. Oh, wait, no you can't, can you? Not now, I mean.'

'Of course she can. She's not an invalid and nor am I. Jérôme, what have you got for celebrating babies?'

'Champagne, ladies: what else could it be?'

Mireille's great dark eyes widened even further when she was told the news.

'Will I still be here when the baby is born?'

'Of course, you will. I want you to be here to help me with it.'

'Like I do with the lambs?'

Thérèse laughed and took her by the hands.

'Yes, but don't allow it to eat grass.'

Mireille's eyes showed that she knew this was meant to be funny but she still seemed unable to laugh, or even smile.

'I know a cradle song. I can play it for the baby. I'll go now and play it. Listen and then tell me if you like it.'

'You wait,' said Lawless. 'She'll play the Fauré berceuse, the one from the Dolly Suite. I'm sure she will. She's always playing Fauré.'

'Not this time,' said Thérèse. 'I've never heard this one. It's very simple and beautiful but the minor key makes it sound a little bit wistful, don't you think? What can it be?'

'I think it's one of her people's lullabies,' said Séverine. 'That's why it sounds sad.'

'Listen,' said Lawless. 'She's singing. I think it's in German. "Sleep my . . something, er, *fiegele.*" I think that means little bird.'

It was a long time after the music ended before Mireille came back into the kitchen. She was clearly anxious to know what they thought.

'It's lovely, Mireille. We've never heard it before.'

'Do you really like it? Can I play it for the baby?'

'Of course you can. Where did you learn it?'

'From my mother. She told me her mother sang it to her when she was a baby. It's very old. When will I see my mother again?'

'One day, Mireille, one day, I hope.'

'Mireille, will you teach me to play it,' said Lawless 'and the words as well?'

***

'What are you doing at the window?'

He breathed in deeply, twice, three times before replying.

'Taking in the morning air. It's going to be a lovely day, warmer than yesterday. I feel like rushing out and rolling in the grass. Want to come?'

'No,' she laughed. 'The dew will make you wet through.'

'We could get wet through together and if we took our clothes off it wouldn't matter.'

'What would Séverine say if she saw us?'

'We could ask her to join us. She'd probably like it. Anyway, she isn't here. Had you forgotten?'

'No, I hadn't forgotten. I wish she didn't go away so much.'

Lawless came over to the bed and bent down to kiss her.

'You miss her, don't you?' She nodded.

'Even though she orders you about?'

'She orders you about as well.'

'I'm a soldier. I obey orders.'

'Oh no, you don't. That's what makes her cross with you.'

'She's not always cross. I remember a whole day when she wasn't cross with me once. It was Thursday of last week.'

'You're teasing me again, you horrible man. Go away and make the coffee. See what Mireille is doing. She could take a flask out to Jeannot. She'd like that. He'll be in the cloup, not far away. That's three nights in a row he's looked after the sheep.'

'Time for me to take a turn again. Sleep out under the stars. Wake up covered in dew. Hm, on second thoughts I'll go for the shelter: might be a bit nippy outside.'

'A minute ago you were wanting to roll about in the dew, with me and Séverine. Coffee: go and make the coffee!'

'Now you're ordering me about. All right, all right, no need to throw things. I'm going.'

When he had gone she reached under the bed and found the basin she kept handy for the early mornings. The sickness was easing a little. Madame Bec had given her a piece of ginger root to suck if she felt really unwell, but she didn't like the taste.

She heard Lawless coming back up the stairs. He always took them two at a time. She slipped the basin back under the bed just in time for him not to see.

'Just had a thought! Why don't we go down to the village on the bikes? You said we needed flour and fresh eggs, if there are any, and some bones and scrag end for Caramelle. And I need some fags. What do you think? Oh, not feeling well?'

'No, no, I'm all right. I'd love that but Dr Vaudet told me I mustn't ride a bicycle now.'

'There I go again, forgetting. You did tell me. Will I ever learn? I'm so sorry, sweetheart.'

'It's nothing. You go. Take Jeannot with you and do the shopping. Ask Madame Janquet if she has any fresh pelardon. I'm dying for some.'

'I can't go and leave you here.'

'Philippe, go this minute and have your breakfast at the café. I'll be fine once I'm up. Mireille will help me with the sheep until you get back. Off you go before *I* get cross with you.'

'You sure?'

'Now!'

'Sergeant, good morning. This is a surprise.'

'Good morning Mr Janquet. I've come for cigarettes and breakfast, if that's all right. Then I have shopping to do.'

'You could not have come at a better time. It saves my having to send word to you at La Commanderie.'

'What about, Mr Janquet?'

'I think we now know each other well enough for us to use first names, Sergeant, er, Philippe. First, you can have rolls and coffee and we'll talk afterwards. Henri will be here shortly.'

'Vabrette? I think I can see what's coming, Jérôme.'

'Eat first.'

With most of a crusty warm baguette covered in fresh butter and fig jam washed down by two large cups of milky honey-sweetened coffee inside him and a Gauloise smouldering between his fingers, Lawless sat back feeling at peace with the world. The boneshaker bike ride down to the village had exhilarated him. He'd had to stop a couple of times to let Jeannot catch up and pedalled the last few hundred metres along the road into the village with the boy balanced on the saddle behind him. Going back wouldn't be so easy—three kilometres uphill most of the way and the groceries to carry. He'd left his own bike in Oxford after the letter came instructing him to report. Was it still in the College cellar? The Head Porter had told him not to worry.

'Be there for you when you get back, Sir. These your room keys, Sir? Thank you. You off now, Sir? Good luck.'

'I think he's dozed off.'

'Christ you gave me a start!'

'You should keep a better lookout, Sergeant,' Vabrette said, grasping his hand in the vice of his own.

'Come into the back room,' said Jérôme Janquet. 'We can spread the map out on the table there.'

'Go on, Henri. Show us what you think.'

Vabrette unfolded the Michelin map and stuck his finger on a place where three red roads converged.

'Right, now here's Mende and here's where the road comes in from Chanac. Now it's the 106 to Florac, there. It's about 35 kilometres from Mende to Florac. Just over halfway from Mende you have the Col de Montmirat, 1046 metres. There it is. See those little roads coming off on either side? I'll come back to them. Now, about a kilometre before you get to the Col there's a bend in the road that you can't see it until you're almost on it, especially if it's misty which it can be early in the morning. That's where we wait. When the lorry comes up to the bend we'll be standing in the middle of the road. We'll be quite safe because he'll be crawling up that steep bit.'

There was a silence while the other two looked at the map and tried to take in what Vabrette had said.

'Then what?'

'They'll find two blokes in the middle of the road with their faces covered and pointing guns at them. That should make them know we're serious.'

'Will they have guns?' said Lawless.

'Not the driver. If there's a gendarme with him, he'll have a pistol but nobody's ever held up this lorry before so they won't be expecting trouble and I can't see a gendarme getting out of bed at that hour of the morning, anyway.' Vabrette gave a loud laugh. 'More likely there'll just be a driver's mate to help unload the bidons. Anyway, what would you do with two guns pointing at you?'

'Keep flying, Corporal, like I always had to. Sorry, sorry, only joking. Why only three blokes?'

'Because Jérôme here will be waiting in the car round the bend out of sight.'

'It is obvious they must not see the car, or me.'

'Shall I go on? Right. We get them out of the lorry, blindfold them and sit them down at the side of the road. One of us, you maybe, keeps an eye on them while I drive the lorry up to where Jérôme and Jean-Pierre are waiting and we offload as many bidons as we can carry. Jean-Pierre should help with that because he's stronger than you. Do you follow me so far?'

'Yes. How long will that take?'

'A few minutes; a bidon holds 20 litres. That's nothing for Jean-Pierre. How many do you think, Jérôme?'

'No more than six strapped on the rear rack. That's all the car can take with four of us in it as well and the hills we have to climb. In fact some of you might have to walk up the steeper stretches.'

Vabrette grinned at Lawless. 'That means you, Sergeant, and Jean-Pierre. You're the biggest. I'm only a lightweight.'

'All right; the bidons are loaded, I'm waiting down the road guarding the driver and his mate. What do we do next?'

'Well, we could leave you there and head off home but you might come in useful later on, so, I come back and prod 'em both in the back of the neck with my gun and tell 'em if they dare so much as fart for the next ten minutes I'll blow their fucking heads off. You say nothing because you still sound too English: remember that. Then we both go back to the car.'

'He doesn't mean it, of course. There must be no violence. The gendarmerie must believe it was only someone stealing petrol. It's become so hard to get anybody might have done it. That's the rule: no violence.'

'*Not yet, anyway,*' Lawless heard Vabrette say under his breath while tapping the map with his finger.

'This is how we get away. I drive the lorry up to the Col with the car following behind. Now, those two little roads: look here on the map. I leave the lorry a couple of hundred metres along this one going to Pont de Montvert while you go the opposite way, towards Montmirat for a bit and wait till I come. We link up with that road down to the bottom of the gorge—it's bloody steep and full of hairpins so I hope your brakes are all right, Jérôme—and . . .'

'And along the river through this place, what is it, Sainte Enimie, cross the river, and up the side of the gorge and back to Saint Chély that way.'

'No, no, Philippe. I can see you have an eye for a map but we must stick to the small roads: too many prying eyes in Sainte Enimie.'

'He's right, Sergeant. We cross the bridge just before Blajoux and take that little road up through Montbrun onto the Causse: plenty of hairpins on that one as well, see?'

'And that's where some of you might have to walk but it's the best way: there will be nobody about on those roads.'

'That's the plan?' said Lawless.

'That's the plan. Don't you like it?'

'Have you ever heard of General von Moltke? He said no battle plan survives contact with the enemy.' Sherwood had said that every time that they took off for a raid.

'Maybe, but at least it's a way of getting at him. After that, well, you're the one who's had most recent contact with the enemy.'

'I think I'm a case in point.'

'That's enough talk,' said Jérôme Janquet. The plan is good enough for me. Are you wth us?'

'I gave you my word.'

'Good. Be here no later than six o'clock on the sixteenth.'

'And bring that Verney-Carron with you,' said Vabrette.

'No. It's too conspicuous. He can take one of mine.'

'Quite right, Jérôme; you think of everything. Now I'm thirsty after all that talk and I don't mean for coffee.'

Despite what Jérôme Janquet had said there was a lot more talk over the beer and pastis before all the details were settled and Lawless remembered he had flour and eggs to buy and something else he could not for the moment remember.

'Philippe, before you go. Come into the other room. I have a camera there.'

'Pelardon, Sergeant; Mams'elle Chevalier always likes the new season's pelardon. I have some here.'

Pelardon, of course, the goat's cheese: that was it. He asked for six of the little white discs. Madame Janquet suggested eight, seeing as how there were now four of them at La Commanderie. There would be plenty more when he wanted them, now that the goats were in milk and that would last into the autumn when the pelardon tasted different because the goats ate chestnuts and acorns then. The flour wasn't as good as it used to be: too much bran in it. The War, that was the trouble. But the eggs were fresh, of course, fresh this morning. Bones and scrag end? No: try Madame Bec. Only butchers sold meat. How was Mams'elle, of course, *Madame*. Good. Such wonderful news. The Sergeant must feel very proud. Until the next time, then.

The sergeant was feeling rather more anxious than proud as he walked in the direction of Bec's shop. Things were happening too fast. Marriage, a pregnant wife and now a highway robbery to contemplate, and all in a foreign country. You had to hand it to old von Moltke. He was bloody well right. Not a single one of these things could conceivably have been foreseen when the Whitley took off for Milan that night in December. A baby and him a *father*! He'd never thought of that, well, yes he had, vaguely: everybody got married and had kids but that was later, after . . . after what? After you were settled in a job. But his job was death. Séverine had said that. She was right. He must have helped kill lots of people and he might kill more. What if one of the men in the lorry put up a fight while he was guarding them? Janquet had said no violence but old von Moltke would have shaken his head if he'd been listening. Séverine was wrong. His job was life: that life inside Thérèse, and, don't forget, Thérèse herself as well. He wanted to spend his life with Thérèse. Can your job be both death and life? Of course it can, because it would have to be. Wasn't there a philosophical flaw in that somewhere?

He passed two women chatting in a doorway. Both smiled and wished him good-morning. One said congratulations. Did everyone in the village know? He smiled at them and took off his cap. The younger one smiled back and smoothed down her hair. Hm.

'Thank you, Madame Bec. That should keep Caramelle happy for a few days. Madame Bec, my wife says she would like to see you again when you have the time. Nothing serious; I think she'd just like to have a talk. I can bring her. She might like the walk.'

'I won't hear of such a thing, Sergeant. Walk indeed! I will go up to see her and Jeannot will take me.'

He left the shop feeling quite different from when he went in. No more uncertainty or philosophical entanglements: things would happen as they would happen. People like Madame Bec who had no uncertainties about anything nearly always had that effect on him. Jack Verrill had been one of those, and Sherwood.

There was no one in the house when he got back but he knew where they would be. A few minutes later he was standing on the rise above the cloup and looking down on them sitting at the edge of the green oval, heads together and completely absorbed in what they were doing; making flower chains, he guessed, and leaving Caramelle to watch the sheep. He gave a shout and they looked up. He waved and ran down the slope to be with them.

PETROL THIEVES

A few days later Séverine walked into the kitchen while the others were at breakfast.

'Is there any coffee left? I've been travelling for two days and I'm just about ready to drop. Jeannot brought me. He's still outside; he says he can stay until tomorrow if we want him.'

Mireille leaped up to embrace her then quickly filled a mug with coffee and ran outside with it.

'Why don't you let us know when you're coming back?' Thérèse said, lifting up her face for the three kisses.

'Because I never know when I'm comimg back until the last minute.'

'You look a bit sunburnt,' said Lawless 'and, hm hm your hair smells of the sea, salty, or is it fishy?'

Séverine pushed him away.'Not as bad as you! You smell like a, like a Frenchman.'

'At last! Thank you, thank you, kind lady,' he shouted, whirling her round in a dance until her feet were off the ground.

Thérèse got up. 'He's just as impossible as ever. Put my sister down, husband, and talk to her while I go and make some fresh coffee.'

Once she was out of the room Séverine sat down opposite Lawless and glared at him.

'That man!'

'What man?'

'Jérôme Janquet!'

'What about him?'

'Do you know what he has done?'

'Look, don't keep asking me questions I don't know how to answer. Just tell me. What has he done?'

'He has told me that I will not be with you when you go to hold up the petrol lorry. I can't believe it! Does he not trust me?'

'Of course he trusts you. If he didn't trust you he wouldn't ask you to go on all these secret visits. I don't know where you go or what you do but it must be important enough for him to need someone who is absolutely trustworthy and that is you.'

'I want to *do* something! I will tell him I must be there. He must change his mind.'

'He's not likely to do that. He is our commanding officer. We all agreed that. Good commanding officers do not change their minds. If they did, the enemy would soon put paid to them. When the commanding officer gives an order, everybody obeys and that includes you. Your father and brothers would have done the same. Look, there will be other times. You'll get your chance.'

Mention of her father and brothers had given her pause, he could tell. She was still seething at the slight, but less sure of herself.

'You must be tired. How long is it since you had some proper sleep?'

'Two days, three, I don't know. There's so much to do and it's not a good idea to stay too long in one place.'

'Was I right? Did you stay by the sea?'

'One lovely day, all day on the beach near Montpellier. That's where I got this tan. Would you believe it: sunburnt in March? I had sand in my shoes for days.'

'I seem to remember you saying you knew some people in Montpellier.'

'Yes, Victor and Jeanette Dumanoir. I stayed two nights with them. Being an advocate he meets a lot of people, all kinds. It's very useful.'

'I'm not going to ask you what you mean by that.'

'I wouldn't tell you anyway. But you never know, you could meet him one day. Never mind all that, tell me what's been going on here. Thérèse looks well.'

'She is. It's such a change. Now she's not so sick anymore, she's up before me, out to see the sheep, make breakfast, start the washing. I have to stop her doing too much. It's worrying.'

'You are an idiot. If she's feeling well, let her do what she wants. She's not an invalid.'

'I know, I know. I fuss too much she says but I can't get used to it, the baby, I mean. What if something went wrong? I don't know anything about babies.'

'Ask Madame Bec. She'll be here tomorrow with Jean-Pierre. He's coming to look at the lambs and sort out the first lot he's going to take away and sell for us. I'm going to bed. Tell Tressie I don't want any coffee. Wake me in time for dinner.'

'She's glad you're back, you know,' he called to her and she went upstairs.

'I know. Are you?'

***

Lawless shivered inside his coat. It was cold on the roadside in the mist 1000 metres up at seven in the morning. Vabrette was sitting on a boulder with his head down and the rifle leaning against his shoulder. Lawless wondered if he could be asleep. He envied the other two who were waiting in the comfort of the car round the corner. Tressie would have read his note by now. All it said was *Ask Sevvie, kisses, Me.* He felt a bit ashamed of letting Séverine do something he had promised he would do.

'What time is it?'

Vabrette hadn't raised his head. Lawless looked at his watch.

'Nearly eight.'

'They're late.' Vabrette's head jerked up. 'Listen, what's that?'

'Something coming up the road; car engine?'

'Shh! Listen. Two-stroke. Shit, it's a motorbike. Into the ditch and get down. He mustn't see us.'

'What about the others? They won't hear it coming in the car.'

'Can't help that. Just hope he doesn't see them in the mist.'

The motorcyclist was too busy peering ahead of him and wiping the moisture from his goggles to see the two figures who were crouching in the drainage ditch at the side of the road. They listened to the crackle of the engine fading slowly away into the distance.

'He's gone. May as well stay here. At least it's dry.'

'Like a fag, Henri?'

'Why not? It'll help pass the time.'

The cigarette lighter flame made a tiny warm glow in the shield of Lawless's hands.

'Are you married, Henri?'

'Why d'you ask that?'

'Oh, no reason, well, do you ever tell your wife about these things we're doing?'

'Don't have to. She seems to know without being told. Women do, you know.'

Both were silent for a while as they drew on their cigarettes. Lawless watched the smoke slowly blending with the mist and said,

'Do you have any children?'

'A daughter. She married a miner. They live in Alès.'

'No son to carry on after you, then?'

'No. Funny thing you should say that. She—she's called Anne—as soon as she could walk she used to like coming into the forge to watch me working. Loved to see the sparks fly. I always had this feeling that she wanted to be a smith, like me. How daft is that? It's a job for a man. Still, I think she could have done it. Her mother would never have allowed it: wanted her to marry a teacher or a doctor. Well, she ended up with a miner. He's not bad. Treats her all right. Bloody well better, I told him.'

'Care for another?'

'Here, have one of mine. What's yours going to be?'

'Mine? Oh, you know, do you?'

'Can't keep that sort of thing secret, Sergeant. Quick off the mark you were! It took us years to get it right. Anyway, well done! I'll stand you a round when we get back to St Chely. Hello, what's happening now? Looks like Jérôme's coming.'

'I don't think they'll be coming now. Something must have happened. The mist is beginning to clear anyway and there'll be more traffic along here soon. We'd better call it off this time and get back home.'

'They can't have got wind of us, can they?'

'No, otherwise they'd have planned to spring a surprise on us. I'll find out. Give me time.'

'Live to fight another day,' Vabrette said. 'Now for that drink, Sergeant: what do you say?'

'Cognac, Corporal.'

***

'That's the car horn. He's early. Have you got everything, Tressie?'

In the courtyard they found Jérôme Janquet holding the rear door of the black car open for the two women to get in. Serge Valentin emerged from the front passenger seat.

'You going too, Mr Valentin?'

'Er, not now, Sergeant. I was hoping to see Mams'elle Chevalier but I see I'm out of luck.'

'Drop you back in the village if you like, Serge.'

'Stay a bit, Mr Valentin. I'd like the company. I'm in charge of the flock today but I'll walk back part of the way with you when you want to leave.'

While Valentin hesitated, there were embraces, the car doors slammed and the engine coughed into life.

'He's a terrible driver,' Lawless said as they watched Jérôme Janquet crashing the gears attempting to reverse. 'I had to keep my eyes shut all the way down to the gorge at Charbonnières.'

Eventually the black Renault ground its way through the archway and out of sight.

'I wonder if it'll get to Florac at all, never mind on time.'

'Has he told you what went wrong two weeks ago?'

'No, this is the first I've seen of him since then. Séverine went to the café the other day but she's being tight-lipped. She can be like that'

'I know. I was there.'

'So you know what happened?'

'It's so stupid. The petrol lorry had a puncture half way between Mende and the Col and their spare wheel was flat. They stopped a motorcyclist and got him to take a message to the Gendarmerie in Florac.'

'Shit! We saw him go by. We were hiding in a ditch.'

'They got the lorry back on the road again and it reached Florac about noon.'

'What a farce! All that time spent freezing up on the hill and just because some idiots didn't check the tyres.'

'It hasn't put him off, you know, Jérôme. He's got it all planned again for tomorrow.'

'You're joking! Nobody's told me anything about that.'

'You're not going; nor am I. He's taking Mams'elle, er, Séverine.'

'Are you serious? Lawless saw Valentin wasn't smiling. 'You are, aren't you?'

Valentin nodded. 'While the ladies are at the doctor's Jérôme will be making some last minute checks with his contacts.'

'Who? Big man with sticking-out ears or a man in a wheelchair?'

'I don't know about them but I know he has someone in the Gendarmerie.'

'Well, well: Séverine. She told me she was going to have a go at him: seems she's persuaded him somehow.'

'He may have let her think that but I think he's testing her. It worries me.'

'Why so? She's pretty tough, you know and I've given her quite a lot of time on the Browning. She knows how to handle it now and you should see her with a shotgun . . .'

'I know all that,' Valentin broke in, 'but haven't you noticed how tired and pale she is sometimes? I don't know what's the matter. She won't tell me.'

Lawless looked at the anxious face. 'You're sweet on her, Serge, aren't you?'

Valentin was flustered. He stared down at the ground, then up again at Lawless with an embarrassed smile but saying nothing.

'No need to be shy, Serge. It's good. She needs someone, especially now that Thérèse and me, well, you know . . . have you told her, does she know?'

'I think she knows. We've worked together. Those times she was away from La Commanderie: I was with her on some of them. We had to pretend that we were married. Yes I'm sure she knows. But I haven't said anything.'

'Why ever not?'

'It was something she said after one of our . . . one of our times together. She said wartime wasn't the time to expect things had to last.'

'Well, she didn't seem to think that applied to Thérèse and me. Tell her, Serge. Make her change her mind. Tell her although you might not expect things to last, you can bloody well hope they will.'

'But don't you see, Philippe, what she might be telling me is that we being together shouldn't get in the way of the other thing, fighting the War?'

'Don't . . . *wait a minute, wait a minute: was that what she thought about me and Thérèse, that we might not last, especially me, but the baby, when there was one, the baby would?* Don't let that stop you telling her. She must feel something for you, from what you've just told me.'

'I don't know; really I don't. I shouldn't have said anything.'

'I had no idea. How long have you known her? When did this start?'

'Not all that long. This is only my second year at the school. When did it start? February; it was a few days after your wedding. Jérôme asked us to go to Nîmes to help with the Jewish children. We came back with Miriam.'

'We call her Mireille. Séverine said nothing about you being involved in that.'

'It's instructions: the fewer people who know, the better. We've done other things as well. The last was in Montpellier. I can't tell you what it was.'

'I know Séverine managed to get sunburnt.'

Valentin gave him a startled look, then laughed.

'You noticed that, did you? We found a very secluded place on the beach.'

'Come into the house. Mireille will make us some coffee. I'll call her down. Whenever she sees or hears someone coming she hotfoots it up into the tower. I'm sure she'd like to see you.'

Mireille allowed herself to be embraced by the schoolteacher; said she was very well, thank you and, glancing at Lawless, replied yes she was happy here, and went off to make coffee.

Watching her go, Valentin said to Lawless that she ought to be a school.

'She's years ahead of her age at mathematics. And she speaks excellent German: did you know that?'

'No, I didn't. She never says much about herself to me although she talks a lot to Thérèse, and Jeannot, of course. She doesn't seem to know much English.'

'It's not enough. Like I said, she ought to be at school, an able girl like that.'

'Why don't you teach her? You could come up here, once a week, say, and give her some tuition. Nobody need know why you're coming and if you think about it, it would let you see more of Séverine.'

Valentin looked doubtful and hopeful in quick succession.

'Do you think I could; would she, I mean Séverine, would she agree?'

'I'll wait for the right moment and suggest it. Ah, here's the coffee.'

'He stayed about two hours after you left. Told me quite a bit about himself. He took his degree at Grenoble, thought about going into the army—his father was an officer, dead now, so is his mother—but didn't pass the medical. He stayed around Grenoble for a couple of years working for one of the professors, looking up references, translating—he knows German and English—card-indexing, dealing with correspondence, all that sort of thing. It kept body and soul together, not much more. One day he was going through some old documents and came across a reference to a pair of obscure Romance poets. He followed it up and became interested enough to start thinking of doing his own dissertation. His professor thought it to be a good idea and encouraged him. He worked at it for over a year. He said he'd show what he'd done sometime. Then it all had to stop.'

'Why, if the professor was helping him?'

'The professor had a heart attack and died in the middle of a lecture. That was the end of Serge's job and his access to the University libraries. Just like that.' Lawless snapped his fingers. 'So he decided to try schoolteaching. He did the training, passed and applied for a post. They sent him to a school near Arles. He hated it: too hot and too humid and the parents were as stupid as their children. He called them *ploucs*, I didn't know that word.'

'It means something like stupid peasant but worse.'

'More like thickhead,' Séverine said.

'Useful word. Where was I? Yes, well he had to stick it for a few years before he had any chance of a move and at last he was offered the job in St Chely. He's pretty sure that nobody else wanted it. But he's happy here. Not so many ploucs, I suppose.'

'You seem to have got on well.'

'We did, sweetheart. I like him. We ended up by calling each other by our first names. Er, he saw Mireille. She made coffee for us. Do you mind, Sevvie?'

'Of course not: they've met before.'

'When was that?'

'I may as well tell you. He helped me get her away. He was good with her parents. He was the one who took care of her brother as well. He went with him all the way on the train to that place in the Velay to make sure he would be all right.'

'He said Mireille ought to be at school. She's very clever, apparently. He knows she can't go, of course but I have an idea about that. Why don't we ask him to come up here once a week and give her some lessons?'

'Philippe that would be really good! What do you say, Sevvie? Shall we ask him?'

'I'm not sure. I'll have to think about it.'

'Well, I'd like him to come, Sevvie. We owe it to her. Don't forget we made her a Chevalier.'

'I'll let you know what I think in the morning. I'm off to bed. I must be up very early tomorrow. I have to see Jean-Pierre about those lambs among other things.'

'How long will you be this time?'

'Back before dinner, I hope. Goodnight.'

'I'll come with you down to the village,' Lawless said. 'Serge is going to let me have a look at his work and he says he has some books I can borrow. I can catch him before school starts.'

'If you like.'

'Sweetheart, I can't tell you how relieved I am.'

'I keep telling you I'm not ill. Perhaps you'll believe me now. I'm more concerned about Sevvie.'

'Why? Perhaps she does look a bit tired but it might be because she's doing so much; all that coming and going. Has she said anything to you?'

'She shuts me up if I ask. She spent quite a lot of time with Dr Vaudet this morning but she wouldn't tell me why, except something about her legs.'

'I can't see anything wrong with her legs, oops! Sorry, shouldn't be thinking about other women's legs.'

'Men are all the same but just in case you start thinking about my legs, I'd better tell you what Dr Vaudet said when I asked him about you and me.'

Lawless sat up in bed and looked down at her in the candlelight.

'How long ago was the last time?'

'A month.'

'Can't be, can it? Seems more like a year to me.'

'I was beginning to think you were tired of me.'

'You were so sick.'

'I was only sick in the morning. There was all the rest of the day, and the night as well. I gave you plenty of hints.'

'Oh God, I don't know what to say. I was, how can I put it, I was worried what this might do to you and the baby.'

'Well now you know you don't have to worry. In fact Dr Vaudet said that women can become more amorous as time goes on; well, he didn't say "amorous" he said demanding. What do you think of that?'

'I think if you put your hand here and I put my mouth there and there, in a minute or two we could find out if he's right.'

'Philippe, are you awake?'

'Mm.'

'About Serge Valentin: was it your idea he should come here once a week, or his?'

'Mine.'

'To give Mireille some lessons?'

'Mm.'

'Nothing else?'

'What else could there be?'

'I don't trust you. But it is a good idea.'

***

'We could take the bikes. You'd get there quicker.'

'I'd rather walk. I like the early mornings at this time of year, all fresh and clean and silent.'

'It's hardly morning yet; more like the middle of the night.'

'You didn't have to come.'

They walked for a while without speaking, stopping occasionally to listen to rustling sounds of small animals hunting or fleeing in the grass, and the distant wailing calls of some night bird.

'That's a stone curlew,' Séverine whispered. 'I love the sound that it makes.'

'It sounds as if it's crying for something it's lost.'

'We all do that at some time in our lives.'

He could think of no answer to that. It was too close to the truth. They reached the bottom of the long slope down from the house before he spoke again.

'Do you remember the snowball? It started as a joke and then we saw you standing there while it headed straight for you, getting bigger and bigger and you didn't move. Why?'

'I can't explain. You wouldn't understand.'

'Try me.'

'Not now. It isn't the right time. I will tell you one day.'

'Sometimes you're so difficult to get throught to. You're,' he stopped, searching for the word, 'you're impenetrable, you know.'

'Impenetrable? Am I? Do you really think so, Philippe? You ought to know better than that.'

It was still too dark for him to see her face but he was sure she was mocking him.

'Yes, you can be; like when I suggested Serge could come to give Miriam some lessons. It's obvious to me and Thérèse but I can't make out what you think at all.'

'I told you I would think about it. I have. I agree. It is a good idea. Now, what is impenetrable about that?'

Before he could think of a reply, she swung round and stood in front of him blocking his way.

'Philippe, you are the one trying to be impenetrable, pretending it was your idea when you were both in on it. I don't mind Serge coming to La Commanderie when he can. In fact, I'd quite like him to. What I do mind is your little manipulations, although you're so bad at it, that it's amusing.'

''Strewth! That's me well and truly told off. What can I say?'

'Say what you think and not what's easier to say.'

'All right. How about this? I know he has feelings for you and I think you have been trying hard not to let us see that you feel the same about him. Am I right?'

'I expect he's told you about us, so, yes, I won't deny it.'

'I knew it. Maybe you thought you'd never find anyone else after, you know . . . didn't even want to; well Serge is different, I'm sure.'

She flung her arms round him so fiercely that he staggered back and almost fell.

'You know so little about people! But I love you.'

'Love me? Me?'

'Yes, for being so young. Now, give me a kiss and let's be going. When we get to St Chely you can leave the gun with me.'

In the middle of his confusion one thought gave him slightly guilty satisfaction: she clearly didn't know that he knew where she was going. Then he began to feel worried about what might happen to her.

***

Séverine was determined to celebrate. Arriving back at La Commanderie late in the afternoon, she looked tired and rather bedraggled but there was an air of quiet satisfaction about her. Carrying her bag on his shoulder was Serge Valentin.

'He's staying for dinner,' she said casually to Thérèse. 'What can we offer him?'

'As it happens, civet; thanks to Philippe here.'

'With mashed potatoes?'

'Of course, and apricot tart to follow.'

'Excellent, don't you agree, Serge?'

'It sounds delicious, especially for one who normally cooks for himself and in effect not too well.'

'Mireille made the tart with the last of the apricots.'

'There should be plenty more in this summerr: the trees are full of blossom.'

'I must change my clothes. I won't be long then we can have *vin doux* before dinner.'

'*Vin doux*? What are we celebrating? I'm intrigued.'

'Tell her, Serge. I think Philippe might have some idea already.'

'She's being very mysterious.' Thérèse's eyes were shining as she looked archly at Valentin. 'Come on, then, Serge. What's this all about?'

'It's nothing to do with me really.'

'Oh dear, that sounds disappointing.'

He looked puzzled. 'No, no, not at all. Everything went off very well.'

Thérèse looked appealingly at Lawless.

'It's time you knew, sweetheart. You remember that morning a couple of weeks ago when I went out early and left you a note telling you to ask Sevvie what it was about?'

'Yes; she didn't say much. Something about an operation.'

'Well it didn't work so Jérôme Janquet set it up again and Séverine went this time instead of me.'

'But what did she *do*?'

'I think Serge is going to tell us she helped steal 120 litres of petrol from the gendarmes. Is that right, Serge?'

Thérèse was speechless, looking horror-stricken from one to the other.

'That's right. Apparently it went off without a hitch. The lorry was on time. Séverine and Henri stopped it on the road. They had masks on and she was wearing men's clothes—they're in that bag—and she tied the driver and his mate up while Henri held his gun on them. She had one of Jerome's. They drove the lorry round the corner, loaded the petrol cans onto Jérôme's car and made off. Oh yes, and Henri left the lorry somewhere on the Pont de Montvert road and shot out two of the tyres just to make sure they would have plenty of time to get away.'

'You two! How can you look so smug? It's awful what she was made to do! She could have been killed. The gendarmes will be here tomorrow.'

'Sweetheart, come here; don't be like that. She's fine. You saw her. She wants to celebrate. Nobody made her do it. She wanted to and she feels proud because she's done something at last to fight back. She was furious when Jérôme left her out the last time. I can hear her coming down. Ask her yourself.'

'Séverine! You told me last night you were going to the village to see Jean-Pierre Bec about the lambs but you weren't telling the truth, were you?'

'I did see Jean-Pierre and we talked about the lambs and I did say 'among other things'.'

'They have just told me your 'other things' were stealing petrol from the gendarmes. And you had a gun! How can you do such a thing? You could have been killed. The gendarmes will come here and arrest you and then what will happen to the rest of us? What about Mireille?'

'Tressie, please don't start crying. The gendarmes will not come here and even if they do, they have no idea who did this. We were very careful not to allow our faces to be seen. They will think that it was just some thieves stealing a bit of petrol to sell on the black market. You are safe and so is Mireille. No, please listen. I have to do this. I have to do something to fight back against what I know is a growing evil. I wasn't going to tell you this but perhaps it will make you understand. Last Friday a thousand Jews, perhaps more, were taken from a prison camp near Paris and put on trains to take them to Germany, or Poland, we are not yet sure. Mireille's parents could have been among them. It's the beginning of something terrible, Tressie, and it's going to happen here one day unless we do something to stop it. You know they're already making preparations. That's why Mireille is here with us. Now do you see?'

'I don't know. I know something's been happening with all these secret meetings and you going away and Philippe hiding that awful gun and bullets and showing you how to fire it but nobody ever tells me properly, even when they say they will. When I don't know, how can I help being worried and frightened?'

'I could have said that it's better if you don't know because then you can't tell but I now think that's wrong. I think you should know as much as we know. What about you two? Yes? See, they're nodding. They agree. From now on we won't keep anything from you, Tressie. And do you know the reason? Because we need your help. No, I don't mean stealing petrol for Jérôme's car—yes, that's why we took it—or using a gun, though I know you're a good shot, I mean keeping your eyes and ears open, helping with plans, just being here at the right time. Everybody in the peloton has their own particular contribution to make and you have yours if you want to be with us.'

'Do you mean all that?'

'Every word.'

'Don't ever treat me like a child again.'

'Good. Now, how about that *vin doux*? Mireille, come in. Have you been listening to us? Never mind, I suppose you're old enough to know if Jeannot is.'

'So this is your room.'

'Not so loud. Their room is just along the corridor. They'll think you're back in St Chely by now. We don't want to disturb them.'

'Mireille?'

'I suggested she sleep in the tower room tonight.'

'She'll know something is going on, won't she?'

'If she does she won't say anything. You can put your clothes on the chair over there.'

'Lovely warm bed. That's a beautiful nightgown. Aren't you going to put it on?'

'It's silk. Thérèse made it for me. I'll leave it off for the moment.'

'Come to bed. I can't wait.'

'Yes, I can see. Just lie back. This is what I like to do first.'

'Is this part of the celebration?'

'The best part: you'll see.'

As instructed, Valentin slipped out of the room before first light and crept downstairs. The others mustn't know, not yet anyway. He was reluctant to go, having seen that Séverine had somehow forgotten to put on her nightgown, but there was barely enough time to cover the three kilometres to the village before school started. He might end up having to run and he was feeling a little too tired for that.

LIEUTENANT GRANDJEAN

'There is a car coming up the hill.' Mireille stood in the doorway looking frightened.

'A car? Is it Mr Janquet's?'

'No. It is different.'

Thérèse pulled her inside. 'Quick! Up to the tower room. You know what to do: take all your things with you and keep quiet.'

Thérèse watched from the window as the car pulled up in the courtyard and two uniformed gendarmes got out. She went to the door, Caramelle at her heels.

One of the gendarmes stood by the car. The other approached her and saluted.

'Lieutenant Grandjean, Gendarmerie Florac.' He pointed his thumb over his shoulder without turning his head. 'Corporal Dolland. You are Mademoiselle Chevalier?'

'Madame Chevalier.'

'*Madame* Chevalier. I see.'

'My sister is Mademoiselle Chevalier.'

'Ah. Is Mademoiselle Chevalier at home, too?'

'No. She is shopping in St Chely.'

'And Mr Chevalier? There is a Mr Chevalier?'

'Yes.'

'And he is here?'

'No.'

'May I ask where is he, Madame?'

'He is out hunting.'

Lieutenant Grandjean looked down.

'Without his dog?'

'He does not need the dog when he is hunting for hares. When he is out, he often leaves her with me. For protection, you understand.'

'Of course. Very thoughtful of him. You have children, Madame?'

'Not yet.'

'I thought I saw a boy in one of the outbuildings as we drove in.'

'That is Jeannot from the village. He helps with the sheep.'

'Jeannot; his father is?'

'Jean-Pierre Bec, the butcher.'

'But no children of your own, Madame, and no other children staying with you?'

'No.'

'May we go inside for a moment, Madame? Take no notice of the Corporal. He will look after himself.'

'Of course.'

It was obvious that the corporal had been left outside to poke around, but Thérèse felt perfectly calm. There was nothing to see. Jeannot would say nothing. Séverine and Philippe were both in the village and unlikely to be back before lunch. She asked the lieutenant if he would take coffee but he thanked her and declined. They sat at the table facing each other. He looked round the room.

'A handsome room, Madame, if I may say so. And this table, oak, very fine.'

'You know something of furniture, Lieutenant?'

'A little, Madame,' he said, looking at the staircase. 'You have a large house. There must be many rooms.'

'La Commanderie has been my family's home for centuries, Lieutenant. There were once many more of us.'

'The Chevaliers of La Commanderie: a proud family and once distinguished, they say.'

'May I ask you how long you have been in Florac, Lieutenant?'

'A month, Madame; why do you ask?'

'Only to wish you welcome, Lieutenant and to say that I hope you will find your new post to your satisfaction.'

'You are too kind, Madame. What can you tell me about the aeroplane?'

The question was shot at her but Thérèse had been expecting it to come.

'Aeroplane? Ah, you mean the English aeroplane that crashed near here. Not very much. We found . . .'

'We, Madame?'

'My sister and I: we found the snow all churned up in furrows near the edge of the gorge. We could not understand what had happened and then Caramelle . . .'

'Who is Caramelle, Madame?'

'Our dog, here, Caramelle: she was digging in the snow and found pieces of metal. We told the Maire, Mr Janquet. I am sure he will have informed the Gendarmerie.'

'Hm, there was a report but no one followed it up until I came to Florac.'

'It was in the middle of winter, Lieutenant. It would have been impossible to do any more in that weather. You do not know the Causses.'

'Well I can inform you something has now been done. We have found more of the wreckage although it seems that much was burned. How did you know it was an English aeroplane, Madame?'

Again the question was rapped out at her.

'Mr Janquet said so. We described the markings on the pieces of metal we saw and he said they were English.'

'What is curious is that we have found no trace of bodies among the wreckage.'

'That is strange. Might the men have jumped out with their parachutes before the aeroplane crashed? My brother Fabrice told me he saw that happen once.'

'You have a brother? Is he here? I should like to speak with him.'

'He was wounded early in the War and died in a prison hospital in Germany.'

'My condolences, Madame. There is one other mystery about this aeroplane. We found a gun turret in the river bed.'

'A gun turret: I am not sure what that is. Why is it a mystery, Captain?'

'Because it contained no guns, Madame; mountings for machine guns but no guns. Now, is that not curious?'

'I cannot say, Lieutenant. I know nothing about machine guns.'

'Have you a car, Madame?'

'We have never owned a car, only horses; many horses in fact, in the old days. Unfortunately, we cannot afford to keep any now. We walk, or use bicycles.'

'The Mayor owns a car, I understand.'

'He does. He has been kind enough to take my sister and me to see Dr Vaudet in Florac when he had business there.'

'Yes. He made himself known to me at the Gendarmerie.'

'Mr Janquet is very serious about his duties as mayor.'

'Indeed. Your identity card, Madame, if you please: a routine procedure.'

'I keep it in my room. Give me a moment. Don't worry about Caramelle. When she is not working with the sheep she acts as guard dog in the house. Stay, Caramelle.'

When Thérèse came back dowstairs Lieutenant Grandjean was sitting exactly as she had left him, with Caramelle sitting beside his chair. He scanned the card carefully and looked up at her face.

'The photograph. Something is a little different.'

'My hair is a little shorter, Lieutenant. I had it cut for my wedding.'

'Ah. I see that this is signed by Mr Janquet and not by the Prefect.'

'As I said, Lieutenant, we are rather isolated at La Commanderie. It is too far to walk or ride to Mende, or even Florac: the hills, you know. The Mairie is authorised to endorse identity cards but of course you know that.'

'And the Mayor was not able to take you, even to the Sub-Prefecture Florac in his car, as you said he did for your doctor's appointment?'

'At the time he had not been given his petrol allowance. It is a little different now, thankfully.'

'Hm, that reminds me: petrol. There was a very serious incident last Wednesday morning, the first of April. A lorry taking petrol from the depot in Mende to the Gendarmerie in Florac was held up by two armed men near the Col de Montmirat. You know it?'

'The Col? Yes but it is many many years since I was there. My brother and I were on our bicycles. I was much younger then . . .'

'Yes, yes, Madame, allow me to continue. The lorry was found abandoned on the Pont de Montvert road with its tyres shot out and six bidons of petrol removed.'

'And the poor men, the drivers, what happened to them?'

'They were abominably treated, Madame: tied up and blindfolded and threatened by one of the men and left at the roadside.'

'Was it cold up there at the time? I expect it was. Those poor men: what a dreadful thing to have happened to them. And no one saw?'

'No one, Madame, or at least, no one is saying. You have heard nothing of this?'

'The only thing I remember hearing about Mende recently was my husband telling me that there had been a big fire there, in a warehouse, I think.'

Grandjean stood up, exasperation plain on his face, and made a move towards the door.

'Thank you for your assistance, Madame. I will bid you goodbye. One last thing: your husband's card and your sister's?'

'With them, Lieutenant: they carry them with them at all times. As we are all required to do. Let me see you to the door. It has been a pleasure to meet you. No, Caramelle, leave the Lieutenant alone.'

'I shall have to see their cards sometime, Madame.'

'I will certainly let them know.'

Corporal Dolland was leaning against the car looking very bored. Seeing the lieutenant approaching, he hastily dropped his cigarette, stamped on it and opened the car door.

Grandjean touched the peak of his kepi in salute to Thérèse. 'Goodbye, Madame Chevalier, until the next time.'

'Goodbye, Lieutenant Grandjean. Walnut: the table is of walnut.'

***

'He was rather nice-looking.'

'Thérèse! I only have to leave you for two mintes and your eyes start wandering.'

'Not as nice-looking as you; more serious, though.'

'Never mind all that,' Séverine said. 'You're sure he doesn't suspect anything?'

'Policemen suspect everybody. It's what they're trained to do. Sounds as if this one's new to the job. He'll be keen to make a name for himself.'

'We must be careful and let Jérôme and the others know.'

'He saw Jérôme had signed my identity card and he saw my hair in the photo was different from now so he doesn't miss much. He asked about your card. What do we do about Philippe?'

'That's one of the reasons we went to St Chely. Show her what you were given, Philippe.'

Lawless took a rather grubby yellowish card from his pocket and unfolded it for Thérèse to see.

'Philippe! You look awful! You look half-dead with your eyes part-closed like that.'

'I never did take a very good photograph. Jérôme says it will do.'

'What does it say here?' She ran her finger down the lines on the identity card. 'Martin, Philippe, mechanic . . .'

'Well, I told you I could mend bikes. I am Phillippe Martin now. I should be able to remember that'

'. . . born 22 December 1920 . . .'

'That's my real birthday.'

'. . . I know. Shut up. Born at Airaines: where's that?'

'Near Amiens. That was Jérôme's idea. Lots of English-looking people live round there.'

'Everything is there,' said Séverine. 'Dates, stamps, signature of the mayor of Airaines and it's been carried around in Jérôme's pocket and rubbed and stained with to make it look well used. And down there, look, change of residence: Saint Chely la Bastide with Jérôme's signature across it.'

'I must say it looks real to me. Where did this come from?'

'I tried asking Jérôme. Something about the same printer who does the posters and the pamphlets for him knowing another printer in Amiens. He wouldn't say any more.'

'Let's hope it fools Lieutenant Grandjean.'

'I don't think we need to go knocking on his door just yet, do you?'

Thérèse thought for a moment. Had she forgotten anything? The canvas bag held bread and pelardon wrapped in a cloth, some thick slices of ham in another, a bottle of sweet cider that Jeannot had brought for them, and a wedge of apricot cake, something that Philippe loved. Should she put in a bottle of water as well? Yes, he was bound to drink too much of the cider and be thirsty and there was nowhere to find water to drink where they were going. What else? Of course, the blanket for sitting on: she could carry that. It was light enough. Was that all? No, take a hat. The sun was getting really warm now and with the sky so blue staying out for the afternoon would dry her skin and give her a headache if she didn't have some shade. He ought to take one as well. He was a bit more weatherbeaten now but that fair skin of his could still burn. She was getting used to the moustache he was growing. He said he wanted it to be thick and bushy and drooping at the ends, like General Joffre's, a real Frenchman's moustache. Séverine made fun of it. She said it was going to be too red and he ought to bleach it to match his hair. Thérèse pulled the string to close the bag and tied the ends in a bow. There were two leather straps for carrying on his back. She went off to look for the old straw hats. Fabrice's should fit him.

They walked slowly down the long gentle slope on the far side of the cloup where Jeannot and Mireille were watching the sheep. The lambs were so much bigger now that you could hardly think of them as lambs any more although quite a few still kept close to their mothers, being firmly butted away if they attempted to suck. The sale of the young wethers had brought a surprisingly good sum, far better than the previous year. Money worries would not be so acute now. Lawless held her arm to make sure she didn't stumble. There was no need but she liked the feel of his hand. She was wearing a pale blue dress that hung loosely from her shoulders just short of ankle-length. The sleeves could be rolled up and usually she wore a belt but near the end of her third month of pregnancy it had become a little too tight.

Halfway down the slope Lawless stood still, tilted back his head and closed his eyes.

'What are you doing?'

'I used to do this when I was a boy.'

When he was a boy. Not very long ago. Not so long ago as when I was a girl.

'I used to look at the hills in the distance and close my eyes and see if I could still see them behind my eyelids and then open my eyes and see if they were still the same.'

'How lovely; and were they?'

'When you first close your eyes they are there, but it's like seeing the negative of a photograph but after a while that fades and when you open your eyes again they are the same as before. That always made me feel happy and thankful.'

'That's a strange thing to say, "thankful", why thankful?'

She thought he looked a little embarrassed when he answered.

'I don't know how old I was, three or four, perhaps. When I went to bed I was frightened to close my eyes for too long in case I couldn't see when I opened them again. It was like a nightmare coming before you go to sleep. So I tried not to go to sleep at all.'

'What did your mother do?'

'She didn't know what to do. She became very worried and even thought of taking me to the doctor. Then she told my grandmother and I was cured.'

'How?'

'My grandmother told her I must have been frightened when I woke up in the dark, so she should leave the light on for a few nights after she said goodnight. And it worked.'

'You like to to keep the light on now, sometimes.'

'That's because I have you next to me. We can go now. The hills are still there.'

Jeannot raised an arm and Mireille waved as they went past, a hundred metres or so away. Caramelle heaved herself to her feet and made as if to come over, but one of them must have said something and she turned back. It was almost noon and the air was beginning to shimmer. Their shoes made the dry silvery grass rustle as they walked. Lawless reached down, broke off a stalk and put it in the corner of his mouth. The root was pale green and tasted slightly sweet.

'We call it Angels' Hair. It's still today but when the wind blows it makes waves run through it.'

'So many more flowers have come out since that shower of rain. What are those red ones?'

'Easter flowers. Look, over there in that hollow: daffodils. Careful, you almost stepped on that orchid'

'I've never seen anything like them before. They're the colour of red wine. Like rubies set in silver in the Angel Grass.'

'It's getting really hot. We ought to find some shade for our picnic. I know just the place.'

She spread the blanket under an isolated stand of ash trees surrounded by eroded outcrops of pink-stained limestone.

'They spend a lot of time together, don't they?'

'Jeannot and Mireille? I'm glad. Without him she'd be very lonely. She's more used to us now but we are older. It's different.'

'You don't think they see too much of each other, do you? He must be nearly fifteen. I know what I was like at his age.'

'And that was so long ago was it?' she said, laughing. 'No; perhaps later but for now she sees him more as a brother and that helps because she misses her own brother so much.'

'Yes but what about Jeannot? It's never easy to work out what he's thinking, or feeling.'

'He's never met anyone like her. I think he's rather in awe of her. I don't think we need worry.'

'All right, if you say so. That was lovely cake. I feel so sleepy. It must be the hot sun.'

'More likely the cider.'

He lay on his back, tipped the straw hat over his face and felt for her hand. After a while his fingers slipped fom hers and his breathing took on the deep slow cadence of sleep. Thérèse leaned her back against the trunk of the ash tree and half closed her eyes.

Papa! Papa, lift me, lift me up! There's a nest in the tree. Lift me up, Papa, I want to see. Please.

Ooh ooh ooh, you're too heavy for this old Papa. Pascal, Léopold, help me lift up this big heavy lump.

Be careful, darling; don't fall.

I can see, Mama, I can see!

He gently wiped the tears from her cheeks and her eyes opened, not seeming to see him at first.

'You were dreaming. Something sad, I think.'

'No, no. I was dreaming about a happy time here, a long time ago.'

'Dreaming of happy times long ago can make you feel sad. Was it here? On a picnic?'

'Yes, a picnic. We came here many times, all the family.'

She was glad he didn't ask her any more about the dream.

'I wonder if Séverine is coming. She said that she might.'

He put up his hand. 'Listen. I can hear a skylark. Do you hear it?'

'I can hear it but I can't see it. The sun is too bright.'

'Skylark, skylark, nice little skylark: that's the first French song I learned to sing.'

'It's a nasty song, at least the words are and it's not French Don't you know any more?'

'Brother James? Is that all right? Or how about Under the Bridges of Paris?'

'It's a sad song if you know all the words.'

'Don't a boy and a girl make love under the bridge? That can't be sad, can it?'

'We can sing it round the piano tonight. Serge may be coming.'

'If he does we could dance as well, all four of us. Mireille can play. Is that all right, dancing, I mean, for you?

'There you go again. You make me cross sometimes. Yes, I can dance but not that, what was it? Jumping . . .'

'Dashing.'

'Dashing White Sergeant, not that. Waltzing, a lovely slow waltz with your arm around my waist.'

'If Serge does come we can have partners in the waltz: you and me and Serge and Séverine, and Mireille can play. I really am thirsty.'

'Well, aren't you lucky? You'll find another bottle in the bag.'

'I know it's an obvious thing to say, but I wish it could always be like this.'

They caught up with Mireille and Jeannot bringing the sheep back for the night. Caramelle bounded up to them, fussed about for a moment and then resumed her place, weaving this way and that behind the flock. The opening lines of Gray's Elegy came into Lawless's mind. He had recited it in full at the Methodist Sunday School Anniversary when he was fourteen to the incomprehension of most of the congregation. He was about to repeat the lines to Thérèse when she jogged his arm and pointed.

'There's Serge pedalling up to the house.'

'Nice soft breeze now to help him up the hill.'

'*En Juin vent du soir*
Pour le grain bon espoir'

'What did you say?

'It's an old Causse saying. "An evening wind in June is great hope for the corn". Mama used to say it.'

Valentin was sitting at the table with a half-empty glass of pale yellow wine and the opened bottle in front of him. There was a tantalising smell of cooking in the room. Séverine was putting something in a large flat iron pan and looked across. Lawless could tell straightaway she was in one of her good moods.

'Philippe, you've caught the sun. Or are you blushing? What have you two been up to? I'll take that.'

She took the bag from Lawless and gave him a peck on the cheek.

'As you were out picknicking all afternoon, I thought I'd make dinner—that's the soup you can smell—then Serge turned up with some trout.'

'Fresh from the river; I had a lucky day.'

'And two bottles of Picpoul: how he came by those, I don't know.'

'Serge, it's lovely to see you,' Thérèse said as he embraced her.

Lawless shook his hand. 'Let me guess: you're staying to dinner. Good. We have plans for you afterwards.'

'So have I,' said Séverine. 'He's going to stay the night.' She gave Lawless a bland look. 'So that he can give Mireille a lesson in the morning. He can have your old room, Philippe.'

'Of course. I hope you haven't tired yourself out on that long uphill ride, Serge.'

'No, no; I got off and walked up the steep bits.'

'I'm glad to hear it. You'll need all your energy tonight.'

'Stop teasing him, Philippe and tell him what you mean.'

'I'm not sure I should.'

'He's being impossible, Serge. He's like that sometimes. He means we are going to dance after dinner, the four of us, and we'll ask Mireille to play. Do you know how to waltz?'

'Madame, even if I did not, with you or Mams'elle your sister in my arms I could do anything.' He bowed to each in turn.

Thérèse clapped her hands. 'Such gallantry! You have your answer, Philippe.'

'I think glasses of Picpoul all round would be a good idea,' said Séverine. 'Then go upstairs to rest if you like. No need to rush. Dinner won't be spoiled.'

'Philippe, you were awful, teasing them like that.'

'I know, I'm sorry. I only do it because I like them both.'

'It was so obvious. It was rather funny, though,' she said, giggling.

'You mean you know what's going on?'

'Of course I know what's going on. I know what a woman is like when she has a lover.'

'You are wonderful, you know. Come here.'

'Not now. It's time we went down to dinner. Later, if you're good.'

Séverine had made a soup from dried chestnuts and mushrooms. It was thick and dark yellow in colour with a smoky taste. It reminded Lawless slightly of kippers. They told him the cevenol name for it was bajanat. He professed to have enjoyed it but the truth was he was becoming rather tired of the taste of chestnuts. Séverine must have sensed this when she said:

'I always think it's nicer with the right sort of mushrooms but you'll have to wait until autumn for them.'

What came next was much more to his taste: grilled trout crisp and scorching hot from the embers, seasoned with thyme, and lying on a pile of stewed sweet onions.

'I don't know know about dancing,' he said. 'I've eaten so much I'm not sure I can get up from this chair.'

'No need to yet. Sit there and have some of the pelardon while I bring the coffee. Serge has something to tell us, he says.'

Valentin glanced towards the door by the staircase.

'Don't worry about Mireille. She's gone to practise. There, she's started. She won't be back for a while. Go on. Thérèse is staying. She knows everything.'

'Jérôme asked me to tell you this. He's arranging a meeting to go through all the details but this is what he's planning. You remember the fire in Mende?'

'I read about it in the paper in Florac.'

'Lieutenant Grandjean didn't say anything when I mentioned it to him but I could see he was annoyed.'

'Who's Lieutenant Grandjean?'

'He's from the Gendarmerie in Florac. He was here a few days ago.'

'Shit! The Gendarmerie, here? What did he want?'

'Calm down, Serge. He's new to the place and came wanting to make his presence known. Some of them are like that. Tressie dealt with him very well. He must have gone off thinking she wasn't quite all there. Still, we shouldn't forget him. He certainly won't forget the identity cards.'

'All right, we'll have to bear him in mind. I'll tell Jérôme. Now where was I? Yes, Mende, the fire: it was started by some of ours. Jérôme knows who. It was a warehouse, one of the Department's depots, where they store all sorts of equipment, spares and supplies for the Police, Gendarmerie, Departmental vehicles, all that sort of thing. It was completely burnt out.'

'Somebody knew what they were doing,' Lawless said.

'Just what Jérôme always says: we need people who know what they're doing. It was part of the campaign; like the petrol lorry.'

'And now you're going to tell us what takes place next in this "campaign"?'

'Two things: another petrol snatch but a bit different this time and a train.'

'A train? Are you serious? What can you do to a train?'

'Derail it,' said Lawless. 'That's what he plans, a derailment, isn't it?'

Valentin nodded then suddenly lifted his hand. The piano playing had stopped.

'Sleep well, Serge? Bed comfortable enough, was it?'

'I'm only taking your advice, my friend.'

'Sorry, I'm sorry, Serge. Take no notice of me. I have this facetious streak in me. It gets me into trouble sometimes. I apologise. You can call me out if you like: pistols at dawn. Do they still do that sort of thing in France?'

'Only if you insult my dancing.'

'Insult your dancing? You made me look like a three-legged cow. I ought to call you out. Where did you learn to waltz like that? Our two women were absolutely smitten. I had to work quite hard later to regain my wife's attention.'

'I had a misspent youth. You are too young to have misspent much of yours yet. I discovered quite early that to be a good dancer, especially at the waltz, is a sure way to find a lady's heart. I could teach you, if you wish. I think you underestimate the number of your legs.'

'I think I have already found my way into one lady's heart.'

'More than one, perhaps. In any case it is also a pleasant way of keeping a lady's heart.'

'When is my first lesson?'

Valentin laughed. 'My other pupil has priority. I want to see how far Mireille has progressed in calculus. Incidentally, my friend, it was most thoughtful of you to ask her to dance last night.'

'Yes, wasn't she good? She managed to prevent me trampling all over her. She was as light as a feather. I wonder if she could get Jeannot to dance.'

'Mm, Jeannot; an unusual boy. A boy of few words.'

'We say that still waters run deep'

'And we say that still waters may simply be stagnant. But not this boy: he has a very active mind.'

'He's a bit young to get involved, don't you think?'

'Perhaps, but he has the gift of being able to make himself inconspicuous.'

'Like some coffee? The others aren't up yet.'

Over the coffee, Lawless pressed the schoolteacher for more details of the Janquet plans. What did he mean by saying the next petrol theft would be a bit different?

'He's thinking that after we've taken as much as we can carry we should make sure the rest won't be any use to the Gendarmerie. He's asked Henri to come up with some ideas.'

'What if we unloaded a lot more of the bidons, took as many as the car will carry and hide the rest? We could collect them later when the fuss dies down. In that way we needn't stage so many hold-ups. The gendarmes can't all be complete fools. They'll change tactics, find some other way of bringing the petrol to Florac or sending an armed escort, or both.'

'That's worth considering. Do suggest it at the meeting.'

'It's what Cavallier would have done.'

'Cavallier? John Cavallier? You know about him?'

'Didn't I tell you? They have a copy of his book here. They couldn't read it because it's in English—can you believe that—so I translated it for them. I'll show it to you. You can correct my French. Now what about the train idea? That's a much bigger job.'

'All he's said so far is something about the comrades at Balsièges. I happen to know that some of them work on the railway. Now, one of the lines coming south from Clermont-Ferrand passes through Mende and Balsièges and goes west to a junction near a place called Meriès—you won't know where that is but bear with me—and that's where it meets the Clermont-Béziers line.'

Valentin sat back and looked at Lawless quizzically. 'Well? Think.'

Valentin the schoolmaster was asking his pupil for deductions from data supplied: just like an Oxford tutorial, Lawless was thinking, except that the college tutor would now be gazing abstractedly down into the quad, or puffing contentedly on his pipe whereas here the pupil was being subjected to a penetrating stare and impatient tapping of fingers.

'Right. I know where Béziers is. It's on the Mediterranean. I know where Clermont is, up in the Auvergne. It must be a main line between the two, passenger and goods.'

Valentin was nodding slightly, but clearly expected more. Troop trains? No: Clermont was in the Occupied Zone and Béziers was in Vichy France. Passengers, then, and goods: what goods? Michelin: that was in Clermont.

'Tyres, machinery. It's a goods line. He wants to derail a big goods train!'

'I think so but let's wait and see.'

'Is this just man's talk or can anyone join in?'

'Séverine, good morning. Have some coffee. It's still hot.'

'I heard you talking about trains. What's going on?'

'Just speculating about what Jérôme meant.'

'And what does he mean?'

'Don't know but I can tell you that he wants all of us this time.'

'Not Thérèse, I hope.'

Valentin made his excuses after lunch saying he had exercises to mark and lessons to prepare. While Lawless was handing him a large envelope containing the Cavallier translation he asked what he thought of Mireille.

'Before long, my friend, she will be teaching me mathematics. Quite remarkable.'

'And German: you said she knows German.'

'We spent half the lesson speaking German.'

'I'll make you an offer. You teach me German, I will teach you English. It could be useful to us both, especially me.'

'Make the offer to her. She speaks far better German than I do.'

Séverine came out and they watched Valentin ride off.

'Found someone you like?'

'I like everyone I've met so far but Serge is different. I can talk to him about other things; things I used to know something about.'

'Before you became a soldier?'

'Séverine, I've told you many times: I am not a soldier; oh, never mind. Yes, before that. Like last night: he was telling me about this 14th Century poet he's discovered who was probably a monk—might have been a soldier once—and wrote the most extraordinary love poetry. He recited a line or two for me.'

'*Tears from your eyes fall into my heart*.'

'You know them! He must have told you.'

'We don't talk only about stealing petrol and how to avoid the gendarmes, Philippe. I told him he ought to go to La Couvertoirade. The library there is full of old books and manuscripts.'

'That's your family house, I mean your other family. Would he be allowed in there? You said you haven't spoken to them for years.'

'That has nothing to do with him. He is a scholar so they would accept him as such. He should go and so should you one day.'

'Surely they are even less likely to accept me. After all, I am married to your sister.'

'But not to me, Philippe; that is the point. You should go.'

'What makes you think so?'

'Just looking ahead, Philippe and,' she said with a smile 'you are a scholar too, are you not? You could go together. Talk to him about it.'

DECEPTION

'I had a visit from Lieutenant Grandjean yesterday.'

Jérôme Janquet said this from behind his bar where he was opening bottles of beer.

'Official?'

'More like busybodying. Wanting to make sure that I'd received the last lot of notices, he said, and why weren't they all up on the board. I said they'd arrived while I was away and I'd only just got round to opening the envelopes that morning. And I said I had a business to run and the Mairie was open only twice a week.'

'He wouldn't like that,' Vabrette said, pouring beer into his glass.

'I don't think he was listening. It wasn't the real reason why he came.'

'Go on.'

'He asked about you, Philippe, and Mams'elle Chevalier.'

Lawless put down his glass. 'What was he after? Oh, yes, I can guess.'

'He said he had not seen your identity cards and why had you not been to the Gendarmerie in Florac.'

'Are we in trouble?'

'I made it clear to him that you had no means of getting to Florac and that you had accordingly presented your cards at the Mairie, as is normal.'

'So he has seen them? Was he satisfied?'

'For some reasom he spent more time examining Mams'elle Chevalier's and hardly glanced at yours.'

'He may be more stupid than we thought.'

'Or more intelligent. I'll make some enquiries. In any case I think it would be wise to present yourselves in person. It would indicate you have nothing to hide.'

'Thérèse is sure he will visit us again at La Commanderie. We can show them to him then.'

'If he gets too nosey we'll have to deal with him,' said Vabrette. 'He might have an accident.'

'Henri, you know the rules of engagement.'

'I haven't forgotten, chief. I don't mean a fatal accident. Let's say serious but not fatal. Base hospital case. What say you, Jean-Pierre?' The big butcher looked at Jérôme Janquet.

'There are other ways if it comes to that. Leave that to me. What's more important is I'm pretty sure he let slip some information without knowing it. I've known for some time he was thinking of switching the route for the petrol deliveries and he asked me what the road was like through Montbrun up onto the Méjean.'

'That's the one we took.'

'Exactly but he can't know that. Henri, where's the map? Jean-Pierre, move the bottles. Now, look. Coming from Mende he would have a short climb up onto the Sauveterre. Then he can take this road down to St Enimie or that one down to Molines. My bet is he'll go for the Molines road; it's not so far. Once he's on the Méjean it's only seven or eight kilometres before he's in sight of Florac.'

'You can't be sure which one he will take.'

'No, not yet, but I soon will be.'

'And when we know that we find the right place to stop him and take the lot, or most of it, like you said.'

Even as he was saying this, Lawless saw Vabrette and Bec shaking their heads. Jérôme Janquet wagged his finger.

'That is precisely what we do not do, Philippe. Lieutenant Grandjean just may be laying a trap for us so we let them go this time, and the next perhaps and when he decides our last coup was a once and only, yes, we take the lot, as you suggested.'

'I get the point but that could take us into July. I thought you were short of petrol.'

'Caution, my friend, and planning: it will be worth the wait. Now, Denise has set a table outside for us. There is leg of lamb for lunch, from one of yours, I think, Philippe. We can discuss the other matter out there.'

Over lunch it emerged that Lawless's and Valentin's speculations about an attack on a train were not quite what Jérôme Janquet had in mind.

'We are nowhere near ready for that. It needs much more planning and besides, permission has not been given, as yet. What we can think of is what the comrades in Balsièges have suggested. Henri, tell them while I fetch another bottle of red.'

'Learn to walk before you try to run. We go for one of the trains that haul coal from Alès up the line to Langogne. Tunnels, bends and viaducts all the way along: lots of places to choose from. One of my Balsièges mates is a driver on that line. Shouldn't be too difficult.'

'What did he mean about not having permission for the other plan?'

'Orders from higher command, Sergeant: there always is one. You should know that. I'm not one for their kind of politics but I've trusted Jérôme for a long time now. He's a good man. Here he comes. Very decent red, Jérôme: my glass is empty in case you hadn't noticed.'

'Well, what do you think, Philippe?'

'I can't really say until I know just what you intend. Is it to be a derailment or do you wish to do some real damage? Have you got any explosives yet?'

'Not yet; we have a contact at one of the quarries but it's taking time. What Henri suggests is what you might call a maximum nuisance attack. He knows the technicalities so let him speak.'

'Right. What we do is take up one of the lengths of rail and get rid of it along with the fishplate—that's the bar that joins one rail to the next—and the fishplate joining the rails on the other side. The place we do it is just at the end of a tunnel so it leaves the train stuck inside on the up-grade. That should make it very awkward to fix. I know just the place. It'll be heavy work but I have the tools and somebody here has the muscle, eh, Jean-Pierre? We need everybody there to crowbar the rail off the track and pitch it down the slope into the river. The train is loaded the night before and comes upline early in the morning—we know the times—so we'll have to do the job in the dark but after—*and this is the tricky bit*—after an empty down train has gone through. Which means we'll have to be quick about it.'

'I think it's a good plan. The line will be blocked, for a day or more. Coal supply is interrupted and nobody gets hurt. What do you think, Philippe? Jean-Pierre?'

The butcher slowly nodded his head. Lawless stared up at white fluffy clouds hanging motionless in a blue sky, tapping his fingers on the table, thinking.

'I hope you realise that once you do something like this Grandjean is bound to link it with the petrol hold-ups and after that life will get more and more difficult for you. There'll be patrols, armed guards, house searches and all the rest of it.'

'Of course, but they will not know where and how we will strike next.'

'Not until they find an informer.'

'We have to face that risk.'

'And once we've found out who it is they'll have to start looking for his replacement,' said Vabrette.

Lawless felt a sudden slight chill in the air. The other three were all looking intently at him and Vabrette's usual smile was missing. Something had changed. He could feel it. He picked up the glass of red wine and drained it.

'Well, hard luck on him.'

Vabrette returned his grin. 'Knew you'd think so, Sergeant. Any chance of a bit of cheese, Jérôme?'

Jérôme Janquet pushed the dish of pelardon towards Lawless.

'More bread, Philippe? No? You're looking serious. Something we should know about?'

'You're sure you want Séverine in on this, are you?'

'I don't see how we could keep her out of it. You know how she blew up the time we didn't take her and she certainly proved herself last time, didn't she, Henri?'

'Steady as a rock. I bet she'd be the same under fire. Make a good 2 IC, I'd say.'

'It's just that she's been away for quite a while now and she can't know what's being planned. Do you know where she is and when she might be back?'

'Soon: don't worry about her. Serge is with her this weekend. All I can tell you is it involves moving some more children and another short visit to Montpellier. I've told her that she can talk to you and Madame Chevalier about it if she wants to. She and Serge will know everything we've discussed today as soon as I see them. When it's over we'll go quiet for a while, let the dust settle, let the gendarmes get bored and careless then we strike again. Just like Cavallier would, don't you think? Serge told me about your translation. I'd like to see it sometime.'

***

At breakfast Séverine announced that the shearers were coming in two days time.

'You do remember that's the day of the next petrol delivery to Florac, don't you? The lorry is supposed to come up through Montbrun and take the D road down to Florac. That's if Mr Mayor's information is right. How does he find these things out, I wonder.'

'But this time we do nothing.' Séverine sounded exasperated.

'Not quite: Serge and I are down to keep a lookout just to see if it really does take that route and whether there's an escort or not. When do the shearers turn up?'

'Dawn, unless they've drunk too much the night before at Chalady.'

'How long will they take? All being well we should be back by lunchtime.'

'They ought to finish before nightfall. They'll want to be paid and get off to the next farm to eat and sleep.'

'Good; I'd like to see them at work. Did you pick up any news while you were away?'

'Only rumours. You never know what to believe but none of it sounds good. Victor, you remember I told you about him? Well, he thinks there's more trouble in store for the Jews. He has lots of contacts and people tell him things—he's a lawyer, you know—and he's now sure camps are being set up for Jews and when they are ready they will all be rounded up and imprisoned. What happens to them then, he doesn't know yet, but he thinks it could be really bad.'

'Can they do anything? What about Mireille's parents? Is there any way they can escape and get out of France?'

'There's no word of them. Victor did say some have managed to cross into Italy, using smugglers' tracks over the Alps. They say the Italians are not as paranoid about Jews as the Germans are.'

'You must like staying in Montpellier. You certainly look well on it. The food must be good.'

'I didn't want to say it, Sevvie, but you do seem to have put on some weight.'

'Look who's talking, my dear sister! I do like it, some of it; Montpellier, I mean. Victor and Jeanette are very hospitable. They have an apartment in the Rue Foch with a balcony and a spare bedroom. They would love to see you. Why don't you go? You catch the train in Florac, change at Alès and again at Nîmes. That's what we do when we go. One of them would meet you at the station.'

'Why don't we, Tressie? Some sea air would be good for you. We could go swimming. I've never seen the Mediterranean. Why don't we try it?'

'Don't look so doubtful, Tressie. He's right. If it's Philippe you're worrying about, well don't. He more or less looks the part now, especially with that absurd moustache.'

'I can't go swimming, not like I am now.'

'Of course you can! Wear a big floppy swimming costume. I did.'

'Where's Tressie, Philippe?'

'She likes to take a little rest upstairs after lunch, half an hour or so. She starts knitting, and then usually dozes off.'

'Let's take a little walk outside, see how Jeannot's getting on with the mowing.'

'I ought to take over for a bit. He's been working such a lot lately.'

'This won't take long.'

They stood for a while on the rise and watched Jeannot at work with the scythe in an area of grass about knee high fenced off from any wandering sheep. Advancing one step after each quarter-circle swing of the blade he sliced his way rhythmically along one side of the patch then, hardly pausing, along the next at right angles to the first. Half way round he stopped, took a whetstone from his back pocket and stroked the blade for a few seconds before resuming the cut.

'He's a lot quicker than me.'

'He's had a lot more practice. He was only ten when he first came here with his father.'

'He looks as if he belongs to the place, don't you think?'

'We need his help. We used to have five men and boys working for us when I wasn't much older than he is.'

'Won't he be thirsty? If it weren't for this bit of breeze it would be almost too hot to do that sort of work.'

'Thérèse will have given him a bottle of half water-half cider.'

'Now we've seen Jeannot using the scythe you might as well tell me why you've brought me out here.'

'I've got something for you.'

'For me? A present from Montpellier?'

'You could call it a present but it's not from Montpellier.'

'How mysterious: can I see?'

She held out her arm and opened her hand for him to see.

'That? A wishbone?'

'From the chicken last night.'

He laughed. 'A wishbone: for me?'

'For us: to break. You promised, remember? The partridge? You cracked the wishbone with Thérèse. I hope you remembered to tell her what it means. You promised. Now it's my turn. Little fingers, little fingers, come on.'

The bone snapped with a sharp cracking sound and Lawless's part flew away.

'Look: I've won!'

'Did you remember to wish?'

'I had my wish a long time ago.'

'What was it?'

'Secret. Can't tell: you know that.'

'You're a funny one sometimes. All right; I'm glad you won. Do you think I ought to go and give Jeannot a breather now?'

'There's something else. Sit down for a minute.'

As he listened to her he grew more and more intrigued and not a little perturbed. She had been to Marseille as well, with Serge and she hated the place, hot, overcrowded: a febrile, heartless place. Go for a coffee at the Samaritaine and sit at one of the pavement tables, Jérôme had said; that's where you hear things. When you've been there a while, someone will join you. Don't look surprised when he does. He'll call you Sara and Stephane. Remember your names. All they heard was trivial chatter, much of it in the thick Marseille accent she could hardly understand and the coffee was awful. They were about to leave when Serge put his hand on her arm. Germans, he had whispered, don't look round. Go to the loo and order two glasses of white wine on the way. She got a good look at them as she was coming back to the table. They didn't look particularly German, but then she had never seen Germans before. Two of them were young men, one blond, fit-looking, smiling a lot, enjoying the sunshine and the beer. Perhaps they were soldiers on leave. Victor had said quite a few came to Marseille and they didn't wear uniform. The third man was different, older, not so robust, paler-skinned. While she was ordering the wine, Serge had moved into her chair where he could hear better. He handed her the newspaper and she opened it while he leaned back and closed his eyes. The wine arrived. She took a sip and tapped him on the hand. He made a show of waking up, said he was sorry, half-emptied his glass and settled back again. She sighed as loudly as she judged realistic and picked up the paper again. The Germans were now deep in conversation with most of the talking being done by the older man but of course she couldn't understand a word. After a few more minutes the two young Germans got up, drained their glasses and strolled away in the direction of the port. She watched them go. They stopped once to take photographs of each other. The older man watched until they were out of sight, then put some notes in the saucer containing the bill and went off in the opposite direction. She noticed he had a slight limp. Serge opened his eyes and sat up. He had just started to tell her what he had heard when a tall man with a reddish moustache called out to them as he threaded his way towards their table. Sara, is that you and Stephane, you as well, he said; I am in luck, and he sat down between them and put his hat on the table. He had long fair hair. She guessed he was about forty years old. He spoke French slowly, a little bit like Lawless but pronounced some words or parts of them differently. She tried to imitate his accent. Lawless wondered if he might be Scottish and decided he must be when she told him the man had given his name—not his real name, he said—as Dunbar, James Dunbar. Drink up, he had said, and suggested they try another café, nearer the port and not so public as the Samaritaine. He ordered tea—oh for a cup of tea, Lawless thought—which they declined. He said he had seen the Germans sitting at the table next to them and Serge told him he had eavesdropped on their talk. Some of it was about how glad they were—the young men—that their unit had been transferred from the Russian Front to France. The older man had said hadn't they heard that General Kleist's First Panzer Army was driving the Russians back in a panic and wouldn't they rather be with Kleist and they looked a bit embarrassed and said they were only obeying orders and would rather be back in action, maybe in Africa. He said what they were doing was important; something about making sure the French police stuck by the agreement. What that was they didn't say. Some places were mentioned, Drancy, or something like that was one of them. It seemed to be about Jews; certainly Jews were mentioned more than once. Dunbar said Drancy was near Paris and there was building going on there, possibly a camp where Jews would be locked up. Dunbar asked if that was all and it was, except Serge said that just before the two young soldiers had left the other man said something to them like they might be back here again one day, if they're lucky. Perhaps he meant more leave in Marseille, if they did a good job in Paris.

'Who is this man calling himself Dunbar? What do you know about him?'

'You could well meet him one day, Philippe. You could ask him yourself.'

'Why would I do that?'

'Because, my dear handsome brother, he could save your life. He is in charge of organising escapes for people like you.'

'Can he be trusted?'

'Who? Dunbar? I don't know but Jérôme must think so.'

'You didn't say anything to him about me, did you?'

'No; why do you ask?'

'Well, I don't know how you're going to take this but I'm not all that sure I want to escape, as you call it. How could I leave Thérèse and you and all this here? And I'm not really keeping out of the war: I am part of Jérôme's campaign, like you. Do you see?'

'Yes, I see but I wonder if you do.'

'What do you mean?'

'None of us wants you to leave, Philippe, but sooner or later you will have to go back; not yet, but one day. Yes, you are part of Jérôme's campaign, and you will do as you promised; we all know that. But this is not your kind of war, Philippe, this little war of theft and nuisance. As important as it is to us—and it will come to serious fighting, as you yourself once said—you were trained for bigger battles than ours and you cannot fight them here.'

There was no arguing against her. She was right. He had been deluding himself, drawing these great open spaces, the clean air and the growing warmth of the sun and the love he had found about him, hiding from the War, covering it up, forgetting it. But it kept breaking in, flooding his mind, sweeping away everything else.

'I want the summer and the autumn. There's so much to do.'

'So do I. And you're quite right: why not start by taking that scythe from Jeannot?'

'See you back at the house. Oh, wait. Rachel: remember Mireille's lamb and Rachel in the Bible? Well . . .'

'I know what you're going to say. I put the Bible out for you to find.'

'You do, er, did?'

'Deception, Philippe; all of us have to deceive sometimes to get what we want. You're no different. Your identity card names you as Philippe Martin, birth place Airaines.'

'Well, yes, all right but there's a good reason for that.'

'There's always a good reason for deception, Philip, or should I say

Philippe?

***

Valentin pulled a Gauloise half out of the packet and offered it to Lawless.

'No, thanks. They might see the smoke.'

'From the road? Surely not; it must be two hundred metres away.'

'Better not.'

'I shouldn't anyway. My cough's getting worse.'

'You should drink more.' Lawless laughed. 'You were down to two bottles last night.'

'Don't. It was very bad wine.'

From the niche in the crags to the west of the road that Lawless had found the day before, they had a clear view of the last two hairpins in the climb up from Montbrun and the level stretch to the crossroads.

'Do you really think they'll get a loaded lorry up that road? It's hardly better than a track. I remember some very hairy stretches lower down.'

'Grandjean is sure to have looked it over. He's not the sort to take anyone else's word for it. Whether he's decided for or against, we'll just have to wait and see. What time do you make it?'

'Just after half past seven.'

'Sun's been up for an hour. It ought to be warmer.'

'Clear sky last night, that's why. It will warm up later.'

'Why ever did we come here so early? They can't get here for another two hours.'

'Grandjean's canny. He might have changed times at the last minute.'

'So he could come even later? If he comes at all.'

'If anything, he'll be earlier.'

They fell silent for several minutes. Lawless watched the last shallow pools of mist slowly disappearing from the hollows as the sun rose higher. It was going to be another hot bright day. Saturday 23 May: what would he have been doing at home? Oxford? A language class in the morning, perhaps, then cricket in the afternoon. The last one he'd played in was against St John's. The White Horse for a pint and some shoveha'penny after dinner and back before the college gate closed at ten or the Dean would fine you. Was Oxford home? It had started to be. Would it be again? God knows—and He's not telling, Jack Verrill would have said. Séverine had told him good and proper where home was for him: Dishforth, Linton-on-Ouse, anywhere they posted him. Home was here, just over that hill and up the rise, where Thérèse was probably baking bread at this moment. Try not to think of leaving her. Just think of coming back again.

'Philippe, why not run through that list of things a German might ask you and what you would reply. It'll help pass the time.'

'All right, but only if you tell me the first sentence of *A Tale of Two Cities* and recite the first quatrain of Sonnet 18. You might turn Séverine's head with that one.'

'I'm waiting.'

'Mm, Halt. Your papers . . .'

'In German, Philippe, German.'

'Halt maken: papieren. Was tun Sie hier?'

'Ich besuche meine Schwester . . .'

'Was ist ihre Adresse?'

'Sie, er, Sie lebt bei dreiundzwanzig Marschall Foch Strasse.'

'Very good but I don't think many German soldiers would like to hear the name Marshall Foch. Remember, if you speak German to them make it sound as if you are trying to be helpful: gives a good impression.'

'Now you.'

'You know, English is such a difficult language. Let me think. 'It was the worst of times, it was the best of times, it was the age of wisdom, it was the age of . . . er . . . age of . . .' Shit! I can't remember. I knew it all last night.'

'It's worth remembering, all of it if you want a good description of what's happening these days. And "best" comes before "worst". What about your Shakespeare?'

'Oh I know that! 'Shall I compare thee . . ."

'Sh! Listen. Can you hear an engine?'

'It's coming. There! An hour early: thinks he's very clever, our Lieutenant Grandjean.'

They watched the lorry labour up the last few metres of the slope and come to a stop when it reached level road. Steam was rising from the radiator cap.

'They ought to keep the engine running until the pressure drops,' whispered Lawless. 'Right, they know what they're doing.'

A black Renault car came into view and stopped a few metres behind the lorry. Four uniformed men got out and one went to tap on the cab window, evidently ordering the crew to get down.

'They're likely to stay put for a while, at least until that engine cools down a bit. That could be useful for us next time.'

'Do we need to stay any longer? We know they've come the way we were told they would. We could get away without them seeing us.'

'Wait a bit longer until we see which way they turn at the crossroads. We need to know if they do take that D road down towards Florac. Remember: Jerome said they could go by Villeneuve? It's farther to go, but you never know.'

Half an hour later they were glad they had waited. The lorry moved on and took the D road as predicted but at the crossroads Lieutenant Grandjean's black Renault took the opposite direction and soon passed out of their sight.

'You know where he's going, don't you?' Lawless said. 'He's heading for La Commanderie. Come on; get the bikes. We don't want to disappoint him. We've got plenty of time to think up a good story and I can point out some of the places that Jeannot and I spotted as good hiding places for the bidons.'

Lieutenant Grandjean was about to get into his car when Lawless and Valentin rode through the archway and into the courtyard. He watched impassively while they propped their bicycles against the wall. Lawless walked across, hand outstretched and smiling apologetically.

'Goodmorning, Lieutenant: it is Lieutenant Grandjean, is it not? Have you come to arrest me?'

'Why should I do that?'

'My identity card, Lieutenant: I have failed to produce it so far, in person, that is. I did leave it at the Mairie with Mr Janquet for a while but here it is now.'

Grandjean took the card without removing his glove and examined it closely.

'Philippe Martin place of birth, "Airaines". Where is that?'

'Near Amiens, Lieutenant; a small place.'

'Philippe Martin": but you were married as Philippe Martyn Lawless, Sir.'

Lawless dropped his voice. 'I knew you would notice that, Lieutenant. It is rather embarrassing for me. Lawless was my real father's name, an English soldier. I never knew him. I think you can guess what happened. After the War my mother married her fiancé when he returned. He was a good man. He accepted me without question and brought me up as his own son.'

'Even allowing you to keep the name of this other man, an Englishman?'

'As I said, he was a good man. I treasure his memory. He knew my mother had fallen in love and could never forget the man who deserted her so he allowed the name on my birth papers to stand. Very few men would have permitted that.'

'You are Martin on this card but Lawless on the marriage papers. That is irregular.'

'Lieutenant, I can only plead embarrassment. Not everyone in Airaines was as understanding as my father, my mother's husband, I mean. The English were not all that popular near Amiens. You can understand why. Having the name Lawless became more and more awkward for me. It was a relief to become known officially as Martin.'

'But the marriage papers, Sir.'

'As you know, Lieutenant, the name at birth is required.'

'Mm; you are a mechanic, I see. From the way that you speak, you hardly fit that trade.'

'Mechanical engineer is what I was training to be, Lieutenant. Then the War came.'

'Ah, yes, the War. Your rank?'

'Gunner Sergeant, 77th; captured near Rumigny when the ammunition ran out. Some of us escaped from the column. It was nearly all over by then. Perhaps you were not part of that. If you were, you'd remember the panzers.'

'And you came here when, December was it? That is some time since June 1940.'

'If you're asking what I was doing all that time, I'll tell you. If you're an escaped prisoner of war in the Occupied Zone, you're always on the run, hiding out, dodging the police, German roundups. It's not a nice life, Lieutenant. And try getting across the frontier, because that's what it is, a frontier, with guards on all the crossing points. I nearly made it twice and the second time ended up in a cell. If it hadn't been for a friendly cop, I'd still be there, or in Germany like the other million poor buggers. At least there's some peace here, for now, anyway and a job of work to do; and a loving wife and family. Are you married, Lieutenant?'

'Take your card, Sir. That will be all for now.'

'Thank you Lieutenant. If you ever need some maintenance done on that Renault, get in touch. It's down a bit on the rear offside; tyre looks all right, probably suspension.'

'Thank you; we have our own mechanics. By the way, I noted you came in on bicycles. May I ask where you had been?

'Trying to find a couple of lost sheep, Lieutenant.'

'Without your dog, again; were you successful?'

'No, Lieutenant; we'll have to go out again,' said Valentin.

'Ah, Mr Valentin, the schoolmaster: do you know much about sheep?'

'Learning, Lieutenant; teachers spend as much of their time learning as they do teaching.'

'Have they gone?'

'I watched them from the tower,' said Mireille. 'They went back the way they came.'

'You should have heard Philippe, Sevvie. Spoke like a native. Grandjean's a suspicious character but he didn't get anywhere. A master of deception, this Englishman, I'd say.'

'I've known him do it without knowing.'

'You were talking such a long time, my love. I was beginning to get worried.'

Lawless put his arms round her and kissed her. 'I was worried too, Tressie. I thought the lunch was getting cold.'

'He's impossible,' said Mireille and they all laughed.

'Say it in German, Mireille. He ought to know it.'

'I do know it: Er ist nicht muglich.'

'Möglich, not muglich. Er ist unmöglich.'

'Do I have to go to the back of the class now?'

'The bit that I really liked was when you said if he'd been at Rumigny he'd have remembered the German tanks. I'll swear he blushed. You sounded so sincere, for a moment I almost believed you'd been there yourself! God, I hope I never have to decide whether you're telling the truth or not.'

'Don't get carried away, you two. People like that Lieutenant never forget anything, especially little humiliations. He hasn't gone away empty-handed. Now he's seen you here, Serge, he'll start wondering why you came; and he's been told things he will be able to check, given enough time. He'll start putting two and two together. That's what policemen do. Let's hope he doesn't come up with four but we're ready for him if he does.'

'Sevvie, do you mean what I think you mean?'

'Nothing for us to do. Henri will see to it. Can we now have lunch?'

'Mireille is taking some for the shearers. She won't be joiming us. She wants to watch them when they start work again. I think she wants to make sure her lamb is all right.'

On the first Saturday morning in June, the petrol lorry repeated its previous journey from Mende heading for Florac and stopped in precisely the same place as before to allow the engine to cool down. Everyone was ready and in place: Vabrette and Jean-Pierre Bec well-concealed behind a thick clump of broom and juniper on one side of the road,

Valentin, Lawless and Séverine in a little ravine on the other. Jérôme Janquet was waiting in the car with Jeannot next to him with the mule cart behind a ruined farmhouse on the road to Poujols in earshot of the double shotgun blast that was to be the signal for them to come.

The lorry driver jumped down from his cab to join his mate for a quick forbidden smoke.

'Grandjean would have their balls for that,' whispered Vabrette. 'Those bidons are leaky. They could blow the whole fucking lot sky high.'

'Time to go?' Séverine asked.

'No, wait. Let them finish.'

'I can hear a car engine,' Valentin said.

A black Renault car came slowly into view round the bend: Grandjean and his three men.

Orders were to abort the holdup if there was an escort.

The lorry crew hastily stamped out their cigarettes and opened the bonnet. A cloud of vapour hid them for a second then drifted away in the gentle breeze.

After a half-hour's wait, the driver fastened down the bonnet lid, got back into his cab and the lorry drew away. Lieutenant Grandjean's black Renault followed a moment later.

'Jérôme, you're a sly old fox, aren't you? You get us out here, all keyed up and all the time you were really hoping there would be an escort and we'd have to let them go. Am I right?'

'Remember your Cavallier, Sergeant. Lead the enemy on; allow him to feel safe. It's what he wants. I think Lieutenant Grandjean is now confident he has found the safe way from Mende to Florac. Next time there will be no escort. And this was a very useful training exercise, do you not think?'

QUICKENING

After days of very sultry weather, dark clouds began building up in the west and gradually drifting across the Causse Méjean. The air became strangely still and oppressive, especially for Thérèse. In the afternoon Lawless persuaded her to sit in their bedroom with the window open and use a fan that he had found in one of the drawers to cool her face.

'You have too many clothes on,' he said.

'I can't strip to the waist like you.'

'Yes you can. There's only me here. I'd really rather like it.'

'No you wouldn't. I haven't got a waist any more. And these are getting bigger as well.'

'Let me get you a drink. Is it often like this in June?'

'No but when it is we are in for a storm.'

'The grass is getting dry. Some rain would be very welcome.'

'Rain, yes, but not hail. The clouds are green and that means hail. Are all the sheep inside?'

'Jeannot and Miriam brought them in. He must have noticed the same thing as you.'

'It's just the wrong time for a hailstorm. It can ruin the apricot crop.'

A sudden blast of cold air swept into the room. Lawless was just in time to stop the window from slamming shut and breaking the glass.

'The shutters! Quickly!'

A vivid flash of lighting that made the room glow a ghostly pink for an instant was followed almost immediately by a shattering crack of thunder. With his ears still singing from the noise Lawless could barely hear the cry Thérèse uttered and tripped over a stool as he blundered towards her in the near darkness. He made out the dim shape of her chair and began to crawl, shouting 'oh God, are you all right, what is it? Don't be frightened, I'm here, oh God,' as more crashing blows of thunder made the floor quiver beneath him. He found her feet, knees, and half rose, trying to wrap his arms around her, still babbling in fear for her. At last he found her hands. They were resting on her stomach.

'Tressie, oh God, are you . . .'

Perhaps she was talking, maybe even shouting like him but her voice came only as a whisper through the deafening drumming of hail that was now beating on the roof and against the walls.

'I'm all right. There's nothing wrong. It's the baby. It just moved.'

The thunder, the shock. It must have jumped in fright and now it's dead. He knew it. It's dead.

'There! It just did it again. Here, feel here.'

He heard her speaking but couldn't understand.

'Philippe, here; put your hand here.'

It wasn't moving. It must be dead. Something fluttered under his hand. He put his head on the roundness and wept.

The squall left them as suddenly as it had struck and swept away across ridge and flat and dry valley leaving behind a thick white mantle of hail that started almost immediately to melt as the sun broke through the clouds.

Lawless threw open the shutters and breathed in the fresh, cool air.

'Look, down there. It's just like I saw it the first time, all white.'

'It won't last long.'

'Well come over here and lean out of the window before it goes. He won't be able to see it, but he may be able to feel.'

'She; it may be she, not he.'

'Or both,' he said. 'Come anyway.'

As if Spring had come again the Méjean turned from fawn to green spattered with yellow, red and blue in a matter of days, giving the sheep fresh grass and Jeannot and Lawless more mowing to do.

'And the desert shall rejoice, and blossom as the rose". That's what my father always said when he planted his potatoes, Jeannot. He always put them in on Good Friday and that puzzled me because Good Friday comes on a different date every year. Did you know that? He said that if it was good for Friday it must be good for potatoes. I think he was joking but I could never be sure. It was a long time before it dawned on me that Good Friday was always a holiday so men had a day off work. I wonder what he's doing now. Have you any idea what I'm talking about? All right, why don't you start at this side and I'll start over on the other? Did you bring the sharpening stone?'

'Good Friday was on the third of April this year.'

'Was it so? You surprise me, Jeannot, knowing that. That means my father's potatoes should have blue flowers on by now; not like those in the grass, but pretty all the same. The ones I put in our kitchen garden have flowers, blue with yellow centres. We'd better get started.'

'Mr Janquet asked if you could go back with me this afternoon and meet him in the café.'

'I'll put my bike in the cart for riding back. Listen, Jeannot, do you know anyone round here who might have a horse or even a pony we could hire? I found a beautiful old trap in one of the outhouses. If it were cleaned up it would be just the thing for Madame to go into the village, or out for a picnic somewhere. She hardly ever leaves the house now.'

'My father will know.'

'Tell him the owner needn't worry. She knows all about horses and so does Mams'elle Séverine.'

'I'm certain: 30 June it is.'

'That's a Tuesday: he's changed the day, the crafty bugger,' Vabrette said.

'And it's only three days away. Will Séverine be back by then, Jérôme? You know the fuss she'll make if we go without her.'

'All I can say is she is expected to be but we must intercept the lorry on that day, come what may.'

'And you're sure there will be no escort?'

'That is what my source tells me and he has never yet proved wrong. Now, you all know what you have to do so I want to move on to the other matter; Henri?'

'The coal train: thirteenth July; it's a Monday. Why then? Because next day is the

Fourteenth and even if the Marshal has banned the parties because he says we're all in mourning—he's right about that, the bastard—he can't stop us having a holiday. So, there'll be nobody to see us take up the rails and no train going up or down that line the next day. You can be sure that they're all be making a long weekend of it, anyway. The first train on the fifteenth is an up train leaving Alès at six in the morning. That's the one that will block the tunnel. Any questions?'

Lawless swirled the wine in his glass. 'If we pull that one off they'll know we're serious. You can expect a lot more visits from Lieutenant Grandjean.'

'The time has come to be serious, Philippe.'

'Does that mean we take the Brownings with us from now on?'

'Only when needed; and that's not yet. After the train we'll lie low for a few weeks. Then we'll see.'

'I had a thought about that,' Valentin said. 'After we've dealt with the coal train is there any way we can spread a bit of misinformation about who might have done it?'

'What about an anonymous letter to the local paper, or the Gendarmerie, saying a car with a, what, a Clermont licence plate was seen going through somewhere, I don't know, somewhere near the railway on the Fourteenth?'

'It's an idea, Jérôme. Why not make it Le Rachas, that's right on the railway,' Vabrette said.

'I'll think about it. Done the right way it might help. Time for a beer, I think. Help me with the glasses, Philippe.'

It was the signal that the discussion was finished. After filling the glasses for Lawless to take back to the table, Jérôme Janquet put a small sheet of paper on the bar.

'A message from England for you. There is only one word. I do not know its meaning.'

Glaramara, Lawless read and looked up.

'It's from my father. Glaramara: it's a mountain not far away from where I lived; before I came here.'

'A mountain? It means something for you?'

'Mm. We went climbing there once. I was about twelve. There's a wonderful view from the top, except we couldn't see it at first. A mist came down and we got lost. I was frightened. He said that we just had to wait until the fog lifted. I thought it never would. But it did; after a long time, it did.'

'And you could see where to go?'

'Yes. I think perhaps he's telling me although he doesn't know where I am he will see me again one day.'

'Where's that beer? Three thirsty men waiting to be served here, Sergeant.'

'Can I send a reply? They only know I am alive; nothing else about what I'm been doing here . . .'

'Sending too much information is dangerous, Philippe. We cannot be sure who may get to know. Your authorities might get the impression you are not making enough effort to return to your duties. But yes, a message can be sent: a very short one, like the last. That is best. One day I hope we will have our own radio; some in the Occupied Zone have them now.'

'Still waiting.'

'Take their beer, Philippe. There is a little more news. The others would like to hear it as well.'

'About time, too; dying of thirst here, aren't we, Jean-Pierre?'

'Come on, then, Jérôme, what's this news you got for us?'

'I have this from the English radio.'

'The BBC?'

'Yes, the BBC, Radio-Londres; not our stupid Radio-Nationale, so you can believe it.'

Lawless was thinking that back in the Mess hardly anyone believed what was said on the wireless especially when you'd been there and seen it but starved of news as he was, he kept quiet.

'Philippe, they said in May the English sent one thousand bombers to destroy Cologne and a week ago another thousand to Bremen.'

I can't believe that. We haven't got anything like a thousand.

'How many did we lose?'

'Cologne? I don't know. Bremen, I think they said twenty five were missing.'

You can double that.

'I saw Bremen burning once.' *And Harper's Whitley and everybody inside it.*

'But this is good news, Philippe, is it not?'

I should have been there.

'Good news? Yes, it has to be.'

'You don't look too sure, Sergeant. Thinking of your mates? Bad thing to do that, think. Drink up, lad.'

He felt Jean-Pierre Bec's hand on his and looked up.

'I think I can find a horse for Madame Thérèse. Soubeyran at Fraissinet has an old mare, well not too old, that was trained to pull a trap. He'd be glad of a bit of cash and he wouldn't have to find forage for her either. Let me see about it.'

'Would you, really, Jean-Pierre? She would love that. She keeps talking about going for a picnic to, damn, I've forgotten the name of the place: it's on the river.'

'Castelbouc. They used to go there on the Fourteenth every year in the old days, the whole family. My mother and some of the other village women used to go along in order to help. My father took them in our cart. The Captain's brother and his family came all the way from Couvertoirade and stayed at La Commanderie. It was just like a fête, so many people there. I was at the last one. That was in 'Fourteen. All us lads swam in the river.'

'That's exactly what I intend to do, my friend. Must be off, Jérôme, and tell my wife the good news.'

'Tuesday. Same time. Same place. Don't be late.'

'Don't forget: tell your lady I'll be along when I can to see to that trap before she uses it. The axles and brake will need some work after all this time.'

'I will, Corporal, I will.'

They listened to him whistling as he pedalled away along the cobbled street.

'Didn't finish his beer,' Vabrette said and drained the half glass. 'You put him back in the right mood, old friend, didn't you?'

True enough, Jérôme Janquet was thinking: he'd even forgotten the reply for his father.

'Jérôme, that day, Tuesday: it could be awkward for me. It's a school day. It might start some people talking if I'm not at school.'

'Give the kids the morning off, Serge. Say you have to go through all the books, or get things ready for the Inspector. You'll think of something. We don't want you not to be with us.'

'Oh Philippe, how wonderful! Do you really think he has found us a horse? A mare, you say? That's perfect. When can we have her? Did he say? Please let us have her in time for the Fourteenth. We can go for a picnic at Castelbouc!'

'You're strangling me. No don't stop. I love to see you so happy.'

'Let's pull the trap out now. Miriam can help. The three of us can clean it up and polish it. Did you find the lanterns? We must have the lanterns. It's so lovely driving back in the dark with the lanterns on. I want it to be like it was when Mama and Papa rode out in it. Come on, let's do it now. Mireille, Mireille, where are you?'

He decided it was not the best time to tell her about Tuesday morning and certainly not about the coal train.

***

'Remember, Mams'elle, just hold the gun on them while Jean-Pierre and I tie 'em up and put the hoods on. And please don't say anything: your voice is too posh. It would give you away.'

'Just you do your job. I know what I have to do.'

In their hiding place among the rocks on the other side of the road Lawless and Valentin were talking about Montpellier. Lawless said he'd finally managed to persuade Thérèse to go on a little holiday and stay at the Dumanoir's flat.

'I wanted to take her away as soon as we'd done this but there won't be enough time before our next criminal outing.'

'You think what we are doing is criminal?'

'Well, yes, don't you? Stealing is a crime isn't it? Not that I care in this case. I was joking in a way.'

'Killing people is a crime. You do that from your aeroplane.'

'I don't like doing it but that's the War.'

'Philippe, when are you going to understand? This is war, our war. It's not as big as yours with your thousand bombers but it's not a joke and I don't feel like a criminal.'

'Sorry, sorry: put my foot in it again. Hey! Listen. They're coming.'

'Masks on. Pull your hat down. Don't let your hair show, Englishman.'

'Masks on,' said Séverine, feeling to make sure that her hair was completely hidden under Fabrice's old hat.

'Look at that: no escort, Serge.'

'Engine overheating as usual. Good thing for us they never think of flushing out that radiator. They're stopping, Jean-Pierre. Come on; a bit further. That's it: just right.'

'Creatures of habit, thank God: stop, get out, light up, have a piss—hope Sevvie's not watching.'

'Not yet, Mams'elle: wait a bit. Want to make quite sure there's no Lieutenant Grandjean creeping up behind.'

'Now!'

They had to be quick. This time they had brought loose hoods to pull down over the men's heads, after gags were tied round their mouths. Vabrette was none too gentle tying their hands behind their backs. He didn't have the time. Bec hauled both of them away from the road and into a clump of bushes and tightened cords around their ankles. He left them propped against tree trunks after making sure that they could breathe and eventually be able to chew away the soft cloth gags. When he got back to the road he found Vabrette in the driver's seat with Séverine beside him. He joined Lawless and Valentin on the back of the lorry.

'Let's hope we get to Jérôme and Jeannot before the engine seizes. Care for a little trip, Mams'elle?'

'Jérôme, there's thirty bidons here. Where are we going to do with them all?'

'Put six in the car. Leave six more here behind the wall and load the rest onto Jeannot's cart. Make sure they're well covered up. You two follow the cart on your bikes and put the bidons in the caves. Mams'elle Chevalier, would you go with them? Jeannot will take you back to La Commanderie after the bidons are hidden away. Jean-Pierre, you come with me.'

'Where are you going?'

'To the dolmen at Les Baumes, Philippe. No one ever goes there. There is plenty of room for six bidons.'

'What about the lorry?'

'Henri will drive it back to where they stopped. We will pick him up there, collect the six bidons you leave here and return to St Chely.'

'You could drop me off near La Commanderie, Jérôme. I promised to do some work on their trap. Won't take me more than an hour or so and then I'll walk down to the village.'

Vabrette refused the offer of lunch, saying he had things to do for Jerome that couldn't wait.

'Can I ask what things?'

'That bloody car of his: we broke a spring on a rough bit of road on the way here. Had to tie her up with a bit of rope. I'll have to forge a new leaf and strap it in and if we're going to have the car ready in time for the train job, I have to get on with it.'

'Well, at least everybody else on the road will be safe from him for a few days.'

Vabrette gave his short sharp laugh, slapped Lawless on the back and hurried off.

Séverine came out to see him go.

'Tressie hardly paid any attention to what we were telling her about this morning. Just as well, I suppose.'

'All she can think about is the trap and the horse Jean-Pierre is getting for us and going on a picnic to Castelbouc.'

'Do you mind?'

'No, of course not. The idea of it has made her so happy. I want us all to go. You and Serge will have to walk up the hills. Henri said hardly anything needed doing to the trap; just some new grease and the brake shoes cleaning and re-setting. He soon had it all done.'

'Did I tell you I found the lanterns? They even had some oil left in them. I thought it might have got too thick so I emptied them and cleaned them out with some paraffin I found. They could do with new wicks.'

'I always wanted to strike the matches and light them but Papa said it was too dangerous and wouldn't let me.'

'You'll have your chance to do it now.'

'I did light one once when he wasn't about. Nearly burnt my eyebrows off when it flared up. He never found out.'

'Naughty little Séverine: doing things she shouldn't.'

'You have to, if you really want to—or need to, Philippe.'

'Like this morning, you mean?'

'I wasm't thinking of that but yes.'

QUERRELL

Séverine put up her hand.

'Sh, sh: listen. Hear that, Philippe?'

'What?'

'That sound, far off: keep very quiet and listen.'

'Bells; sheep bells. Jeannot must be moving the flock.'

'Too far away and wrong direction: not our sheep. We've been waiting for that sound. They're very late this year.'

'You're going to have to explain this to me. Who's very late this year?'

'The shepherds from the plains in the south. They bring their flocks up to the Causses in early summer. It's called the transhumance. Most of them stay on Mount Aigoual. The grass is very good there and it's cooler because it's so high. A few still follow the old Aubrac trackway across the Méjean. There used to be many more. Last year there were only three; still, they had over two hundred sheep with them. It sounds as if they are coming at last. I'm not sure why they're so late.'

'"Transhumance"? I've never heard of it. Do they stay here? Can we spare the grass for them?'

'It's our tradition to be hospitable. Papa used to have food and beer taken to the men after they had settled their sheep for the night, and that's usually quite late. The dogs look after them after that. They have some beautiful dogs. I like the white ones best. The name is patou. We haven't much to offer them but some soup always goes down well. And their dogs, we'll find something for them. They'll be off again tomorrow. They'll go back to the trackway near Chamblon and down to the bridge at St Enimie, then up the other side of the gorge onto the Sauveterre. We'll give them some coffee in the morning and see them off.'

'No problems with our own sheep?'

'Not if you mean what I think you mean: every animal has its owner's special mark.'

'What a slog it must be, coming all that way up here; something my uncle never has to do. His sheep stay out on the fells all year except for shearing and lambing times.'

'It's always good to see them again. We make them welcome for a night and in return we hear their news of what's happening in their part of the world. That's always interesting and especially these days. They don't miss much. And they are a help. Roland Querrell—he's the leader, master shepherd some would call him—knows everything there is to know about sheep. He always has a good look through our flock and if there's anything amiss he'll see it and let us know and as often as not put it right himself.'

'Should I keep out of the way? He'll wonder who I am and what I'm doing here.'

'He wouldn't ask and he wouldn't tell. You ought to meet him. Find out if he sees through you. Oh, if there's one we must keep out of the way, it's Caramelle. She's in season and they bring some lovely dogs with them. One dog is as many as we can feed in the winter.'

'Is Serge still with Mireille? Will he be staying?'

'He said not but once he sees the shepherds are here he'll want to stay and eat with us all.'

'Séverine, you know, you and Serge haven't said a word about what we did this morning. How can you be so calm? I'm still shaking.'

'It's what you grow used to, Philippe. We would be the same in one of your aeroplanes. Anyway, try not to let it show if Grandjean puts in an appearance.'

***

Thérèse decided the night was warm enough to eat outside in the courtyard and sent Lawless and Valentin to look for boards and trestles she said were somewhere in the barn. There was no need for tablecloths and other niceties, she said: they would be rustic tonight but candles would be needed because the shepherds always came after sunset after their sheep had been settled down, so bring the brass candleholders from the chest in the storeroom.

What Séverine had casually referred to as soup turned out to be an immense iron dish of steaming thyme-pungent rabbit stew, so heavy that Lawless and Valentin had to carry it to the table, followed by a similarly-sized tray of potatoes that the shepherds had brought and Thérèse had baked in the oven. After his second plateful of rabbit and potatoes, Lawless leaned back in his chair to let it all settle and watched fascinated as the three shepherds slowly and silently demolished what was left, finally wiping the dish and their plates clean with their bread. A basket of sweet ripe apricots and a plate piled high with pelardon were brought out by Mireille and more bread for the cheese by Jeannot, whom Lawless had not noticed until that moment. One of the shepherds fished a large wedge of cheese out of his pocket and put it next to the pelardon. It was pale in colour with a thick brown rind and tasted sweet and slightly peppery. No, it didn't have a name. It was just a cheese his wife made from ewe's milk. The dark bits in it? Juniper berries and herbs from the garrigue.

A fringe of the moon was appearing above the roof of the tower when Querrell asked whether it was permitted to smoke, adding thank you, Madame, no they would not take coffee but yes, a drop of vin doux would be excellent for the digestion. By this time Mireille and Jeannot had disappeared and the faint sound of the piano was coming through the open window of the salon. Was all this real, Lawless was thinking as he watched the shepherds puffing on their short pipes lit from the candles and his wife so beautiful in the moonlight, yes, *his wife* with his child growing inside her, quietly talking to her sister who had kissed him so hard those two times, and the schoolmaster who was also a petrol thief dozing over his glass of vin doux? Had he himself really nearly frozen to death not all that far from the place where he now sat in the warmth of a still summer night, smoking a Gauloise; he, who had buried all his crewmates near the river and was now one of a French gang planning to derail a train a few days hence? He had to be mad, or dreaming, perhaps both. It was the War; yes, the War where madness was the only reality and just for now it wasn't all that bad, was it? It was truly astonishing what you could get used to. Wasn't that what Séverine had said?

'If you permit, Madame, Mams'elle, we will say goodnight and leave you. The meal was excellent and we thank you.'

'You are sure you will not sleep in the barn? I think there are not many rats.'

Querrell smiled. 'You are most kind but, as you know, we must sleep close to our beasts. The shelter near the cloup suits us very well.'

'There will be coffee in the morning for you before you leave.'

The three men briefly bent their heads to the women and shook Valentin's and Lawless's hands.

'I will walk a little way with you, Mr Querrell.'

They came to the edge of the slope where they could just make out below them the blurred patch paler than the shadow that was the flock gathered in a circle. A bell sounded faintly as some animal stirred. The moon was high now, large and bright.

'Do you ever move them by night with a moon like this?'

'It's three nights past the full. Never at night: they would lack strength the next day. Do you know your stars, Sir?'

'The North Star, there,' Lawless pointed, 'and Vega up there: does it look blue to you?' He turned right. 'Arcturus, the red one and down there, that must be over Aigoual, Antares, that's red as well.'

'You seem to be someone who has used stars. We follow that one, the Pole Star, or leave it behind us when we return.'

'Has Mams'elle Chevalier said anything to you about me?'

'She has. I was surprised.'

'Why?'

'You speak our language so well and in the dusk it is not easy to see your face or your hair.'

'How do I smell?'

'Smell?'

'Yes, smell. Do I smell like a Frenchman?'

'Jacques, did you hear that? What do you think? Does he smell like us?'

One of the other shepherds came a step closer, stretched his face forwards and sniffed like a dog.

'Well?'

Jacques inclined his head slightly one way then the other.

'He can't tell,' Querrier said and started to laugh.

Lawless laughed with him. 'That's all I wanted to know.'

He went with them as far as the flock. A large white dog with a big bushy tail got up as they approached, making faint rumbling noises in its throat.

Querrell said something quietly and the dog went back to its place among the sheep.

'I thought he was one of the sheep at first.'

'He is, almost. He was born among them and he'll eat and live with them all his working life. He knows you're with me now, so you're all right. But he'll keep watching you while you're here, and so will the other two. I didn't see Mams'elle's dog.'

'Just as well. If she had got out I think your three would have had other things on their minds than your sheep.'

'Some advice. You're too ready with a joke. It's an English way. I remember them near Reims in July '18. The Germans used gas one night. We passed through some English in a wood near a river. There wasn't much that we could do for them; no time, you understand. One said to me *Go on Frenchy, breathe on the buggers. Garlic's stronger than mustard.* The gas, you know.'

Lawless waited for him to go on, thinking he was right. Jack Verrill was like that. It hadn't really occurred to him he was too.

'It's an English way, not a French way. It could give you away, where you are going.'

'Where am I going, Mr Querrell?'

'You know. If you want to fly another aeroplane, don't leave it too long. Every day there are more Germans in the south, in the towns, Marseille, Montpellier and others. None of them in uniform, but you can tell.'

'Do they smell different?'

'Did you hear what I said? It's not the Germans that will find you out; it's the French who work for them. One day you won't be able to tell the difference.'

'You're more than just a shepherd, aren't you, Mr Querrell?'

'I've said enough. When the warning comes, don't hesitate. And when you go, follow the old trackways whenever you can and you won't come across the wrong sort of people.'

'I'll need a map.'

'No you won't. You know enough about sheep to see where they've been. Menhirs and dolmens are the signposts, seven of them between St Enimie and the Jonte.

'I'll remember.'

'Time for us to sleep; up again at daybreak. Can you find your way back?'

'Now who's joking? Good night.'

Thérèse needed her sleep these days, so he got up as quietly as he could and took his clothes with him into the corridor to dress. He found Mireille in the kitchen making coffee.

'Guten morgen, Mireille. Wie stehen Sie heute?'

'Guten Morgen, Herr Lawless. Ich bin sehr gut vielen Dank. Mochten Sie einen Kaffee trinken?'

'Ich danke euch, aber ich muss einigen zu den . . . er, shepherds.'

'Einige, not einigen; Shepherds is Hirten.'

'Sheep, sheepdog?'

'Schäfe, Schäferhund, or Hütehund but that's more like guard dog.'

'You are good, aren't you? It's time you learned some English: not now, I have to take the shepherds their coffee.'

'Let me come with you. I want to say goodbye to the Schäferhunden.'

They found the sheep jostling each other to get at a water trough that two of the shepherds had to keep filling with buckets carried two at a time on a shoulder yoke all the way from the courtyard pump. Querrell sprinkled a few crystals of salt in each bucket. They stopped for a few minutes to drink the coffee while it was still hot.

'We've had a look at your sheep while we were doing our own. Nothing for you to worry about: they're in good shape. There's one blind in one eye but there's nothing you can do about that. That girl: she wasn't here last year. Is she family?'

'Mireille? She's staying with us for a while.'

'Hm. I've never seen our dogs go so daft about anybody as they do about her.'

'It's the same with Caramelle: that's our dog. She's teaching me German.'

'Where did she get that?'

'Mother, grandmother, I don't know. She's French.'

'Could be useful for you one day. I picked up a few words in Germany in '19. Not that I could use any of them in front of a young woman. Have you finished there, Jacques?'

Seeing his friend nod back, Querrell picked up his backpack and thrust his arms through the straps.

'Time to be off, my friend. I'd like to be over the other side of the gorge before it gets too hot and up on the Sauveterre before sunset. Do you think she'll let us have our dogs back?'

He gave three short sharp whistles echoed by the other two men and the dogs went back to their places on the outside of the flock, a little reluctantly, it seemed to Lawless.

'I'll take the buckets back.'

Querrell held out a big brown hand. 'We could get on, you and me. If you ever want a job, let me know.'

'Joking again, shepherd?'

'I'm allowed, but not you, remember? No, not this time: I could like you English now you're fighting the Germans again. Would you believe it, somebody I met once said my name was English? A shaft for a crossbow, he said. Can you believe that? Hallo, there she goes,' he said and pointed. 'She knows the way.'

Lawless saw one of the sheep plodding away from the flock in the direction of the gorge, the bell hanging from her neck clanking its distinctive note. Chivvied on by the three dogs, the others slowly began to trail slowly after her.

'Thank the ladies for us, Sergeant. Will you be here when we come back through?'

'Who can say?' Lawless said, but any reply there might have been was lost in the bleating of sheep and the tinkling of bells.

'I don't know how much he told you,' Séverine said. 'He seemed to open up to you which is a little unusual.'

'We have a common enemy. He more or less said as much.'

'I didn't like the sound of some of the things he had to tell and not just the treatment of the Jews. The police are a lot more active, more people are being stopped and asked to produce their papers, more arrests, more house searches, police cars patrolling in places they've never been seen before. There are rumours that some sort of special force called the Milice is being planned to search for people who are causing trouble for the authorities.'

'You mean, people like us?'

'Yes. We've hardly started but there's much more disaffection in the big towns and it's growing. I knew that already from what Victor and Jeanette told me in Montpellier.'

'Grandjean must have had his orders.'

'Undoubtedly but at present he hasn't enough men or vehicles and he's new to the Causses. We have a little time yet.'

'I wonder how much we really have. Something Querrell said worries me. He said there were so many more Germans in the south with so many French working for them that you soon won't be able to tell the difference. What can he mean?'

'He means that when the Germans decide it is necessary they will attempt to force us all to work for them.'

'What do we do?'

She looked at him in surprise. 'We carry on,' she said quietly, 'and on, until we finish them or they finish us. Isn't that what you would do?'

Twenty four raids and he had survived them all. There would be another twenty four and more after that, if . . . That was how it worked. She was right.

'Any news of the horse? Sevvie, what's wrong? Are you all right?'

She had given a sudden agonised gasp and bent double, clutching at her stomach. He took hold of her as she swayed and lowered her onto the grass where she kept gasping and screwing up her face in pain.

'What is it? Can't you breathe? Lie there. I'm going for Thérèse.'

She caught his hand as he started to get up. 'No, don't. Don't frighten her. It's going, ah, ah, not so bad. I'm all right. Indigestion. I haven't eaten anything. I'll be all right in a minute. Don't look so scared. I've had it before. It only lasts a minute or two and, there, it's going. I'm better. Help me up. Let's go in. They'll be wondering where we are. Don't say a word, now.'

'Sevvie, listen, you've been overdoing it: all those times away, travelling all over the place, not getting enough sleep, then these hold ups. It's too much of a strain. Have a rest. You mustn't go on that train thing. Leave it to us.'

'Stop fussing. You're just like Serge. I'm not listening to you. If you want to be useful, make some coffee and drop the subject. I can hear Tressie coming down.'

THE TUNNEL

'Philippe! Philippe, where are you? Jeannot's just told me about the mare. We can have her at the end of the week. She's a chestnut, he says, about twelve years old. Philippe! Are you there?'

'Here! Coming.'

Lawless emerged from the barn, hot and dusty with grass sticking out of his hair.

'Nearly done. Where's Jeannot? He said there was one more load.'

'Never mind the hay. The mare, Philippe, the chestnut mare, did you hear what I said?'

'Something about the end of the week. When? What day?'

'Saturday, he thinks; in the morning. Jean-Pierre will bring her. We must look out all the tackle and clean it and see if anything needs repairing. Philippe, isn't it marvellous? We'll have a horse in time for the Fourteenth! Castelbouc, just think of it! Give me a kiss!'

'Hey, hey, look out!'

He staggered backwards into the barn, falling onto a pile of hay and pulling her down on top of him.

'Philippe, stop it now; let me go. Jeannot might see us. Help me up.'

'You've got hay in your hair. Let me pull it out. Remember that time when I threw the straw down and covered you? You were so cross. You looked beautiful then. Like now.'

'I know that tone of yours. You've had your kiss for today.'

'What about tonight? All right, all right; ooh, that hurt! Saturday, did you say? Doesn't leave much time: we have things to do on Monday. Did Séverine say anything to you?'

'She's told me enough.'

'Did she say anything else; about her, I mean? I don't think she should come with us. It's going to be hard work and she doesn't seem as fit as she was. Why don't you tell her?'

'She won't take any notice or me, or anyone else. You know that. You will have to look out for her.'

***

'Well, if we do pull it off, it will be the last one we do for a long time, or so Jérôme said. Which reminds me. About that holiday in Montpellier: can we decide on a date?'

'I can't think of that now. All I want is to have our horse and go to Castelbouc and all the other places I want to to show you. It's going to be lovely, Philippe! I'm so excited.'

Even Séverine said that they had done well although she had forbidden any touching up of the paintwork, saying that only Serret in Florac had the necessary skill for that. Lawless, Mireille and Jeannot had spent the better part of two days with brush, sandpaper, cloth, water, vinegar, linseed oil and saddle soap cleaning and polishing until the trap and its iron and brass work and tackle gleamed in the Saturday morning light, waiting for the Jean-Pierre Bec to arrive with the mare. Lawless's final task was to scrape and brush years of lichen growth from the four stone steps of the mounting block in the courtyard so that Thérèse and Séverine might not slip as as he handed them up to their seats. The brass lanterns were full of new oil and the whip once wielded by their father had been found in a cupboard and now stood in its holding tube ready for whoever first took up the reins.

'You really have only two days to get to know the horse, let alone seeing how she behaves with the trap.'

'Jean-Pierre knows what he's doing. He wouldn't bring us a horse that isn't well used to it.'

'How long is it since you took it out? It must be years and years.'

'I can't remember. When was it, Tressie?'

'1930. We had only the mare left and we kept her until Fabrice had had his 21st birthday. Then she had to go. Do you remember her: Angel? We had her from a foal. I cried when she was taken away.'

'Angel, yes, of course I remember her. She was a chestnut as well. Fabrice learned to ride on her.'

'So it's twelve years since?'

'Philippe, you fuss too much. It's not something you forget, how to handle a horse; or a trap for that matter.'

'I was thinking about Thérèse.'

'I'm well aware of that but we're not talking about riding—although maybe that too, later on; after you know what.'

'All right, I'll shut up. I know next to nothing about horses but at least I can pull the trap out here all by myself. Wait there.'

'I can't understand how anyone who lives in the country, even if it's England, knows nothing about horses; can you, Tressie'

But Thérèse wasn't listening. She was watching Lawless emerging from the barn between the long curved shafts of the trap, a hand on each, and walking as easily as any horse. He drew level with the mounting block and carefully lowered the shafts to the ground.

'No, no, Philippe: tilt it backwards, onto the support rod. You'll damage the shaft ends like that.'

There was the unmistakeable clatter of a horse's hooves and Jean-Pierre Bec appeared through the archway leading the chestnut mare.

'Oh look, Sevvie! She has a star on her forehead: a white star. I was so much hoping for that.'

We're just like the Israelites worshipping the Golden Calf, Lawless thought as he joined everyone else clustering round the mare.

'Apples,' he said. 'Here, I brought some. That's one thing I do know about horses. They eat apples.'

'You feed her. Palm flat, remember.'

The wrinkled velvety muzzle with its few spiky hairs brushed his palm lightly before the apple disappeared. He had to admit that it was a rather thrilling feeling. He stood back for Mireille to offer the second apple and stroke the white star under the horse's forelock.

'That's enough for now,' Séverine said. 'What do you think, Jean-Pierre? Shall we hitch her up?'

'No, not yet,' Thérèse protested. 'Let me have her. I want to walk her round the yard, and talk to her and show her the stable. Give me the reins, Jean-Pierre. What's her name?'

'Fleur, Madame, and she *is* one, don't you think? Here you are. Don't worry, Sergeant. I rode her all the way up here. She's as gentle as a lamb.'

'Will you teach me to ride, Mams'elle?'

'I can show you how to take her out with the trap, Mireille, but as for learning to ride, why don't you ask Jeannot to show you? He was riding before he could walk.'

Lawless was seeing them all rather like creatures in another world, but a world he clearly would have to get to know; if he knew what was good for him. He must ask Jeannot to teach him to ride too. That should please Thérèse and perhaps even Séverine. There was one other very good thing about the horse: it would take Tressie's mind off what he and the others were going to do on Monday night.

***

'Where is it you said we're going?'

'Le Rachas. There's a railway viaduct crossing the lake and the track goes straight into the tunnel mouth on the other side. There's a little road close by where we can park.'

'I didn't now you had a lorry.'

'I don't. This belongs to a mate of mine. He's a mason; let's me take it if I have something heavy to shift. He thinks I'm getting a load of timber for firewood. I am, I mean we are: I know where there's a pile just off the road. If anybody asks where we're going or where we've been, that's our story.'

'Henri, you think of everything.'

'Have to, Sergeant, if you want to survive.'

'Where are we now?'

'Should reach Chazeaux soon.'

'I haven't seen the others' lights since we turned off the, what was it, the N88; have you, Jean-Pierre? Are you sure Jérôme knows the way, Henri?'

'He ought to but if he gets lost and doesn't turn up, it's up to us three to do the necessary. Ah, lights: that must be Chazeaux.'

No one was about in Chazeaux. Hardly anyone stirred out of the house after dark in this part of the world.

'Is it much farther now?'

'Six, seven kilometres to Chasseradès. We turn right after the cemetery and take a single-track road that joins the D906; say another seven. After that, seven or eight kilometres to the tunnel. I'd say about an hour altogether, maybe a bit less. If this old bugger keeps going, that is. It needs a bloody decoke.'

There were some trees at the side of the road where they could park the lorry out of sight. The tunnel mouth was down a slight slope no more than twenty metres away.

'Get the tools out of the back while I take a look. And keep the noise down. The houses are only about two or three hundred metres away. I can see a light so somebody's still up.'

Any hopes they might have had for a cloudy night were disappointed. The waters of the lake and even the railway lines glittered in the bright light of a near-full moon. The houses of Le Rachas were in clear view. As Lawless looked, the single light in the village went out.

'Catch hold,' Bec said from the back of the lorry, handing down a crowbar. 'Watch out: it's pretty heavy.' A second crowbar, two big long-handled box spanners and four sets of heavy lifting tongs followed.

'Might as well start taking the tools down seeing as there's nobody else here yet. I'll take the spanners if you bring the lanterns and the hammer and oilcan then we'll both come back for the rest. I hope Henri's remembered the matches.'

They found Vabrette near the tunnel mouth kneeling by the track and feeling along one of the fishplates. He looked up when they arrived.

'We could be in luck. These nuts are fairly new so with a drop of oil they should come off easier. There'll be too much light here in the morning so just to be sure the driver doesn't spot something wrong with the track we'll go further down where it'll be darker. Have the others turned up yet? No? Let's get on with it. I'll take the lantern and this box spanner and make a start while you fetch the other stuff.'

By the time Bec and Lawless came back with the other tools Vabrette had removed the four nuts on one of the fishplates and had made a start on the next.

'Here, Jean-Pierre, you take the nuts off this one while we spring the bolts out of the other. Did you bring that oak shaft? Good, we don't want to wake up the whole bloody village when we hammer out the bolts. Sergeant, hold it steady on that end while I give it a whack.'

The nuts of the fishplates on the rail opposite were older and much harder to turn but eventually after much straining and sweating they came off.

'Time for a breather and a fag, I think,' Vabrette said. 'Sergeant, would you mind going up and seeing if there's any sight or sound of the others? You'll find a couple of bottles in the toolbox.'

Lawless scrambled up the rocky slope and and back to the lorry. The viaduct across the lake, or river, he wasn't sure what to call it, was stone-built with four graceful arches. There was a building at the side of the track halfway between the end of the viaduct and the entrance to the next tunnel that he could plainly see to the right of the village. It was all very quiet and peaceful in the moonlight. Then he heard a dog start to bark somewhere and at almost the same moment he saw the dim lights of a vehicle turning onto the little road leading to where he stood by the lorry. It had to be Jérôme, didn't it? What if it were a police patrol come to check the viaduct? What if it were Grandjean himself? The lorry was well hidden from the road. All right: back to the tunnel and tell the other two.

'I think they're coming.'

'About bloody time: did you bring the bottles?'

A few minutes later Valentin appeared at the tunnel entrance.

'Séverine wanted to come down but I persuaded her that the slope was too steep and she'd be more use standing guard by the car.'

'Is she all right?'

'You know what Jerome's driving is like. We nearly came off the road on one of the bends near Chasseradès. I think she'd rather go back with you. Is there anything left in that bottle?'

'Can we get him to give Grandjean a lift one day? Scare the shit out of him?'

'Come on, let's finish the job,' Vabrette said. We've done the easy part except for the spikes holding the track onto the sleepers. They need to come out and then there's the hard part: lifting the rails. They're going to weigh about 500 kilos each, so it's a good thing you got here, Mr Schoolmaster. Are you feeling strong?'

'Henri, I was thinking about those two rails. Why not just lever them to the inside of the track? When the train comes off the rails they're going to be underneath it or a truck, aren't they? That makes it even more difficult to shift. It's going to be a hell of a sweat lifting and dragging them out of the tunnel to chuck down into the river and even if we could do it, we might make enough noise to wake up somebody or some dog in the village: not a good idea. What do you think?'

'Why didn't I think of that? Have another drink, Sergeant. We don't need the clamps, the bars will do. None of us is going to get a hernia after all.'

'All done, Jérôme: time to go home. If you like, I can take everybody else back: save you the bother and they can help me load the firewood I've been promised. Mams'elle, you can sit in the cab with Serge and me.'

'I've done nothing worth doing tonight, Henri.'

'Yes you have, Mams'elle. You stood guard: most important job for a soldier. Everybody else in the squad relies on the picket.'

'Good idea, Henri, taking the others home. It gives me a chance to go back a different way, through Cubière. There's someone there I need to see. That was good work tonight, my friends. Mams'elle Chevalier, tell Philippe what I was saying to you, will you?'

Two hours later the firewood was all loaded and they were ready to set off again.

'Who do you think he knows in, where was it, Cubière?'

'Hm. I know a quarryman who lives there. Makes you think, doesn't it?'

Caramelle was standing behind the door, wagging her tail, when they crept into the silent kitchen.

Lawless whispered, 'Caramelle, good girl; want to go out?' but Caramelle went back to her rug.

There was a jug of cider on the table covered with a cloth.

Lawless held up a glass. 'Care for some?' Séverine shook her head.

'A little milk if there is any handy.'

He found a full can in the half-cellar where they kept the milk cool and filled a glass for her. She was sitting at the table as he had left her. She seemed not to notice when he put in the glass front of her.

'You look worn out. You ought to be in bed.'

'I'm too tired to sleep.'

'I'll warm that on the oil stove for you and put some honey in it. My mother says that's the best thing for making you sleep: sweetened warm milk.'

She took a few sips, holding the glass in both hands and said something he couldn't catch before drinking a little more.

'What was that?'

She looked up at him. 'I was thinking of Mother's milk: you said your mother made it for you.'

'Drink it up and then I'll see you to bed.'

'I hope you see your mother again, Philippe. I wish I could see mine.'

He put his arms round her and kissed the top of her head. He didn't really know what to say.

'Don't be sad, Sevvie. You overdid things tonight and you're exhausted. I'll help you upstairs, even tuck you up, if you like. Think about tomorrow. We're all going to Castelbouc in the trap: us, Serge, Jeannot, everybody. All your happy memories will come back; you'll see.'

'Oh Philippe, you can't imagine how hard it is not to be able to do all you want to do any more.'

'Well, you don't have to do any more like tonight, not for a long time anyway. Why are you looking like that?'

'Something Jérôme told me to pass on to you. I'm so tired I almost forgot.'

'Oh God: not another petrol raid, is it? When?

'No it's another train: wait, not like tonight. Jérôme wants us to meet some people coming on a train. He says he needs you to go and either me or Tressie. He hasn't said where or when as yet.'

'I won't even think about it now. Come on: upstairs. It'll be light soon.'

'At last: I'd just about given up calling you. It's getting late. Jeannot's going on ahead with the chairs and the picnic baskets and the rugs. If you hurry, you and Serge can ride with him.'

'Serge and I thought we would take the bikes and follow the trap. I quite fancy freewheeling down that road to the bottom of the gorge. You ought to take parasols: it's going to be hot.'

'They're already in. Tell Jeannot he can go. I think he has everything we need. Madame Bec is with him. She always used to go with us. She takes care of the food and Jean-Pierre and his dog are out there somewhere with the sheep.'

'What have we got to eat? I hope there's some strawberries.'

'Leave that basket alone! Wait and see.'

'Serge said he would bring his rods. Ah, here she is. Morning Mams'elle Chevalier: just in time for coffee. Sleep well?'

'Like an innocent child, thank you, Sir. With hot milk, if you please.'

Lawless was amazed. Last night she had almost dead on her feet and she can't have had more than three or four hours sleep yet here she was looking as fresh as a daisy and clearly enjoying the sweet warm drink.

'Hm. Just what I needed. Now then, are we all ready? Where's Mireille?'

'Outside, with Fleur and the trap. She helped Jeannot with the harness earlier. I wouldn't be surprised if she has Caramelle with her.'

In fact Mireille was sitting on the driver's side, holding the reins and looking as if it was something she had been doing all her life. She dropped the reins and moved to the rear passenger bench when the sisters came out.

Thérèse and Séverine were wearing long white summer dresses and carrying wide-brimmed straw hats, each with a flower in the band. Lawless handed them from the mounting block into the trap, Thérèse second into the drivers's seat. He remembered seeing something similar to this scene in a French film his father had taken him to see: a countess and her daughter being helped into a carriage by some flunky with a powdered wig. Was one of them played by Danielle Darrieux? He couldn't remember.

'Serge isn't here yet.'

'You three go on. I'll wait for him. We'll catch you up.'

Thérèse shook the reins and told the horse to walk on. Mireille waved to him as the trap rolled through the archway and was soon out of sight.

'Try the brake before you go down the hill,' he called but they were too far away to hear.

Valentin was late. He'd slept in, he said, and then he couldn't find the rods until he remembered he'd left them in the school storeroom and it was quite a stiff ride up the hill from the village; no wonder he was in a sweat.

'Stick your head under the pump and we'll get going. You'll cool down on the way to the crossroads: it's nearly all down hill. What's that clinking in your sack?'

'My contribution: I know you'll like it.'

They caught up with the trap at the crossroads where Thérèse had stopped to allow Fleur to rest. Lawless was worried about the steepness of the road down past Montbrun to the river and said so.

'Are you sure the brake works?'

'Of course it does. Henri made sure of that and we've been testing it on the way to here. The road isn't all that steep anyway because of all the hairpins. We take it slowly and stop two or three times on the way down. There's no need for you to worry. We know this road.'

Half an hour later they reached the bottom of the hill and stopped just short of the bridge to rest again. The women took off their hats and stepped down to stretch their legs in the shade. Looking back, Lawless wondered how trees could grow so thickly and cling so firmly to the gorge's craggy walls that seemed almost vertical. Across the river it was quite different, with shrub and grass-coated slopes, just as steep, rising to the lip of the Sauveterre. The river was deep near the bridge and thirty metres wide with a shingle beach on the far bank. It was still early, barely nine o' clock, but sunlight was now slanting across the gorge as far as the other side, and the still air was becoming warm and humid. The river's clear waters looked very inviting.

'You can see Blajoux over there. We follow the road along this bank now. Can you fill the bucket for Fleur to take a drink before we go? It's level all the way to Castelbouc: soon be there.'

In the distance, in shadow, it seemed to be part of the cliff face, a huddle of stone pillars like those rearing out of the dry plains of the Méjean. Closer to, he could see dark patches that were windows with their dull brown shutters, open on the shady side now that it was morning. Castelbouc clung to the side of the gorge above a curve in the river, its houses poised to topple in, he thought, if the earth should ever shake. Now he could see ivy-patched walls and rosebushes which were spotted pink with blooms and a narrow cobbled street that snaked between stone steps and gable ends and away out of sight. It was an impossible place, impossibly beautiful; who could have thought of putting it there?

'Thérèse, is it real or just magic?'

'Yes, it's real,' she said and took his hand. 'And magic; come and see our picnic place.'

It was a little grassy field sprinkled blue with chicory flowers and shaded by chestnut trees on a broad ledge above the river. Downstream the river ran straight for a short stretch and then began curving until hidden by the trees. The water was dark and deep on this side but shallowed quickly on the other into a sandy beach. White streaks on the hillside high above marked the road that led downstream to Sainte-Enimie, Thérèse told him. A collapsible table had been set up in the shade and Madame Bec was taking plates and glasses from a large basket, helped by Mireille and Jeannot.

'Is there a place where we can dive in? Not you,' he said, softly stroking her now unmistakeable curve.

'I can show you where I used to jump in with Fabrice. He had to hold my hand or I wouldn't do it. Séverine used to dive in but we never told Mama.'

'I think I'll wait until it's in the sun. Do you know if Serge can swim?'

'I don't think so. But Jeannot can, I'm sure. You haven't brought a swimming costume.'

'Who cares? If anyone does, they can look the other way.'

'I won't care,' she said with a giggle, 'but what about Sevvie and Mireille?'

'That depends on how interested they are. Is there a fig tree in the village? I could be Adam and use one of its leaves.'

'Two,' she said, still giggling. 'Big ones: don't forget your backside.'

Séverine and Valentin came over from the trees where they had been tethering the horse with a rope long enough to allow her to crop grass in the field or stand in the shade, as she chose.

'What are you two laughing about?'

'Oh, just something Philippe was saying about fig leaves.'

'What's so funny about fig leaves? Oh, yes, I can guess. I know the way his mind works by now.'

'I was offering to be modest. There is something about a river on a hot day that makes me want to take my clothes off and dive in. Tressie said you would show me the place. Now?'

'In a little while. What we all need now is something cool to drink. Madame Bec makes the most delicious lemonade.'

'While that's coming I'll but the wine in the river to keep cool,' Valentin said, ' if you'd set out the chairs and rugs under the trees, would you, Philippe?'

Somehow, Madame Bec had managed to keep the lemonade cool. It was sweetened with honey that had a faint flavour of thyme. Jeannot brought them tall glasses filled to the brim and then went off with Mireille to stand barefoot in the shallows playing ducks and drakes.

'Sevvie,' Lawless said quietly, 'haven't you forgotten something? Sunday was the Twelfth. Isn't that when . . .'

'I know, Philippe. I hadn't forgotten but we were so busy with the horse, apart from other things, so I thought today, when all that was over, today would be a better day.'

'Can I be part of it?'

'Of course: you must. You are family now. I've written the words down for you. Just before lunch: that's when Papa always said them.'

There was a shriek of triumph from river. Mireille had sent her pebble skimming across to the other side, beating Jeannot's best try.

'Is something wrong, Sevvie?'

'No, no,' she sniffed, a lace handkerchief at her face. 'Don't mind me.'

'What is it?'

'I did the same as that once. Léopold was furious that I beat him.'

The diving place was only a two-minute walk away from the field. There was a little clearing in the trees fringing the riverside and a ledge of rock overhanging a blue-green pool where the river ran slow and deep along its concave bank. The top storey of a house peeked above the treetops. Shutters were drawn back on the shaded wall and a bright blue curtain trailed from the open window.

'It's always three or four metres deep here, quite safe for diving,' she said. 'I've done it many times.'

'Will you come in as well, Sevvie?'

'At any other time I would, Philippe. But I can't these days. Don't ask me why.'

'Pity. Like I said, I can't resist it. I'm going in.'

How different he looked from that first time she saw him clearly without his clothes when she had helped Thérèse wash him in the kitchen after the crash. Six months of hard work in the open had grown smooth swelling muscles in his back and arms and his skin was the colour of almond shells.

Stripped down to his pants he glanced over his shoulder at her, grinning.

'No fig leaves; I'll have to make do with these.'

'I can hear the others coming. Once he sees you in the water Jeannot is bound to join you.'

He was floating on his back with his eyes closed, drifting languidly downstream when a wave splashed over his face and Jeannot twisted beneath him supple as an otter and surfaced on his other side. Lawless pushed his head under only to feel hands grasp his feet and pull him down. They surfaced at the same time and started splashing water at each other. Jeannot broke away and started upstream with Lawless in pursuit. It was harder than he expected. The water might be moving slowly but it was deep with a stealthy force that seemed not to hinder Jeannot but caused him to work hard. He was glad to reach the shallows and followed Jeannot onto a sand spit on the far bank where they both stood shaking the water from their hair and feeling their skin dry and grow warm again in the sun.

Thérèse felt Séverine's hand take hers and squeeze hard.

'I was thinking the same: Fabrice and Thierry.'

Mireille could stay silent no longer.

'Can I go in?'

'Can you swim?'

The girl slipped out of her skirt and a second later dived in causing hardly a ripple.

'Is there anything that girl cannot do?' Valentin said, shaking his head.

Madame Bec had everything ready for them, even towels for the swimmers. There were cold chicken and spicy sausages and new crusty baguettes, baskets of tomatoes and apricots and cheeses wrapped in cloth. Valentin brought wine bottles from the river, sprang one of the corks and began filling glasses with pale yellow wine.

'What's this, Serge? There's no label on the bottles.'

'Special wine, made by someone I know. He lets some of his friends have the odd bottle. Try it. What do you think?'

'It's nectar. Where does your friend live? Can we raid his cellar?'

'There's only this one bottle: a glass now and another with the Roquefort. Ladies, you're not drinking.'

'Dr Vaudet said I'm not supposed to now. Well, perhaps a little sip just to taste wouldn't matter.'

'The same for me, Serge. It's too hot for drinking good wine.'

'Oh dear, have I done the wrong thing?'

'No, you haven't,' Lawless said. 'More for us. Should Jeannot and Mireille have a little, Séverine?'

'Yes, and Madame Bec as well, for the toast: now is the time. Have your glasses ready.'

This is supposed to be a picnic, Lawless was thinking; *my hair is still damp from swimming. Jeannot hasn't put his shirt back on yet. Mireille is wearing a little crown of daisies. Who made that for her? There are blue butterflies everywhere. Thérèse looks so happy. Is Sevvie really going to do this?* She was.

'Papa would never have believed that France would one day be betrayed again by those sworn to uphold her honour. I am glad he did not live to see these times. The traitors have different names now. No more Mercier, Billot, or de Boisdeffre and their like. We have Darlan, Bousquet, Laval and Pétain.' She spat out the name again, 'Pétain, to despise and defeat, and we shall, never fear, we shall do that. Philippe, I want you to read the words.'

He had half suspected it when she had given him the sheet of paper. Was it because she saw him as head of the family now? He cleared his throat and looked at the expectant faces.

'I am honoured to be asked to do this. With your permission I will speak first in English and then in French and I do this because together once more we fight against a common enemy.'

I have only one passion, to cast light, in the name of humanity which has suffered so much and has the right to happiness.

Je n'ai qu'une passion, celle de la lumière, au nom de l'humanité qui a tant souffert et qui a droit au bonheur.'

He was conscious of everyone looking at him, Thérèse proudly, Valentin with a little nod of approval, Madame Bec smiling, Jeannot solemnly, Mireille wide-eyed. And Séverine? Trustingly? He felt as if she believed he had made a vow.

Séverine raised her glass.

'Liberté, Egalité Fraternité. Vive la France!'

For a moment Lawless thought that they might be about to sing the Marseillaise but no, the ritual part of the day was over as far as Séverine was concerned and she turned her attention to the table. Jeannot and Mireille wandered off upriver chewing on chicken-filled baguettes while the others sat with their plates in the shade and watched large iridescent blue dragonflies darting over the grass or approaching to hover almost within reach, inspecting the bowls of strawberries and raspberries with their large bulbous eyes. Libellules—dragonflies, he loved the sound of the French word. Wondering idly if he could stay awake long enough to finish the glass of Muscat Valentin had given him to go with the salty Roquefort cheese, Lawless turned to speak to Thérèse but her eyes were closed, like those of Séverine. He put his glass down beside his chair, decided this was not the time to light a cigarette, lay back and tipped the brim of his hat over his eyes. The soft rippling sound coming from the river and the hypnotic murmuring of insects remined him vaguely of a piece by Fauré his mother used to play, or was it Debussy? Before he could decide he was asleep.

JEU DE BOULE

Lieutenant Grandjean was dissatisfied. On orders from above, the usual celebrations for the Fourteenth, Bastille Day to some, had been banned and the day had been decreed a Day of Mourning, like the Eleventh, but not as a day of triumph. The singing of the Marseillaise, in particular, was not permitted. There were plenty of notices on display informing citizens of this ruling and yet during his routine walk through the streets he had distinctly heard the sound of voices joined in singing and although he was tone-deaf, he recognised enough to know the law was being broken. There were plenty of people about, after all it was a fine day, but no matter where he looked, nor among whom he questioned, could he identify any culprits and such a thing dissatisfied Lieutenant Grandjean. He decided to drive to St Chely la Bastide. No one in that small out-of-the-way place would expect a visit from him on this day of all days and surprise sometimes paid off. As well as that, he could not rid himself of the nagging feeling that the mayor of St Chely knew more about these infernal thefts of petrol than he was letting on. Mayors heard things and during the sort of subtle enquiry that Lieutenant Grandjean prided himself he knew how to conduct, might let useful information slip out. Then there was the Chevalier family. They were known to the mayor: there was a report that a week ago they had both visited the doctor, Vaudet, that was his name, in the rue du Pêcher, driven there by the mayor himself. Two birds with the same stone? No, three: Lieutenant Grandjean permitted himself a thin smile at his own witticism. Evening would be the best time; after the pastis when they were all playing boule.

The others were still sleeping in the shade when Lawless woke suddenly, trembling from the flash and burst of flak starboard of his turret, only to find the sun hot on his face and bumblebees buzzing round the plate at his feet. He got up quietly and walked down to the river's edge to scoop up water to cool his face and arms. Standing up again, he half-closed his eyes, letting the sun dry his skin. Upstream, he could see two figures in the shallows walking slowly in his direction, Mireille and Jeannot on their way back, he supposed. The sun was now close to the top of the great wall of the Sauveterre. Down here they would soon be in shadow, but the air would stay warm. When would they have to start for home? Should he go for the bucket, or should he bring Fleur down to the river to drink?

'This is a perfect day for Madame Chevalier, Sergeant.'

'Ah, Madame Bec: I didn't notice you there.'

'And for Mams'elle, of course; they both wanted so much to come here again.'

'Like old times?'

'As you say. Those were wonderful times when they were little girls. I remember so well.'

'You came too, with the whole family?'

'Oh yes, we had so many there was hardly enough room in the shade for all the chairs and tables and parasols. We had to use another place to tether all the horses. Such games they had, leapfrogging and tennis and the boys diving and swimming and the Captain joining in everything: wonderful times, Sergeant.'

'And it never rained, Madame Bec? It always seems to rain on picnics in England.'

'No, Sergeant, I never remember it raining. The best time was the last, in 'Fourteen, it was. I was very young. We had the biggest party ever. The family from La Couvertoirade all came over. I remember the Captain's brother Alexandre: such a fine-looking man. Not quite as tall as the Captain, but very handsome. They lit a fire in a special iron basket, and the little boys and girls were allowed to toast marshmallows. Mams'elle Séverine burnt her tongue. It hurt, I could tell, but she wouldn't cry, not our Mams'elle.'

'I can believe it. And that was the last time any of you came on a picnic here, you say?'

'After the Captain and the boys didn't come back, well, Madame Chevalier, old Madame Chevalier, that is, well she just couldn't bring herself to come any more. I think they tried to persuade her but she hadn't the heart. Such a shame, Sergeant: everything changed after that.'

Lawless waited. He could see she had something else to say but was unsure how to put it, or embarrassed, he didn't know which.

'I hope you won't mind my saying this, Sergeant, but you coming has made such a difference. Just look at them, sleeping like babies, they're so happy. It makes me frightened.'

'Frightened, Madame Bec, why frightened?'

'I'm sorry, Sergeant, but I feel it: it's like it's too good to be true, too good to last. I'm sorry,' she said, going on in a rush, 'but you will take care of her, won't you, Sergeant, you will look after them and the baby, you will, won't you? I can't bear to think what would happen if you didn't come back. They've lost so many they loved, I don't know what they'd do if they lost you as well.'

There was such anxiety in her voice he hesitated, uncertain as to how he should reply.

'Thinking about it keeps me awake at night, Madame Bec. Every time we fly we never know if we will be coming back. But believe me, if I do live through this war I will return here.'

***

'Lieutenant Grandjean: fancy seeing you here! Not working while everyone else is on holiday, are you?'

'The Gendarmerie is never off duty, Mr Mayor.'

'And a good thing too, Lieutenant. I hear there's been more trouble.'

'Precisely what is it that you have heard?'

'Can you hold on just for a moment, Lieutenant? This is our last throw and if I don't shoot Sébastien we're done for.'

'Shoot Sébastien?'

'That boule dead in front of the little pig: it's Sébastien's. I must shoot it out of the way with mine. Do you not play boule, Lieutenant?'

'I have no time for games.'

'Pity; you can learn a lot about people by the way they play games. Here goes.'

Left knee bent, right leg trailing behind, back almost horizontal, head up and eyes fixed like a hawk's, Jérôme Janquet drew back his arm, paused for balance and lobbed the wooden boule high. A silent crowd watched its flight and descent almost exactly onto the top of target boule, glancing it away with a sharp clacking sound and coming to rest in precisely the same spot. There was an audible murmur of appreciation all through the onlookers, of a perfect throw.

'We call that a silver boule, Lieutenant.'

'So you have won.'

'*We*, Lieutenant, my team: yes, we have won. You will take something?'

'A glass of water, if you please. It is a warm evening.'

'I have put some tables in the shade outside the café. We will not be disturbed.'

Lieutenant Grandjean put down his glass after a few sips.

'You have heard something, you said.'

'A mayor hears many things, Lieutenant. Most are nonsense or harmless tittle-tattle. One must listen but not always take the stories seriously.'

'Go on.'

'I heard that there had been another theft of petrol.'

'Who gave you this information?'

'Gossip in the café one evening; I don't know who exactly. The place was full. Is it true?'

'I tell you this in confidence: yes, there has been a theft.'

'Another? These criminals must be caught, Lieutenant. Who knows what they may do next?'

'Enquiries are being made. Steps are being taken. If anyone has information it is their duty to inform the Gendarmerie.'

'Well, since you mention it, Lieutenant, I don't know if there's anything in it, but a friend of mine told me he had seen a suspicious car on the road near Le Rachas.'

'When was this? I must ask your friend's name.'

'Saturday last, he said: Costain, Louis; lives at Cubière. He goes fishing. There are good stretches in the Chassezac for brown trout, so he says. You know, the Chassezac, near Le Rachas where the viaduct is? I must say I like brown trout but I'm no hand at fishing; are you, Lieutenant? Now, if you want a real sport . . .'

'Yes, yes, what did he see that made him suspicious?'

'Car nearly knocked him off his bike, he said, and never stopped.'

'Is that all?'

'No, he was on his way home when they came flying out of that little road near the lake that joins the D 906; nearly flattened him like I said, and charged off up the road in the Langogne direction. Three of them in the car, he said, and he did catch sight of the car plate; didn't see it all but it was a 63. I don't need to tell you, that's a Puy de Dôme number plate; might be Lyon. Don't see many of them around here.'

'Nothing else: any other numbers, letters, make of car?'

'No letters but the two first numbers were 13 and it was a Citroën 11CV, black. He remembers that because he always wanted one.'

'This could be very useful; thank you, Mr Mayor.'

'Anything I can do to help, Lieutenant: you have only to ask.'

'There is one other thing. I had assumed the Chevalier family would be here, but no: elsewhere perhaps? '

'Now I can tell you that for certain. They are all at Castelbouc. It is their favourite picnic place.'

'Jeannot says that there's a nice still pool not far upstream and the fish are rising. How about taking the rod and trying our luck?'

'What about the ladies, Serge?'

'They've walked into the village to see some old friends. We have an hour or so.'

'You mean you haven't done this before?'

'Only as a kid with a bent pin on the end of a piece of string.'

'I can't believe you English sometimes. Have you no rivers where you come from?'

'We have but the fishing usually belongs to someone else.'

'You need another Revolution. Since 1792 the fishing and hunting here have belonged to the people. All you need is a permit from the Mairie.'

'Well maybe the War will change all of that for us.'

'You mean it?'

'We can only hope. Go on, show me how you do it.'

'The best bait for trout on this river is the sort of thing they hunt themselves, nymphs of mayflies and dragonflies. But there isn't time to find any of those so we'll use these flies that Jean-Pierre makes.'

'How does he do that? They look just like real insects.'

'Let's hope the trout think the same. This is a good pool, long and quiet and not too deep. The hook goes through the body, like that and this bit of thin copper wire wound round it helps the nymph to sink slowly towards the bottom. Now, stand back and I'll cast.'

He seemed to give the rod only a slight flick but the line leaped six or so metres away and after briefly skimming the water the nymph slowly disappeared below the surface.

'A few seconds to let it settle, then we wait. The water at the bottom moves slowly. If nothing bites when the line comes level with us, we try again.'

It took half a dozen casts before there was a bite where the pool began to go shallow and the line ran quickly upstream as Valentin let the fish take it freely at first then gradually slowing it with the reel and drawing it in as it turned downstream. They had no net but held fast in the shallows, the fish was easily lifted out. It was light brown with some darker stripes on its sides. Valentin weighed it in his hand.

'Brown trout; a kilo near enough. There must be others in there.'

His luck was in and in quick succession he caught three more, smaller but still worth keeping. Clearly pleased with his catch and feeling generous, he handed the rod to Lawless.

'Your turn: hold it like this.'

No matter how much he tried and Valentin demonstrated, Lawless could not get the hang of it and when his last throw—cast would be the wrong word—snagged somewhere among boulders near the bank, Valentin took the rod from him and sent him to find the hook and free it.

It was in a little pool between two stones stuck fast under the weed. Pulling had no effect so he ran his finger and thumb down the line under the water feeling gingerly for the nymph. The hook was lodged firmly in the top of something pliant and spongey: half-rotted driftwood or rubbish of some sort washed down by the Spring floods, he thought, as he prised it free. It was a sodden leather glove, or what was left of one, a flying glove, standard issue to bomber crews.

Valentin wondered what was taking him so long to find the hook. In fact he didn't seem even to be searching for it, just standing near the riverbank looking down at something in his hand. He went to see.

'Let me do it, Philippe. I know how to get these things out. I think we ought to be going back. The others will be wondering what's become of us. I'll keep that for you, if you like. We can put it with the other things under the stones when we can find the time.'

'I don't know whose it is. It can't be Jack's or Ernie's. They were burned. Doesn't really matter any more.'

'Let's go, Philippe. They'll be waiting for us.'

There was a place for making a fire, blackened flat stones laid in a square, and soon flames were leaping cheerfully in the gathering twilight. The air was still very warm and scented with thyme and lavender, but a fire outdoors draws everyone close and they came to stand near, holding their out hands to its heat. Lawless held back at first; fire was too much on his mind. Thérèse had seen that stillness in him often enough to know he was lost in a different sort of darkness and that what usually could free him from it was her closeness and her touch.

'As if there wasn't enough to eat already, now we have fish,' Séverine said. We need lots of big leaves to wrap them in and let them bake in the embers.'

'Will fig leaves do?'

'Can't you think of anything else?'

'Yes: drink. Where's Serge? My god, there's a light moving about on the river!'

'That's Serge, looking for the wine he left cooling in the stream.'

'Jeannot, go and help him. If you can't save him at least make sure you save the bottles.'

He's all right again, she thought and kissed him on the cheek.

There were only a few mouthfuls each but fish never tasted so good, Lawless said, especially with Madame Bec's bread and Valentin's white wine, Picpoul again.

'Leave room for the strawberries. There's some Muscat left to go with them.'

'And marshmallows: everyone must toast marshmallows. Jeannot has peeled sticks for us.'

'Careful you don't burn your tongue, Séverine.'

'Who told you that?'

'Just a wild guess.'

Lawless lay with his head in Thérèse's lap, watching the glow from the embers lighting her face. He had a feeling almost of timelessness, as if only the occasional flicker of flame reflected in her eyes marked the minutes passing.

'I don't know how to tell you what a wonderful day this is, Sweetheart. I never want it to stop.'

He saw her lips open and knew she was smiling. On his cheek he could feel a softer warmth coming from between her thighs and thought if only the others were not there, he might make love to her in front of the fire, as they made love on the night they were married. She had said they could, if they were careful. Tonight, when they were back in their own bed? It would be too late: tomorrow, then. At least it was dark enough for no one to see if he touched her breasts. He lifted his hand.

No one seemed to be making any move to pack up and start for home. Madame Bec sat with her head down on her breast, clearly fast asleep. Jeannot and Mireille were close to the fire, poking sticks in the embers and blowing on the glowing ends, and trying to raise a flame. Séverine and Serge's chairs were empty: perhaps they had gone for a stroll in the moonlight. The moon had risen high enough to turn the river into glinting stretches of silver below the deep shadow of the Méjean's wooded cliffs and the bare grey walls of the Sauveterre.

'They're coming back.'

'Shouldn't we be getting ready to go? I don't want to but we can't stay here all night.'

'Yes, we can. We're staying in Castelbouc, with someone who wants to meet you. It's all arranged. There's a piano and Mireille says she is going to play for us.'

'Is everyone staying? What about Fleur and Jeannot's mule?'

'Yes, everyone and there's a stable for Fleur as well. The mule can stay out as usual.'

Lawless woke to the smell of coffee. Opening one eye he saw Thérèse standing by the window, fully dressed with a cup in each hand.

'Everyone else is up and about. No coffee for you unless you get up now. Come and look.'

He dragged himself across and took the cup she held out. He realised now that this had to be the house with the blue curtains he had seen the day before from the diving place. There were the blue-green depths of the river, way below and further upstream a boat with two people in it was crossing to the other side. The early morning breeze was fresh on his face and the coffee hot on his lips. She was very close and very beautiful. How they had loved last night.

'We have to make an early start. It's going to be another hot day. Drink up. There's new brioche and apricot jam downstairs. Don't be long.'

Before he could take her in his arms and tell her how much he loved her, she was gone.

'Where is everybody?' he mumbled with his mouth full.

'Jeannot and Mireille are getting the trap ready, Madame Bec and Serge are loading things onto the cart and Séverine is on the terrace talking to Madame Lamphier. Philippe, it's nearly eight; please hurry.'

'Coming, coming; where are my shoes?'

Madame Lamphier remained in her chair and raised her hand as Philip approached. At a loss as to whether to shake it or kiss it, he compromised by holding the tips of her long fingers for a second and giving a slight bow.

'Madame.'

'Charming, the English, Séverine, don't you think? Sit with us for a moment, Sir.'

Lawless pressed his lips lightly three times to Séverine's cheeks and sat down.

'Ah, I see he follows the local practice. He must know you really well by now, my dear.'

'Can any man ever know a lady really well, Madame?'

'We occasionally allow them to think so. If it suits our purpose.'

'Philippe is endeavouring to turn himself into a Frenchman, Justine.'

'Despite the colour of his hair and eyes?'

'Hence the moustache, Madame.'

'Hm. Abundant and not a little rustic but your French is good, very good.'

'Less so than your English, Madame.'

'Is he not a flatterer, Séverine? I like that. It is so long since I was flattered. My father saw to it that I had the best teachers, Sir, and sent me to stay with a family in Cheltenham, for the accent, you know. Regrettably I never visited Oxford.'

'Last night you mentioned living in London.'

'Yes, for a few months while my husband was military attaché at the Embassy before the War. I met many young officers there. Some stayed with us later when they had leave. That was while we were in Paris, my husband's duties being mainly liaising with the English military. I seem to remember one young man in particular, extremely good-looking and with a rather strange name; Smallwood, I recall.'

'That's a coincidence: one of my tutors in Oxford was called Smallwood.'

She seemed not to have heard him, only smiling and saying, as if to herself,

'There was nothing small about him: he must have been almost two metres tall. Séverine, tell me something about the child who played for us last night.'

'She is in our care. We think her parents must have been arrested because there is no news of them.'

'Would I be right in thinking she may be Jewish?'

'She is.'

'Is that not hazardous for you?'

'We must do what we can, Justine.'

'Ah, yes, the Code Chevalier. I can hear your father's voice in yours. Is there any way in which I may help?'

'There is an inquisitive new Lieutenant of Gendarmerie in Florac. If he becomes too suspicious of us would you take her in?'

'Of course. But Séverine, her playing is exquisite. She should be at the Conservatoire. Impossible now, of course, but when better times come she must apply.'

'Thérèse thinks so too and she should know: you remember Pascal? Philippe feels the same, don't you?'

Before he could reply, Thérèse herself appeared, hat in hand. Lawless saw she had put fresh flowers in the band, sprigs of pink geranium. Sensing it was time for them to leave,

Madame Lamphier rose from her seat.

'I think you look radiant, my dear, you and your sister both. It has much to do with this young Englishman, Thérèse, I am certain; in fact it is obvious to see. Now be sure not to leave it so long again before you give me the pleasure of your company. And you, Sir, since you have now become a member of the family I think you may embrace me and I may call you Philippe.'

She was as slim as a girl and tall enough for him to need hardly to stoop at all to touch her cheeks with his, and twice only as he suspected she had hinted earlier might be more proper. Her dark eyes were searching his face and her slightly roguish smile had gone.

'The Chevaliers are not like other families, Philippe,' she said softly enough for the others not to hear. 'I should know. I hope you understand what you have done. You should go to see the Uncle.'

What is it about these two, Séverine and now Madame Lamphier, he was thinking; they both possessed some sort of power that could make him feel like a small boy again.

'Ah, I think I can hear the others coming to say goodbye. She is already a beauty, that child, Séverine. Remember what I said. If she has to take refuge with me, do not worry. Janquet calls this a safe house.'

'Jérôme Janquet, our mayor?'

'That Janquet, yes; we are in touch from time to time.'

'And what does he mean by a "safe house"?'

'A place the authorities would not suspect of harbouring a fugitive.'

'And you have had some stay with you?'

'Oh yes, several: until arrangements have been made for them to go elsewhere. One was an Englishman, a soldier, nothing like as charming as Philippe. He had dirty finger-nails. He was here for two weeks in May. I put him in the hayloft above the stable. A man who said that he was a blacksmith came in an old lorry to take him to catch the train to Béziers and that was the last I saw of him.'

'Jérôme has never said anything of this to me.'

'Why should he? Perhaps I should not have told you.'

As they were letting Fleur and the mule drink at a roadside trough before beginning the homeward climb to Montbrun Lawless asked Thérèse how they came to know Madame Lamphier.

'She is of the family, a distant relative on Papa's side, but a Chevalier through and through. They have owned that house and a great deal of land for centuries. Mama said they owned the castle as well: you remember, the ruins on that rock in the woods above the village? She was a great beauty: you can still see that, can't you? . . .'

'No more beautiful than you, with those flowers in your hat. Mm. Mm.'

'Stop it. She married very young. He was an officer, Captain Lamphier, Christophe Lamphier, quite a lot older than she.'

'She said they were in London for a while. He was at the French embassy.'

She giggled. 'Séverine said she was sure he was a spy. Justine used to tell us about all the scandals and the parties and balls they went to and the gowns she wore and when they went to the races and sailing on yachts. She told us she was once introduced to the Prince but he was too short for her, she said. Sevvie and I used to laugh about how she was so tall she could look down on the Prince's head!'

'She said a curious thing to me. She was talking about your family. She said she "should know". What did she mean by that?'

'We think she was Uncle Alexandre's lover. Sevvie heard Pascal telling Léopold he'd seen them together when he went to get something from the house at the last picnic. She must have had many lovers. The Englishman, Smallwood—? Sevvie told me Mama said he was one of them. There was a scandal that was hushed up and she had to go away for a while.'

'Did anyone else know? What about her husband? Wasn't he at the picnic?'

'I don't know if he knew and perhaps he did not care. Oh yes, he was there, rowing Sevvie and me on the river in a boat most of the afternoon. It was sad, you know. Mama said he was something very important during the War and he was at lots of the meetings they had in Paris to decide about the peace. And in the middle of it all he suddenly died.'

'He died: what of?'

'The influenza. Mama was so frightened that we would all get it.'

'I've just remembered! She said I "should go to see the Uncle". That's Alexandre, isn't it, the one who lives in La Couvertoirade?'

'Yes. I always liked him in spite of everything.'

'Sevvie said I should go, too. And so did Serge, because of his library. What do you think, Sweetheart?'

'I think you should go. It could help heal some old wounds.'

PASSENGERS

'Serge will be staying with us during the school holidays,' Séverine announced at breakfast. 'You two could take the trap and help him bring up his things and do some shopping at the same time.'

'I'll go and see what we need. I know we're short of flour and oil.'

'It's Friday today,' Lawless said when Thérèse was out of the room. 'I can't wait to hear what's happened about the tunnel.'

'If we were successful they may keep quiet about it until the line is cleared and then pass it off as a minor breakdown. The authorities will know this was sabotage, not like some petty thieves stealing a few cans of petrol to sell on the black market, and it would look bad for them.'

'Should we expect another visit from the Lieutenant?'

'I do hope so. We have the perfect alibi for the Fourteenth.'

'It was wonderful, the whole thing, even helping push the trap up that last bit of the hill. It was like, how can I put it, like living in a different age. It must have taken you back. Madame Bec told me about your picnics there.'

'Hah! So that's how you know about my burning my tongue on the marshmallow,' she laughed. 'Yes, it was wonderful but if you want to know the truth, Philippe, there were moments yesterday when I thought my heart would break.'

There were tears in her eyes. He stretched out his fingers to wipe them away.

'No, please, that would make it worse. Give me your handkerchief.'

He passed it to her without a word. She dabbed her eyes, sniffed, sighed and looked up at him again. The smile was back, just.

'No more of that. What did you think of our cousin? Tressie and I always called her the Chatelaine; not to her face, of course.'

'I should like to meet her again.'

'Be careful, young man. She is very seductive.'

'Then she is no different from the other Chevalier women I know.'

'She had said you were a flatterer. What else did she say? I heard her whispering to you.'

'She said I should see your Uncle, the one at La Couvertoirade. People keep telling me the same and I would like to, one day. But first I want to take Thérèse to Montpellier. Can we do that? In fact why don't we all go, the four of us?'

'See what Jérôme has to say about the tunnel first. And do you remember I told you he wants us to meet someone on another train? Once we know where and when that is, we can decide on dates for going to Montpellier.'

***

'The Lieutenant turned up on the Fourteenth, while we were playing boules. I got him to admit about the petrol being stolen and then I fed him the story about some mate of mine being nearly knocked off his bike near the lake at Le Rachas by a suspicious car with Lyon plates and he swallowed it.'

'So what do we do now, Jérôme?'

'Act as if nothing has happened and wait for Henri. I'm expecting him this morning.'

'We want to go on the train to Montpellier for a couple of days holiday. It would be good for Thérèse to get away. You know, paddle in the sea, eat ice cream—if there is any to be had—that sort of thing. Serge and Séverine want to come as well but she says we can't fix a date until we know what you want us to do about meeting somebody on a train somewhere. What's it all about?'

'We'll wait until Henri gets here. There's something important you should know and I want everyone to be here when I tell you. That's a very fine trap you have out there. It's been years since I saw it being used.'

With Thérèse still deep in conversation with Madame Bec about things he suspected they did want him to hear, Lawless decided to call on Valentin and persuade him to take a break from packing and come to the café. The look on Henri Vabrette's face told them something had happened

'. . . my mate says there's been pandemonium in Alès and all the way up the line. Ah, there you are Sergeant. Come and join us. We've something to celebrate, eh, Jérôme?'

'We have, Henri, but not quite so noisily.'

'Have you been to see for yourself?'

'No fear; been keeping well away, I have. I get all this from my mate from Balsièges. He's one of the drivers. Couldn't understand what was going on when he turned up for work: all up-trains kept in the station yards, all down-trains delayed, and nobody saying what the reason was. When he asked, he was told to keep his mouth shut or else. . . It soon came out when he talked to one of the track maintenance crew. Problems with the line, they said, didn't take long to fix. That was it, but why all the secrecy? Happens now and again on that line if they're out of spares or there's a tree come down, that sort of thing.'

'Didn't take long to fix? A bloody train derailed in the tunnel! What was he talking about?'

'My mate said nothing about a derailment.'

'I don't understand,' Lawless said. 'We all know that the lines were taken out. If there wasn't a derailment what caused all that fuss, pandemonium you called it?'

'Don't ask me.'

'What I can't understand is how they've managed to keep such a thing quiet for so long.'

'Everybody was told if the word got out they'd all get the sack and you don't want to lose your job these days. You'd never get another one.'

'Why don't we make sure people know?' Valentin said. 'Have a few posters printed, put them where people can see and let them spread the news. I was thinking of the wording, something like "Citizens! Hunt down the criminal railway saboteurs of Le Rachas! Help your Gendarmerie in their search!"'

'Very stirring, Serge, but I think that might sow more unwelcome suspicion in our Lieutenant's mind. Best let the news seep out slowly. Mayors talk to each other, remember. When people do find out they will wonder why the Gendarmerie tried to keep it quiet for so long and ask whether there could be anything else they ought to be told. Now, listen carefully and don't interrupt until I've finished. Then you can have your say. First, I have been instructed to tell you that what you did at Le Rachas has been seen as a very successful piece of work and you can feel congratulated. Traffic on an important line was disrupted for a considerable time and the authorities have been severely embarrassed. Secondly, you deserve an explanation of why there was disruption but no derailment.'

'This had better be good, Jérôme. We took a big risk that night.'

'Sergeant, let me remind you that you were present when it was agreed that I am the commanding officer here. You have your orders and I have mine. In your big war you fly where you are told and drop your bombs as instructed. You are not always, if ever, told why. In our little war, it is the same except this time, as I was saying, I am able to give you an explanation of why things were done as they were. Understood?'

'I'm listening.'

'The Occupied part of our country is under the control of a foreign invader whose treatment of our citizens worsens by the day. Violence against such an enemy and those who support him is fully justified. Here, it is different: we disrupt, we spread dissent, we undermine authority as best we can but we do *not* harm our own loyal citizens. If we do, we will lose all our support—active or passive—and then we will be lost. If things change, and they may, then we will act in the same way as our comrades in the North and, as you know, we have the means to do so.'

'I am still not clear what you are saying, Jérôme, but would I be right in thinking you, or your superiors, did something to prevent the derailment?'

'An anonymous telephone call to the railway authorities giving them just enough detail and just enough time to alert the system and deal with the track was all it took to prevent what could have been a possible train crash with heavy loss of life. Le Rachas is on one of the main lines from Paris to the Mediterranean, Philippe.'

'My God, Jérôme, you ran a hell of a risk. What if they hadn't listened?'

'There are ways of making them know when a message is serious. And, just in case, we also alerted Lieutenant Grandjean. He was in no state to ignore messages like that.'

'Jérôme,' Valentin said with a frown, 'why was all that trouble taken? What did it achieve? Trains delayed a bit, some track to repair, is that all?'

'You are right, Serge, that would hardly be enough but think: they now know what we could do, *if we wanted*, and they will never rest easy again. As Henri said, we have cause to celebrate. I will bring the cognac.'

In silence they watched him disappear into the café.

'What do you think, Henri?'

'Chain of command, Sergeant: always the same. Poilou never gets told until afterwards, and not always then. He has a point though. I like the thought of those buggers biting their nails and wondering what's coming next.'

'Gaston de LaGrange: you'll like this, Philippe. Health! Now, to other matters' Jérôme Janquet went on quickly before anyone could demur. 'Henri, anything about the passengers?'

'Two, the lady says. I saw her yesterday. They'll be on the afternoon train to Béziers on the 24th, that's next Friday. It makes a short stop at Sévérac. That's where you meet them.'

'Now, Jérôme, tell me what this is all about? Who are these 'passengers', what do we do with them and who is this 'lady'?'

'The passengers—we always call them that—are men like you, escaping from the Germans and trying to get back to England. Our people help as best they can, hiding them, getting them onto trains or some other way of travelling and giving them money and papers. That's what I am asking you to do.'

'Give them money and papers?'

'Yes and further instructions.'

'Why me and why Séverine?'

'Because you speak English and can drive—at least I hope you can drive—and Mams'elle Chevalier, well she is who she is as you'll find out if there is any difficulty. And she knows the way to Sévérac. I may as well tell you who the "lady" is since you already know her: Madame Lamphier of Castelbouc.'

'So Madame Lamphier is one of your people?'

'It might be nearer the truth to say she regards us as some of her people.'

'I'd like to go too, Jérôme.'

'Not this time, Serge; could be difficult if one of Grandjean's patrols stopped you and started asking questions. If Grandjean happened to be there he certainly would smell a rat.'

'I count on you to make sure she's all right, Philippe.'

'More likely she'll make sure I am. Oops, here comes my wife. What do I tell her, Jérôme?'

'As little as possible, Sergeant: I leave it up to you.'

'No other news, you know about . . . messages . . .? Nothing? Oh, well.'

***

'The road along the river is better but this way is much shorter, about forty kilometres or so, I should say. There's a good bridge over the river at Les Vignes; that's about half way.'

'You have the money and the papers?'

'Of course, in this envelope and I know what we have to tell them but you do the talking. Can you remember?'

'When they get to the ticket barrier at Béziers they both turn and make a fuss of waving to somebody who is getting off the train behind them. Then they show their tickets to the ticket collector. A man wearing a straw hat with a black band on it will be waiting for them and will raise his hand when he is sure he has recognised them. He will say his name is Gérard and he has a taxi waiting for them. They need say nothing.'

'Don't drive so fast, Philippe. You're making my teeth chatter.'

'What time is the train?'

'You haven't forgotten already, have you?'

'No; just testing you. It's due at 13.07. If it's like our trains it will be late.'

They drove along in silence for a while. A man swinging a scythe in a fenced-off patch of long dry grass took no notice of their passing. Sheep were grazing in the angel hair with no one apparently guarding them. Perhaps there was a sheep dog lying down out of sight somewhere, keeping an eye on them, as Caramelle was often left to do.

'Shall I open the window? It smells a bit of petrol in here.'

Séverine seemed not to hear. The breeze coming into the car was warm on his face. He wondered if they might be able to have coffee at the station, or lunch. No one had mentioned it when they left St Chely. It was a decent car, a Primaquatre Jérôme had said when asked; the one with the bigger engine because of the hills. Why it went so badly when Jérôme drove, Lawless couldn't understand. Perhaps he'd never learned. That reminded him of something he had decided he would do if he ever got back to England: re-apply for pilot training. He'd had enough of freezing rear turrets, the most dangerous place in the plane. Yes, be a pilot. Sherwood said it was just like driving a bus. Or was it Verrill who said that? He was beginning to forget.

It was shady and cooler where the road ran through woodland but sunlight flickering through the leaves made it harder to see clearly ahead. A sheep charged across the road in front of the car causing Lawless to swerve and stamp hard down on the brake.

'I should have warned you,' she said. 'There's a big farm just ahead, Masselac. They have good grass but not very good dogs and their sheep wander all over.'

'I'm sorry. I wasn't paying attention to the road. Do you want to stay here for a minute?'

'No, stop at the bridge. The road starts going down soon, lots of twists and turns.'

Sometimes ahead, sometimes out of the corner of his eye, he could see the wooded lip of the gorge with its grey ranks of pinnacles and rock towers eroded into fantastic shapes. He fancied he saw a pair of hooded lovers, one gazing down on the other looking up, arches and caves, an alert hound's head, candles, goblets, and above them, soaring and wheeling in the sky, the black ragged specks of birds he knew to be vultures. What better place could there be to hide away, secure from your pursuers than on those heights and among that chaos of wind-worn rocks? Cavallier had known that.

'After the bridge we turn left then sharp right and follow the road up the hill. There used to be a sign for Le Massegros but it may not be there now.'

With the sun hot on their backs they leaned their arms on the iron railing of the bridge and looked upstream. The water level was low, with hardly any flow over a rather tumbledown weir visible on a bend beyond the village. The riverbanks were thick with long dry grass speckled bright red with poppies. The air was still and heavy and the village seemed fast asleep. She seemed to be in an unusually relaxed mood.

'You can't quite see from here but just upstream from that far bend the river squeezes through a very narrow part in a kind of long waterfall. It's called the Pas de Souci. Fabrice once turned over in a canoe trying to paddle through it.'

'Hurt himself?'

'No. Thierry was with him and pulled him out.'

Lawless hesitated then said, 'Do you know where Thierry is now, Sevvie?'

She didn't answer at first. 'On the other side from the top you can see almost all the way up the gorge. It's called the Point Sublime, a very good name for it. I went there with Thierry one afternoon. We climbed up a very steep little path from St Hilaire. No, I don't know what's become of him. You could ask his father when you go to La Couvertoirade.' She turned to look at him. 'You will go, won't you? I would like to know.'

'Yes, I'll go but after we've been to Montpellier.'

'Let's get this over first. It's time we were going.'

The signpost for Le Massegros was missing, but the road was clear enough, snaking its way this way and that up the face of the Sauveterre. By the time they reached the village, steam was rising from the filler cap of the radiator, and Lawless stopped by a fountain in the square to let the engine cool before refilling.

'It's so different here. I never thought it would be like this. You look that way over the gorge to the Méjean and there's another world, empty, stony, silent except for the wind and here it's all fields and farms and sheep bleating everywhere.'

'Which do you like best?'

'I'd give all of this for one cloup on the Méjean. I mean it.'

'Would you fight for it, like your favourite, Cavallier?'

'Isn't that we are doing?'

'The real fighting hasn't started yet, Philippe. That's what you told me. Remember?'

He was about to reply that you had to start somewhere but seeing her expression decided to refill the radiator instead.

'Go left here. I want to give you a surprise.'

The road was hardly more than a cart track winding along a little valley and shaded by overhanging chestnut trees.

'Stop. Look down there. What do you see?'

'A ditch with puddles and a grassy bank. Not a bad place to sit in the shade. If we had anything to eat, that is.'

'It's the source of the Aveyron.'

'Is that the surprise?'

'No, that comes in a minute.'

'Sevvie, why are you telling me all these things: Pas de Souci, Point, what was it, Sublime, now this?'

'For when you come back to live here, Philippe. You need to know these places.'

'Of course, sorry, I should have thought of that.'

'Now, go slowly, just round this corner. There!'

A kilometre away across dry brown fields the fawn-coloured walls and two remaining towers of a half-ruined castle crowned the summit of a conical hill. Houses climbed its sunlit slopes to stop abruptly at the base of the lower ramparts. Above were other long walls, one with a wide gateway and those higher with rows of empty rectangular window spaces.

'Sévérac le Chateau,' she said.

'Can we go see, the chateau, I mean? There must be a wonderful view from up there.'

'Another time perhaps. We have work to do. The station is round to the west.'

They arrived with a quarter of an hour to spare. It was too hot to wait in the car and there was nowhere to sit in the dusty square in front of the station. Lawless held open the creaking double doors of the entrance to allow Séverine through into the passage past the empty ticket office onto the platform. She wrinkled her nose at the smell of the shabby waiting room and found a bench further along the platform, thankfully in the shade. A wooden walkway crossed the track to a central platform patchily covered with tufts of dry grass and weeds. Lawless looked northwards along the track, the direction from which he presumed the train would come. There was a building he thought might be a signal box about two hundred metres away on the other side of the tracks and a little further beyond one of the lines curved away to the west. He listened but could hear no sound but the rustle of a dry leaves stirring on the platform surface.

'Nobody here,' he said. 'Are you sure this is the right day?'

'Someone will turn up soon. There's a policeman about somewhere. That was his bicycle leaning against the wall. Sit down. You'll draw attention to yourself.'

He sat on the bench beside her. A flock of tiny birds hurtled overhead twittering excitedly and just as quickly disappeared. Insects hummed as they hovered around the few tired flowers among the weeds. Everything smelled hot and dusty.

'It's late,' he said, showing her his watch. 'Look: 13.10 now.'

'The policeman has come back. He's watching us. Say something to me.'

'Hear that sort of singing sound, very faint? That's the lines. It's coming all right. Who's that?'

'Station master.'

'I can see it now.'

'Remember: they've been told to step down and look round for someone meeting them.'

'And we act as if we are all relatives, I remember.'

The carriages passed slower and slower and finally the train came to a halt. Lawless was surprised to see so many passengers on it and waited anxiously for one of the doors to open and hoping it would be only one. The stationmaster went to speak with the drivers but the policeman stood where he was, surveying the train carriage by carriage.

'There they are, third carriage along, looking this way. Give them a wave. Why on earth are they dressed like that?'

One man had stepped down onto the platform while the other remained standing on the step. Both were wearing dark trilby hats and long coats. They must have been very hot. Seeing Lawless and Séverine approaching, the one on the platform raised his hand in a tentative wave.

'Wave again. Come on, quick. We haven't much time. Don't forget to embrace both of them.'

Lawless grabbed the first man by both hands and gave him smacking kisses on both cheeks. The man stiffened and started back.

'Don't act so fucking English, you fool!' Lawless hissed at him while Séverine clutched the other man to her and ruffled his hair before kissing him loudly and bursting into tears very convincingly.

'Here: there's two thousand francs and papers for the two of you in this. Shove it in your inside pocket now. Don't let that cop see you doing it! Put your arms round me; go on, try to look upset. You're supposed to be on your way to a funeral. And take those stupid heavy coats off. It's summer down here. Now listen.'

Smiling all the time Lawless gave the man his instructions and made him repeat them.

'You'll have to tell your mate what I said when you're on the train, but not while anybody else can hear. Right? Shit, that's the whistle. Hug me again and get back on.'

'You English, mate?'

'What do you fucking think?'

'You don't look it. Not with that fucking moustache.'

'Thank god for that. Now, get back on and good luck.'

'Same to you, mate. Sure you don't want to come with us?'

The door was closing as the train drew slowly away. One of the men leaned out of a window and waved. Séverine buried her face in Lawless's chest and sobbed loudly. Lawless held her tightly as he watched the train pass under a bridge, curve away to the right and disappear. He looked at his watch. It had all happened in four minutes. The train made other stops on the way south, but they would have to fend for themselves at those before they reached the comparative safety of Béziers station. How long would it be before they got back to England: if they ever did? Lawless found himself wondering how he would get on if he were the one on that train.

'Your papers, Sir.'

'Papers? Ah, of course. Here.'

'"Martin, Philippe" . . . "Airaines" . . . not from round here, Sir?'

'No, born in the North. My wife and I live near St Chely.'

'This is my brother-in-law, Officer. Here is my card.'

'Ah, Chevalier, Mams'elle Séverine, of La Commanderie. I see. Those men on the train, Mams'elle, may I ask who they might be?'

'My nephews, Hervé and Robert. It is very sad, Officer. They are travelling to be present at their uncle's funeral in Lunas, not my brother, you understand, their mother's brother and they are also representing my sister and myself because we cannot travel at present, if you understand me. Perhaps you saw my brother-in-law giving them our letters of condolence.'

'In fact no, Mams'elle but I fully understand that must have been why you met them at the station here.'

'You are very understanding, Officer. Now, after all that emotion, I do feel a little tired. Would you mind if we made our way to the Station Hotel for a little rest and some refreshment?'

'Not in the least, Mams'elle, Sir. Do you know the way?'

'Oh yes, I know it well. We have stayed there on occasion, although more often with the de Laurents. Goodbye to you.'

Lawless put down his glass of rosé. 'I don't know how you do it. You had him eating out of your hand. Is there really a de Laurent family in Sévérac?'

'Naturally. You could never get away with inventing something like that. If you have to deceive, Philippe, always base your untruths on something that is true. If he did happen to mention meeting me to Solange de Laurent she would say, of course, she knows me and what a pity it is that she has not seen me for some time.'

'He fairly melted when you looked up into his eyes and said you could not travel at present, *if you understand me,*' Lawless said, mimicking her voice. 'What did you mean by that?'

'You really haven't noticed yet, have you? Always the seductress, isn't that what you think of me?'

'It seems to be in the family. Not that I have any objections, *if you understand me.*'

'Now you're flirting with me. I think we had better change the subject. Have you chosen?'

'What is aligot?'

'A mixture of melted cheese and potato and cream purée, commonly eaten with sausages but in this restaurant you will have roast pork.'

'Just the thing for a starving sheep farmer like me: I'll have it. And you?'

'Trout Meunière. The trout will be fresh from the Aveyron.'

Lawless looked round the dining room. Most of the tables were occupied and all had small posies of flowers in slender china vases in the centre. There was an occasional sound of cutlery on plate and a hum of quiet conversation. Glasses were being re-filled from time to time by a young waiter. Lawless left the choice of wine to Séverine, saying that he would like to try something local. When the waiter had gone off with their order, Lawless took a morsel of bread from the basket and smiled across the table.

'Still warm: is there really a war on, Sevvie? Look around us.'

'I know what you mean, Philippe, but yes, oh yes, there is a war on. Jèrôme told me things before we left that he said you should know, very bad things.'

'Tell me.'

'Not yet. Eat first. After all, you are in France. Isn't that the sort of joke you English would make?'

'Live for the day, you're saying. My tutor in Oxford said that, in Latin, of course and then she added something else.'

'She? You were taught by a woman?'

'Yes, the one I'm thinking of. She taught me quite a lot. She said live for the day and plan to do the same tomorrow.'

'I think she was very wise. Ah, here is our lunch.'

***

'Take the little road on the left.'

'St Georges . . . something . . . can't read the rest?'

'Not all the way. I'll tell you when to stop.'

He drove slowly along a rutted stony track for a kilometre or so hoping the springs could take it and passed a rundown-looking farmstead at the side of the road.

'Stop here. Now we walk, not very far.'

'Why are you bringing me here? Is this the Point Sublime?'

'Wait and see. We have to climb up that hill. I hope I have the legs for it.'

She had to stop for breath well before they reached the top of the rise.

'Look,' he said, 'this is a game I used to play with my mother when we were hill-walking at home.'

He put his hand on her back just above her waist and pressed hard.

'Now, up you go.'

'That's amazing,' she gasped. 'I feel as if I'm floating. Close your eyes before you reach the top.'

Suddenly the wind was blowing on his face and he felt her take his hands and turn him round.

'There, you can open them now. Look straight ahead, not down.'

He saw the Méjean stretching away into the hazy distance like a brown and green cloth creased and puckered here and there with winding dry valleys and small rock-streaked hills.

'What does it make you feel?'

'Free,' he said. 'It's so enormous it should be overwhelming but it makes me feel free.'

'Fabrice found this place. He said the same as you just did. He told us that he could see Mount Aigoual from here and we had to come and see it as well, Tressie and me. We couldn't see it no matter how hard we tried. I think he was imagining it but that doesn't matter.'

'Perhaps he did see it, or rather a mirage of it. On very hot days such things can happen. You don't have to be in a desert.'

'I never thought of that. He could have seen it after all.'

'So we are on the Point Sublime, are we?

'No. This is higher. I wanted you to see the Méjean. People go to the Point Sublime to look down into the gorge. You can't feel as free down there.'

'Castelbouc?'

'Yes, Castelbouc perhaps. But that's for other reasons.'

'What were you going to tell me, something Jérôme had said?'

'I don't know if I should. I'm afraid it will spoil your mood.'

It was bad news, very bad. Thousands of Jews, men, women and children living in Paris had been rounded up and herded like animals into a cycling stadium and kept there for days in the most awful conditions with no food or water before being sent off to prison camps.

'And who did this? The Paris police. Not the Germans, though they must have ordered it: our own police.'

Her voice was quiet but there were tears in her eyes, from anger or despair he could not be sure. She turned away from him to look again towards the Méjean. The wind blew her hair across her face.

'How could they do such a thing, such a cowardly, terrible thing?'

'Does Mireille know?'

'No and she must never know; not that, Philippe.'

'Wouldn't it be better if she did know? She's so acute, Sevvie. She notices everything, how we look, what we say, what we don't say, every nuance. She will know there's something we're not telling her and she won't stop until she finds out what we're hiding from her.'

'I can't tell her, Philippe. I couldn't bear to see the look on her face when she hears.'

'Thérèse can tell her. We should ask Thérèse. She will know how.'

'I want to go now.'

'Not just yet. Remember what we were saying about feeling free when we looked across the gorge and over the Méjean? Don't say anything, just look; find the farthest-off point you can make out and keep looking at it and then you'll feel all the freedom between here and there. I promise you: you will.'

He stood between her and the wind and held her close with his arms around her and across her breast. After a long time, though not as long as he would have liked, she said she was better now.

'We ought to go. Jérôme will be getting anxious about his beloved old car.'

THE NETWORK

Jérôme Janquet put two cups of coffee on the table and sat down beside Lawless. It was Saturday morning, the day after the drive to Sévérac le Chateau. Thérèse had allowed him to handle the trap all the way to the village this time and had now gone off to do her shopping. He knew that she would also spend time with Madame Bec. He suspected most of the talk would be about babies.

'If all went well at Béziers station yesterday, they should be on their way to Perpignan in a couple of days.'

'Then where?'

'That's not my business but Spain, I suppose, somehow. I don't really know.'

'And what if they were picked up by the police at Béziers? They didn't strike me as very bright and I don't think either of then had a word of French.'

'A police cell in Béziers and then on to the gaol at St Hyppolyte. That's where they keep the runaways. They could be there for weeks before someone gets them out.'

'Is there someone who can do that?'

'I've heard there is but don't ask me who because I can't tell you. We, or rather you two, have done our job and that's enough.'

'Was Madame Lamphier in on this?'

'She is part of the network. That's all I can say. Now, stop asking questions and listen: you'll be glad to hear this. Christian Tollaincourt was in Florac this morning . . .'

Tollaincourt, Lawless thought, Tollaincourt: name rings a bell; then he remembered, Tollaincourt, one of the names on the War Memorial plaque.

'. . . are you listening? Christian, drops in here every day, you must have seen him. Anyway, he was in Florac and the news is now all over the town.'

'You mean about the tunnel being blocked?'

'What else? Everybody he met was talking about it. The police and gendarmes have been knocking on doors and questioning people, the ones on their list, the ones they always chase up when anything happens. I told Christian to let everybody in the village know as well. You can be sure that Henri has been spreading the word where he lives. I haven't seen the paper yet but it's bound to be a headline story. I expect Grandjean will be along here soon. Unless he's been called in by his superiors in Mende to explain himself, of course.'

'You must be feeling satisfied, Jérôme: yesterday Sévérac and now this. Sounds to me as if this could be a good time for us to slip away for that little holiday in Montpellier; get out of the way, if you see what I mean. I think you said something about lying low for a while?'

'Hm, you may be right. If Grandjean does decide to make a visit I should get to know when and I could be on the road to Florac station with you four while he is on his way here. Yes, now I come to think of it that would be a very useful thing to do. Ah, good morning Madame Chevalier. Perhaps you would like coffee?'

'And Jérôme says he can take us to the station.'

'We can't leave Mireille on her own while we're away.'

'Jeannot would be there and Caramelle . . . all right, all right, I'm not thinking straight. How about Madame Bec: would she stay? It would only be two nights.'

'Be quiet a minute. I'm trying to think. What if we could get Mireille to Castelbouc? We could take her in the trap. She would be safe there with Justine. Then Jeannot and maybe Jean-Pierre could look after La Commanderie. If it were at a weekend Jean-Pierre would not be at work and we could give him a nice bedroom, nice enough for Madame Bec as well. I'm sure she would like that. We would have to give them something for their trouble. Let me think about that.'

'Tressie, you are a marvel. You've got it all worked out.'

'It would be lovely to see the sea again.'

'And paddle and go in a boat and swim, perhaps. And eat ice cream. I can't wait.'

'I'll just go back and see Madame Bec and then let's go home quickly to tell Sevvie and Serge. There's a lot to do.'

'You haven't said anything to Mireille yet, have you? About you know what.'

'No and a good thing too, now all this has come up. It can wait until we get back from Montpellier.'

'While you're seeing Madame Bec I'll talk to Jérôme . . . and have a large glass of his red while I'm about it,' he added but that was after she had left.

***

'Can I take the reins along here? You promised.'

'All right but only as far as the top of the hill. Ho! Fleur.'

'Are we going to Castelbouc again?'

'Yes; just for two nights while we are away.'

'So I'll be safe?'

'Yes and because Madame Lamphier wants to hear you play again.'

'Can I swim?'

' Let's see what she says. Now, concentrate on what you're doing.'

'You will stay for lunch,' Justine Lamphier said as if the matter was already decided. 'Call the child down, Thérèse, if you would. I left her choosing one of my peignoirs for her swim. Perhaps you would go with her? You know the place in the river that I use.' She turned to Lawless. 'I go in occasionally, Philippe but only at dusk as I prefer to wear nothing when swimming.'

Mireille appeared trying to look nonchalant in a white lawn robe slightly too long for her. Justine drew the lapels closer and tightened the belt a little.

'Charming,' she said, 'A little daring but you have the figure and colour for it. Now off you go, you two. Back within the hour.'

Passing Philip as he held the door for her, Thérèse gave him an arch sideways glance and whispered,

'Be careful, my Love. She's been dying to get you on her own.'

'I am waiting, Philippe. There is something you want to ask me?'

'I'm not sure that I should.'

'Then of course you must ask and after that I have something to show you.'

'Tell me about the uncle. If I am to meet him, as Thérèse hopes I will, I should like to know what to expect.'

She regarded him evenly and long enough for him to wonder if he might have offended her.

'You can expect the courtesy appropriate to a member of the family.'

'In spite of the long estrangement?'

'You had no part in that and he will have no preconceived opinion of you. You are both scholars and soldiers: useful and important things to have in common.'

'Thérèse hopes old wounds may be healed. As for Séverine, all she said was I should go because of her uncle's library.'

'Séverine and Alexandre are two of a kind: each too proud to be the first to hold out the hand that both long to offer.'

'How do you know this?'

'He is still my lover, Philippe. Surely they have told you that?'

The look on his face was her answer.

'Listen to me, Philippe. As my husband might have put it, you are a new piece on the Chevalier board and you have already changed the game; as Alexandre well knows. Don't look so surprised. I told him about you after the picnic. We often write to each other and meet from time to time. Lovers do, Philippe. The last time was in the week before you and Séverine had your rendezvous with the passengers at Sévérac. We had to make sure the arrangements were in order.'

'Please, you're going too fast. Uncle Alexandre knows about me, now I hear you were the ones who planned the Sévérac rendezvous . . .'

'Solange de Laurent found out about trains and times and so on. We had to make sure the arrangements would work.'

'My god! You are all in it, aren't you, all in the network?'

'We play our part, Philippe. As do you. How did you find the food at the Hotel de la Gare, by the way? Do you really like aligot?'

'You even know what I ate. Was it the waiter who told you?'

'No, the owner. But, Philippe, listen, these are unimportant details. What is important is that you and Alexandre come to terms. I have made it clear to him that this rift has lasted long enough. Closing it will not only bring the family together again but it will also strengthen the network. The matter is now in your hands.'

'I never fail to be amazed by you Chevaliers.'

'Absence of guile is one of your most appealing qualities, Philippe. Now, let me show you my portrait. I keep it in my bedroom.'

'Alexandre wanted me looking as if I had just come from swimming. We had to keep it our secret while my husband was alive.'

' It's like a Renoir. Who was the painter?'

'A young man, hardly known. Lost in the War. Does it still look like me?'

'Yes, he's caught the lights in your hair beautifully and that downward glance.'

'And the rest?'

'Well, you're not . . .'

'Look away. This won't take a moment.' There was a rustle of silk falling to the floor. 'Now, what do you think?'

Sounds of the piano being played came from a room below.

'They must have come back early. Oh dear, we spent too much time talking, Philippe.'

'I don't think you have changed at all, Justine.'

'Can we stop here for a bit, Tressie? That hill seemed a lot steeper than last time I helped push that trap.'

'Take Fleur out of the shafts first and I'll give her a rub. She can graze over there while we sit and have a drink. Justine gave me a bottle of wine for you and some Badoit for me.'

Lawless lay on his back and looked up at the cloudless sky. Good flying weather: not if there were any 109s on the lookout. No need for radar: they could see you from miles away. Why did he have to think about them? Why not? They'd be there when he got back. The sound of liquid being poured made him open his eyes and sit up.

'Glasses too? She thinks of everything, doesn't she? Mm, nice; more please.'

'Philippe: it's Chablis. Don't gulp it. Now, all through the lunch you two kept looking at each other. What has she been telling you?'

'Well, she was very revealing, er, what I mean is she told me all sorts of things you might know but I didn't. She is part of the network as they call it, you know, with Jérôme and us and—did you know this—your Uncle Alexandre?'

'No, I didn't know, but I'm not surprised. He must have been deeply ashamed of what happened in 1940. Did she say anything else about him?'

'Not a lot—he is her lover, by the way: you were right about that. You'll be glad to know she has told him that it's time the family quarrel was sorted out and—I have no idea how I can do this—she's told me I'm the one to change his mind.'

She was quiet for a moment, looking into her glass and pressing her lips together in the way she did when thinking hard.

'You'll talk about regiments and wars—that's what soldiers always do when they meet—and about old books because obviously you're there to see what he has in his library. Take your translation to show him and ask him what he thinks of Cavallier's story. Only after that do you talk about the network—he will be expecting it. He will know about Sévérac, and Justine will have told him what else you have done . . .'

'Active service, we call it.'

'Yes, so when you tell him you think that the network can never be fully effective unless everyone in it, *especially members of the same family*, can trust and rely upon all the others I am sure he will take you seriously. Don't think he won't see what you are up to: it's for you to convince him it has to be done. Who knows? He may simply be waiting for someone to say what he wants to hear.'

'Justine said something like that. You're not all that different from one another, you Chevaliers, are you?'

'Are you saying I am like Justine?'

'You are more beautiful.'

'Hm. Did she show you her portrait?'

'The one in the salon?'

'No, the other one. The one in her bedroom.'

'Which other one? Tressie, there's something else I thought might help to sway your uncle's feelings: our baby.'

'Oh, Philippe, I was hoping you would say that.'

'First birth in the family since which one? Fabrice, a long time ago. Family line goes on: wouldn't that be important to him?'

'It was when we all thought Séverine and Thierry would . . . He is all alone now. Aunt Anne-Marie died years ago. We only heard long afterwards. He has no grandchildren, no one.'

'There's Justine; no chance there now, of course.'

'She has no children. That's how she kept her figure. Look at me.'

'Willingly. Unbutton your dress.'

'You're terrible, you terrible man!'

'Impossible?'

'Now, yes. Perhaps not when we get home. Call Mireille. Help her put Fleur back in the shafts.'

MONTPELLIER

There was no gendarme or policeman at the station in Florac.

'All busy searching for those vile criminals who blocked the line to Clermont,' Valentin said with a smile of relief.

'Jérôme must have a very good spy placed in the Gendarmerie if he knew in advance that Grandjean would be taking the long road to St Chely this morning. Who do you think it is, Séverine?'

'I have no idea and if I did I wouldn't say. You know the rules. I expect he intends to call in on us.'

'He won't get much out of the Becs. Oops, We're moving. How long to Alès, Serge? These seats are very hard.'

'You can never be sure. About an hour to Sainte-Cécile, less if no one flags the train down on the way and we aren't held up behind some train hauling timber. It's a junction so we could have to wait there a bit for the fast train to pass through, now that they can again! Don't worry: we won't miss our connection to Montpellier.'

'I wish I'd brought a cushion.'

The two-carriage train trundled along its narrow track through cuttings and tunnels up the valley of a little river that Thérèse told him was the Mimente, going steadily at first, and then gradually slowing as it climbed through forests of chestnut trees loaded with bunches of spikey nuts.

Valentin pointed out several stretches of the river he said were good for fishing while Lawless resigned himself to an autumn and winter of yet more chestnut-packed meals. They heard the squeaking of brakes taking hold and felt the train jolting as it slowed. With some difficulty Lawless pulled down the window and looked out.

'We're stopping. There's a sign but I can't read it.'

'Cassagnas halt. The land of Cavallier, Philippe,' Séverine said.

'There's a chap getting on the train with a dog and three sheep.'

'He'll be taking them to Sainte-Cécile,' Valentin said. 'It must be market day. It's slow going now up to the col then downhill all the way to Sainte-Cécile.'

'You know St Cécile is the patron saint of music, don't you?'

'Of course; everyone knows that.'

After a rattling and wildly swaying ride down from the col, Lawless was in dire need of a walk up and down the platform at St Cécile d'Andorge to settle both his nerves and his stomach. Although the valley—of the Gardon, Valentin told him—was not much wider, and the steep hillsides just as thickly forested, there was a different feeling and smell to the place that Lawless recognised but could not identify.

'Coal,' Valentin said, 'from the mines further down the valley. The coal trains come through here on their way up north: the ones we hoped to stop at Le Rachas, remember?'

'There're a couple of policemen over there looking at us. No, don't look round. The ladies are coming.'

'Are you feeling any better?'

'Yes. Thank you, Sweetheart. See the policemen?'

'It's all right: they're talking to the driver.'

'I hope they arrest him for speeding.'

'We thought we had better let them see us with you: to make you look more respectable.'

Back on the train Lawless said despite its name he didn't like St Cécile d'Andorge very much and Séverine replied that Cavallier hadn't liked it much either, because it was one of the few Catholic towns in the Cevennes and Rolland had attacked it and burnt it. That set him thinking again about his translation as the train clattered down the line to Alès. He would take it—not the book, Alexandre Chevalier was bound to have his own copy and surely could read English—to La Couvertoirade after Serge had finished with it. There were several things he wanted to ask about the Camisard leaders. They had fallen out in the end, Cavallier and Rolland. Comrades can become enemies when trust is lost. There was a lesson in that. What was it Vabrette had said? Yes: *you have to trust your mates but don't be so sure about the higher-ups.* Hemsworth, in Yorkshire, that was the place he'd been thinking of, and the other colliery villages round about. Railway trucks and black spoil heaps: coal everywhere and the smell of it.

Valentin looked at his watch and ran his finger across the timetable notice. 'Change at Nîmes. There's only a short wait, eight minutes.'

'Lots of police here,' Lawless said, looking along the platform. 'I hope I don't look like a train wrecker.'

'Take Tressie's arm and stroll towards them, Philippe. Pregnant ladies don't usually associate with train wreckers.'

'They don't know who they're looking for anyway,' Valentin said. 'Look: that must be our train coming.'

It was strange, almost unnerving, to feel oneself racing across a flat plain with so many houses and fields and trees being snatched out of sight as the train rushed over and under bridges, closed on a river—not clear like the Mimente but sluggish and muddy brown—and swung away again as if in search of, of what: more little fields of dry brown grass, station platforms gone in an instant, vines in rows, a lorry on a road to chase and pass? This was a foreign land, hot, blurred, indifferent, not one where he belonged. It was worse in the station at Nîmes, so big, noisy, busy, bewildering. Thérèse was looking around, wide-eyed. Séverine and Serge seemed quite at ease, being experienced travellers. Lawless felt relieved and foolish at the same time as he had as a child when his mother finally found him wandering, lost in the crowd at the seaside.

Through an archway he caught a glimpse of an avenue of trees stretching away from a square with people sitting at tables in the shade. Two policemen stood by the ticket collector at the exit gate as passengers handed over their tickets.

'Platform 2 for Montpellier,' said Valentin. 'Come on, we only have a couple of minutes.'

Lawless was sure the policeman at the gate was going to stop him after he showed his ticket, but no, he seemed more interested in two pretty, long-haired girls who pushed past. When they were all finally sitting in the carriage, in much more comfortable seats he realised, he found himself shaking. Sometimes he was like that walking back to the debriefing room after a raid. Five minutes after leaving Nîmes he was asleep with his head resting on Thérèse's shoulder.

'There's Victor!' Thérèse cried, waving frantically.' Victor, Victor!'

A man with short black hair and wearing a white open-neck shirt was chatting and laughing with the policeman and ticket collector at the end of their platform. He must have heard Thérèse calling and turned round to wave back.

'Come on, Philippe! You must meet Victor; oh, it's so long since I last saw him!'

She pulled him by the arm, half-walking, half-running. When she reached the gate she flung her arms round the man's neck and hugged him as if she would never see him again. He held her close, looking over her head and smiling at Lawless. Valentin and Séverine came up and he gently disengaged himself from Thérèse's clasp, embraced them both and turned to Lawless.

'Victor, this is Philippe. You know we're married, don't you? Six months ago.'

'And one week,' said Lawless.

'And one day,' she laughed, wagging her finger at him.

'So long? An old married couple, eh, Philippe? You are a very lucky man. You've snatched this beauty from under my nose, you rogue.' He lowered his voice. 'Listen, I told them that I was meeting you. Let me have your tickets and go through. They won't stop you.'

They waited in the concourse while Victor Dumanoir had their tickets clipped and exchanged more banter with the policeman.

'He knows everybody and everybody knows him,' Valentin said.

'How much does he know about me, Sevvie?'

'Probably more than you think, Philippe. Victor, where have you left Jeanette?'

'Making lunch for us. I've got a car outside. The porter will bring your bags.'

A large gleaming black car with sloping back radiator and wave-shaped mudguards was parked outside the station. It was wide enough for Valentin to sit between the two women in the rear seat. Even the Air Marshal who had once come to inspect the squadron at Topcliffe had not arrived in a car like this. Lawless supposed a man who knew everybody might well own such a beauty.

'Sit by me, Philippe. You haven't been to Montpellier before, have you? I would give you a tour but Jeanette will be waiting. This is a Panhard in case you're wondering. I've only had it for a week. I'm looking after it for a, let's say a client, who had to leave rather hurriedly. Everybody comfortable? Right we go up here—Rue de Verdun—not too much traffic at this time of day. Now, look right, that's Place de la Comédie—it's the real city centre. The opera house is there, good cafes, nice place for a stroll in the evening, never know who you might meet . . .'

'Including some you wouldn't want to meet,' came Séverine's voice from behind.

'Quite so, but worth the risk. We go up this street, Rue de la Loge, lots of shops as you see and there's a covered market: you go in there.'

'There's one in Oxford.'

'What?'

'A covered market.'

'Really?'

'Yes, I sometimes go, I mean I used to go, for breakfast: bread and dripping.'

'You eat bread and dripping? For breakfast?'

'Well things were a bit short in England. Not like here: it looks just like peacetime.'

There was silence after that until the car slowed down at the end of the street for a turn left.

'Rue Foch,' said Dumanoir. We are about half way along.'

The graceful five-storey houses of fawn-coloured stone made the long straight street seem narrower than it really was. Lawless was reminded of similar streets in Paris, except here some of the balconies with their elaborate ironwork were festooned with pink and white oleander and bright red geraniums in terracotta pots. At the far end of the street was a ceremonial arch with a tall central gateway through which Lawless could just make out an equestrian statue of someone.

'Here we are,' Dumanoir said, drawing the car into the kerb and switching off the engine. 'That's our very own little Arc de Triomphe you're looking at.'

'Who's that on the horse?'

There was a snort of disgust from the back seat. 'The monster that betrayed Cavallier. Victor, how can you stand having that staring down at you whenever you leave the house?'

'I rather like the colour, Sevvie. Let's go up.'

Lunch was simple but welcome and delicious, sautéed chicken and salad with cheese and lemon soufflé to follow. Jeanette Dumanoir exclaimed over the pelardons Thérèse had brought. She was slim and elegant in a pale blue skirt and white blouse with a deep Vee neckline and elbow-length sleeves. Spectacles hung from a gold chain round her neck and Lawless thought that she looked particularly attractive when she put them on. They had coffee on a veranda overlooking a courtyard two floors below where the early afternoon sun was shining on water tumbling from a fountain into a white stone basin.

'You can stay here tonight—we have plenty of room,' Dumanoir said, 'see a little of the town later on and come back for supper. I expect you might like an early night. Or you could go straight on to our place by the sea, be by yourselves and listen to the waves or do whatever else you have in mind. It's up to you.'

Before anyone else could say a word, Thérèse burst out, 'Oh, I want to sit outside one of the cafés in the Place de la Comédie and drink wine—even though I shouldn't—and watch the world go by! Philippe, say yes: you'll love it.'

'Well, there you are. Who am I to say no?'

'That's settled then. How about a little rest until it gets cooler? Jeanette?'

'Yes, I'll show you the rooms. They overlook the street but it's quiet during the afternoon in summer.'

'Care for a cigarette on the balcony before you go up, Philippe? Don't worry, I won't keep him too long, Tressie.'

Valentin, who said he had given up smoking—again—picked up the suitcases in the hallway and followed the three women up a flight of stairs.

'Do you own all of this?' Lawless looked round and nodded in the direction the others had gone.

'We'd like to; may do one day. No, it's on a long lease. Our bedroom is on this floor and we both have studies. Jeanette is a teacher, did you know? Upstairs is mainly for guests, bathrooms, a salon, that sort of thing.'

'There's another floor above that, isn't there? Is that yours, too?'

'You notice things, don't you? No, it's empty but we do have access. It comes in useful on occasions.'

Dumanoir did not explain why and Lawless thought it better not to ask. He fumbled in his pocket and brought out the untidy packet of Gauloises.

'Try one of these.' Dumanoir held out a familiar-looking white and blue packet.

'They're English! Where do you get them?'

'From someone I know. Where he gets them I have no idea. Gibraltar, maybe, North Africa . . .'

'North Africa! How on earth . . .'

'The Germans have nearly reached Alexandria in Egypt, Philippe. They captured huge amounts of supplies on the way and some of the cigarettes have found their way here.'

'You're joking.'

'I am not joking, Philippe. The news is very bad, not only from Africa but Russia as well. The Red Army is in full retreat again.'

Lawless looked at the smoke writhing upwards from the cigarette between his fingers. Outside the sun was shining brightly and the faint breaths of air wafting up from the courtyard carried the scent of jasmine. Lunch had been so agreeable, so civilised, full of chatter and joking—how happy and excited Thérèse was to be with her old friends again; and Séverine, he had never seen her so content and, yes, so beautiful, before. And he, well, they had soon made him feel part of it all and he joined in the chaffing and even flirted mildly with Jeanette next to him. In the late afternoon when it was cooler and people came out to see and be seen they would sit under the bright awning of a smart café in that great gleaming square with its fountain in the centre and sip white wine or rosé and criticise or admire the artists with their easels, or ask what the opera was this week, or tell more stories of old times, or simply sit and drink and look around. And tomorrow? The sea, the beaches, the sun going down as the fishing boats went out, sinking into another bed and making love and sleeping and not dreaming. It was just like peacetime: he had said that to them in the car, hadn't he? He stubbed out his cigarette. It didn't taste right.

'I can guess what you are thinking, Philippe. Don't judge us too harshly.'

'I don't, Victor. It's myself.'

'Fresh as a daisy,' he said. 'You look fresh as a daisy. They're waiting for us downstairs. Victor says why don't we walk: it's not very far.'

'Do I look all right?'

'All right? All right! You look gorgeous, pink cheeks, soft red lips, big dark eyes . . .'

'I mean this,' she said, sliding both her hands over her stomach.

'That's the best of all. Let me feel. Is he awake; or is she awake? Or are they both awake?'

'You're impossible.'

'I know. Don't you love it?'

'No wine, thank you. It's not good for me. I want ice cream, though, lots.'

Séverine opted for the same and Lawless could not resist when he saw the tall flared glasses brimming over with swirls of strawberry and vanilla ice cream set down on the table, each with its floral napkin and long-handled silver spoon. It was so cold it made his teeth ache and the others laughed at his screwed-up face.

'Is something wrong, darling? Don't you like it?'

'No, no,' he said wincing *and remembering or was he imagining: shivering cold and something icy and sharp in his throat that made him cough and retch and his head to ache?* . . . No, I'm not used to it, that's all. Hm, better now; god, it's delicious.' Through half-closed eyes he saw the waiter slip a piece of paper under the bill he placed in front of Dumanoir.

'Oh dear, the man over there: one of my clients. I'd rather not bore you with him. I'd better not let him see me. Excuse me for a moment, would you mind?'

'Victor, darling, ask them to bring us more wine, and an extra glass for Philippe,' Jeanette said as Dumanoir made his way towards the café entrance. The folded bill remained on its plate but the slip of paper was no longer there.

'Does Victor have many clients, Jeanette?'

'I sometimes think that he must be the only lawyer in Montpellier, Philippe. He's always busy. He must have made a special effort to spend so much time with us like this.'

'Sorry to leave you by yourselves for a minute. I have to, you know . . .' Lawless stood mouthing *loo* silently to Thérèse.

'Straight through to the back; the door sticks,' Séverine said, giving him a certain kind of look.

There was no sign of Dumanoir in the café. Lawless looked enquiringly at a waiter who silently pointed to the rear of the room where Lawless found the door marked 'Toilette'. Next to this, slightly ajar was another door with frosted glass panels. Lawless pushed it fractionally further open and recognised Dumanoir's voice speaking to a man seated at a table, listening and nodding his head. His fair hair was rather long for a man of his age, about fifty, Lawless guessed. He thought he heard Dumanoir say something like 'tomorrow, then, or the day after; I can't be there but Jeanette will,' then there was the sound of a chair's legs scraping as someone stood up so he pushed hard on the toilet door and went inside.

The others were all standing up when Lawless got back to the table.

'Philippe, there you are. We were just thinking about a little stroll, along as far as the Opera.'

Stopping here and there to greet or be greeted by people he evidently knew, Dumanoir lagged behind, finally catching up with the others as they stood in front of the Opéra-Comédie. It had three wide entrances but the doors were closed. Above were three huge arched windows and above those a balustrade with statues and a clock enclosed in what looked like wings of stone. In the space in front of the entrances were tables and chairs shaded by parasols.

'It's been burned down three times,' said Dumanoir. 'Let's hope this one lasts.'

'So long as the English don't drop bombs on it,' Séverine breathed in Lawless's ear.

'What do you think, Philippe?'

It reminded Lawless of a railway station he had once seen but where, he could not remember. He thought the library in Peckwater Quad was more beautiful even if the stone wasn't as clean as here.

'Imposing,' he said. 'Is it open tonight?'

'Closed for the season; re-opens in the autumn, although we haven't seen a programme yet,' Jeanette said. 'It's later than usual. Things aren't as certain these days as they used to be.'

After supper Dumanoir apologised and said that unfortunately he would not be able to take them to their seaside place tomorrow. Something urgent had come up that he had to deal with but of course Jeanette would go with them. Lawless asked where it was.

'Palavas, Palavas-les Flots.'

'Is it far?'

'Fifteen kilometres: there's a train.'

'I feel like some sort of film star in this dressing gown.'

'Come to bed, Philippe. I'm so tired. What are you doing there at the window?'

'Just watching the sunset. It's all apricot and red.'

He heard a door close somewhere in the street and casually looked down just in time to see the black Panhard pull away from the kerb and drive off in the direction of the Place de la Comédie.

It was a funny old black tank engine with three shabby green carriages that might have been standing in a railway museum were it not for the smoke that was pulsing from its tall funnel and steam hissing round its wheels. A family with children and two or three other people were already seated in the first carriage so they went to the last to be on their own. A whistle blew, wheels raced and grated and with a shudder and loud clanking noise the train began to move. The city was soon left behind and the train rattled through drab marshland in the middle of which it stopped briefly at a small station with the name Lattes on a platform notice to allow a solitary man to board and carried on until it reached a narrow weed-covered causeway that crossed an immense shallow lagoon stretching out of sight on both sides. A narrow bridge carried the track over a canal running inside the lagoon along its entire length. Lawless had a brief glimpse of barges with smoke drifting upwards from their chimneys and people cycling along the canal towpath. Seconds later he felt the engine's speed slacken and the train slowed to a stop in the shade beside a very low and rather short and dusty platform.

'Serge, what was all that water we crossed?'

'Over there it stretches all the way to Agde and the other way as far as the Rhone mouth. Different parts have different names; here it's the Étang de Pérols.'

'Hm, I can smell the sea. Do you know that chap?'

'What chap?'

'The one who got on at Lattes. I thought he was looking at you. He's gone now.'

'I didn't notice anyone.'

'This is our hideaway,' Jeanette said. 'It's only a cabin really but it's nice inside—and bigger than it looks.'

It was only a few metres from the beach, a solid-looking single-storey wooden cottage with a red tiled roof set among drooping green branches covered with the pink dusty-looking flowers of tamarisk that gave it some shelter from any onshore wind.

'Five minutes from the baker's, ten seconds from the sea: we catch the rainwater. There's a big tank at the back with a filter. If it gets low a man comes from Palavas with a tank on his lorry. There's even a little shower room and loo. Don't worry: it flushes. We have a septic tank. Come in.'

It was as comfortable and simple and well equipped as Lawless guessed it would be, having seen how the Dumanoirs did for themselves in the Rue Foch. While Jeanette was showing Thérèse and Séverine the other rooms he went out again, pushed through the tamarisks and found himself on the edge of a smooth yellow sandy beach that sloped gently to the edge of the sea less than a hundred metres away. The Mediterranean, at last—and as blue and calm as it was in Cézanne paintings he remembered, with a sky above that was just as blue but a tiny bit pinkish and hazy. He closed his eyes and let the sun begin to make his skin tingle from its heat. The waves made a faint hissing sound as they crept over the sand. He could smell salt and seaweed and very faintly, wood smoke.

'Philippe! Where are you? Jeanette's leaving.'

'The train leaves in half an hour, Philippe. If you come with me there's just time enough to show you where the baker is and a little restaurant we know where you could have supper tonight. No need to bother about lunch. I packed a basket for you. You'll find wine and beer in the store room.'

She leaned out of the carriage window to say goodbye.

'You've made her so happy, Philippe. I can't thank you enough. I'm very fond of Thérèse, you know. I thought it would never happen for her, being married—and a baby as well. Have you thought of names?'

'Nothing decided: we keep thinking of new ones and arguing. One thing is certain: there'll be a Chevalier family name among them.'

'Séverine as well and Serge: I'm so pleased. You know, she's told me….'

The stationmaster's whistle squealed and her voice was lost in the answering blast from the engine. He must remember what she had said: six o'clock tomorrow evening at Montpellier station. Victor would meet them. He marched off along the lane back to the cottage with his baguette under his arm, feeling very French.

Of course, there were parasols in the storeroom, big ones with pink and white stripes and steel pointed shafts for ramming deep into the soft sand and chairs and a collapsible table for setting out the food and wine. They sat in the shade, with the waves not quite reaching their feet and ate paper-thin slices of dry-cured ham and melon and ewe's milk cheese that Valentin said must have come from the Pyrenees.

'Have you been there, Serge?'

'Once, after they turned me down for the Army. I wanted to get as far away from Grenoble as quick as I could and prove to myself they were wrong so I went climbing alone in the Pyrenees, as high as I could go and I didn't care where. I got lost and wandered about and then the clouds opened and I saw a col and thought if I went down the other side there might be a village or a hut or somewhere to stay. When I got there I could see nothing but scree slopes and rocks and more peaks further on. I felt I must be in Spain.' Valentin stopped speaking and he smiled.

'Go on, Serge. What happened next?'

'I was wrong. I was very tired so I sat down behind some rocks out of the wind and I must have dozed off—I know, shouldn't do that in the mountains. When I woke up there was a man looking at me: must have been trying to decide if I was dead before he went through my rucksack. He shook his head when I asked him where I was in Spanish. It turned out he spoke Catalan but he did know some French and told me where I was: just inside Andorra! He must have been a smuggler . . .'

'Very useful people, smugglers,' Séverine said, 'especially these days.'

'Why he took pity on me I don't know. He must have thought I was mad. He kept looking at me and tapping his head but he beckoned me to follow him back down the way that he'd come and after a few minutes he showed me a sort of track I'd certainly never have found myself and said if I followed that I would get to a road. He was as good as his word and if he hadn't been I wouldn't be here now drinking this rather good wine of Victor's.'

'Don't stop there, Serge. Tell us the rest of the story,' Thérèse pleaded.

'Another time: I want to swim. How about the rest of you?'

Lawless jumped up and seized Thérèse's hand. 'Come on, Sweetheart, you loved it last night in the moonlight and you did, Séverine, admit it, wet dress and all. Oh, all right then, at least come for a paddle while we swim, no getting out of it, lift those hemlines up: there's nobody watching.'

'We didn't bring the towels.'

'Afterwards: I'll go for them afterwards.'

Sand was still sticking to his feet when he opened the door of the cabin so he began shuffling them on the mat set there for the purpose.

'Enjoy your swim?'

'Christ! Who are you?'

'Friend of Victor's—and Séverine's. I sometimes come here.'

'Wait a minute, you were on the train, got on at that place, what's it called . . .?'

'Lattes.'

'Yes, Lattes.' *Longish fair hair, faint accent.* 'You were the one talking to Victor in that bar in the Place Comédie, weren't you? The two of you were arranging this. You're Dunbar, aren't you? I've heard of you.'

'Not too much, I hope. Hm, Dunbar, that's the name I go by. By the way, it's the Place *de la* Comedie. Better get it right, if you want to pass as a Frenchman.'

'Why are you here?'

'Listen, you've obviously come for something to take back to the beach, so I haven't much time. I know all about what you and the others are doing up on the Méjean. Don't look so surprised. We're on the same side: ask Séverine and Serge.'

'Don't worry: I will.'

'And quite right too. Don't take anything on trust from a stranger. Now, there's one thing for you to know and one thing for you to do. Your life may depend on the first and a lot of other people's on the second. No, let me speak. Leave your questions to when I've finished. First thing: you are going to have to get out of here at some point, no matter what you think your obligations are because, believe me, you will be caught eventually if you don't. And there's another reason that you know without my having to tell you. When the time comes, you will be told and you will then do *exactly as instructed.* Understand, Sergeant? *Exactly.* Consider it an order from a superior officer—Captain in the Seaforths, if you want to know—that you get away.'

'May I ask why am I so important . . . Sir?'

Dunbar looked exasperated for a moment and then said calmly,

'Because of what you are, Sergeant; someone of value to your Service and also because of what you will be taking with you.'

Lawless remained silent, expressionless.

'Aren't you going to ask what it is?'

'I expect you're going to tell me anyway, Sir.'

Dunbar's face relaxed into a grin. 'All right, Philippe—that's right, isn't it? This isn't a First Year Oxford tutorial. All I can tell you at the present is that you will be carrying very important information: too important to be sent by the primitive signalling systems we are cursed with here. You know the expression "by hand of officer only"? Well, we haven't any officer as well equipped as you are to pass as a Frenchman, so,' he said, his grin becoming almost mischievous, 'a Sergeant Gunner from Kendal will have to do.'

'Thank you, Sir,' Lawless said, smiling back at him.

'You're a cheeky sod. It could get you into trouble one day.'

'That's what Querrell said, Sir.'

'Hm, Querrell, yes, I expect he'll stop over with you again on his way back south. Listen to what he has to say.'

'I will, Sir. I think we got on quite well together. The towels, Sir: they'll be getting cold waiting for them on the beach.'

'Why are you standing there, then?'

'Well, you haven't told me when and where I'm to be given this very important information . . . Sir.'

'Oh, yes. You're planning to visit La Couvertoirade some time soon, aren't you? Alexandre Chevalier will have it for you. When, I don't yet know. You'll be told. Now, off you go. Don't keep the ladies waiting.'

'Sorry I took so long. I found a chap in the cottage who wanted to tell me something. He seemed to know everything about me.'

'Oh, Dunbar: Victor said he was coming. I saw him get on the train at Lattes.'

'Séverine, why don't you tell me these things?'

'It's best to wait and see if what you're told will happen actually does, Philippe. Serge, hold the towel up while I take off this wet dress.'

'How would you like to go to the cinema tonight, after supper? It's «Mayerling»: Danielle Darrieux, Philippe? Charles Boyer, Tressie?'

'Victor, how lovely! Oh yes, let's all go. It's our last night.'

'We can walk there; and eat ice cream in the street on the way back.'

'Let the others go on ahead, Philippe,' Victor said. 'I don't want Tressie to hear this.'

He's going to ask me about Dunbar, Lawless thought as he watched the others walk along the platform to the waiting train.

'When you see Jérôme Janquet, tell him he's got the go-ahead for Balsièges. Just say that. He'll know what to do. And see that he gets this envelope: it's urgent. It was good to meet you at last, my friend. Séverine was right about you. I know we can trust you now. Give my best to Alexandre when you see him, and to Justine. Watch your step there,' he said, half closing one eye. 'I know what I'm talking about.'

On their way to the station, Lawlesss stared through the car window, trying to see as much as he could of the bustling streets and shops and cafes and even the posters on the noticeboards all the way to the station so that he might remember everything about the careless time that they had enjoyed in this sparkling city that seemed so far away from the War. He turned once to say something to Thérèse but her eyes were closed. Was she dreaming of the cottage or their love-making on the bed he had made as soft as he could on the beach, or the ice cream, or the film last night? No, not the film with the sad ending because she was smiling: the beach, then.

Thérèse snuggled up close to him and took his hand as the train pulled away from the platform.

'You seemed to get on very well together, you and Victor. I'm so glad. What do you think of Jeanette? Very pretty, very chic, no?'

'Charming. Very good cook, too.'

'Pff! I know what you're thinking. I don't mind. You're with me now. Wasn't it wonderful? I'm going to remember these past three days as long as I live.'

'So am I, my love, so am I.'

ALEXANDRE CHEVALIER

It was his turn to act as shepherd which meant little more than sitting in whatever shade he could find or failing that, pulling Fabrice's floppy straw hat further down over his eyes and letting Caramelle do the watching. It left plenty of time to think although that wasn't too easy with everywhere he looked—grass, tangled rocks, far-off hills—blurred and shimmering in the heat of a late August afternoon. So his thoughts came and went piecemeal, like shreds of paper from torn up letters fluttering past in the wind—no word from Jérôme, perhaps he's away . . . no one does anything in August in France . . . what was that about Balsièges....Serge said something about it once . . . vultures up there . . . two of them, circling, quartering the sky . . . they'd spot a Messerschmidt miles away . . . bees never stop, not even in August: there's one burrowing into that blue flower, only the tip of its arse showing . . . does a bee have an arse . . . Grandjean, what's he up to these days . . . no word yet from Jérôme . . . Séverine said let the enemy think you've gone away, then . . . Séverine in that wet dress . . . sure she's putting on a bit of weight . . . still makes you tingle a bit when she looks at you in that way though . . . hope Tressie's going to be all right . . . time to see the doctor again Madame Bec said . . . need Jérôme's car . . . must have dozed off . . . where's Caramelle, oh, all right, she's there . . . wouldn't like to get on the wrong side of Dunbar . . . shoot you without a thought if he had to . . . *exactly as instructed* . . . officer talk . . . *army* officer . . . give his best to Alexandre . . . next week Serge says, before school starts again . . . Justine as well . . . Justine next to that portrait, without a stitch on . . . bloody hell . . . don't even think about it . . . not about Sherwood either or Jack Verrill, not for ages . . . what was in that envelope for Jérôme . . .

Mireille found him fast asleep in the meagre shade of a straggly box tree with Caramelle at his side. She had to tap him on the shoulder three times before he woke and took the bottle of cider held out to him.

'Danke schön, Fräulein Chevalier.'

'Bitte schön, Herr Lawless. Serge, Herr Valentin, sagt, wenden Sie sich bitte an das Haus zu kommen.'

'The house, er, das Haus?'

'Ja. Ich werde den Schafen bleiben. Jeannot kommt.'

'Waren Sie mit einer Mathematikstunde?'

'Nein, ich werde das Klavier zu spielen.'

Lawless got to his feet and stretched his arms wide.

'Ich mehr . . . er . . . spiele . . . shit! I'd better speak French: I ought to play more. What were you playing, the Gymnopédies? You play them so well, much better than I do.'

'Ich mehr spielen sollte. No, the others, the *Gnossiennes.* Mr Valentin says they are dances from an ancient palace in Greece.'

'I think he may have meant the composer imagined them so. Oh, there's Jeannot coming. I'd better go. It might be urgent.'

Valentin was waiting in the courtyard with the bicycles. Ten minutes later they were sitting outside the café in St Chely waiting for Madame Janquet to bring the beer.

'The station at Balsièges.'

'But Jérôme, we suggested that once before and it was turned down.'

'This is different, Serge, and a lot simpler: no one gets hurt but plenty of trouble is caused. What we do is destroy the signal on the line from Mende to Le Monastier.'

'Why not one on the main line down from Neussargues, or the signal box? That would cause a lot more trouble.'

'Because this is a trial to see if it can be done, and to find out any problems before going on to something bigger. Standard military procedure, Serge.'

'Listen to the Sergeant, Serge. He knows what he's talking about.'

'How do we do it?'

'We blow it up, Philippe.'

'Your friend at Le Bleymard: he's finally come through as he promised?'

'Louis? Yes: dynamite and detonators. Henri can tell you the details.'

'Gelignite, not dynamite, Jérôme. I'm to pick him and the stuff up on the tenth and bring him here.'

'What kind of detonator, Henri?'

'Fuse attached; ninety seconds a metre burn; that's enough to give us about three minutes to get away.'

'How far can you run in three minutes, Corporal?'

'I could cover a kilometre if I knew two sticks of gelignite were just under my arse but you and Serge are going to be waiting for me and Louis only a hundred metres away.'

'Mind you don't trip up. So we're part of it as well, are we? Not Séverine? She won't like that, Jérôme.'

'Mams'elle Chevalier will be elsewhere, Philippe; without Serge here as Henri said because school will have started well before then. All right, that's enough for now. All we have to do is wait for Louis Costain. Oh, by the way, you will be the driver, Philippe. You will use my car. Please be careful with it.'

'You couldn't let us have it for our trip to La Couvertoirade, could you? We plan to go at the weekend.'

'Hm hm, no, too risky, I think. I'm becoming a little worried about informers. I know that the Gendarmerie in Florac is getting quite a lot more anonymous letters these days. I'm sorry, still, fit young chaps like you: a bicycle ride like that is just what you need. Good exercise.'

Vabrette and Valentin started an intense discussion about which was the better stream for trout, the Mimente or the Chassezac so Lawless went inside to look for the local paper.

'Glad you came in, Philippe There's something I was wanting to tell you. It doesn't concern the other two, although it might; Henri I mean, not Serge.'

'Is it about La Couveroirade, Jérôme?'

'Partly, but mainly Castelbouc and Madame Lamphier. We are not certain yet but we have been warned there may be danger coming their way and if that is so we shall have to deal with it or the whole network could suffer.'

Jérôme Janquet's tone and the serious frown on his face sent a chill down Lawless's spine. Nothing like this had been said before. He thought of Thérèse and Séverine, my god, yes and Mireille and suddenly the carefree times seemed over and a long way off, just like that cold feeling he used to get when the afternoon briefing revealed what a bloody dangerous target they'd been assigned and the banter and the boozing in the pub the night before vanished from his mind.

'You remember the passengers you met on the train at Sévérac? That went well. They have been sent further on their way like all the others before them but now it seems that someone may have talked. We don't yet know who or how much was said but we expect the network is soon going to be tested.'

'How?'

'Everything is being done to find out but so far all we know is it is something to do with passengers.'

'In that case shouldn't you cancel Balsièges?'

'No. Look at it this way, Philippe. If we are successful there our enemy will think we are completely unaware that we are being sought and are easy prey for whatever action they have in mind. No, we stick to our plan and wait for them to show.'

'What about us and La Couvertoirade? Should we put that off?'

'Again, no. Chevalier will have ideas once he sees the message from Victor Dumanoir that you are taking.'

'I am?'

'Yes, there was a separate envelope for him in the one you brought for me.'

'I'm beginning to get used to these things going on behind my back.'

'It has to be like that, Philippe. I am sure you don't tell me everything you get up to. But believe this: whatever is important for you to know will always be told to you.'

'I'll hold you to that promise, Jerome: as soon as you find out what this 'test' as you call it, is going to be, I want to be the next to know.'

'You have my word. Now, let's go outside before those two come to blows about trout streams. I don't think Serge would have much of a chance.'

***

'You still look tired, Tressie. Why don't you rest? I'll take the trap to Castelbouc for Mireille. Jeannot will come like a shot if I ask him.'

Thérèse was secretly relieved not to be asked to go. Montpellier had been a delight but the journey home was very tiring, especially the jolting ride from Alès to Florac.

'Don't forget the nosebag for Fleur. Jeannot knows where it is. And the bucket . . .'

'I know, I know: don't fuss.'

'Embrace Justine for me.'

'Tell the men where I've gone when they come back.'

'Sevvie, you'd better hurry before Philippe gets back or he might want to come with you. And you know what Justine is like.'

Don't worry. I'm off.'

'They're young, my dear. Let them have a little time to themselves. They look charming together under the almond tree, don't you think? She's been so good. I have loved having her here. I think she must have tried on every one of my dresses and she eats like a horse. How she stays so slim, I can't imagine. And such a pianist! She played for me every night. We even attempted a duet or two but she's so much better than me. I could see she was being very patient. She should have a teacher; yes, yes, I know, impossible. No one must know about her. Now, tell me about Montpellier. I want to know everything.'

'Tressie loved every minute and so did I . . .' Séverine told Justine all about the sights in the Place de la Comédie, and seeing *Mayerling* at the cinema—"How I wept when I saw it!' Justine cried—and the ice cream they ate and bathing at night at Palavas les Flots and it all took a long time because Justine asked countless questions. Only at the end did she mention Dunbar and what Lawless had said about him.

'I know something of that. Alexandre and I are in touch, you know. We see each other from time to time.'

'You remember Philippe is going to see him.'

'Yes. That will be important. I also know what Victor asked Philippe to take to La Couvertoirade and as one of the network you should know too. It was Alexandre himself who said that, Séverine. I can see from your face how much that means to you. Our information is still incomplete but this is what we know so far.'

Jeannot drove the trap all the way back to La Commanderie, scarcely able to conceal his delight in having Mireille at his side. Séverine sat on the bench behind, almost oblivious of the journey home. There was so much to think about and plan for from what Justine had told her, especially one of her last remarks.

You can't keep any secrets from me, my dear. I am really delighted and I am not surprised. But you must be very careful and look after yourself.

***

'You did say 90 kilometres, didn't you? That's going to take me all day and a good bit of tomorrow. Where do we sleep?'

'It's true, then: I've heard the English don't really like cycling.'

'It was handy having a bike in Oxford. It's very flat there.'

'Well, if it's any comfort, except for one stretch its mostly flat or down hill all the way to La Couveroirade.'

'Don't tell me about the bit that's uphill.'

'It's best to get as far as we can before the sun really warms up so let's go. And don't make so much noise. You'll wake the others up.'

Pedalling across the Causse with Valentin pointing out the menhirs and dolmens on the way and scattering a flock of sheep when they turned a corner in a hamlet he was told was Hures was quite fun but skidding and braking round endless hairpin bends on the descent into the valley of the Jonte river would store up nightmares for him, Lawless was sure. He insisted on stopping in Meyrueis to search for a café and calm his nerves over coffee with cognac in it. There were hard-boiled eggs and rolls and sausages on the counter that helped raise his spirits further and by the time they left the little town with fresh baguettes in the saddlebags Lawless felt all was well with the world, for a while anyway. The road out of Meyrueis hugged the right bank of the river Jonte and they dawdled along it in the cool of mid morning, occasionally stopping to stare up at some particular pinnacle or cave that Valentin knew by name in the seemingly endless vertical cliffs looming over the gorge. Lawless thought he had better ask.

'Do you come for fishing here as well?'

'Not bad for trout. There are quite a lot of coarse fish, perch and such for those who like that sort of thing. I don't come much. You know the waters I like best.'

'Look—down there. I think the river's disappeared.'

'Where? Oh, there. It flows underground quite a way except when there's a lot of water coming down. It's usually very low at this time of the year.'

An hour later they came round a bend and there before them was another vast gorge yawning wide on their right. A high stone bridge arched across this new river that joined the Jonte and they stopped to look over the parapet.

'Well, you know this one river, my friend. At least further up you do. Castelbouc is forty kilometres upstream from here.'

And Sherwood and Verrill and the others? A bit further on. 'What's this place?'

'Le Rozier; that's Peyreleau on the other side.'

'Pretty names. Time for another coffee? Or a beer?'

'There's nowhere here. It's only an hour to where we turn off this road. I know where we can get a drink there and some lunch as well, if we get a move on.'

'I'm going to walk up most of that,' Lawless said, eying the road that wandered from side to side up the ever-steepening southern wall of the valley as if desperately searching for an easier way and never finding one. 'I'll see you at the top.'

'The climb is worth it; I promise you. It's clear today: you'll be able to stand on one Causse, the Larzac and look across three others, the Sévérac, the Sauveterre and the Méjean.'

'Promise me a sit down and a drink and I'll believe you.'

'You English! Think of Cavallier: know your country. Even I who have never been one know a soldier should do that.'

He's right; but my legs ache. 'I'm coming.'

The sun was now very hot on his back but a little breeze was helping to dry the sweat that soaked his shirt. Valentin swept his arm round in a half circle from north to south.

'What did I tell you?'

Half-remembered lines of poetry by Keats sprang up in Lawless's mind, something about Stout Cortez with eagle eyes staring at the Pacific, silent, upon a peak in Darien. He felt like that now. It was like an ocean, the Causse, through scrubby brown, not blue, and spotted with greenery, dwarf box and broom and splotched red with poppies, not white-topped waves but its surface gently swelled and troughed like an ocean; and it had islands, only these were twisted and buckled pillars and piles of rock, not coral atolls. But most of all, like an ocean it was immense.

'Did you hear me?'

'What? Oh, yes, yes, you were right.'

'Look, down there, the gorge, all the way we came.'

'I don't want to look down there. I like it better up here. There aren't any walls, I mean cliffs, shutting you in.'

They cycled slowly through a silent dusty village that was all shuttered windows and time-eroded massive walls and half-ruined towers, where nothing stirred in the glaring heat except an indolent dog lying outside one doorway that raised its muzzle for a second and then decided they were not worth the effort of following or even barking at.

'Templars were here first, then the Hospitallers, then, well you know the rest: priests, farmers, shepherds, hunters, miners in the valleys. That's the history of the Causses. There are quite a few places like this: you'll see.'

'I won't be sorry to see the back of this one. That dog looked as if it was the last thing left alive here.'

'This is the turn,' Valentin said, peering at his map, 'about five more kilometres and we're there.'

'Serge, I've no idea where he lives or what he's like. He may not even know we're coming.'

'Oh he'll know we're coming all right and if he's anything like the other Chevaliers we'd better tread gently, certainly to begin with.'

'Hm, Justine said something like that. She told me the Chevaliers were not like other families.'

'Justine, is it? Reveal any other secrets, did she?'

'I don't know what you mean.'

The road to La Couvertoirade soon degenerated into little more than a meandering lane of loose pebbles flattened in two parallel tracks by cartwheels and bordered with straggly shrubs coated in orange dust. Wilted grass and weeds and piles of sheep droppings filled most of the space between the tracks. Fearing damage to the tyres, the two men ended up walking most of the way.

Their first sight of any human activity was a windmill crowning a small reddish bare-topped hill.

'Well, at least someone's alive, Serge. The sails are moving.'

A few moments later they caught a glimpse above the bushes lining the lane of red tiles and grey stone.

'More walls and towers, Serge. How do we get inside?'

'There must be a gateway somewhere.'

'Careful: there may be archers on those walls just waiting for the likes of us.'

'Are you ever serious? Better not be like that when we meet him.'

'There's the gate, at the bottom of that square tower.'

There was a cobbled passage through the gothic gateway that branched into streets either side of a tall house with a set of stone steps climbing up to a bolt-studded door. They stood for a moment, undecided as to which way to take or whether they were already looking at the house they sought.

'Follow me, gentlemen. You are expected.'

The speaker was already walking away from them along the left hand street evidently assuming they would follow without question. He led them round corners and through dark narrow alleyways and finally out into a small square half in the shadow cast by a large stone house with grey tiled roof that stood on its own mound close to the town wall.

Deeply worn stone stairs led up to a doorway taller than the portal that led into the town.

'Machines there, gentlemen. I will see to them.'

Despite his limp their guide was quicker up the steps than they could manage and had opened a massive studded door and was standing straight as a sentry by the door-post waiting for them catch up. Despite the heat of the day he was hatless and wearing a blue military tunic buttoned to the throat and with the left sleeve sewn up short at the elbow. Standing in profile and staring straight ahead with his bushy moustache bristling he might have been one of Napoleon's Old Guard, without the shako.

'Inside gentlemen—straight along the corridor—door at the end—knock twice and wait.' Lawless recognised the tone and pushed Valentin inside.

'Enter.'

There were two doors in the room, the one they had just opened and the other in the wall to the left, and two tall windows opposite with shafts of sunlight slanting through narrow gaps in heavy curtains. The rest of the wall-space as high as the ceiling was hidden by books of every size and thickness and type of cover with more, filling bookshelves standing inside the room and stacked in unsteady looking piles on the floor.

Alexandre Chevalier was staring down at a table that was covered with papers and yet more books, several of which were open. He turned towards them, bowed imperceptibly to each man but made no move to shake hands.

'I am Alexandre Chevalier. You have come some distance.'

Lawless remembered to say he was enchanted to make his acquaintance.

'Philip Lawless.'

'Serge Valentin, enchanted.'

Again the imperceptible bows. Alexandre Chevalier murmured to each that he was enchanted too.

'Ninety kilometres. On bicycles.'

'A taxing journey on such a hot day. Sylvestre will show you where to wash. There will be some cool lemonade waiting for you on the terrace.'

'Hand me that towel, please. They all have that look about them, don't you think, the Chevalier men? Tall, wiry, long straight nose, sharp eyes looking directly at you—have you seen that portrait in the bedroom at La Commanderie, the one of the soldier, and the photo of Fabrice? All the same.'

'Thérèse isn't like that. Different hair.'

'She takes after her mother, Serge. Séverine has the look, though. Better get a move on; that drill sergeant won't like being kept waiting.'

In fact only Alexandre Chevalier was standing on the terrace, indicating a table where two glasses of pale cloudy liquid awaited them. Lawless took a sip. It was cold and delicious.

'Sylvestre's wife makes the lemonade. I doubt if you will see her. He serves at table.'

'It's very good,' Valentin said.

'Everything she makes is very good, as I feel sure you will discover at dinner which, by the way, we take at six-thirty. I hope you will forgive my leaving you to your own devices until then. Sylvestre will be here shortly to show you to your rooms. He will have already taken your belongings there. Ask him for anything you may need.'

'We have two packages for you,' Lawless said. 'One is from Victor Dumanoir and the other is from me, or rather, us.'

Alexandre Chevalier looked enquiringly at him and waited.

'It is my translation of Cavallier's "Memoirs . . . of the Wars of the Cevennes" . . . improved by my friend Serge, from a copy in English given me to read at La Commanderie. Doubtless you have copies in your library but should you have a moment to glance through what I have done, I should greatly appreciate it. I will ask Sylvestre to bring both packages to you.'

Chevalier regarded him gravely for a brief moment then gave his almost imperceptible nod of the head and left the two of them to continue with their lemonade.

'What do you think?'

'So far, so good: he's impressed by your French. I didn't see him wince once. Let's hope he finds that you write as well as you speak.'

'If he bothers to read it.'

'Oh, he'll read it all right. Doing that is part of his assessment of you, and me, I suppose. It was a good move to start with Cavallier and slip in a mention of La Commanderie. He will have noted that. It's what he would have done himself in your shoes. Now we have to play the rest of our cards in the right order: the network . . .'

'Justine has been in touch with him about me, I know.'

'Oh, I'm sure she has. Do you think she told him everything?'

'I'll ignore that. I hope you find a chance to bring up the work you've been doing on the poet.'

'We'll see. You know as much as I do about him now.'

'We are sure it's a he, are we?'

'Of course we are sure! What a stupid question.'

'Just asking. Smarten yourself up, man. I can hear Sylvestre coming. I fancy a bit of a lie down before dinner; what about you? I hope there's a view over the wall.'

'Your rooms are on the floor above, Gentlemen. Follow me.'

Sylvestre rapped out information as he led them along the corridor towards the staircase.

'Dining room here. Music room off.'

'Music room? Is there a piano?'

'There is an instrument in there, yes. Not been played for a long time now, not since, well never mind that. Salon there: not used since Madame died. Study. Documents Room. Gun room. Right, up we go.'

'Whose is the portrait?'

'Colonel's father. This one: grandfather. That one: great grandfather; see the ship? In the Navy, he was. Along here: you there, Sir, and you in there, Sir. The Necessary's along the corridor at the end. I see you have a watch, Sir. What time do you make it?'

Lawless looked at his wrist. 'Five-thirty.'

'Same as mine,' Sylvestre said, holding up a large silver pocket watch up to the light. 'Never misses a second, this doesn't. Six twenty-nine at the dining room door, Gentlemen. Try not to be late.'

There were four places set for dinner. Alexandre Chevalier noticed Lawless glance towards the end of the long oak table.

'Sylvestre still insists on setting a place for my wife. I do not object. He was devoted to her. I hope you find your rooms comfortable.'

'Perfectly,' Lawless said while Valentin nodded vigorously in agreement. 'I have a fine view over the walls and across the Causse as far as the horizon. I could not have wished for anything better. The Knights must have had a keen eye for country.'

'In all respects: not only to see who was coming and going, and how many—we are here on the ancient road from Millau to Lodève—but also for what could be grown and what could feed here, on the Causse and in the valleys too.'

'On the face of it and I speak from a depth of ignorance, some things seem to have changed little since their times. I feel myself now more of a sheep farmer, or shepherd rather, at La Commanderie than a student at University.'

'Or Sergeant Gunner in the Royal Air Force?'

'No, not more than that. The training and . . . what followed . . . have made certain of that.'

Consommé was ladled by Sylvestre from a large tureen into white bowls that Lawless recognised as Limoges porcelain. Chevalier made a slight gesture with one hand and Sylvestre returned from the sideboard with lighted candles in silver holders for the centre of the table. Conversation lapsed as the soup was consumed. When the bowls had been removed and large plates set in their place, the host spoke again, changing the subject.

'I have had time to read some of your translation and I am not unimpressed. Contrary to what you said earlier, there is no copy of Cavallier in my library. The one you have used was once on my shelves but my brother Aristide requested loan of it in the summer of 'Fourteen. In the circumstances, I thought it best not to ask for its return.'

'Because he did not return; nor Pascal, nor Léopold, your nephews.'

'That is so.'

'Would I be right in thinking that you left the book with him on the day of the picnic at Castelbouc when all the family met together for the last time?'

Chevalier remained silent, nodding very slightly and slowly, his eyes bearing the far away look of someone feeling once more the bittersweet pain of a treasured memory.

'Perhaps he intended to take it with him when he left with his men: something to remind him of home, perhaps, or give him courage. My father once told me . . .'

'Your father who was at Maricourt. The King's Regiment attacked at Maricourt alongside mine.'

'How could you know . . .?'

'Janquet: he answers to me.'

'I see. I suppose from that so do I, so do we, Serge and myself.'

'Does that disturb you?'

'Certainly not,' Valentin broke in—rather hurriedly, Lawless thought; and better not, given that faintest hint of menace in Chevalier's tone.

Sylvestre arrived to busy himself at the sideboard, carving portions from a rosemary-sprigged rack of lamb which he then carried on warmed plates to the table, serving his master first and following up with a dish of onions, tomatoes, red peppers and potatoes that had been roasted under the meat.

'You will take wine. He usually brings a Rhône for lamb. What is this, Sylvestre?'

'Gigondas,' said Sylvestre, on his way out of the room.

'Please try it. I do not drink wine with food, except occasionally with the cheese.'

Again there was a lengthy silence except for the sound of cutlery on china and the discreet brush of lip on glass as the meal continued.

'To return to your translation, I detect two hands or voices in it, one with more edge to it than the other. Experience of war in the field—in your case, in the air—sharpens the pen as much as the sword.'

'But leaving less time for reflection, for evoking the complexity of emotions?'

'Reflecting too long on what one has done in war can bring more pain and shame than one can bear, Mr Valentin. But I concede that in the translation where the two voices sing their appropriate parts the duet is richly in tune. I apologise for overworking the metaphor so blatantly.'

For the first time they saw a smile appear briefly on Alexandre Chevalier's face.

'How do you find the Gigondas?'

'On reflection, richly complex,' said Lawless, joining in the laughter that followed.

It turned out that conversation was not discouraged over the cheese, at least not on this occasion. Lawless by now was familiar with pelardon but had to ask the names of the other two cheeses on the board that Sylvestre thrust under his nose.

'Roquefort and what Sylvestre calls "house cheese". Try all three. I will be surprised if I am wrong in predicting to myself the one you will find most to your taste. You need more bread. Sylvestre!'

'Coming, coming; already bringing it.'

'Madame's bread: it may still be a little warm from the oven.'

'Madame is a very fine cook, as you said. Thérèse, my wife, would find stiff competition here. But I think she might run a close race.'

'She will have been well taught by her mother; that I do know. Now, tell me, in your view which is the best cheese?'

'The Roquefort is too salty for my taste; the pelardon I very much like but the best is the "house cheese": delicious. What about you, Serge?'

'I am with you: the smoothest and sweetest I have ever tasted.'

'There you are, Sylvestre. Say to Madame that she has gained two more devotees.'

'Never doubted it myself. I'm going for the dessert.'

'Mr Valentin, I understand you worked for a while with Kellerman in Grenoble.'

'For almost three years.'

'On the Romance poets?'

'No, no: as his assistant. I had barely begun on the poetry myself when Professor Kellerman suddenly died—in the middle of a lecture. It was some time afterwards that I came across a reference that intrigued me: no more than a few lines—not in the original of course—of love poetry in one, perhaps two hands, possibly—again you see the uncertainties—connected with a monastic house.'

'Intriguing indeed. I had a brief correspondence some years ago with someone, evidently a scholar, writing from Berlin. He preferred to remain anonymous—I now realise for reasons that have since become tragically clear. He touched on the same possibility as yourself, but I was very sceptical, even rather dismissive. Love poetry was the field of troubadours and surely forbidden to monks. I have since moved somewhat from that position. Despite my coolness he sent some of his evidence, and further references some of which I followed up, made little progress and put aside for another occasion. Somewhat later, more followed, including several pages in the original. My anonymous correspondent added a note saying he was sending the material for safekeeping as he doubted he would ever be able to work on it himself. It was the last I heard from him. I hope he may have survived; some of the lucky ones did by escaping to England or America. It may be the time has come to take the matter up again. I warn you, however, that it will not be easy for me to find that correspondence. You have seen the state of my library and believe me it is immaculate compared with the other places where my documents are kept. I should say that I did discuss this mystery also with a colleague—one more by correspondence than personal contact—in . . .' and here Chevalier turned to look at Lawless, 'Oxford: Granville College, if you know it.'

'You give me considerable hope,' said Valentin, an eager smile on his face, 'and I can hardly restrain my impatience to hear more from you.'

'Patience is for young men, Mr Valentin. They have more time left to endure it than those older.'

Sylvestre returned carrying a silver tray.

'Ah, dessert. Madame makes excellent tarte tatin and crème caramel.'

'Lemon soufflé tonight,' sniffed Sylvestre, bringing round the ribbed ramekins. 'Best eat it quick before it flops. Strawberry sauce in the boat—for them as likes it.'

With the final spoonful of the soufflé melting in his mouth Lawless watched as Sylvestre put no longer needed items from the sideboard on his tray, took a box from a drawer beneath and went through a door leading onto the terrace. He was back a moment later, picked up his tray and left the room.

'It's remarkable how well he manages with only one arm and that limp. Has he been with you long? A family servant?'

'Sylvestre was what the English would call a Sergeant-Major in my regiment. A machine gun burst at Maricourt gave him the limp. He lost his arm at Mount Kemmel in 1918.'

'I keep hearing the name Maricourt, from Jérôme Janquet and Henri Vabrette and now here, yourself and Sylvestre.'

'The regiment was there. Some of us who were left were at Mount Kemmel too. So were some of your father's King's Regiment. In that place by then we were one army in effect.'

'My father hardly ever spoke of what he did.'

'Understandably. If you would like to smoke we will go onto the terrace.'

On the terrace Alexandre Chevalier offered them cigarettes from a mahogany box.

'Dupont, Gitane; English on this side.'

'English? Not from North Africa?'

It was getting dark by now but Lawless could just catch the faint smile that came onto Chevalier's face.

'No, I promise you, not one of those. These are from Gibraltar.'

Lawless, reassured, took one, using his own lighter for it and the Gitane chosen by Valentin. Chevalier did not join them. The terrace faced west. A red glow on the distant horizon showed where the sun had gone down. A few stars were showing in the clear but rapidly darkening sky: red Arcturus low down ahead, Vega, pale blue, further to the south. He identified them automatically, without thinking. Training. He'd said that earlier, hadn't he? The sky was huge but no more so than the Causse.

'Do you ever think about them, the Knights?'

'Constantly. Who could live in this land and not feel their presence?'

'I've thought a great deal about them since I came to La Commanderie and I'm beginning to realise how little, how very little I know about them.'

'You have all of my library at your disposal to find out.'

'Thank you. I mean, why did they settle here at all, on the Causse? It's so remote and so barren. Why build all these massive towers and walls? Who were the enemies they feared?'

'No one: they feared no one. The Templars were always in the van, the Hospitallers the rearguard: the most dangerous places in any column.'

'That's exactly what I mean! The Crusades: that is where I have always been led to believe was their place. So, why here, why spend so much time and effort and, yes, money here?'

'You are thinking too simply. If you are to be a scholar you must read, Lawless, read. For instance, La Commanderie is a misnomer; *maison forte,* what I believe in English would be called a fortified manor house, would be nearer the mark. The Commanderie established by the Templars was Ste-Eulalie, fifteen kilometres from here. This place was one of its dependencies, La Commanderie one of its smallest. Ste Eulalie was the centre of administration and worship, so important that it even had a library, of forty books, some say. Imagine such wealth of learning for the times. The land was worked to produce almost everything they needed—at least while the Order kept to its founder's rule of piety and frugality—and it was good land in their hands. What we may believe is that in those times the seasons were gentler so that the crops and animals farmed were sufficient to feed many more people than is the case now. We have a mill at La Couvertoirade. You will have seen it on the hill outside the town as you approached. I have yet to locate mention of it in any of my documents of that time but I feel sure it rests on a site chosen by the Knights.'

'That makes them sound more like managers and farmers than soldiers.'

'Think, Lawless. What lies behind you when your aircraft takes off on a raid? Adminstrators, managers, suppliers, mechanics, armourers, cooks, clerks, drivers; the list is endless and without such support no fighting man could carry out his orders. This and many places like it together formed the base that provided the common soldiers as well as the Knights and their train and kept them supplied all through their campaigns. That is why they came here and stayed so long.'

'Then left, or rather were dispossessed and others took their place.'

'Know your Heraclitus, Lawless: nothing is permanent except change.'

'Change must have been what established the Chevaliers here and once established they seem to have spent a lot of time and blood resisting the inevitable: further change. I hasten to say that I admire them for that, especially now.'

'I am glad to hear it. In effect, that first change was less radical than has been supposed. The Rules of the Hospitallers had important aspects in common with those of the Templars. Each influenced the other. And if one comes down to everyday matters, life had to go on, whoever was in charge: the crops to be planted, the animals to be fed and the settlements and their defences to be maintained and strengthened—as I could show you tomorrow if we have the time. It is worth remembering that the common people are known to have continued calling the Brethren Templars long after their Order had been suppressed and their commanderies turned over to the Hospitallers. As time went on, land and farms were leased and families established themselves where Knights and monks once ruled, and some of the founders of those families may well have once been Knights or even monks. Names in those days often derived from a man's position or his work, as I am sure you know. Which makes your name an intriguing one, Lawless.'

'My sister-in-law wishes me to add her family name to mine and my wife mine to hers.'

'Your tone suggests to me that you are seeking my opinion. I see no reason why both their wishes should not be met. You may not be aware of this but it will not be the first time that an Englishman gained some title to land in the Causses.'

'Séverine told me that we were here as bands of routiers, interested only in loot.'

'She is correct. English raiding parties were one of the reasons why the Hospitallers rebuilt and reinforced the walls of this town and others but as part of a treaty forced upon the French when they were on their knees, much of this province was ceded to the English, happily only temporarily; but here you are.'

'If you will forgive me,' Valentin intervened, 'I think I will go to bed. The excellent dinner and the journey are having their effect. I wish you goodnight.'

'Goodnight to you, Valentin. If there is anything you need, ring the bell for Sylvestre.'

'Wait for me, Serge' Lawless turned to Chevalier. 'I feel rather tired myself: not used to long cycle rides . . .'

'Stay a moment. Your friend was being tactful, I think, leaving us to talk of family matters.'

'You probably know that he and Séverine have become rather close and he has been living at La Commanderie during the school holidays.'

'I do know but it will not lead to his becoming a member of the family, as you have become. I know my niece. He is not the man she would marry.'

Lawless felt his heart beat a little faster. Was this the moment? Should he tell Chevalier what Thérèse had told him about Séverine and Thierry, and Fabrice? He might order them both to leave. No: etiquette would forbid such abruptness. He would just go all silent and remote and there would be a cool goodbye in the morning; no more talk of the library or those fragments of poetry Serge and he both wanted so much to hear about. To hell with it, perhaps the Gigondas was helping, but this is what he'd come for: to try to heal old wounds. He couldn't let Thérèse down.

'I know about Séverine and your son. Thérèse told me the story. Where is Thierry now?'

There it was: the silence, the not looking at him as if he were no longer of any interest or even existed. He'd better apologise and just leave. Some people would never change.

'Some weeks ago there was a battle at Bir Hakeim in the desert. The Legion's 13th Demi-Brigade helped hold off the German advance for sixteen days. Eventually the survivors broke out and made contact again with a British force. Thierry was with the 2nd Battalion during the siege. That is all I know.'

'On my second raid over Germany the aircraft nearest mine was hit by flak. The starboard wing caught fire and she went into a dive. Only two parachutes opened. I had no chance to see how far down they went; not far, I thought, because the flak was so intense. Back at the base she was recorded as lost and all the crew missing, presumed killed. Nearly six months later the Squadron Commander received notice that one of the crew had survived and was in a prisoner of war camp in Germany.'

'I am glad to hear that. Thank you for telling me, Philippe.'

Here goes, Lawless thought. 'Mr Chevalier . . .'

'Alexandre, Philippe; I think we are close enough now for us to be less formal.'

'I'll try to remember that . . . Mr . . . Alexandre . . . do you believe old wounds can be healed?'

'We both carry them, Philippe: what do you think?' Again the faint smile, more easily seen now that the moon had risen.

'I think they should be.'

'And so do I. I am so pleased that you came. A little cognac while we go over a few other matters?'

It was after midnight before Lawless got to bed and another hour going over in his mind all that Alexandre Chevalier had told him before he fell asleep. The plan for the signal at Balsièges was a good one: element of surprise, quickly done, small risk, significant effect. *A wasp sting, Philippe; sharp prick, prolonged soreness.* Details of the danger to the network Janquet had mentioned were a little clearer now. It was known that a security service agent posing as an escaping British officer would be one of the 'passengers' travelling on the train to Béziers: when, it was not yet known, but probably quite soon. The man would not know where he would be contacted nor if money would be given him or a safe house found to stay—he would simply have to wait and see—but the information could be conveyed to him by one of the network once he was actually on the train and out of touch with his controllers. The provisional plan was that he would be met at Sévérac le Chateau and there dealt with as judged appropriate. There might be other agents on the train keeping watch on him, but the network should have become informed of that in good time, in which case no approach would be made either en route or at the terminus in Béziers

Lawless would have to be involved because only he would be able to identify inconsistencies in the man's behaviour in impersonating a British officer. There was one particularly dangerous possibility: the man might actually be British, someone who had been turned somehow and was now collaborating with the security service. Efforts were being made to find out more.

'The network is growing, Philippe, but slowly. We are fortunate in having a few well-placed informers but we do need more active recruits who must have particular skills.

Until we can find them the few we have are being asked to bear a heavy burden and run increasing risk. That is why after the two operations we have been talking about, you will be stood down for a while.'

'Why me? I survived twenty bombing raids in as many weeks. A few ambushes and hold-ups hardly compare with that.'

'That is not the point. In the air you were anonymous to your enemy. Here, on the ground the more you take part the greater the risk you will become known for what you are.'

'I'm prepared to take the risk.'

'Perhaps, but the network cannot, as others have found to their cost. Believe me, anyone arrested is sure to receive the most severe interrogation. We believe the real enemy, the Germans, are providing some of the interrogators and they are very ruthless professionals. No one doubts your courage but you do not have the training to withstand their kind of questioning. And remember, Philippe, you have dependents, especially the one yet to be born. They would not be immune. I could not allow it.'

'Does that mean there will be nothing more for me to do?'

'Yes, but later: a very important task. One that only you can carry out.'

'I know the rules: 'do not ask. You will be told when the time comes'. But have you thought about the Brownings? I am the only one who has used them in action—Henri Vabrette perhaps could handle one, and Séverine has been shown how they work by me: isn't it about time to bring them into action?'

'Think of them as a secret weapon—element of surprise, overwhelming firepower when least expected. The right time will be when the enemy thinks he has superior strength. That time has yet to come and when it does you may not be here, so training others can be your task.'

'Séverine . . .'

'Séverine has been given other assignments elsewhere. La Commanderie will not see her for some time. Which brings me to my letter for her and for Thérèse. I think you know what it will say. It will explain everything and I hope it will heal the old wounds for which I alone, and not the Chevaliers of La Commanderie, am responsible. It will be ready in the morning and I wish you to be my courier because without your coming here it might never have been written.'

'I'm worried about her, Philippe. She told me she doesn't know how long she will be away.'

'Don't let it upset you, Sweetheart. She has Serge with her for the weekend and after that she'll be safe with Victor and Jeanette. You have to admit the two of you have been so much happier since you had the letter. She was dying to tell Victor all about it, I know.'

'I know, I know. It was wonderful. I don't know how you did it, Philippe. If only Mama and Fabrice could have known.'

'It wasn't me, Sweetheart. It was you. I could see it in your uncle's face when I told him what you had said and knowing that he is soon going to be a great-uncle must have finally convinced him it was time to do something. I think he quite approved of my translation as well.'

'You haven't seen his letter yet, have you? You must read what he says near the end. Oh, I can't wait to tell you! He says if Thierry does not come back from the War, everything he has, the whole estate, everything, will be left to his two nieces, that means Sevvie and me, and our children and he is instructing his notaire to change his will to make that clear.'

'My god! He doesn't do things by halves, does he?'

'But poor Thierry, he must come home, he must; especially now the family is all together again. But if . . .'

'He said something about Séverine that makes me think, but no, never mind, I can't be sure. Go on, what were you saying?'

'Uncle Alexandre said if Thierry does come home he will still see to it that La Commanderie is safe and we will not be short of anything we need. And Philippe, he wants to see us again! He's invited us to go to La Couvertoirade and stay after the baby is born and if he can find time he may come here before.'

'Come here, you. No, I don't care who's looking; I want to hug and kiss you. You can't believe what a load that takes off my mind. Tressie, what are you doing? Ooh, I like that. What have I done to deserve . . .?'

'Don't look round. I've just seen the Lieutenant going past the gate.'

'Grandjean? Did he see us?'

'I'm not sure. He glanced this way.'

'That's the only way out of the station. Leave it a couple of minutes then we'll go. He may be on his way back to the Gendarmerie anyway.'

Lieutenant Grandjean seemed to be reading the station noticeboard when they came out into the street. He smiled his thin smile and tapped the side of his kepi with his baton.

'Madame, Mr Chevalier. Seeing someone off?'

'My sister, Lieutenant, as it happens; visiting friends.'

'And you are not accompanying her this time, Madame?'

'So much work to do on the farm, Lieutenant—getting in the hay, always things to do with the flock; some of us are not so lucky.'

'All work and no play, Lieutenant.'

'Sir?'

'Yourself, Lieutenant; you never seem to have any time off.'

'The Gendarmerie is never off duty, Mr Chevalier.'

'Chasing villains, keeping us all safe. We owe you a great debt, Lieutenant.'

'Solving crime is only one part of one's duty, Sir. Preventing it is the more important part of one's work.'

'Well, we mustn't keep you from your duties, Lieutenant. It was a pleasure meeting you unexpectedly like that.'

'With your permission, Madame, I will walk a little of the way to the café near the Mairie with you. You are going there as usual, I take it, Mr Chevalier?'

'In fact, back to Doctor Vaudet's surgery, Lieutenant. I have something to pick up from there.'

'Only a moment of your time then, Madame. Am I right in thinking that the shepherds on their way back south from the Aubrac will be passing by La Commanderie again? Near the end of the month, is it not?'

'They usually come our way. We are never sure precisely when they will arrive. I am intrigued to see you have become interested in our old country ways.'

'Whatever goes on, Madame Chevalier, whatever goes on. It's all part of getting to know one's territory, finding one's way around. I understand the leader shepherd, Querrell, is a veritable mine of information—about the countryside. I must try to catch up with him. Madame, Mr Chevalier: good day to you.'

'Nice touch that, tapping his cap with the baton. Didn't do that before. He must have seen it in a film somewhere.'

'Be serious, Philippe. I didn't like the way he was talking, hinting about this and that.'

'He's always like that, trying to make you think he knows more than he does.'

'Maybe; I'm not so sure. In any case you must let Jérôme know and Querrell, somehow. Jérôme might be able to get a message to him by one of the farmers on the Sauveterre. Then he could take one of the other trackways across the Mejean if he wants to and not come by us at all. That would spoil the Lieutenant's little game.'

'I'd miss meeting Querrell again but I'm sure you're right. I didn't know you had to go back to Vaudet's surgery.'

'I don't but I wasn't going to have Lieutenant Grandjean with us at the café when Jérôme turned up.'

Lawless looked at her admiringly. 'Clever old you! I wish I could think of things like that. What did Vaudet say? Séverine went in with you. Did he see her as well?'

'I am fine. Everything going well, he said. He looked very pleased; with himself or me, I couldn't be sure. Probably both. Séverine was in with him a long time but when they came back into his waiting room they both seemed happy enough. He's given her the name of a doctor in Montpellier, she said. I think it must still be something to do with the veins in her leg but she didn't say.'

'I can see Jérôme coming. A quick coffee, or a drop of something else and then we'll be on our way. You can put your feet up when we get back.'

'Don't forget to tell him what I said.'

Serge Valentin reappeared on Sunday evening saying he had cycled all the way from Florac. He was reassuring about Séverine, saying that he had left her at Victor and Jeanette's flat going over maps, looking up timetables, making lots of notes and generally being a kind of clerk as far as he could see, so they shouldn't worry about her. He said he would do an hour of mathematics with Mireille after supper if she wanted and then go to bed if they didn't mind because he had to be up early in the morning to get to the village in time for school opening.

When Lawless came down to the kitchen to make coffee for Thérèse the door was open and he could hear the sound of a bicycle pump squeaking outside.

'Lucky to catch you: I was just off. Message from Jérôme—didn't want to say anything last night, you know why. It's on for Thursday night. Be at the café at eleven. You'll be driving.'

'Shit, not Jérôme's car. There's likely no oil in the sump. And I don't know the way.'

'I'll be in the front.'

'Well, I hope you can see your way in the dark.'

'Cat's eyes, that's me,' Valentin grinned, wiping his spectacles. 'Turned him round, didn't you, the old man at La Couvertoirade? My guess is it was the Cavallier translation, refined by me, of course. Couldn't have been your looks, not with that moustache.'

'He knows class when he sees it. Now bugger off and confuse a few more young minds.'

***

Thursday, 10th September was a moonless night, ideal for illegal activities but nerve-racking for anyone driving an unreliable vehicle with dim lights over unfamiliar and badly maintained roads with all three passengers constantly arguing as to which was the best way to go. No one was more surprised than Lawless when Vabrette finally jabbed a steely finger in his back and said

'Here, turn right. You can go through the back street. Station's on the other side of the village.'

'I can hardly see a bloody thing.'

'Keep going. You're nearly there. Along here, there's some trees hanging over the road at the end.'

The car crawled in first gear along a track full of potholes with the engine making a noise that Lawless felt must wake up everyone in the village but when he reached a dark stretch under the trees and switched off not a sound could be heard outside.

'Right, you wait here while Louis and me do the signal and start up as soon as you see us running back.'

'What if somebody comes?'

'Well, bloody well think of something! Sit on his knee and pretend you're having a shag. Got every thing in the bag, Louis?' Right, we're off.'

'This is too close to Mende,' Valentin said. 'Jérôme should have gone for Chanac.'

'He must have his reasons. Maybe it wasn't his idea. Maybe whoever did decide wanted it to be close to Mende for sending some sort of message. I don't know. We just follow orders.'

Valentin stayed silent. Lawless wound down the window, letting in cool night air. They seemed to be taking a long time out there. He wondered how the French signals worked. Perhaps like the English ones. He remembered reading somewhere that some of the earliest railways in France were built by English engineers. The first train journey he ever made on his own was to Oxford to sit the examination papers. His father took him to Oxenholme by car and bought the return ticket. As he got on the train it was beginning to snow. He could see his father now, waving him off, snowflakes settling on his hat. Oxenholme—Preston—Crewe—Birmingham Snow Hill. Walk across the city centre to find New Street station, worrying if he would get there in time. Birmingham—Leamington Spa—Banbury—Oxford. Oxford in the snow was freezing cold. He hadn't expected that . . .

'They're coming back! Start up!'

Lawless fumbled on the floor for the starter handle—Jérôme's battery never held much of a charge. He almost fell out of the car, managed to get the handle in first time and swung, hearing a loud backfire bang just as Vabrette and Costain arrived breathless back at the car.

'Backfire,' he said; 'try again,' and started to engage the crank handle.

'Idiot! That was the charge going off. You asleep or what?' Vabrette started laughing. 'She's already running. Get in.'

He had been driving for a good five minutes before he felt compelled to break into the chatter and sniggering coming from the back seat and say something.

'It must have been an echo. I thought it came from behind.'

'Only thing that came from behind was Louis here farting, eh Louis?'

'Well, all right, you've had your joke but did it work?'

'Oh it worked all right. I saw it come down straight across the track, neat as could be. Louis's a dab hand he is, aren't you, Louis?'

'Turn here,' Valentin broke in. 'Jérôme said to go back a different way'. 'Take the road round Ste Enimie and cross the river at Castelbouc. You know the way after that, I think.'

'Castelbouc, did you say?'

'Don't raise your hopes, driver. No stopping off. I've got school in the morning.'

'And we both have to get to work, Sergeant, so put your foot down.'

'Serge,' Lawless whispered, 'does he ever say anything; Louis, I mean?'

'Probably never gets a chance with Henri there. Or maybe he's deaf: too many explosions in the quarry where he works. Keep straight on here.'

Thérèse murmured something in her sleep and turned over as Lawless slid carefully into bed, keeping as far away from her as he could. He lay awake for a long time, thinking over something Alexandre Chevalier had said to him when he handed back the Cavallier manuscript.

Cavallier knew where to go when he decided to escape. There were secret ways, Huguenot roads with guides and safe places to rest, known to the Camisards and others before them who had fled the Catholic tyranny, some of them no more than sheep tracks through the hills and mountain passes of the Luberon and the Drôme and over the Vercors to Grenoble and on to Switzerland where they were safe.

'Byways like the shepherd's trackways are always best for those needing to escape notice. You

might bear that in mind next time you come to La Couvertoirade.'

Why had Alexandre said that? Lawless determined whenever he went to La Couveroirade again he would travel by car.

He was sitting at a table outside a café in a square bright with sunlight and full of people coming and going. Séverine was saying something to him. The Webley shouldn't be lying on the table between them for everyone to see. What was she saying?

'Coffee for you, sleepy head.'

He sat up in bed and took the cup Thérèse was holding out to him.

'Oh, I needed that. Thank you, Sweetheart. I was dreaming.'

'Where did you get to last night, Darling?'

'Me? Last night?'

'Yes, last night. Something woke me up. You weren't there but you were next to me when I woke again this morning. Downstairs Mireille told me she heard the squeaking noise the bicycle pedal makes and thought someone might be stealing it. She didn't go out because she's been told not to let anyone see her. Remember your promise? Tell me where you were, please.'

There was no getting out of it. Rather shamefacedly he told her all about what happened at Balsièges.

'But I've been told I only have to do one more thing and then I'm free; like going on long leave. So I'll be here all the time after that.'

'One more thing? Is it dangerous?'

'No, no, I'm sure it won't be. I haven't been told everything yet but I think it's another of those arrangements to meet somebody on a train: like the time I went with Séverine. Remember? That wasn't dangerous at all.'

'And when is it?'

'I don't know that either but it might be soon. I hope it is. I'd like to get it over with. As soon as I know, you will too and I'll tell you everything. I'm sorry I kept last night's thing from you. The trouble is I keep being warned not to say anything about what's going on in case it gets to the wrong ears.'

'You're not saying my ears are the wrong ears, are you?'

'Oh god, no! Damn, I keep saying the wrong things. Your ears are lovely, gorgeous, both of them. Long soft lobes: I feel like biting them. Can I? No? How can I make it up to you, then?'

'It's too early in the morning for what I have in mind but there is something else: you and Serge—oh yes, we know he went with you; Mireille heard him swearing—can come with me to Castelbouc at the weekend. Justine will know a reliable farmer on the Sauveterre who can warn the shepherds about Lieutenant Grandjean. It will be another nice long bicycle ride for you.'

'That's very thoughtful of you, Sweetheart. Is there any chance of a swim at Castelbouc, maybe some fishing for Serge?'

'We'll see if there's time. Breakfast should be ready soon. I asked Mireille to scramble some eggs. I know that you like them. Oh, Jeannot says the grass on the other cloup is ready for mowing and two sheep have gone missing. Looks like a busy afternoon for you, Darling.'

***

'Another beer, Jérôme. I've been slogging away all day mowing grass and looking for two lost sheep and I'm absolutely parched.'

'Did you find them?'

'What? Oh, the sheep: yes. Well Caramelle did. Both of them were tangled up in a thorn bush. Is there anything more stupid than sheep?'

'I can think of a few people I know.'

'Me too. Like a fitter we had who kept breathing in too much of our oxygen, just for fun, he said. He wouldn't stop so I reported him to the MO, the squadron doctor, not the snowdrops—police—because he was a good fitter. Doctor told him his bollocks would drop off. That stopped him.'

'Philippe, before you ask, I am sorry but there is still no message for you from England. The news does not get any better. Radio-Nationale repeats German boasts about panzers reaching the Russian city of Stalingrad and an English raid on Dieppe being smashed and thousands killed on the beaches.'

'That sounds very bad, Jérôme.'

'There's something else and in a way it's worse for us because it's closer. We've known it was coming because of what has been happening in the Occupied Zone. There's now a law for the "use and guidance of the work force"—that's what it says—making all men aged between 18 and 50 and, listen to this, women, yes women from 21 to 35 subject to any work that the authorities deem necessary. It won't apply to me but it will to you, and even Madame Chevalier. It's conscription, Philippe, and you can be sure France isn't the only country you might be sent to work in.'

'Is it happening now?'

'Already in some parts, so we hear.'

'Will the people stand for it?'

'Plenty of them will, for all sorts of reasons but some certainly will not. When you think about it, it might help us find recruits. A lot of people have relatives or someone they know in the country, or in the mountains—like around here—and will hide away with them. And some of them could be very useful to us. —so long as we're careful.'

'What do you think we should do?'

'Nothing different for now. Just sit tight. It will take them a long time to do anything about it.'

'What about Grandjean? Isn't it the sort of thing he would like to do?'

'I don't think so, at least not yet. We have a feeling he's waiting for something to happen where and when he thinks it will, then he'll pounce. After that, I don't know.'

'I've got that feeling you're leading up to something. Am I right?'

'I can't hide much from you, can I? You're just like your uncle-in-law, or any of the other Chevaliers for that matter. Yes, Madame Lamphier . . .'

'I'm going to see her on Saturday, with Thérése and Serge.'

Jérôme Janquet stared at him in surprise. When he spoke he sounded somewhat taken aback, even a bit huffy.

'So you already know, do you?'

'"Know", Jérôme? I have no idea what you're talking about. Thérèse asked me this morning to take her on Saturday to see Justine, Madame Lamphier. Serge will be coming as well. It's something about getting a message to a farmer up on the Sauveterre to let Querrell and his shepherds know that Grandjean may be looking for them when they come back from the Aubrac, which is some time soon, I believe. Now, what were you going to say?'

'All right, I understand. From what you say you were told at La Couvertoirade you now know more about that danger to the network I was talking to you about earlier. Madame Lamphier has received more of the information needed to deal with it and she has been asked to pass it directly on to you without my being given any of the details. That's all to do with not spreading information too widely, and I approve of that, as you know. I thought for a moment you had been told without my knowing.'

'Am I expected to deal with this, er, situation by myself?'

'You will have Henri with you if necessary. I can at least tell you that.'

Lawless looked long and intently into his empty glass. That old pre-raid prickly feeling began to creep over him.

'I think I'd better have another beer, Jérôme. No, make that a cognac. And a beer.'

'In that case, I'd better tell Serge what I think Querrell could do and who might give him the message. Serge will remember it better than you ,but I'll tell you anyway, to be on the safe side. Listen, I will make sure that Grandjean is waiting on the trackway at the edge of the Méjean above St Enimie. That's the way Querrell would normally come, but he could take the road downriver past the big bend and up onto the Causse towards Caussignac—I don't suppose you know where that is. Doesn't matter. From Caussignac there's an old road and trackway all the way down to Meyruies. He's bound to know the way. After that he might head towards Mont Aigoual; who knows? Grandjean can sit chewing his fingernails as long as he likes: he'll never catch sight of Querrell or his sheep. On the other hand, knowing Querrell, I wouldn't put it past him just to walk straight up to Grandjean and ask him what he wants.'

'I can remember that last bit. Better be going: thank you for the beers. Very nice cognac.'

***

'Sweetheart, before we set off I must tell you Jérôme has some suggestions for Justine about the shepherds and says she will have information and instructions for me about that last thing I told you I have to do before I stop doing that kind of work. I'll tell you as much about it as I'm allowed, don't worry.'

'Darling, *what* she tells you worries me less than *how* she does it, but thank you.'

'Justine worries you? I can't think why. Oh, I see. Well, you needn't worry about that. It's Serge she's interested in, not me.'

'Serge as well, I shouldn't wonder.'

Castelbouc was as sun-drenched and drowsy as he remembered from the picnic in July. A young man whom they had not seen before led Fleur and the trap away into the shade somewhere and the same silent woman from the village showed them into the salon. Thérèse subsided thankfully into a soft armchair and took off her hat. Lawless walked out onto the balcony and looked down at the river. The deep pool they had dived into before looked even deeper and just as inviting. Valentin wandered round the room lowering his nose over the vases of flowers and idly picking up a journal or a book from one or other of the tables and putting it down again. Everyone was hoping for a cool drink.

'My dear Thérèse; let me embrace you.' Justine Lamphier, graceful as ever in a cool primrose suit. 'You look really wonderful. Do you not have that charming girl with you this time? I was so looking forward to hearing her play again. Mr Valentin, there you are: what a pleasure. And Philippe: where is that man? Ah, as I thought, on the veranda, of course. Come inside, Philippe. I hear Clothilde approaching with the drinks. Now everyone may choose and Philippe will serve. Now, I want to hear all your news before we go down to lunch.'

After lunch: omelette, salad and peaches from the orchard with a bottle of chilled Vouvray—'the last, my friends; we shall see no more until these terrible times are over'—Justine Lamphier suggested Thérèse take a little rest in her bedroom while she talked with the two men on the veranda where they could smoke cigarettes if they wished. After Thérèse had left them, Valentin said would they mind if he took his rod and had a few casts in that pool where he had had some sport in the summer.

'How tactful of them both, don't you think? Are you sure Thérèse is not just a tiny bit suspicious I may have designs on you, Philippe?'

'Do you, Justine?'

'Philippe, what a thing to say! And after you so charmed Alexandre.'

'I was uncouth. Please forgive me. Is that really what he said?'

'He said that if you survive this War the world of diplomacy would beckon but lose you to the world of scholarship. And you were not uncouth; artless, rather. In the young artlessness has the charm of sincerity. In the older, well, that is another matter.'

'In your presence, Justine, and in Alexandre's I do sometimes feel out of my depth.'

'Awareness of that can be the beginning of sophistication, Philippe.'

She sat with her hands in her lap, looking at him with her head tilted slightly to one side and the faintest of smiles bringing tiny lines to the sides of her mouth. He could think of nothing to say.

'Dear Philippe, you really have no idea how attractive you are to women, have you? And many men, too, I suspect. In other circumstances I would take the greatest pleasure in seducing you but,' and here she stood up and took his hands in hers, 'that must wait until some other time—if ever. We have different matters to concern us now. Oh dear, perhaps we should wait a few moments while you compose yourself?'

Eventually, once his pulse had slowed sufficiently, he was able to stammer out what Thérèse and Jérôme Janquet had suggested should be done about Querrell and the shepherds. Justine pursed her lips as she thought.

'Dorier of Le Cros is the man. Querrell will pass the night on his land before coming down to Ste Enimie. It will not be necessary for you or Mr Valentin to climb all the way up to the Sauveterre. Dorier brings his wife to the market in Ste Enimie every Monday. I will send Albert there with the message for him by word of mouth only. Good, that disposes of Lieutenant Grandjean's plan. I suspect there will come a time when we shall have to dispose of him too. You look shocked, Philippe. There is more to this war than stealing petrol and knocking down railway signals.'

'I did bring my machine guns to Alexandre's attention.'

'Of course you did. It is my turn to apologise to you. You have much terrifying experience of war. I apologise. There: is that acceptable?'

She leaned over to him and pressed her lips briefly on his. He thought to say 'for now', decided against and smiled weakly instead and nodded, then noticed her eyebrows raised and wondered if that meant she might be a shade disappointed. Before he could do something about it, she began speaking again in a lower and very different tone.

'Now, to the other and more serious matter. Alexandre has explained to you in some detail the attempt planned by the police to trap the network into revealing its activities. It seems the German pressure may have been applied. We now know the real name and the assumed name of the agent and the train on which he will travel. He will be expecting a member of the network to make contact with him at some time during the journey to Béziers and he will not be disappointed. You will be the one.'

'Might there be plain clothes police on the train keeping him in sight?'

'Our information is that he will travel alone. We did consider luring him off the train on the pretext of hiding him in a safe house—in fact here—and disposing of him. Vabrette would have seen to that. In the end it was decided that the time for such extreme measures has not yet come and in any case there is a danger that the trail could be traced back here. The plan is now simpler. This is what you will do.'

Lawless listened intently for five minutes while Justine Lamphier described the plan of action. He was then made to repeat the details to her, was put right in one or two places and when he had everything correct was told to commit everything to memory and on no account to keep any reminder notes or any written account whatsoever. It reminded Lawless of briefings by the Wing Commander before a raid. Justine had something of the same matter-of-fact terseness.

'Thérèse, there you are again. More rested, I hope. Was my room cool enough for you? I know: shall we have some tea? I have a little left. Philippe would like tea, surely, wouldn't you Philippe? With lemon? Of course not: milk for the English. Clothilde will bring it onto the terrace. I shall leave you two to yourselves for the moment.'

'Well?'

'Well what?'

'You spent nearly an hour together. What was it all about?'

'I have to go to Béziers on the train'

'Why?'

'I have to meet a man on the train at Sévérac and see that he gets to Beziers.'

'Is that all?'

'No. I have to make sure that he is met by the right person when he arrives. Then I come back. We can use Jérôme's car again but make sure we leave it with Madame de Laurent while I am on the train.

'Who is this man?'

'Thérèse, Darling, I ought not . . . oh, well, why shouldn't you know? I did promise. I haven't been given his real name. He will be travelling with false papers. I have to deal with him as an escaping British officer, something like those other two. I needn't even talk to him much. In fact I shouldn't. All I have to do is make sure he gets there. After that I go into retirement: back on the farm.'

'When do you have to go, Philippe?'

'Week after next: Thursday. I'll be back the same night. Don't worry. Everything will be fine. It's all been worked out. Nothing can go wrong.'

'Darling, something can always go wrong. Of all the people you should know that.'

'Sweetheart: look what came of it. I met you and we made him, or her inside there.'

Holding her close and kissing the top of her head, he suddenly thought of something else and whispered:

'Oh, I forgot, Sweetheart: I have to take two of the bikes with me. I hope they'll fit in Jérôme's car.'

Justine Lamphier paused outside the room, glancing in at them. They did look so sweet, embracing each other like that, oblivious of anything or anyone else. Naturally, it made no difference to her determination to make sure that he should do as he had been instructed, nor to her other feelings about him.

'Cou—cou,' she called, before coming in. 'Tea is ready and there are some strawberries. Mr Valentin has not yet returned.'

As September wore on the days were still warm, but when the sun went down the evenings could be cool enough for a light sweater to be worn. Two thunderstorms in the middle of the month had again revived the grass and Thérèse grew more and more confident that the haylofts would be full enough to feed the flock right through the winter. There would be a glut of apples this year, enough to last in store until March perhaps, and not counting the dried apple rings that she ought to be thinking of making next month. As for chestnuts, Philippe had said gloomily he had seen branches already near breaking off with the weight of fruit. She smiled at the thought. He would have to eat them anyway. They would get through the winter more easily this time. It had been a good year. And now there was always Uncle Alexandre. They would not go short. If only Sevvie were here. She hadn't thought she would miss her so much. Time to get supper ready. Oh, she had forgotten: Mireille had said she would make it tonight and afterwards they would play duets together. The baby was very active these days—and nights, sometimes. They still had not decided on names, at least not all of them. Philippe and Serge were outside somewhere: stargazing perhaps now that Mireille had found Papa's old telescope in one of the greniers. Philippe had told her names of lots of stars. She was feeling rather sleepy with Caramelle's head warm on her feet.

Lawless waited until the last notes of the Chopin nocturne faded away before knocking and then opening the piano room door.

'Querrell is here. He won't stay but he wants to say hello.'

Mireille jumped to her feet.

'Does he have his dogs with him?'

'One, I think, outside. The others have to stay with the flock.'

'Philippe, at least tell him to sit down for a moment. I'm coming.'

Querrell was standing just inside the door of the kitchen with his fingers ruffling the long hair hanging over Caramelle's eyes.

'Mr Querrell, welcome indeed! Please sit down and have some wine or coffee if you prefer. Mireille put the kettle on, please.'

'Madame Chevalier, I hope you are well. I don't have much time. We think there are some foxes about near Caussagnac so I have to get back. But, yes, thank you. Who could resist some of your coffee?'

'The Aubrac, Mr Querrell: was the pasture good this year?'

'Well enough, Madame. I have known better, but well enough. And you, a good summer?'

'The best for some time. At least something has gone well this year.'

'And something even better still to come, if you will forgive my boldness.'

'Oh, this,' Thérèse laughed, putting her hand on her middle. 'When you are next this way he—or she, perhaps—will be able to crawl after your lambs.'

'I wish that might be so, Madame Chevalier, but it is not certain we will come by this way next year. Nothing is certain these days, except, I am sure, a fine son or beautiful daughter in your arms before much longer.'

'Philippe, a glass for Mr Querrell. The cognac.'

Thérese shook her head in response to Lawless's offer and watched the three men raise their glasses.

'To better times, Madame, and to a son or daughter whom one day I hope to carry on my shoulder.' Querrell put down his glass. 'May I be permitted?' He embraced Thérèse and pressed Mireille's hands in his. At the door he turned and nodded his grizzled head to Thérèse.

'Thank you, Madame. We had no time for wasting on that policeman.'

'We'll see you on your way, Roland. Coming, Serge?'

Querrell's big white dog sidled away when they stepped out into the courtyard and kept its distance behind them as they set off in the direction of St Chely.

'A quiet night, Roland, but then it usually is up here.'

'Quieter than a night not long ago in Balsièges, I hear.'

'Hm. Was it quiet in the Aubrac?'

'Not as quiet as last year, more comings and goings. Even noisier further north where there is better organisation like in Clermont. There have been many more arrests but no lack of others to take their place. Before long the Germans will lose patience and step in and I am not the only one to think that. They must have had plans to drive further south and laid them aside after the armistice. They must have taken them out again if there's anything in the rumours I was hearing.'

'What rumours?'

'More vehicle movement than usual on the other side of the border, heavier traffic on the railway, roads closed then re-opened then closed again. Something is up. You should be on the lookout.'

'I'll pass it on.'

'I already have but there's no reason you shouldn't say I've been talking to the two of you. I turn off here.'

Querrell stopped and to Lawless's surprise instead of the expected handshake embraced first Serge and then him.

'Listen,' he said, 'you've both got yourselves into some dangerous work but if anything you are the one at greatest risk, Sergeant. There's always somebody who will talk or be made to talk. It's only a matter of time and you may not like it but not everybody likes an Englishman, especially one who looks as if he might get his hands on a nice bit of French property. What I'm saying is be ready to move very fast if someone tells you. Here, take this—no, don't open it now—it might help if the time ever comes.'

Querrell pushed a large stiff envelope into Lawless's hand. Lawless fumbled, almost dropping it.

He started to say will we see you again but Querrell was already striding away into the darkness with his dog at his heels.

'Who knows?' they heard him call. 'But I'll remember you.'

The dog was the last thing they saw, a white blur moving down the slope.

'Rolland,' Lawless said, 'he fought on after Cavallier escaped, Serge.'

'And died fighting, my friend.'

***

'My car is all ready for you, Philippe. Please take good care of it. There's a full tank, at least I think it is: the gauge seems to have stopped working. Perhaps you could mend it.

You are on your own this time. Serge has school and Henri isn't needed now. In any case it doesn't do to be seen together in the car with the others too often. The wrong people might notice.'

'Querrell said something along those lines. Which people?'

'Can't always tell: just people. Better play safe. Now, you drive to Sévérac. There's a map in the box, if you need it. Go to Madame de Laurent's house, 26 Rue du Chateau and leave the car there. She will give you further instructions.'

'Is that all?'

'It's all you need for now. Isn't it time you were going?'

'Just checking what you said about petrol in the tank. Good enough. Give her a swing, will you? No, wait; on second thoughts I'd better do it.'

Lawless secretly prided himself on his memory of roads travelled and his sense of direction. Years of long walks in the Cumberland hills with his father had taught him to store landmarks and turnings in his head. He took the same road for Sévérac he and Séverine had followed in July. He somehow expected a sheep to charge across the road in front of him near Masselac as had happened before and when it happened again wondered if it could have been the same one. The rock pinnacles standing like sentinels above the gorge had the early morning sun on their backs as he wound through the twists of the descent to the river where he had stood on the bridge with Séverine while she told him about Fabrice and Thierry and the Pas de Souci. He didn't stop this time. There was still no signpost for Le Massegros but he remembered the turn and was soon on the long slow second gear climb through the hairpins up the eastern face of the Sauveterre with the sun behind him. The engine was running well and there was no sign of steam from the bonnet as he drove through the village's empty street. Jérôme must have filled the radiator this time; Henri had probably reminded him or done it himself and topped up the oil. He was sorry not to have Henri's company on this journey. What had Justine meant by 'extreme measures' when she said Vabrette would have seen to disposing of the very man he was now going to meet on the train? Would Henri do that? Yes, he would if it had to be done. Without noticing it he drove past the source of the Aveyron that Séverine had shown him, swung round the corner and saw the chateau of Sévérac sunning itself on the hill.

No one had told him where the Rue du Chateau was—only that it was half a kilometre from the station—but surely the name was some indication. He drove slowly into the town and after a few experimental turns realised he was lost. No one was about. Too early in the morning: in a French town anyone who had to go to work had already left. Everyone else was keeping to the house. A bakery: bound to be one open somewhere. He tried a few more short narrow streets. Clearly he was in the wrong part of the town. He chose another at random and suddenly found himself in a square with a slab-shaped stone memorial in the middle and, yes, a café on the other side. I'm losing time, he thought: risk it. He drove round the square, parked the car outside the café and went in.

'Good morning. Rue du Chateau?'

The man behind the bar with the Gauloise in his mouth glowered at him from under the bushiest eyebrows Lawless had ever seen. He took so long to answer Lawless thought he must be trying to decide if Lawless's moustache was bigger than his own.

A jerk of the head showed a decision had been made.

'Turn round. First right. Straight on: one hundred metres. First left: can't miss it.'

Number 26 was halfway along the street, a large stone built house of three storeys with tall windows and freshly painted shutters. Lawless guessed the wide arched entrance at one side with its gates fastened back led into a rear courtyard. He decided to waste no more time and drove straight in. As he was getting out of the car a woman watering flowers in a row of terracotta vases turned and looked towards him.

'Madame de Laurent?'

She put down her watering can, approached him for a closer look and then pointed towards a door that was half open.

'Come inside. You have just enough time for some coffee while we talk and then you must go. The train is due in forty minutes.'

He sat in a chair next to a window opening onto the courtyard. The scent of roses came into the room. It was silent except for faint sounds of crockery being moved. Madame du Laurent reappeared carrying a round tray with a coffee pot, cup and saucer on a lace cloth.

He had been expecting someone like Justine, or Séverine perhaps but this woman was more like a schoolteacher he had had in the Infants school with her spectacles down on her nose and her greying hair pulled back in a bun.

'There is no sugar. Would you like honey?'

Lawless said no and took the proffered cup of black coffee.

'I have got into the habit of not using names but I think each of us knows who the other one is,' she said with a smile.

Lawless gave her in return what Thérèse called his deliberately boyish smile.

'I hope one day I may use yours. I know it is a particularly beautiful one.'

'Hm. Justine was right about you.' She kept the smile nevertheless. 'Drink your coffee and listen carefully. One or two things have changed as a result of our latest information. You are looking for a man of thirty, well built, clean-shaven and wearing a dark blue jacket, open-neck striped shirt and grey trousers. He will have a small brown leather suitcase, and probably keep it between his knees or in the rack above his seat if there is room. He has a cap but it may be rolled up in his pocket. His hair is dark, almost black and cut short. He does not smoke. He may have a copy of a French newspaper with him—we do not know which—as part of his disguise. His real name is Pierre Alain, but of course he will not use that. He will be travelling in the second coach after the engine. Can you remember so far?'

'The important details: appearance, brown case, newspaper, yes.'

'Very good. In ten minutes you will start for the station. Take one of the bicycles you brought and follow the man riding on the other. He will leave his at the station for you. Do not speak to him. Buy a return ticket to Beziers. Here is enough money for it and some to spare and this envelope has the money for Mr Alain in it. Have your papers ready to show. The porter will help you put the bicycles on the train.'

'Why am I taking two bikes with me?'

'One is for you and the other for Mr Alain. Now, this is the most important part. Both of you must get off the train at Magalas, not stay on to Béziers.'

'Magalas.'

'Yes watch for the sign. You tell Mr Alain that it is safer to get off there and cycle into Béziers because the main stations are under surveillance. Outside the station you will be met by someone you will recognise. That is the completion of your task. Leave Mr Alain with that person, cycle into Beziers and catch the next return train.'

She made him repeat her last set of instructions, nodded her approval and stood up.

'Goodbye and good luck.'

He looked back at her from the doorway.

'Who is he pretending to be?'

'Allan, Captain Peter Allan.'

'Allan, Peter; Alain, Pierre. Very thoughtful: easy to remember.'

Lawless managed to keep the other cyclist in sight all the way to the railway station, pausing for a few moments in the square while the man propped his bicycle against the wall that was near the entrance door and walked away. Lawless had been expecting to have to show his papers but the ticket clerk hardly glanced up as he pushed the requested ticket across the counter. To his relief, because the policeman there the last time might have remembered him, he found he had the platform to himself. Still ten minutes before the train was due. To steady his nerves he ran through his instructions, trying to picture in his mind Madame de Laurent's face as she had spoken to him. Grey jacket and blue trousers? No, idiot: the other way round. Think of something else: it'll all come back to you when you need it. You hope. For something to do he started pressing the brake handles and squeezing the tyres. One of these bikes was going to be left at Magalas. He wished the bloody train would come. What if it was late and the flic turned up? Remember: you speak hardly any English. But does our man speak French? Some officers might. All right, work on that one: listen to see if any of his French has an English sound, or, of course, the other way round. He heard the strange singing noise. It was coming. Christ! He'd not felt this excited and nervous since that first take-off with a full bomb load.

It was nearly three hours to Beziers, say a quarter of an hour less to Magalas: plenty of time to calm down and get used to the train before he started looking for Alain. He chose an empty compartment in the second carriage, leaned back in his seat next to the window and watched the rolling countryside glide past. He began counting the tunnels and gave up after the sixth. He felt the train begin to slow as the brakes went on and a descent began. The train passed through a halt with a sign . . . Vez . . . he could not catch the rest of the name; then another tunnel, still going down, and another and then a long curve in the track taken even more slowly and into a deep valley between a road and a river, quite a wide one with little fields on the other side. It looked vaguely familiar. Yes, they must be not far from Millau. Time to make a move and find him in case the carriage filled up. He patted his pocket to make sure the envelope was still there.

The next compartment was empty. Two women, mother and daughter perhaps, were chatting in the one after that. The younger woman looked up as he passed. A man by himself in the next, smoking a pipe. Two men sitting in the one after that, on opposite sides, one near the door and the other by the window. Was it him, next to the window: blue jacket, cap stuffed in pocket, short black hair: no sign of a newspaper though. The other man was reading one. Oh yes, brown suitcase on the rack above the window man. That was Alain: had to be. Lawless slid back the door and went in.

'Good morning. Excuse me.'

The man reading the paper made no sign of hearing but leaned back to let Lawless pass inside. The window man looked up, nodded and turned back to look out of the window again.

'A fine day. Should be getting into Millau soon.'

The window man nodded again without speaking. The other looked up suddenly then folded his newspaper and looked at his watch. Lawless hoped like hell that meant he was getting out at Millau. Anyway, his French must be sounding all right.

A few minutes later the train came to a halt in Millau station, a larger and slightly less dilapidated place than Sévérac. Two policemen were strolling along the platform looking in the carriage windows. Lawless stared up at the brown suitcase on the rack opposite while they passed by. Carriage doors slammed as several people got on. Two women came along the corridor, glanced in and went further on. A whistle sounded and the train began to move.

'Looks as if we've got the carriage to ourselves.'

Again the nodded acknowledgement but Lawless felt sure he was being inspected.

'Going far, are you?'

'Béziers.'

'Not a bad place. I go there now and again. Quick visit, this one. Something might come of it. Work, you know: not easy these days. You have to go if there's even a small chance. Did you see those two cops looking in all the windows? Makes you think they must be after somebody, doesn't it?'

'It is possible.'

'Staying long in Béziers, are you?'

'Not long.'

'Me neither. I know the buses. I could tell you the right one for anywhere you want. How about a drink at the station bar?'

'Someone is coming to meet me.'

Rencontrer. That was odd. A Frenchman would use *chercher.* Perhaps that was his way of making Lawless think he was English. Try again.

'Oh, too bad. Never mind. Look: that other chap left his paper, there, in the corner. Anything in it?'

The man hesitated, then leaned over, picked up the folded newspaper and made as if to hand it to Lawless.

'No, just tell me if there's anything worth knowing about. I've broken my reading glasses.'

The man paused a moment then opened the newspaper scanned the front page. Lawless noticed he took quite a while before saying anything.

'What's new?'

The man looked up at him and started to turn the pages.

Quoi de neuf. He doesn't know what it means! He's looking for page nine.

'Some local news. "Police have arrested a suspect in the affair of the damaged signal at Balsièges station" . . .'

And he pronounces Balsièges like the Siege of Leningrad.

'. . . Hervé Lacoste, gardener, of Rouffelac"

'You're English, aren't you,' Lawless said.

'What are you saying? I am French! I will report you to the police!'

'Listen, we may as well speak English because your French is terrible. You can stop pretending. I'm here to help you. We know who you are. You're Peter Allan and you're an escapee. Am I right?'

The man stopped spluttering and grinned at Lawless.

'All right, mate. Like they say, it's a fair cop. Now what?'

'Look, I have to make sure or we could both get into trouble. Just a couple of questions and if you answer right, I'll tell you what we have to do.'

'Fire away.'

'Your rank and regiment, please.'

'Captain, Seaforths.'

Seaforths: Dunbar's regiment!

'Where were you captured, and when?'

'Dunkirk, er June 1940; third of June, I think. Everything was a mess. I've forgotten the dates.'

'And you've been on the run since then?'

'Yes, moving from place to place. Hiding away when the police came round.'

'Did you say which battalion?'

'No, well, the Second. Lost a lot of men.'

'You must have. I'm sorry.'

'Have I passed?'

'Oh, yes, of course. All in order. Oops, we're slowing down. Must be coming into a station.' Lawless pressed his face against the window. 'Tournemire. Better wait to see if anybody gets on.'

'Lovely country round here,' Lawless said as the train gathered speed. 'The Causses, you know. All these old castles and things: like everybody says, the true France.'

'Very interesting: you were saying?'

'All right. I've got some money for you,' Lawless said handing Allan the envelope given him by Solange de Laurent. 'You have 500 francs in there for expenses. You'll also need train tickets, I expect, as well as other things. Got all the right papers, have you? Can I see? Good. Can you ride a bike?'

The man jerked his head back in surprise. 'A bike? I haven't got a bike.'

'I put two on the train: one for you and one for me. Don't worry. You won't have far to ride.'

'I thought . . .'

'You thought we were getting out at Béziers. I know. Well, we're not: too risky. Béziers station is crawling with cops. Can't afford to have you picked up there, can we? Or me. No, we get off at Magalas and ride into Béziers. We'll be met there or maybe even at Magalas. We'll see. Now, what do you think of that?'

'I don't know. I suppose it sounds all right.'

'You'll be fine: in good hands; nothing to worry about. It's all arranged.'

'Do we stop anywhere else?'

'I doubt it: non-stop all the way to Magalas now, I'd say. We can enjoy the ride, or sleep, or just chat. Anything you want to ask me?'

'Your English is very good. Where did you learn?'

'Oh, I spent a lot of time in England before the War. Went to school there. Where did you live? Let me guess: Scotland. You were in a Scottish regiment. Where in Scotland? I went there once on holiday: Edinburgh. Anywhere near there?'

'Yes near there. A little place: you wouldn't have heard of it.'

'Fine city, Edinburgh.'

In fact the train made one brief stop, at Bédarieux. Some bags were thrown out of the luggage space in the last carriage but no one got on or off. The countryside was now very different: rows and rows of vines and olive trees almost everywhere it seemed.

Magalas railway station was on the outskirts of the little town. No one seemed interested enough to make an appearance when the train drew in. Lawless and Allan, suitcase in hand, alighted from the carriage and walked to the rear of the train and retrieved the bicycles. Lawless was on tenterhooks again as they walked back along the platform to the exit. Would he be stopped and asked for his papers and would Allan seize the chance to denounce him to a guard or a gendarme? He felt sure Allan must be at least a bit suspicious of him. Then again, who was supposed to meet them outside and how would he know where to look, or wait? What on earth should he do if there was no one there: bike into Beziers? And do what when he got there? He didn't know the way in any case.

There was a car parked on the other side of the space in front of the station. Lawless heard the train's klaxon give out its high-pitched hoot and waited to see what happened. The passenger door of the car opened and a woman got out. It was Séverine in a bright-coloured loose summery dress. She put on a white straw hat with a red band and walked towards the two waiting men, smiling a welcome.

'It's too hot for cycling,' she said, 'so we brought the car. Stay here,' she said to Lawless. 'We shan't need you any more today. Wait for your pay.'

Without saying a word to Lawless Allan walked meekly to the car with her and got into the back seat, putting his suitcase beside him. Séverine sat in the passenger seat in front and Lawless saw her turn and start speaking to Allan. A man got out from the driver's seat and strolled across to Lawless.

'He'll be watching us,' Dunbar said, 'so take this envelope. Only for show: there's nothing in it. Well?'

'He's not French, speaks it badly; he's English. Calls himself Allan, Peter Allan, Captain. Says he was in the Seaforths at Dunkirk . . .'

'Silly bugger: they were at St Valery with the Highland Division. I should know. Bloody cheek, saying he's a Seaforth. Don't you laugh.'

'Pretends he's Scottish and lived near Edinburgh but he's got a faint Brummy accent. He's a bloody fraud. Watch out: he may have a gun in that suitcase.'

'Don't worry about us. We'll deal with him. He's a police plant all right. Maybe they turned him; maybe he wanted to turn. Some do it for money. Difficult to say at this point but we'll find out. Don't hang about here. Take one of the bikes; find a café somewhere. But remember: back here for the afternoon train in an hour. If you miss that there's a five hour wait for the next.'

'They were wrong, you know, the network. I was told he was French and pretending to be English. It could have been very awkward. '

'Nobody's perfect, my friend. No harm done was there? Not to you, anyway. I do wonder who gave him the idea of saying he was a Seaforth. Off you go now.'

Lawless paused long enough to see Dunbar get back into the car and hear some of what he was saying to Allan.

'You'll be fine now, old chap. We'll see you're all right.'

The idea of a drink cheered Lawless up. He had been feeling rather flat after all the tension and excitement and then finding Séverine treating him as if she had never seen him before. Of course he knew that was deliberate in front of Allan but it still got to him. He found the Café du Midi open in a side street off the Avenue de la Mairie and ordered a glass of red. He felt suddenly hungry and realised he had eaten nothing since early morning, and that had been only a piece of bread and some tepid coffee. Was there anything, he asked the woman who had served him. She shrugged: omelette, merguez, perhaps some potatoes. He ordered all three and peaches. He drank the harsh red wine, knowing that he shouldn't on an empty stomach and a hot day. It was sure to make him drowsy. When the food came it was substantial and surprisingly good. He asked if there was another wine, a little more, you know . . . and smiled at her. Her look sized him up for a moment and when she returned it was with a half-litre carafe of deep red plummy bottled sunshine. She gave the slightest nod towards the curtained doorway behind her and put her finger to her lips: evidently he was being favoured with a forbidden drop of the boss's private store. The wine did make him drowsy. His head was drooping over the empty plates when he felt a touch on his shoulder. The woman had placed two cups of coffee and a small bowl of sugar on the table. She sat down on the chair opposite and they both looked at each other over the rim of their cups as they sipped the strong sweet drink. He noticed she had taken off her apron and brushed her hair.

'I have a train to catch,' he said.

'How long?'

'Twenty minutes.'

'You have a bike. It's only two minutes to the station.'

'Won't he hear?'

'No. He drinks a whole litre of that at lunch time.'

He had five minutes left to get back to the station and pedalling along the dusty deserted streets he felt something like he had that day heading back to College after being rewarded by the Granville don for his examination success, but with an added frisson of guilt. He hoped she wouldn't take his leaving too many notes on the table the wrong way. That wasn't what it was about. They both knew they would never see each other again.

The other bike was still leaning against the station wall when he skidded to a stop. He could hear the train coming. He snatched his ticket back from the stationmaster and rushed along the platform to fling the bikes into the rear luggage space just before the whistle sounded. There was no time to get to the front carriage. Why bother? He opened the nearest door and almost fell into the corridor as the train started to move.

A young man in the standard blue overall worn by French workmen was lounging outside the station entrance at Sévérac when Lawless emerged. Without saying a word he took one of the bicycles from Lawless and rode off, waving an arm for him to follow. He had disappeared by the time Lawless rode into the de Laurent courtyard but the bicycle had already been put in the back of Jérôme Janquet's car.

The tea offered by Solange de Laurent helped slake his thirst and clear his head.

'He doesn't say much, does he, the bicycle man?'

'Following orders. I assume all went as planned?'

'Not exactly but in the end well enough.'

'What do you mean, "not exactly"?'

'The man was English, not French as I was told.'

'I see.'

'It might be advisable to find out whether that was a genuine mistake or was the trap more subtle than we thought?'

'I imagine our friends who met your train will already have that in hand. Have you five minutes before you leave? Someone is here to see you; in the salon.'

Justine Lamphier was standing by an open window looking down into the courtyard. The late afternoon sun was streaming into the room.

'What does the scent of roses do for you, Philippe?'

'It reminds me of tea on the College lawn at Oxford.'

'For me, Versailles: the perfume of Roseraie de l'Hay.'

'Is that the scent fom Solange's roses?' Her cream-coloured dress was made diaphanous by the sun. He could see a faint shadow of her body through the silk.

'No, it is not a rose for growing in courtyards. It needs to be free. I have had a visitor at Castelbouc, one I have been expecting for some time: Lieutenant Grandjean. A social call, he said.'

'He is persistent.'

'Dogged.' '*Ténace*': she made the word sound distasteful. 'I had hoped you might call on me again but perhaps it would be unwise for the moment.'

'Jérôme said today was my last assignment, at least for the time being. I am now on leave.'

'Then perhaps this will not be the last time I see you.'

'I have no plans to go anywhere. There is plenty to do at La Commanderie but if you should need anything, if the Lieutenant becomes too inquisitive, Castelbouc is not far away.'

'That is reassuring but I think I know how to deal with Lieutenant Grandjean. He has a fatal flaw: he lacks imagination.'

'I should be going; Thérèse will be worried if I am late. I haven't told you anything about what happened today.'

'Later: what is important is that you are here now and that surely means the day went well.'

He could not resist that look, the one the artist had caught, twice. He put his arms around her and felt her hands draw his face down to hers and eventually release him and push him gently away.

Lawless had expected there would be few, if any, mornings for getting up late or afternoons lying under a tree reading but had not been aware how full the final days of September and, it seemed, all of October would be. The last of the grass had to be mowed, left to dry, tossed with a pitchfork and left to dry further and eventually carted back to the barn in bales and hoisted into the lofts. Potatoes had to be dug—and there seemed to be more than they could ever eat—and put into clamps. At the weekends Jeannot hauled one load of logs after another from the woods and all had to be stacked in just the right way for the air to keep them dry before sawing. The despised chestnuts, piling up on the slopes of the gorge had to be gathered, although he managed to persuade Jeannot and Mireille to do most of that work in the evenings before the light faded. Serge was some help on a couple of the days he had off school in the middle of the term but disappeared for the rest of the break, saying he had to see Séverine in Montpellier, or Marseille, he wasn't quite sure. Then there were the ewes. Séverine had long ago arranged the tupping time, making it later this year than last, but the two rams had to be brought from Masselac and that meant going with Jean-Pierre Bec all the way there and back in the cart. The ewes had needed extra feed and careful inspection in preparation for running with the rams and watch had to be kept to stop any rough handling of a ewe or fighting between the rams. It all took a lot of time and as October wore on Thérèse was able to do less outside or with the sheep. To Lawless's great relief MIreille took on more of the role of housekeeper. She seemed never to tire and always to be able to find time to play for them in the evenings.

One day they drove in the trap to the edge of the gorge to look at the autumn colours now decking the woods.

'I remember the very first time we did this,' Thérèse said. 'I think I must have been three. Papa said we had to go because all the leaves were turning gold and we must see them before they fell. I thought the ground would be covered in gold and I asked him if we would be rich now and could I have a pony. Mama said we should gather some and press them in a big book and they would last for ever.'

Lawless put his arm round her shoulders. 'All mothers do that. I still have some in one of my books at home.'

Mireille ran off, saying she was going to gather some gold as well.

They watched her kicking her way through the carpet of red and gold leaves followed by an excited Caramelle snapping at them as they flew over her head. Lawless picked up some of the best and promised Thérèse he would press them in the Cavallier book when they got back to the house

'I suppose you wouldn't like to creep into the shelter with me? It's not far away. Only joking, Sweetheart: we could have a look in from the outside, though. I'm very fond of that place.'

Later he said, 'I know! Why don't we go to the café tomorrow morning?' We haven't been for a long time. We can have coffee, maybe some lunch and you could see Madame Bec.'

'I'll drive the trap,' she said.

Mireille heard them and looked up. 'Croissants. Please bring me back a croissant.'

'As many as you like.'

'Two, then; and one for Caramelle.'

Jérôme Janquet fussed over Thérèse like an old hen, bringing out a softer chair, holding it for her while she sat down, ostentatiously wiping the table in front of her and beaming all the time.

'Sit here, Madame Chevalier. How good to see you. It is too long since you were last here. Would you like a rug over your knees? No? Well, yes it is warm for so late in October. And are you well? You must take care of her, Philippe; remember now. What can I bring you? Do you still take coffee? Of course: stupid of me. Coffee then: our best, and croissants?'

'I love this,' Lawless said, looking at the brown jugs, the larger full of steaming with coffee and the smaller with warm milk, and the basket of fresh croissants on the table. 'Sitting outside a café on a sunny morning with a beautiful woman opposite me and just about to bite into a warm croissant. Do you know, I have never seen a croissant in England?'

'What do you eat for breakfast?'

'On the base, bacon and eggs, every morning, and tea, always tea; never coffee like this.'

'The base?'

'The airfield.' He looked at his watch. 'I'd be asleep if I were there now.'

She saw that far away look in his eyes again. Moods change quickly when you're so young, she thought, and felt a great surge of love for him, wanting to hold him and tell him not to be sad, not to miss that other home. Come back. I'm here. Look at me.

'Mm mm, she certainly makes good coffee, Madame Janquet. Do you think I've know her long enough to call her Denise?'

'See if she blushes if you say it. Then you really will know if you have a way with women.'

'I don't think I dare. Another croissant?'

'You eat it. I must go and see Madame Bec. We have a lot to talk about and Jeannot told me she wants to show me the baby clothes she's been making. And that reminds me. There's a job for you: the cot. Mama used it for all of us; the last one was Fabrice. It's been put away in the storeroom for, ooh, what is it, thirty years? It might need some work.'

'What colour should I paint it? Pink or blue?'

She laughed, that chuckly laugh he loved so much. 'I don't know. You decide. No, don't get up. I can look after myself.'

'Half pink, half blue,' he called after her.

Jérôme Janquet sat down beside him

'Soon, eh?' He said, as they watched Thérèse making her way carefully along the cobbled street.

'End of next week, we think. She's so calm, Jérôme. Are women always like that? I keep waking up in a panic, wondering what to do.'

'When the time comes, you'll be told. Vaudet's a good doctor and Marie Bec has helped more women having babies than anybody else in St Chely. They all go to her. All you have to do is be there and keep the house good and warm.'

'It's warm enough today.'

'There's a change in the weather coming. Soubeyran, remember him, the man from Fraissinet whose horse you have? He was here yesterday; told me he smelt it coming and all the birds were flying south. We'll have snow, he said.'

'Do you believe all that stuff?'

'He's been right before.'

'I'll tell you something, Jérôme. I've found cloud covering the target when we'd been told it would be so clear we would see everything and then a week later seen moonlight shining on night fighters coming at me when they were all supposed to be grounded by bad weather. That makes me very suspicious of anyone claiming to know what the weather will be. Don't believe anything until it happens.'

'By then, Philippe, it may be too late. Keep the house warm and your tyres hard. Listen, there's been some good news, at least, it sounds good. A big battle has started in the desert and it looks as if the Germans are being pushed back.'

'I've been hearing aircraft flying over these past few nights: I wonder if that's anything to do with it. You haven't asked me about the passenger on the train; why not?'

'No need to. You did well—and with those two men we sent up to be shown how to use the gun. You'll be left alone now: happier things for you to take care of.'

'Anything more about the Lieutenant?'

'Funny you should mention that, no, except his car seems to keep breaking down. Stops him getting about as much as he used to. I can't think why they don't look after it better in Florac.'

'Well, well. I heard from Jeannot about the explosions in the railway yards at Alès. Something about the piston boxes on two engines.'

'Hm, yes I heard that. Nothing seems to be safe these days.'

'Jérôme, you're being very cagey. Something's going on: what is it?'

'I might tell you, if I knew. There's nothing definite, lots of rumours about more Germans being seen around in Marseille and Montpellier, even Nîmes and that's not so far away. I heard those aircraft as well: they could have been German or they could have been yours. We just don't know. All we have been told is to keep our ears and eyes open and be ready. Ready for what, I should like to know.'

'Roland Querrell told me the same. From what he said I'm sure he thinks the Germans are up to something. If you're right about that fighting in the desert it could be they're preparing to move more troops there. All I hope is they don't come this way.'

'So do we all, Philippe. I've often wondered why they stopped where they did.'

Thérèse insisted she could take the reins on the way home.

'Madame Bec has made some lovely things for the baby, Philippe. I want to show them to you when we get back.'

'Are some of them wool? Jérôme told me the weather's going to change and we might have snow.'

'Wool and cotton and towelling and wait until you see what I made with some of the silk left over from my nightgown.'

'You've been knitting for weeks now. How many clothes does a baby need?'

'Madame Bec says you can never have too many.'

'Tressie, if it snows will the doctor be able to get here?'

'It would take a lot to stop Doctor Vaudet, so don't worry.'

'I can't help it, sorry. How do we let him know when it, when, er, things start to happen?'

'You go to Jérôme and get him to telephone.'

Thérèse had called it a cot but it stood on curved rocking bars so it was really a cradle with inward sloping sides and ends. Whatever it was called, there was no need to paint it; in fact that would have been wrong because it was made of polished mahogany with carvings of lambs on each end panel and five names with dates, the Chevalier girls' on one side and boys' on the other, in the order they were born. Lawless made sure that there was room for at least one more. It needed no more work than a thorough dusting and polishing up with beeswax. Mireille asked, please, if she could do it. She helped him carry the heavy box down the stairs to the bedroom, Thérèse having said it must be next to her side of the bed until the baby was old enough to move into the nursery next door. Lawless was now left to get on with work outside, or with his translation, or whatever else because his wife and Mireille now occupied themselves for most of the day in cleaning, dusting, changing curtains and bedclothes and going through piles of baby clothes and chattering all the time about whether the room should be re-papered, or the carpet changed and how Lawless must make sure the chimney was clean so it wouldn't smoke and harm . . . Lawless crept out and busied himself with the sheep. Caramelle seemed to suspect something different was going on and slunk about the house sniffing in all the corners and creeping upstairs to see what was going on there.

'Let's go down to the café,' Serge said. 'They don't need us here.'

'Tressie hopes Séverine will be here for the birth.'

'She told me she'll do her best to come and let Jérôme know as soon as she can; then we can meet her at the station'

'God, I hope she makes it. Let's go. No, wait a minute; help me in with some more logs. The weather's turned bloody cold. I've got to keep the house warm.'

The first fall came during the night. Lawless woke to find the room quiet with that strange silence snow brings. The bedroom was still warm. There were some embers in the fireplace that he blew into life, piling kindling sticks on the redness and willing them to catch. After a few minutes flames began to lick up the sides of the larger logs he piled on.

'Oh, lovely, Philippe,' her sleepy voice came from the pile of blankets and quilt, 'I love to see a fire in my bedroom. Come to bed and rub my back again, please.'

'It's snowing. I hope it doesn't lie.'

'It may not because the ground is still warm from the summer, Mm, a little further down, yes, there. Not so hard. Now across.'

'Is that enough? Would you like some coffee now?'

'Lots of milk and some honey in it.'

The snow had gone by midday and the sun shone brightly in a hard blue sky. Jeannot came into the kitchen as Thérèse was putting potatoes into a pan of water. He took it from her and hung it from the hook over the fire.

'Jeannot, shouldn't you be going home? I'm sure your father has things for you to do.'

'My mother said I must stay here and make myself useful.'

'As if you ever did anything else! All right: lunch will be in half an hour. I know you like fish so you can have some of what you caught with Serge.'

Lawless knew that meaningful look that Jeannot sometimes put on for him.

'Let's take at quick look at the sheep. Mireille's out there with Caramelle.'

With the snow gone the sheep had found enough grass in the cloup to last them the afternoon. If the weather held, Lawless thought, they might be moved further down towards the trees. Mireille was pacing round the flock, with Caramelle at her heels. Lawless supposed that she might be doing that to keep warm but you never knew with Mireille. She might be working out some problem in spherical geometry that Serge had set her, or one she had thought up on her own.

'What's on your mind, Jeannot?'

'I found another box of bullets.'

'You haven't! My god, Jeannot, how do you do it?'

'The sangliers had been digging down near the river. You can tell by the way all the leaves have been scattered about. I brought it to the house. It's in the barn. Mr Valentin didn't see.'

'Too preoccupied with fishing. You're a bloody marvel, Jeannot. How old are you now, nearly sixteen? You know what? I think it's time I showed you how to fire the gun. What do you think?'

The smile on Jeannot's face was his answer.

'I'll have to ask you father first, and Mr Janquet.'

It began snowing again after dark. Jeannot went home after helping to bring up the flock. Weather seemed to have no effect on him. Not all of the snow had disappeared by the following afternoon. The ground was getting colder.

For three days the skies were clear and blue and the nights frosty. The summit of Mont Aigoual glistened white with a capping of snow. Lawless cycled to the village with a rucksack on his back for flour and oil—and sugar, if there were any. In the café he asked Jérôme Janquet about what he had said to Jeannot.

'If Jean-Pierre agrees, so do I. Now Philippe, I heard this morning on the English radio that the Germans have been completely smashed in the desert. Full retreat. Your English army has won a victory. There were French soldiers fighting as well, of course.'

'Are you sure, Jérôme, really sure? We've heard that kind of story before and then it all changes and the Germans turn everything round again, like in Russia.'

'All I can say is that it sounded different this time and the stupid Radio-France is very quiet.'

Despite himself Lawless's mind was in a whirl. Could it really be true, after all this time? What now? The Germans never give up. They'll be pouring reinforcements into the desert. Could the Navy stop them? Are there any bomber squadrons in Gibraltar? He was so out of touch: he knew nothing. He had a sudden thought.

'Jérôme, you said French troops. Alexandre Chevalier told me his son Thierry was with the Legion, Second Batallion. Was anything said about them?

'Philippe, you know how it is. They never name a unit involved in any action.'

'Even so . . . I must go home quickly. Jérôme, will you speak to Jean-Pierre about Jeannot for me?'

'You must do that yourself.' I know he is at home.'

Jérôme Janquet must have already spoken about Jeannot and the gun to Jean-Pierre Bec, knowing the butcher would need time to think and, more important, to see what his wife thought. The outcome was that both agreed the boy should learn the workings of the Browning but for the time being remain as scout for the network. Later, they would see.

'I'll find time to show him tomorrow when he comes up. Thank you and thank you also for being so helpful to my wife. Oh look: snowing again. I must be going.'

'Winter's come early this year,' Madame Bec said. 'Just a few moments, Mr Lawless.'

'Please call me Philippe . . . er, Denise.'

She blushed a little. He could tell she was pleased.

'Philippe . . . about the snow . . . babies know nothing about snow or any other kind of weather. They come when they decide to be born. Just in case . . . this is what you need to know how to do.'

'Was there any sugar?'

'I could have only half a kilo this week, Sweetheart. It was rationed in England but that's the first time I've known it run short here.'

'Oh, Philippe, that's because you haven't been doing the shopping. Still, we have lots of honey.'

'Jeannot is coming up tomorrow to go through the flock with me. We marked all the ewes we are pretty sure stood for the rams but there are one or two we're not sure about so we are going to examine for estrus. He has sharper eyes for it than I have.'

'We owe him—and Mireille—so much, Philippe. I don't know how we can ever repay them.'

'Sweetheart, you are saving Mireille's life and as for Jeannot, well, he just does it because he wants to. He idolises you and Séverine. And, of course, Mireille, but that's different. At least, I think so.'

'How was Madame Bec?'

'I know what you're getting at. If you really want to know, we're Denise and Philippe now and she did blush.'

'I see. Another fair damsel added to your list of conquests.'

'Hardly that: she could break me over her knee. She did give me something, however.'

'I'm not sure I should ask what that may be.'

'A lesson in childbirth. I just hope I can remember but my fervent hope is that Dr Vaudet will deal with it all.'

'Or . . . Denise!'

'Don't be like that. Listen, Sweetheart, Jérôme told me some good news about the war in the desert. The Germans have been badly beaten and they're retreating. And he said the French troops had a part in it. Maybe Thierry was there and maybe your uncle Alexandre will hear from him again. What do you think?'

'I daren't think about it, Philippe. It might make me hope and . . .' She fell silent. He knew what she was thinking. 'But it would be wonderful for Séverine, if only . . .'

***

The Whitley was on fire, going down, engines screaming. He couldn't find his parachute. A hand was gripping his shoulder trying to pull him out.

'Philippe, Philippe, wake up.'

Thérèse was standing at the bedside. *Thank god, he was all right.* 'What is it? What's the matter?'

'Philippe, it's the baby, I'm sure it is. I feel it here.'

He jumped out of bed. He felt very calm. The room was warm, well warm enough. That was good. There was plenty of wood for the fire, to blaze it up. She was having pains. He face showed it.

'Sweetheart, sit down.'

'No, I have to walk. It's all right, I won't fall.'

'I'll make up the fire, bring you something warm to drink.'

'No, Mireille can do that. Go call her. Then go quickly to the village and ask Jérôme to telephone Dr Vaudet. And then go for Madame Bec. Oooooh! No, I'm all right. Go bring Mireille.'

He rushed upstairs and banged on Mireille's door. The handle turned and through a crack and he saw big dark eyes in a frightened face. The door opened and she stared at him in surprise at first then quickly nodded her head and disappeared inside. A few seconds later she came out wearing the blue dressing gown Séverine had given her, slipped past him and ran downstairs. When he came back into the bedroom he found the two of them walking slowly round the room arm in arm.

'I'm all right now, Philippe; you can go.'

Upstairs all the curtains had been drawn to help keep in some warmth, and the house was almost in darkness. In the kitchen Lawless squashed his hat down over his head and shrugged himself into a thick overcoat. Wrapping a scarf round his face, he opened the door and stepped out into a veil of silently falling snowflakes. He decided that cycling was worth the risk if it gained a few minutes and dragged one of the old boneshakers out of the barn. He fell off twice on the slope down to the road but the snow was soft and he ignored the bruises. Bursting into the café he found Jérôme Janquet behind the bar holding the telephone receiver to his ear.

'Right. Yes. Grandjean, you say. Are you certain? Tomorrow night. Wait. He's here. I'll tell him.'

'Philippe, listen . . .'

'Never mind that. Phone Dr Vaudet now, immediatley! The baby, tell him he must come!'

It took so long: getting the bloody operator to wake up, then repeating the number, twice, three times, then more silence as Jérôme Janquet, receiver clamped to one ear looked at him impassively, and waited and waited for a reply. Vaudet must be out, or asleep, or dead, no, there was a distant faint quacking noise from the telephone and Jérôme Janquet spoke, *Madame Chevalier, baby arriving, come as quickly as possible; La Commanderie; yes it has been snowing but much less now; yes I will tell him; yes it is urgent;*

thank you Doctor Vaudet. Lawless was hopping from one foot to the other, frantic with impatience.

'Cognac. Drink it: all of it. Good, now get back to your wife. Vaudet will come here as soon as he can. I will call Denise Bec. Jeannot will bring her in the mule cart. Wait: tell Madame Chevalier that her sister is arriving tomorrow night with Serge Valentin. Be here at nine to meet her. Do not forget: at nine. Now go.'

He left the bicycle at the bottom of the slope and made the climb on foot. The snow had stopped by the time he reached the house and he was tingling hot with the effort. Mireille met him at the door

'Quick, quick; the pains are coming all the time.'

She held him back at the foot of the stairs while she pulled off his sodden overcoat and hat. He raced up two steps at a time, pulling the wet scarf from his neck and letting it fall behind him.

Thérèse was lying back in the bed, her hair straggled and damp with sweat and her face crumpled with pain, or effort, he couldn't be sure.

'Oh, Philippe, you're here at last. Mireille has been wonderful . . .'

He knelt beside the bed and took her hand.

'We phoned Doctor Vaudet. He said he would be here as soon as he can. Is it very bad? What can I do?'

He body tensed as another pain seized her. She gasped and squeezed his hand so hard it hurt.

'It's too late. I'm all wet. The baby's coming. I can feel it. '

'Madame Bec . . .'

'No time. You, Mireille, now, please, please.'

There was a warm humid smell, a bit like the sheep pen when the new lambs were born. He wanted to shout that he couldn't do this; he didn't know how; he would hurt her, kill the baby. She was pleading with her eyes. Mireille was beside him, looking at him. He couldn't run away now. He gently slipped out one of the pillows so that she could lie back more comfortably. He nodded to Mireille to take off the sheet and ease Thérèse's nightgown above her hips. He helped her raise her knees and spread her legs. That seemed to lessen the pains a little. He held her hands and smiled to her to squeeze hard, harder. She rolled her head from side to side.

'My back hurts.'

He drew her forwards and holding her with one arm used his other hand to rub her back slowly, up and down and across. He felt her tense again.

'Push down, Tressie. I'll hold you. Push now. Keep on pushing down.'

He looked up for Mireille. She was at the foot of the bed, watching Thérèse very intently. He saw her eyes open wide.

'The baby: I can see the baby!'

'Is it moving? Is it coming out? Help her.'

Again the strong warm animal smell and sounds, squelching, slippery sounds and panting noises from Thérèse. Mireille was leaning over her, doing something with her hands.

'The head: I can see the head, looking down, coming out, now, turning round.'

Thérèse gave a long loud half gasping, half straining cry and Lawless felt her go slack in his arms.

'He's here! I can feel him, all wet and warm and his eyes are closed. Look.'

Thérèse struggled, trying to sit up. Lawless held her.

'Give him to me, give him to me.'

Mireille had wrapped the wrinkled red little shape in a white towel and laid it on the bed.

'He's a boy, a little boy and he has lots of hair. I must clean his mouth and eyes first. Then you can have him.'

Very gently, but quickly, she dabbed and wiped the tiny puffy lips and tightly closed eyes and when she had done, picked up the glistening reddish shape with the lolling head and splayed arms and legs and held it towards Thérèse's outstretched hands. Before she could touch him, the baby spluttered and began to cry, tiny squeaking sobs. Thérèse held him close to her breast as tears ran down her cheeks and dropped onto his head.

Lawless was silent, dazed, still automatically massaging Thérèse's back, unable to take in what had happened, what he had seen but still could hardly believe.

'The cord, Philippe: we must cut the cord. Philippe, the cord.'

Mireille's hand was on his arm, stopping the massage. He looked blankly at her and then at the long whitish wrinkled tube twisting from under Thérèse's arm down towards her thighs.

'Take him. Be careful. It's all right, Tressie sweetheart. Soon be done. Lie him on his back. Have you got the string? Scissors?'

'All here, all clean. Tie here. Good. And there. Now cut: in between. Now we wrap him up and give him back to Mama. Wash him later when the rest is done. I will get warm water.'

The room felt different, calm, all the rush and smell and panic and pain gone. Thérèse lay back on her pillows with the baby clasped softly on her breast, looking up, tired but smiling at Lawless. All kinds of thoughts were racing through his mind and the only ones that mattered were that she was all right and the baby was breathing. He could see its lips fluttering.

'Look at him, Philippe? Is he not beautiful?'

'I can see him and he is and so is his lovely mama.'

Mireille reappeared carrying a basin and jug and more towels hanging over her arm.

'Philippe, everyone will soon be hungry so please go and make something to eat. There is a rabbit casserole to heat up. You do that while I wash the baby and help Thérèse and come when I call you because there will be things for you to take away and bury in the ground. And then we will all eat and watch the little boy being fed by his Mama.'

They both looked at Mireille and then smiled at each other. It was clear who was in charge.

'Oh, and before you go, make up the fire. The room must be kept warm.'

'Yes, Ma'am. Call me when you need me.'

He was astonished to see that it was still daylight but sure enough, by his watch it was still only three o'clock. He felt as if he had been in the bedroom all day but it was barely six hours since he had arrived back from the village. Babies, especially first babies were supposed to take ages, days to be born. Hadn't Madame Bec—Denise, he smiled—told him that could be so? But not his son—his son! Oh no, he had been in a hurry. His son, what was his name; no, what would be his name? Shouldn't they weigh him? People always talked about how much a baby weighed. There were some scales in the kitchen. He would take them up to the bedroom. God, he felt so tired. What was it that Mireille had said? That's right: a casserole to warm up. At least he could do that. He put some more sticks on the fire and began to stir the iron pot hanging over the flames. It had just started to simmer when the kitchen door was thrust open and it seemed the room suddenly filled with people.

Dr Vaudet, hatless and bag in hand, hastened up the staircase closely followed by Madame Bec. Jeannot came across, took the ladle from Lawless's hand and began stirring the pot.

'Sit down for a minute, Sergeant and let them do what they have to do,' Jean-Pierre Bec said, closing the door behind him and coming over to sit at the table opposite Lawless. 'Jérôme said he wanted to tell you this but your mind was on other things,' Bec said, casting a glance upstairs, 'so he asked me to let you know. Two days ago the Americans and the English made landings at Oran and Algiers and we think Casablanca as well. There was some fighting but most of our men have now gone over to their side. Darlan is dead. Jérôme says the Germans are now trapped.'

Lawless was silent. He could hear what Bec was saying but it was difficult to take in when what he wanted to know was what was going on upstairs.

'Did you hear me, Sergeant?'

'Yes, yes. That's very good isn't it? What are they doing up there? I ought to go see.'

'Leave them, Sergeant. The doctor takes a little time. Listen, yes it is good news but Jérôme has heard something else, something very worrying.'

'Worrying, what do you mean?'

'He says he must tell you himself when you go to the café tomorrow to meet Mams'elle Chevalier. He told me especially to remind you about that.'

Lawless stood up. 'I hadn't forgotten. Is that everything? I really must go see.'

At that moment Dr Vaudet appeared on the landing above and all three sets of eyes in the kitchen stared up at him. He trotted briskly down the stairs and strode over to Lawless beaming broadly and seized him by the hand.

'My congratulations, Sir! Yes, yes, very good, very good. Healthy little chap, hungry too, yes. Your wife is very well, Sir, very well; tired yes, but that is not surprising. She must sleep a little if she can. A good birth; no complications; nothing to concern us. No. You have an excellent little midwife up there, Sir; one of the family, I suppose, yes. Said it was just like a little lamb being born. Ha! Can you believe that? I understand you also played your part. Hm, unusual, but needs must sometimes. The good Madame Bec will do everything necessary now, eh Bec? No, no, no: no time to eat. Must be off. Other calls to make: broken leg in the village. Ice on the cobbles, you know. Yes. Bec, may we go if you please? Goodbye to you, Sir. I will call again in three days, or immediately if anything, but not to worry. All is going very nicely. Yes, yes, you can go up now. Bec, are you ready?'

When Lawless entered the bedroom, Denise Bec came up, kissed him on both cheeks and left without a word closely followed by Mireille carrying a towel-covered basket. The room was warm, softly lit and quiet and Lawless had his first sight of his wife feeding his son at her breast.

Some time later when Thérèse and baby were sleeping, Lawless went downstairs, found the basket and buried its contents in a deep hole he dug well away from the house. Jeannot would have done it if asked, he knew, but this was something he needed to do himself. When he returned to the kitchen the table was set for four. He opened the bottle of red wine.

'Time to wet the baby's head,' he said to the mystification of the other three.

Late in the afternoon, the next day, Thérèse said she wanted to sit by the fire. They watched the flames dancing up from dry logs Jeannot had brought in. He said it should smell sweet because it was apple wood. Lawless had a glass of red wine in his hand. Thérèse said she would not drink while she was feeding the baby so Madame Bec was supplying her with warmed milk and honey.

'Yesterday frightened me a bit, Sweetheart, but today feels like the best day of my life.'

'He looked so funny when you put him on the scales.'

'Three and a half kilos: is that big for a baby? And he didn't wake up.'

'Not too big, but it did feel like it at the time,' she laughed.

'You are sure you're all right, aren't you? Nothing, you know, nothing . . .'

'Some things but they're all normal Madame Bec says. You haven't changed your mind about his name, have you?'

'No: Alexandre Aristide Duschene Lawless Chevalier sounds rather grand to me. I like it, even if it is a bit long. What shall we call him, Alex?'

'Wait and see. Uncle Alexandre should be pleased. I only hope Sevvie is as well.'

'Ah, yes. You remember she's arriving tonight and Jérôme wants me to go down to the village to meet her? There was something else Jean-Pierre said.'

'What about?'

'He didn't seem to know. Said Jerome wanted to tell me himself. I wonder if it could be a message from my father. It's been a long time now.'

'That would be wonderful, Philippe. You can send a reply about the baby.'

'Well, I don't have to be there until nine. I'll go down with Jeannot; put the bike in the cart in case there isn't enough room with Sevvie and Serge coming back as well. What was that? Is he all right?'

'Oh he just makes those little noises. All babies do. Leave him. He'll wake up soon enough and shout for food. You'll see. Just like a man. Don't forget to take the Family Book when you go. It's in the drawer. Jérôme will need to write in his name and date of birth.'

LA COUVERTOIRADE

Jérôme Janquet was leaning over the bar reading the local paper when Lawless walked in. The fuggy smoky warmth of the café was welcoming, after the sharpness of night air outside.

'I'm sorry, I'm a bit late. Had to help bathe the baby.'

'It's all right. They haven't arrived yet. How is he, the little one and Madame Chevalier?

'Mother and child doing well; that's what they say, isn't it? Both were asleep when I left. Oh, I've got the Family Book here for you to fill in and I've written his names and date of birth on this sheet of paper.'

'Thank you. I'll see to it.'

'Anything wrong, Jérôme? You're rather quiet.'

'No, nothing, well, yes, you ought to know: there is something badly wrong. Look, have a drink first and we'll toast young Mr what is it,' he said, studying the sheet of paper, '*Alexandre Aristide Duschene Lawless Chevalier*. Very fine names, all in the family. Splendid. To the new Chevalier, a long and happy life.'

'Phew! That's just what the doctor ordered, Jérôme: Gaston de Lagrange again?'

'Only the best for the young man. Is that package for me?'

'No, something I thought I'd let Séverine have; a sort of present for her coming back to stay for a while.' Lawless pushed the wrapped up Webley into the deep pocket of his overcoat. 'I've left my bike outside and there's this rucksack Jeannot said was for you. I don't know what's in it. Now what's all this bad news you were on about?'

'Sit down a minute while I put this bag behind the bar. Your coat and hat can go with it. We'll have a beer.'

'Your health.'

'To yours. Now, Jean-Pierre has told you about the landings, yes?'

'Yes, wonderful news. They're on the run now; at least in the desert they are.'

'That they are but they're also on the run here, or they soon will be.'

'The Germans? What do you mean, 'on the run here'?'

'We've had news that one army has starting to move from the west, along the Spanish border and another south from the centre, heading this way and down the Rhone valley: infantry, tanks, everything. There's talk of advance motorcycle patrols already near Toulouse and Brioude. They're invading, Philippe, taking over the whole of France!'

'Bloody hell! Are you sure? Why do that? And why now?'

'Algiers, Oran: the landings, Philippe. They want to make sure that your lot don't head for Marseille as well.'

'What do we do? The network . . .'

'There's nothing we can do, not yet anyway. We haven't enough men, or the right sort of weapons or explosives, nothing like enough. This is the German Army, Philippe. They'll do what they like.'

'Jérôme, I'm so sorry. Poor France.'

'Don't feel sorry for us! We don't need your pity! We need your guns and your bombs and your men. That's what we need!'

Lawless had never seen him angry and frustrated like that. He watched the mayor jump to his feet and pace around the shabby room swearing out loud and slapping his hands together in a fury.

'You can have my machine guns and all the ammunition and me to work one of them whenever you want.'

Jérôme Janquet turned and came back to the table, looking down at Lawless. He was trying to control himself but his eyes were still wild.

'We need more from you than that, Sergeant, much more.'

'I don't understand. What more can I do? Go on, tell me.'

'Oh . . .' the mayor swung away from the table, burning to say something, Lawless could see, but unable to bring himself to do it. 'Nothing, nothing. Leave it until they come, Serge and Mams'elle. Have another beer.'

Lawless judged it wiser not to try persuading him any further. Jérôme Janquet went out of the room returning a few minutes later with a plate of thickly sliced sausage, cheese and bread. He was calmer, almost his old self again.

'If we're going to have to wait a while and drink more, you need something in your stomach. You'll be glad of it afterwards.'

Séverine and Serge Valentin walked into the café an hour later. Lawless heard a car drive away after they came in but no one said whose it was. She was all bundled up in heavy loose clothes and looked tired as usual. Serge hovered round, clearly concerned about her but not daring to say anything. She kissed Lawless warmly and clung to him as if she needed some of his strength.

'I can see by the look on your face something has happened.'

'A boy, Sevvie, a lovely little boy. Born yesterday. And he's strong and Tressie is all right, dying to see you. She's so happy you're back.'

'That is the most wonderful news, Philippe. Come here.' She put her arms round him and kissed him again, a long and lingering kiss. 'Another Chevalier at last; a much needed and loved companion. And his name?'

'Alexandre Aristide Duschene Lawless Chevalier.' What did she mean, "companion? For her? Mireille? Who? Never mind. She had looked surprised at the 'Alexandre' but her expression showed she understood why and she was greatly pleased by 'Aristide', he could see.

'Good strong family names. I approve: very wise, Philippe. Uncle Alexandre will be most pleased when you tell him the news.'

Serge Valentin shook his hand and said how delighted he was. He looked as if he had something on his mind; Sevvie perhaps, as usual. They all sat round the table and wine and more beer and food was brought. The talk was all about the German invasion. One thing was clear: the campaign of nuisance was over. This was now a war.

'In that case,' Lawless said, 'I think you should have this, Sevvie. No need to open it now. It's something that you have seen before.'

She took the package containing the Webley and put it in her own bag without saying a word. He felt sure she knew what it was.

The café door opened and Jeannot looked inside.

'Time we were going,' Serge said. 'It's getting late.'

Lawless stood up with the others.

'Not you, Philippe,' Séverine said.

Lawless laughed at her and made for the door. 'What do you mean, not me? I'm coming with you, on the bike if there's no room in the cart.'

'No you're not, Philippe. We can't allow it.'

'Have you gone mad? What are you talking about?'

'It's too dangerous, my dear handsome brother: for you and for all the network. You have to leave. There is important work, vitally important work for you to do. Listen, you knew this time would come, you often said it would and now it has.'

'I'm not listening to you. I must go back to the house, to Tressie and the baby. Do you know what you're saying? He's only a day old. You, Jérôme, Serge, tell her she's mad!'

Both men were looking at him but neither of them spoke.

'Sit down and listen to me, Philippe, please. Let me explain. Give him another cognac, Jérôme.'

'I don't want another cognac. I want to go home. You're all mad.'

'Don't we have a good reason to be mad, Philippe? The Germans have now stolen all of France from us. Do you know what that does to people like us? I'll tell you: it makes us even more determined to get rid of the whole lot of them in any way we can and, listen, in ways that you can, you English with your bombers. You, Sergeant Air Gunner Lawless Chevalier in your bomber, not that wreck in the gorge, but a new one you will fly from England to burn German cities. You can't stay here any longer now the Germans are everywhere. They'll catch you, oh yes, they will: somebody, somewhere will betray you, Englishman and then what will happen to Tressie and your new little son and Mireille and everyone at La Commanderie? I'll tell you: execution for hiding an escaped English soldier or prison camp where it's so bad they will die anyway. Don't think for one moment any of us would get away. They'll torture you until you tell them everything. They are very good at that. You cannot stay a single day longer.'

'Sevvie, please, it's me, Philippe. Jerome, Serge, speak to her.' Lawless felt tears filling his eyes. He couldn't bear the thought: today had been so happy, so wonderful and now the people he thought were his friends, the ones he's risked being arrested with, had turned on him and wanted rid of him. Look at their faces.

'Sevvie's right, Philippe,' Serge Valentin said. It's a terrible thing to say, but you must go, if only for Thérèse and the baby's sake.'

Lawless looked desperately at the other man. 'Jérôme? Tell her. Please.'

There was profound pity in the mayor's eyes but his voice was firm.

'I am sorry, Philippe but there is no other way. Think of your family and think this also. You will return to them when all this horror and hatred has been washed away by people like you. I do not like saying this but there has also been an order from Dunbar. If you do not return to England you will be court-martialled as a deserter and in time of war you know what that means.'

They were implacable, sorry for him, but implacable. He could see no way out. He felt shamefully weak. How could any man leave his wife and baby one day after he was born? The threat of court martial meant nothing to him. To hell with Dunbar. But the idea of Tressie being dragged off to die in a prison camp and the baby with her because of him was unbearable. And he could come back. He would come back. Alexandre Chevalier and the others would look after his family.

'Can I just see them one more time?' He knew what they would say.

'Tressie will understand. Remember how strong she is. She has little Alexandre and Mireille and all of us. She will understand when we explain.'

'At least let me write something to her.'

They gave him a sheet of paper and a pencil. His heart was so full all he could think of saying was:

> *I love you and I love our little Alex. I have to go. Sevvie will explain everything. I love you and whatever happens I will come back. Please understand and forgive me. I will come back. Kiss him for me as I kiss you.*

He read it over. It was so flat, banal but his whole being was in it. He hoped she would see that and the spots where his tears had fallen on the paper.

They embraced him in turn, Jean-Pierre, Serge, and lastly, Séverine. She held both his hands and looked long into his eyes

'Courage, Philippe. You have given us so much hope and you are part of us, Tressie and me for always. Nothing can ever change that now. You are going where you should go as any good soldier must and when the work is done, you will come back to your family as any good father would.'

Then they were gone and he was left in the dim light of the shabby café staring at the closed door with a terrible tight feeling in his chest, abandoned, miserable and lost. Jérôme Janquet looked at the hunched shaking shoulders and knew there was only one thing to do.

'Philippe, listen to me. There's no time to lose. Grandjean has told me they are coming for you.'

Lawless looked at him with red haunted eyes. 'Grandjean? He's coming for me?'

'No, not him: he is warning you that others are on your trail. He sees that the Germans are the real enemies now and he has joined us. He has made sure you have a little time to get away before the others come for you. Do you understand? All right, this is what you must do. You have to get to La Couvertoirade where arrangements have been made for you. Put your coat on and your hat and this scarf. It will be cold where you're going so I've given you some gloves. Now here, the rucksack: there's bread, sausage and cheese and wine in it and some spare boots and socks and a sweater. Have you cigarettes and matches? No? Take these and my electric torch. What's most important is the map Querrell made for you in that envelope. I have it here, don't ask how I got it. Look, he's marked the way you go. The roads are full of patrols, probably even Germans by now so you have to take the shepherds' trackways. You're lucky there hasn't been too much snow. If you miss your way, look out for the menhirs. They'll put you back on the trail. Use the bike as far as you can. It should get you to Meyrueis before anyone's about. After that, you'll be on foot. Remember, keep to the map and don't talk to anybody if you can help it. Make out you're deaf or stupid and most people will leave you alone. Just to be sure you know where to go, let's have a quick look at Querrell's map.'

Jérôme Janquet started stabbing his finger at the words written on the map. Lawless half-listened thinking inconsequentially that Querrell's italic script showed the hand of calligrapher.

'There's Meyrueis, then you follow the track that climbs all the way up to that place, Malbosc. See it? Malbosc.You keep on south, always south—Dourbies—La Rouvière—heading towards Mont St Guiral—he's put a triangle marking it—the track keeps to the western slopes and descends—Le Jaoul—La Roujerlet—reaches the Col de la Barrière and drops down to le Luc. After that it's a five kilometre easy walk on to La Couvertoirade.'

'God, Jérôme, it's an awful long way and I feel absolutely shattered. I can't do this.'

'Yes you can, you bloody well can! Cavallier would have done it, and you can do the same. It's not much more than fifty kilometres and Jeannot is going with you as far as the top of the gorge above Meyrueis. On the bikes that takes less than an hour. He's in the kitchen wondering what's happening. It's time you were going. The flics could be here any minute. I'll help you on with the rucksack. You can find somewhere to lie up for a rest, maybe near Dourbie, and with a bit of an effort you could be having breakfast with Alexandre Chevalier the day after tomorrow.'

He turned and yelled at the door leading to the kitchen.

'Jeannot! Here! Time to go.'

***

The moon was a slim curving scratch in a clear black sky bright with stars. It was very cold and Lawless was glad of the gloves. He shook his shoulders to settle the pack on his back and set off.

'Not that way, Sergeant: this way now.'

Jeannot led the way along paths and tracks he seemed to be able to find effortlessly but Lawless could hardly see. There were patches of ice where puddles had been and where there was grass he could hear the frozen tufts crackle under the tyres. After perhaps twenty minutes a faint light showed ahead. 'Village,' Jeannot hissed and swung left apparently heading across a rough field but actually along the narrow but smoother line of a sheep track. With the village out of sight again Lawless called for a brief halt, wanting to scan the night sky, see which way they were heading. Polaris was at their backs, Orion near the western horizon on his right: south then. The going became easy with not much in the way of hills to climb. Jeannot pointed left, then right. 'Menhirs; good signposts.' Straining to see, Lawless could just make out two dark shadows standing a few metres to either side. The pace quickened a little as the trail began to lead downhill. Lawless tried the brakes and the front wheel skidded. Careful next time, he thought. A kilometre further on with the trackway now on a steeper downhill slope Jeannot stopped to wait for Lawless to catch up.

'Down there, Look.'

Far below Lawless saw a cluster of dim lights that flickered as he looked.

'Meyrueis. I leave you here. The road is steep but after one turn is straight.'

Lawless looked at the green glow of the pointers on his watch. Midnight: they had been riding for fifty minutes. A bit quicker than Jérôme had said, he thought: I'd like him to know that. Lawless dismounted and laid the bicycle down. He slipped the pack from his shoulders.

'I've said it before, Jeannot: how do you do it? Never mind, I wouldn't understand. I don't know what to say to you, except thank you and I hope to see you again when, well, you know when. You will look after them: I know I don't have to ask you that. I can't say any more. Shake. Now, off you go.'

'Mams'elle asked me to give you this.'

Lawless took the envelope and put it in his pocket.

'Thank you. I'll look at it later.'

'Safe journey, Sergeant.' Jeannot stood to attention and produced a fair attempt at a salute. Lawless returned the compliment and looked round for his pack. When he straightened up Jeannot was nowhere to be seen.

Lawless suddenly realised that for the first time in nearly a year he was really on his own. He sat down with a great aching emptiness inside him and began to sob. He tried to stop them but the images flooded his mind, Tressie laughing, at the piano, her delight with the horse, all of them dancing, the hot lazy days by the river at Castelbouc, Tressie frightened—oh god, that hurt—Tressie covered in straw, Tressie with the baby at her breast—that drove a knife into his heart . . . more and more the pictures came. How long he sat there weeping, even sometimes smiling through the tears, he didn't know. His watch told him ten minutes when his eyes became unblurred enough to see the time. He felt strangely, guiltily better. Was it grief, or loneliness? Try to forget, not for long, but long enough to get going again.

In places the road down into the gorge was so steep he had to get off and walk. Jeannot had told him to cross the river on the first bridge he came to because the Gendarmerie was near the one further downstream. Meyrueis seemed jammed into one of the narrowest and coldest parts of the valley: very different from the last time he was there, in the summer with Serge eating hard-boiled eggs and sausage and drinking beer in the café. Go round the back streets, Jérôme had told him. Easier said than done in the dark but for a little time trying to find the way took his mind off what he was leaving behind. Keep the star at your back, head south. Padding through one narrow street he heard noises behind a door and caught the unmistakeable smell of bread baking: baguettes being produced for next day's breakfast, memories of St Chely.

At the end of the baker's street he came onto a narrow stone-surfaced road with many potholes leading out of the town. It seemed unlike the sort of road Querrell would have recommended and a quick look at the map in the light of Jérôme's torch showed he had put a cross over what was obviously this road and drawn his line a hundred metres or so to the west following a small stream. Seeing the dark shape of hills rising where the track would lead, Lawless decided it was time to abandon the bicycle and see if he still had his fell-walking legs. After a fairly easy uphill pull in which he crossed the other road twice he found a signpost whose finger pointed south. To his astonishment torchlight disclosed the faded letters MALBOSC on it. He was on the right track, such as it was. The hillside steepened as the road twisted its way through dense wood cover and he decided to try what his father had called their very own light infantry drill of marching for half an hour and resting for ten minutes. What also helped was an urge that had come over him to drive on, to put distance behind him and memories too, at least for as long as he could.

It was ten kilometres to Malbosc and all uphill. However, the effort ensured he was no longer cold; in fact he had soon taken off the heavy coat and tied it on top of his pack, though finding it necessary to don it again when he stopped. He checked the length of the marches and rests meticulously with his watch, chanting as many lines of Shakespeare as he could remember, and panting French songs and take-off and landing drill and anything else that might keep up his walking rhythm. He promised himself bread and sausage and wine when he reached Malbosc and sleep, most of all sleep, if he could find somewhere to hide. He was sure it must be near daybreak when he saw a dark huddle of buildings ahead. It had to be Malbosc. There was no other place on Querrell's map where he judged he must be by now. He crept past what was surely a farm from the smell and plodded on. There had to be a place to rest somewhere. He almost blundered into it before he realised what it was, a shepherds'shelter. Back aching with exhaustion he crept in, dragging his pack after him. He looked at his watch: five o'clock. He leaned back and fumbled for the cord that closed the pack but was asleep before he could pull it loose.

It was shelter, but a bad place to choose, bringing back memories as soon as he woke that were precious but now unbearably painful and he had to force himself to stay inside at least long enough to eat and drink his wine without the risk of being seen. Getting out again was not easy, stiff and aching as he was. Once you're up, get going, his father always said: if you're stiff, walking will ease it away. After putting on dry stockings he heaved up the pack and forced his arms through the straps. Time? Eleven. Six hours sleep; six, perhaps seven hours left to nightfall. He looked at the map. Could he make the twenty kilometres to the Col de La Barrière? Although it was cold, the sky was clear and best of all, there was no wind. This was different country, wooded ridges, rounded slopes of rough grass and clumps of gorse still yellow with blossom and tall thistles with tufted blue tops: not too hard going but there was a gorge to cross and beyond that a fair sized mountain marked St Guiral with a triangle by Querrell. To his relief he saw that the trail ran some way below the summit on its western side. Where he now stood the line was well marked, no doubt by many sheep hooves and men's boots over the years. He could hear the cooing of pigeons and the tapping of a woodpecker in the woods behind him and as he set off a chaffinch started up somewhere. He tried imitating the chipping and scraping call and finally got a response.

There was no way of avoiding the village marked on the map as Dourbies. The trail wound down a bare rock-strewn hillside towards its close-packed pale grey houses with their steep-sided dark roofs and its tall slim church tower set among leafless trees above the little river in its narrow gorge. Lawless decided to brave it and even stop for coffee in the café should there be one open. He had bad luck and good luck: the café was closed and the streets empty. It was the time of day when no one stirs from the house in France. The same was true of La Rouvière, a much smaller place that he passed through half an hour later. Ahead lay a steady slog up the boulder-covered lower slopes of St Guiral into the forest that spread down from the summit but still the trackway was clear and with what was left of his bread and cheese and the last long pull of Jérôme's red inside him Lawless resolved not to stop again until he had that granite peak behind him and he could see his way to the Col de la Barrière.

It was still daylight when he reached the Col, where the trail finally emerged from the woods and crossed a road much larger than any he had seen since leaving Meyrueis. He scratched away the moss covering a stone pillar at the roadside and made out the name Le Vigan with below it an arrow pointing east. The map showed he still had nearly five kilometres to go before he reached Le Luc but there was no more climbing to do and he reckoned he could get there before dark. He ate his last bit of sausage and risked a drink from a little stream before setting off again and feeling almost cheerful enough to start whistling.

Le Luc turned out to be a handful of single storey houses seemingly built of granite boulders. Some had stone-slabbed roofs and one was thatched. Lawless approached as dusk was falling and saw lights come on in some of the windows. He felt suddenly tired, too tired to look for a shepherd's shelter floored by mouldy straw and smelling of sheep shit. He banged hard on the door of the first house in the village. It opened to reveal a man with a lighted lantern in his hand. The man held it up to shine on Lawless's face.

'Take off that hat. Let me have a good look at you.'

'Good evening, Sir. Can you direct me to La Couvertoirade?'

'Come in. We've been expecting you, Englishman.'

A fire blazed brightly in the chimney place and the room smelled pleasantly of wood smoke. The lantern carried by the man and another on the mantelpiece did little to lighten the shadows in the rest of the room. A dog, that could have been the twin of Caramelle, raised its head from its place in front of the hearth and eyed him briefly before resuming its doze.

'Put that sack down by the door and sit yourself by the fire.'

Lawless did as he was told and stretched out his hands to the warmth. A door creaked somewhere in the gloom and a woman came in. She had a scarf over her head and he could not make out whether she was young or old.

The man jerked his head towards Lawless. 'It's him. Bring him something to drink while I get the cart.' The dog heaved itself to its feet and followed him out into the darkness.

Sounds came from the shadows in the back of the room: the creak of a cupboard door opening, the faint clatter of knife, or fork on plate and liquid poured from a jug. The woman came over and handed him a plate of bread and soft cheese and a beaker. She was younger than he had guessed, not much older than Mireille and her eyes shone in the firelight.

'Thank you, Madame.'

'Mams'elle, Sir.'

'Thank you, Mams'elle.' He raised the beaker to her. 'Health. Hm, very good; much needed. May I ask your name?'

'Clémence.'

'A very pretty name, Mams'elle.'

'You are the Englishman?'

'One of them, Mams'elle,' he smiled.

'I have never seen an Englishman before.'

'We are not very different, Mams'elle.'

'But you are very tall, taller than my . . .'

The door opened and the man came in followed by his dog.

'Drink up. You can eat that on the way. The cart's outside and ready.'

Lawless swallowed the rest of the rough red wine and stood up.

'Where are we going?'

'Mr Chevalier's house: where else?'

At the doorstep Lawless turned and raised his hand to the girl. She made no response. The door closed and she heard cartwheels begin to roll outside.

'Safe journey,' she said and put the empty plate and beaker on the table.

'Lie in the back and cover yourself with that blanket, just in case we see somebody.'

It suited Lawless. His mind was too full of his own thoughts to want a conversation. Wounds brought shock and numbness that could last for hours and he had seen it happen, more than once. The pain came later. It always did. That was what he was beginning to feel now.

An hour after leaving the house in Le Luc the cart drew up at the gateway he had entered once before.

'You get out here. Sylvestre should be waiting for you somewhere inside.'

Lawless climbed down painfully and felt in the cart for his pack. He reached up to shake the driver's hand.

'Thank you. What is your name?'

'Names don't matter. We won't be seeing each other again.'

Shouldering his pack, Lawless walked through the great arched gateway of La Couvertoirade. He recognised the upright stance and the limp of the figure that came towards him.

'Good to see you again, Sylvestre.'

'You're a bit later than expected.'

'Sorry about that. It was quite a long walk.'

'Hm. You'll need a bath. Supper's keeping warm.'

'Who was that man who brought me?'

'Nobody. One of the peasants.'

It was wonderful, a tub full of steaming hot water, a block of Marseille soap and a large sponge. Lawless lay back soaking, feeling the tiredness and stiffness seep out of him. A sharp rap on the bathroom door and a few brisk words jerked him out of his liquid doze.

'Supper. Five minutes.'

There was game pie in a square dish and mashed potato, rich in butter. Sylvestre poured red wine from a decanter that he then placed on the sideboard next to an empty bottle with the label Chateau Mont-Redon. Cheese did not appear but the hoped-for lemon soufflé did.

Sylvestre cleared all the plates and cutlery away and without being asked placed a sizeable glass of cognac in front of Lawless.

'You'll be wanting an early night. Same room as before. Everything's set out for you there. Lantern's on the table outside. Lights out in half an hour.'

'Mr Chevalier?'

'They'll see you at breakfast. Eight o' clock.'

'My compliments to the cook.'

'Hm.'

Once in his room Lawless decided to have a cigarette before going to sleep. He opened one of the windows to let out the smoke. It was a clear night, brilliant with stars. The Causse looked dark grey in starlight. Trees and shrubs had no shadows. Was Thérèse looking at the stars too? Or was the baby crying to be fed? He wanted to picture the scene and yet not even to think about it. He felt guilty, helpless, hopeless and lonely all at the same time. When would he see them again? Would he ever see them again? Cold air was pouring into the room. He tried to think of it as taking off on a raid. He'd always got back somehow. So far, he reminded himself. It didn't work. His cigarette was dead. He closed the window, turned down the wick of the lantern and got into bed, pulling the sheets over his head.

What had Sylvestre meant, saying *they* would see him at breakfast?

***

Three places were set. There was a basket of crusty warm rolls and brioches covered with a napkin, a pat of butter and a variety of conserves and honey in little porcelain dishes. Alexandre Chevalier sat at the head of the table, coffee cup in one hand, turning over sheets of paper with the other. He looked up as Lawless sat down and gave his grave smile.

'Sleep well?'

'Like a log, thank you.'

'Good. You have a long journey ahead of you. Tell me, how did you leave my nieces and of course, my little nephew or perhaps little niece: if I have one yet, that is. Well, I hope.'

Lawless struggled to reply. 'Thérèse was sitting up in bed and looking well and happy. He, your little nephew, was asleep in his cot beside her.'

'He? A boy: is he named?'

'Alexandre Aristide Duchesne Lawless Chevalier.'

Alexandre Chevalier repeated the names softly as if to himself. Lawless could see he was greatly pleased.

'The family is finally reconciled in him. Let me shake your hand. You have brought us a new generation of Chevaliers.'

'And Séverine is there with them.'

'She must rest a while, at least until she recovers.'

'She takes on too much.'

'That and now . . .'

'Philippe, my dear. Here you are. Come and embrace me.'

Justine Lamphier stood in the doorway with her arms opened in greeting.

'Mm, mm: you smell like a Frenchman but fortunately one of the cleaner kind. I will sit opposite you and you shall tell me all about your adventures.'

'Thérèse has given birth to a son, Justine.'

'Philippe! Is this true? When?'

'The day before yesterday.'

'The darling. I wish he might have been born in happier times. Does he resemble you or his mother?'

'It's difficult to say. Tressie thinks he has my mouth and her nose. I don't know how she can tell.'

'Alexandre, we must go see this wonderful and longed for arrival as soon as possible. Perhaps I might be his godmother.'

'He carries my name and that of his grandfather, my brother,' said Chevalier.

Justine Lamphier gave Lawless a look that he could only read as roguish.

'Impeccable, Philippe; so correct and so diplomatic.'

'We chose his names together, Tressie and I; with Duschene and Lawless too.'

'Lawless,' she said, seeming to lick the word as she spoke it. 'I love the name, so debonair, almost insolent.'

Sylvestre stumped into the room carrying a silver coffee pot. There was silence as he filled everyone's cup.

'It's on the sideboard if you want any more,' he said and stumped out again.

'Eat your breakfast like a good boy, Philippe. You need your strength, though I must say you have now given ample proof of that.'

'The brioches are delicious,' Lawless said with his mouth half full.

'Try the garrigue honey. So healthy for a young man.'

She took nothing but black coffee, accepting a second cup from Lawless after he had finished eating.

Alexandre Chevalier looked at his silver pocket watch. Lawless sensed a change in mood coming.

'We must move quickly, Philippe. All has been arranged. There is money for you and new papers with a different identity. You have a little time to read through them.'

'And I will help you learn all about your new self,' said Justine Lamphier.

'The train to Béziers makes a brief stop at Montpaon; the station is 18 kilometres from here.'

'Alexandre does not drive, so I will take you there. You will have a suitcase and different clothes, of course.'

'You have already made this journey once, Philippe and as before you will be met.'

'At Magalas, I suppose.'

'Just so. The rest of your journey is the responsibility of the person who will meet you there. You can have complete confidence in him.'

'All of this must have taken some time to organise, Alexandre.'

'It was anticipated. The German invasion simply made it more urgent that you escape, not only for the safety of the network and your loved ones but even more importantly for what you will be taking with you back to England.'

'Dunbar said something about that and you too when I was last here. Can you please tell me now what it is I have to do?'

'You will be carrying two sealed packages which must be delivered to an address in London. That is all I can tell you.'

'What address?'

'I cannot tell you that, either.'

'I cannot know what is in the packages and I cannot be told the address where I must take them. I'm confused.'

'Philippe,' Justine Lamphier put her hand over his. 'If you knew what was in the packages and you were caught, even if you were able to get rid of them, the Germans would find out everything about the network and much more besides. Many people would die.'

'All right, I can see that but how do I deliver these packages if I have no address?'

Alexandre Chevalier selected a page from the papers next to his plate and handed it to Lawless.

'When escaped men return to England they are always interrogated by an officer about their activities since they went missing. You must ask him for permission to telephone your family to tell them you are safe and well. What you *will* do is telephone the number on that sheet of paper. A voice will ask for the code word that is written next to it. You will say the word and repeat it twice. The voice will not speak again but you may carry on talking as if your father or mother had replied. The packages will be collected the same day.'

Lawless looked at the paper. The telephone number had six digits. The code word was Birnam. Chevalier and Justine Lamphier watched him intently as he read. He looked up.

'Birnam: the only Birnam I know is in Macbeth. Why Birnam? Sorry, shouldn't ask.'

'Fix the number and the code word in you mind, Philippe, and then give the paper back to me.'

'What about the packages?'

'They are already securely hidden in the suitcase that I told you about. Now,' said Justine Lamphier, rising from her chair, 'shall we go through your new papers together and play question and answer?'

An hour later she declared that he was word perfect.

'You are a very quick learner, Philippe. You must have pleased your professors at Oxford. Philippe Martin, mechanic, of Airaines near Amiens has become Claude Vallon, student, from Brioude. How strange: they look the same, even of the same age. They could be twins. I don't see you as a Claude, but there it is.

And what is the purpose of your journey?'

'I am on my way to stay with a family my mother knows in Narbonne to give lessons in English to their daughter and help her with her piano.'

'English?'

'Yes, she has examinations next year.'

'Names, address?'

'Dr and Mrs Deluze, 21a rue Cuvier. It's not far from the Lycée Beauséjour.'

'Excellent. I think that will do. What is the time? Eleven already? The train leaves at thirteen hours. You must change and pack your case. You will find your new clothes in your room.'

'Where is Alexandre?'

'In the library writing letters. He wants you to post some for him in Magalas.'

He was just about to pull the shirt over his head, when she came into his room and closed the door behind her.

'Justine! What are you . . .'

'Sh, Philippe. We have only half an hour. I just wanted you to have something to remember me by. You wouldn't refuse me that, would you?'

Alexandre Chevalier came to the top of the steps outside the house with them to say goodbye.

'I wish we had had more time to talk about other things than the war, Philippe; your interest in Romance poetry, for instance. Your ideas on how metre may subtly illuminate the poet's real leanings in his treatment of opposing passions, religious or carnal, when the words and phrases that might otherwise be used are forbidden by the conventions, have given me pause for thought. They are scholarly and deserve pursuing. I have looked out some material that could be of interest to you whenever better times come. Remember that. Goodbye and a safe journey. Those you love are in my care.'

Justine Lamphier took Lawless's arm as they walked through the winding cobbled streets to the main gateway.

'How do you see yourself, Philippe: as a Templar or a Hospitaller? I think, yes, a Templar, tall and severe leading the van, intent on conquest.'

'I feel more like Cavallier when he decided he had to make a run for it.'

She stopped, suddenly serious. 'Oh no, Philippe: you are only exchanging one danger for another.'

Sylvestre was standing by the car just outside the gateway.

'Suitcase in the boot. Lunch in the basket on the back seat. You take care now, remember.'

'Why don't you drive, Philippe? It would look more normal in these parts.'

They embraced decorously, as an aunt and nephew might, outside the little station at Montpaon. She had said that it would be less conspicuous than on the platform where there just might be a gendarme on duty. He took his suitcase and lunch basket out of the car and she handed him the ticket that had been bought some days ago, she said.

'I'd better go inside.'

She smiled. There were no tears in her eyes but they were sad.

'Yes, go quickly now. Remember me, Philippe. I will always remember you.'

FLIGHT

The train entered a long tunnel shortly after leaving Montpaon. When it emerged, he took little notice of the countryside passing by or the stops the train made. He had seen it before and there was too much on his mind. A few people got on at Bédarieux but none came into his compartment. From time to time he looked at the basket on the seat beside him but didn't feel like eating. He wished the train would get to Magalas. At least that would give him something to do and stop him thinking of La Commanderie.

It was late afternoon when he got off the train at Magalas. There was no policeman on duty and no one in the ticket office. He left his ticket on the unattended counter and went outside. No one would believe the Germans had just invaded southern France: everything was the same as when he was last there, that is nothing was happening. He heard the sound of a car horn hoot once and took no notice. It hooted again and this time he remembered that odd coughing sound. He walked over to the car that was parked under a tree.

'Get in,' said Dunbar. 'Put those things on the back seat.'

'Where are we going, Béziers?'

'Narbonne: 21a rue Cuvier, not far from the Lycée Beauséjour. You know it, don't you?' Dunbar looked across and grinned at him.

'Is it safe there?'

'Safer than Béziers, I can tell you. Bloody Germans all over the place there. Most of 'em don't even know where they are. Complete bloody chaos. Of course it's safe. It'll take us about a couple of hours, because we'll be going by the back roads. There could be a curfew, so we have to get a move on.'

Dunbar parked the car near a bend in the rue Cuvier east of the city centre in Narbonne. He produced a key for the street door and they climbed a spiral stairway to the first floor.

'We're staying here tonight,' Dunbar said, unlocking a door numbered 21a. 'The Deluzes are away for a few days, so we have the place to ourselves. What have you got in that basket? Jolly good: and a bottle of Chablis? They do you well at La Couvertoirade: no need to go out then. Germans have probably eaten everything anyway.'

When all the food from the basket had been eaten and the last glass of Chablis had been poured, Dunbar sat back and offered Lawless a cigarette. It was an English one.

'We have to be up early tomorrow. You've got a long day ahead of you so get plenty of sleep if you can. Don't need any money do you? Good.'

'Where am I going?'

Dunbar looked at him in surprise. 'Spain of course. It's still the best way out. We've sent plenty like you that way in the last two years but you're a bit special, aren't you? We've had to make different arrangements for you. I was going to put you on the train for Perpignan but that wouldn't be such a good idea now so we're off to Foix in the morning, all along back roads again. It takes a fair bit longer but it should be safer.'

'Then what?'

'We've built up a group in Foix and most of them know the mountain tracks well because most of them are smugglers. We keep them well paid. One of them, I know him and he's a good man, he'll take you up into Andorra. There is a border, but it's France for all intents and purposes. He'll find you a Spanish guide, no doubt one of his mates in the same business, and one way or another he'll get you to Barcelona. There is a Consular officer in Barcelona and he will arrange your transport to Gibraltar. Then it's up to the Navy or your own outfit to get you back home.'

'Serge got lost in the mountains in Andorra.' Lawless told Dunbar Valentin\s story about a smuggler finding him and setting him on the right track to safety.

'Could have been one of ours, but I doubt it if he didn't ask for money. Listen, Philippe: sorry about that court martial thing. Shouldn't have said that, seeing what you were going through.'

'It wasn't that that persuaded me to do this.'

'I know. Good man. Time for bed,' Dunbar got up and yawned. 'Still,' he said, grinning, 'court martial offence getting married without your CO's permission. King's Regulations: did you know that?'

Dunbar said that they should make an early start and find somewhere on the way for breakfast. Just before leaving the flat he gave Lawless a backpack like the one he had left behind in La Couvertoirade, telling him it had his mountain kit inside. Lawless expected to see German patrols or troops manning barriers but there were none on the roads that Dunbar took. Early morning hazy sunshine promised a mild day near the Mediterranean although Dunbar told him to expect snow in the mountains. The road wound an up and down course through fields, many of them ploughed and olive groves and vineyards where the vine leaves were turning yellow, and gradually climbed the farther west they drove. Signposts indicating right to Carcassone, Rivesaltes and later Perpignan to the left went by without a word from Dunbar. Lawless's stomach began to claim his attention.

'You said something about breakfast.'

'Soon; I want to get over the Col before we stop. There's a place I know down the hill from there.'

Past the Col du Paradis 622m as the sign said, the road snaked down through scrubby fields and stands of oak and beech for another five or six kilometres until the keep of a castle with four corner towers came into view.

'Arques,' Dunbar said. 'This is Cathar country, if you know anything about them.'

'They had the same sort of trouble with a Pope as the Camisards did. Cavallier would have sided with them, I bet. Interesting that the Templars didn't seem to have too much against them, though.'

'I wouldn't know anything about that but I do know where you can get a decent cup of coffee here.'

Lawless breathed in the unmistakeable smell of coffee and Gauloises and wondered if this might be the last time he would have the pleasure. They sat at a table well away from the window. The man who came over from the bar evidently knew Dunbar well although he gave Lawless a sharp look.

'Morning François. Don't worry about my friend here. He's all right. Speaks good French, though, so mind your manners.'

The man grinned and swept the table top perfunctorily with his cloth.

'A big jug of your strongest and the rest. We're hungry.'

The coffee came first, coal black and steaming in a litre-sized brown jug. It was the real kind and there was sugar too. Three spoonsful in the first cup and Lawless immediately felt better. Fresh bread, butter, slices of ham and cheese and sugar dusted rolls followed. François went back to his station behind the bar and started the ritual polishing of glasses.

'Any Germans been through here?'

'Not yet. A patrol went through Quillan: motorbikes and a couple of trucks. They asked the way to Perpignan! I would never have believed it; I thought we'd done for the buggers in 1918.'

'We will again, François, you wait and see. They'll soon be kicked out of Africa.'

'Means more of them over here.'

'Well, we'll have to do something about that, won't we? What's the weather been like?'

'Snow above 1200 metres on this side I've heard, but the sky's clear. Should be all right if you get going soon.'

'We'll be off then. Thank you, François. I'll drop in on the way back.'

Dunbar put a note on the table and they got up to leave. At the door, Lawless turned and said thank you for the best breakfast he had had in days.

'Good luck; you watch out now.'

'When I told you we were going to Foix,' Dunbar said, after they had been driving over narrow, twisting roads for about half an hour, 'I didn't mean the town itself. A few kilometres to the south there's a safe place that is just off the road to Tarascon where we gather until the guides turn up. That can be a few days and we've had as many as ten in the group waiting to cross. As I said, you're different so you'll be on your own with the guide and set off as soon as we get there.'

'Are you sure he will be there?'

'He'd better be,' Dunbar said grimly, or I'll shoot the bugger when I see him next. He knows that.'

'That reminds me. Any news of our friend Allan?'

'Who? Oh, him. No; at least none that need bother you.'

They left the low ground far behind them and drove in silence for an hour along empty side roads through a river valley with mountains on both sides higher than any Cumbrian fell Lawless had ever climbed. It was almost midday when Dunbar spoke again.

'We turn off soon and cross the river just outside Tarascon. It's about another twelve kilometres.'

It turned out to be market day in Tarascon with people crowding the main street and blocking all traffic. Dunbar swore under his breath as he wound his way through the side streets until he found the way at last to an old stone bridge arching over a river. Lawless saw from the sign on the parapet that it was the Ariège.

'Soon be there now,' Dunbar said.

'That railway line just after the bridge. Where does it go?'

'Over into Spain through a tunnel. Early on some people tried it, but it was always a problem. Bloody uncooperative border guards, and you had to change trains. The Germans are bound to be there now so it's a write-off. Pity, it would be a lot more comfortable than walking. Now, it's not far along here.'

There was a tumbledown barn near the road a few kilometres further on. One of the big double doors was open and Lawless could see ragged bales of dirty looking straw haphazardly piled up inside. Dunbar saw him looking rather apprehensive.

'Perfect,' he said. 'Nobody ever gets suspicious of a barn with an open door. Come on. Bring the bag. I'll handle the case.'

There was a smell of mouldy straw in the draughty cavern-like space. Lawless put his bag down and looked round.

'Nobody here yet.'

'He'll be around somewhere, probably watching us to see if we've been followed. He'll be along. You'd better get ready for when he turns up.'

Lawless watched him open the suitcase, take a knife from his pocket, slice away at the lining of the lid and take out two thick sealed envelopes.

'These are what you're taking to England and believe me, it's more important they get there than you do. Right, while I have a gander outside hide these and get out of those clothes and put on what's in the bag, and I mean everything, scarf for round your ears, hat, gloves, the lot. I don't want you getting frostbite up there like the buggers that went up the Port de Siguer last January.'

'I know about frostbite,' Lawless said. 'Remember I was a rear gunner flying over the Alps.'

In the rucksack was the mountain kit Dunbar had mentioned: boots, socks, thick trousers and belt, heavy working shirt, woollen roll neck sweater, scarf, gloves and a peaked cap. There was also a thigh-length coat with high collar and deep pockets and what looked like a British Army issue groundsheet that Lawless put back into the bag. He had just finished dressing when Dunbar returned and handed him a cloth bag he had taken from the car boot.

'Bread, cheese, sausage and dried apricots in there and water bottle, full; and this.' He held up a half bottle of brandy. 'You might need this where you're going.'

'I think our friend has arrived,' Lawless said, nodding past him towards the door.

A short stocky man in a well-worn sheepskin coat and a flat cap came slowly, warily towards them. He carried a heavy walking stick with a pointed end and had a haversack slung over one shoulder.

'Juan,' said Dunbar, 'this is my friend.'

Lawless offered his hand but the man stood back, searching Lawless's face with his deep-set black eyes. He made no reply when Lawless spoke to him in French but his eyes showed he must have understood.

'Does he always inspect people like that? Will I do, you think?'

'He's all right, just likes to be sure. He understood you. He's Spanish; had to get out of Spain when Franco won because he's Catalan. That's his first language but he knows enough French. Comes with the job.' Dunbar turned to the man, switched to French and prodded him in the shoulder. 'Doesn't it, Juan: comes with the job, I said: your job, merchant?'

Juan's face creased into a sly grin and he held out his hand. Lawless took it. It was surprisingly warm and soft.

'It's two o' clock,' Dunbar said. You should be able to get quite a way before it turns dark. He'll have his own food but I expect he'd like a nip from that bottle now and again.

He won't say much but when he does talk, listen hard. It will be for your own good.'

'Do I have to pay him? I have money.'

'No. He's had some on account and he gets the rest when I hear that you've reached Barcelona. Now, unless you have anything else to ask, it's time you were going. Good luck. You know what you have to do.'

Juan's eyes followed Dunbar's car until it was out of sight then he turned and walked rapidly away from the barn, beckoning Lawless to follow him.

***

The path they followed was very like one of the shepherds' trackways in the Causses. Lawless imagined it had the same purpose. It wound up the wooded mountainside, avoiding hamlets of white-walled houses lower down and contouring the steeper slopes headed in the direction of a peak on a high ridge covered in snow that was tinged pink by the late afternoon sun. After two hours of steady climbing they rested on bare granite slabs below the peak on its southern side where the snow was not so deep. Lawless offered Juan the water bottle but the guide shook his head. He looked west to where the last rays of the now invisible sun made the ridge tops glitter and stood up.

'Two hour,' said and put his clasped hands up to one cheek. 'Sleep'.

Lawless was feeling strong and in high spirits for the first time in days. The months of hard work in the fields and barns and the fifty-kilometre route march—as he described it to himself—from Meyrueis to La Couvertoirade were paying off. There was still light enough to see and the view was breathtaking: valleys and ridges green with forest or heath or grey where the rock lay bare ran down from the southern snow-capped peaks to the now dimly-seen dark groove where the Ariège cut its course downstream towards Tarascon. It was Cumbria on a far grander scale. Juan gave him little time to savour the sight and set off again without a word.

It was quick slip and slide down into the darkening cold valleys and slow, sweaty slog up the sides of the ridges but always ahead rose the now not so distant white peaks to beckon them on. Lawless began to wonder where they would stop for the night. Juan's two hours were almost up. It was more like three hours had passed when the dark figure ten metres ahead of him suddenly stopped and pointed down the valley. A dimly flickering light was showing. Lawless had no idea how far away it was. In the silence he heard the sound of running water.

'We go there, Juan?'

'No. This way.'

The running water that Lawless had heard was an icy stream he almost fell into as he slipped on one of the stepping-stones that crossed it. On the bank above was a dark shadowy mass he thought might be a huge fallen boulder but turned out to be a rough wooden hut with sagging roof. When he reached it, the door was open and Juan was already inside fumbling around in the gloom. The tiny flame of Lawless's lighter revealed him with a short thick piece of candle in his hand. It was not much but when lit somehow it made the hut feel warmer, much warmer, Lawless realised, than the freezing darkness outside. It was time to open the bottle of brandy.

They shared each other's food. Lawless preferred Juan's cheese and said so. As for the sausage: no, far too spicy and pungent but to be polite he swallowed hard and forced it down. Juan had olives and Lawless the dried apricots. After such a day, it was a feast. Hot coffee would have been wonderful but after all, there was more brandy. Juan accepted a Gauloise and lit it from the candle. Smoke from the two cigarettes brought back a fleeting memory of the Café de la Place. Now sleep. There were some dirty-looking sacks half-filled with straw in a corner. A goose down-filled mattress could not have been more comfortable.

'Sunrise tomorrow,' came Juan's voice from the other corner. 'We go.'

Before the sun penetrated the valley snow that had drifted down during the night had a hard crackling surface and thin plates of ice fringed the sides of the stream. Bread, cheese and the last of the apricots were hastily swallowed and washed down with cold water and they were on the trail again at seven according to Lawless's watch, following the valley of a tributary to the stream by the hut. He felt stiff to begin with but that soon wore off as he worked hard to keep up with a man he guessed was at least twice his age. Two hours steady climb up the valley with Juan allowing no stops longer than enough for Lawless to catch his breath brought them to a wide boulder-strewn col with great scree fans on either side tapering up towards immense white peaks. There Juan did allow a ten-minute rest which they took sitting with their backs against an upright stone pillar that Juan said was a signpost between two valleys. He pointed back over his shoulder.

'There, France. This way, Andorra,' he said nodding to the south.

'How far?'

Juan held up two fingers, added a third, then folded it back. Lawless took him to mean two, perhaps three kilometres. It was a very stiff climb made slower by thickening snow and Juan's stopping from time to time to slide his pointed stick slowly into the snow and listen intently as his gaze carefully swept the slopes, side to side and up and down. The second time he did this Lawson asked him why.

'Avalanche. Make no noise.'

The three-kilometre climb took three hours and looking back from the col and feeling the strain as he did, Lawless was amazed that they had made it in so short a time.

'Where are we now, Juan?'

The Spaniard took a couple of steps forward, pulling Lawless by the arm with him.

'Andorra,' he said with his broad creased grin.

'Andorra! How do you know? There's nothing to say.'

'Feel different.'

'You're right. Let's get going. I like this country.'

It was now easy going at last. Lawless could see the trail that was weaving its way down the side of the valley to join a larger road far below. In what seemed no time at all the trail became more of a cart track with a few primitive looking cottages and shacks in snow-covered rough fields on each side. A church spire came into view and where the track joined the metalled road was a sign saying Soldeu. Lawless turned left towards the houses but Juan pulled his arm and shook his head.

'Bad people there. Escaldes better, this way.'

Escaldes was twelve kilometres away but they passed the last five sitting in an ancient open-backed lorry on a heap of muddy swedes that were being chewed by two young pigs. The driver, clearly someone on very good terms with Juan, dropped the two of them at the bottom of a hill outside the town. By this time Lawless knew better than to ask where they were going. He shouldered the rucksack and tramped after his guide, hoping there might be somewhere they could eat before the day was over.

The side street they followed opened into a small square. Juan pointed to the other side.

'I leave now. You go there, see?'

He was pointing at a shabby looking building distinguished from the others by having a larger window and a sign over the door saying Café del Sol.

Lawless hesitated. Juan gave him a push.

'Yes, waiting. Jenaro, waiting for you. Go.'

'You're not coming in?'

'No.' Juan turned to go.

'Wait. Here, take this. It's all I have to give you.'

The Spaniard accepted the half-full bottle of brandy with a nod of thanks and Lawless managed to shake his hand.

The café owner, Jenaro—Lawless never found out his surname either—showed not the slightest surprise on seeing him, simply gesturing for Lawless to follow him into a back room where there was a table and chair and a bed in the corner. Food was brought later by an old woman with greying hair and a dark southern face: a loaf of bread and a bowl of hot stew that was mainly beans, pork sausage and tomatoes, a bottle of wine and another of dark green olive oil that she indicated was for drizzling onto the bread. Lawless was so famished that he felt he could eat the lot before she had left the room. The food and wine made him feel sleepy and as no one else seemed to be coming to see him he lay down on the bed without taking off his clothes and fell asleep

He was woken by a hand shaking his shoulder and sat up quickly to find the man Jenaro standing over him. It was now evening and someone had put a lighted lantern on the table. Jenaro spoke good French with a strong Midi accent. He told Lawless he had worked for years in various bars and on the docks in Marseille but decided to return to Andorra after the German invasion in 1940.

'You will sleep here tonight. Tomorrow my brother takes his cheese and meat to the market in Santa Julia de Loria in his van. It is more difficult now, the escaping, since the Germans came south. Some say they will invade Andorra as well. I do not know. It is difficult. The police have taken the house we used to have but there is another. My brother will take you there and you will wait for the man to come from Barcelona.'

'What man is that?'

'From the British consul in Barcelona.'

'How long must I wait for him?'

'I do not know. I am sorry but it is difficult. But you will be safe in Santa Julia.'

'Jenaro, I thank you for doing all this for me. It puts you in danger. One day I hope I can repay.'

'The Fascists! I hate every one. Franco! I shit on his face! You have been fighting them or you would not be here so you are a friend. Give me your clothes. My mother will clean them and bring you more to eat later. Now, you are still tired. Go back to sleep.'

After three days hidden away in the attic of a dingy house in one of the back streets of Santa Julia de Loria where he saw no one but a middle-aged woman who brought him food from time to time but could speak neither French nor English, Lawless felt he would go mad with boredom or frustration or both. He decided he must get out and at least walk a few yards along the street and to hell with being stopped and questioned by a policeman. He put his few things and the remainder of his last meal in his rucksack and crept downstairs with his boots in his hand. There seemed to be no one in the house but him. He stopped in the grimy passage to put his boots on and opened the door onto the street. Standing on the step with his hand raised to knock was a short round-faced man in a smart coat and trilby hat. They stared at each other for a moment and then the man held out his hand.

'Hello, old chap. You must be Sergeant Lawless. Name's Davis, Harold Davis: HM Consulate Barcelona. Sorry to have kept you waiting. Had a flat tyre; all fixed now.'

The drive to Barcelona took nearly four hours. In the car Davis handed Lawless a sheaf of papers including what he called an Emergency Certificate that would guarantee his identity with the Spanish authorities: most important, not to lose it on any account.

There was some delay at the border into Spain when Davis became engaged in a lengthy discussion with some armed policemen, at one point being escorted into their guardroom. Eventually he emerged looking distinctly annoyed, climbed back into the car and sat drumming his fingers on the steering-wheel rim until the flimsy barrier was dragged aside and they could drive on.

'They're getting rather tiresome since the Germans took over Vichy. Don't want to antagonise them, I suppose. One chap I was taking through, an Australian, seemed to take against them for some reason. I only just stopped him in time from socking one of them. That would never have done, oh no. It cost quite a bit more than usual to calm them down and let us through. Shouldn't blame them too much: never seen so many Germans before. All over the place, they are. Can't mistake them.'

He was an affable man, chatting during most of the journey about life in Spain and his visits to prisons where the Spaniards kept escaped men—he referred to them as 'prisoners of war'—before eventually the Consulate secured their release. Some had a bad time whereas others were well treated; it all depended on the guards. Lawless was damned lucky to make the trip over in so short a time: two days. Some people had taken weeks, getting frostbite or losing the guides and having to go back down somehow and try again later. Some never made it at all and must be still under the snow on the mountains somewhere. Lawless must have found a gap in the weather; the snow could be metres thick on the high passes at this time of year. Did he think Spain would join in with the Germans? No: Franco liked to play both sides against each other and now with the recent news from North Africa and Russia, things were beginning to look as if the Germans were in trouble. Still, you never knew what they would do next. But Lawless mustn't worry, oh no. The Vice-Consul had been working personally on his case. The Embassy in Madrid knew all about him. He would be all right. It would just take a bit of time. With this anodyne reassurance in his mind, Lawless gradually drifted off to sleep.

'The Consulate's in the middle of town,' Davis said. 'Busy sort of part, so we've put you up in a discreet little hotel in a quieter street. I'll see you in and then I'll have to leave you; sort out the car for Madrid and a few other things. This one's not too reliable—though, she seems to have done all right this trip. Hotel Esmeralda, can you believe it? Soon be there now.'

Davis dealt with the papers at the reception desk and accompanied Lawless up to his room at the back of the hotel. It was a welcome change from the primitive hideaway in Escaldes. The sheets were spotless and there was not the slightest hint of lumps in the mattress.

'No, don't come down. They'll bring you a tray with some dinner. The wine's not too bad, usually a Rioja. Have you got enough cigarettes? Have some of mine. They're Senior Service. Right, I'll be off. Should be in touch with you again tonight. Somebody will come up and tell you there's a telephone call for you. Ah, sorry, I forgot.' Darcy fished in his briefcase and came out with a newspaper. 'Thought you might like something to read: copy of The Times. I'm afraid it's a few days old. Do you do crosswords?'

Spaniards stay up late, even in winter. At midnight Lawless could still hear voices and movement below. The dining room and bar must still be open, he thought. He got up to open his door after he heard knocking. The porter told him he was wanted on the telephone at the desk.

It was Davis's unmistakeable voice on the other end of the line.

'Seven o' clock sharp tomorrow morning. Black Citroen opposite side of the street. Watch for the lights flashing. Come straight over and get in. No need to go to the desk. Everything's paid for.'

The line went dead.

Lawless hardly slept. He kept looking at his watch. Finally he got up, put on his coat and sat at the little desk with the reading lamp on, and found the page with the crossword. He was pleased with himself, having solved six clues—the last one, eleven letters, 'fishy kind of pattern', obviously herringbone—before he felt too cold to go on and got back into bed. Still he could not sleep. Thoughts of La Commanderie tormented him.

The Citroen was a fast car and Davis a driver in a hurry, but it still took twelve hours with brief stops on the way for coffee, a snatched lunch and more coffee to reach Madrid. With Davis to hand and the correct papers, including his own RAF pay book, Lawless was allowed into the Embassy without too much fuss. He was astonished at what he found. The place was crowded, not only with men and women who were quite obviously Embassy staff, but many others wearing odd clothes, some of them service uniform, or parts of it, wandering about looking bored or lost and clearly getting in the way of harassed secretaries and attachés. Even the gardens were being used for accommodation. Wooden huts had been installed on what must once have been pristine lawns or jealously tended flowerbeds. The whole place was seething, noisy commotion, rather like a street market, and quite the opposite of the smooth, quiet process of diplomatic business that Lawless had expected.

'I don't know how they put up with it,' Davis said as they pushed their way along a corridor. 'I hope to God I don't get drafted here. Some of them do nothing but complain, you know. You'll have to put up with it, I'm afraid. At least you've got a share of a room on the top floor and there's a lavatory near, you'll be glad to know.'

'Now I'm in and they know who I am, what do I do next?'

'Wait to hear what train you're on, old chap, and hope it's soon.'

'Wait: I'm getting used to that. Look, Davis, I don't know how to thank you for all you've done. I hope I see you again one day.'

'You never know, do you? Might be in Oxford if I ever get to a Gaudy after the War.'

'I'm not sure about that.'

'Oh yes. You'll be there. You've got Oxford written all over you. Anything else I can do?'

'There is one thing.' Lawless took an envelope from his pocket. 'One of the secretaries let me have some paper for this. It's a letter to some people back in France. I wonder if you might see your way to getting it through? I don't want to put you to any trouble but it's rather important.'

'Can't promise, old chap, 'specially with what's happened recently but leave it with me. I'll see what I can do.'

A week later, by which time Lawless was beginning to think he would rather be over Bremen again with a night fighter lining up on him than spend another hour in this turmoil, he was told by a harassed-looking military attaché he was to be taken to the railway station at eight the next morning and put on a train for La Linea.

'You're going to Gibraltar, my lad.'

ENGLAND 1942

D'YE KEN JOHN PEEL?

He had known there was a squadron of Halifaxes based at Leeming but now he was looking at one close up for the first time and it was huge. He could stand under the wing without stooping. Four massive inline engines and bristling with guns, it looked solid as a rock.

'No bomb-aimer this trip, so you can have his seat,' the pilot said. 'I'm told you're a gunner anyway, so should suit you.'

'I used to sit at the other end.'

'Believe me,' said the pilot, 'they look the same whichever way they're coming at you but with a bit of luck we won't meet any this time.'

Lawless was relieved that they hadn't asked him who he was or where he'd come from. He had read somewhere that the sudden loss of a limb didn't bring immediate pain. Numbness came first and could last some time. It was the body protecting itself somehow. But the pain came later, always. And afterwards you could feel the lost limb even though it wasn't there anymore. He was feeling like that now. Being on his own for a few hours just looking out at the clouds or the sea, not talking to anyone: that was what all he wanted.

'Up you go, then; along there. Frank will tell you where everything is.'

Frank was the flight engineer. After showing Lawless where to put his parachute, fix his straps and plug in his oxygen and intercom, he said there were thermoses of coffee and plenty of sandwiches stowed aloft. Lawless only had to ask.

'Best if you stay back behind me for take-off. Just in case, you know: bad place to be in, down there, if the Skipper takes a wrong turning. Hang onto something. You'll be all right.'

With everyone aboard and all doors and hatches closed, the pilot and flight engineer began running through the pre-start check-list that Lawless could only partly hear.

'Undercarriage uplocks disengaged. Check above. Batteries connected. Ground flight switch to flight. Controls unlocked. Aileron controls unlocked, rudder and elevator. Flaps pressure. Test flying controls, Autopilot, Supercharger. Gateway this is Halifax ZY 244 requesting permission for startup

'ZY 224 you have permission for start-up.'

'Starting port outer engine . . . now.'

Lawless heard the loud clatter and coughing of the starter motor and a propeller beginning to turn, clatter louder, surge and begin to hum.

'Port inner . . . now . . .' More clattering and humming.

'Starboard inner engine . . . now . . . starboard outer . . . now . . .'

The whole aircraft was now vibrating as all the four engines settled into smooth synchronised running.

'. . . bomb doors closed . . . flaps . . . engineer check if oil pressure and temperature ok . . . both chocks away . . .

'Gateway, this is Halifax ZY 224, request taxying instructions.'

'ZY 224, runway 26. QFE One Zero Zero Four.'

'Roger Gateway runway 26, taxying now.'

'Compass normal . . . flaps 20 degrees down . . . all crew with me.'

Lawless recognised the pilot's way of asking each member of the crew to report status in turn. Lawless saw the flight engineer glancing at him and could tell that he was replying but could not hear what he said.

'Gateway, this is Halifax ZY 224, request line-up 26.'

'ZY 224 clear to line up . . . wind Two Seven Zero, 15 knots.'

Lawless felt the aircraft turn as it faced the runway and heard the engines surge with power and the Halifax seem to strain against its brakes.

'Ready take-off.'

'Clear take-off.'

'Rolling now.'

Lawless was pressed back harder and harder as the Halifax accelerated down the runway and lifted smoothly into the air much quicker than he remembered the Whitley ever having done.

'Raising flaps . . . 165 knots indicated . . . fuel booster pump off . . . turning Two Seven Zero . . . climbing to 2000 feet . . . navigator give me course and distance . . .'

The flight engineer raised his eyebrows to Lawless and jerked a thumb forwards. He struggled past towards the nose of the aircraft to take up his position for the flight.

The single gun in the nose was a hand operated Browning ·303 that Lawless needed no explanation of how to operate. He settled himself on the padded seat that apparently folded down into a sort of mattress for the bomb-aimer to lie on prone when he was working his bombsight as the aircraft approached its target. He switched on the intercom. It was all coming back to him with an eerie but curiously comforting familiarity; even the smell of his leather mask.

'Fifteen thousand feet . . . levelling off.'

The rear gunner and mid-upper gunner requested permission to test their guns and Lawless heard the familiar rapid thumping. He was the last to be given permission and tilted his Browning down and fired two bursts. There it was again, the unmistakeable shudder running through him as he pressed the firing bar. Guiltily, he was beginning to feel at home.

The aircraft flew west for almost an hour before turning sharply and eventually settled on a more northerly course. With the pilot's permission, Lawless unstrapped and unplugged himself and crawled up to the flight engineer's table to look for some of that coffee. The flight engineer bellowed into his ear.

'You'll see nothing but clouds or sea until we're almost there. Don't want to fly over France, do we? Not now, for sure.'

'How long before we get there?' Lawless shouted back.

'Six hours or so, if the wind does what we've been told.'

'Where do we land?'

'Bicester. Know it?'

'Played cricket there once in 1941. Lost.'

'Not far from London, isn't it?'

'Near enough. Who made this coffee?'

'It's better than you'll get in Bicester.'

When the crew reported to the debriefing room the officer in charge looked Lawless up and down, consulted a list on his desk and called over a Flight Sergeant who was standing near the door.

'Room 46, Sergeant.' The officer looked up at Lawless. 'Follow the Flight Sergeant.'

'Sir, may I request permission to telephone my family? It's almost a year since they heard from me.'

The officer looked at him steadily for a moment, looked down at his list again and then sighed.

'All right. Flight, take him the phone box in the corridor. Listen to what he says. Be brief and don't say where you are calling from. Off you go.'

The Flight Sergeant lit a cigarette and leaned against the wall as Lawless picked up the receiver and waited for the operator to answer and gave her the number he had memorised. A voice answered within seconds. Lawless put on a happy smile for the Flight Sergeant's benefit.

'Hello Dad! It's me, Philip. How are you?'

The voice asked him to state the code. Lawless replied, 'Birnam' and repeated the word after being asked again. The phone went dead at the other end but Lawless kept talking.

'Yes, it really is me! I'm back. How's Mum? Listen, Dad, I have to go. Tell you all about it when I see you. I'll be in touch again. Give Mum my love.'

He replaced the receiver. The Flight Sergeant didn't seem to have noticed anything unusual. If asked, Lawless would have told him Birnam was a sort of silly secret game he and his father played.

The Flight Sergeant rapped smartly on the door of Room 46, opened it and stood aside to let Lawless go in first. An officer was seated at a desk, writing. After a moment or two he looked up.

'Sergeant Lawless reporting, Sir.' Lawless remembered: officer seated, without cap, no salute and felt stupidly pleased with himself.

'Thank you Flight. That will be all.'

The door closed behind the Flight Sergeant and Lawless was left still standing at attention, alone with the officer whose sleeves bore the insignia of a Flight Lieutenant.

'At ease. Lawless, Sergeant Air Gunner, is it? Been away quite a while, haven't we, Lawless? Right, well park yourself there and let's hear all about it.'

Lawless sat on the hard wooden chair in front of the Flight Lieutenant's desk and looked round the room. He had seen many like it. Cream painted walls turning dingy yellow, scuffed lino-covered floor, grey standard issue filing cabinet, in tray and out tray on the desk, picture of the King in RAF uniform on the wall behind; but no windows. That was different.

'Let's start at the beginning. RAF Topcliffe, 8th of December 1941, 1800 hours, you take off; target, the Fiat works in Turin. And that's the last anybody hears of you.'

The telephone at the Flight Lieutenant's elbow started to ring. He ignored the first few jangles then frowned impatiently and picked up the receiver.

'Collinson. What? Yes, he's here. What? Will you repeat that? Are you sure? All right, but it's very irregular. Yes, yes. Of course I understand.'

He banged down the receiver and glared suspiciously at Lawless.

'It seems we'll have to do this later. Someone else,' he said distastefully, 'is coming to see you. It's all very unusual.' He pressed something underneath his desk and a few seconds later the door opened and the Flight Sergeant marched into the room.

'Flight, you're to take Sergeant Lawless here to the mess and see that he has something to eat. Let him spruce up first. He looks as if he's been sleeping in his clothes for days. Then he's to wait in Room 50 with all his kit until called. Stick by him at all times, do you understand? Don't let him out of your sight. And you, Lawless, do something about that bloody awful moustache, will you? Now, get out.'

'Christ almighty! What's got into him?' the Flight Sergeant said to Lawless out in the corridor.

'No idea, Flight.'

'Somebody fucking heavy's just trodden on his fucking toes, mate.'

It was about two hours after Lawless had made his telephone call that the door of Room 50 opened and two men in civilian clothes came in. Two hours was long enough for someone to have driven quite fast in the dark from London, Lawless thought afterwards; or from anywhere else about sixty miles from Bicester, for that matter.

'Sergeant Lawless?' said the taller of the two men.

'Yes.'

'I'm Johnson, this is Robinson. Got everything with you? Good. We'd better be off then.'

Robinson turned to the Flight Sergeant and showed him what looked like an official warrant card. 'It's all right, Flight Sergeant. He'll be going with us now.'

'Thank you, Sir. If it's all right by you, Sir, I'd like to have Flight Lieutenant Collinson say so, Sir.'

'Of course. We'll wait while you fetch him.'

There was silence in the room until the Flight Sergeant reappeared. He seemed oddly pleased.

'That's all right, Sir. He says it's all right by him for you to leave, Sir. I'll see you out.'

'No need, thank you, Sergeant. We know our way. Johnson, bring Sergeant Lawless's bags with you, will you?'

No one questioned them as they left the building and got into a large black car that was parked outside. It was too dark for Lawless to see the number plates but not too dark for him to know it was not an RAF car. At the main gate an armed sentry stopped them at the barrier. Two other sentries with rifles at the ready stepped smartly to either side of the car. Johnson handed a leather wallet out to the first sentry who looked at it in the light of his torch and went back to the guardroom. He quickly re-emerged, handed back the wallet and signed for the barrier to be lifted and saluted as the car drove away.

'Where are we going,' said Lawless from the rear seat.

'London,' replied Robinson. 'Do you know it at all? Not all that far from Oxford.'

Lawless yawned. It had been a long day. He settled back in the rather comfortable leather seat and was soon asleep.

Lawless never knew the name of the place in London where he was taken in the early hours of the morning by the men who called themselves Robinson and Johnson, until much later. When he got out of the car in the darkness and was being hurried across the pavement, he had an impression of a long tree-lined street of very large houses with all their windows blacked out and that was all. He had been wondering what was coming next; some sort of interview with an officer who would want an account of what he had been doing; that was sure, but he hoped he might be allowed a few hours sleep first.

Johnson, or was it Robinson—one of them anyway—quickly disappeared with Lawless's bag of meagre belongings. The other handed him the small parcel containing the envelopes he had been given in La Couvertoirade and pointed towards a wide marble staircase at the end of the hall.

'Three flights up, I'm afraid. I hope you're not too tired. There's a lovely view from the top; in daylight, of course.'

Yet another interview room, Lawless thought. What number would it be this time. Dim lighting and wartime neglect could not entirely hide the quiet opulence of moulded ceilings, panelled doors and marble-tiled landings and passages they passed on their ascent to the top floor. They stopped at a door that was no different from any of the others and had no number.

'Here we are. Don't bother to knock. Just go in.'

Lawless did as he was told. To his surprise, the room was brightly lit. The white walls were bare of any picture or map but there was a thick maroon carpet on the floor. He noticed a small wooden table and chair against one wall and a large desk in front of the heavily curtained window opposite. Behind the desk sat a man in a dark suit with glasses and thinning hair, who looked up and rose to his feet as Lawless came in.

'Sergeant Lawless, please take a seat. I won't take up too much of your time. I expect you would like to get to bed. I think you may have something for me.'

Lawless placed the parcel on the desk and sat back. The man carefully unwrapped it and took out the two envelopes, glanced at them briefly but made no attempt to open them.

'Birnam. Good. Well done.'

He opened a drawer in his desk and locked both envelopes inside. That done, he looked up at Lawless with a smile.

'Now, Sergeant, what we used to do with people like you was give them a sort of questionnaire to fill in; details of their comings and goings, how they were captured or shot down, how they escaped, anything useful they saw on their travels, people they met, all that sort of thing. Information, Lawless, information that's what we need; build up a picture of what's going on over there, what they're up to and what we're up against. We need it and chaps like you can give it to us. But we found it didn't work as well as we hoped, so we've started trying another tack: letting people write down their experiences, tell their story in their own way and so far we've found that we are learning more that way. A bit surprising sometimes though, when you find the most unlikely people don't know how to spell or even write the King's English. Don't expect that sort of thing from you, of course. Now, you take this pad and pencil away with you and write down everything you remember, everything, and we'll have a talk about it tomorrow, or the next day, or as long as it takes.'

The interview was clearly at an end. Lawless got up, wondering what came next.

'Oh, yes, outside; someone will show you your room. Goodnight to you.'

Johnson—or Robinson—took Lawless to a room on the same floor and asked him if he would like a cup of tea or a sandwich. Lawless thanked him but said no. All he wanted was to sleep.

'Bathroom two doors along; toothbrush and so on in there. They'll bring you breakfast about eight. Goodnight.'

They don't seem to know whether it's night or day, thought Lawless. Or maybe they don't care. The room was small and bare except for the essentials; chair, table with reading lamp, plain wardrobe, bed against the wall. Perhaps it had once been a maid's room. His bag lay on the bed. Someone had put a pair of striped pyjamas, a towel with toothbrush round tin of dentifrice and a safety razor next to it. Lawless decided to leave washing to the morning. The bed proved more comfortable than it looked.

He was roused by a knock on the door and sat up in time to see a woman come in carrying a tray that she put on his table. She gave him a quick glance and left without speaking. The scent of fried bacon made him feel suddenly hungry. Two eggs, as well, toast and a pot of tea under a tea cosy: he sat down in his borrowed pyjamas and made short work of everything. When he came back from the bathroom, washed, shaved and with teeth cleaned at last, to find the tray had gone. In its place were the writing pad and pencil. With nothing else to do and nothing to read he set to work. It all came back to him as clearly as if he were living the events over again. In two hours he covered twenty pages with few pauses to think.

Everything, the man had said. Well, he was certainly not going to get that. Names, for instance: some they would certainly know, like Davis's and others they might know or would find out anyway. So Alexandre Chevalier and Janquet and Dunbar were mentioned and, after a little thought, Victor Dumanoir and Lieutenant Grandjean. He had to say where he had stayed and that the two women were from the same family as Alexandre but he decided to keep quiet about his marriage to Thérèse and the arrival of Mireille at La Commanderie. He included accounts of the exploits with the railway line and the signal and assuming the way that Allan had been dealt with must surely be known to them, he included that too. He ended with as much detail as he could remember about his escape and was particularly complimentary about Davis. Reading through what he had written he wondered whether to mention the recovery of the two Brownings and the ammunition and decided against. He added a final note on where the remains of the other members of the Whitley crew had been buried.

At 12 o'clock the same woman who had brought him breakfast reappeared with a tray of lunch. Lawless had always enjoyed steak and kidney pudding and apple pie and custard; solid stuff after the delicacies provided at Alexandre Chevalier's table, but welcome nevertheless. Johnson came in just after he had finished, left a day-old copy of the Times for him and took away Lawless's script.

The date on the Times was 28th November. The German army in Stalingrad was surrounded with no hope of escape, he read. Toulon, he saw the name on a headline: the French fleet in Toulon had been scuttled on the orders of its admiral. The article said it was to prevent the Germans from capturing some powerful ships. He wondered why they had not seized the warships earlier. It was not like the Germans to miss such a chance. Before he could read any more, the door opened and Johnson came in again to tell him that he would be needed sometime in the evening to talk about his report. That set him thinking again about what he had written and about the occasions when Alexandre Chevalier and Séverine and others had urged him to tell the full story of what the network had done and was planning to do and of the urgent need for help, with the supply of weapons, explosives, radios and many other things. Only he had a chance of convincing the English authorities, they had said, because he had been there and seen what the real situation was. He realised his first account did not do justice to their pleas. Someone had to be told—but not the men who had been questioning him so far. The solution came to him in a flash. He sat down, re-opened the pad and began writing rapidly.

Johnson came for him after supper. By then Lawless had his pile of script folded out of sight in his inside pocket.

'Johnson, could I ask a favour? There's a letter I'd like to send but I don't have an envelope. Could you let me have one?'

'We'll stop in my office on the way.'

He was in luck. Johnson looked in his drawers but for once it turned out he was out of envelopes.

'Can't it wait?'

'It's to a senior officer. Of course, I'll hand it over to your boss as soon as I see him but I get the impression he would prefer to have it sealed up; like that package I brought back from France.'

'Hang on, then. I'll get one from one of the secretaries. Wait here and don't touch anything while I'm away.'

There was a telephone on Johnson's desk. It was worth the risk. He lifted the receiver, and asked the operator for an outside line. When she said he was connected he dialled the telephone number that Alexandre Chevalier had given him. A voice asked him for the code. He gave it, repeated the numbers when asked, said the word Birnam and then quickly

'Lawless—confidential report resistance network for Birnam in interrogator's possession shortly—urgent you collect fastest—Lawless.'

He replaced the receiver just in time before Johson re-entered the office with a packet of official buff envelopes in his hand.

He expected to be questioned in detail but when he was back in the numberless room the man in the dark suit made only a few desultory remarks and said what he had written seemed to be a very full and clear account. Lawless wondered if this might be a tactic and that when he was off his guard there would be a sudden sharp demand to come clean on something important they knew about and he had left out; but no, apparently that's all there was. He could go and finish the Times crossword. That did make him think. Did they know that Davis had given him that copy of the Times in Barcelona and asked him if he did crosswords? Evidently they did not. Oh, one other thing, the man said: normal routine. The doctor would see him in the morning; just to see if everything was all right.

'Will I be able to go after that, Sir?'

'Yes, yes, all being well: keen to get back to your squadron, eh? See the doc first and then you'll be given all the necessary. May be in touch again later, but that's all for now. Goodnight to you.'

'I've added a few pages to what I wrote earlier, Sir.'

The man looked rather surprised but took the envelope from Lawless, glanced at it and put it in his drawer.

'Thank you. I'll look over it later. Anything more? No? Goodnight to you.'

As Lawless was walking to the door, the telephone rang. He heard one side of the conversation as he paused in the doorway,

'Yes—just now—he's leaving—what—now?—all right if you say so'

but not what the voice on the other end of the line was saying, although he guessed what some of it might have been,

Has he given you the follow-up to his report—where is he—bring me what he has written—now—that is what I said—thank you so much.

Back in his office after taking Lawless's envelope to another room in the building, the man sat for a while thinking over the past few minutes' events. That was one very smart young man, he thought, especially his writing Birnam on the front of the envelope and over the seal on the back as well and ensuring there would be insufficient time for anyone to unseal the envelope with all the care necessary to avoid detection before the call came in from 'upstairs'. He was wasted as a gunner in the RAF. There were possibilities there: ought to keep track of him. Now how did he get hold of that envelope? Must have a word with Johnson about that. He lifted the receiver.

It was midnight before the official known as Birnam finished reading Lawless's additional report. Chevalier's and Dumanoir's letters provided valuable accounts of the network's activities directed against the Vichy regime in their parts of southern France. Chevalier's was particularly interesting in its predictions of Vichy's counter-resistance strategy, including the likely recruitment of a paramilitary force to carry it out. That must be taken seriously. After all, Chevalier had proved right in his prediction some time ago of a German invasion of the Unoccupied Zone if the situation in North Africa became critical. But what Lawless had done was more enlightening in its credible on the ground description of the actual people involved in the fight; their thinking, their methods, their resolve, yes, but also their desperate need for hardware—weapons, explosives, radios—if ever their campaign were to become really effective in inflicting serious damage on the Vichy and, more important, German machines. The allusion to the old Camisard guerrilla leader Cavalier's being promised help from England in his fight against the French king, only to be disappointed, was a telling point: it must be different this time. Birnam underlined some passages and jotted down a few points as reminders for the summary and recommendations to be put before the Plans Committee at its next meeting.

It was clear to Birnam that Lawless's first report of his experiences in France and Spain was incomplete and deliberately so. People he named were obviously those he expected to be known about already. There must have been others playing important roles who remained anonymous. The single page letter in the envelope with his first name on it was signed by one of these and what it said was very revealing. In fact it altered the whole picture not only as far as Lawless's stay in France was concerned but also what arrangements about his activities in England ought to be considered. Birnam thought for a moment: a phone call using the scrambler or a confidential letter? Neither: it had to be face-to-face. The Group Captain would be at the next meeting in London of the committee reviewing future operations. He might be persuaded to have lunch somewhere private after the meeting. Birnam knew just the place.

The envelope itself showed no sign of having been opened before it reached Birnam's desk so Lawless cannot have read the single page letter it contained. He must remain unaware of it, at least for the time being. Birnam locked it in the drawer that contained the most secret documents.

Chevalier evidently had the highest opinion of Lawless's potential as a scholar or he would certainly not have entrusted to the those fragile pages of old manuscript to Birnam with the request that they be kept for the young man as pristine material for research should he survive the War. Birnam knew enough about the period to recognise that the verse had very unusual features, only some of which Chevalier had noted in his covering letter. London was not the safest place for such things these days. She resolved to take the manuscript back to Oxford when she returned there for lunch with the Group Captain.

The doctor was a friendly old man smelling faintly of pipe tobacco and probably brought out of retirement for jobs like this. He asked Lawless to strip to the waist and listened to his heart and lungs with a well-worn stethoscope, looked in his mouth and peered at the whites of his eyes.

'You look in good shape, young man, better than some I've seen in here. Have you been working on a farm? Where did you get that tan, eh? Drop your trousers. We'll have a little look down there; just make sure you haven't caught anything nasty where you've been. Don't look so surprised. You wouldn't credit how many I've seen. That looks all right. Now, just cough for me. And again. All right, pull 'em up. We're finished. Sit down a minute while I fill in this form, then you can go.'

'You mean I can just leave, Sir?'

'Yes, as far as I'm concerned. I can pass you as fit for service. That fellow waiting outside will give you all the paperwork you need. You have your pay book, have you? Good. You'll be due a fair bit of back pay, I expect. Ask him if you can have a voucher. You look as if you need some decent clothes to travel in until you get a new uniform.'

Lawless found Robinson outside the doctor's room. He thought of asking after Johnson but Robinson seemed in something of a hurry.

'This is your travel warrant and this is an identity card which you can show to any policeman who asks for it. You still have your issue pay book, I believe. Shouldn't really have had that on you but we'll overlook it this time. You can show it as proof also.'

'The doctor said I could ask you for a voucher against my back pay. I can't really go about in these clothes any longer and my uniform was lost.'

'Hm, did he? Oh, all right, I'll make one out for you. You'll have to sign for it and the other things. You have been given seven days leave and then you report back to your squadron at, where was it?'

'It used to be Topcliffe.'

'Ah, yes, Topcliffe. There've been some changes there. Where will you take your leave?'

'My parents live in Kendal.'

'Kendal, yes; now I think that's everything.'

'Could I telephone home from here?'

'Ah, well, leave it for now. There's a young woman waiting to see you. She'll deal with all that.'

'A young woman; who is she?'

'She says she's your cousin Anne.'

Lawless was puzzled. Why would Annie have come to London to meet him?

'Where is she?'

'Wouldn't come in; said she would meet you outside. Got everything? Right, well good luck.'

***

Annie was standing on the pavement smoking a cigarette. It was the first time Lawless had seen her doing that. She looked much more grown up, dressed in a smart knee-length coat and wearing a wide-brimmed hat. She looked every bit as pretty as he remembered, no, more so.

'Annie! What are you doing here? Give me a kiss. How are you? How are Uncle John and Auntie? I must find a phone box and let Mum and Dad know I'm back. Have you seen them recently? I've been given a week's leave and a travel warrant so we can go on the train together. Annie, I can't think why you've come here but it's lovely to see you. You're very quiet. What is it?'

There were tears in her eyes.

'Oh, Philip, haven't they told you? Oh, that is cruel of them. Uncle Bert and Auntie Louie are dead, both killed in the air raid on Manchester.'

Manchester? What were they doing in Manchester?

'Philip, are you all right. Did you hear what I said?'

'Yes, yes, I'm all right. I think I am. It's very cold. Do you feel cold? Can we go somewhere?'

She put her arm in his and led him away down the long street with its stately houses and its plane trees bare of leaves. There was a sign at the end with its name, Kensington Palace Gardens, but neither of them saw it and neither of them spoke again until they were sitting in a Lyons Tea shop with cups of tea going cold on the table in front of them.

She told him what had happened and his eyes never left her face as she spoke, although she wondered from the distant look in them whether he heard all that she was saying. It hadn't been a heavy raid, not like the one at Christmas in 1940 when the cathedral was bombed and the whole of Piccadilly was set ablaze. They said some of the German bombers had been aiming for the factory where they made the Lancasters but some of the bombs fell a long way off target. One was a direct hit on Uncle Bert's cousin's house where they were staying for his birthday and everybody inside was killed. She told him the date when it happened. He tried to remember what he was doing that day, but couldn't. Not that it made any difference. Now he knew why his dad had never replied to his last message; if it ever got to him.

'I can't think, Annie. I don't know what to do.'

'Come home with me, Philip; I mean to our house. You can stay with us. Mum and Dad want you to.'

His Uncle John was waiting for them with his old car when the train reached Oxenholme station. As a farmer he had a petrol ration. He shook Lawless's hand but didn't say much. It was the way they had in Westmoreland but Lawless felt his uncle's sympathy for him. And he had lost a brother; that was part of it; and a son, too, Colin. Where would it end?

'You look cold, lad. Best be getting home by the fire. Your auntie's looking forward to seeing you. It's been a long time. How long have you got?'

'A week, Uncle John.'

'You'll be all right. We'll go up and take a look at the house later, when you want.'

They gave him Colin's room to sleep in. He lay awake for a long time, all kinds of thoughts whirling round in his head, until there was a soft tapping on his door and Annie slipped into the room in her nightdress.

'Are you still feeling cold?'

He nodded, yes, he was. She took off the nightdress and got into bed with him. It was a long time before they made love but when they did, he felt a little bit warmer and told her. She knew it wasn't love. It was need. But when you think about it, is there much difference?

It was three days before Lawless felt able to go back to the house in Kendal. Annie went with him on the bus. He couldn't bring himself to open the front door, so Annie did it, using the key that her father kept. The house was cold but tidy so he guessed somebody must go in from time to time to see everything was in order. He wandered through the rooms, picking up ornaments and putting them down, looking at the photographs and the embroidery work of his mother that hung framed on the walls. He ran his finger over the top of the piano, leaving a trace in the thin layer of dust. He had learned to play on this piano, his mother at his side, beating time herself because she disliked metronomes. He lifted the lid of the keyboard, saw the familiar name John Broadwood & Sons in gilt letters and touched the keys, C sharp—E sharp—A: a Chopin chord. No, that was wrong: C sharp—E natural—A. Thérèse had showed him his mistake. Tressie, oh god, he was losing everything.

'Let's go, Annie. I can't stay any more. I'll come back another time.'

'You need a drink,' Annie said.

They went to the Black Swan in Allhallows Lane. His mother had never approved of pubs but his father had taken him there on his eighteenth birthday, telling him not to breathe a word about it when they got back home. They were lucky. The landlord remembered him and said he was sorry to hear about his Mum and Dad and he'd had a delivery of a few bottles of whisky only yesterday. It seemed a good idea on such a cold day but it didn't make him feel any warmer, even after a second glass. This was a different sort of cold feeling. He now knew what it was and it had nothing to do with the temperature outside. It was a rather frightening feeling but he knew it would stay with him and he wanted it to stay. It was the need for revenge.

'Christmas coming on,' his aunt said that evening when they were sitting in front of the fire after supper. 'You're very welcome to stay with us, Philip. Annie would like you to, wouldn't you, Annie?'

'If he plays for us.'

'I don't know, Auntie. I have to report back by Monday night and I've no idea when I'll get another leave.'

'Well, you let us know. We're having a goose this year.'

'Do you think you might give us a tune, Philip? That piano hasn't been touched since, well, you know.'

I know: since Colin left and was shot down over Dunkirk.

'I don't suppose you've been doing overmuch piano playing where you've been, but I won't ask. I know we shouldn't ask where you were and what you were doing.'

'I did try to sending messages home, Uncle John but I never heard if they got there.'

'One did, your Dad told me. All it said was "D'ye ken John Peel?" Not much, but we knew it must have been you. We did laugh. Just one sheet of paper in a brown envelope that looked official, your Dad said.'

'Go on, Philip,' Annie said, 'play something for us. Doesn't matter if you're out of practice.'

He managed a few tunes that he knew they liked and some Schumann that he found in a book that must have been Colin's. He did think of some of the music his mother used to play but thought they wouldn't like it and he couldn't bring himself to play it anyway. They clapped when he finished and stood up.

'You haven't forgotten how, Philip,' Annie said. 'You must have been playing while you were away.'

'I did have a chance, now and again.' He couldn't bring himself to tell them, especially Annie, anything about what had happened in France

They were lovely people. They tried their best to make him feel at home. He could tell from the way she looked at him that Annie would come to sleep with him again and how could he stop her? But now, all he really wanted to do was get away and back to Topcliffe, to that other very different life.

***

'I won't ask where you've been for the past year,' the Flight Lieutenant said. 'I don't want to know. It says here that you've been passed fit for duty and that's good enough for me. You can draw new uniform and kit from the stores: see the Flight Sergeant at the desk outside. He'll tell you which hut you're in. And ask him where you can find Pilot Officer Chester. You'll be in his crew, if he likes the look of you, that is. That's all.'

'Sir, may I request to see the Commanding Officer?'

'Already? You've only been here five minutes. He's got too much to do without that sort of thing.'

'Sir, it is important. Personal matter, Sir.'

The Flight Lieutenant stared up at Lawless. He knew the man had survived 24 raids in old Whitleys, now, thank God, soon to be taken out of active service, so he supposed that should count for something.

'Oh, all right then. Request noted. You'll hear in due course.'

Pilot Officer Chester had been a student at Sheffield University on an Engineering degree course before his call-up. He was almost a year younger than Lawless, a tough-looking Yorkshireman who had been on the University soccer team.

'What's your name?'

'Lawless, Sir, Sergeant Gunner.'

'Your other name?'

'Philip, Sir.'

'When we're in the aircraft, we don't use ranks or surnames. I'm Tony and you're Philip, right? This is Harry. He's the navigator, God help us. You'll meet the others before the day's out. You ever flown in a Halifax?'

'Once: Gibraltar to Bicester. Before that, 24 raids in Whitleys'

'Twenty four, eh? That's more than us, isn't it, Harry? We're on our twelfth. You ever been hit?'

'A few times; shot down over France. It took a while to get back.'

'Listen to that, Harry. We've got a real airman here! Only joking, Philip. Welcome to KY 262, our pride and joy. We call her Sheffield United. Harry here will take you aboard and show you what's what. You're our new mid-upper gunner. Don't ask what happened to the last one. Canadian: he only lasted two trips, but the turret's had new panels fitted and been thoroughly cleaned, you'll be glad to know.'

'I was rear gunner on Whitleys.'

'Well, it's a step up for you, then, isn't it? Warmer and not so lonely. Like I said, Harry will show you round and this afternoon we'll all go up and do a few circuits and bumps, you know the sort of thing, and you can get yourself used to your guns. Tonight's op has been cancelled because of weather over the target. Could be on again tomorrow night. We'll see.'

'Where was it?'

'Don't know. They didn't tell us. Our bet was Bremen. Ever been there?'

Chester noticed the look on Lawless's face and decided to drop the subject.

Two weeks later he was ordered to report to the Commanding Officer on the following day. In those two weeks KY 262 took off on two operations, one mine laying off the Danish coast and the other a bombing raid on Frankfurt where the weather was so bad they never saw the target at all but bombed anyway. Chester said he had heard it wasn't just the bad weather that was keeping them grounded. There was a lot of reorganisation going on higher up and certainly the number of operations was much lower than earlier in the year.

Walking back to the huts after a cross-country flight for testing navigation and wireless equipment, Chester nudged his arm.

'What's all this I hear about you being sent for by the Groupie? Been a naughty boy, then?'

'No more than you have. Perhaps he wants to invite me home for Christmas dinner. Don't worry, I'll let you know.'

'Talking of Christmas, we're having a bit of a celebration down at the pub. It's been a bit dull lately. We need to liven things up. You play the piano, don't you?'

The Group Captain was reading a file at his desk when Lawless marched into the office. He glanced up, signed for Lawless to stand at ease, and closed the file.

'You wanted to see me; personal matter, you said.'

'Yes, Sir.'

'Well, out with it.'

'Request to transfer to pilot training, Sir.'

'Hm, it says in your file you applied before and your request was turned down. Why was that?'

'I was told there were enough pilots at that time but not enough air gunners, Sir.'

'And you think circumstances are different now, do you?'

'Mine are, Sir.'

'I see. That's why this is personal, is it?'

'Yes, Sir.'

'Lawless, I read your aircraft went missing on a raid on Turin in December 1941 and that it was almost a year afterwards that you turned up in Spain. I'll leave for the moment asking you what you were up to all that time but if your request is something to do with what happened then, it had better be good.'

'My parents were killed in a raid on Manchester, Sir. I only found out when I got back to London.'

'Go on.'

'This may sound a bit histrionic, Sir, but I want to do more to get back at them, the Germans I mean, for what they've done to me and I think I can do more as a pilot than I can as an air gunner. And, Sir, I did learn to fly with the University Air Squadron.'

'Oxford, wasn't it? Sit down, Lawless.'

The Group Captain put his elbows on his desk and his hands together under his chin. He looked Lawless steadily in the eye.

'I don't think that you're telling me everything, Lawless. I get the feeling something else has happened to you, maybe after you were shot down. But we'll let that be. Are you sure about this? Pilot Officer Chester says you fitted into his crew right from the start and you're a good gunner. It's a crew that works well together and one of my best. They would miss you.'

'Yes, Sir, I do know that but I still hope you will consider my request.'

The Group Captain thought for a while, still with his shrewd eyes fixed on the boy in front of him—nearly all of them were boys now—then seemed to make up his mind.

'All right, Lawless, there are things in this,' he said, tapping the file in front of him, 'that need following up but I'll see what might be done. Now, you must let Pilot Officer Chester know immediately. I would not want him to find out by accident or rumour, d'ye hear?'

'Yes, Sir, thank you, Sir!'

The Group Captain waved his hand and Lawless sprang to his feet.

'There's something else, Sir.'

'What now, Lawless?'

'It's my pilot, Sir, in the Whitley; Flight Lieutenant Sherwood.'

'What about him? He was killed in the crash, wasn't he?'

'Yes Sir, but I found his cap. I thought his parents might like to have it, Sir.'

'Hm, it's been some time now. It could upset them all over again. Are you sure?

'Yes, Sir. If I could give it to them, I think it might help. But I don't know how to find out where they live.'

'That would take a while and you don't have the time; later, much later, perhaps. Let me have it with a letter from you and I'll see that it gets to them.'

'Yes, Sir. Thank you, Sir.'
'Dismissed.'

The Group Captain sat back in his chair and reflected on his lunch with Birnam in that oak-panelled room in Oxford where they usually met. Funny how things fitted together sometimes, he thought: Lawless himself had just come up with the perfect answer to Birnam's concern about him. Canada was the ideal place for pilot training. He would be well out of the way for most of the next year at least: if he survived the operations still to come.

Lawless did not get leave for Christmas—that was spent on the base with long sessions in the local pubs—but he was granted four days over New Year to prepare himself for his departure for Canada, sailing out of Liverpool and bound for New Brunswick.

Lying in bed with Annie on his last night, he thought back to last New Year's Eve when they all danced and he drank too much and ended up drunk and snoring on the kitchen floor and on New Year's Day morning he had his worst hangover ever, although it didn't stop him having to go out and see to the ewes. There he had told them all about frumity eating and first-footing but here he had done it all again, just as he had every other New Year's Eve for as far back as he could remember. In a couple of days he would be leaving all of them again and going even farther away this time. He would keep sending his letters. Maybe they would have a better chance of reaching La Commanderie from Canada. He hadn't had any replies so far.

'Philip, when you were over there did you meet anyone?'

'Lots, well, quite a few.'

'I meant anyone, you know, special.'

'Special? Yes, there was one. She was very special.'

'I knew there was someone. What was she called?'

'Caramelle. She was a lovely big sheepdog and she saved my life.'

She banged her fists on his chest. 'Sometimes I could kill you!'

Later she whispered sleepily in his ear. 'Will you write when you're over there?'

'Yes,' he said. 'I'd already thought of that.'

ENGLAND 1943

LUCKY STRIKE

In September 1943 Liverpool still showed the effects of German air raids in the early years of the War. One of the docks where an ammunition ship had exploded in 1941 was still an unusable ruin. Lawless had grown used to the open, unspoilt, un-threatened spaces of Canada. The rubble and wreckage which he could see from the rail of his ship as it edged carefully towards its berth were grim reminders that he was now back in a very different country. He had been hoping Annie might have come to meet him after he landed but no one he knew was there, only a breezy corporal sitting at a desk with two bored-looking aircraftmen behind him in a bare and dingy room where returning RAF personnel were directed to report.

'Pilot Officer Lawless? Right, Sir, these are your papers, travel warrant, identification; sign please. Thank you; transport for Lime Street station at the end of the dock, Sir. Have you any kit still on board? No? Good: you can toddle along straightaway, then, Sir. Here, you, carry this officer's bags; get a move on.'

I'm back, Lawless thought. 'Any chance of a cup of tea somewhere, Corporal?'

'At the station, Sir.'

The tea at the smoke-filled station buffet was terrible, almost as bad as his first taste of insipid Canadian coffee. He put the mug down half-full and looked again at his papers and the travel warrant that stated his destination as Selby, changing at York. There should be RAF transport at Selby for the airfield where he was to join the newly installed Heavy Conversion Unit for Halifax bombers. It was a fine cold morning. He felt himself looking forward to the train journey across the Pennines: anything to get away from this place.

***

'Have you any idea what we're supposed to be doing?

'Getting to know each other, I'd say.'

'Ah, you sound as if you've done this before. By the way, my name's Kendrick, Richard.'

'Lawless, Philip Lawless. You could say that. I was based at Topcliffe; air gunner on Whitleys.'

'Whitleys, eh? I thought they were . . .'

'Yes, withdrawn: it was some time ago. Navigator, are you?'

'For my sins. They found out I'd done some Maths. You've got your wings, I see.'

'Canada, flying Ansons.'

'Me too: Mark Fives. Fancy a drink?'

It's the best way, Lawless thought: find out for yourself who you can get on with and team up with them. After three days of being crowded together in briefing room or hangar for airfield and aircraft familiarisation lectures and demonstrations and beery sessions in the bar in the evenings, they had the makings of a crew.

The next twelve weeks were one long exhaustive series of practising circuits and landings; emergency procedures with one engine shut down, then two; simulated mechanical breakdowns; blind-flying practice; defensive manoeuvres against enemy fighters; practice bombing from different altitudes; more circuits and landings; gunnery practice out over the North Sea; baling-out drill; take-offs fully loaded with all ammunition boxes charged and five tons of sand-filled casings in place of the real thing; more bombing practice, again over the sea and using dummy bombs; cross-country flying at different altitudes and much more instruction and practice in the air and on the ground until every man began to wonder if there could possibly be anything else to learn. Then, with 150 hours flying time behind them they were allowed to take up a great big Halifax bomber all on their own.

It was the only flight one of the new crews ever made. Perhaps someone made an elementary mistake, or the hydraulics were faulty but the twenty-ton bomber attempted a crash landing with its undercarriage up and all the crew still on board. None of them survived the fire. Lawless's aircraft had been listed next to fly, but had to wait until the afternoon for take-off when the runway had been cleared.

There was a brief passing out parade and short speech from the Commanding Officer which they could hardly hear because the wind was making so much noise. It seemed they were being wished good luck on their new postings that were listed on the board in the briefing room. Lawless had the distinct feeling that they were being hurried on to make room for the next intake that was arriving the following day.

He had a letter to send, one that had been on his mind and his conscience for days. His own son's first birthday was now several days past. There had been no chance of buying a birthday card, one with a picture of flowers on it or a happy fat little cherub. A letter, his first father's letter to his son would have to do. His mind went blank with sadness and longing. What did Alexandre look like now? Could he walk? Did Thérèse tell him about his father who was a long way away but was coming home one day? What could he say that would tell of his love and longing and hope and, yes, fear? He started to write.

Everyone was granted 72 hours leave that for some was barely enough time to get home, say hello and catch the train straight back to their new squadron. Lawless decided to take the train back to Oxenholme and telephoned his uncle to see if he could be met at the station.

'I can't tell you where I'm stationed, Uncle John, but it's not all that far from the sea.'

'When will we see you again, Philip?'

'I don't know, Auntie. I'll write.'

In the kitchen when they were washing up after supper Annie said,

'Shall I come in again tonight?'

After they made love and he was lying beside her again she was quiet for a long time. Lawless thought she must have gone to sleep.

'I can't do this with you anymore, Philip. I love you but I don't think you've noticed that. You're very kind and you know how to make me feel good but you don't give yourself; I can feel it. I think you must love somebody else but I know you won't say.'

'Annie . . .'

'No, listen. I want to tell you. When you were away all that time in Canada I met somebody. It was at a dance and he was on leave. He's in the Navy. He's really nice, Philip. I'm sure you would like him. He's called Andie, Andrew really, Andrew Burns. He's asked me to marry him and I said yes, Philip. I've told Mum; not Dad yet.'

'Annie, I'm really happy for you. You deserve somebody better than me, really you do.'

'You have changed, Philip; inside, I mean. Do you know that?'

'I do know, Annie. A lot of us have.'

'Andy's different. I have this feeling he won't change and I know he loves me. Him and me, we haven't done this, Philip. I think he's shy.'

'Listen, Annie: I'd like to give you and Andy a wedding present. I want to give you our house in Kendal. I don't need it. I don't think I could ever live there again, anyway. It'll be yours. No, I won't listen. I've made up my mind. I'll get a solicitor to draw up all the papers and I'll do it as soon as I can; before . . .'

Lawless left it at that. She would know he was going to say *before it's too late.*

***

In its first operation on the night of 3 December 1943, Halifax KN 342 D was hit in the lower side of the starboard wing five minutes after it had dropped its bombs on Leipzig. Dickie Dent, the rear gunner had seen a shadow in the cloud below him, thought it might be a night fighter but could not depress his guns enough to fire on it. The engines kept running smoothly but Lawless felt the controls going heavy in his hands. He called for the flight engineer, Ernie Gibbons to come forward and lend a hand in case the strain on his arms became too much. The rest of the crew reported no visible damage except for Leslie Proud, the wireless operator who said his instruments had gone dead. Unless the problem could be fixed the Halifax would be unable to signal base when the need arose. After a further half hour of steady flying, Ernie Gibbons tapped Lawless on the shoulder and pointed to the fuel gauges. The needles had fallen back more than they should. Lawless asked the navigator for a course and estimated distance back to base. Gibbons rolled his eyes when he heard the numbers.

'Listen, all of you. We might have a little trouble making it all the way back. If there's anything you can throw out let Ralph know and he'll deal with it. That doesn't apply to ammunition. You hear that, Dickie? John? Keep parachutes handy everybody.'

'I can't swim, Skipper.' That was the mid-upper gunner, John Brent.

'Tell him to jump now, Skipper. Lessen the weight.' That was Ralph Henderson the bomb-aimer.

They always make jokes when they're scared, Lawless remembered.

'Can you take hold here for a bit, Ernie, while I flex my hands? Let me know when we cross the coast, Richard. English coast, if we get there.'

'Should be crossing the coast now, Skipper.'

'Still on course?'

'Still on course, Skipper; fifty miles, approx.'

'There's something bloody wrong here. What is it, Ernie?'

'Can't tell, Skipper. Could be hydraulics.'

'Oh Christ.'

The starboard's inner engine coughed, started up again, coughed and died. Lawless pressed the lever to stop the propeller from windmilling. The starboard outer engine shut down without warning.

'Get up here Ralph! Everybody, bale out now. Now!'

'If you're staying Philip, so am I,' Kendrick said. 'You need someone to show you where to go.'

The others bundled out as fast as they could, leaving a howling gale sweeping through the aircraft.

'Runway! There it is!'

Lights on—a bit of flap—keep her nose up—throttle back as she touches—he was Sherwood now—steady—Jesus Christ! Bloody undercarriage stuck!

KN 342 D pancaked in a wet field 100 yards short of the runway at a speed of 140 knots, enough to take her through the perimeter fence, onto the runway and slew sideways to collide with a stores building another hundred yards away to the left. The aircraft broke in two just behind the mid-upper turret. Both men left inside when she hit the ground had put their parachute packs in front of their faces and their safety harnesses held fast. They both survived with only extensive bruising to show. Ambulance and fire wagons were not needed. There was virtually nothing left in the fuel tanks but vapour. Halifax KN 342 D was later declared a total loss.

Late in the afternoon with the MO's permission, Lawless and Kendrick limped across to take a look at her. A dozen ground crew mechanics were swarming all over, retrieving bits of equipment. The Flight Sergeant in charge marched up to them and saluted.

'Looks a bit of a mess, Chiefie.'

'A bit of a mess? I give you a brand new Halifax aircraft worth forty five thousand bloody pounds and the first time you take her out you fucking well break her in two. Sir!'

Lawless's bruises had turned yellow by the time another aircraft became available for his crew. They had two days to get used to her before the next operation was called. She was not new and had clearly spent some time in the repair workshops where she had had new engines installed and numerous patches fitted in the port side of the fuselage below the mid-upper turret. To Lawless they looked the right scatter for 20mm cannon rounds.

Accompanied by Ernie Gibbons, Lawless made a thorough investigation of the aircraft before signing the Form 700 taking responsibility for Halifax FB 160 B and handing it back to the Flight Sergeant.

'Please don't break this one, Sir. We haven't all that many left.'

'Tell the fucking Jerries that, Chiefie,' Ernie Gibbons said.

On the way to the briefing for the night's operation ,Dickie Dent said they ought to give her a name.

'When we get back, Dickie. We'll have an idea what she's like by then.'

The target was Frankfurt. Everybody groaned when they heard but they always did. The forecast was for clear skies and light wind. There would be diversionary raids to draw away the night fighters. It was to be a big attack, over 600 aircraft. That brought more low groans. The more aircraft streaming quickly over the target, the more collisions and more danger of being hit by bombs falling from aircraft higher up. Never mind the fighters and the flak.

They were lucky to be placed near the front of the bomber stream. It meant less chance of being attacked by night fighters that would need time to get into position. That was on the way out. On the way back it could be a different matter.

Again the weather forecast proved wrong. The target was almost completely obscured by cloud. Target indicators dropped by Pathfinder aircraft ahead of the stream seemed to be scattered widely. Ralph Henderson released the bombs as close as he could judge to the centre of the city and Lawless made an immediate sharp turn away to port.

'Steer Two Seven Zero, Skipper. Put your foot down.'

'Fighter! Fighter! Dive left! Go!'

Both gunners opened fire. Whether they saw a target or not they knew it was a good way of frightening off a less than determined fighter pilot. Lawless saw tracer streaking past his starboard wing.

'Can you see him, Dickie?'

'JU 88; he must be over and past you.'

'John?'

'Never saw him, Skipper.'

'Well stay awake everybody. He may be back. Going home.'

Whether it was the same fighter or not, they never knew, but a few minutes later the inside of the fuselage was lit up by a great flashing light and sparks flew into the cockpit. Lawless heard hammering tearing noises from somewhere above and behind him. Even with his mask on he could smell cordite. Instinctively he put the Halifax into a dive.

'Anybody hit? Ernie, you OK? Get back and see.'

'Port outer, Skipper; fire.'

Lawless increased the power. Higher speed might dowse the flames flashing from the engine.

'He's following us down, Skipper.'

'Get onto him Dickie! You as well John!'

The night fighter got his burst in just before the eight guns in the two turrets blazed away at him. Lawless felt the Halifax stagger under a heavy blow somewhere at the rear and yaw sharply to starboard. She needed Ernie's hands as well as Lawless's on the controls to bring her back on course.

'I got him! I got him!' Dickie Dent yelled. 'Look at the fucker go!'

'There, Skipper, your side.' Ernie Gibbons took one hand of the controls and pointed.

Lawless looked left and saw a long streak of flame plunging down, two, three hundred feet below. It suddenly ballooned in a bright orange silent explosion shedding glowing sparks that faded as they drifted into the darkness.

'You lovely bugger, Dickie. All OK at your end? I felt something hit us.'

'Bloody great bang underneath. I think he hit the tail wheel.'

'I'm sure I hit him as well, Skipper,' John Proud said.

'See him, John?'

'Single engine job; 190, I think.'

'All right, everybody. We're still a long way from home. Stay awake.'

'Fire's not out, Skipper.'

'Shut it down Ernie. Maybe they won't see us so easily and save us some fuel.'

'We need to, Skipper: gauges a bit low.'

'Oh Christ, not again.'

The damage report on Halifax FB160 B listed 15 holes up to one foot in diameter in the port side of the fuselage aft of the mid-upper turret and twelve corresponding holes on the starboard side; two perspex panels in the mid-upper turret shattered; port inner fuel tank pierced and empty; port outer engine damaged by fire and not repairable; tail wheel missing.

Lawless had somehow managed to land the Halifax, and held her on the undercarriage long enough to keep the tail from grounding until she had almost stopped. While they were in the air John Brent had not mentioned the cannon shell that flew through his turret nor the wound to his shoulder caused by Perspex fragments from the shattered panels. Lawless told him he had disobeyed standing orders and bought him a beer.

The crew were still standing by the aircraft looking at the visible damage when the Flight Sergeant alighted from his 30 hundredweight with his team of fitters. He stood with his hands on his hips looking along the Halifax from nose to tail and back again and shaking his head.

'What do you think, Chiefie?'

'All I can say, Sir, is that some fucking people have all the fucking luck.'

'That's the name, Skipper,' Dickie Dent said. 'Why not call her Lucky?'

'From the state she's in,' said Kendrick, 'Lucky Strike might be more apt.'

'Lucky Strike she is,' said Lawless. 'Can you have that painted on with a lightning flash for us, Chiefie?'

The Flight Sergeant finished his examination of the damage the next day. On Form 78 he concluded by deeming Halifax FB160 B repairable on site, assuming a replacement engine available. Other problems turned up during test flights and she was not declared ready for operations until 19 January 1944 but was grounded again the next day when a testing showed up problems with oil pressure in the replacement engine. No other aircraft being available, Lawless's crew did not take part in the raid on Berlin that night. Two of the squadron's Halifaxes failed to return.

'Lucky we missed that one, Skipper.'

'Keep your fingers crossed, Dickie. There's a whisper going round we'll be going there again soon. My round, I think Richard?'

'I'll get them in, Philip. Why not give us a tune?'

ENGLAND 1944

Lawless found that he got on well with Kendrick, the navigator who told him he had been at Stowe public school. He showed no surprise when Lawless said he had been at a grammar school.

'Couldn't get into Winchester so my dad decided somewhere a lot newer might suit me better. It was all right: played a lot of cricket and nipped off to Oxford now and again. It's not all that far from Stowe.'

'So why did you choose Cambridge?'

'Good for Maths.'

'But you told me you were reading History.'

'They let me change after the first term. History's better. You get more time to think—and play cricket. I wanted to get a Blue.'

'Now I understand why they made you a navigator.'

'Well I don't understand it. Usually if you know how to do something they put you in a job where what you do know is absolutely irrelevant.'

'All right Pythagoras, let's see how good your Maths is. I've been told that the chances of a new crew surviving the first five ops are ten times lower than a crew with more ops behind it. How does that leave us?'

'Crafty, aren't you? I know what you're getting at. You've done two ops with us and you told me 24 in Whitleys, 26 in all. Do your ops help all of us, or do our two bring you down to our level: that's it, isn't it?'

'You could look at it that way, yes.'

'Well it's not Maths, my dear old Skipper; it's statistics and that makes it too boring to think about. I'll get them in.'

While Kendrick was at the bar a sudden thought came to Lawless: he had actually done 28 ops counting the two in Chester's crew. Thirty ops made a full tour and that meant six months off as an instructor. Two more to go: perhaps he should put in a request. Become an instructor: on what aircraft? Whitleys—nobody needed them now. So what would he do in those six months? Desk work; train air gunners; sweep up offices? It was fantasy. He decided to keep quiet and see what happened.

'Here you are; get that down. You look as if you've worked it all out. Listen, how about a bash in Cambridge when we get leave? I know a few girls there. Or Oxford if you like: hundreds of pubs.'

'I'll think about it.'

Lawless's instincts and the rumours he heard were right. Well before the briefing he had a good idea of the likely target from Ernie Gibbons who usually hung about when fuelling-up of the aircraft was in progress and knew that full tanks meant a long trip and these days that meant Berlin. The place had been raided so often by now; there was an obvious pattern. It had to be Berlin.

'Full, you say? Let's hope it's a lighter bomb load. It must mean a big diversion, not going straight across.'

'Less trouble on the way there, Skipper,' Ernie said, not sounding very convinced.

Lawless grew more and more apprehensive as the day progressed. Bad weather reports led to take-off being delayed twice and the squadron did not receive orders that the raid was on until nearly midnight. A long restless day behind them and a long flight ahead meant tired crews. However, the diversionary route seemed to have served its purpose, at least as far as Lawless's squadron was concerned, because they saw no enemy aircraft and only sporadic flak on the long approach to Berlin.

It was very different when they eventually got there. As Lawless set the Halifax on its bombing run the cockpit suddenly lit up, went dark and flared again a second later. He saw two Lancasters on fire, one on each side, less than a hundred yards away. As he watched, the port wing of one broke away between the two blazing engines and fell, twisting round like a log in a current. The other flew on as if the crew had seen nothing wrong but suddenly exploded in a massive red and white ball that hurled glowing shreds towards Lucky Strike but to Lawless's great relief falling below her as she passed by.

'Steady; steady; left a little; steady': the bomb-aimer's litany chanted on all approaches sounded again in Lawless's ears.

'Flak got 'em both.'

'No, flak's too low down; fighter somewhere.'

'Christ! There's another. It's a Halli. Isn't that Bill's? Somebody's jumped.'

'Right a little; steady; hold there; steady. Bombs away.'

Relieved of five tons of metal and explosive Lucky Strike bounced upwards nearly a hundred feet.

'Fighter, fighter! Below astern! Dive left, dive!'

Dickie Dent's four Brownings shook the Halifax as he hosed away at the fighter now above and behind him after Lawless's diving turn. John Brent joined in from the mid-upper turret.

'He's gone! He's gone! I saw flashes on him. I must have hit him.'

'Could have been his exhausts, Dickie.'

'No; definite flashes; on a wing maybe.'

'Port inner, Skipper; look.'

'What is it, Ernie?'

'Revs up, oil pressure dropping: he must have hit us.'

'I didn't feel anything.'

'You don't if it's an engine.'

'Well at least it's not the new one.'

'No, but it's on the same wing. Should shut it down, Skipper; it could catch.'

Lawless tried to think. *One engine dead and another suspect.*

'Richard, give me a straight course back home. Bugger the Denmark trip. We'd never make it.'

A few moments later Kendrick's calm voice sounded in his ear.

'Steer Two Eight Zero; estimate two hours plus to Dutch coast.'

'Two Eight Zero it is. Shut it down, Ernie. Listen, everybody, usual thing: trouble getting home. Can't climb on three engines so keep your eyes open. We could meet some of them on the way back.'

There was some desultory flak as Lucky Strike approached the Dutch coast, but the gunners were well off target. The sky was clear of night fighters all the way; the chase was on far away to the north. Lawless held to the same course until Henderson in the nose caught sight of the English coast ahead.

'Let 'em know who we are, Les. I don't want us being tagged by a Beaufighter.'

Leslie Proud started repeating the identification codes of a damaged friendly aircraft every thirty seconds until eventually he received a signal to fly on. Ten miles from the field he radioed the control tower that they were coming in on two engines. From five miles out Lawless saw the runway lights come on.

Lucky Strike touched down on its home airfield at eight o' clock on a cold and drizzly morning and taxied slowly to its parking position in the dispersal area, followed closely by a fire engine and ambulance. The port outer engine died on the way.

'Seized,' Ernie Gibbons said, shaking his head. 'That bloody oil pump again.'

On the ground, even in the half-light they could see the cause of the trouble. The port inner engine had two neat holes in the rear of the cowling.

'So he did manage to get a couple of twenties into her, Ernie?'

'Christ knows what they did inside 'cos there's no sign of them coming out anywhere. How it kept going at all after that I've no idea.'

They found scattered holes in the port side fuselage that Lawless said must have come from fragments flying from the exploding Lancaster. No one remembered hearing any impact.

'She needs two new engines, Skipper and that's going to take some time because Chiefie told me they're running short of this type.'

'Two, you say?'

'Two: I don't know about you but I don't want to go up again with that bloody port outer. You tell him.'

'Here's the truck. Come on, let's get the quiz game over with. I'm bloody freezing.'

At the debriefing Lawless told the Intelligence Officer that they had seen a Halifax go down in flames over Berlin and thought it was Bill Tremlett's. That was confirmed later in the day. Tremlett was the Squadron Leader. The senior Flight Lieutenant was put in temporary charge pending the arrival of a replacement. Two other of the squadron's aircraft also failed to return.

Lawless learned that Lucky Strike was withdrawn from service and parts of her used as spares but that was some time after the next raid which was ordered for the following night. Lawless was told of this late in the afternoon and that they were on the list to fly.

'Can't go, Sir. No aircraft.'

'Oh, we've got a replacement for you. Brand new Mark III. Should be enough time for you to get used to her in the morning.'

'If they carry on treating us like this,' Dickie Dent said, 'I'm going to have a word with my shop steward.'

'The truck's waiting outside. Let's go and meet our new lady friend. We've got five hours to get to know her inside and out before the armourers have their turn.'

'I wish you wouldn't talk like that, Philip,' Kendrick said. 'It gives me disturbing thoughts.'

The target was Berlin again. The announcement brought more audible groans than usual.

The Wing Commander held up a hand for silence and said the Germans would not be expecting such a quick return. Their fighters and flak units would still be recovering from the last battering. *What about us?* Outward route the same as last time, a bit further south—they wouldn't expect that, either. *Fat chance!* The return route was more direct with a slight diversion south of Brunswick. The forecast was for clear weather over the North Sea, some patchy cloud over the target area and quarter-half moon on the outward flight. None of that sounded very promising to the listeners. Take-off would be at 1800 hours. Synchronise watches now.

The Station Commander added his words of encouragement. Berlin was being battered to pieces but the Commander-in-Chief wanted no let-up. Good luck.

Eight of the squadron's Halifaxes, all that could be mustered, took off as scheduled. Replacement crews for those lost on recent raids had not yet arrived.

Fifty miles north of Berlin Dickie Dent suddenly shouted he'd seen something, wasn't sure what, a sort of shadow aft and below his turret and catching up.

'Corkscrew left now! Hang on everybody,' Lawless yelled and put the aircraft into a steep dive to port. Henderson, readying himself in the nose for the bombing run, screamed, 'fighter, starboard, firing, gone!'

Lawless started the standard climbing turn to port, misjudged, and made it too steep and felt the Halifax start shuddering. Christ, he thought, she's going to stall and pressed the control column forwards. Instead of dropping her nose and gaining speed the Halifax tipped until its wings were almost vertical. Everything not bolted on or securely tied began to fall down. The wireless operator who was not belted up fell with them. Lawless shoved the control to the right to raise the aileron and try to roll her back upright. After an agonising delay during which he prayed the night fighter was not coming back for another try, she responded and went into a shallow dive. After that it was a simple matter to bring her gradually up into a climb to regain the right altitude for the bomb run.

'You could make a fortune as a stunt flier after the War, Skipper,' Kendrick said.

There was cloud over Berlin but large patches were already on fire so Ralph Henderson aimed for the hottest looking part. There was a lot of flak coming up and Lawless saw three aircraft go down, all Lancasters, he thought.

It was a relief to leave the red glow behind them and set course for the Dutch coast. It seemed a good time to open a thermos flask and have some coffee and call up Henderson the bomb aimer.

'Les, what did you see?'

'Twin-engine job, 110, I'm pretty sure.'

'And he went past us?'

'Like shit off a stick. Funny thing, tracer was going up, not straight ahead.'

'He must have been in a climb.'

'No, straight and level, what I saw of him.'

Certainly they were all tired and still shaken after Lawless's aerobatics in escaping from the night fighter. Perhaps they were for once less alert than they might have been because of the so far quiet return flight. Lawless knew that one of the most dangerous parts of the flight back could be after they left the Dutch coast and he kept moving and stretching and turning his head this way and that to keep himself wide awake. He could not ensure the others did the same, even if he occasionally used the intercom to contact them. A second's loss of concentration was all that was needed.

Again the attack came from astern and this time the night fighter fired first. The burst was high and over the port wing but close enough for Lawless to catch a glimpse of red glowing streaks just outside his port panel. Lawless dived right hoping that the mid-upper gunner had seen the fighter and would swing his turret round and fire after him. Dickie Dent should now be wide awake and able to deal with anything more from behind. He heard John Brent's Brownings fire a long burst. There was no sign of flashes or fire ahead. John must have missed him.

No one needed Lawless to tell him to keep a sharp lookout. They were now flying in faint moonlight and that fighter had missed a good chance earlier. He might fancy another try. When he did come back he came in on the starboard beam, a very unusual tactic, probably going for a longer target. It was a bad decision in the event because John Brent happened to be facing that way as he traversed his turret and immediately opened fire when he saw the shadow. The fighter opened up at the same time. Dickie Dent saw the tracers flying in opposite directions and when his guns came to bear he joined in.

Lawless felt hammering blows raking the whole starboard side of the aircraft, and the fuselage filled with sparks and flying pieces of metal. A fraction of a second later, there was a tremendous jolt at the rear and she veered sharply right, almost wrenching the steering column from Lawless's grip. Ernie Gibbons shouted that the starboard inner engine had been hit and glancing across Lawless saw a burst of smoke start from the top of the nacelle followed immediately by a spurt of flame. Ernie shut down the engine without being told and the flame disappeared although the smoke spread out in a thick black trail.

'He's going, the bastard's going! Look at that! Boom!' Dickie Dent was obviously still alive and signalling the downing of the night fighter. There was no response from the mid-upper turret.

'Les, are you there? Can you see anything? Can you see John?'

All right, Skipper; got a few splinters in my hand. Wait a minute. I think John's been hit. There's some blood.'

'Ralph, Ralph, come in. Get up there and have a look at John. Everybody get hold of your 'chutes. We may have to ditch.'

In the last few frantic minutes the Halifax had lost a lot of height and was still heading down. Lawless hauled back on the column, more in hope than expectation and to his amazement she responded and began a slow climb.

'How far, Richard? Richard, you there?'

'Here, Skipper.' Kendrick's drawl always had a calming effect but this time it was slower and sounded tired. 'Steer Two Eight Zero; 50 miles. Should see coast . . . soon.'

'Skipper, John's arm looks bad. I've put a tourniquet on. He's unconscious, hanging in the straps. Think he got a bang on the head. Turret's a mess.'

'Keep an eye on him Ralph. Get him down when you can. Help him Les.'

'Four thousand feet and holding Skipper.'

Maybe we'll get there, Lawless thought.

'Could call up one of the Yank fields.'

'Too risky, Ernie. They get a bit edgy. No, I'm going for home. Les, send the ID signal.'

'That engine's burning inside, Skipper. Look at the smoke.'

'Les, when we're in range tell the tower we're on fire, three crew injured. ETA, Richard?'

'Wait . . . 08:30, give or take.'

'Send that, Les.'

Kendrick's voice came on again. 'Can you put your foot down, Skipper? It's rather draughty in here.'

As soon as the Halifax stopped rolling the fire truck screeched to a halt alongside and the crew hosed foam on the smouldering engine, covering the whole starboard wing. An unconscious John Brent and a protesting Les Proud—'it's only a few scratches, Skipper'—were shoved into the ambulance and driven away.

'You should have gone as well, Richard. You look a bit groggy.'

'Just a bang on the chest. I'll be all right.'

Lawless turned to the waiting Flight Sergeant.

'Sorry about all that, Chiefie. A 110 hit us and took the top off the rudder. I couldn't get out of the way.'

'That's all right, Sir. You're not the worst. I'm glad you brought her back. Everyone's back this time.'

Everyone was back but the Halifax Chiefie had referred to had crashed on landing. Five of its crew ended up in hospital and two never flew again. John Brent was one of six others who were taken to the sick bay.

The Wing Commander told them that it had been a very successful raid causing widespread damage. It was believed an SS Barracks had been hit and three bridges were down.

They listened in silence, not really caring what he said. They were still too tired and shocked and worried about John and Les. It had been a very near thing this time.

In the evening Lawless said he was going to see how John and Les were getting on in the sick bay.

'I'll come with you,' Kendrick said. 'There's a rather interesting Staff Nurse there.'

Leslie Proud was sitting up in bed with one hand heavily bandaged. He told them he was being discharged the next day and expected to be sent home on sick leave. He had not been able to see John.

The Staff Nurse said Sergeant Brent had been transferred to hospital at Halton. She could not say much about his injuries except there was worry about his arm that had become badly infected and the blow to his head was affecting his sight.

'You go on, Philip,' Kendrick said outside. 'I just want to have a word with that nurse. I'll see you in the mess.'

Some had half expected it, but all aircrew were surprised when they were granted seven days' leave.

'Richard, you ought to see the MO. That's a huge bloody bruise and you're wheezing.'

'I smoke too much, that's all. Should give it up. No, I'm staying on. I might be transferred if I report sick. I'm not leaving the crew. I know John got clobbered but we all got back alive. We've always done that, so far, no matter what. I've got this feeling we're lucky, Philip. It must be you: you're lucky. Lucky Lawless. It's important. Napoleon knew that.'

'That's rubbish. You said it was all to do with statistics. Remember?'

'What about it? We're still here. That's what matters. Now, where are you going? I have to put in a couple of days at home, see the old Mum and Dad, but afterwards, what about that bash in Cambridge?'

'I don't know. I've got relatives whom I could stay with but I haven't decided yet. Might do some walking in the Lakes.'

'Too healthy for me. If you change your mind and fancy Cambridge, leave a message with the Porter at Corpus. He'll know where I am.'

He hadn't been all that serious about the Lakes. He had no boots and no proper weatherproofs with him. His old kit would be in the house somewhere but he didn't want to go back there or to his Uncle's farm where he could have borrowed some, sure enough. But it would be too awkward there with Annie. He didn't know what to do. On impulse he decided to go to Oxford. Perhaps there would be a room in the College. At least it was somewhere he knew.

The train journey took all day. He went by York, Sheffield and Birmingham. Walking from Snow Hill station through the cathedral square to New Street for the Oxford connection brought back memories of 1939 but it was very different now. Some of the Cathedral windows were boarded up and the grass looked untended. There was evidence of air raid damage everywhere. Is this what it's like in Bremen and Essen, he thought. He had looked down on the fierce glow of the fires there and it was probably much worse.

It was getting dark when the train drew into Oxford station. The platform was crowded with people, many in uniform, shivering and stamping their feet as they waited for late trains. Among them were quite a few American airmen in uniform. Lawless recalled there were bases near Oxford; he knew one was Grove and there was Bicester. He couldn't remember any of the others.

There was no chance of a taxi if Americans were about. He set off to walk up Hythe Bridge Street into town. The windows in all the houses were now blacked out.

The College gate was closed so he pulled the bell chain and listened for the familiar faint clanging in the Porters Lodge. He had to pull twice more before the wicket gate creaked open and the porter peered out.

'Good evening Lewis.'

'Mr Lawless? You back then, Sir? Haven't seen you in an age.'

'I've been away, Lewis and now I'm back, in the RAF, as you see. No, of course you can't. Can I come in?'

'Well, I don't know, Sir; there being a War on. Most of the College is closed down.'

'I'm on leave, Lewis, and I haven't anywhere to stay. There's no chance of finding a hotel at this hour.'

'There's some officers in some of the rooms in Garden Quad. Convalescing, they are. It's like a hospital now over there; nurses and doctors and such coming and going. Maybe there's a room at the top of a staircase not being used. I'll see if the key's still here. You'd better come in, Sir.'

Half an hour later Lawless was installed in a cold dingy little set at the top of Staircase XI. At least there was a bed and it was made up and the sheets felt dry. Perhaps someone was expected. Well, hard luck.

''Fraid there's no coal, Sir. It's on ration.'

'It's all right, Lewis. I've got my greatcoat if I get too cold.'

'Do you want a call in the morning, Sir? I've got a boy as helps me.'

'Not to worry. I'll get myself up.'

'Goodnight, Sir. Nice to see you back.'

'Goodnight, Lewis and thank you.'

'Oh, Sir, one thing: the Bursar's away at the moment, or I wouldn't have been able to do this without asking him.'

'I'll remember that.'

'If I were you, Sir, I'd go down and mix with the others for breakfast in the Hall. In that uniform they won't know the difference.'

It was only after the porter had left that Lewis saw a covered plate on the battered wooden table. Under the cover was a bacon sandwich.

A handful of men, all in Army uniform, including one in a wheelchair, were eating breakfast at one of the long polished oak tables in the Dining Hall. After some mildly curious looks, they took no further notice of Lawless, except to pass him the teapot when he asked. A boy in a white jacket brought him a plate of scrambled egg and sausage and placed a rack of toast on the table by his cup and saucer. There was no butter put plenty of marmalade, Cooper's, he was pleased to see. He ate everything not knowing what he might be able to find for lunch. He had been given the usual special leave ration card but that did not guarantee there would be any food available.

After breakfast he took a walk in the gardens where he saw some uniformed nurses sitting beside men wrapped up in blankets against the chill, or pushing others slowly along the gravelled paths in wheelchairs. The sun began to emerge from the early morning mist and feeling fit and rested and his stomach full he decided to go out into Broad Street, walk along the Turl and head down to the river.

'Pilot Officer Lawless, I do believe.'

He turned to see who had asked. The tall woman in a black hat with drooping brim and smart black coat seemed familiar; her deep voice even more so.

'Dr Smallwood. Good morning.'

'Good morning to you. Now what might you be doing in Oxford, if I may ask?'

'I'm on leave so I thought I'd come up and see if there was anyone about that I knew.'

'And so you see one. How long are you staying?'

'I don't know. The porter let me have a room last night, emphasising that the Bursar was not around. I may go on to Cambridge. One of my crew told me he would be there.'

'I am sure your room is cold and quite inadequate for a serving officer on leave. You must stay with me. No, please do not decline. You know where I am. We shall have supper together. Shall we say at seven? A bientôt.'

He watched her cross the Broad, walk past the crumbling heads of the Emperors on their pillars outside the Sheldonian and go up the steps of the Clarendon Building.

Well, well, he thought: Lucky Lawless. A bientôt? Why had she said that?

When he woke up, his watch showed 8 o'clock and she was gone. The impression of her head still showed on the pillow next to his and there was a trace of her perfume in the room. He saw the note she had left on the dressing table when he came back from the bathroom.

Makings of breakfast in the dining room—certain books perhaps to your liking in the library—suggest the Randolph for lunch—back by six for wine —play the piano if you wish.

The note was not signed. *How did she know he played the piano?*

He spent the morning in her library, a room where the walls were hidden behind hundreds of books. The Romance texts, in particular, drew his attention. Several were in Occitan, including Spanish and Italian variants he had not seen before. There was a shelf of doctoral theses mostly in English but with some bulky German and French works too. How Chevalier and Valentin would have revelled in this collection. Leafing through one in French, his eye was caught by a section on the analysis of dialect words and phrases in different metrical forms. He looked for paper to make some notes on the references and then stopped himself. How could he follow this up? Not now. Later—if, always if—when there was time; it might mean returning here. Would that be such a bad thing?

Without warning all the memories came back—and the guilt and he sat down and wept because no one else was there to see. He made himself dress and go out. The brightness of the sky lifted his spirits a little, enough to be going on with. He did not feel like lunch, not even at the Randolph, so he decided to go to the river and walk along the towpath to look at the college barges. A pair of swans closed on the bank, hoping perhaps he might have something to throw to them. Not to miss the chance ducks came scurrying across the surface. The barges were empty and silent, some of them covered in tarpaulins. The peacefulness of the water and the view across the Meadows to Christchurch and Merton skirted by the old city wall soothed away some of his torment and brought back a little of his appetite. And something else, difficult to put a name to, some sort of resolve, a recognition that what he was looking at was worth keeping and keeping in mind to return to when.... yes, but when? He retraced his steps and went through the Memorial Gardens into St Aldate's. One of the pubs was still open. There was only mild beer on offer but the landlord said there were some pork pies if he wanted one. Did he like mustard?

He wandered back along a crowded Cornmarket Street, past the Clarendon Hotel that seemed to have a lot of uniforms going in and out. Had it been commandeered? The square tower of St Michael at the North Gate stood as tough looking and aloof as ever. He had never been inside. He quickened pace. He felt like playing the piano and not just pub tunes this time.

He was still playing three hours later when she came back.

'Don't let me stop you,' she said. 'I much appreciate the subtleties and innuendoes of Satie. I can still hear you while I change.'

He stopped playing and turned round on the piano stool when she came back into the room with a tray holding a decanter of pale yellow wine together with a dark bottle and two glasses.

'I seem to remember you say that you liked sherry. I did wonder at the time whether you were simply being polite. I have to confess that unlike so many of my colleagues I do actually prefer a sweeter wine and I am lucky to have a little of this excellent madeira left.' She held out the bottle for him to see. 'It is a 1920 Blandy's. You should try it. Unless you prefer the amontillado?'

Anyone might think this is a game, Lawless thought, but conversation in Oxford really could be like this. If it was deliberate, intended to draw him away at least for a little time from the routine dreadfulness of his other life, it was working.

'Madeira sounds very interesting.'

'You may find some similarity with certain sweeter sherries. Some do. Both are rather seductive wines.'

She slipped into French and over two glasses each of madeira they talked about Romance literature. Not surprisingly it turned out she was expert in Occitan. She complimented him on his French, saying that she could detect no trace of English accent when he spoke though there was occasionally something of the Midi. Conversation paused when they heard the sound of a college bell tolling.

'The chaplain still conducts a short evening service,' she explained. 'At present there is no suitable organist nor choir; hence no Evensong. However, we now know it is seven o' clock and I promised you supper. Come with me into the kitchen. You can help with the omelettes.'

'I know how to crack eggs.'

'Without that knowledge there can be no omelette,' she laughed.

Their lovemaking was more leisurely than the previous night. Then it had been simple, almost business-like although oddly he had found that very arousing. This time she permitted him to undress her and use his hands and tongue in the gentle but insistent and exploratory ways that Justine Lamphier had taught him in that unforgettably intense half hour at La Couvertoirade.

'*Ars amoris*, Mr Lawless: where might you have learned such skills?'

'As an officer and gentleman, Ma'am, my lips are sealed. For now, that is.'

'And a wit too,' she smiled and became more serious. 'I sense some conflicts in you, nevertheless. If speaking about them may be of help, I am an experienced listener as you may recall.'

The intuition of women: Annie had sensed it and now this astute, sophisticated woman twice her age had detected something of the same. But she, like Annie, was touching a part of his life he could not yet bring himself to reveal to anyone else. There was the other part.

'I'm not sure I should say this but now I feel I can to you.'

It was academic habit, perhaps, that attentive look she assumed, head slightly tilted, one eyebrow raised, awaiting information or opinion, reserving judgment.

'It's difficult . . . I don't want to sound defeatist . . . I'm not . . . none of us is . . . but . . . we . . . we sometimes wonder . . . where we're going . . . is it working, what we do, I mean . . . we go out . . . come back . . . some don't . . . we know that's going to happen . . . and every time . . . every time it's the same . . . and we're told we hit them hard but how can we be sure—the flak is just as bad the next time—and the fighters. I'm sorry . . . I shouldn't. Forget everything I said.'

'No; go on.'

'You know, this morning I went out and walked along the towpath, down from Folly Bridge. I wish I'd had something for the ducks. And I looked across the river and the Meadows—have they been digging trenches there? And there was the cathedral spire and Merton tower and the wall and this odd feeling came over me: I wanted it to stay like that, always, and, I don't know how to say this; it was just worth it, worth keeping. Can you see what I mean? But how can we, I mean us, when we don't seem to be making any difference?'

'Someone of my acquaintance is an engineer. It may surprise you to hear that my friend is a woman. She works on properties of metals. Trying to explain the significance of her experiments she once handed me a piece of wire—copper, I seem to remember. She told me to bend it, this way and that and observe what happened. You will, of course know. It became hot and eventually and quite suddenly broke in two. Metal fatigue, she said and went on to say something about loading and unloading and grain interfaces and critical crack size, all of which was lost on me. But the point is that not much seemed to change until suddenly it did and the thing broke.'

'It could happen that way to us; some of us.'

'No, not to you, or you would not have said 'some of us'. It will happen to them. And it will happen to them, the Germans. When it does—and I have no doubt that it will—those things you love will have been kept safe by what you do.'

They talked on into the night until during a pause they heard the college clock striking midnight. She sat up in the bed and stretched her arms.

'I must be in London tomorrow; early train: committee meetings all day.'

She looked down at him and smiled, glad to see less tension in his face.

'I think, however, we could find time time before sleep, for you to unseal your lips.'

'You've got that look on your face,' Kendrick said, 'nackered and pleased with yourself at the same time.'

'You just look nackered.'

'Well, I had a strenuous time in Cambridge.'

'I can believe it. You're still wheezing a bit.'

'Ah now, about that. Always do what Mama tells you to do. I went to the family doc and know what he said? Cracked sternum—breastbone to you—gets better on its own.'

'You can't go up yet, surely?'

'Can do. Doc checked my heart and lungs and signed me off fit for duty and I have a note from him saying so.'

'I'm not sure. You ought to see the MO.'

'Is that an order, now you're a Flying Officer? Come off it. You need me.'

'All right but you're not to join the snow-clearing squads. That is an order. Hell, I'll be late! Wingco's called all pilots in to tell us about new crews and aircraft. I want to see Chiefie afterwards; find out what's happening about our kite.'

'I'll come with you for that.'

'Chiefie, how did you do it? She looks as good as new. You didn't by any chance find my thermos?'

'We found a lot of things that you left behind, Sir but only one thermos and we put that in the scrap hopper.'

'Why did you throw it out, Chiefie? That thermos was a Christmas present from my aunt.'

'Didn't think you would have any further use for it, Sir, seeing as it had a 20mm hole right through it.'

Heavy rain turned the snow to slush and persistent low cloud covered the airfield making flying impossible and leading to the postponement of an operation against Berlin to the next night. It was postponed a second time when the weather failed to improve. Delays like this could unsettle even experienced crews and the squadron had eight new crews bringing it up to strength.

John Brent's replacement as mid-upper gunner was a quietly spoken dark-haired 20 year old from Barra in the Outer Hebrides called Gillis MacNeill. Lawless suggested a get-together in the pub for him to meet the rest of the crew.

'I don't drink, Sir.'

'You don't? Ah, well, you could have something else, lemonade perhaps?'

'It's the public house, Sir. My mother might get to know.'

'I see. Would it make any difference if she were told you had been given a direct order by a superior officer? We are sometimes compelled to do things in wartime that we would never do in peacetime, don't you agree?'

'I don't know, Sir. She has her opinions.'

'Why don't we just try it out for once? If it were summer we could sit outside but as it is, well, you understand.'

'Yes, Sir.'

'Good; the bus will be outside the gate at six. We all meet there. Good, that's all, Sergeant.'

'Thank you, Sir.' MacNeill saluted and turned to go.

'Oh, er, Sergeant MacNeill: Gillis, isn't it? Off parade and in the air, we don't normally use ranks and surnames in this crew, right?'

'Yes, Sir. Thank you, Sir.'

This is going to take some time, Lawless thought after MacNeill had left. Still, he looks all right and he did come out top of his course.

At the bar in the Dog and Gun Kendrick took the cigarette Lawless offered him and said,

'He doesn't say much, does he, our new gunner? Do you think he knows enough English? They mostly speak Gaelic up there in the Hebrides.'

'You're a Cambridge man: you could give him lessons. No, he'll be all right; and he must be good if his report is anything to go by. That's what matters most.'

'Well, I just hope he uses words the rest of us can understand when he sees a JU 88 coming in. Now, about this name.'

'Save it for the rest of them to hear. They've got the dart board and he's playing.'

'We've got a marksman here, Skipper,' Dickie Dent shouted over the din after MacNeill ended the last of three winning games against another crew by throwing an impeccable double top.

'Thank god we've got one at last,' Ernie Gibbons said, dodging Dickie Dent's swing.

Kendrick hammered on the table with his fist.

'Quiet please. Gentlemen, we have a christening to arrange. But first, we must choose the name. So may we have suggestions? Right, while you're all thinking I'll tell what I suggest and I may add this is based on deep thought and much experience.'

'We're listening.'

'I suggest Fine Leg, for two reasons. First, the cricketing reason: fine leg is where the most difficult chances are taken, and certainly that applies to us. Secondly, the morale reason; think of the picture: sheer silk stocking, short skirt, a hint of knickers. It's enough to put lead in anybody's pencil.'

Kendrick sat back smiling confidently. Lawless asked for other suggestions. MacNeill was the only one to stay quiet.

'Right, now we'll take a vote.'

By a majority of one they backed Ernie Gibbons's suggestion and Halifax L 142-J became Lucky Lady.

'Where did you learn to play darts like that, Gillis?'

'It's the first time I've played, Sir. Dickie showed me what to aim at and all I had to do was throw.'

'Right.'

***

All the squadron's Halifaxes took off next day in the early evening. One turned back after twenty minutes with a fault in the hydraulics that prevented the undercarriage from lifting. The rest climbed steadily and eventually joined the bomber stream on the now familiar northern route, heading for Denmark. The German defences detected the first aircraft when they were still over the North Sea but the first attacks took place over the Baltic and continued, increasing in intensity all the way to Berlin. Green flares that must have been dropped by fighters appeared in parts of the bomber stream.

'Letting their mates know where we are,' Ernie Gibbons said.

On the port side Lawless saw pieces flying off a Halifax's wing and tracer streaking from the rear turret guns. The fire spread across the wing and the Halifax fell away in a steep dive towards the sea below. Only two parachutes appeared.

Dickie Dent opened fire minutes afterwards yelling dive, dive. Lawless lowered flaps slightly and pushed the control column forward. It was a tactic for dealing with an attack from behind and below they had discussed before the raid. Lucky Lady's speed fell away as she headed down. Seconds later a shadow passed overhead. MacNeill was waiting with his turret trained forward and immediately fired a long burst that first shattered the tailfin and then smashed into the cockpit of a twin-engine fighter causing fragments to fly back dangerously close to Lawless's starboard wing. The fighter went into an immediate vertical dive and exploded with a vivid white flash two hundred feet below.

'Bloody good, Gillis! First time out, first one down!'

'110,' Dickie Dent said. 'See the antenna on the nose?'

'Evens up the score,' said Henderson. 'Oh god, who's that?'

Less than a hundred yards to port tracer was streaking outwards from both turrets of a burning Halifax. They could not see any fighters. The fire spread across both wings, but the aircraft kept flying steadily on its course. Lawless felt himself willing the crew to jump. The guns stopped firing and still the Halifax flew on. Perhaps everyone on board was dead. He hoped so.

'Pull over, Skipper. He could still have a full load on.'

Lawless turned away to starboard, fearful that any moment there might be a collision.

'It's Harry Pearson, Ernie. Christ!'

The fire must have reached the tanks of the burning Halifax and she disappeared in a cloud of flame that almost instantaneously erupted in a huge explosion as the bomb load went up. Lucky Lady was almost overturned by the shock wave and went into a dive that dropped her two thousand feet before Lawless could bring her back under control. It was vital to regain height before reaching the target and not become an unwitting target themselves for the rain of bombs soon to start falling from above.

Not for the first time Henderson had to release his bombs over an area where a dull red glow showed dimly through the thick cloud cover that shrouded Berlin. Lawless had the familiar slight feeling of relief that they had managed to do what they had come here to do and continued on the same course, waiting for Kendrick to signal the 90 degree turn that would set them heading west and for home. Searchlights and flak continued to search for them but the night fighters, probably out of ammunition and low in fuel, left them alone until the Dutch coast where as usual the German controllers had fully armed fighters with fresh crews waiting for tired and shocked crews. Lawless counted six bombers hit, either exploding or catching fire and plunging down, two of them into the sea. Lucky Lady was unmolested and made good time with a strong following wind but her crew's hopes of an early landing and breakfast were disappointed. The control tower ordered Lawless to keep circuiting the airfield until wreckage had been cleared from the runway.

At debriefing Lawless reported the Me110 shot down by MacNeill and seeing Flight Lieutenant Pearson's aircraft blow up fifty miles north of Berlin.

He was told he was mistaken. Pearson had made it back, just. It was the wreckage of his Halifax that had blocked the runway. He and the mid-upper gunner had survived, but the rest of the crew were missing, possibly baled out. There was always hope. There was no sign yet of two other of the squadron's aircraft with new crews. Lawless was about to say perhaps it was one of them they had seen blow up but kept quiet. What was the point? Anything could have happened.

Three days later, after several delays and changes of take off time, nine Halifaxes of a still depleted squadron finally took off at 21 00 hours on a cold dry night and set course straight for Berlin where the bomber stream would turn sharp south towards Leipzig.

'A chance to get some of our own back,' the Wing Commander had remarked at the final briefing. What he meant was that Leipzig was an important centre for aero engine manufacture and body assembly plants.

'The wind forecast is wrong again, Skipper,' Kendrick said. 'It's coming from the north and they told us we'd have a headwind.'

'Any suggestions?'

'I can work out dog legs for you follow to stop us getting over target too early.'

Lawless tried to think. Maintaining his present speed could mean reaching the target area thirty or forty minutes ahead of time and it was unlikely that there would be any target indicator flares for Henderson to see where he should aim. On the other hand, dog legging increased the chance of collisions in such a large bomber stream as well as offering a slower target to night fighters.

'Les, how's the set working?'

'Can't tell yet, Skipper. There's likely to be too many big ears listening out for the signal. Need to be nearer target before it's safe to switch on. It was working all right on test this afternoon.'

It's a calculated risk, Lawless thought. No it's not: you don't know the odds.

'Richard, we're going on. Could get too messy if we start wandering about. Get us as close as you can.'

'You're the boss, Skipper.'

And the boss can kill you all. Fingers crossed Ralph can make the set work.

The map on the wall at briefing had showed several rivers converging near the centre of Leipzig. Lawless could remember only one name, the Pleisse. Their radar worked best where water and land were in contact but the rivers were nothing like the size of the Rhine.

'Steer Two One Zero; sixteen minutes to go, Skipper.'
'Two One Zero; turning now. What do you see, Ralph?'
'Nothing Skipper; blacker than a mule's arse,' the bomb-aimer said.
Dickie Dent's voice came on. 'Somebody's catching it way behind. I can see two flamers going down.'
Simultaneously Lawless and Ernie Gibbons saw white flashes in the sky ahead.
'Flak about our height. Must be 88's.'
'Somebody's got there ahead of us.'
'Five minutes.'
'Bomb doors opening. All yours, Ralph. Les, are you on? What's it looking like?'
'Fuzzy; hang on, tuning. Bit better now.'
'Talk us in, Les. Ralph, you listening?'
'Must be the river, I think.'
A vivid white flash lit up the ground below and was gone in an instant.
'Steady; steady; steady. Bombs gone!'
Not waiting for any word from the wireless operator, Henderson had aimed for the white flash.
'Steer One Nine Zero.'
'One Nine Zero; turning now.'
A flak shell burst fifty feet below the port wing, tilting it violently upwards and shaking the whole aircraft.
'Something's hit us, Skipper; port outer: oil pressure dropping.'
'Two minutes to turn,' Kendrick said.
'Lanc on fire, going down, 500 yards aft.'
'I can't see anything, Ernie. She feels all right.'
'No pressure, Skipper. Shutting it down or she'll burn.'
'Steer Two Three Zero . . . now.'
'Turning Two Three Zero. How's fuel, Ernie?'
'Enough for three.'
'Going home. Eyes skinned everybody.'

'Where are we, Richard?'
'Dutch coast 30 minutes.'
'Fighter, fighter, port side,' Macneill shouted and immediately opened fire.
Lawless saw sparks flying off the starboard wing of a single-engine fighter about a hundred feet away, heading in the opposite direction to theirs. Macneill's tracers followed the German as it hurtled on and blew up with a bright orange flash that dazzled Dickie Dent and sent fragments flying past his turret but did not prevent him excitedly reporting a 109 down and out.
'He's a fucking dead shot, that boy,' said Ernie Gibbons.
Lawless nodded in agreement. 'I'm glad he's on our side. Richard?'
'And I was hoping for a quiet night. Dutch coast five minutes.'

Once they had crossed the English coast Lawless reduced speed and began a slow descent to 3000 feet. Les Proud reported hearing other returning aircraft asking for landing instructions. Lawless told the tower they were coming in on three engines.

'Straps tight on, everybody and brace yourselves. This could be a hard one. Get out and away from her as soon as you can when she stops.'

Lucky Lady rolled to a stop at 07 00 hours precisely. The Halifax had a reputation as a fairly easy aircraft to get out of in an emergency and Lawless's crew took full advantage this time.

'You got an unexploded bomb in there?' the driver of the fire wagon said.

'No,' said Kendrick, 'but there is rather a bad smell.'

They were the first crew home and six others followed over the next hour. That left two of the nine that had set out for Leipzig but they never did return.

With Lucky Lady's new port outer engine installed and flight tested Lawless led five of the squadron's aircraft during the last week of February on two mine-laying operations to Kiel Bay on the north German coast. Not having to face the intensity of flak or the swarms of night fighters they had encountered over Berlin was a welcome relief to the crew. Lawless knew, however, that these operations which they called gardening did carry a risk. Everyone knew of the occasion when a Stirling had been blown out of the sky when the mine it dropped had exploded on contact with the waves.

On the return flight from the second operation they were fired on by a flak-ship, though to no effect.

'That was very uncivil of him,' said Kendrick. 'We weren't doing him any harm.'

By now they had gathered from the BBC broadcasts of losses and stories from other crews in squadrons on the satellite fields that the raid on Leipzig had been a very bad night. Lawless was finding it difficult to sleep and noticed differences in the crew. Gillis MacNeill remained his usual imperturbable self and Ernie Gibbons just got on with his work but Henderson and Proud seemed to have lost their appetites and even Dickie Dent was quieter than he used to be.

'Are we all getting a bit edgy, Richard? What do you think?'

'I think I'd like another pint.'

When Lawless came back from the bar Kendrick had his thoughtful look on.

'They're pushing us, Philip. Do you know we have replaced almost a whole squadron in the past few weeks? I certainly don't want to see the word Leipzig up on the ops board again. I just hope they know what they're doing. Drink up. It's the only way.'

On the first of March they were despatched to Stuttgart and a week later to Le Mans to destroy the railway yards.

'Nice change that,' said Kendrick, 'seeing a bit of French countryside. Of course, you've been here before.'

'Long time ago, on the way to Italy.'

Frankfurt followed next, another week later. It was a hard one. Two of the new crews were lost and Lucky Lady had a tank—fortunately empty—punctured and the wireless and the landing gear hydraulics put out of action. Lawless readied the crew for bale out when they crossed the English coast but by some sort of miracle Ernie Gibbons got the hydraulics working again—with sticking plaster and a hand pump, he claimed afterwards—and Lawless was able to make a heavy landing with one of the tyres in shreds. One bright spot was that another JU 88 was blown out of the sky with both gunners claiming half each. The other bright spot was that the repairs necessary kept them off the list for yet another Berlin operation that took place five days after Frankfurt.

The Dog and Gun was very quiet, even for a Wednesday night. Lawless and Kendrick sat at one of the corner tables near the fire, half empty pint glasses in front of them.

'What's happening?' Kendrick said. 'Two of them writing letters, or so they say—I believe Gillis; he writes nearly every day to his mother, but not Dickie. Les and Ralph wanted an early night and as for Ernie, where is he?'

'Working on his matchstick model, he told me. They were all a bit quiet on the Essen trip. Nobody likes the Ruhr.'

'Is that where we went? Essen? You know, I'm getting to the point where I can't tell one from t'other. One more before we go?'

While Kendrick was ordering the beer, Lawless glanced at the daily paper lying on the next table.

'RAF batter Essen again', the headline said. He didn't bother to read the article. He knew he wouldn't recognise the raid that it described.

'Play you 301 for a quid?' Kendrick said. ' I fancy my chances against you but I wouldn't play MacNeill for money.'

'He doesn't gamble.'

'We all do, my friend: every time we take off.'

On the way back to the airfield on the late bus Lawless said there was a rumour that a big op was on for tomorrow night.

'Where to?'

'I don't know but a longish trip I heard'

'God, not Berlin again. Anywhere but there.'

NUREMBERG

Battle orders naming the aircraft and crews for the operation were posted in the crew room at noon. Lucky Lady—known officially as LZ 620—was on the list.

Rather than the usual ritual groaning a puzzled murmuring rose from the assembled crews when the chosen target was announced: Nuremberg. It was to be a big show, a maximum effort job with nearly 800 heavies, not counting the diversionary raids designed to draw off the night fighters. The weather forecast was favourable: cloud cover on the outbound route but clearer skies over the target. The bomber stream would keep tight formation and all the bombing had to be concentrated into less than half an hour. Engineering works, tank factories, ball bearing and electrical equipment plants made Nuremberg an important target and the time had come to do something about it. So they were told.

Lawless glanced down and saw the lights of the flare path shrink into fuzzy yellow points as the Halifax climbed steadily through thin swirling mist towards its allotted cruising height of 22000 feet. The first searchlights started looking for them as they crossed the Belgian coast east of Ostend. Yet again the weather forecast was inaccurate. The moon was near half full and the skies were clear. Vapour trails streamed from some of the higher-flying aircraft. Lawless saw something he had never seen before: scores and scores of bombers, some very close, seemingly motionless in the night sky with moonlight glinting on wing or turret. Bomber's moon, he thought. Oh Christ.

'See that?' Dickie Dent said. 'Fucking hundreds.'

'Never mind them,' Lawless snapped. 'We're not the only ones that can see them.'

'Tail wind a lot stronger than we were told, Skipper. You know what that means.'

Lawless knew well: too early arrival over the target and flying around in the flak: Leipzig all over again. The more alert navigators would have noticed it and their pilots would be deciding whether or not to start dog-legging. Before long the bomber stream would start losing its tight formation and once that happened, the night fighters' task would become that much easier. It started sooner than he expected. A Lancaster suddenly appeared, crossing their path no more than a hundred feet ahead.

'See that? No dog-legs, Richard. Too risky. I'm starting weaving and wagging.'

It was a manoeuvre they had used before and many other experienced crews did the same. Lucky Lady began changing course slightly from starboard to port and back again, at the same time dipping and rising as she flew on. The theory was it made it that more difficult for a night fighter to keep the target in its sights. It would not shake off a really good enemy pilot but that was a chance they had to take.

'Namur, Skipper; steer Zero Eight Five.'

'Zero Eight Five, turning now. How're we doing?'

'Fifteen minutes ahead of time; estimate distance 400 miles.'

'Keep awake, everybody.'

Bomber's moon; Thérèse had asked him what it meant. Don't think about that.

'Say something, Skipper?'

'Nothing, Ernie. They're spreading out a lot. Can't see so many now.'

'There's one, Skipper; starboard beam. He's caught it.'

They watched a Lancaster bank sharply with one wing ablaze and dive almost vertically trailing flames. Dickie Dent came on shouting he had just seen an explosion on the ground. Kendrick logged time and position of the crashed Lancaster and height when first observed.

'Fire on the ground ahead, Skipper; no, two fires.'

They were too small for ground targets being hit. It had to be two downed aircraft; British or German, who could say?

There were many more to be seen in the next two hours as well as explosions in the air, above, below, to either side. The bomber stream had spread over fifty miles wide and the night fighters enjoyed almost free play. After logging twenty sightings Kendrick gave up. He was the least superstitious of men but he was good at estimating odds.

Lawless was thinking it was always the same: you see bombers being hit but hardly ever the fighters out there hitting them.

'I don't like this. Starting banking search. Now.'

Lawless pushed over the control column and the Halifax banked right, flew on about a mile—long enough for everyone to have a good look out—then righted and banked left. No one reported a sighting. Five minutes later, during the next search, Ernie Gibbons had just reported another Halifax two hundred yards away to starboard, when he gave a loud incoherent yell and there was a harsh clattering noise and a rush of wind behind his seat.

'The fucker fired on us! I saw the flashes from his mid-upper!'

'Take his number, Ernie. Report him to the police when you get back,' said Kendrick.

'Steady. You all right, Ernie?'

'Nearly shit myself and its draughty back here now.'

'Think yourself lucky it wasn't a JU 88, Ernie,' Henderson said. 'He wouldn't have missed you.'

'Change of course, Skipper. Steer One Three Zero. Nuremberg next stop.'

'Turning One Three Zero. Now. I don't think I will stop when we get there. Haven't got the time.'

Make jokes. Try to keep your hands from shaking. God, his mouth was dry.

'Is there any coffee, Ernie? Get up here, will you?'

'Five minutes to target, Skipper.'

There was a lot of flak ahead, bursting high; heavy stuff. Dickie Dent stopped himself just in time from opening fire on a twin-engine black shape that flashed past his turret trailing glistening stripes behind.

'Mossie scattering Window, Skipper. Bloody close.'

Inside the Perspex nose of the bomber, Ralph Henderson was adjusting the controls of the bombsight mechanism, occasionally squinting at the crosshairs of the sight itself on its small square platform. There were scattered clouds over the target area but they had reached it almost on time and Henderson could make out some target markers through gaps in the mist and cloud. Fires were already burning but seemed rather scattered. The red glow was turning orange as green marker flares mingled with the incendiaries. Flak was bursting at their level but far enough away not to shake the Halifax off course.

'Bomb doors open, Skipper.'

Lawless pulled on the lever and felt the slight check and stagger of the aircraft as the two sets of doors yawned open. He felt his heart beat faster. It was something that started after he had heard the story about a Lancaster that had just opened its doors in time for an 88mm flak shell to burst inside the loaded bomb bay. The Lanc had disintegrated, taking with it two others flying nearby. It might have been only rumour—how could anybody have even seen, let alone know an 88 had hit—but it affected him nevertheless. Anything could happen.

'Reds and greens; hold her like that.'

'Two minutes,' said Kendrick, calm as ever.

'Left, left, steady.'

The Halifax rocked and tipped as flak shells burst dangerously close, flashing vivid lights in to the cockpit and turrets.

'Bugger; bring her left, left, more, steady, steady.'

For Christ's sake, get on with it Ralph!

'Right a little; steady; steady. Bombs gone.'

The Halifax leaped upwards, lighter by four tons. Sometimes this caused collisions with aircraft above. Not this time. Lawless steadied the controls.

'Get a picture, Ralph?'

'We'll see when we get back, Skipper. I'll stay down here for a bit.'

Henderson knew every pair of eyes was needed for look out on the way back. The nose was a dangerous place to be but not as much as the gun turrets. Some night fighters went for them first.

Lawless turned the bomber away from Nuremberg onto the new course given him by Kendrick. Four hours to go: it seemed a long time.

'I don't know about this one, Skipper. The fires seem scattered all over the place and none of them very big.'

'Nothing we can do about that, Richard. Going home same way, weaving and wagging.'

An hour into the homeward flight Dickie Dent opened fire without warning and Ernie Gibbons, sitting in the do-pilot's seat said he saw pieces flying from their port wing flaps.

'JU 88,' Dickie called. 'Came in sudden from port side. Think I hit him. Maybe scared him off.'

He seemed to have been right. The Halifax flew on without further trouble for the next two hours. Lawless knew better than to let his hopes rise. He started a new series of banking searches. On the second banking to the left the mid-upper turret opened fire aft.

'Twin engine 110, I think. Saw some strikes,' said MacNeill in his precise soft voice.

'Confirm that,' said Dickie Dent. He hasn't gone away. Down there somewhere.'

Lawless could almost feel the tension in the Halifax. That was a clever determined pilot out there.

'Corkscrew left, go!' yelled the rear gunner.

No, he's expecting that. Lawless instinctively wrenched Lucky Lady into a right diving corkscrew, and the BF 110 hurtled overhead with a stream of tracer flying upwards from behind the cockpit and sparks flying from its starboard wing, where MacNeill had somehow managed to hit it.

Lawless brought the Halifax upright and level.

'Where's he gone, Dickie? Gillis?'

'Can't tell, but he was giving off smoke.'

'Belgian coast ten minutes, Skipper.'

Lawless felt the tension tightening in him again. He tried hard not to think they might get away with it this time. Again.

'Port wing, Skipper. It's stripping. I can see the rods.'

'Engines?'

'No trouble. Fuel a bit low.'

'Buckle up everybody.'

The port side flap refused to lower but Lawless got her down with a terrific jolt and some emergency braking as she slewed off the runway sending the flare path lights flying and showers of sparks from the starboard wing tip ploughing through the concrete. For a few seconds there was silence and nobody moved. Then there was a quick rush for the escape hatch. Snow was falling but none of them noticed.

At debriefing Lawless reported the target had been bombed in spite of the cloud cover and one BF 110 damaged on the homeward flight. He mentioned the odd thing about tracers shooting at an angle upwards from the rear of the cockpit, yes, *upwards*.

He was the second one to report that, the intelligence officer told him. The debriefing went on longer than usual, the gunners being questioned much more than usual. As they left the hut Lawless had an uneasy feeling that the raid had not gone as planned and they were being blamed for it.

It was very quiet in the Mess as they ate breakfast.

'Lots of fried eggs spare,' said Kendrick. 'Fancy another?'

Lawless shook his head. He had had trouble getting one down.

'I've got a bad feeling about this one, Richard.'

'So have I. Never mind, cheer up. We managed to get her beaten up enough for us to have a few days off while Chiefie puts her right.'

'She got us home, Richard.'

'And you, old lad: Lucky Lawless; told you so.'

They had more than a few days off. Nuremberg had been bad; maybe the worst night ever, so far. The squadron itself lost four aircraft, three over Germany and one written off after crash-landing on an American base in Norfolk.

Over a week passed before Lawless saw on the notice board in the crew room that they were down to fly again.

'Lille,' Kendrick said. 'That's France: do you think they've made a mistake or is there nowhere left in Germany to blow up?'

'It makes a change, Richard and it's not so far to go.'

'Railway goods yards, eh? Railways are good for navigators: just follow the tracks and there you are.'

'So you'll have no excuses this time.'

'Now, now, Flying Officer Lawless DFC, Sir. You could be of some use to us this time if we have to jump: as an interpreter.'

Lawless had been informed the previous day of the award. It had cost him a sizeable portion of his last pay in the Dog and Gun.

It was another bomber's moon but Lucky Lady avoided the flak and never saw a night fighter the whole flight.

On their return in the early morning the Chiefie congratulated Lawless on his decoration and on the fact that for once he had brought his aircraft back intact.

Their next two operations, two days apart, were targets in France and Belgium, and again they were railway yards. The squadron lost one aircraft on the Tergnier raid but all crews returned unscathed from Ottignies.

Lawless could see, if only from their renewed interest in the Dog and Gun, that the crew had regained some of their confidence and energy after the last three fairly uneventful operations. After comprehensively beating two other crews at darts, largely due to MacNeill's unerring aim, they sat round the table with refilled pints in good spirits and, to Lawless's surprise, started arguing good-naturedly about where they would be going next.

'Railways,' said Dickie Dent. 'It's got to be. We've done three in a row now: bound to be another railway yard. Do you know any others in France, Skipper?'

Oh yes, but we're not likely to go there. At least I hope not.

'Me? Rouen: I went there once when I was a boy. Amiens's another place. Then there's Paris. All French railways go to Paris.'

'Oh please don't let them send us to Paris,' Kendrick said. 'Think what a mess we'd make of the place.'

During the laughter that followed Lawless was thinking. The targets were all in northern France—except Ossignies in Belgium, but that wasn't far from France. Something was going on.

'Gardening,' said Ernie Gibbons. 'I fancy a bit of gardening. Always did like gardening. You should have seen my sweet peas.'

They all laughed again. That was a good sound, a good sign.

'They've got railway yards in Germany, don't forget,' Leslie Proud said.

'Bugger off, Les. Don't put a damper on the party. They won't send us there again.'

But they did. At briefing two days later the crews were told the target was Dusseldorf in the Ruhr.

'Just like old times, Kendrick said. 'Nasty place, bags of flak and the sky full of JU 88s all thirsting for blood. Not that I've been there, of course.'

'I have,' Lawless said. 'I can't quite remember when but I can remember what it was like. It is a nasty place.'

They were both right. The sky over Dusseldorf was clear and the enemy ready and waiting. The bomber stream became scattered, and quickly penetrated by both twin and single engine night fighters well before the target was reached. Lucky Lady came under fire just as she started the bomb run but the fighter's aim was off, probably because both rear and mid-upper gunners had spotted him at the last moment and caused him to veer away when they opened up. He did, however, manage to put a number of 20mm cannon shells through the port wing just missing the outer engine.

Ralph Henderson continued giving his instructions to Lawless as if nothing had happened. Lawless wondered if the bomb-aimer had noticed anything other than the cross on his bombsight.

Kendrick logged eleven bombers shot down, mostly on the way to the target. Lawless was pretty sure that at least two were from their own squadron.

It was another tricky landing. The damaged wing unbalanced the aircraft, and she came down hard. The fire wagon was waiting but not as it happened for them. Another Halifax had signalled it was coming in with an engine on fire.

The ground crew did a remarkably quick job of repairing the damaged wing and Lawless signed the form accepting Lucky Lady as fit for service three days later. On the same afternoon at briefing they were informed of the night's target.

'I shouldn't have said that out loud,' Kendrick said. You know about not going to bomb Paris? Somebody was listening and now look what I've done.'

'Villeneuve-St Georges; it's about ten miles from the centre of Paris. Think you can find it?'

'Met says it's going to be a clear night, ha ha. I'll look out for the Eiffel Tower.'

Ralph Henderson claimed to have planted his bombs exactly on the target markers. As Lawless turned the Halifax away to start the homeward run there was a huge explosion at the southern end of the railway yards. He thought it must have been an ammunition train that went up.

During the day after their safe return Dickie Dent learned that he had been awarded a DFM and all aircrew were given 72 hours leave.

'Where are you going, Richard?'

'Not sure; home perhaps. The old Dad's not too well. How about you? Come if you like.'

'Thanks anyway. I think I'll just loaf about here; catch up on some sleep; maybe go to York one afternoon.'

DAFFODILS

It was still cold at the end of the month and the snow had changed to sleet and rain. Lawless spent the first two days of his leave sleeping and eating, gradually becoming bored and restless, a new feeling that unsettled him. He decided to catch a train to York. His memory of the place was hazy. He did recall eating hot buttered teacakes with his mother in a café somewhere in a twisty old cobbled street where the upper windows hung out over the lower ones, and high walls with battlements but not much else.

The train was held up outside the station for half an hour. Lawless could see why when he finally stepped down onto the platform and had to struggle through the crowds, mainly of men and women in uniforms of all kinds filling the platforms as they waited for their trains. He gave up thinking about a cup of tea when he saw the length of the queue outside the refreshment room. The station had been badly damaged in a German raid in 1942 and work was still in progress on relaying track and repairing the roof and buildings.

He found a street that led into the town and asked a passer-by the way to the Minster. The directions were complicated and he was soon lost until by chance he stumbled into a street which he vaguely recognised as the one where he had eaten the teacakes. There was a café but it was closed and the windows were shuttered. 'For the Duration', the tacked on notice said. Asking again for the Minster he was told to keep going, bear right then left and he would be looking at it.

Inside was all dim, quiet, calm, cathedral hush. The larger windows were boarded up and patches on some of the walls showed where pictures had been taken down. A boy in a white surplice was lighting some candles with a taper and many of the pews had people sitting in them or kneeling praying. Perhaps there would be a service soon. Lawless sat in an empty pew and leaned back to look up at the soaring vaulted roof of the nave. It seemed as high as the clouds. The organ sounded a few exploratory chords and then began the first lines of a Bach fugue that he immediately recognised as one he had sometimes heard in the College chapel. He felt calm enough now and thought if he stayed longer he might even fall asleep. He got up and walked quietly through the massive doorway onto the paved square outside. An old man was walking slowly about on the green nearby occasionally stooping to pull out a weed. He told Lawless it was possible to walk along the city walls.

There was a sloping glacis outside the wall covered in grass where clumps of daffodils sprouted in full yellow glory. They were there in the angel hair grass with Easter flowers and orchids on the Méjean where he had lain beside Thérèse under the shade of the ash trees on that hot day in —could it be two years ago? And never yet had there been a reply to any of his letters. He could not bear to go on looking at the yellow flowers.

He hurried back to the crowded railway station and saw the next train was due to leave in five minutes. He found a corner seat in a smoky crowded shabby compartment and sat down and closed his eyes and tried not to think except about getting back to the base and the squadron, the only places where he felt able to think of something else.

Kendrick was a day late in returning from leave.

'You'll be for it,' Lawless said.

'No; the Wingco was told.'

'Well, come on, where were you?'

'Saw the old Dad and mother. He was feeling better.'

'And?'

'Well, it's all hush hush, so of course I'll tell you everything. If you let on I'll deny saying a word.'

'Scout's honour.'

'London: can't tell you quite where because it was a place that looked like all the others. There was a committee wanted to see me.'

'A committee? What sort of Committee?'

'All civilians—though one of them looked as if he would be more at home in a uniform. Six of them ranged along a table and me sitting opposite: a bit like that picture of the Roundheads frightening those two children in front of them. Only two of them spoke. The others just sat there listening.'

'What did they want? Have you been doing something stupid?'

'No, no, well, nothing they would know about—I hope. No, it seems they got to know about my doing Maths at Cambridge and they had the idea I could be of more use to them than risking my life—and others'—navigating Halifax bombers.'

'But you stopped doing Maths after a year.'

'Yes but I suppose that it's like riding a bike. Just get on again and it all comes back to you. Anyway, they want me to join one of their teams and work on some very secret wheeze they've come up with. And sorry, I can't tell you what that is. Pain of death, they more or less said.'

'But you obviously know what you're expected to do.'

'Oh yes, and they spent a lot of time going into whether I could do it, one of them, that is. They didn't say who he was but I think I know: theoretical mathematician as weird as hell but a brain from here to there. He put me through it while the others sat and watched. We covered sheets of paper with equations and argued quite a bit.'

'What about the others?'

'Like I said only two of them spoke. The other was a woman, 40-odd, very smart even in a tweed suit: *very* good figure. Reminded me of somebody but I can't think who. She asked me quite a lot.'

'About mathematics as well?'

'No, oddly enough she wanted to know what I'd done in History and why I switched. Do you know, by the end of it I think she rather fancied me?'

'You always say that about women.'

'Before or after, old lad, either will do.'

'I can't believe this, Richard. Are you telling me you'll be leaving the crew?'

'I'm sorry, Philip but yes, it does. I hate to do this but they made it very clear I had no choice.'

'Oh, Christ, what are we going to do?'

'Meet up at Fenners after the War when I go out to bat against the Australians. And afterwards at Lords.'

‘Fuck off; are you ever serious?’

‘All the time, mon ami; I just don’t look it, that’s all. Come on and let’s have too much to drink; all the lads as well. I’ll be gone tomorrow. Good news about Dickie, don’t you think?’

‘He deserves it. All of them do, for what it’s worth. You should have got something.’

‘You’ll be next. Mark my words. Were the daffodils out in York?’

Lawless was given news of his promotion to Flight Lieutenant the following week after Lucky Lady had completed two more raids on French railway installations on consecutive nights and a gardening trip planting mines off the Danish coast. Climbing the ladder fast, they called it. One of the reasons for it was the speed at which gaps kept appearing further up

Everyone knew by now that D Day must be coming soon. It made sense from all the raids on French railway yards as far apart as Boulogne and Orleans and mine laying off French Atlantic ports. Fewer bombers were being lost. All the squadron's Halifaxes had returned intact from the last four operations, something that boosted confidence among the newer crews. They were being told at every briefing that Mosquito night fighters specially assigned to deal with German nightfighters would accompany the bombers and others would be jamming German radar and attacking night fighter bases.

'Just so long as they keep out of our way,' Dickie Dent said. 'Remember that Mossie over Nuremberg? Left scratches on my turret, he did.'

'Well something seems to be keeping the JU 88s away so maybe it's them. I'm beginning to like France. At least it's nearer. Be different over Germany, you bet.'

Lawless kept silent. He was watching Lewis Gorman, Kendrick's replacement. The young pilot officer had completed four ops without seeing a single German night fighter and only distant flak. Did he know he was one of those statistics: still only a one in ten chance of surviving until the next op? What did that mean for the rest of us? Kendrick would have pulled a face at such a question. Lawless missed him. They all did. Never in a flap, always coming out with a remark that made them laugh: everyone felt better when he was around. Young Gorman was proving good at his job but he was no Kendrick and he hadn't seen any real action yet. Mustn't let him think that. He'll get better and we need him. If only he would join in a bit more. Always sits with Gillis, neither of them saying much. At least Gillis is good at darts.

'Fancy another, Lewis?'

'I haven't finished this one yet.'

'I'll have it, Skipper,' Dickie Dent said.

'Ralph, you silly bugger, why did you say that last night?'

The coming night's operation was to be yet another railway marshalling yard. But this time it was Aachen in Germany and there was no shortage of night fighters to meet them long before they reached the target.

Any doubts that Lawless may have had about his twenty-year old navigator were dispelled that night. Gorman stolidly logged the information for nine bombers shot down on the outward flight, one of them exploding two hundred yards to starboard and showering them with fragments, and still managed to bring Lucky Lady to the target on time despite all Lawless's corkscrewing and wagging and weaving on the way. They were attacked twice by night fighters on the return leg but both were driven off by the gunners. Gillis MacNeil claimed hits on a JU 88. Gorman calmly logged the types of attacking aircraft, positions, altitudes and results of defensive fire, even asking MacNeil how many strikes he had observed.

Lawless's crew was first back, followed in quick succession by nine more of the squadron's Halifaxes one of which was lacking most of its starboard rudder.

'They must have been sticking close to us, Skipper,' Dickie Dent said. 'I wonder why.'

'Perhaps they recognised a good navigator when they saw one.'

'He'll do,' said Ernie Gibbons. 'All he needs now are some lessons from Gillis.'

Two of the squadron's aircraft were lost on the operation, one shot down by flak over Aachen and the other brought down by a night fighter intruder only fifty miles from the airfield.

As Station Commander the Group Captain was present at all briefings before operations where he was always last to speak, quietly emphasising the importance of the target and always sounding genuine in his encouragement and wishes of good luck. Everyone knew he had been through this sort of thing himself, especially in the early days of the War when he flew Wellingtons in daylight raids that were almost suicidally dangerous. No matter what the time of day or night he was always there to see them take off and they knew he was not far away when they returned, but careful to keep out of the way of the ambulances and fire wagons. His height made him an unmistakeable figure. Not remote but not casually approachable, he was, for want of a better word, trusted. Lawless was surprised to receive an order that Flight Lieutenant Lawless was to report to the Group Captain's office at 13 00 on the day after the Aachen raid.

'Sit down, Lawless.'

'Thank you, Sir.'

'New navigator, Gorman: getting on all right is he?'

'A bit quiet, Sir, but he's coming on. He did well on his first real raid.'

'Aachen, yes. You had trouble on the way. Still, a good job was done. They are all real, Lawless.'

There was silence for a moment or so. He's thinking about the two we lost but I bet he won't say anything, Lawless thought.

'He's not Kendrick, Lawless, but he's a good man. I expect you to make something of him.'

'Yes, Sir.

A longer silence followed.

'Twenty two operations behind you, Lawless; on Halifaxes, that is.'

'Yes, Sir.' *When was he going to get round to it?*

'I have someone from a Ministry coming tomorrow, specifically to see you he says. I have no idea what it's about but knowing those people it could be a bit of a problem. Any ideas?'

The Group Captain fixed Lawless with a very piercing stare.

'Not a clue, Sir.' *Christ, what was it all about?*

'Well there's nothing I can do about it now. You will have to see him; 14 00 tomorrow in the room along the passage. I don't know his name.'

'We're down for the op tonight, Sir.'

'You'll be back in time. Good day to you, Lawless.'

***

The last time when we went to Paris,' said Ralph Henderson, 'we blew up that ammunition train.'

'They must be sending them to Trappes now, Ralph. Make sure you don't hit Versailles. See that he gets there, Lewis. We wouldn't want your namesake's palace flattened.'

Versailles. Louis the Sun King. Cavallier. Why was he always being reminded?

They flew all the way in bright moonlight only to find patchy low cloud covering the target area. The flak was very heavy with many close bursts rocking and shaking the aircraft as Lawless started her on the bombing run.

'Time on target now,' said Gorman.

'On the markers; left, left, steady, steady. Bombs gone.'

As she lifted, Lawless swung Lucky Lady sharply to starboard simultaneously increasing the power only to be half blinded by the violent flash of a flak shell exploding directly ahead. The centre panel of the perspex windshield disintegrated spraying sharp-edged fragments everywhere. Lawless felt several hit his chest and helmet but his oxygen mask and goggles protected his eyes and most of his face.

'You all right, Ernie?'

Amazingly Ernie Gibbons had happened to be bending down to retrieve a screwdriver when the shell fragment struck and the pieces of shattered windshield had passed over him. No one else had been in range.

Kendrick would have said something like it was going to be a draughty ride home now. Lawless resisted the urge to imitate him. Everyone at the front of the aircraft would soon see the ice starting to form on every metal surface.

Lewis Gorman logged two Lancasters shot down and a single radial-engined night fighter, probably a FW 190, flying past Lucky Lady about 100 yards away to starboard firing at an unseen target somewhere ahead. Tracers from MacNeil's guns followed the fighter for three hundred yards before it blew up and disappeared.

Everyone except the gunners in their heated suits found it more than usually difficult to get out of the aircraft when she finally came to a halt on the parking perimeter at 14.30 hours. Lawless was treated for minor cuts on his forehead. The MO found it hard to believe that none of the crew had frostbite. Chiefie's men had a new Perspex panel installed by eight o' clock in the morning and Lucky Lady was declared ready for operations the same night.

An aircraftman woke Lawless and told him the time was 12.35. That left enough time for him to have a leisurely lunch in the Mess and a cigarette and some coffee afterwards before his meeting with the mysterious visitor.

He had been expecting one man but there were two of them waiting for him in the room along the passage from the Group Captain's office. He knew them both: the man in the dark suit sitting behind the desk in the house in London and Robinson standing in front of the window.

'Pilot Officer Lawless, please sit down; we meet again.'

'Flight Lieutenant.'

'Flight . . . ? I beg your pardon. Flight Lieutenant Lawless.'

Lawless put his cap on the desk and sat down. The two men looked at each other.

'Noisy places, airfields: all those aircraft; on the ground, flying overhead.'

Lawless said nothing.

'Hm, yes; well, I don't suppose you know what this is about?'

Lawless shook his head.

'I'll come straight to the point. Always the best thing, don't you think?'

Lawless remained wooden-faced.

'Yes, well, the thing is, we have a little problem and we thought, who can we ask and then we came up with you. Lawless can help, we thought.'

Lawless crossed his legs and waited.

'I *am* sorry. Please, if you would like to smoke . . .' The man raised a hand and twiddled his fingers, 'Robinson.'

Robinson started forward, feeling in his coat pocket.

'No thank you.'

'No? Well now, the thing is this. We know a little about your activities in France after your aircraft went missing.'

'How little?' Lawless said.

The man frowned then quickly smiled again. 'Enough to know that instead of trying to escape you became involved with the Resistance. Is that correct?'

'I became aware of it. Everyone did.'

'More than that, Flight Lieutenant, more than just aware. We know something of their activities and you, we think, do so too.'

The man suddenly thrust his face forward and glared at Lawless.

'Gerard Janquett! You know that name!'

'Everyone did: *Jérôme Janquet*. He was the mayor of the commune.'

'Vabrett!'

'Local blacksmith. He went everywhere; shoeing horses, mending carts, ploughs, everything a blacksmith does. It's a farming area.'

'Give me some other names!' They know practically nothing, Lawless realised.

'I was a shot down airman in a hostile country. Anyone could have turned me in to the gendarmerie. I had to keep out of the way so I met very few people.'

'But you did know some: Janquett and Vabrett, for example.'

'I've told you that.'

'You haven't told us what they were doing, like blocking a main railway line, destroying signalling systems and a lot more serious things like blowing up bridges and ambushing German patrols and shooting up German convoys.'

'I know nothing about ambushing German patrols and attacking German convoys. But what's wrong with that? The Germans invaded what was Unoccupied France and they fought back. We would do the same to an enemy. A least that's what we were told to do if they ever came here.'

'What is wrong with it, Flight Lieutenant, is that they are not conforming to the plan. Yes, the Germans must be harassed and attacked so that when the invasion comes their power to resist will be seriously weakened. We are already supplying arms and equipment to those groups who are following the plan, the instructions from London. These people, Janquett and Vabrett and their like refuse to be part of the planned campaign. They go their own ill-disciplined way and that will not do. You do realise they are communists?'

'Many living in that part of France are communists but not the sort who take orders from some foreign central command. They have a long history of resistance to central governments who have tried to oppress them for centuries. They are very independent people who think and act for themselves. That's their idea of communism.' *Idiot, I'm talking too much. No, these are the idiots. Calm down.*

'You seem to know a good deal about how they think, even if you do not know many of their names. Enough for you to be able to help us.'

Lawless thought it better to keep quiet this time.

'Yes, well, this is what we have in mind. You know the place—you were there for nearly a year after all—and at least some of the people who are proving to be awkward. We want you to go back there and deal with them, persuade them to stop what they are doing and come into the tent, as it were, follow orders. They will trust you. Then all would be well. Of course, if they refuse and carry on as they have so far, well then, we—you—would have to think of other ways of dealing with them. Permanently, you understand. I hasten to say you would have our backing and anything you need, in the way of equipment.'

'How would I get there?'

'Ah, good! Easy; we have 'planes going there nearly all the time now—Lysanders, even big ones, like yours, parachuting equipment and people in. All the time.'

'When?'

'It has to be soon. I'm sure you must know what's coming, almost any day now. We have to do everything possible to stop the Germans sending reinforcements to the front, wherever that may be. But it has to be done in the right, coordinated, disciplined way. Like the way your attacks are planned, one might say. In about a week's time.'

'A week? That's not very long to prepare.'

'For anyone but you, I would agree but you have knowledge of the ground. Now, what do you say, Flight Lieutenant?'

'I am on an operation tonight. Our equipment, oxygen supply, scores of things like that, they all need testing before we're ready. Then there's the final briefing: so much to do.' Lawless made a show of consulting his watch. 'I'll think about it. I'll let you know.'

'We should like to know now.'

'I can't do that. I need to think about it. I'll let you know.'

'Very well. We can give you forty-eight hours. And, Flight Lieutenant Lawless, please understand, no one else is to know about our conversation in this room.'

'Could prove an awkward bugger,' Robinson said to his companion as they drove back to London.

'Yes. We may have to apply some pressure. Special pressure. Can we find out more about those women?'

As soon as the men had left, Lawless went straight to the Group Captain's office and requested an urgent meeting.

'Can't be before the morning, Sir,' the corporal said. 'I'll note it down.'

It was a new kind of target: coastal batteries near Calais where the Germans had installed several 300mm guns in massive reinforced concrete emplacements. The weather was poor with thick cloud covering the coast and obscuring the markers but at least it kept the fighters away. There was plenty of flak coming up but the gunners must have been firing blind and apart from some buffeting Lucky Lady was undisturbed. Ralph Henderson said he could not be sure where his bombs landed but probably nobody else could either. The Halifax touched down at 03 00 hours and the crew were in their beds by 05 00. It had been one of the quietest nights they had had for weeks, except for the pilot. Lawless had too much on his mind to be able to get any sleep. He was relieved when an aircraftman came at eight o' clock to tell him that the Station Commander would see him in half an hour.

'Out with it, Lawless. I haven't much time.'

'Well, Sir . . .'. Lawless took a deep breath and told Group Captain Smallwood everything that had passed between himself and the two men who had called to see him yesterday.

'They said at the end, Sir, that I was not to repeat anything that had been said to anyone else.'

'So you saw fit to tell me.'

'Yes, Sir; as my Commanding Officer.'

'Go on.'

'I simply can't do what they ask, Sir,' Lawless replied and went on to tell the Group Captain in great detail why not.

He was still feeling anxious when he finished speaking, but also greatly relieved. He had been forced at last to tell someone the whole story of his time in France and now he began to realise what a great strain it had been keeping it all locked up inside him for so long.

The Group Captain looked down at some papers on his desk for several seconds, clearly not reading them, and then straight up again at Lawless.

'You gave them the guns from your aircraft.'

'Only the two that were serviceable, Sir. And 2000 rounds: it seemed the right thing to at the time.'

'Hm. You must have things to do, Lawless. I'll think about this. Carry on.'

'Sir.'

The Group Captain watched the door close behind Lawless and picked up one of the telephones on his desk. He heard the connection, pressed his scrambler button, dialled a number and listened.

'Yes.'

'Tomorrow's meeting at High Wycombe ends at noon. Can we have lunch?'

'One o' clock.'

The line went dead.

Just before he left Bomber Command Headquarters near High Wycombe where progress on the planning of the D Day landings was discussed, the Group Captain had a brief telephone conversation with the Wing Commander on his station and learned that all the aircraft despatched to bomb the bridges near Coutances and railways leading to the Normandy beaches had returned without loss or damage. Preparations for the next attack on road and rail targets near Fougères were proceeding to plan.

'On Wednesdays very occasionally we have lamb chops; sadly, not this week. However, Oxford sausages can be good. Your driver will be having the same, probably with chips. Please help yourself.'

For dessert there was apple tart made with dried apple rings and custard.

'Coffee? It's American. I'm afraid we've run out of sugar but there is saccharine.'

The Group Captain shook his head.

'I expect that you know why I have come to see you, Winifred. It's about Lawless. Some of your people—at least it sounds like your people—have fastened on to him because of what he got up to in France. You must know the people and the sort of things he was involved with and I don't suppose you told me everything. That doesn't matter. What does matter as far as I am concerned is that they are threatening him in all sorts of ways to make him agree to be sent out there again and bump off the group he was connected with and all because they're communists and refuse to obey orders from London. He told me straight he won't do it and for very good reasons in my opinion.'

'What do you want me to do about it, Robert?'

'Call 'em off. Apart from his own reasons I can't lose this man, Winfred. He's by far the best and most experienced pilot I have left. He's done more than fifty ops. His own men swear by him and the new crews look up to him. They believe he gets them back. They call him Lucky Lawless. I know, I know, it's foolish but it's the kind of thing that keeps them going. And every time they complete an operation they are that little bit better the next time. Without Lawless I would have a serious morale problem with the squadron. I tell you if someone doesn't put a stop to this, I'll go to the C-in-C—and soon.'

'There will be no need for that. This is the chance I have been waiting for to do a little bit of long overdue cleaning up. You'll keep your Flight Lieutenant.'

'Squadron Leader: I'm putting him up for it. That's how much I think of him.'

'Though I don't suppose that's the sort of thing you tell *him*,' his sister said with that teasing smile he knew she put on when he had been overdoing the elder brother senior officer bit.

Robert Smallwood looked at his watch.

'Time I was going. I'd like to stay a bit longer, look round the gardens, but . . .'

'I know. D-Day has come at an awkward time.'

They both laughed.

'You know what I mean. I have to be back for the final briefing—and to see them off again tonight.'

'Tell him something before he goes.'

'I'll give him the nod.'

He thanked her for lunch, kissed her on both cheeks and left.

She looked down from her window and watched the tall upright figure of her brother striding across the quad to the porter's lodge where his driver was waiting. She put a finger to her face where he had kissed her. He must have first learned that embrace all those years ago in Paris. She wondered how much Lawless had told him: about his marriage; about meeting Justine and Alexandre? Robert never mentioned Justine. Perhaps it was too painful to remember the scandal—and the child that died.

She went into her office and sat at her desk. She should be in London at six and the trains could take as much as three hours these days. She lifted the telephone receiver and put it down again.

What to do about those two? Send then both to St Chely la Bastide by Lysander to deal with Jérôme Janquet and Henri Vabrette themselves? That would be amusing but perhaps excessive. Northern Ireland then: counter-infiltration along the border. That was it. She took out her pen and began to draft an order. She headed it Operation Icarus. Icarus: someone else who had flown too high for his own good.

Robinson came into the office and said that he had cleared his desk and was ready to go. There was an escort waiting for them in the corridor. The man in the dark suit snapped the locks shut on his brief case and looked up.

'There's one thing we can do to that bastard before we go. We can keep making sure none of his letters gets to France.'

In the first three weeks of June 1944 Lawless and his crew completed ten more operations of which the last two were attacks on Flying Bomb launching sites inland from Calais.

Lawless thought he knew what was coming when the Wing Commander sent for him.

'Thirty ops, Lawless; Squadron Leader now and DFC. Pretty good.'

'Yes, Sir; thank you, Sir.'

'Call me Arthur, Philip: no need for formalities at the end of a tour.'

'Er, yes, Arthur.'

'Good crew you have there; looking forward to some leave, I shouldn't wonder.'

'I think they've started packing, Arthur.'

'Not MacNeill and Gorman, I hope,' the Wing Commander laughed, 'they haven't done their thirty yet.'

'No, no, of course not, Arthur.'

'Know where you're going when you leave us, do you, Philip?'

'Not yet but I expect it could be instructor at the HCU.'

'Heavy Conversion Unit: I always think of it as *Halifax* Conversion Unit, eh? Not so exciting as the last few months, eh, Philip?'

'You could say that, Arthur.' *Why was he laughing so much? It's not like him.*

'Yes, well the thing is, Philip, how can I put this? It leaves us a bit short, the Squadron I mean, if, I mean when you leave.'

I should have known it. Here it comes.

'You see, we're still down two crews since the last op and we've two unserviceable, and with you going as well, it leaves us well, under strength for this very important op and we're being pushed very hard from up top to put on a good show. So you see how it is.'
'I don't know, Arthur. I'm not bothered about myself but there's my crew. They're just about nackered. It's a lot to ask.'

'I know, I know and I wouldn't ask anyone else. Tell you what: see what they say. If it's no, I'll understand. If it's yes, there could be a Mention in it, or better.'

'I don't know if that would sway them, Arthur, but, all right. I'll ask, but I won't put any pressure on them.'

'No, no, no, nothing like that.'

'What is it and when?'

'Railway yards: full of tanks and ammunition wagons and it's not all that far off, east of Paris. They mustn't be allowed to get to Normandy. And it's on the Marne, easier than some to find. Tuesday night. Don't let on about it yet.'

'Does the Groupie know about this; us going I mean?'

'He'll be informed, of course; if you decide you're up for it.'

'I can't promise, Arthur, but I'll see what they say.'

'Good man!'

Lawless felt like kicking himself all the way to the huts. Why on earth had he agreed to this? Why on earth had he said he wasn't bothered about himself? Well, to be honest, he wasn't. Over the past year he had been trying to force himself to think of nothing but the job: flying a Halifax full of bombs to Germany and dropping them on some miserable shattered town and getting back home so that he could do it again the next night if he had to and keep on doing it. And now, what else was there to do? The War would never end. His work was death. Séverine had told him that. This is what he did, cause death. But wait a minute; what about the crew? Ernie and his sweet peas and Dickie Dent wanting to get married: what about them? Bloody idiot! He'd really dropped them in the shit. Lucky Lawless: the one they all trusted. Now look at him. Oh fuck.

They listened in silence to what he had to say. He could tell by the look on some of the faces that they had been half suspecting something like this when they heard he had been with the Wingco. MacNeill and Gorman listened impassively. They would be going anyway, in another aircraft or in Lucky Lady with a fill-in crew. The others looked at each other, not knowing what to say. He knew what they were thinking. It was Ernie Gibbons, as always, who spoke up for them.

'It's a bugger, Skipper, but if you're up for it so are we. That right, lads?

The others nodded, all looking at Lawless as they did but not saying anything.

Oh god, trusting me again, poor sods.

'Mind you, Skipper. It's only this one. Understand?'

'Yes, Ernie; only this one.'

It was not quite a bomber's moon but bright enough in a cloudless sky for him to see at least half a dozen other bombers hanging motionless in the clear night air, just like that outbound flight to Nuremberg. For some reason the letter from Sherwood's mother came into Lawless's mind.

. . . next to his photograph on the desk in his bedroom. Thank you so much, because of you we now know where he is. Michael often spoke of you. God keep you safe in these terrible times . . .

'Extra sharp lookout everybody. I want to see them before they see us this time.'

'Oil pressure problem, Skipper: port inner.'

'How far to go, Lewis?'

'Eighty miles, Skipper.'

'Keep an eye on it, Ernie. Do what you can. I'm not turning back now.'

'It's getting too low, Skipper. Think we're losing coolant. I'll have to feather the prop.'

The Halifax began gradually to lose height.

'Lewis?'

'On course; fifteen minutes, Skipper.'

Lawless saw yellow flames stream from the wing and quickly disappear..

'What the hell's that, Ernie?'

'Exhaust stubs blown. Must be bloody hot.'

'Dowse it, Ernie; quick as you can.'

Ernie Gibbons pressed the fire extinguisher control for the port inner engine and cut off the fuel feed. Lucky Lady was now down to 9000 feet and flying on three engines.

'All yours, Ralph,' Lawless said to the bomb-aimer.

Still no night fighters and hardly any flak. They must all be asleep. Or hammering some other poor sods. Get 'em out, Ralph, then I can haul her back up again.

'Steady, steady . . . bombs gone.'

Lawless banked and turned on full power as the Halifax leaped up.

'Course please, navigator.'

'Steer Three One Five.'

'Three One Five. Climbing now. What's it look like now, Dickie?'

'Like Bonfire Night. Bang on, Ralphie.'

Lawless gradually nursed Lucky Lady back up to ten thousand feet, but she would go no higher. Everything seemed to have gone according to plan so far, he thought: no fighters, no flamers going down, target well and truly plastered.

'Keep looking everybody. That was the easy part.'

'South coast ten miles, Skipper.'

He could see a white line ten thousand feet below; could it be waves breaking on the shore or the white cliffs?

'Down there; where are we Lewis?'

'Isle of Wight, Skipper. New course: steer Zero One Five.'

'Zero One Five. Check IFF, Les.'

The wireless operator confirmed the Halifax's friendly aircraft signal was on and working.

'Last leg, Ernie; everything OK?'

'That engine's still hot. There's something wrong.'

'Fuel off?'

'Done that. Maybe there's a leak.'

'Try the extinguisher again.'

'It's empty. '

'Well it's not far now. Fingers crossed.'

The port inner engine started pouring out smoke when Lucky Lady was still fifty miles short of her home airfield. Lawless brought her down gradually to five thousand feet.

'Send a Mayday, Les. I'm not risking it, Ernie. Get your 'chute on. Listen everybody, we are close to home and when you land, you can catch a bus. Now, this is serious: everybody out now. Now!'

'I'm not jumping, Skipper.'

'Yes you are, Ernie. Out now: that's an order. When you've all gone I'll turn her out to sea and bale out.'

A damaged Halifax was easier to escape from than a Lancaster and the crew dropped through the escape hatch without fuss one by one. Ernie Gibbons was the last to go, giving Lawless a thumbs-up as he went. Lawless counted six parachutes open and slowly drift down.

Fifty miles; less now, Lawless thought. That engine's not on fire. I can bring her down. I know I can. Sherwood did. Two thousand . . . one thousand. Good girl.

Damaged bombers returning with tired crews could be at their most vulnerable as they approached their own base, especially if it were not too far from the sea but Luftwaffe night fighter intruders had become rare by the summer of 1944.

With the runway lights now visible and concentrating on getting Lucky Lady down all by himself, Lawless had no warning of the JU 88 swooping down on him from above and behind. The German pilot was a very experienced man who knew the value of conserving his ammunition. Six 20mm cannon shells were enough to set the whole of Lucky Lady's starboard wing ablaze.

Too late to jump now. Sherwood got her down. Oh, Tressie.

The station crash report said that Halifax L142-J crash-landed on the runway with the starboard wing on fire at 03 40h and the pilot, Squadron Leader P.M. Lawless DFC, still at the controls. Six other members of the crew came down safely by parachute and reported to base over the following twenty-four hours. The aircraft was subsequently declared to be a total loss.

Lawless's DFC had been approved the month before. The Group Captain determined to recommend him now for an immediate DSO.

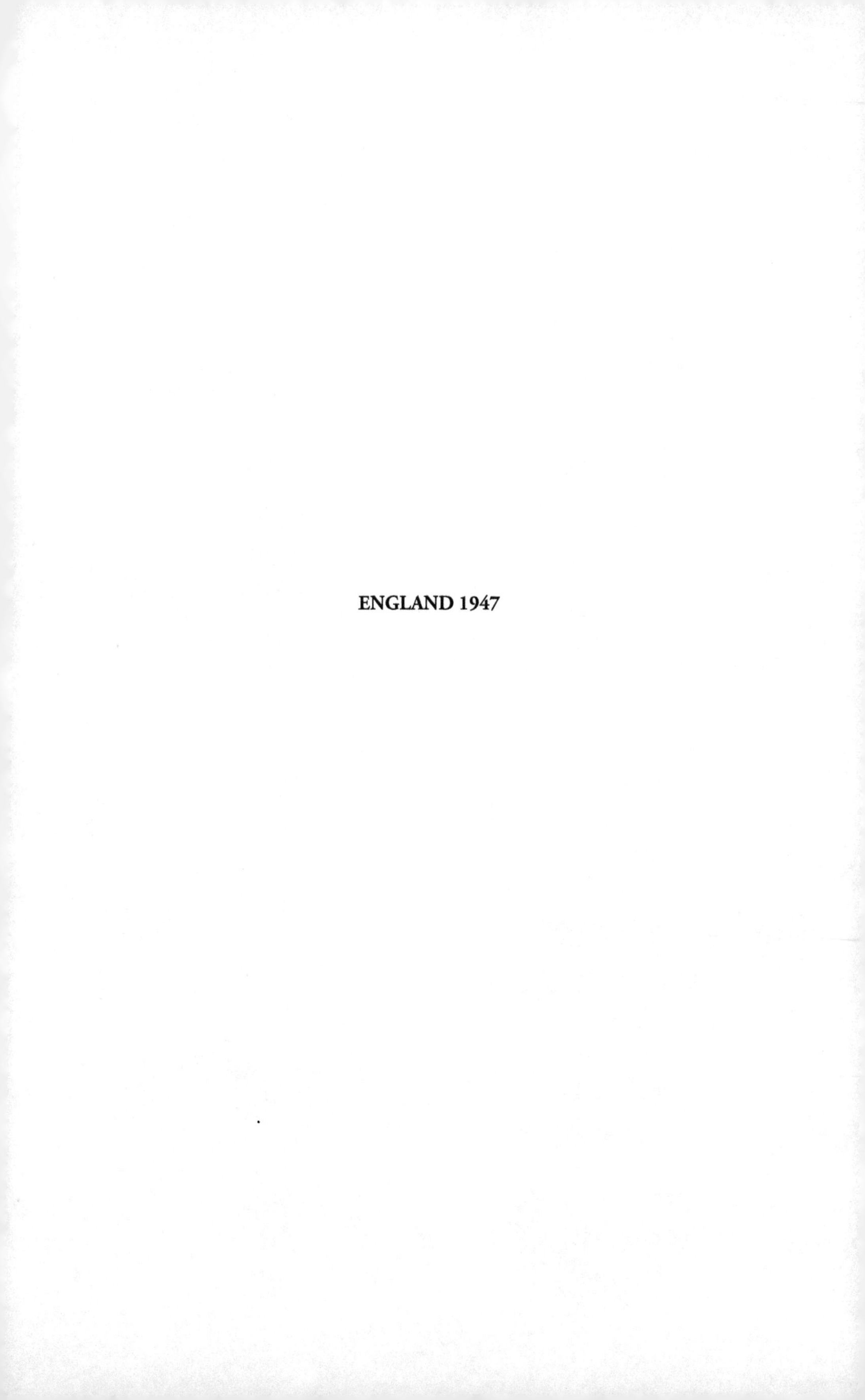

ENGLAND 1947

THURSDAY'S CHILD

Nursing Orderly Corporal June Wheater's day began at 06.30h when her alarm clock woke her in the WAAF living quarters of the military hospital outside Oxford. She washed and dressed quickly, checked her appearance in the mirror and left the chilly dormitory for the even colder outdoors. Hoping no senior officer was about so early to spot her, she dashed across to the mess hall for breakfast. It was important to be there on the dot to be sure all the bacon had not gone and also to finish eating in enough time to have a quick fag before reporting to the ward.

'You still on surgery?' her friend Lucy asked.

'No. I've been switched to long-term care. First day today.'

'I've done that. There's some pretty sad cases there.'

The Sister left June to do the routine jobs: straps not too tight, pulse, under-arm temperature, feeding tube, catheters and fluid levels. Everything seemed in order and ready for doctor's rounds. She lifted the clipboard from the bed's end rail to make her entries and read the patient's name and date of arrival in the hospital. The other nurse in the staff room had told her they called this one The Oldest Living Inhabitant but she was still surprised to see how long he had been there: since the end of June 1944. That was not far short of three years; and it appeared that not once had he woken up. She looked at him lying there all still, breathing slowly, arms by his sides—as if he was just asleep. There was a scar on his forehead, probably from the crash but all his other wounds and broken bones had healed long ago and the burns had been on his back where you couldn't see them. June knew a bit about comas from her training; how they could open their eyes but they didn't seem to see you and how they might move their hands and mumble or even say things but this one didn't show a flicker. The doctor would be coming on his rounds soon and she had others to see to. Better check his pulse again.

She couldn't loosen his grip on her hand and he was staring straight up at her. She just managed to reach the bell push and shout 'Sister!' at the same time.

***

'Are you a relative, Dr Smallwood?'

'No, doctor. The Sister will tell you I have visited him regularly almost since the time he arrived here but I am not a relative.'

'His next-of-kin is apparently an uncle who lives in the Lake District somewhere. He hasn't been here for some time now, I believe.'

'His cousin, a Mrs . . .' the Sister looked at her notes . . .'a Mrs Anne Burns was here to see him two months ago, doctor. He doesn't seem to have any other relatives.'

'I simply wanted to ask how he is now that he's awake again. I am sure he knows who I am but he says hardly anything, even when I mention things I know used to interest him greatly. They seem to mean nothing to him.'

'It is a something of a mystery, I confess. So many of these young men were terribly injured, not only physically but mentally too. He is a bit unusual in that he has made a very good physical recovery, some might say a miraculous one, except that he appears to remember nothing whatsoever about the War. Oxford, yes, when he was here as an undergraduate—perhaps you knew him then—and he knows where he is now. But nothing, he remembers absolutely nothing in between. Extraordinary.'

'What can be done, doctor?'

'Well, we want to keep him here for a little while longer. We need to be sure about a couple of things before we let him go. Then I'm going to send him to a young neurologist colleague of mine who has done a lot of work on the effects of head injuries.'

'Does he have a head injury, doctor?'

'Not that you can see. But there is something wrong inside; something missing.'

'Does your colleague work in this area? I should like to keep up my visits if at all possible.'

'Oh yes, he's not too far away. Just up the hill from you, one might say. Sister, could you let Dr Smallwood have the address on her way out?'

***

'He knows that you're here. I did as you asked and he said I could tell you anything you wanted to know. I must say, not many of my patients would have done that.'

'I have no intention of prying into his condition. I simply wanted to know whether there is a name for it.'

'Selective memory loss: I'm not sure I'm comfortable with that. It implies some measure of *deliberation*, choice if you like and that can't always, maybe not often, be the case. Lacunar amnesia is another term.'

'Meaning some sort memory gap.'

'Yes, yes; sounds more objective. There are other names, psychogenic amnesia, dissociative amnesia, circumscribed amnesia and so on, all with slightly different symptoms. He's not the only case I've known but he's certainly the one with the most closely *defined* gap: the War. Outside that, his recall is more or less normal.'

'I suppose it must be the result of the crash.'

'That's the thing you'd obviously start with but it doesn't get us very far in discovering the actual mechanism inside the brain that responds to the trauma by causing the gap. Does his brain not want to remember certain things or can't it help forgetting them? Is it like a line of pencil writing rubbed out but leaving the faintest of marks that one day the brain might be able to discern—remember—or has a whole bit been cut out and as it were thrown away? Simply don't know. Not yet, anyway, until we've found out an awful lot more about what goes on in here,' the young man said, tapping the side of his head. 'Or is he simply hiding it all for some reason of his own and making a fool of us? I do not think so. Not this man.'

'Nor do I and I think that I know him quite well. What happens now?'

'I'd like to go on seeing him and he's agreed to come and help. I say 'help' because I've got really rather interested in him and I'd like to try some new ideas; see what happens. I was at a conference in America earlier this year and . . . but you don't want to hear about that. What happens now? Well, as far as I'm concerned there's no reason why he shouldn't get on with normal life. The medics will want to keep up with him I expect and as I've said so do I. Do you know what he can do?'

'He is still technically a serving officer in the RAF but once the medical and neurological reports have been submitted and accepted he can expect to receive an honourable discharge from the service on medical grounds.'

'Yes, but then what?'

'It's only my opinion but I think he should return to being an undergraduate and continue where he left off when he was called up. He is still a Scholar of his College, after all. They would be glad to have him back.'

'What a good idea! He won't be far away, then, will he?'

She got up to leave.

'Thank you. You have been most helpful.'

'Not a bit. I hope we meet again, Dr Smallwood. He's waiting for you in the garden. Oh, by the way, nearly forgot. Not a good idea to bring the subject up with him, not yet, anyway; one day, perhaps but not yet. Could do harm; could set him worrying too much. You will remember that, won't you?'

'Yes, don't be concerned. We have many other things we can talk about.'

***

'It was a terrible winter, Philip. You didn't notice any of it, of course, but it's spring now and the floods have gone down. Why don't you go and spend some time up in the Lake District with your aunt and uncle? He has a sheep farm, doesn't he? You could help with the sheep. You must have learned something about them when you were a boy. You need a break from Catalan syntax. Do some walking on the hills. Recite Wordsworth as you stand above Ullswater.'

Lawless jumped out of bed and walked about the room reciting 'Daffodils' while she watched him.

The scarring on his back was still plain to see, but they had done a very good job on the burns on his arm and hand at the Queen Victoria Hospital and now that all his hair had grown back the scars across his scalp were invisible. He walked well, but his right hand had a slight tremor. Lucky: that was what his crew had called him. Was he really lucky? Yes and no, she decided.

'I recognise the words but I cannot see you as Wordsworth like that.'

'Like what?'

'Without your clothes on.'

'Now tell me truthfully, what do you prefer, clothes or poetry?'

'That depends.'

Lawless was nervous to begin with about going back to the Lake District. He felt that there was such a gap between his own life and that of his uncle and aunt that he wondered how much they would have left in common, how much they could have to say to each other. It was the sheep and the dog that eased the way. They immediately brought back memories of his childhood and he began to feel a little bit at home again.

'I think she remembers you, lad.'

'I think she does, Uncle John,' he said stroking the collie's head. 'Nell, good girl, you remember me don't you?'

'It's Kitty, lad; Nell's pup. We don't have Nell any more. Come yourself in. Your Auntie's made such a tea for you.'

'I can't eat another thing, Auntie. I'd burst if I had another slice of custard.'

'You look as if you need feeding up. There's hotpot for supper. I know you like that.'

'In that case I'd better go out for a bit; walk some of it off.'

'I'll come with you, lad. She won't let me smoke my pipe inside any more.'

They walked without saying anything along the farm lane to a gate that led into a field where sheep were grazing. It was a mild evening with clear skies and no wind. This was always known as one of the more sheltered valleys in the Lakes. It wasn't as green as he remembered it. Lawless watched the sheep and lambs moving slowly about for a while.

'You used to have more than this, Uncle John. Have you got some up on the fells already?'

'No, this is all we've got left. It was the winter: worst for a hundred years, they say. I've never seen so much snow and it came late as well. We had scores of 'em buried in all that. Couldn't get up there, see; it was so deep and drifted. Terrible. Everybody lost a lot, some of 'em nearly everything.'

'Can you manage?'

'Have to, lad. Start building up again. Takes time though.'

'I'm sorry. I'm here to help for a bit, if you want. Just tell me what to do.'

'Aye, thank you, lad. We'll see.'

They started back towards the house.

'Annie might come tomorrow, Philip.'

'Annie? It's such a long time since I saw her. I can't even remember when it was.'

'She did come to see you when you were in hospital. We did as well, once.'

'Did you?'

'Didn't they tell you? You were asleep; in a coma they said. So we sat there for a bit and your Auntie talked to you, and held you hand, but you never moved.'

'And Annie came as well?'

'Aye, not so long ago but she said you were just the same.'

'I'm sorry, Uncle John. I never knew.'

'Never mind, lad. You're here now. You'll see her tomorrow like as not.'

'Uncle John, I ought to tell you. I can't understand this or explain it, but I just can't remember anything about the War. Nothing. It's all a blank. So I might not understand what you're talking about sometimes. That's already happened quite a lot. They tell me that I did this and I did that and I was with these men and those men and none of it means anything to me. I didn't even know I was made a Squadron Leader and got the DFC and DSO. But it must be right because I have the medals. They're in the place where I've been living in Oxford. You'll have to forgive me. One day it might all come back. I just don't know.'

'Now then, now then, don't get all upset. It doesn't matter. You're here now and that's what matters. Come on; let's get back. Evenings are still a bit chilly.'

He walked along the lane again the next day with Annie and the little girl in a pushchair.

'She likes to see the lambs.'

'How old is she, Annie?'

'Thirteen months; twenty fifth of April last year she was born. Thursday it was.'

'I was born on a Thursday.'

'Thursday's child has far to go, Mum says.'

'She'll go far with a name like Margaret, Annie; and blonde hair like that.'

They walked along in silence and then she said,

'Dad told me what you said, Philip, about not being able to remember anything. I did come to see you, you know, in the hospital. They let me in when I told them who I was. You were just lying there, still, like you were asleep. I wondered what was going on inside your head. They said talk to him and I did. I told you about me and Andy getting married and about Margaret. But you just lay all quiet, as if I wasn't there. It made me feel frightened, Philip but they said not to worry. You were all right. But you weren't, were you?'

'Now I am, Annie. I'm helping your Dad and I'm going back to Oxford in October.'

'I'm glad, Philip and I want you to know I'm happy, with Andy and little Margaret. I really am.'

He didn't know what to say so he took her hand and pressed it. She let him hold it for a few seconds and then gently took it away.

'I want you to meet him, Philip. I know you'll like him. He's so nice with Margaret. He loves her, talks about nothing else. He's done a lot in the garden. You ought to see. When he came out of the Navy he got a job in a garage, Johnson's in Kendal. They put him in charge a year later. He told me one day he'd own it. I don't know about that though.'

'He will, Annie. Just wait and see.'

'There now, she's woken up just as we got here. Here you are, Margaret. Look, little lambs playing. This is your Uncle Philip.'

***

Lawless wrote to the Dean asking if he could come up early as he needed to find somewhere to live before Term began. He received a reply saying that there was no need since he would be living in College for his Second Year and as a Scholar had already had rooms allocated to him. He arrived as instructed in Oxford on the Thursday before Michaelmas Term and went first to the Lodge in search of his keys.

'Mr Lawless, back again then, Sir.'

'Can't stay away, Lewis.'

'I was expecting you earlier than this, Sir. 1946, I thought it would be.'

'Well, you know how things are, Lewis.'

'Yes, Sir. Sometimes I do and sometimes I don't. The Dean's given you your old rooms: Garden Quad, Staircase 1.'

'Is Harris there now? I wrote saying that I was coming up.'

'Harris isn't with us any more, Sir. He didn't come back from Burma. Your Scout's a new man, Payne.'

'Lewis, that suit you're wearing. Are you . . .?'

'Yes, Sir; Head Porter now.'

'Congratulations. Did Plowman retire?'

'You could say that, Sir. He dropped dead in Hall, just after Grace was said, which is nice in a way. You haven't asked, Sir but your bicycle's ready whenever you want to collect it.'

As far as he could judge his rooms had not changed since he last saw them at the end of June in 1941. Same dark red curtains; same faded Axminster carpet with the same threadbare patches; same oak table with the same ink stains: even the slightly dusty smell of the room was the same. Nothing had changed. Lawless felt curiously relieved. And *at home:* he felt that too. This was where he belonged.

He sifted through the envelopes and cards on the table. Chapel card, invitations to drinks from various Presidents of various University clubs seeking new members, a reminder from the Proctors that undergraduates were forbidden motor vehicles whilst in residence, notice of the first Junior Common Room meeting of the Term; and many more, most of which ended up in the wicker wastepaper basket by the fireplace. He kept the Senior Tutor's and Modern Languages Tutor's cards giving the times of his meetings with them on Friday morning and the Domestic Bursar's reminder that his Ration Book should be deposited in the office on arrival.

He contemplated lighting his fire, decided to save his coal ration for the colder, damper days that would surely come and sat down in the same old scuffed leather armchair and opened the envelope bearing the crest of Granville College.

'As I am to be your tutor for your chosen Option I think we shall have to be more professional and certainly more discreet in our relationship.'

'Of course; I understand.'

'In Term our weekly meetings will be purely academic.'

'In Term, naturally.'

'I shall be out of Oxford for most of the Christmas vacation. Do you have plans?'

'If I can persuade the Dean to let me stay up I should like to spend most of it in the libraries, with a few days over Christmas in the Lakes with my aunt and uncle.'

'I will add my support to your request. Come to see me for a reading list after the end of this Term. We can review the Term's work over some wine. I normally take small reading parties to Cornwall in the Easter and Long Vacations, all quite informal. You would be welcome.'

'Thank you. That sounds delightful. First tutorial, five o' clock on Tuesday you said?'

'I did. Good afternoon, Mr Lawless.'

In one respect it was an advantage to have a mind uncluttered by any memory of wartime experience. He suffered none of the nightmares, the panics and sweats brought on by sudden loud noises, the guilt of being a survivor, the violent reaction to a fancied slight, the difficulty of simply getting down to schoolroom work, obeying orders from elderly stay-at-homes most of *whom just had no idea of what it had been like.*

On the other hand it meant he had nothing to offer when the conversation turned, as it occasionally did after the third drink, to Alamein or the Rhine crossings or the Russian convoys. Noticing this, the odd one might have wondered if he had been a conchie but most accepted there were those who could never tell anything of what they had seen or done. It was the piano that made him one of them. He would always sit down and play, or try to play anything they asked. The Chaplain had given him permission to practise on the chapel Steinway for the Provost's Christmas party in the Lodgings.

And there was the work. He immersed himself in it like a parched traveller in the desert plunging into an oasis pool. He loved the silence of the Bodleian and the feel and smell of the old books, unaware of time passing and always the last to be told to leave. He never missed a class. He agonised over the essays, re-writing, re-phrasing, refining—he hoped—the argument and adding footnotes until the very last minute before he had to leap on his bike and pelt up the road past the War Memorial to Granville College.

He paused and looked up at her enquiringly from time to time but she never interrupted him until he had finished reading. The silence continued as she thought. Then came the dissection of his argument and the demonstration of his misunderstandings of crucial parts of the texts. Finally, as he was scribbling his notes and crossing out whole sentences, he heard the word he was hoping for. However.

'However, I commend your bringing in the passage from Berlinguer: most apt and not in the reading list. He develops the point in a later paper that he circulated but has not published. I will loan you my copy.'

As the Term progressed the dissections became less comprehensive and as he was reading his last essay he noticed from time to time she was nodding approvingly. He sat back and waited. The silence was short. She actually smiled briefly.

'Thank you, Mr Lawless. I think that we have begun to get somewhere with this subject. I have nothing to add. Now, while you cast your eye over this reading list you will take away for the Vacation, I will bring the wine.'

She came back carrying a tray holding two glasses and an unopened black bottle. 'Perhaps you would care to draw the cork? Happily I have come across another bottle. Do you remember it?'

Lawless looked at the wine label.

'Sherry I remember very well but BUAL—1920—Blandy's—MADEIRA. No, I'm sorry; I don't remember this.'

'I think you will. Sip it slowly. We have about an hour before I must be in the SCR before dinner.'

'Only three quarters for me: Scholars have to be at dinner on the last night of Term. And I have Provost's Collections afterwards.'

She put down her empty glass and got up from her chair.

'Oh, I think that should be enough time, don't you?'

'Very satisfactory tutor's report, Lawless,' the Provost said. 'You seem to be getting on very well with Dr Smallwood.'

'Yes, Provost, I am learning a lot from her.'

'Pretty demanding, I should say, eh?'

'She does work one hard but I like what we're doing, Provost.'

'Settling in all right, are we? Long time away, what was it?'

'Seven years, Provost,' put in the Dean.

'Seven years? Was it indeed? A great deal has happened in that time, Lawless, lots of changes.'

'When I came up again I felt as if I'd never been away, Provost.'

'Really? Well, that is remarkable. Well done, Lawless; Happy Christmas to you. Oh, wait, you are going to play for us, aren't you?'

'Is he all right, Dean?' the Provost said after Lawless had left. 'By all accounts he had the devil of a rough war.'

'He's physically sound, according to the College doctor but can't remember a thing about it.'

'Can't say I even pretend to understand but it doesn't seem to affect his work. I've never read such a commendatory report from Winifred Smallwood before. Racing certainty for a First I should say, if he goes on like that.'

Lawless found a card for him in the Lodge from the Dean. He would have to vacate his set in College for the vacation but there was a room for him in the College annexe in Holywell.

On the train to London Winifred Smallwood was debating with herself what to do about Lawless. Not remembering the madeira might be a small thing, but it was symptomatic of the lack of any progress at all in his regaining his memory of six lost years. It was seven months now since he had left the hospital. Probably, he was still seeing the neurologist, psychologist, whatever he was, but that seemed to be having no effect. Was it premature to expect any change? Did it matter? After all, he was happy and his work was outstanding. Best leave well alone? Was there anything his doctor did not know and should know that might help, open up some understanding? There was the letter that only she had read and one other person, not Lawless, knew about. There was no need to show it to the neurologist. She would keep it in the files she was having transported to Oxford as she cleared her desk in Kensington Palace Gardens. She could remember everything it said. It was worth a try.

The letter brought to mind Alexandre Chevalier and Justine and then, naturally, her own brother. It was unlikely that Alexandre knew anything of what was in the letter but it was now a long time since she had had any news of him. It was impossible for her to travel to France to see him, pleasant though that would be. She smiled in reminiscence. Perhaps he might be persuaded to visit Oxford again. There was much they could discuss. But no, there was Lawless to consider. It would not be prudent. Justine would certainly not stay quietly at home. And that could be rather awkward, her brother having just recently been promoted Air Vice Marshal and established in the Air Ministry in London. She knew he would advise against her revealing the contents of the letter to anyone so she decided not to make any mention of it at lunch and talk only about the Governing Body's invitation to her to become the next Principal of Granville College. But, yes, she would speak to Lawless's neurologist as soon as she returned to Oxford.

'Dr Smallwood; good to see you again. Please sit down.'

'Am I to think of you as neurologist or psychologist, doctor?'

'Ah. It confuses some of my colleagues but I like to think of myself as labouring in both fields. Our understanding of human behaviour and mental functions-and their disorders—cannot ultimately succeed without practical knowledge of the nuts and bolts and wiring of the thing in here responsible for them,' the doctor said tapping his head.

'Thank you for clearing that up.'

'Not at all: what can I do for you? I suspect this concerns Squadron Leader Lawless.'

'It does. I am assuming your professional commitment to complete patient confidentiality when I tell you what I and I alone know.'

'You have my word.'

She proceeded to tell him in detail what the letter contained. Almost before she had finished he jumped up from his chair and began to walk about the room, occasionally stopping to ask a question or verify something she said. Finally, just as she was beginning to feel irritated, he sat down abruptly in front of her and looked at her very intently.

'This could, possibly, conceivably, could explain a lot. It is most interesting. It gives me a great deal to think about.'

'I could say the same but what I should like to know is what will you do with it.'

'Do? Do? Well nothing of course. Not a word. It would be extremely dangerous, cause possibly great distress, overwhelming guilt, shock. No. It must be kept from him at all costs. This is a very, very slow process, Dr Smallwood. We must tease him gradually out of this blankness that he may well have unknowingly created for himself, or somehow find the physical lesion, scar, break whatever it is that is responsible for the block. There is so much that we do not know.'

'It sounds to me as if this will take a very long time.'

'You are right. But as the cliché has it, time is the great healer. He will recover. I am sure of it and it will be mainly through his own efforts—assisted very patiently by us. Fascinating. Fascinating.'

COMPLEX NUMBERS

Lawless saw very little of the other residents in the annexe: an Australian Physics research student who spent most of his time in the Clarendon and a couple of South African law students one of whom was training for the upcoming Blues match at Twickenham. There was a pokey kitchen where he could make tea, boiling the water on a gas ring, and almost nothing else. His room had a one bar electric fire that had hardly any effect on the chill. The College kitchen was closed for the vacation but he found the British Restaurant in the Woodstock Road near the Radcliffe Infirmary, a warm and cheerful place where he could have toad in the hole or steak and kidney pie for a shilling. Medical students thronged the place and he took to having the odd pint with them in one of the pubs nearby. He was perfectly happy to be on his own for most of the time. The Bodleian was marginally warmer than his own rooms and it stayed open until 10 pm. It was where he spent most of his time, working through his vacation reading list and following up all the references and many of the references in the references. He began to develop an idea for a short paper, a 'note', or more portentously, a 'communication'. He decided to work on a draft, and see what his tutor thought of it.

'Where've you been all this time, Sir? The Head Porter said reprovingly. 'You haven't picked up any of your post since the end of Term. One of 'em must be important because there was a phone call from a Doctor Hemming for you.'

'What did he say, Lewis?'

'He wanted to know where you were and I said I hadn't seen you for days.'

'God! I clean forgot I was supposed to see him.'

'You're working too hard, Sir, forgetting everything. It isn't good for you, sitting all that time in the Bod and I don't know where else. You'll be worn out by the time Term starts.'

'I'd better phone him up. Can I use your phone, Lewis.'

'Not working, Sir. They're sending somebody to fix it, the Bursar said but I don't know when. Now why don't you get on your bike and ride up there to see that doctor? Exercise would do you good. It's a nice day, for once.'

'I might just do that, Lewis.'

'And before you go, Sir, sign the book will you? I don't know yet whether you're staying up over Christmas or going to Timbuktu.'

Lawless looked again at the letter from Westmoreland inviting him to spend Christmas and New Year with them. He was in two minds whether to say yes, or make some excuses and stay in Oxford and get on with his draft and other texts he had turned up in the Bodleian that had not been on his reading list. There was a particular volume that he felt he must read. It was in German and although he had been surprised to find how much he could follow it was not good enough and would require long and patient work with the dictionary to uncover the vital evidence he needed. No sooner had he decided he would stay in Oxford over Christmas than he discovered that the Bodleian closed on 20 December and did not reopen until after the New Year. That still left two days and then he would go.

In the end he wished he had stayed in Oxford. He was made welcome, fed wonderfully—no rationing here, not at Christmas his aunt said—helped bring home the ash Yule log and played carols while everybody sang round the piano. Just like old times, his uncle said but it wasn't really. Too many people who would have been there in the old days were missing from the party. And Annie was different. He sensed the tension when they were in the same room together. She said very little to him and once simply stared at him and left when he asked if anything was wrong. He was sure something was coming when Andy suggested the two of them take Margaret along the lane to see the lambs.

'Give the women a bit of peace,' he said.

'More like getting out of helping with the washing up,' Mrs Lawless laughed.

They walked slowly along the lane in silence while the child chattered and squirmed around in her pushchair. Stopping at the gate, Andy lifted her up and sat her on the top bar with his arms round her.

'I was in the Med most of the time,' he said, not looking round. 'Did you ever get to fly down there?'

'I don't recall, Andy.'

'I was in destroyers; ended up Leading Wireless Mechanic. Torpedoed twice and survived both times. I was lucky.'

'I've been told I was but I can't remember a thing about it.'

'Look, lovie, there's a black one, there, there, black one. Look!'

The child pointed and squealed with laughter, shaking her head from side to side in delight.

'I try not to remember it but it keeps coming back. You think the Med's warm but it isn't Phil, I can tell you. Ooh, ooh, Margaret you're a big lump!'

The child began to jump up and down in her father's arms. He lifted her off the gate, set her on her legs on the ground and crouched beside her, holding her steady. He looked up at Lawless.

'Know what kept me going that second time? Thinking of Annie: somebody to come back to. I couldn't let her go. Do you know what I mean?'

'I know what you mean, Andy. You're a lucky man: still lucky.'

'Even more, Phil, even more, now that we have this one. We can't have any more, see.'

'I'm sorry.'

'No need to be: we're all right, just the three of us. Aren't we my little pet?' he said lifting the squealing child high above his head.

'I think I'd better be going back before the New Year,' he said to Annie while Andy was putting the pushchair away. 'I've got such a lot to do. I hope they won't mind.'

'It's for the best, Philip.' Her eyes were moist as she looked up at him. 'No, don't.'

He let his hand fall from her shoulder and put it on the child's curly head instead.

The pubs in Oxford must have had an extra delivery in time for New Year. Those still on their feet at midnight in the King's Arms roared a version of Auld Lang Syne as Lawless clumsily banged it out on the piano. He drained what remained in his glass and headed quickly for the Men's.

***

'If I may ask, Dr Smallwood what is your interest in my patient?'

'Since I became Principal I have had to cut down on my teaching and he is my only pupil and the only one in his year working for his special subject in an area where I have some expertise. He has an uncle and aunt in Westmoreland where he spends a little time but for most of the year he works in Oxford.'

'Where you, as one might say have taken him under your wing.'

'That is an exaggeration, Dr Hemming. I would say rather that I keep an academic eye on him, and for good reason. He is quite the most gifted student I have ever taught. He is producing exceptional work, some already of publishable quality. In fact we have recently submitted a contribution to a very prestigious journal, something I have never done before with a co-author who is still at the undergraduate stage of his career.'

'As I am sure you are aware, Dr Smallwood, gifted students are not unknown in this establishment.'

'But how many of them continue to perform their work without interruption and lead otherwise quite normal lives?'

'I take your point. Among the unusual he is the most unusual in my experience.'

'It is not paradoxical that one with so capacious a memory should have no recall of almost a quarter of his own life?'

'It might be. It might be. I do wonder whether we may have some form of compensation here. Putting it crudely, is that capacity to some extent enabled by the memory gap of six years?'

'Might that not imply that were he to regain some or all of the lost memory his level of scholarly work would diminish?'

'Not necessarily, otherwise I should have to consider abandoning his treatment. No, our memory can be a source of inspiration even though we may be unaware of it. We should continue our efforts at unearthing Mr Lawless's.'

'You used the word "treatment" earlier. May I ask what form that takes?'

'You appreciate I cannot go into detail. Suffice it to say that I introduce certain words into our conversation, certain references, the odd question—all carefully chosen beforehand—and note reactions.'

'I may inadvertently be doing something of the same during our tutorials.'

'Then should you observe some reaction you consider relevant perhaps you could keep note?'

At the end of his last tutorial of the Hilary Term Lawless told his tutor that her suggestion of asking the College for a travel grant to visit the Institute in Heidelberg in the vacation had proved successful.

'Hoffmann is there now. He was one of the few in Berlin who escaped the Nazis and went on to the United States after a short time in Cambridge: where I met him in fact. I will write to him that you are a student of mine.'

'It means that I shall miss your reading party.'

'It's more important that you see Hoffmann at this stage in your work. You can come to Cornwall in the Summer Vac.'

'Off to Heidelberg, I hear, Lawless.'

'Yes, Provost. I leave next week.'

'Well I'm sure you will make good use of your time there. Mustn't waste the College's money, eh?'

'We shall need a report on what he has done, Provost,' the Dean put in, 'and I intend writing to Professor Hoffmann to ask for his impressions.'

'We know about your French, of course Lawless but how's your German?'

'Ich weiss dass eine ausreichende Menge, Herr Provost.'

'Ah, well that sounds all right. Good day to you, Lawless.'

On the night before he was due to leave Heidelberg Lawless went on the off chance that he might get a seat in the opulent hall of the Old University for a chamber music recital given by students of the Music School. He managed to find the last empty seat in the back row. As the four musicians were tuning their instruments he heard two girls in front of him whispering to each other.

'Ich weisse die erste Geigerin,' said the blonde one.

'What's his name?'

'Shh. Sie beginnen.'

So, the other one was English.

In the interval they both stood up and looked around.

'Funfzehn Minuten, Iche brauche einen Schluck Wasser.'

'Ich auch. Ich werde mit dir kommen.'

Hoping there might be beer as well as water Lawless followed them out.

He should have known. There was only water. He saw them standing near a doorway sipping from their glasses and made his way across.

'Hello, do you mind? I though that I heard someone speaking English. Sorry. Entschuldigen Sie mich Fraulein.'

'I speak also English.'

'Ah, do you? They're very good, aren't they, the Quartet, do you think?'

'Yes, good, I think; not excellent but good.'

'Are you students here? I'm only on a short visit. Leaving tomorrow.'

'I am medical student. My friend is . . .'

'A mathematician.'

'From here? I mean, doing a degree here?'

'No, for one term then back home.'

'Where's home?'

'Cambridge. And you?'

'The other place,' he said smiling.

'Was ist das anderen Ort, Jane?'

'He means Oxford, Gisela. Which college?'

'Beaumont. Yourself?'

'Girton.'

'Sorry, I should have said: I'm Philip Lawless. I've been here for two weeks working in the library and seeing Professor Hoffmann two or three times.'

'Professor Karl Hoffmann?'

'Yes, in the trade he's known as the King of Romance Philology. My tutor put me in touch with him. Can I ask your names?'

'This is Gisela Wolff and I'm Jane Carstairs.'

A bell sounded, summoning the audience back to their seats. The second part of the recital was an early Haydn quartet unfamiliar to Lawless. The two girls slipped away as soon as the applause ended and before Lawless could suggest they had coffee somewhere. Jane Carstairs: all he could remember afterwards was that she was quite tall and didn't say very much. And she had short fair hair. He thought he might send her a card of Oxford when he got back.

'He let you see the de Cabestany text?'

'We read some of it together. I wasn't very good.'

'Remarkable. You seem to have impressed him.'

'I can't think how. He doesn't say a great deal.'

'Hoffmann bases his judgments on the questions you ask.'

'He didn't answer some of mine.'

'He would be leaving you to find out the answers to those for yourself. Good, your time was well spent. Did you meet anyone else?'

'No, not really, well, I met a girl; two in fact.'

'Did you now? You have your thoughtful look on. Tell me about them.'

'It was at a chamber concert in the auditorium in the Old University.'

'I remember it so well. Mercifully Heidelberg escaped the bombing; as did Oxford, of course.'

Lawless seemed not to have heard what she said.

'One was a German student and the other was English, from Cambridge; a mathematician she said.'

'Go on.'

'Well, that's about all, really. We only exchanged a few words during the interval. I didn't see them leave.'

'Chance encounters often stay the longest in one's memory. Now, about this essay of yours.'

He paused at the door. 'I did wonder if . . . if she might come on the reading party?'

'A mathematician?'

'She speaks very good German and . . . and when I mentioned Professor Hoffmann's name she seemed to recognise it.'

'And so may have absorbed some of his learning by a form of osmosis? Does she have a name?'

'Carstairs, Jane Carstairs: she's at Girton.'

'Girton, you say. Then I shall consider it.'

'You had a visitor while you were out, Sir; a Mr Kendrick.'

'Kendrick?'

'Yes, Sir. Said he was passing through Oxford so he thought he'd look you up.'

'Kendrick, Kendrick. I don't remember anyone called Kendrick, Lewis.'

'Said he knew you, Sir.'

'Did he leave an address?'

'No, Sir. He said he was going away for a while but he'd get in touch again when he was back.'

***

A party of six students assembled at Oxford Station one evening in the middle of August for the start of the long journey to Cornwall. Their instructions were to get off at Gwinear Road station on the Exeter-Penzance line, and wait for the train to Helston. At Helston there would be a bus to take them on to Coverack. Times for the bus were uncertain, but when they eventually arrived in Coverack, they could telephone the number supplied and someone would come to collect them. It was important to take food and drink for the journey and above all, not to forget their ration books. Swimming costumes were optional.

A dozen or so Navy personnel boarded the train with them at Gwinnear Road and were picked up by a lorry waiting at Helston but there was no sign of a bus at five o'clock in the morning. It was warm and already bright daylight. A little way from the station they found a meadow full of flowers and fell asleep in the shade of an elm tree.

Lawless was woken by the sound of a motor horn. He looked at his watch: eight o'clock. He struggled to his feet and hurried over to the gate. An ancient bus was standing outside the station, streams of black smoke drifting from its exhaust pipe. He waved and shouted at the driver who was standing outside his cab smoking a pipe. The man beckoned him to come. He hurried back to the others who were all still asleep and shook them awake.

'Come on, get up. It's here!'

Half an hour later the bus deposited the party near the harbour wall in Coverack. Boats were tied up or riding on the calm water and the air was full of the smell of salt and fish. Out beyond the harbour the sea was as blue as sapphire with the tops of little waves sparkling in the sun. Bleary-eyed and hungry they blinked in the bright light and waited for something to happen.

'You must be the party from Oxford. Bring your stuff. I've got the trailer parked up by the Post Office. The others arrived yesterday. We'd better be quick or they may have eaten everything.'

The driver of the tractor hauling the trailer introduced himself as Christopher Smallwood—'one of the nephews'—and explained he had just been demobbed and was down on holiday for the rest of the summer before starting his first year as a medical student.

'Are there any more of you, family, I mean?'

'Droves of us. We all come here in the summer. We've had the place for centuries. You must be Lawless. Aunt Winifred said that you were older than the others.'

'I bloody well feel it after that journey.'

Young Smallwood laughed.

'I know. It's terrible. We used to drive down here before the war. Can't get the petrol now, of course. You can always go in for a swim when we get there. That should wake you up.'

'Breakfast then bed for me; besides, I forgot to bring a costume.'

'We don't usually wear them here. Soon be there now.'

The house was built on the west side of a shallow valley where the slope levelled out about half a mile from the sea. It was a big old rambling place with barns and stables set among trees and surrounded by tumbledown stone walls. The valley had a small stream winding down to the sea and almost hidden by dense green growth of gorse, blackthorn and ivy.

The tractor pulled up outside the front of the house and everyone crawled stiffly down from the trailer.

'It's not easy to see from here but there's a path down the valley to the cove. Nice clean sand but quite a few people use it. We have our own private one round that point. It's only a few minutes walk. Let's go in. I can smell the coffee. You must be starving. No, leave your stuff here for now.'

'Now I'm not going to introduce everybody to everybody,' Winifred Smallwood announced. 'You all know who I am and now you know Christopher. It's up to you to find out who the rest of you are. Tea and coffee and sausages and other things are on the sideboard. Help yourselves. After breakfast Christopher will show you the sleeping quarters. Sort yourselves out. After that do whatever you want. Drinks before dinner at six.'

After the sorting out process Lawless found he had a small bedroom at the top of the house to himself. He wondered if the others thought he was too old to share with one of them. From his window he had a view all the way down the valley to the sea. Two people were making their way along the path towards the house. He could see only the top half of their bodies because of the thickness of the shrubbery they were pushing through. He watched until they came closer and saw both were girls and must have been swimming because they had towels round their necks. They were laughing about something. One was a slim girl with short fair hair. So Jane was here already. He felt suddenly very happy. He lay down on the rather hard bed and found his place in the copy of Proust he had been told to bring.

For then the die is cast, the person whose company we enjoy at that moment is the person we shall henceforward love

Swann was hooked; no doubt about it, he decided and fell asleep.

It was not so much a reading party as a talking party, Winifred Smallwood explained, and the talking could be done at any time but especially during and after dinner. And it was also a swimming and a walking party, and if anyone liked drawing or playing the piano, then it was that kind of party too. And, last but not least, it was a working party because wood had to be chopped for the stove or there would be no hot food and the vegetable garden had to be weeded and watered or they would all suffer from a lack of vitamin C.

'Now that's understood,' she said, 'to Proust. Was Swann really in love with Odette?'

'Infatuated, I'd say.'

'What about the others, the Princess and the needlewoman and . . .'

'He falls in love with any woman he finds attractive.'

'Fancies them all, more like.'

'You can't love two women at the same time.'

'Or two men.'

'Love or be *in* love: it's different.'

'I don't think Odette ever loved Swann. How can you get bored with someone if you really love them?'

'Swann's a terrible snob. How could anyone love a snob? They only love themselves.'

Winifred Smallwood watched them arguing, talking over each other, sitting back looking pleased or irritated, all with something to say but not always knowing how to say it in a way that would silence the opposition. Love, you could always rely upon love to get the thing going. It was their age, of course. Come to that it was anyone's age. Lawless had said little. Why was that? The girl, of course: Jane. She was on his mind, not Swann. Oh Lord. What now?

Jane spent most of her time with the other two girls. They all shared the same room. Then one morning when he came down early for breakfast he found her in the kitchen by herself stirring a pan on the stove.

'What is it?'

'Scrambled eggs.'

'Shall I make some toast?'

'If you like. Put the kettle on for tea first.'

'Is there any butter?'

'In the pantry, keeping cool.'

She put two plates of scrambled eggs on a tray and carried them into the dining room. Lawless followed with the butter and slices of toast in a toast rack.

'I like lots of pepper,' he said. 'Hm, very good; just soft enough.'

'Did you mean it when you said that you can't love two women at the same time?'

He took a sip of tea. 'I think so. I mean, perhaps you can love someone and be *in* love with someone else at the same time.'

'Only if you didn't know it.'

'What, be in love and not know it?'

'Yes, why not? You could simply not know that what you are feeling is being in love.'

'That's interesting. In the stuff I'm working on with Dr Smallwood—well, I say I'm working on it but she's the real expert—early Romance poetry, the poets—troubadours some of them—express sentiments of love in a stylised, refined way that's said in some cases to be a disguise for their real feelings and hopes. It's a sort of code but often very beautiful. Now, do they love or are they in love without knowing it?'

'Doesn't a poet always say what he or she really means?'

'Ah, like a mathematician perhaps? What kind of mathematics are you interested in?'

'Pure mathematics. I work on complex numbers.'

'You're going to have to explain that to me. I find all numbers complex.'

'A complex number has two parts to it. One part is real and the other part is imaginary.'

'That's enough for me. It sounds rather like what I was talking about.'

'Well, either the real part or the imaginary part can be zero. Where does that leave you?'

'Lost,' he said. 'Would you like to go swimming this afternoon?'

'There's a walk along the cliff path to Kennack Sands and a picnic this afternoon.'

'Tomorrow, then?'

'Tonight: we're all going for a midnight swim in the cove.'

'Tell me some more about complex numbers.'

They left their clothes in piles well out of reach of the incoming waves and ran over the firm damp sand towards the sea, shrieking at the chill of the water and splashing each other in excitement. Lawless stumbled in last. The moon was four days from new, a waxing crescent giving little light, something that Lawless was grateful for: the scars on his back would not be seen. He glimpsed pale patches in the dark sea, shoulders and arms moving as they swam. He waded out until the water was chest deep, feeling its pressure on his ribs, stood with his toes just reaching the bottom, and looked up at the stars. He heard splashes near to him and something touched his shoulder.

'Which is which? I know the Pole star.'

'Antares . . . Altair . . .Vega,' he said, pointing. 'Red white and blue: very patriotic. Vega's in the Lyra constellation; that means a lyre.'

'I've never been able to see what any of them is supposed to be.'

'Orion's the easiest to believe but he doesn't show until later in the year.'

'Where did you learn all this?'

It was disturbing to have her so close and naked and not be able to see her. Despite the chill he felt himself hardening.

'I don't know; from my father, I think. If we were out too late walking and the stars started to show he said we shouldn't worry because they would guide us home.'

'I'm getting cold,' she said, 'back to the beach.'

She was a good swimmer. There was hardly a splash as she slipped away. The others were all towelling themselves and dressing when he found them. He was glad of the large towel and darkness.

Someone had brought a torch and they followed the flickering light back to the house, laughing when they slipped or squealing when the gorse brushed against them.

'I've brought my violin,' she whispered as they were going in. Would you like to play a duet?'

'I'd need the music and lots of time to practise.'

'I know just the thing and I brought the music.'

He couldn't get to sleep, thinking of her, close and whispering in the hall below; close to him unseen but naked in the waves. He got up, walked to the window and lit a cigarette, blowing the smoke out into the soft night air. It wouldn't go away, that feeling of wanting to see what couldn't be seen when they were standing in the sea talking about the stars. He knew he wouldn't sleep. He could do one of two things to take that feeling away. Trembling a little and feeling rather guilty but unable to stop himself he walked as quietly as he could down the stairs and along the corridor and knocked softly the door at the end.

Winifred Smallwood was sitting up in bed reading by the light of a candle. She put the book on her bedside table and took off her spectacles.

'I was wondering where you had got to,' she said.

On the last day of the reading party there was always an entertainment after dinner. Everyone was expected to take part, singing, playing, acting, reciting, whatever they chose to do. The hostess saw to it that there were cider and beer enough, and some wine, to ease pre-performance nerves.

Things began with a mock admissions interview in which one of the girls, astonishingly convincingly dressed and made up as Winifred Smallwood, tried in vain to get a puzzled young man with more than a passing resemblance to Lawless to explain why he wished to read French when he had actually applied for the vacant post of gardener, that brought screams of laughter and set the tone for the evening. A dripping wet Wordsworth with a broken umbrella came next, glumly reciting 'Daffodils' in a strong northern accent, making mistakes, forgetting the lines and starting again until finally a female voice screeched 'William! Come in you daft bugger, you'll catch your death!' and he trudged off muttering 'Dorothy, Christ, I wish she'd leave.' There was a brilliant pastiche of Proust with a vamping Odette and moustachioed Swann eyeing each other over their shoulders as they slowly circled round a bed reciting the lines of 'My old man said follow the van.' Lawless and Jane Carstairs' performance of a Fauré berceuse was the only serious act of the show and brought it to a close.

'I don't suppose for one moment that you'll take any notice of me when I say get an early night,' Winifred Smallwood said with a smile. 'But if you don't, I hope you sleep well afterwards.'

'You were very good,' Lawless said to Jane as she picked up her violin case, 'even when I fluffed that bar. I'll do better another time.'

'Weren't Swann and Odette hilarious?'

'Do you have a boyfriend?' he blurted out without thinking.

'Not anymore,' she said and went upstairs.

He watched her go. What did that mean? Not now but there was one, or never again?

'I'm coming to Cambridge some time after Christmas,' he said as they got on the train at Helston station. 'There are some texts in Trinity library I need to see; only copies of course. Do you think we could meet up? I can let you know when.'

'I don't see why not.'

She sat with the other girls on the London train and all there was time to say to her was goodbye when he had to change at Southampton.

ENGLAND 1948

CAMBRIDGE

Lawless wrote several letters, some of them quite long, to Jane, after the Cornwall reading party. Her replies were fairly short, saying little about herself or what she was doing. Work, she said, was taking up so much of her time but she was enjoying it. In one letter she did tell him that she had been reminded of that night he had identified the stars when she went to a lecture by quite a famous Cambridge astrophysicist who had a theory about how the chemical elements had formed. Some of them had to come from massive explosions of stars and she was trying out some ideas as to how complex number theory could be applied to some of the processes involved. He sent her a Christmas card with a picture of a page of an illustrated Romance manuscript on it and got one back of the Three Wise Men on their camels looking up at a pointed star. Inside it she had written, 'Is That One Next?'

'Three days at most,' Winifred Smallwood said when they were finalising his visit to Cambridge. 'You won't need more than that and there's still plenty to get through here in the run up to Schools.'

'I haven't found anywhere to stay yet. I wrote to Trinity to ask if I might have a student room—it's my sister college—but I haven't heard anything. Still, I expect I can find something when I'm there.'

'You haven't forgotten the reason you are going to Cambridge, have you Philip? The texts, they are the reason.'

'Of course; why do you ask?'

'I think you know. Listen to me, Philip and please do not think I have any ulterior motive for saying this. Are you sure she is the right person for you?'

'It's nothing serious. She was very nice in Cornwall—and we got on very well learning that duet. That's all. Besides, she's far too involved in her work. And so am I.'

The Australian research student he had got to know in Holywell gave him an address in Cambridge where he said he had once stayed while doing some work at the Cavendish. He had finally heard from Trinity that there was no room available at this time in the Term, so he decided to give it a try. He set out to walk along the river. Crossing one of the bridges he heard his name being called from behind.

'Lawless! Philip Lawless! Hey, Philip!'

Before he could turn to see who was shouting he felt a hearty slap on his shoulder.

'Lawless! It is you! Where have you been all this time?'

He turned round and saw the broad smile on the good-looking face gradually fade.

'Philip, it's me, Kendrick! Don't you recognise me?'

'Kendrick? The Porter said you came to the College. I'm sorry, there's some mistake. I don't know any Kendrick.'

'Come on, Philip, you must remember me. I was your navigator. Remember the old Halifax Squadron, all those hairy fucking nights over Germany? Ernie Gibbons, remember him? Dickie Dent? Dead Shot MacNeill? Lucky Lady, our very own kite? I heard you pranged her. Come on. Wait, wait a minute, you don't, do you? What's happened to you?'

'I don't know. They tell me that I did all kinds of things and I ended up in hospital and didn't come out until 1947 and I cannot remember a single thing about any of it.'

'Come on, we need a drink.'

In the pub Kendrick told Lawless he had once visited him in hospital so he knew about the coma. Ernie and Dickie had been as well, he knew, but none of the others. They hadn't come back from one of the raids on flying bomb sites.

Lawless listened and believed all he heard. He had the feeling that this man would not make anything up. But no matter what he was told, none of it evoked any memory at all and he had to say so.

Kendrick took a long swallow and sat back looking at Lawless with a faint resigned smile on his face.

'All right. What's past is past. What's now is the need for another pint before we both have to go.'

Kendrick came back with two pints of bitter and sat down again.

'We're lucky to get these. They quite often run out.'

'Are you working in Cambridge? I don't know what you do.'

'Nor do I sometimes. I thought the War was over in 1945. Now, I'm not so sure. No, I don't live in Cambridge. In fact I'm not far away from where you are now.'

'Really? Where?'

'Can't say, my old warrior. Not allowed. But not too far away that I can't drop by now and then.'

'So, why are you in Cambridge? You've just told me you were here, at Corpus. Did you finish a degree?'

'Oh yes, they let me do that in my spare time.'

'Who were "they"?'

'The people I worked for.'

'I give up.'

'Look, Philip, I'd like to tell you but I can't: more than my life's worth. I worked in a place not far from here that nobody talks about and now I work somewhere else.'

'That you can't mention either.'

'It's a weird world, Philip, make no mistake about that. The War was simple compared to this one. That's enough about me. Tell me about you. Have you met any interesting girls? You have, haven't you, you old Lothario? I can tell by that look on your face. Come on who is it? Is that why you're here?'

'No, well not really. I'm working on some old texts in Trinity library.'

'That's very interesting. But where are you *sleeping* and with whom?'

'I haven't found anywhere to sleep yet and she's a mathematician if you want to know. Complex numbers, she told me.'

'Is she now? I ought to know her if she's into that.'

'Oh God, I hope not. Jane Carstairs; that's who she is. She's at Girton.'

'She's a Final Year undergraduate, isn't she? Yes, we, I mean I, know about her. Very bright; very, very bright: you've picked a real winner there.'

'I can't understand the first thing about what she does. She tried to explain but it was like a foreign language.'

'I thought you were good at those. Pure Maths: same words but with a totally different meaning.'

'She's no good at Catalan.'

'Well, there you are. You can speak to each other without either of you knowing what the other is talking about. Listen, you can bunk in with me while you're here although I have to be off tomorrow.' Kendrick lowered his voice to a whisper. 'Going to the States for a bit. Salivating at the very thought of some really big steaks.'

Kendrick was gone when he woke up. He found some dried milk and tea and a few slices of bread and a half-empty jar of what looked like home made plum jam. After breakfast he went to see the Librarian at Trinity College and worked there until the library closed at nine o' clock. As he was leaving the college the Porter said a young woman had left him a note earlier in the day.

'Meet you at the Lodge at seven tomorrow. Come and have supper.' It was signed 'Jane'.

In her Final Year she shared lodgings with two friends in a house in Thornton Way not far from her College. They were just in time to catch a bus to get there. Each girl had a bedroom and they all shared a sitting room and a small kitchen.

'Hannah and Chrissie are both away for the weekend,' she said. 'That means the baked beans are all for us. Cut the bread, will you? You'll find a toasting fork by the gas fire.'

'I met a man whom I used to know called Kendrick today; quite by chance while I was crossing the bridge, Clare Bridge, is it? He said something that made me think he might know you.'

'Kendrick? Oh yes, I remember him. He was at the meeting of the Scientific Society I told you about in my letter: that lecture on the origin of the chemical elements. I asked a question and he came up afterwards and we talked about it for a while. I think he must be a mathematician, judging by some of the things he said.'

'Did he ask you what you were thinking of doing after Finals?'

'Everybody asks you that at this stage. I said I was going to do research. Here in Cambridge.'

'What did he say to that?'

'Something about hoping to hear how I was getting on if we should meet again. Why are you asking all these questions, Philip?'

That was the first time she had used his first name, he realised with surprise.

'No reason. I'm sure he's all right. I'm staying in his place while he's away. Apparently I used to know him very well at one time.'

'You do say the oddest things sometimes. Look, I've found some of Hannah's mother's cake. Would you like some? There's nothing else for pudding.'

She was much easier to talk to than in Cornwall. Like him she was an only child. Her father had been quite a lot older than her mother and died when Jane was only four. Both her parents had been teachers, her father teaching Physics and her mother Latin and

Greek. It was her mother who encouraged her music and she had taken Grade 8 violin by the time she was fourteen. She wanted to do the Diploma but her school said she must concentrate on her work if she wanted to get into Cambridge. She was not yet seventeen when she won her Scholarship. Her PhD was already arranged. All she had to do was get her First.

She stopped talking for a moment and looked at him.

'You must have been in the War,' she said.

'Yes, I must have been.'

'That's where you knew Mr Kendrick.'

'So he tells me.'

'There you go again, being odd. Still, if you don't want to talk about it, that's fine. I'm going to have another look in the cupboard. I think I saw a sherry bottle hidden away behind the tea caddy.'

There were some clinking sounds and she came back with a bottle and held it up to the light.

'About a quarter full; Chrissie won't mind. Oh dear, coming from Oxford, you probably only drink sherry *before* dinner.'

'I'll drink sherry anytime,' he said 'I must have got into some awfully bad habits during the War.'

The sherry was all drunk and the gas had gone out because they had no more coins for the meter.

'I ought to be going,' he said.

'The last bus left ages ago. It's raining and you haven't got a raincoat.'

'Have you got an umbrella?'

'We only have one and Hannah's taken it. You can stay here, if you like.'

'If I do, can I sleep with you? Can I?'

'I don't see why not. There's nobody else in the house.'

They looked at each other and both burst out laughing at the silliness of her answer.

'You really had to think about that, didn't you?'

'I always think about everything I do, Philip.'

It was the first time a man had made love to her, and she never fully relaxed while it happened. Lawless tried to be as gentle and as gradual as he could. It was a long time before he felt she was ready for him. She cried out once but quickly put her hand to her mouth to stifle the sound. Afterwards she lay silent beside him for a long time. He stroked her hair.

'I love the colour of your hair,' he said.

'It's dark. You can't see it.'

'Oh yes I can. Shining in the Cornish sunlight. I can see it now.'

She turned over on her side and her breasts brushed against his chest. He could feel her looking at him.

'I'm sorry. I didn't know what to do.'

'It's never easy, the first time. You were wonderful.'

'I wasn't. I know I wasn't. I will be; I hope.'

'I hope you will, because I want to marry you. Will you marry me, Jane?'

'Yes, yes I will. But only after Finals.'

'Of course; first things first. I've got mine as well.'

'It's a promise. Shall we try again? Can you do it again so soon?'

'I'll do my best but you'll have to help. Where's your hand?'

***

He saw her again early in the summer when he was persuaded to fill in at the last minute when someone dropped out of the College cricket team going to play its annual game against Trinity. She came to watch the last few overs of the game where Lawless carried his bat for 34 runs, while the last man was out with ten runs still to get. He was foolishly pleased to see her sitting outside the pavillion and raised his bat to her.

'Well done,' she said. I saw you hit a four.'

'We really wanted to win. It's the first time the game has been played since 1939. We came close but not good enough.'

'But it's the game that counts, isn't it, not just winning?'

'Not where I come from,' he said with a grin.

'I'd ask you back to the flat but we're all revising like mad. My first paper's on Monday.'

'Never mind. I ought to be working as well. I only agreed to come with the team because I hoped I'd have a chance of seeing you.'

'When does your coach leave?'

'When the pubs shut. They have a bit of a party in Trinity and then head off on a pub crawl. The Trinity men have to wear gowns, of course but not us. We look like civilians.'

'You ought to be going with them.'

'Can we go for a walk along the river? Just a little way; I don't want to keep you away from your sums.'

She slapped his arm. 'You know I don't do sums. This isn't arithmetic. We need to be quick if we're going to have that walk.'

'Give me a few minutes to change. I'll ask them to take my bag with theirs when they leave.'

They walked along the same stretch of the river as far as the bridge where he had met Kendrick, holding hands most of the way.

'You have to go that way now,' she said. 'Trinity isn't far away. Your friends will be expecting you. I can catch a bus back to the flat.'

'It's been lovely seeing you again: a perfect end to the day. I don't want to go. I'd much rather, you know . . .' He didn't finish saying what he was going to say.

'It is odd you didn't recognise Kendrick, don't you think? From what you said about him you two must have known each other very well.'

'I'll tell you all about that—or as much as I can remember—when we have time. Can I kiss you goodbye?'

'I don't see why not,' they both said at the same time and laughed.

Then she kissed him quickly on the lips and walked away.

'Let me know what happens,' he called after her but all she did was lift one hand and kept on walking.

Out of nowhere the thought came to him that neither of them had yet said 'I love you.'

Early in July Lawless received a brief telegram from Jane that he did not understand. He thought perhaps Dr Smallwood could explain it and left a note in Granville lodge asking if he could see her. It would be the first time since the end of the previous Term, the rule being that an Examiner should not tutor a candidate in the final Term before the examination.

'Star-Star-I, the meaning is clear, Mr Lawless. Miss Carstairs has secured a Double First Class Honours degree and more than that, one that in Oxford would be deemed a Congratulatory First. You may not be aware of this but she will actually be able to take her degree since Cambridge has at long last accorded women academic equality with men. Perhaps you should reply in some appropriate way.'

He thought long and hard about what to say and at last wrote 'Congratulations-Pythagoras-Jealous' on the telegram form.

The following day he received a letter from the Clerk of the Examination Schools requesting him to attend for a Viva. Full academic dress should be worn.

Oh, Christ, a Viva: the last thing anybody wanted. That meant he was borderline. He must be. He was in for a gruelling by the Examiners. He could think of countless errors and omissions in his papers. Which would they fasten on? How many? With a Second he would never be accepted for research. He was sure of it. Schoolmastering: that's all he could look forward to, or the Civil Service. No, they demanded a First. Hopeless.

He ground out his cigarette on the pavement and went into the marble-floored hall of the Examination Schools.

'Mr PM Lawless?' The clerk looked down his list. 'May I see your letter, Sir? Thank you. Room Fourteen, Sir. Knock twice on the door and walk straight in.'

The seven Examiners were all there in full academic dress, gowns, hoods and caps. Winifred Smallwood, Chairman of Examiners was in the centre of the line. On the table in front of them were piles of examination scripts.

As one, the Examiners rose to their feet and applauded. Lawless didn't know what do so he just stood there with the mortarboard that was too small for him perched on top of his head and a foolish nervous smile on his face.

Winifred Smallwood, smiling broadly spoke for them all.

'Congratulations, Mr Lawless. We have only one question of you. Is it to be Cambridge, or All Souls?'

Still in a daze he wandered along the street in the direction of the General Post Office.

The telegram clerk looked at the form Lawless pushed over the counter.

'Just one word, Sir?'

'Yes, just one. SNAP.'

GRISEDALE TARN

'I remember another occasion when I congratulated you on your success in an examination; with sherry, I believe.'

'And not only sherry.'

'Yes, you were very sweet; rather hasty but very sweet.'

'Thank you for introducing me.'

'Philip, I hope you are not being arch. It ill becomes one who has graduated . . .'

'To madeira. This is a particularly fine . . .'

'North Oxford talk does not impress me. Put the glass down. I do not want you spilling that very expensive wine over me. Yes, that's better.'

'I don't know how to set about preparing for the All Souls Examination.'

'I think that you should put it out of your mind completely and go off somewhere. Go walking, somewhere mountainous or by the sea; make yourself physically tired, not mentally exhausted as you undoubtedly are now. Come back in two weeks and we will talk about it. Ask Peter Grierson to go with you. You seemed to get on well with him on the reading party. He likes climbing and he's at a loose end, waiting to go into the Army.'

'I doubt if I could drag him away from his girlfriend. I could ask Jane.'

'Do you think you should? She may not wish to be distracted from her work.'

It was not the first time she had given the impression that she had misgivings about his feelings for Jane—or Jane's for him, perhaps. He wasn't sure. She couldn't possibly be jealous. Hadn't she made it clear in a quite matter-of-fact way that their enjoyment of sexual intercourse together was a perfectly natural part of their acquaintance with no commitment from either party?

'There's only one way to find out.'

'Very well. Two weeks at the outside. Now, I have something very important to show you.'

Jane replied to his letter saying she was happy to go walking with him but could spare only a week.

He could think of only one place to go and wrote to his Aunt asking if he could come to see them and bring a friend with him. Her reply, unusually quick in coming, was slightly puzzling. She had to dash off the letter she said because they were very busy but it would be all right and she would explain when she saw him.

'We're all upside down at home, lad. Wait 'till you see it. No. I'll let your Auntie tell you what's going on. It's nice to meet you, Miss. I'll put your things in the boot.'

'Jane, Mr Lawless; call me Jane, please.'

'Philip, you didn't tell me you were bringing a young lady. I'll have to make another bed up. Isn't that just like a man, my dear?'

'It's all different, Auntie. You've taken the pictures down and the parlour's full of packing cases. Are you moving?'

'You'll be thirsty after that long journey, so sit yourselves down while I make a pot of tea. Then I'll tell you all about it.'

'We're moving to Australia.'

Lawless was thunderstruck. 'Both of you?' he said stupidly. Going to Australia?'

'Emigrating,' his uncle said, packing up and emigrating.'

'Annie's coming as well and Andy and our Margaret. We're all going.'

'I can't believe it. You've lived here on the farm all your lives and Grandad and his dad before that. Lawlesses have always been here. I just can't believe it.'

'It was Annie's idea at first. She wants a different life, not so much for herself but for Margaret. And Andy can get a job. They want mechanics out there. He wasn't so keen at first because he has a good job now in Kendal but then he thought about it and all that sunshine and everything and he changed his mind.'

'I can see that in a way but what about you? Why do you want to go?

'Well, we didn't want to see our family split apart and thousands of miles away from each other and Margaret's the only grandchild we'll ever have and we want to see her grow up.'

'I'm sorry, Auntie, I didn't want to upset you. I understand.'

'And I'm not getting any younger, Philip,' his uncle said, 'and I've nobody to take on the tenancy when I retire so it's the end of the line, if you see what I mean. I'm no too old to find another job out there, so they say. Australia's full of sheep, you know.'

'I think it's a very good idea,' Jane said. 'It's a new country.'

'Thank you, love. It's nice of you to say. Would you like another biscuit? They're home-made.'

'So, where are you going? Which part of Australia?'

'It's called New England, Philip. We're going to live near a town called Armidale. It's hilly, like here and it doesn't get too hot. I couldn't stand it in those deserts.'

Are you saying you've already got a house?'

'No, we have to rent first and then we'll see. Annie's been doing all the writing and form-filling and seeing about passports and medical tests and all that and we've all been to London to Australia House and been seen by the people there. So it's nearly all arranged now.'

And it only costs ten pounds for each of us to go. It might not be as much for Margaret.'

'When are you leaving, then?'

'At the end of the month, Philip. We would have told you earlier but we knew you were busy with all of your examinations.'

'I still hardly know what to say. I will miss you.'

'And we'll miss you, won't we John? And I know Annie will. But, you never know, we might be back one day for a holiday and see how you're getting on, and if you've got a family and you could always come out to see us.'

'Auntie, you were always the optimist. I'm sure you'll all get on really well. Good luck.'

'I think that deserves a drink to celebrate, I mean us going and you doing so well in your exams and then seeing this young lady for the first time. Mother, is there any sherry?'

Their offer to help with the packing after breakfast was politely refused. They were told they were on holiday and not there to work. If there were something they could do, they would be asked. It was going to be a nice day, so why not make the most of it? They could take the bus to Grasmere and walk up the old packhorse road as far as the col. It wasn't far down the other side to Grisedale Tarn and they should have a lovely view of Helvellyn. It would make a nice day and there would be rabbit pie for supper.

'They're such nice people, Philip. You never told me about them.'

'I'm sorry. I should have done but I haven't been in touch with them for quite a while. How are your legs? The first bit gets quite steep and the last bit as well up to the col. In between it's a stroll.'

She made him stop several times on the way up, not to rest, she said, but to see the views down to Grasmere and a glimpse of Rydal Water.

'Wordsworth lived there,' he said, 'Grasmere.'

'And his sister; nobody mentions her much.'

They sat on the col eating cheese sandwiches and seed cake and looking down at Grisedale Tarn.

'It's so blue, isn't it? I never expected that.'

'I once swam in it and I was blue when I came out. It was bloody freezing. I believe it's because it's very deep. It was a lot warmer in the sea in Cornwall. Do you remember that night?'

'I know what you're thinking but you can stop it.'

'Pity we have separate bedrooms and the floorboards creak.'

'Did you hear what I said? We are here to look at the view.'

'I am. You have lovely hair and your eyes are bluer than the waters of Grisedale Tarn.'

'I think it's time we were going down. I want to walk round Grasmere.'

'Good idea. It's too bright up here. You might catch the sun.'

'What does that mean, "catch the sun"?'

'Get sunburnt: you have that sort of skin.'

She sat on the grass at the lakeside while he lay on his back beside her with his eyes closed against the sun and chewing a stalk of grass.

'What did your uncle mean about not having anyone to take on the farm after him? He was looking at you when he said it.'

'After Colin was killed he began thinking that I might take it on one day.'

'Colin?'

'Their son, Annie's brother; he was shot down over Dunkirk.'

'What's Annie like?'

'Very nice, very pretty, same age as me. She lives in Kendal in what used to be my parents' house. I ought to say goodbye before they leave.'

'Why don't we go to see her? Kendal isn't far from here.'

'I think it would be better to see them off at Southampton.'

He's being a little evasive, she thought. He's not telling the real reason.

'It isn't that I don't like the farm. You might not believe it but I know quite a lot about sheep. Still, I couldn't have been a farmer. I wasn't cut out for it. I knew that as soon as I got to Oxford.'

'Where are we going tomorrow?'

'Let's see what the weather's like in the morning. Then I'll tell you.'

'It's going to be another lovely day. You are lucky, Philip.'

'People keep telling me that, Auntie. I think I must be, sometimes.'

'Where are you going then today?'

'Jane said that she's feeling stiff after climbing yesterday so I thought we'd take the ferry across Windermere and walk through to Hawkshead.'

'I'm sure she'll like it. It's a pretty place. And it's an easy walk by the lake.'

The day grew very hot so halfway along the road past the lake they decided to climb a little way up the slope and sit in the shelter of some trees. From there they could see men in boats on the lake fishing.

He took her hand and felt her softly squeeze his but when he ventured to put it up to her breast she pushed it gently away.

'I don't understand, Jane. Don't you want to make love?'

'Not now.'

'You mean not here? Later then tonight; like we did in Cambridge?

'No. I can't. It's difficult. Can we go back down to the lake?'

She had started down the slope before he got to his feet. He felt confused, rebuffed and then it occurred to him what the reason might be. She was too embarrassed to explain.

'Wait for me!' he shouted and started after her.

An hour dawdling along the shore, playing ducks and drakes when they found flat stones, picking reeds to plait into curved whips to flick away the flies and stopping to look through the hazy sunshine at the fishermen sitting idly in their boats out on the lake took an hour or more and then they reached Hawkshead. Up one of the cobbled streets of whitewashed cottages they found a teashop that had homemade scones. More than once as they were walking he thought she had been about to say something and thought better of it. When the scones had been eaten he asked her how her work was going.

'Very well; I've been given an Award.'

'Already? You've only just started.'

'No, silly, it was for my Finals results.'

'Well congrats; they haven't given me anything yet.'

'I have to tell you something, Philip. I don't know how you'll take it.'

'Is that why you were, er, shy when we were sitting under the trees? I'm sorry. You don't have to say. I do understand.'

'No you don't. The Award: it's for me to go to America.'

'America? Where? For how long?'

'Princeton; von Neumann is there. It's for one year but renewable.'

'But what about your degree work at Cambridge?'

'It's applicable, so I can carry on with that. They gave me leave when they heard about the Award.'

'So you are going?

'In a week's time.'

'Oh, I was hoping we going to be able to spend more time together, visiting each other's places. I have work I can do in Cambridge. Still, if it's as good as it sounds you must go.'

'It's too good a chance to miss. I'm so excited, Philip.'

'Who is von Neumann?'

'It would take too long to tell you how much he's done in mathematics—and physics as well. He is a genius. Thank you for being so understanding. Now, tell me about those papers Dr Smallwood is giving you for your own work.'

'You might find it a dry subject so let's have some more tea and scones first.'

She was more relaxed after she had told him about America and he was so encouraging. As the warm dry days went by they roamed the hills and rowed on the lakes and one day he even persuaded her to attempt what was for her a quite tricky scramble on Scafell Pike. Think of it as a problem with complex numbers, he said; rocks are real and falling off them is only in your imagination. She forgave him when they reached the top and she could see the view. There were some kisses and handholding but no suggestion of lovemaking. Her mind he accepted was on what she could see and on what lay ahead for her. On the way back to the farm on their last day he asked her if they were still going to be married.

'I'll stick by what I said,' she replied.

'I thought you said there were nine pages of text,' he said.

'I thought so too and then I realised one was thicker than the others and it turned out it had another adhering to it. The Bodleian spent a week taking them apart.'

'So whoever gave these to you, can't have seen the fifth page.'

'Evidently not. What are you looking at?'

Lawless picked up a magnifying glass and peered closely at the fifth page lying on the table in Winifred Smallwood's study.

'I'm pretty sure this is in a different hand, lighter in touch. The letters are slightly smaller and look here, there is a longer tail to the q and here and here, the f is not always crossed. I have a feeling that this is a reply, or part of one, to the message in the other four. There's another odd thing: the letters are sloping a little. Look. What do you think?'

'Very good: I should have seen that. I've done a rough translation of the first four pages with a few comments I'll give you but then it's over to you. Which is what the donor specified.'

'Do you know who it is? Is the provenance trustworthy?'

'The donor asked to remain anonymous to you. Don't ask me why. And yes, these are unquestionably genuine.'

'It's an amazingly generous gift: an original Fourteenth Century text that no one has worked on before. I wish I could thank him, or is it her?'

'One day, perhaps you may. Now, can you drag your attention away from your thesis material for a moment or two and talk about the All Souls Examination?'

It had the reputation of being the most difficult academic examination anyone—any man that is, because women were not accepted as candidates—would ever, could ever, attempt. Evidently, his College had confirmed that he was suitably qualified to enter, because he received a letter from The Warden of All Souls requesting his attendance in academic dress in time for the first Special Paper which would start at 9.30 am on Thursday 23 September. The dates and times of the other four Papers were also listed. There was no point in getting worried or nervous about it. He may have little or no chance of success, but come what may, he did have ten pages of pristine Romance text to work on for the next few years. He decided to enjoy the experience of the Examination, not be scared of it.

'You have a month or so to prepare,' she said.

'Minus two days: there's something I have to do before I begin.'

The P&O liner carrying migrants to Australia left Tilbury early in the afternoon. Lawless waited out of sight until he saw his uncle come to the passenger rail and scan the crowd on the quay below, obviously looking for him. Lawless shouted and waved like everyone else, wondering if he would be seen. It was Annie with the child in her arms who spotted him and called the others. As the tugs got to work, the ship began to edge away from the dockside and everyone waved their goodbyes, Annie lifting the child's hand for him to see. He watched until the ship stood well out in the river and he could see none of them any longer. He had two hours to catch his return train to Oxford and barely made it to Paddington on time. As the train left the station he realised with something of a shock that there was no one left of his family in England but him.

'Don't try to be too clever. They want to know if you know anything worth knowing and whether you can show that it is worth knowing—and another thing: that there will be more to come.'

'I've been thinking about the single word question paper.'

'Last year it was "Vulgarity". The year before there was a choice of three. There's no way of knowing what it will be. Some say it's a test of whether you can be entertaining at High Table or in the Common Room.'

'What do you suggest?'

'The same as for any examination: read the question carefully and write down the answer.'

On the reverse side of the envelope there was a small imprint of a yellow shield with a red chevron and three red five-petalled flowers. The letter inside invited him to attend for an interview with the Warden and Fellows at 8pm on Friday 29 October.

'Two vivas in one year,' he said when telling Winifred Smallwood of the letter.

'Well the last one didn't take very long. This one should be over in half an hour and they will be asking you some very pointed questions about what you wrote. Can you remember anything? We could do some of practising if you like.'

'I answered one that said "Why go to war?"I think I wrote quite a lot—which is odd because I can't remember anything about what I might have done.'

'Does that matter?'

'I think it must. I could have done terrible, questionable things.'

He was not asked about his answer to the question on war. He felt he handled one Fellow's querying of his views on the differences between Templar and Hospitaller administration in Provence quite well but was less certain of his dealing with another's criticism of his dismissal of the idea of a papal monarchy. Perhaps he went on too long about the vernacular in certain 14th Century texts but no one seemed to mind.

He received a letter with the same crest by special delivery the same evening. In it the Warden wrote that the College was glad to offer him an Examination Fellowship with a tenure of seven years and if he accepted, he would be elected Fellow on Monday 27 October.

'Well, congratulations, Philip. I never had the slightest doubt you would get there.'

'I could never have done it without your help.'

'Nonsense. I know that I can now pass on the torch. I see you as the next occupant of the Chair of Romance Philology which would be, let me see, yes in six year's time: just about right.'

'A stipend, rooms in college, membership of the Governing Body . . .'

'And access to the best wine cellar in Oxford. You'll be dining in for the first time after your election. That should be quite interesting for you. You will meet some rum characters. Now, we should celebrate your launch onto the choppy seas of academia.'

'I've brought this bottle of Blandys.'

'You're learning, Philip. Have you written yet to Jane? This could make a difference, you know.'

'I doubt it. Her work comes first. I should tell you: she said she would marry me when she has finished her PhD. Don't you approve? You don't look very pleased.'

Should she tell him now that it was impossible? Tell him about Séverine's letter and about the wife and child he had in France? No sudden shocks, that rather garrulous doctor had decreed. Give it time. When would be time enough?

'My being pleased or not is irrelevant. Her being on one side of the Atlantic and you on the other—and I am sure she will find the option of renewal of the Award irresistible—means you will see very little of each other. Your areas of work are similarly far apart.'

'Perhaps it's the distance between our research which brings us together.'

'There are other kinds of distance than that and the geographical.'

'I'm not quite sure what you mean.'

'I've said enough. This is no time to risk dispute. I see your glass is empty. Oh, I forgot: I didn't ask you about the one-word question. What was it?'

'Self-indulgence.'

***

In the Common Room after dinner, the Warden took Lawless to one side.

'Very glad you're now with us, Lawless. You're the only Prize Fellow this year, you know. Squadron Leader was it—your rank? DSO and DFC?'

'I was lucky, Warden.'

'Yes, I suppose that must have been part of it, but only a part. I wanted to tell you that I have a guest coming to dine on Sunday who says he knows you. In fact he tells me he was your CO: Smallwood, Air vice-marshal Sir Robert Smallwood. Of course, you know his sister, Winifred Smallwood, Principal of Granville.'

'She was my tutor, Warden and now my supervisor.'

'You're lucky again there, Lawless. She's the foremost scholar in her field. I hope you'll be dining in next Sunday. Now, we did find your analysis of the Hospitallers' acquisition of Templar possessions in the Gévaudan quite intriguing. Do you know what one of the Fellows said? He said it was almost as if you had personal experience of it: the time he meant. Now, what do you think of that?'

'I'm glad I was so convincing, Warden.'

'This is an unexpected pleasure, Robert.'

'I was coming up to dine in All Souls tomorrow but I got the news late last night and thought I'd tell you in person. Is there a guest room I could have?'

'You can stay in the Lodgings with me of course. What "news" are you talking about?'

'Things have been moving fast since the Brussels Treaty last March. The Americans are coming in, at least I hope to God they are, and I'm being sent as part of the delegation to Washington early next week. There's a real chance of an Atlantic treaty with them and Canada in if we can pull it off and that could mean another posting for me, possibly in Paris.'

'Should you be telling me this?'

'You're joking. It will be all over the papers soon, anyway.'

'Paris, eh? I can see why you're interested. Tell me more.'

'Later. I'd really rather like a drink. Have you any scotch?'

'Scotch? You really *are* interested.'

'I hear they've elected young Lawless to a Prize Fellowship. I imagine he'll be there on Sunday night.'

'Ah, in that case I must talk to you about him.'

Winifred Smallwood re-read the last paragraph of the aerogramme her brother had sent her from Washington just before Christmas.

> *'I met young Lawless at the All Souls dinner as I expected; just walked up to him and said hello. He looked all right, finding it a bit strange (who wouldn't in that place!) but starting to settle in. They've given him a pretty nice set of rooms overlooking the High. He showed me that old manuscript you mentioned; went on and on about it, in fact. I did as you said and never let on what I knew about France but I talked a bit about the Squadron and some of his chaps. He was very polite and listened but didn't say much except he had met one, Kendrick, his navigator who's over here somewhere. All the time I was talking he looked as if he was listening to a story about other people's lives, not his and I don't think he recognised me but there was one funny thing. When we met he lifted his arm as if he was going to salute me, then dropped it and shook my hand. What do you think of that, stirred a memory, or not? Worth telling that doctor of his?'*

Squashed in at the bottom of the single page of blue airmail-weight paper was a PS.

> *'Had a brief note from J I clean forgot to tell you about. Seems A isn't too well. They're completely in the dark about all this.'*

'J' and 'A': Justine and Alexandre; not the sort of news that she wanted to hear. Should she pass on the matter of the half-finished salute to Dr Hemming? He had asked her to let him know if anything significant happened. Perhaps it was purely a conditioned response, instilled by training. But then, it appeared that he hadn't been introduced to Robert by name, simply met him face to face and something inside him prompted him to start to salute. And there was Jane and the intended marriage and on top of all that he was just at the beginning of his research on the manuscript, in fact his whole academic career. Should that be put a risk? For the first time in her life—no, the second but that was long ago and still too painful to think about—Winifred Smallwood felt she was losing control.

***

'So . . . he saluted, or nearly did; how very interesting. But then he stopped halfway; even more interesting. A response—and a reaction to the response: something in the subconscious makes him acknowledge an authority and then something else immediately—not in the subconscious?—tells him his response is inappropriate. It is a connection between two circumstances, past and present and one of them must be some aspect of memory and one that can be connected only with the time in his life that concerns us.

'It seems very little to be going on with.'

'Nothing in this case is insignificant, Dr Smallwood.'

'Very well. Now what significance would you attach to his telling me he intends to be married? Not immediately I hasten to say, but in the not too-distant future.'

'Ah. I should say given what we know, that would pose a grave dilemma.'

'I take it he has not told you of this himself.'

'No indeed and I wonder why not. We do touch on matters of, what shall I say, relations between the sexes.'

'You need not be over-delicate with me, Dr Hemming. I may be unmarried but I am fully aware of the needs and behaviour of young men. The question is, what should be done about the "dilemma"? I should add I do have another contingent interest in the matter.'

'I can see no easy solution. It would be far better were there to be no marriage, no second marriage that is, but that appears unlikely.'

'There is just a possibility it might not happen—if certain predilections prevail.'

'I am not quite clear what it is that you . . .'

'A woman senses feelings a man may not. I think the young woman—despite her promises and what she may have done—may prove not to be the marrying kind.'

'I understand they will be apart for at least a year.'

'Time and opportunity to reflect—and chance, let us never forget that, chance of meeting others who make one realise the truth about oneself.'

'I see. He does speak warmly of yourself. Forgive me for asking this but I judge it to be relevant. How would you describe your relationship with Squadron Leader Lawless?'

'If I am to answer that I should expect what I say to remain confidential between ourselves.'

'Indeed; you have my assurance.'

'I should say that our acquaintance—which goes back some eight years—is normal and satisfactory in both academic and personal ways.'

'Thank you. You mentioned another "contingent interest".'

'By that I mean his work, his research. He is in possession of some unique material that in his hands will open up a radical new understanding of the subject. I expect him to produce an outstanding doctoral thesis that will form the basis of an OUP monograph that will remain the standard work indefinitely. It would be disastrous for scholarship if that were to be lost because of revelations of his past.'

'Scholarship or truth, Dr Smallwood?'

'Scholarship is truth, Dr Hemming.'

GERMANY 1949

In one of her aerogrammes Jane wrote that she had met Richard Kendrick again. It had been at a seminar when he queried something the speaker had said, and when his point was contested, went up to the blackboard and altered the terms in an equation that everyone including the speaker eventually agreed made it much more robust.

'After the seminar he came and introduced himself to me as another Cambridge mathematician. He said he knew you in the War but he wouldn't say anything else about you or what you both did. That makes two of you. He wouldn't say what he was doing over here either, only that what I was doing was very interesting. How he knew about my work I have no idea. All rather mysterious!

I'm going on a trip to Virginia with a friend of mine here. She's called Ainslie Anderson (hints she's descended from a Civil War General) and she's very well off and sporty. We play a lot of tennis on one of the indoor courts. You ought to try tennis. I'll be coming to Cambridge for the last two weeks of Easter Term, then it's back to Princeton (I'm renewed!) for the summer and Cambridge again for a short time in Michaelmas (it's called the Fall here). It's a way of keeping up my residence.

Hope your work's going well. How's Dr Smallwood?'

He would tell her when he replied that his work was proceeding very well and he was going to Heidelberg again to try out his ideas on the great Hoffmann. He had composed a 'communication' for publication and Dr Smallwood was going through it for him. She was in Paris at present staying with her brother who was something very important in the new Treaty thing. He was thinking the title for his communication could be something like 'Gender identification by textual analysis and graphology: some misconceptions': what did she think? He couldn't get the hang of tennis but he was in a cricket team, not for the College, a pub team: the Pheasant in Keble Road. It looked like being a good summer. And he missed her.

He saw her on only two days of the two weeks she spent in England in the Easter Term and as she was living in a College annexe there was no chance of spending a night with her. She had a lot of work to get through and visit her mother who was unwell, she said.

'Have you told her about me? And that we're going to get married?'

'About you? Yes, of course. She wants to meet you when she feels better.'

'I'd like that. What does she say about us getting married?'

'I haven't mentioned it to her yet.'

She told him all about her holiday with Ainslie, driving along the Blue Ridge and visiting Civil War battlefield sites in the Shenandoah Valley. She would have liked to stay in some of the campgrounds on the Blue Ridge, especially the one called Otter Creek because she liked the name, and sleep under the stars, but Ainslie insisted they drive down to the nearest town each night and stay in the best hotel and as she was paying for it all Jane didn't mind too much. They went as far as the Smoky Mountains where they saw a black bear one day and got ticks. Ainslie said they had to get into the shower together so they could pick them of each other's legs. Compared with her adventures Lawless had little to tell except that his visit to Heidelberg had been postponed.

'It means I'll be able to come and see you off at Southampton. I don't go until the day after.'

'Don't bother. You'll have too much to do getting ready yourself. Let me know if you meet up with Gisela.'

'Gisela?'

'You remember—Gisela Wolff, the girl I stayed with in Heidelberg? You met her at that concert.'

'Oh, yes—medical student, wasn't she? That was the first time I saw you.'

'And here we are. Life is odd, don't you think? Talking of which, you'll have to show me around All Souls one of these days.'

Hoffmann was not the stereotypical German Herr Doktor Professor, autocratic, remote, demanding complete silence in his lectures and having his own personal entrance to his department building. He was in fact rather jovial and informal, enjoying a joke—the more suggestive the better—and speaking impeccable English with the slight American accent he had acquired at Harvard during the war years.

'You want me to say what I think of your "communication", Herr Lawless? I think the time is fast coming when I shall have to ask you what you think of mine! Publish it! Tell Winifred I say so. She sometimes does what I suggest—not everything, you understand. She can act the very proper English lady, eh?

'Publish—after you have thought about that point I made, eh? Now, I know you have not much time left but I have been pondering, yes pondering your remark about line 56 in the Cabestany text which some fools suggest may be a forged insertion. I will not even say their names! You know who they are. I think you make an important point. Now what do you think of this?'

An hour later the Professor's telephone rang. After ignoring the first few rings he snatched up the receiver and barked 'Hoffmann!' His expression immediately changed and he listened in silence for about a minute before whispering,

'Tut mir Leid meine Leibling. Natürlich. Sofort.'

'My wife,' he said, looking rather apprehensive. 'I am late. I have forgotten her drinks party. I must go immediately. Excuse me.'

Lawless got up to leave. Hoffmann was already looking a little more cheerful.

'My respects to Winifred and to Leveson and Clayton in your College in Oxford but do not believe a word Andrews says. He is the worst kind of idiot because he does not know it. Auf Wiedersehen, Philip. Go out tonight. Drink some wine before you leave Heidelberg!'

Lawless had come to like standing on the old bridge over the river, just to look down at the clear water slowly swirling under the arches or up at the red-walled castle on the hillside surrounded by dense green woods.

'Lawless, Philip!'

'He turned at the sound of the woman's voice.

'Ah, so it is you. You remember me?'

'Fräulein Gisela Wolff; guten Abend.'

'Good evening, Herr Lawless. We will speak English so I can learn more. You are again in Heidelberg.'

'Yes. I have been working with Professor Hoffmann and tomorrow I return to England.'

'Good. I am glad.'

'Glad because I am going?'

'Of course, no! Glad because you have time to come to my house tonight where we have a little party of some friends. Yes?'

'Yes. Now I am glad also.'

'I will write the address,' Gisela Wolff said, taking a small pad from her bag. 'You must come at, let me think, yes: nine of clock.'

'Shall I bring a bottle of wine?'

'Of course no. We have many bottles of wine and some beer also.'

The house was in a rather run-down part of the city where many students had lodgings. Lawless could hear the music as soon as he turned into the street. He banged on the door several times without any result so pushed it open and forced his way in. It was the sort of party that he remembered from his first year at Oxford; crowded room, dim lights, drifting wreaths of cigarette smoke, loud Dixieland music competing with a confused babble of voices male and female and alcohol flowing freely everywhere you looked. Someone thrust an opened bottle of Löwenbräu into his hand and shouted something that he could not hear let alone understand. Drinking from the bottle he looked round, peering through the smoke to see if Gisela Wolff was there. A tall girl with short-cropped blond hair and very red lips wormed her way towards him and put her arms round his neck, closed her eyes and puckered her lips.

'Wo ist Gisela?'

The girl opened her eyes, looked at him reproachfully and pointed across the room. Before he could move she kissed him hard on both cheeks and turned away. Lawless pushed his way through the crush. Every girl seemed to be fair-haired. He tapped the nearest one on her back. When she turned he thought it was Gisela but could not be sure because of the heavy make-up and low-cut black dress, quite unlike her usual appearance.

'Very good. You find us,' she shouted above the din. She looked at him closer and laughed. 'Ah, you have found Gabi! I think she likes you.'

He put his hand to his cheek. It came away smeared with bright red lipstick. He fumbled for a handkerchief, but Gisela stopped him.

'No, no. She will kiss again if you take off. Come.'

She pulled him by the hand through the crowd and into a kitchen, pushing aside a couple clasping each other in a tight and noisy embrace. She took the beer bottle from him and poured him a tumbler full of pale yellow wine from a large jug.

'Now we drink together good wine,' she laughed, pouring a second glass for herself. 'Skol!'

'Cheers!'

'Yes. Cheers. Drink all and take one more. We begin long before you come.'

The wine was quite sweet and very strong. Remembering parties with medical students in Oxford he suspected something powerful from a laboratory might have been added to it. Be careful, Lawless, he thought; you haven't eaten since lunchtime. Did she read his mind?

'Here is bread and some sausage if you want.'
He ate the few crusts and scraps left as she watched him and talked.
'Jane writes sometimes letters to me from America. You see her?'
'Not long ago. I saw her twice in Cambridge.'
'Not many times, Philip. I call you Philip? Yes.'
'Yes, please do. I wish I saw more of her. She likes you, I know.'
'Yes, we like and she also like this girl in America.'
'Ainslie? Yes, she tells me about her. They went on holiday together.'
'Yes, she tells me many things. They live in one apartment.'
'Oh, I didn't know that.'
'Like me here. Gabi is with me.'
'That must be fun . . .'
'Listen, the music. I like this one. Come, we will dance. Bring your wine.'

Dancing, if it could be called that in such a dimly lit crush, meant being very close to the one whom you held on to and from time to time finding it was someone else you were holding and not infrequently holding up, until as happened you eventually found the one you had started with. And by then several more glasses of the insidiously strong wine had been drunk and all kinds of questions had been asked and all kinds of suggestions had been whispered into not always unresponsive ears. Gisela's face appeared mistily in front of him, saying something.

'Philip, Philip. You will play us the piano. I know you can play. Play now.'

He felt himself being pulled across the room. There seemed to be fewer people now but it was still not easy to find the way. Hands pushed him down onto a chair and he found a piano keyboard in front of him. He could not think of a single thing to play so took a long swallow of wine from a glass someone held to his mouth and began to improvise, running his fingers up and down the keys. It seemed to work and after rippling through chords and arpeggios in different keys, mainly minor, he played some rags that came automatically to his hands, what little Dixieland he remembered and finally settled down to the blues. He felt rather than saw the faces looking down at him from behind the piano and the dancers behind him shuffling slowly round the room. He didn't know how long he went on or how late it became. He was completely absorbed in his playing and the last wine tumbler stood untasted on the piano top until finally he felt a hand on his shoulder. It was Gisela's.

'All have gone now, Philip. Some sleep on our floor. It is now too late for you to go. You are not German so police can arrest you in the street at night. You stay with us, Gabi and me.'

'God, what time is it? I have to catch a train at ten.'

'We will wake you with the clock. Come now.'

He backed hurriedly out of the room when he saw Gabi standing in front of a long mirror wearing nothing but her stockings.

'Christ, sorry!'

'No, no, Philip; go in here. We have only this one bedroom. '

In the morning after a hurried cup of coffee, Gisela walked with him along the street to see set him in the right direction.

'Er, Gisela, you won't say anything to Jane about us last night, will you?'

'No, Philip and Gabi will not. Do not fear. But I think Jane is not angry.'

'You cannot know that.'

'Oh yes. I know Jane, Philip. We feel last night much scarring on your back and Gabi see a penetration wound of your leg. She thinks you were a soldier in burning tank. Is so?'

'Something like that; a long time ago, I think.'

'You go this street now. Auf Weidersehen bis zum nächsten Mal.'

ENGLAND 1951, 1952

WINTER JASMINE

In August of 1951 Jane wrote to Lawless saying she had submitted her thesis and hoped to have her viva before Christmas. Lawless replied saying that he still had a long way to go with his. They agreed to take a few days holiday together and found a Bed and Breakfast place with a weekend free near Cromer on the Norfolk coast. As expected they had to take separate rooms. After breakfast they walked along the shore to Sheringham and took the old train as far as a halt on the Heath and wandered along the paths and through the heather and bracken trying to identify the flowers and birds and eventually finding a hidden little patch of long grass among the heather where they could sit and eat their sandwiches.

It was a hot still afternoon with the air full of the sound of bees and she put her hands palms down at her sides and leaned her head back with her eyes closed, letting her hair fall down and the sunlight fall on her face and neck. He could not resist cupping her breast with his hand and pressing his lips to her throat.

'Philip, please, no.'

She didn't seem angry, only rather sad he thought.

'I wanted to make love to you. I still do.'

'I want us to wait.'

'How long? I don't know if I can.'

'Until we're married.'

'But that's such a long time away, Jane.'

'As soon as my thesis is accepted. That's what we agreed. Three months, four at the most: is that too much to ask?'

'It's been three years already, Jane.'

'Then three more months doesn't seem so long, does it?'

'It makes me wonder sometimes if we will ever be married.'

'I gave my promise, Philip, and we agreed.'

''We agreed, we agreed'; I *know* we agreed! What I don't understand is that you let me make love to you once and I must wait for years until the next time. Why? And, please don't say "we agreed" again.'

'I've had a lot of time to think.'

'And what conclusion did you come too?'

'That I do like you and I will keep my promise and you have some butter on the end of your nose.'

She smiled and then laughed out loud. 'And now your mouth's wide open and a bee is about to fly in.'

He knew that she was running away from the argument and he knew he was too weak to stop her, to tell her to hell with it: it's over and let's go home but he couldn't because, blast it, they had agreed. He struggled to say something but she was still laughing, knowing she had him confused and helpless.

'Let's talk about something else. Tell me about Heidelberg. Did you see Gisela?'

He had a wild urge to tell her yes, he had seen Gisela, all of her, and all of Gabi as well and made love to them both, one after the other in the same bed and what did she think of that? But what he said was,

'Only once. She invited me to her flat with a few friends and we had some nice wine. I was leaving the next day. She sends her love.'

***

He was standing at the window looking down into the High as he usually did when trying to shape the precise phrase he needed when the telephone rang.

'Philip, it's me! It's over, the viva and I've passed! I've just come out. I'm so relieved. They want me make only one tiny little alteration. I'm not sure they're right but I didn't want to argue. So it's done!'

'Jane love, that's marvellous. Congratulations. Are you . . .'

'I'm coming to Oxford tomorrow. Where will you be? I'll tell you all about it.'

She sounded very excited, almost breathless.

'Tell me when your train gets in. I'll meet you at the station.'

'11.32. Wait . . . ' he heard the sound of women's voices . . .'have to go. Some friends have come with a bottle . . . 'bye . . . see you tomorrow.'

He wasn't expecting her to fling her arms round him and hug him tightly, but she did in front of everybody on the platform and then chattered all the way to the College in the taxi about who the examiners were and how serious they looked at first and that was only pretence, because almost straightaway they said she had nothing to worry about and all they wanted to do was ask her a few questions and she was in there for only an hour and mostly it was about what she was going to do next and where she should publish, and on and on . . .

'Philip, what a lovely room. You are lucky. Look down there: you can see all the way up and down the street. You need some flowers in here.'

'Would you like a drink? I've got a bottle of champagne. The wine steward says it's very good.'

'Hm, yes please. Thank you, Philip. You are very good to me.'

'Here's to you and the great thesis. Have you got it there? Can I see it?'

He looked at the title in gilt letters on the front cover. The only parts he recognised were the words 'probabilities' and 'amplitudes' and the rest was a mystery to him. He turned over some of the pages. There were very few words other than, 'let us assume', 'then', 'it follows' and line after numbered line of equations.

'I'll read it later,' he said, smiling. It's very short, fifty pages. Shouldn't take me long. Mine looks like going into two volumes; if I ever get it finished. A refill? Then we'll go out for lunch at the Mitre. It's just up the street.'

'Why not here?'

'This is All Souls: ladies, you know. I told the porter you were my cousin.'

'Philip! I would never have thought it of you.'

'I'm full of surprises. Just you wait.'

'I can't wait. I'm absolutely starving.'

They had roast chicken and potatoes and sprouts which Lawless didn't like so Jane ate them. There was ice cream with the apple pie that followed.

'I've found somewhere for you to stay,' he said.

'Oh, Philip, I can't—I have to go after lunch. I'm being met at the station at three. It's about my job. I have to go to a meeting, a sort of interview I think.'

'I didn't know you had a job'

'I didn't want to tell you until it was certain. It sounds very interesting. I'll be working mainly in London but going to other places now and again. One of them is near Oxford. Might even get a chance to go to the States again.'

'What about? . . .'

'I know what you're going to say and the answer is yes, we can get married now.'

'Oh Jane, sweetheart. I want to kiss you.'

'Here? In the restaurant?'

'Yes, why not?' He leaned over the table and touched her lips with his. 'When?'

'When you like.'

'No, when you like. Say a date.'

'Twenty third of January,' she said, as if at random.

'Twenty third it is. Where?'

'My mother wants it to be where she lives.'

'That's fine by me but there's something I have to tell you. Do you mind if we keep it a secret? I'm not at all sure the College would approve.'

'I thought there would be something like that but I don't mind. No one will know until we're ready to tell them—except my mother and the Registrar, of course and a witness.'

'A Registry wedding? You don't mind not having a long white dress and bridesmaids and walking up the aisle?'

'Too expensive and too much fuss. No, all I want is a nice bright frosty January day.'

'And me?'

'Yes, you can come as well. Heavens, look at the time! I have to fly.'

A black car was waiting for her outside the station. She waved from the rear window as it drove away and turned right to take the Botley Road west out of Oxford. He had thought that she would be taking the London train.

***

Winifred Smallwood hoped that the relief which she felt when Lawless told her that the marriage would be kept secret did not show in her face.

'I suppose I must congratulate you, Philip and we should celebrate, though not with madeira on this occasion, do you think?'

They drank the single malt that she normally reserved for her brother's visits.

'Now, the problem is, where will you live? The College is out of the question and it would be a pity to move out when your rooms are so convenient for your work.'

'Well, she has this job in London and it involves quite a bit of travel as well. We thought that she should find a flat and I could stay there from time to time. It's not ideal but it's the best we can come up with. After I finish the DPhil we can think of something else.'

'I'd say that you have at least another year before that can happen.'

'I was thinking two. I don't want to rush anything. Hoffmann's sent me some new stuff that will take a lot of going through. I might have to do some rewriting. I'll show you later.'

'Perhaps it's for the best that you're not together all the time. You can have your marriage but also both of you can get on with your work undisturbed. Now, so that I do not inadvertently let any cats out of bags, I intend to forget everything you have told me and not even ask where and when. Show me what Hoffmann has sent you.'

When he had gone she sat and wondered whether she should give Dr Hemming a call. She decided to leave things as they were.

***

The old man who tended to her mother's garden acted as witness at the Registry Office. Jane carried a small posy of winter jasmine. Lawless had a sprig of the same in his buttonhole. The ceremony lasted only a few minutes and afterwards they went back to her mother's house for tea before catching the train to Ely for the one night of honeymoon that was all Jane's imminent departure for America could allow.

It had been too long a wait, too much anticipation, too much expectation on his part; too much apprehension, perhaps, on hers. It was a deed that each knew had to be done but hardly an act of love. Afterwards she lay close to him and he liked that and eventually they fell asleep.

They got up late and had a leisurely breakfast. He had thought it might be awkward but she talked away about Cambridge and the papers she was writing from the thesis and the new job.

'What will you be working on?'

'Partial differential equations of very high pressure variation systems.'

'Sounds very interesting. Is it about explosions?'

'Why did you say that?'

'No real reason. I had to say something or you might think I was completely stupid. It's an old Oxford trick.'

She laughed. 'I'm annoyed it worked on me. Tell me about yours.'

'A woman's hand.'

'I know you're working on some old manuscript. Is it to do with that?'

He nodded.

'Well, which hand is it: left or right?'

'You know, that's a very good point. I never thought of that. We should live together, don't you think? We could help with each other's work if nothing else.'

'Yes, let's,' she laughed, 'but now we have to go. The London train leaves at 11.25, remember?'

'I wish I was coming with you, he said as she leaned out of the window. Take care of yourself.'

She leaned further out to kiss him. 'When I come back,' she whispered, 'I'll try harder, I promise.'

'Don't try, love, just let yourself go.'

ENGLAND 1954

ACKNOWLEDGMENT

Winifred Smallwood looked out of the window. It was late afternoon in November and already almost dark outside. Lights were coming on in undergraduates' rooms all round the quad. Lawless would soon be arriving for tea. He had said he had something to tell her and she had an idea of what it might be. She hoped he would not be late, especially this time. The envelope with the French postmark and the handwriting which she remembered so well lay open on her desk in front of her. She picked up the single page and began to read for the third time.

> *My dear Winifred*
>
> *I expect I shall be dead when you read this, my last letter to you. The doctors have finally given up on me, washed their hands literally and metaphorically. Of course, there never could be any cure but they have to keep up appearances. I should not complain. I have had the most tender care from my niece and the young women and, naturally, from Justine, especially when the news of Thierry came at last.*
>
> *As I write, I am sitting in my library surrounded by my old friends, my books. Some, too many, I have not yet read, nor will I now. Life has proved too short as it always does. But I find comfort in knowing that my most precious possession—among my books—has inspired what you say will be the masterpiece that I once hoped I would create.*
>
> *I have faithfully followed your wish not to reveal what became of my son-in-law, neither where he is, nor what he has become, trusting that for the time being it is the better course. The pain has lessened, though not passed. I doubt if ever it will pass but the boy is a fine boy with a likeness to his father and that is great comfort to his mother. The girl will be a beauty—is already—and entrances audiences with her playing. I have made sure they will lack nothing and the schoolmaster is now part of the household which is of benefit to the education of the young and perhaps in other ways to my niece.*
>
> *I am becoming very tired and writing exhausts me, but I must say one thing more. After being too long apart because of my foolishness and deceit we came together again, my very dearest Winifred, in the cause of France. Believe me when I say that for me it was also the rediscovery of our love.*
>
> *Now, like the English poet all I can hope for is to cease upon the midnight with no pain but to the end I will always suffer from the pain of the pain that I caused you.*
>
> *Alexandre*

She still had his very first letter and all the others that followed and every time save once he had written in English while her replies were in French but now, at the end, as with the first, he chose French because he felt for her as he had that first time.

The beautiful girl who played so well: who could that be? The Jewish girl they had sheltered; she played the piano. Of course, it must be her.

She recognised Lawless's knock on the door and put the letter down.

He embraced her as he had been permitted to do for some time now.

'You were expecting me, weren't you?'

'Yes, why do you ask?'

'Nothing, it's just that you looked as if you were far away. Did I disturb you?'

'Just a letter from an old friend.'

'From France, I see. Anyone I know? Sorry, I shouldn't ask.'

'It's from your benefactor, the one who sent the text.'

'Well, when you hear what I have to say you'll tell me it's time to write and thank whoever he or she is.'

'I think the wish for anonymity will remain.'

'Are you sure? Well, you know best. I hope I will find out one day. Now, look: my thesis, two volumes of it. These are for you. I have one set and the other two have been sent to the Clerk of the Schools for the Examiners. I can't tell you how I feel, free in a way but starting to worry.'

'I can understand. I am unsure as to how I feel myself at this moment.'

'You know, everything I have done I owe to you.'

'Be anything but humble, Philip. It is unbecoming a scholar.'

'Oh. Well, in that case may I simply say thank you and then we can have tea and after that I'll think of some other way to express my gratitude and respect.'

'Nor does pomposity, Philip, even when assumed. I seem to have run out of tea.'

'Madeira would do, if you have any.'

As she was refilling the glasses she asked him when he had last seen Jane.

'In September. She was over for a few days, mostly in Cambridge but we did have two nights together in the London flat.'

'And before that?'

'Let me think, it was just before she went to America again. She was working at that place near Reading, she told me. It seems to be one of those secret Government places, so she can't say much about what she does there. 'Calculations' is all she says when I ask her. I would have been a bit fed up at not seeing much of her except it was during that time when I got completely bogged down and had to come crawling to you for help. Do you remember?'

'I remember. Philip, how many times and days have you and Jane been together since you were married?'

'Ten, maybe twelve days altogether, I'd say.'

'Ten or twelve days in two years; you can hardly know each other.'

'We do write quite often, tell each other what we're doing. When I say ten or twelve times together I mean with each other, in the flat or somewhere. But I *see* her more than that when she's here, in the day.' He paused and looked at her. 'No, you're right, it's not very much is it? But we have been very busy, both of us.'

His voice trailed off. He looked down at his glass, crestfallen, puzzled.

'Philip, look at me. Is all as it should be between you two? You know what I mean, don't you?'

‘Of course! Yes, it is.’ he fell silent, closing his eyes and clenching his fists. ‘No, it isn’t. I don’t know what I’m doing wrong,’ he muttered looking down at the floor.

‘Have you told her? What does she say?’

‘I’ve tried. Perhaps I say the wrong things, misread her mood; want too much, want her too much. I ask her if there’s anything wrong, have I upset her or been too demanding and she says no and she does like me and likes being with me and talking and telling stories and . . .’

He stopped again, shaking his head and looking anxious and bewildered, not meeting her look.

‘But not really wanting you to make love to her, is that it? Makes excuses, says not now but later and then there’s another reason not to? Is that what she does?’

‘No! Well, yes, sometimes.’

‘Most of the times?’

‘No! All right, yes. We have made love—once, but, oh, I don’t know, it seems as if she’s only letting me, not wanting me. Do you think I should ask her if there’s something wrong with me, or with her? Would it be an idea to see a doctor? A woman doctor?’

‘That is the last thing you should suggest.’

‘I do like her, you know; I love her and I know she likes me. She says she does . . .’

‘Usually when you suggest something more?’

‘You seem to know more about her than I do.’

‘I think I do, Philip. You haven’t noticed the several times I have tried to imply that marriage to Jane might not be the thing for you, or for her. Heaven forbid, I don’t want to sound superior or patronising but most men, especially young men, do not see or worse, refuse to accept the message that certain women are sending out. I am going to put this rather bluntly because each of you has gifts that are too precious to risk losing through misunderstanding. No, listen to what I have to say and then you can storm out and refuse to see me ever again if you wish. Jane does like you, I am sure of that. If she did not, she would never have suffered your company in the first place. You yourself said that it was distance that brought you closer together. It was a nice conceit but with more truth in it than you knew. The closeness is because you like each other, respect each other’s abilities, enjoy each other’s company. The distance is between your emotions; to put it plainly, your sexuality.’

‘I don’t want to lose her. What am I to do?’

‘It is not simply up to you. The two of you must be open with each other. If you both want this marriage to continue, it can work, but not in the way our society claims to be conventional. The French have a name for it. You must have heard, or at least read of le mariage blanc. If you wish to keep Jane that is what you should accept.’

‘When I first asked her, why didn’t she say no? I would have accepted that.’

‘I wonder if you would have. You can be very appealing, Philip. Very few women would want to disappoint you.’

She watched him thinking, more than once seeming about to say something and then deciding against. She waited.

‘I do want us to last. There are so many things that we like doing together. Perhaps I, perhaps we should do as you say. It’s just . . . it’s whether I can stick to it. I don’t know. I thought she might change as we got to know each other better, but it hasn’t happened. Now, after listening to you, I can see that that part of us won’t, can’t change.’ He looked up at her with an expression that was almost pleading. 'But I want it. I can't help that. What can I do? It's how I am.'

'I know that. You should not feel ashamed. What can you do? I will tell you. You will say to Jane what you have just said to me and she will understand. And in time you will go on finding fulfilment of that side of your life elsewhere. And she will understand that too, sooner or later, because she will be feeling the same herself.'

'Isn't that deception?'

She could see that her point had struck home but he was still struggling with it, looking for difficulties.

'Not if you both have decided that is how it shall be. We are not talking about infidelity, Philip. We are talking about acknowledgment. I have said all that I have to say on the matter. It is for you to decide. Now, shall we turn a few pages?'

***

Lawless knew the stories of the theses that had been accepted virtually unchanged for publication as monographs by the University Press and the old joke that the most distinguished monograph was one that sold not a single copy. For him his thesis was hardly more than an entrance to the subject. There was infinitely more waiting to be discovered and distilled into what he already had in mind: the definitive work. There were two years of his All Souls Fellowship to run: perhaps enough to compile the first two volumes. That would be his target. Target? Was that a suitable word to choose? First, there were papers, communications to write. Winifred Smallwood had suggested three at least from the thesis.

'The spectacular does not impress all examiners,' she said. 'Some suspect it of showing off. But both of yours must have seized on it, judging by what you say. I think that it must have particularly attracted Hoffmann—I was relieved when the Board supported his nomination; there can still be difficulties with securing visas for Germans—and Tyndale surprised me with his approval. It verged on the enthusiastic. Perhaps Hoffmann played a hand there.'

'He can be very persuasive. There was one point where Professor Tyndale made some remark and Professor Hoffmann demurred and they went at it like dogs over a bone, completely ignoring me. I just sat back and watched.'

'And did you listen?'

'It wasn't easy but I did catch some of it. I think they agreed to a draw and turned again to me. What I really want is your opinion.'

'On the text and what your interpretation means? Your proof of a female hand in the dialogue is as clear and convincing as checkmate in chess. It may have been suspected before—if so I do not know where—but you are the first to identify it. Remarkable, a woman poet writing in what is clearly correspondence with one of the monks, in the precinct of one of the houses and with a passion that almost burns the words. Remarkable, perhaps most interestingly in how much it reveals of your own understanding of women.'

'I can't believe that. They are a mystery to me. What I really want to do is identify her. I am sure I am right about her being left-handed. The handwriting experts weren't a lot of use because they knew nothing about Fourteenth Century script but Sinclair was, you know, the palaeographer at King's. I've got an idea that her name is in the text and so is his—and I think he's her lover—and there must be clues. I'm just not seeing them. It's like a code.'

'Have you thought of asking Jane? She knows a lot about the right sort of mathematics.'

'Do you think so?'

'Without a doubt. I used to know mathematicians in that field, cryptanalysis. Put the problem to her.'

'You know it was she who put me on to the left handedness?'

'Well, you rightly acknowledged it. How are things between you these days?'

'Could hardly be better; I think you know what I mean. She's in London for a month. I go at weekends.'

'I am very pleased. I thought there were fewer lines on you forehead.'

'It's turning out as you said that it might. She's told me about this friend of hers in America, Ainslie something, er, yes, Ainslie Anderson and I don't mind. I would never have believed it but I don't mind. There's a chance she may be coming over. I'm quite intrigued to meet her.'

'And what about yourself?'

'Do I need to say?'

'Not if you don't want to but I suspect even the search for the Fourteenth Century mystery woman will not take up all of your time.'

'You know me so well, don't you?'

'Can one ever say that about anyone? What do you know about me, for example, Philip?'

'Well, for a start I know you are quite fond of Madeira.'

ENGLAND, FRANCE 1956

A FRENCH WEDDING

'It's gone: the whole manuscript. I've just taken it along to the Press and handed it in. God, what a relief to see the back of it! I feel like a drink.'

'Come round,' Winifred Smallwood said. 'I have an hour free between meetings,' and put down the receiver.

'Congratulating you is becoming a habit with me. Here's success to Volume One. Knowing you, I expect you've already started on Volume Two.'

'Thank you. Mm, this is very good. What is it?'

'Condrieu. My brother sent me a rather extravagant present.'

'I've brought a copy of the dedication page.'

This entire work is dedicated to Winifred Smallwood, Principal of Granville College, Oxford, without whose constant guidance, scholarship and friendship it could never have been undertaken, let alone achieved

'They say it will take at least a year. You will have the first copy.'

'I am touched. If the Press meets its promise it will come out just at the right time.'

'You mean at the end of my Fellowship?'

'That too, but more importantly in time for the Electors for the Chair to meet with Volume One available to them.'

'You're not serious, are you? I'll only be 36. There are far more senior people than me.'

'Your only serious competitors are Tyndale and Hoffmann. Tyndale is too old and Hoffmann would never leave Heidelberg. I should not be surprised if the Electors simply offer you the Chair.'

'Professor of Romance Philology: I suppose you have to give lectures.'

'Twenty or so a year, I should say; hardly a back-breaking duty. There's an inaugural, of course. You might think of using the search for the mystery woman poet, if you and Jane have tracked her down yet. Have you?'

'Getting close—oh, I have to tell you: her mother died last week and her funeral is on Monday. I'll be going with her of course.'

'Please give her my condolences. Has she now taken up that permanent post with the Ministry?'

'The week after next. She will be staying at the Atomic Energy Research Establishment where she's been off and on for what seems years now. They have accommodation there; pretty basic, but at least it's something. We have our minds on a place in Oxford for us both to live after my Fellowship ends. I'll have to look for a job. I can't just live off her.'

'I must not be late for my meeting, Philip.'

'I'm sorry. I'm going on a bit. When can I see you again? I want to go through the comments you made on the syntax paper.'

'I'm away for a few days after the end of Term. I'll be in touch.'

Winifred Smallwood made a mental note to ask her secretary if all the travel arrangements for going to Paris had been confirmed and picked up her papers for the Tutorial Committee meeting.

Robert Smallwood had waited for what he judged to be a reasonable period after Alexandre Chevalier's death before he made the journey alone from Paris to Castelbouc to propose to Justine Lamphier. She asked him to allow her twenty four hours to decide her answer. They had dinner together and he slept alone in one of the guest rooms that looked out over the river. He set out for Paris early in the morning, planning to arrive there in time for her telephone call.

'All you have to do is say yes, or no,' he said.

Two days later he wrote to his sister with what he considered to be the good news.

> *. . . and she has said yes. I fell in love with her the first time that I saw her in Paris in 1914 when she was newly married to Christophe. We spent one weekend together before I was sent to the Front and I did not see her again until the end of the War when she told me for the first time of the child she lost, our child. I think you know my feelings for her have never changed, not even when she chose Alexandre rather than me after Christophe died but of course I could do nothing about it until now.*
>
> *My posting at SHAPE Headquarters has been confirmed and my role will be as much diplomatic as military. I am sure that you will agree she will make the most wonderful hostess there but that is incidental. What is infinitely more important to me is that I, and I hope she, may spend the years left to us rediscovering the love we first found so many years ago.*
>
> *Knowing of your own attachment to Alexandre, I hesitate to ask you to be present at our wedding but I hope you will agree to come and be one of the witnesses. It will be a very small and private affair in the Mairie of the village where a house was provided for me at the time of my appointment. If you do come I will arrange to have you met in Paris and driven there.*
>
> *Please do come, Winifred. Justine wants this as much as I do. In fact she suggested it before I had the chance to say.*
>
> *Your loving brother*
>
> *Robert*

The letter was handwritten and the envelope bore the postmark of a commune she later found out was on the Seine south of Fontainebleau.

The mayor wore his smartest suit and freshly pressed sash and was on his best official behaviour at the brief ceremony, conscious of the considerable honour of officiating at the marriage of an obviously very senior officer—was he not always accompanied by a uniformed driver and a young lieutenant, present here in civilian dress? And to such a beautiful aristocratic French lady. And the other imposing lady, the officer's sister, as beautiful in her own way, spoke to him in impeccable French without the slightest hint of English accent. The postmaster and the schoolteacher had both been eager to stand as witnesses. The mayor had prudently sought the schoolteacher's advice on the pronunciation of English names.

'Monsieur Robert Smallwood, prenez-vous pour épouse, Madame Justine Lamphier?'

They returned to the house to drink toasts in champagne and as Robert Smallwood was refilling the glasses his aide came in to say HQ was on the line.

'It can be hours when that happens,' Justine said. 'Bring your glass with yourself if you wish, Winifred and we will take a little walk by the river.'

'Did I see a Gendarmerie car go past on the road a moment ago?'

'Yes, they have regular patrols and there are others we do not see. We are under constant surveillance, Winifred. But you and I are both used to that, in our different ways, are we not?'

'I have left that world, Justine.'

'Can one ever leave such a world? The past always beckons to one out of the shadows. Do you know why I asked Robert to give me twenty four hours to make up my mind about whether to marry him or not? It was not that I lacked the desire. It was because of you. I wondered if you would see me as again taking from you someone who was very dear to you.'

'And what made you decide to accept him nevertheless?'

'I did so because I love him and also because in a way you had taken someone whom I held very dear away from me. I read Alexandre's letter to you, Winifred. He showed it to me before he sealed the envelope. At the end he loved you as he did at the beginning. So, we are the same, you and I.'

'I realise now why I came, Justine. But I am left without Alexandre and you have Robert.'

'He will always be your brother, Winifred. That will never change and I am glad. And think of this: you have our young sergeant with whom I did fall in love.'

'Philip? Did Robert tell you this?'

'Of course not: he did not have to say anything. I can tell, Winifred.'

'Shall I tell you something, Justine? I wish you had been on my staff in those dangerous times.'

'Then we are friends? Yes? Embrace me, Winifred. We can weep together.'

They turned back in the direction of the house.

'Robert has said nothing to me about Philippe. What can you tell me about that young man?'

'Nothing, I am afraid, that would not cause greater distress to those who have waited for him to return to them but I will tell you this—and it is only for you to know. He was so gravely injured when his aircraft crashed and burned that he was never expected to survive. He did survive but remained unconscious for almost three years. After he woke from the coma he quite quickly regained his physical strength but . . .'

'Please do not tell me that his mind has gone.'

'Not his mind: his memory; he remembers nothing of the War; nothing; not his comrades, not his actions, not his time in France, not his escape, not his return to England. And, I am deeply sorry to tell you this: neither you nor any member of the family nor comrades he left behind. The gap in his memory is remarkably precise. It encompasses only the part of the War in which he served. We know this because he remembers me as his tutor before the War and again from the time when I visited him in his convalescence.'

'It is inconceivable.'

'It is true. He has become a great scholar and will be greater but the gap in his memory of those times is profound and as far as the doctor who attends him can perceive it is permanent.'

'What can be done?'

'It is the hardest thing to ask but I beg you to say and do nothing. He would not know you if he saw you. He did not recognise Robert who was his Commanding Officer, nor the closest of his comrades. Think what the same reaction might do to others who have been close to him. Think what such a confrontation would do to him, what guilt it would ignite in him. Let all their lives continue in the refashioned way they are. Only he could restore what once was and he cannot do that without his memory being restored. And there is no prospect of such a miracle.'

'But if it should happen, what then, Winifred?'

'Then I have not the slightest doubt that he would put everything else behind him and he would return to you all.'

'What little faith I had disappeared in that First War but I think I will try a small prayer and see if anyone listens.'

'And is that all you will do?'

'Yes. You have persuaded me. I have enough sorrow. There is no room for more.'

ENGLAND 1957

THE CHAIR

The tall urbane looking man in the casual but impeccably cut dark tweed suit came towards him to shake his hand as Lawless was ushered into the Vice Chancellor's office in the Clarendon Building.

'So good of you to come, Dr Lawless. Please sit down would you?'

'Thank you, Vice Chancellor.'

They looked at each other across the wide expanse of a mahogany desk. The Vice Chancellor's gaze was amiable but keen.

'I have been looking through the first volume of your Monograph. We had it on the table at the last meeting of the Delegates of the Press—I chair the meetings, as you know. Sales have been good, very good for a monograph. The second volume is in press, the Secretary said. There's even been a rumour that you're thinking of a Dictionary. You seem to write remarkably quickly, if I may say so.'

'I think it will be quite some time before the next volume is ready, Vice Chancellor. As to a Dictionary that would be a very long term undertaking but one is needed.'

'Quite. I was interested to see a section by Winifred Smallwood in the first volume.'

'She is the authority in that particular field, Vice Chancellor—and in many others.'

'You know she has just been made a Fellow of the Academy?'

'I saw the announcement. One might say "at last".'

'Yes, yes. Well, to business. You are no doubt aware that the Chair of Romance Philology has fallen vacant by reason of retirement. The Electoral Board met last week under my chairmanship and came to a decision. I am authorised to advise you that the Board is minded to offer you the Chair. Before the offer could be made official it is important for me to be able to report to the Electors that you would accept it. You may have a week to consider.'

'I do not need time to consider, Vice Chancellor. I am honoured that the Electors should consider me suitable and I will accept their offer as soon as it is made.'

'Excellent. I shall report back without delay. You must be thinking this is timely: I understand your Fellowship along the road terminates at the end of Term.'

'I think I must be very lucky, Vice-Chancellor.'

'Not lucky, Lawless: worthy. You wouldn't have been asked otherwise. Unless you haven't already done so, you can read up the duties in the Statutes but they will be enclosed with the letter of election, of course. One of them is an inaugural. Any ideas of a topic—off the top of your head, of course; wouldn't keep you to it.'

'Hm. "The Dark Lady of the Text"?'

'Sounds a bit Shakespearian. Sonnets 127 to 152, I seem to remember.'

'You mean it's been done before? That is a pity.'

They both laughed and the Vice Chancellor went to open the door and ask his secretary to bring in some coffee.

'The prospect of being back in your old College as Professorial Fellow must please you.'

'Oh yes. They were vey good to me as a DPhil student. I wouldn't have been able to work in Heidelberg without their help.'

'Heidelberg: lovely place. I know Freiburg better; spent a few years there. That was a while ago. They turn out a good side at cricket; Beaumont College I mean, not Freiburg. Do you play?'

'When I've had the time.'

'Perhaps we shall face each other on a wicket one day.'

'You play at a much higher level than I do, Vice Chancellor.'

'No need for flattery, Lawless. The offer's been made.'

***

Lawless decided to leave telling Jane about the Professorship until after her mother's funeral, thinking it might help dispel some of the sadness that he knew she was feeling. The service was in the little church of the village a few miles from Cambridge where Dorothy Carstairs had lived the last forty years of her life after her husband died leaving her to bring up Jane on her own. There were no other relatives present. Like her daughter, Jane's mother had been an only child and her father's only brother had been killed in Flanders before his nineteenth birthday. Apart from Jane and Lawless the only mourners were a handful of people from the village who had been her mother's friends.

After the burial in the churchyard they stood near the grave for a while as the vicar talked a little to Jane about how good a friend to the church her mother had been, always doing the flowers and, of course playing the organ. She would be greatly missed. The mourners came in their turn to shake hands, pay their respects, offer their condolences and then leave in that quiet, relieved way mourners do. Lawless stood by her side as Jane looked down at the posies and wreaths of flowers and fern lying on the mound of freshly turned soil. He thought of taking her hand but decided it might be better to leave her undisturbed with her thoughts and memories. He could hear the soft cooing sound of pigeons in the elm trees and felt a vague memory stirring: pigeons in a graveyard somewhere else. There must be hundreds of graveyards all over the country with pigeons in the trees. No, this memory was different. It irked him to find he couldn't place it. Yes, perhaps that was it: the Lakes. Going out with his father to follow the farmers when they went shooting pigeons to keep them off the wheat. Or was it?

'Shall we go back?'

This time he did take her hand and they walked out of the graveyard and down the narrow overgrown lane back to her mother's house in the village.

'I've got all her things to go through now. When she knew that she was dying she told me she had seen the solicitor and made a will and apart from some money for the church everything would be left to me. She was very careful Philip, and she said she was making a complete inventory of all her things. I don't know if she ever finished it.'

'The solicitor will know.'

'I do want to keep the piano. I learned to play on this one. She taught me from the start. It's a good one, a Broadwood. The violin came later but she found just the right teacher for me. She must have had to pay quite a lot. I don't know where we can put it, never mind the other things. There's hardly any room in the flat. I suppose everything will have to go into store.'

'No it won't. We can put everything you want into a house in Oxford.'

'Don't be silly. How could we afford something as big as that?'

'Because I'm to be the next Professor of Romance Philology and the salary will be enough to rent one, maybe even buy one, if I can persuade the bank to give me a loan.'

'Philip, you pig! You kept it from me all that time.'

'Only a few days and for a very good reason, don't you think?'

She put her arms round him and squeezed hard.

'Yes, you really can be very sweet. And yes, I am thinking.'

'What about? Wallpaper, curtains, garden shed . . .?'

'Shut up; I'm calculating. Yes, we can do it; with both our salaries we just might buy . . .'

'Three bedrooms, one for each of us and one for visitors . . .'

'Better than that: there's this house as well. It's very nice and very close to Cambridge. Lots of people might be interested.'

'But don't you want to keep it? You were born here, weren't you?'

'Yes, I was and I have lots of happy memories but I don't want to live here and I couldn't anyway because of the job.'

'You could rent it out.'

'No. The best thing would be to sell and with the extra money we can buy a bigger place, somewhere really good in Oxford.'

'Whatever you say.'

On the train back to Oxford the next day, as Lawless was watching the fields slip by and the telephone wires swoop up and down along the track and thinking of the Dark Lady, he suddenly realised who she was and turned to Jane to tell her.

'Philip, what happened about your parents' house in Kendal?'

'Annie and Andy lived in it after they were married. Didn't I tell you that?'

'Yes, but what did they do about it when they emigrated?'

'I don't know. I suppose they must have sold it.'

'I just thought it might have been yours and you were letting then live there.'

'I don't think it can have been. It was my parents' house and then it was theirs. It can't have belonged to anybody else in between.'

'I'm surprised you aren't at all curious about it.'

'I'll write to them and ask. Now, I have to tell you: I know who she is.'

'Who?'

'The Dark Lady. I know who she is. It's just hit me and it's all because of your idea and your cryptanalysis. I know her name!'

'Well, are you going to tell me?'

ENGLAND 1958

GHYSLAINE DE VÉZELINS

'. . . my warmest thanks to Dr Jane Carstairs for her acute observation that the word "hand" which we use somewhat routinely when referring to a writer and his or her style has the implication when the script is handwritten that the hand used may be the right, or the left. Since left-handedness is an attribute of only some ten per cent of humans, recognition of a left hand at work will materially narrow our search for the identity of the writer.

Palaeographic methods and textual analysis—and here again, I acknowledge both Dr Carstairs' remarkable cryptanalytical findings and Dr Sinclair's observations—are of considerable help but for identification purposes we need something more, something personal, and I suggest we find this in more than one instance in the text.

On page two, lines twelve and thirteen we have what I believe is significant evidence that our writer is not only a woman, but a woman who uses her left hand. An illustration of these lines is on the screen. Those familiar with Occitan will know that I am offering a somewhat free, but I maintain reasonable translation, when I read these words as:

"closest to the heart the hand that guides the needle threads my pattern surely as the pen my words."

No man in those times would do needlework. The hand closest to the heart is the left hand. We have here a woman who works at her embroidery or threads her tapestry with the needle in her left hand, the same hand that she uses to write.

There are other clues to her lefthandedness. Here on page four we have:

"as tight as bound the hand to heart side I am bound to yours."

Forgive the literal translation but this must allude to the practice of binding a child's left hand so as to compel it to use the right—a practice I believe unwisely continues in some places to the present day. Notice moreover how she is bound to the other's heart side, that is, in love.

So far, I hope, so good: how much farther may we now go? The colour red finds mention eleven times in the text in more than one form and more than one context. I will not enumerate all the instances by page and line number—these will be listed in the published version of this lecture—but quote only three.

First, the sun at close of day is described by a phrase that means "blush of red gold": one might say "orange" although I suggest "blush" evokes the red flush seen on the skin of some apricots, a fruit, I have been informed more likely than the orange to be found in the upland region whence this manuscript comes, the High Causses. My informant has also remarked that sunset in that part of France often has a delightful apricot hue.

Secondly, there is red as in the colour of blood. Our writer refers to drawing her own blood, a tiny bead on the finger by the accidental prick of her needle—it would be the finger of her right hand of course—and though painful it is as nothing compared with the pain and the blood on the brow of the crucified Christ nor, and here we have a very significant allusion, nor with the pain of and the blood shed during the torment. The grammar shows clearly that this blood and torment are not those of the Christ but of the person addressed in the text. Someone has been tortured. Remember also that red is the colour of fire.

Thirdly, there is red as applied to the colour of hair, in particular the darker red we call auburn. The relevant line of the text is unfortunately damaged but I interpret the word as describing dark red hair from the rather mysterious phrase (as I have reconstructed it) "gathering up the autumn broken fall", which I see as harvesting chestnuts that display such colour when the husk splits open. The chestnut, as is well known was in past times a food staple in the Causses, as in the Auvergne. So I suggest this is a metaphor of hands lifting, perhaps fondling or running through the dark red hair of the writer. Whether I am correct in this I admit is arguable but there is no doubt that the reference is to the woman's hair being red.

Our writer is a woman who uses her left hand and has red, probably dark, red hair. Each of these physical attributes is uncommon, and perhaps possession of both may render a person doubly distinctive. Have we enough now for identification? With one more piece of evidence I think we do.

As a student I was fortunate enough to make several visits to Heidelberg where Professor Karl Hoffmann was kind enough to give me access to the manuscript archives of his department. By one of those happy chances that can occur when one is searching for something quite different, I came across an illuminated volume that at first sight seemed to be an early Book of Hours. The illuminations were few but good in quality and from one particular illumination I assumed the book was of the kind a husband, in this case possibly a minor nobleman (a soldier, judging from the sword at his side) might have presented as a gift to his wife on their marriage. I show this illumination on the screen now. You see a couple seated in rather simple chairs on either side of a table on which there is some sort of vessel and to the side is a priest making the sign of the cross, blessing the union, one supposes. The lady, you will see has red hair—dark red—and in her hand holds what is undoubtedly a pen. She holds it in her left hand and in the way some left handed people do with the wrist bent at a right angle and the fingers holding the pen at a slope. This grip normally causes the written letters to incline to the right and we see a clear tendency for this in the text. Having looked at this for a little while—because it is an unusual thing to find—I resumed my study of the other volumes I had come to see.

These details I recalled when I began considering what should be my subject for this lecture. Dr Carstairs could tell you how I announced this rather abruptly on the train one day. First, I wrote to Professor Hoffmann and asked him if he knew of the manuscript and whether the names of the knight and his lady in the illumination were known. On receipt of his reply I went as soon as possible to Heidelberg to see and confirm for myself what he had said.

The knight, as I think of him for reasons that will become obvious, is Guillaume de Brussac and the lady is Ghyslaine de Vézelins.

We know something of Guillaume de Brussac. He went on the disastrous Eighth Crusade (or Seventh, depending on your point of view) when he must have been a very young man but by the time he married Ghyslaine, much to his benefit since she was an heiress, he was over sixty. The marriage was not blessed with children and the blame was fixed on her—as was almost always the case. Could the superstitions and prejudices against left-handedness and red hair also have had something to do with that? In our text there are other references to discords in the past that culminated in what was nothing less than confinement in the "house of Servant Sisters", described bitterly in the text as "winter in time of summer" so it must have been hard to bear.

Now, of Ghyslaine we know something of what she looked like and we know she could write—why otherwise would she have a pen so prominent in her left hand? But can we say she was the author of this poetic text? Her name is French of course, but of old Germanic origin and etymologically derives from "pledge" or "vow" or "hostage", all meanings that are related. These words all appear in the text; "pledge" five times, "vow" seven, and "hostage" two. The first two are in earnest statements of assurance to the person addressed. The word for hostage is used for two opposing conditions of the writer: as one confined and under threat in the "house of the

Servant Sisters" and as one made hostage to another by her love for that other. In the code of these pages I contend she has all but signed her name.

Let me say a little of what became of her and how this poem, this lament, came to be written. It is a sad story . . .'

'Congratulations, again; I think you carried it off very well,' Winifred Smallwood said as they each raised a glass to the other after the lecture. I liked the informal style. So many of these inaugurals tend towards obscurity or pomposity. Oh, here comes the V-C. I'm going to speak with Jane. I will catch up with you later.'

'Well Lawless, I think you will have set a number of people thinking afresh about all of that and a good thing too, if I may say so.'

'Thank you, Vice Chancellor. One always has hopes.'

'Now tell me Lawless so that I have things straight, are you saying that this lady—and I think you make a persuasive case of identifying her—was put away by her husband for not producing an heir? Was there nothing else?'

'I suspect that was a pretext, one that would be just about acceptable at the time, but not the only reason. I think Guillaume found her too much of a handful: much younger, more intelligent and better educated than he was. It is very unlikely that he knew how to write whereas she was clearly very skilled and a poet too. Given what we know happened later it is not unreasonable to suspect her behaviour caused concern, perhaps even scandal. Guillaume could not take any more drastic action for fear of repercussions from her family but putting his wife out of the way of temptation would not have been an unprecedented act for a husband in those times. It could be given out that it was her wish to enter the company of holy women.'

'Yes, I see. But it didn't work, did it?'

'No but the affair at least wasn't public knowledge, that is, not until the very end and even then known by very few.'

'One of whom betrayed these two lovers. Who could that have been?'

'So far I have not been able to find out. There may be clues in the manuscript that I have yet to decipher. The betrayal could have been for any one of many reasons: genuine moral outrage, jealousy, revenge, money, someone saving their own skin. It was a very disturbed time. The Order was being suppressed and its possessions sequestered or transferred to the Hospitallers who may have assimilated many of the Knights that did not simply pass into obscure retirement. But some did not escape the stake for their so-called heresies and that was surely the fate of our knight.'

'Hence the "red sacrifice" that you pointed out. As you say it is a sad tale.'

'At first I thought the poem was a dialogue between the lady and her knight because he is actually given words to say. It is a lament of course but now I see it also as a recollection to keep as a comfort in her later age and there could be one spark of optimism.'

'I don't recall much of that in your address.'

'I did not include it because I still lack proof—again a matter for decipherment—but the phrase that puzzles me is in the line after "red sacrifice". It is "his blood passes through the flame"; the word "passes" can also mean "survives" or even "escapes". This may be an unwise guess that I shall have to discard, but I think it could mean that a child lived on after its father's death.'

'The knight's child?'

'Yes, the child of the chevalier, the word used twice earlier in the text.'

'I am impressed, Lawless. I am intrigued by mysteries and their solutions, as you may know. I look forward to the publication. Judging from the mass of detail you gave, you must know that part of France very well.'

'It's all from my reading. There are very good and relevant works.'

'You sounded more as if you've lived there yourself.'

'I should like to see the Causses some day, Vice Chancellor.'

'So you should. Now, is that young woman speaking to Winifred Smallwood who I think she is?'

'Dr Jane Carstairs, yes Vice Chancellor.'

'You must know her well by now from all that work together.'

'I do, Vice Chancellor. She is my wife.'

'Well for God's sake man, introduce me.'

THE YEARS THAT FOLLOWED

NORTH OXFORD

The house that they bought had become shabby and the gardens neglected after the previous owner, a retired don, had lost his wife and with her much of his interest in life and finally died leaving it to an only and estranged son who lived abroad and had no wish to keep it. But it was large and a few minutes walk from the Cherwell and easy cycling distance from Lawless's place of work and the College. Jane still had to make the early morning journey in the staff bus to the Research Establishment south of Oxford where she had recently been moved up to Deputy Group Leader. Her promotion meant more pay and they began to think of buying a second-hand car for her so that she would not have to suffer the spartan accommodation made available for times when the experiments ran late and the analysis of results later still and the last bus back to Oxford had long gone. They decided they would do the redecorating themselves and started planning a complete redesign of the garden that would need extensive clearance before any new seeding and planting could be started. They moved in early in autumn and gave themselves a deadline of 15 July the following year, after all Lawless's examination duties would have been fulfilled, for a housewarming party on what they hoped would be a decent new lawn or, if wet, in the freshly painted and papered ground floor rooms in which guests could drink their white wine and eat their canapés and watch the rain refresh the lawn outside.

Territories were established without too much dissent. The ground floor was common and of the two largest bedrooms on the first floor Jane chose that at the front of the house overlooking the quiet no-through road and Lawless the rear overlooking the garden. Jane declared the bathroom to be unusable until completely modernised, and made larger, by knocking down the wall between it and the adjacent third bedroom. Lawless said he would accept it as it stood once it was modernised and why did she not turn the fourth bedroom into a bathroom for herself. That would leave a bedroom spare for guests. She agreed so readily that Lawless suspected she must have had that in mind to begin with. There were rooms enough on the second floor for a study and library space for Lawless, a second guest room and another for storage; anything left over would have to go in the attic.

'You know that this is going to take years, don't you?'

'Well we'd better make a start at the weekend,' she said.

'There's going to be a huge bill for plumbing,'

'Oh I know someone in Chemical Engineering who'll be very happy to do it for us and rewiring as well. That has to be done as soon as possible or we'll all be electrocuted. We won't have to pay him, just keep him fed and and watered.'

'I think I need some help like that with the garden.'

'Ask Alice Layton, three doors along. She's quite an expert.'

'I can't just knock on the door and ask someone I don't know if they'd help me dig out some old roots.'

'No, but I'll ask her husband Peter to pass the message on. He travels on the same bus as me.'

Alice Layton called round in the afternoon a few days later, bringing her spaniel with her.

'I hope you don't mind dogs,' she said. 'I don't like leaving her in the house. She gets lonely and starts yapping. The neighbours don't like it—they're all cat people if they're anything. She won't be any trouble; probably just go to sleep under a tree. Now, Jane told Peter that you needed some help. What is it you want me to do? Shall we go round the back and take a look?'

'Come through. Be careful in here. The paint's still a bit tacky.'

'Oh dear,' she said as she surveyed the garden from the steps leading down from the french doors. 'I see what you mean. It must have been beautiful once but look at it now. I think the best thing to do is make a start on identifying what's here. Have you a notebook? You can put things down as I tell you what they are and when that's done we can decide what ought to stay and what has to go.'

'Lead on. You know all about plants, I take it.'

'I read Botany here. I always liked the fieldwork but this is splendid. I've never had a jungle to explore before.'

After two hours of exploration the listing —provisional, she said—was finished and she accepted the offer of tea.

'I'm very grateful to you for giving up your time. I wouldn't have known where to start. I can dig, though and I'm quite good with a saw.'

'You have one or two real treasures hidden away out there but there's a lot of clearing to be done. I'm happy to give a hand if you do the heavy work.'

'Are you sure you have the time? I was thinking of having a word with the College gardeners.'

'You've got me interested. It's quite a challenge, bringing such a lovely old garden back to life. I've been looking for something to do now that the boys are away at school and Peter works such long hours. I expect it's the same for Jane. I've been applying for jobs but nothing has come up so far. So, I am available.'

'Marvellous. What can I do now?'

'Wait until I come back with a plan and then be prepared to work hard and spend money.'

As she was leaving with the dog he said,

'You know, I'm sure you remind me of someone but I can't think who.'

'I remember us passing each other in the road when you and Jane came to have your first look and we said hello.'

'No, longer ago than that. When were you here as an undergraduate?'

'I came up in 1939; just after the War started.'

'That's when I came up. Could we have met, I wonder.'

'Could be. A lot of water has flowed under Folly Bridge since then.'

Pulling the garden roller which he had borrowed from the College up and down the new turf was heavy work in the heat of late May. He stopped to take a breather under the walnut tree and watched Alice coming across with a glass in each hand.

'Cold lemonade,' she said. 'The best thing on a hot day. Let me do that.'

He took the glasses from her and she dabbed the sweat from his forehead with his handkerchief.

'I've just remembered where we met,' he said. 'I don't think I behaved very well then, do you?'

Because she smiled it seemed perfectly natural to take her to bed after that.

'Can we do this again sometimes?'

'I think so,' she said. 'You were a great deal better this time than you were in 1939.'

It was a perfect Saturday afternoon in July for the housewarming garden party. The Vice Chancellor came with his wife, and was very affable with everyone.

'Charming, Lawless; how on earth did you manage all this in such a short time?'

'Our neighbour, Dr Layton, Vice Chancellor; she is the real creator. She designed and chose almost everything. All I did was to follow her instructions. Would you care to meet her?'

'I would indeed. She could teach my gardener a thing or two.'

Jane took Lawless over to meet some of her colleagues from the Research Establishment. One of them said a chap called Kendrick had been on a short visit and had asked for a message to be given him.

'Did you know, Jane? You never said.'

'I'm sorry, Philip. It went clean out of my head. Yes he was with us for a week.'

'What was the message?'

It was about, er, Rob, what was the name?'

'Someone called Dickie Dent. He said that you would know him. Bad news: he was killed in a car accident.'

'I'm so sorry, Philip. I should have remembered. Was he a friend of yours?'

'I'm trying to think, Jane but I can't recall anyone of that name.'

'Rob, are you sure you got the name right?'

'Quite sure, Jane. It was Dickie Dent.'

'Show me round, Philip,' Winifred Smallwood said, taking his arm. 'Alice Layton told me there's a very fine late flowering clematis on the wall of the summer house.'

'You know her then?'

'She was an undergraduate at Granville. I didn't have much to contact with her because she was reading Botany, the only one in her year in fact.'

'She must have got a First because she went on to do a DPhil.'

'She did and she was President of the JCR and played tennis against Cambridge.'

'Well, well; she's never mentioned any of that to me.'

'Perhaps you have too many other things to talk about. This really is a most beautiful clematis. Perle d'Azur, isn't it?'

'I think so. Alice will know.'

'You must have spent a lot of time together doing all this work. It's a complete transformation.'

'Winfred, you are being slightly arch. If you are hinting at what I think you are, then it's true.'

'You didn't need to say anything. Forgive a little gentle teasing. I'm very glad for you. Only my dear, don't let it appear too obvious. Shall we re-join the others? People may talk.'

As they went to the table to have their glasses refilled, she said she had gone through the proofs of his inaugural as he had asked.

'We can go over them together when you like and you can tell me what you think of my comments. Why not come on Thursday and stay to Dinner? We can go through the proofs afterwards. It shouldn't take too long.'

'Winifred, look at me. How did you know Jane was going to be away for the next fortnight?'

'I asked her and she told me.'

'Philip, I've been trying to catch you to tell you my good news. I heard this morning. I've got a job! It's in the Botanic Garden, mainly general sort of work but they say I could have some time to start up my genetics research again if the Professor agrees. They read my thesis and the two papers I wrote and they're interested. I'm so excited.'

'That's wonderful, Alice. When do you start?'

'In a fortnight but that's not the only thing. I mentioned the job to Winifred Smallwood a few minutes ago and quite out of the blue she said the new Senior Tutor at Granville was keen on increasing their science entry—she's a biochemist—and the Governing Body would discuss her proposals next Term. Winifred says that the College has had botanists in the past—well, they had me—and might be inclined to take it up again and in a bigger way. She said she would keep me informed. It's all very confidential, by the way.'

'I'm good at forgetting. Jane's always telling me so. You know, if you're lucky you could be the Fellow in Botany at Granville one day.'

'Please don't say that. I hardly dare to think.'

'When can I see you again?'

'You've been seeing me almost every day.'

'You know what I mean. When?'

'I don't know. The boys are here now and they hardly leave me a minute free. They are going to stay with my mother for a week or two but as soon as they've gone there my job starts. I'm not trying to make excuses. It's been lovely with you but all of a sudden my life has changed and it's such a chance. I won't be a bored North Oxford wife searching for something to do much longer. Oh shit, I'm sorry, I didn't mean . . .'

'I know you didn't.'

'We'll find a time. I promise.'

That night as he was taking off his clothes Jane came in and sat on the side of his bed.

'You've caught the sun again. Your nose is a rather pretty shade of pink. What happened to that very smart hat you had on when the party started?'

'Never mind the hat. I wanted to tell you how happy I am. The party was lovely and all because of the garden. Everybody said that it was gorgeous. You have been marvellous Philip, doing all that work.'

'Don't forget Alice. She was the brains behind it.'

'And you were the brawn, well, muscle or sinew anyway. I hadn't realised how brown you were.'

'When no one was looking I took my shirt off.'
'Yes, you must have done; like now.'
'Jane, you have a very strange look in your eye.'
'What? It's my grateful look.'
'Now wait, do you mean . . .?'
'Of course it's what I mean. Now take the rest off. Quickly, in case I change my mind.'

Was he dreaming or did he really hear her say:
'I don't mind about you and Alice, Philip. 'I'm glad for both of you.'

HOFFMANN

Some months later Winifred Smallwood telephoned Lawless to say she had received a letter from Heidelberg

'Hoffmann's retiring. I have been asked to contribute to his festschrift. I expect you have too.'

'Yes, a letter in this morning's post. Will you go to the Symposium?'

'I think that I will. We could travel together. It would be a good chance for a meeting about the Dictionary.'

'He's a phenomenon. He's been sending me batches of material every month. I wouldn't have believed someone of his age could have such energy.'

'Be careful what you say, young man. Of all people you should know that age does not eliminate all of one's capabilities.'

At the end of the Hoffmann symposium a reception was held in the same Great Hall where Lawless had first met Jane. Hoffmann took Lawless's arm and steered him away from the throng of Sekt-sipping speakers and guests.

'I see the Rector is monopolising Winifred.'

'He has an eye for an attractive woman.'

'I was sorry to hear that you will not be coming to Oxford to receive your Degree in person.'

'No more than I, my dear Lawless. An honorary degree from Oxford is an honour indeed and the thought of spending a little more time with that magnificent woman before I die would be, could one say, "gilding the lily"? I think I may not have that the right way round: you know what I mean. Perhaps "having one's cake and eating it?" No, that sounds a little vulgar in this instance. But as you see now, I am in no fit state to make the journey. These damned sticks always get in the way and I am continually forgetting where I have put them. I will devote my time to the Dictionary. You are organising it very well: two volumes to be published by the Oxford University Press. I hope I live to see the day.'

'You will. I haven't finished with you yet.'

Hoffmann laughed and slapped him on the shoulder and then looked serious.

'You know, Lawless, what I have never been able to understand is how you can have such knowledge of our subject and of the region without ever having been there. You have truly a deep feeling for it. Where has that come from? That old text that you have so meticulously interpreted: it originates there. I know who sent it to Winifred. We spent time together there. It was long ago and we were very young. Has she not told you?'

'She said the donor wished to remain anonymous.'

'Perhaps there may come a day when you can ask her. Ah, here she is.'

Winifred Smallwood came up and took Hoffmann by the arm.

'I have managed to escape. Your Rector is a very persistent man. Now leave Philip to circulate and come with me. You promised to show me the paintings.'

'You see how it is, Lawless? An order I cannot refuse. Remember what I was talking about. You should go and see for yourself.'

'Now, Karl, where were you telling Philip he should go and see for himself?'

'The vineyards at Schriesheim.'

'I don't believe you.'

'You said that to me when I told you Alexandre would leave you; and he did.'

'But he came back to me, Karl; in his way he came back.'

'I was always there, Winifred.'

'I know, my dear, and now here we are. And we shall sit together at the concert this evening.'

***

Lawless had come to regard his half yearly appointments with Dr Hemming as he did his own research: the systematic and persistent accumulation of information that one day would lead to a convincing interpretation. He did, however, have less faith in his own medical case than he did in his own research.

'Anything since we last met? I don't think so, except—I don't know if it's important, but sometimes music. No, it's nothing.'

'No thing is nothing; in the sense of having no meaning. Music: please tell me what you were thinking.'

'Music is part of my life. I play in a chamber group with my wife and we go to concerts when she has the time. It's happened more than once: a phrase, a bar or two, just a few notes.'

'Music for some is the most powerful stimulant of memory as smell is for others. Please go on.'

'The other day I turned on the wireless. It was a Chopin nocturne—I can't remember who was playing—and suddenly one of the chords sounded different from the way I play it. That's ridiculous of course because I do make mistakes but it sounded like an echo in my head.'

'You said it has happened more than once.'

'Yes, with a Satie Gymnopédie—the second. The same feeling, a kind of echo but of what I don't know. What do you think?'

'You must have heard those pieces before. Did the echo sound then?'

'No. It has happened only recently and then only when I heard the music by chance. When I play it myself on the piano, nothing like that happens.'

'It may be you are hearing the echo of someone else playing in the past. I should be interested to hear if it happens again and how often. Is there anything else you want to tell me?'

'More and more I have the feeling that some people know more about me than I do myself: you, for example.'

'I know only what people are prepared to tell me, like you. I listen; occasionally I ask questions but mainly I listen.'

'How do you assess me now. Am I making progress?'

'I assess you as one who has adapted to difficult circumstance. Progress? I see what you have just told me as significant.'

'I think losing memory or a particular memory is as sad and wounding as losing someone you know.'

'I would not argue with that.'

***

Karl Hoffmann, as he had hoped, lived long enough to see the publication of the first volume of the Dictionary in 1970, and Lawless and Winifred Smallwood made a special journey to Heidelberg to present him with his copy. In the same parcel was a copy of the third volume of Lawless's monograph that had appeared the year before. He sat for a few moments looking at the two dark blue books, then drew his wheelchair up to the table and put his hand on the Dictionary.

'Will you open it for me, please?'

Lawless picked up the heavy volume and turned to the page he knew Hoffmann would wish to read first, the page with all the categories and meanings of the word 'love'. He placed it carefully on Hoffmann's knees and the old man traced some of the lines with his finger.

'Such weight knowledge has, my friends. Greater than the weight of guilt.'

'You have nothing to feel guilty about, Karl.'

'If that were true I would be alone in the world. I fled my country. There lies my guilt.'

'If you had not, you would never have survived.'

'So many did not because they could not leave as I did. I see their faces. Sometimes I write down their names. And there were countless, countless others I never knew.'

'Someone had to survive, Karl and why not you?'

'That is my guilt, Winifred: the guilt of the survivor. However,' he said looking up with the old impish smile on his face, 'had I not, you and I and this young and quite promising scholar would not be here together looking at our work. Or going out to dinner tonight at a restaurant with a view of the river and the castle on the hill, so we will put aside guilt for a few hours, yes?'

SOUTHERN STYLE

During the year after publication of the Dictionary and his election to the British Academy, Lawless received many invitations to lecture or conduct seminars including several in the United States, all expenses paid. He was able to persuade the University to grant him sabbatical leave in the last term of the academic year. With the Long Vacation to follow he would have a long period in which to accept some of the invitations and also push on with Volume 2 of the Dictionary.

'I was due to retire this year,' Winfred Smallwood told him, 'but the College has asked me to stay on for another three years. I can't imagine why.'

'I can, and I hope you agree. What would I do without you?'

'Well you have Jane. And there's always Alice, although now she's one of our Fellows it might be seen as verging on the incestuous.'

'Oh, that's all over with. We are still friends but nothing more now.'

'It's very wise to keep one's friends. You never know when you might need them. I was thinking of going to visit my brother and his wife. They continued living in France after he retired. They have a very pretty place not far outside Paris and she still has the big house in the Midi. Why don't you come and bring Jane? They have plenty of room.'

'When would that be?'

'After the end of the year—next July.'

'I would have loved to come but we shall be in the States. I'm giving some lectures and Jane said she was being sent over as well to some place in California for a month. Rather lucky really.'

***

Dear Philip

I haven't written for a long time and I'm sorry to send you some bad news. Dad died in his sleep yesterday. The doctor thinks that it was a heart attack but they have to do a post mortem and Mum feels awful about that. We never knew anything was wrong. He was working with the sheep on the neighbour's farm only the day before. I can't believe he won't be there anymore. He wasn't very old, only 70 last birthday. Margaret is very upset and keeps asking where Grandad is. Andy is very good and does everything we need. He has a good job now and we have a new house in Armidale. That's why there's a different address on this letter. I wish you could have been closer when it happened. Dad always liked you and so does Mum.

I will write again and tell you all that happened but I can't write anymore now. We hope you are doing well at Oxford and Andy sends best wishes.

Love

Annie

'Is anything wrong, Philip? You look unhappy.'

'It's my uncle John. You remember him, don't you from that time we spent in the Lakes?'

'Yes, I do; a very nice quiet man. He called me "Miss".'

'He's died. I always liked him as well. He was a sheep farmer, a hill farmer really. I used to help with the sheep, especially at lambing time.'

***

After a hectic week in which he lectured at universities in New York, Washington, North Carolina, and finally Charlottesville, Lawless was glad to be met at Roanoke by Jane and Ainslie and settle down in the rear seat of an immense Cadillac to doze all the way along the Shenandoah Valley until they reached the Anderson mansion near Lexington.

It was very hot in Virginia in July but the colonial style house with its pillared portico, marble floors and huge high ceilinged rooms had a welcome coolness.

'You must be very tired, Philip. You could rest for a while before dinner or take a swim if you like. We cool the pool to 70 in the summer.'

Ainslie Anderson was tall and blonde with blue eyes and had a figure that the fashion magazines would have described as willowy, though with somewhat more prominent breasts. Her movements had a casual, easy grace and she always wore white, except occasionally jeans or riding britches and a cream blouse when she rode. For driving she wore sunglasses but never in the house or grounds, preferring a wide floppy brimmed hat of finely plaited straw. Her manner, like that of so many Virginians, was friendly and confident and her accent entranced Lawless. She also clearly entranced Jane.

Someone had thoughtfully left a pair of swimming trunks still in its wrapping and a soft cotton dressing gown on a chair by the pool. Seeing no one about, Lawless quickly stripped, put the trunks on and slid into the water at the deep end. It was wonderfully cool. He was not a good swimmer, in fact did not actually like swimming, preferring to paddle a bit and then float on his back, or do a little lazy side-stroke. No one was there to disturb him. He almost fell asleep.

Eventually he climbed out feeling very refreshed, stepped out of the trunks and started to dry himself with a very large soft white towel.

'Hello there; you must be Philip.' The voice might have been Ainslie's, but it wasn't. 'Don't mind me. I won't look.'

He hurriedly put on the dressing gown and shuffled off the damp towel.

'Sorry about that.'

She turned round smiling, looked and raised one eyebrow.

'Shouldn't you . . .?'

'Sorry, sorry.' He hastily tied the cord round his waist.' Yes, Philip, Philip Lawless. How do you do?'

'I love that English phrase: "how do you do?" How do you do what? I always think. I'm Shannon. How do *you* do?'

'Ainslie's sister: you look alike. You have longer hair.'

'He notices. Would you like a drink?'

'What are you offering?'

'You may be expecting a mint julep.'

'I'm afraid that I don't like the taste of mint.'

'No problem. I had in mind a margarita.'

'I have no idea what that is.'

'Try one and see what you think. I make a very good margarita. We'll go outside. It's cool and shady under the maple tree.'

'That is a remarkable drink. How do you make the salt stay round the rim?'

'I keep half a dozen glasses chilled and ready in the freezer. Have another.'

'Thank you. This is a beautiful place. How old is the house?'

'Pretty old, about 1830.'

'It must be a lot of work keeping it as beautiful as this, all the lawns and trees and flower beds, as well as the house itself.'

'We have a Mexican couple, Cesar and Paola. They're at the beach right now with the parents so we're looking after ourselves. All the yard work is contracted out. Mother supervises.'

'And what do you do all day?'

'Right now, not much: ride a little, swim, read. I'm on vacation. When I'm working I run the Alumni Office at Denniston.'

'That's a women's college, isn't it?'

'Yes, near Staunton. I know what you do: famous Professor at Oxford, world authority on Occitan, editor of all sorts of things. You don't look old enough to be all that.'

'I'm older than I look but I've lived a blameless life.'

'You're kidding: blameless life with a name like Lawless?'

'How do you come to know about Occitan?'

'I'll have you know that I do have a degree, Sir, from UVA and apart from that you get to know all kinds of things in an Alumni Office.'

'What kinds of things?'

'Well, for instance, we have an alumna who works on Creole languages and would you believe it, thinks she may have found Occitan origins for some words in Creole. She is in Guadeloupe as we speak, doing her field work.'

'You must let me have her name and where she works. I could ask her if she might care to contribute to the Dictionary. I knew Huguenots had colonised and raided in the Antilles so it had to happen.'

'Why not go there yourself one day? Talk to her about it. It's very beautiful. We were there a couple of years ago on a short vacation. Can I sweeten that drink for you? One more before dinner? It's rather a special one before the other two set off. You can try some Virginia wine.'

'What other two? Set off where? To the beach?'

'Jane and Ainslie; didn't they say? No, not the beach: to Hot Springs for a few days, leaving early in the morning. It's about a fifty mile drive.'

'Leaving us here on our own, are they?'

'I think that was the idea. In case you were wondering, I should tell you that I am not like my sister.'

She sat on the edge of the bed and offered him a glass of chilled orange juice.

'You were still sleeping when they left. I waved them off.'

'Come back to bed. There's no one else in the house. We won't be disturbed.'

'I have a better idea: the pool. No need for bathing suits. Then we'll have breakfast and after that, we'll see.'

She swam without a bathing cap, letting her hair float all round her as she lay on her back. He said she reminded him of Millais' painting of Ophelia.

'She was drowning and had her clothes on.'

'I was thinking of the way your hair is floating.'

'My hair: is that all you were thinking about?'

'I must admit, no. Can I dry you when you get out?'

'Only if I can do the same to you. Deal?'

'Philip, where did you get those scars on your back?'

'It must have been in the War. My turn now.'

Wearing only their dressing gowns they sat in a room off the kitchen that Shannon called the sun parlour and ate breakfast Southern style, biscuits with gravy, cheese grits, buckwheat pancakes with syrup and rather weak coffee. Lawless found it all fascinating, except the coffee.

'You did all this yourself?'

'Every good Southern girl knows how to cook. Momma teaches you,' she said in a stage southern drawl. 'Eat up. We got places to go.'

'Can't we first . . .?'

'No. We have tonight and three more days for that. I'm going to show you the battle-fields where mah Great great granddaddy fought and bled for the South.'

***

The table was laid for breakfast when Lawless came down. Jane came in from the kitchen with the toast rack and coffee pot, a sheaf of letters from the morning post under her arm.

'Three for you: one from Germany, and two for me. Pass the butter, please.'

Lawless handed her the butter dish without raising his eyes from the newspaper.

'There's an interview with Winifred on her birthday in the paper.'

'How old is she?'

'It's her eightieth'

'Impossible. She didn't look a day over sixty when we saw her last week.'

'I know she's eighty. I send a card from us both the day before yesterday. It must be ten years ago since she retired from Granville.'

'Is there a party for her?'

'Drinks, this evening at her house. I have a present for her. Now, I never knew that! It says here that she was engaged in secret work during the War.'

'Does it say what?'

'No, she's still not allowed to say.'

'I bet she would tell you, if you asked.'

'Her kind doesn't let on about things like that. Anyway, read it. It's very interesting. Did you know she was England Junior Girls' tennis champion or her father got the VC in the Great War? Are you listening?'

She was reading one of her letters. She handed it to him without saying anything. It was quite short.

'Jane! That is wonderful! A Senior Research Fellowship at Granville: you're going to accept, aren't you?'

'I might well if they would hold it over. I have one more year at the Establishment and there's a lot to finish off.'

'No need: with an SRF you could carry on with what you're doing. If the Authority would let you, of course.'

'They might, that's true. I'd still have my security clearance.'

'Did you know this might be coming?'

'There were some hints. I think Winifred may have had something to do with it.'

'She'd never admit it, even if you asked. Anything important in your other letters?'

She was reading one very attentively.

'Yes; it's from Ainslie. She's buying a house in England. She always said she would like to live by a river and she's found one near Maidenhead.'

'Why? They have that lovely big place near Lexington and I know she has a flat in New York. Ah, could it be she wants to be nearer you?'

'We've talked about it from time to time. I did tell you once but you can't have been listening. It would fit in well with my leaving the Establishment. She says that Shannon would be part owner. That should please you.'

'Shannon has been very helpful with giving me contacts.'

'I'm sure she has. What time is Winifred's drinks party?'

Lawless's letter was postmarked Heidelberg. It was from the Rector of the University himself. He regretted to inform Herr Professor Lawless that their distinguished colleague Herr Professor Hoffmann had suffered a stroke and was unconscious in the University Medical School hospital.

Winifred Smallwood had received a similar letter. They drank to the health of Hoffmann without much hope that it would have any effect.

'I booked two tickets from Heathrow,' Lawless said. 'I expected that you would want to go. I have something for him.'

'Thank you. I should like to be there.'

Hoffmann never regained consciousness. Lawless left Volume Two of the Dictionary on his bedside table. Inside the cover was a note from himself and Winifred dedicating the volume to Hoffmann. Lawless quietly went out of the private room, leaving Winifred seated at the bedside holding the hand of the dying man.

***

Lawless was sorry but not greatly surprised when Jane told him she would like to live with Ainslie in the Maidenhead house during the vacations.

'You can come any time you want. There will always be a room for you. I know that you like Ainslie and you get on well together. And we'll come up to Oxford for the rehearsals and other things and stay the odd weekend—in Term as well. I have to attend the College meetings. And we can have some dinner parties for all our friends. I don't want to lose contact.'

'I'll miss you, but of course you must do as you want. I wouldn't dream of trying to stop you. It's what we both knew could happen.'

'Shannon is bound to want to come again. She says there are quite a few Denniston alumnae in England and Europe and she wants to organise meetings with them. One of them is the wife of the Ambassador. I think Shannon has her eye on her.'

'It will certainly be a pleasure to see her again.'

'She plans to be in England in July for a few days.'

'She is very welcome to stay here if she wants; stop me feeling too lonely.'

'I expect she will but I ought to tell you, Philip, that she's going to get married when she goes back. Ainslie will be bridesmaid, of course, and I know we will both be invited.'

'You don't think it would be a bit awkward if I were there?'

'Philip, don't be so old fashioned.'

'I'll think about it.'

She came up to him and put her arms round his neck and looked up into his eyes.

'I'm not leaving you, Philip. I wouldn't do that because I think so much of you and you have been the sweetest and most understanding man. And I do love you.'

He kissed the top of her head and then the tip of her nose.

'And I love you. And Ainslie and Shannon and that girl in the teashop . . . but most of all and really only you.'

'You are a pig but sometimes you do say the nicest things.'

'I know. Rehearsal tonight at eight: remember?'

KINGFISHERS

'Can you tell me about it, Justine?'

'It all happened so suddenly, Winifred. We had lunch on the terrace—it was such a warm afternoon—and we talked about those few days we had together in Paris before he had to leave again for the Front. Exquisite times, Winifred, snatches of happiness, mad wonderful moments. How we laughed. You had them too, Winifred, with Alexandre, I know.

After lunch he always read in his study, or wrote: I think that he has been making a book from his memories. After this quiet time we would take a little promenade by the river to watch the fish rising, or the birds. There are kingfishers living in the banks. He loved to see them dive. He was late coming out of his study so I knocked on the door and there was no answer. Asleep, I thought, so I went in and he was lying back in his chair—the one behind the desk by the window. He looked very peaceful. He was breathing but I could not wake him. I telephoned the Pompiers and they came very quickly with the nurse. It was only some minutes before he was in their ambulance and on the way to the hospital. I followed with the nurse in her car.'

'The doctors would not tell me very much, Justine, only that they were doing everything they could.'

'He has to breathe oxygen. Always they look serious when they speak with me. It is his heart, Winfred. They have not said so but I think he will die.'

'We must have hope, Justine.'

'Yes, hope: what else do we have but hope and memories?'

'Shall we walk by the river?'

'Yes. If we see a kingfisher we can tell him.'

'The farmer on the other side of the river was turning the grass yesterday. There will be lots of hay this year. Can you smell it, drying in the sun?'

'What will you do, Justine if . . .'

'If Robert dies, you mean? I am not sure. We both came to love this place, but I may not be able to live here without him. I think I will go back to Castelbouc. Do you remember it? We all swam in that deep pool below the house and Robert and Alexandre fished in the river for trout. Robert caught more and I think Alexandre was not too pleased.'

'But being a gentleman he congratulated Robert.'

'Yes, yes he did. I remember. Anne-Marie had eyes for Robert but Alexandre did not notice.'

'Because he had eyes for you, my dear.'

'And you.'

The two upright elderly ladies stood silent for a while looking across the river to the hayfields but not seeing them, only the other river and the young men laughing and splashing in the water.

Justine Lamphier took Winifred Smallwood's hand.

'When I go to Castelbouc, will you come to stay with me? And perhaps bring the young man whom we both love? There are kingfishers in the river.'

'He should come, Justine, but I think he is not ready yet. I must tell you this. A letter addressed to him came accidentally into my possession many years ago.

'You read it, of course.'

'Of course and I think you too have a right to know what it says but this is not the time for him to know. When I tell you the contents I think you will agree. If and when he regains his memory and resolves to return to France he shall have it before he leaves on condition that he does not open it until he is here.'

A VIRGINIA WEDDING

Lawless and Jane both attended Shannon's wedding which was a very grand affair with a bishop officiating and a marquee bigger than any Lawless had ever seen, on the mansion's lawn for the wedding breakfast. The ceremony was held in the early evening when the air was a little cooler. Looking round at the smartly dressed men and the exquisitely gowned women chatting in their Virginia and South Carolina accents while sipping their champagne and bourbon, Lawless could not help thinking that were the dress to include a few grey-blue tunics and swords and some floor-sweeping white gowns and fans, he could well be in a scene from *Gone With The Wind.*

Shannon sought him out to introduce her new husband who shook him painfully hard by the hand, addressed him as 'Sir' and said he was honoured to meet the Professor from England.

'Shannon has told me a lot about you, Sir,' he said smiling politely while questioning Lawless with his eyes.

'Nothing to my discredit, I hope.'

'Nothing at all,' Shannon smiled, squeezing the young man's hand. 'I never give away a secret. It's essential in my profession'

'Has your wife told you how helpful she has been with my research?'

Shannon put a gloved finger lightly on his lips.

'Now Philip, no talk of work today, please. We are all here to enjoy ourselves. Let me take you to meet my mother.'

Speeches, most of them lacking any wit or the kind of scurrilous revelations Lawless would have expected at an English wedding, and numerous toasts followed dinner. Later, as the guests strolled about the grounds or rested in the house, an orchestra began to tune up in readiness for the ball that was to follow in the marquee where the tables and chairs had been cleared away and the hardwood flooring swept clean for the dancers. In a more remote part of the grounds in a smaller marquee a Dixieland group was already strumming away for the younger and more energetic.

Lawless was ashamed of his poor dancing skills but Shannon's mother was polite and managed to avoid serious injury.

'My daughter speaks warmly of you, Professor Lawless.'

'She was most hospitable on our last visit to your beautiful home, Mrs Anderson and took me on a fascinating tour of the battlefields.'

'I am so glad. Your country was a good friend to the South during the War Between the States. I should like to visit if I can persuade my husband to travel by sea. I have a fear of flying. Now that Ainslie has found a house in England—I think not far from Oxford, is that so?—I should welcome your showing me your beautiful city.'

'I would be my pleasure, Mrs Anderson.'

'Jane, I don't think I can stay on my feet much longer. They all have such good manners: would anyone think it impolite if we were to slip away?'

'It's dark enough. Shannon is sitting over there. Ask her where you're to sleep. Ainslie and I are going for a swim.'

Shannon was surrounded by young men but he managed to catch her eye. She told him he had a room to himself at the top of the house. Paola would show him where.

Two days after the wedding, Lawless was back in Oxford leaving Jane behind to attend two conferences and spend the rest of the summer touring with Ainslie. They planned to return together in October for the beginning of Term.

JANE

Ainslie Anderson telephoned Lawless to say that Jane would not be attending the College meeting as she had lost her voice and would he pass her apologies on to the Principal because she could not speak herself.

'I don't think it's serious, just a slight case of laryngitis.'

'Tell her to keep warm and gargle. Let me know how she gets on.'

Two days later Ainslie telephoned again.

'She still has no voice, Philip and the odd thing is her temperature is normal and her throat isn't sore. She's not really unwell, only a little tired. It doesn't stop her working.'

Lawless spoke to one of the medical Fellows in at lunch.

'Hm. Find out if she has a cough or gets breathless or has pains in her chest or shoulders—and has she lost weight? Any of those: call her doctor.'

Lawless rang Ainslie in the evening and told her what his colleague had said.

'She doesn't like me asking her, says that I am making a fuss. But I'll find out.'

'She hasn't got a cough but the other things, yes, all of them.'

'I'm coming in the morning.'

'She can't be feeling herself, Ainslie or she wouldn't have agreed to my taking her to see the doctor. You will come too?'

'I'll drive, you give the directions.'

She was in with the doctor for a long time. When they finally emerged from his consulting room the doctor said he had arranged a consultation at the Churchill Hospital in Oxford for the following afternoon.

'I'll pack some things for Oxford,' Ainslie said.

'The room should be all right for you,' Lawless said. 'It's been kept clean and tidy since you were last there.'

The consultant at the Churchill said that he wanted to carry out some more tests. He had asked for the results to be expedited and his secretary would telephone with another appointment as soon as they were ready.

Lawless knew she must be frightened when she asked him and Ainslie to be with her when she saw the consultant again.

She had an aggressive form of squamous cell carcinoma with secondaries and the consultant said he was very sorry but it was inoperable because the tumour was large and too close to the aorta. He would prescribe medication for the pain.

To the inevitable question that Jane wrote down herself with a firm hand he replied,

'Three months, perhaps a little more.'

He read the words Jane wrote next and gave her a smile that seemed to Lawless to be one of admiration but no certainty.

'I'm sure you can manage that,' he said.

Lawless took a look at the sheet of paper.

Time enough to finish my last paper was what she had written.

The paper was finished, sent to the journal, and accepted with very few required changes, before the three months was up. Lawless brought the proofs to her room in the hospice and she even managed painfully to write the necessary alterations.

Ainslie and Lawless were at her bedside when she died two days before Christmas in 1988, the year before Lawless was due to retire and Winifred Smallwood celebrated her 86th birthday.

***

Although she had not lived in it for any length of time over the past few years, the house in Oxford seemed much emptier to Lawless now he knew that Jane would never be there again. There were signs of her everywhere: the bulky PC she had abandoned when she acquired an early laptop with a touchpad in America was the most obvious but the coffee cups, scrabble board, small garden fork and the kitchen whiteboard's magnets with mathematical symbols were just as poignant reminders of her. She had had a habit of leaving reminder notes for herself. He found one saying 'remind Philip haircut', another 'Ainslie birthday', a third with scribbled equations. He put them in his pocket. He was used to having breakfast by himself but now he missed her holding the paper with one hand and a slice of toast in the other.

The crematorium had been crowded at her funeral and many had to stand in an antechapel or outside. More people than he could remember sent letters of sympathy and condolence. Winifred Smallwood and Ainslie sat on either side of him, as her favourite Schubert was played. Shaking hands with everybody afterwards and trying to listen to their sympathetic words took a very long time. He did not feel the cold until everyone had gone, everyone, that is, except Winifred and Ainslie who drove them back to the house, leaving Winifred at her flat in north Oxford.

'Can I fix you something to eat, Philip?'

'I'm not hungry, Ainslie, but if you look in the pantry you'll find a bottle of Chablis Jane left. She loved Chablis and I feel thirsty. How about you?'

'Where are the glasses?'

Ainslie was grief-stricken but controlled, he could see. Her eyes were moist and she kept a Kleenex ready in her sleeve. She keeps talking to keep herself from thinking, Lawless thought. They drank to Jane's memory, once and then again with another glass.

'I loved her, Philip.'

'I know.'

Could you love a woman who was your wife for thirty years and hardly ever shared your bed? He could; not in the way he had loved others, although he never lost that desire for her, but simply for her and what she was—what she had been. They finished the bottle.

'Can I stay tonight?'

'Of course. I'd like you to. The bed should be aired. I'll find you some towels.'

'I mean can I stay with you tonight? I can't face being by myself. We both loved her, Philip. We could share her love between us.'

ENCORE

'I long ago made an effort to forget my birthdays but I think I should make an exception for this one and I want to you share it with me.'

'I'm intrigued. I know it's what people are beginning to call a "special" or "significant" birthday but what do you have in mind?'

'It's not the actual day, but it's near enough: Encaenia. Have you seen the list of honorands?'

'I haven't been to the ceremony for years: put off by those terribly uncomfortable seats in the Sheldonian and that dreary organist. Who are receiving degrees?'

'The usual grandees, but there is a Nobel laureate and most importantly as far as I am concerned, Reinhardt.'

'Miriam Reinhardt? I have every record she ever made. No one plays Schubert like her. Sublime is the only word. I'll certainly go to the ceremony.'

'Then we shall go together. As a past Principal I am usually given a comfortable seat. As a mere Professor you may have to be content with the gods if you're not there early. In the evening she is giving a recital. By way of thanks to the University, I expect. We must not miss that.'

' How Jane would have loved that! She revered Reinhardt. I can't believe it's been now four years since she died.'

Lawless watched the tall silver-haired woman in her soft black academic cap and Doctor of Music's cream coloured robe with the crimson sleeves pace slowly towards the Chancellor to shake his hand and receive the scroll of her degree. Lawless felt the urge to applaud but he knew it was not the custom for this occasion.

At the garden party in the grounds of the Vice Chancellor's college, Reinhardt was surrounded by so many admirers that Lawless was unable to approach her.

'Don't worry,' Winifred Smallwood said. 'You'll have a better chance at the reception after her recital. It's for a chosen few and I have seen to it that we are among them.'

It was a relatively short recital, appropriate after a long and tiring day. Reinhardt began with three impromptus and after a short interval played Schubert's last piano sonata. The silence that followed as the sad, reflective chords faded away was almost tangible, as if the audience could not bear to let the music leave them. They would not let her leave either, continuing to applaud until she finally took her seat again for an encore.

The first notes of the Satie echoed in Lawless's head more insistently than ever before as his mind fought to explain why these simple plaintive sounds should move him so deeply.

The reception after the recital was in All Souls so Lawless knew exactly where to go. He waited with Winifred in growing impatience while others monopolised Reinhardt until he saw she was looking over their heads in his direction. She smiled, making excuses as she left the group and came towards him. Winifred Smallwood poked him in the back.

'Philip, don't just stand there. Go and congratulate her.'

She reached him before he could take a step and took his hand.

'Philip, Sergeant: it is you, isn't it?'

The Satie, that face, and the voice, echoes in his head. He felt a massive tightness in his chest.

'Philip, it's me.'

He could barely whisper, 'Mireille? Mireille, Mireille.'

The guests watched in polite academic astonishment as an Emeritus Professor and a great pianist embraced each other with tears running down their cheeks.

Winifred Smallwood took charge, taking the Warden aside by the arm and telling him quietly but urgently that Dr Reinhardt and Professor Lawless had not seen each other for many years and had exchanged some sudden and upsetting news. She was sure that he would understand that they needed a private place for them to talk undisturbed for a little while. When the matters had been dealt with, both would undoubtedly return to join him and the other guests.

'The Library: the door is unlocked but no one will be there at this time of night. Lawless will know the way but since he appears to be in a very emotional state perhaps I should ask the Dean to go accompany them.'

'I know the way to the Codrington as well as anyone, Warden. With your permission I will go with them myself. Perhaps you would explain to the guests what is happening.'

'Thank you. I am very grateful, Winifred.'

'Philip, are you listening? Give me a few moments with Dr Reinhardt, while I explain a few things to her. Wait for us in the alcove: the desk with the light on.'

Lawless was looking dazed and in no state to speak. She had to repeat what she had just said before he seemed to take it in and walked slowly away.

'May I call you Miriam? Thank you. I am Winifred Smallwood, retired Principal of Granville College.'

'I saw you sitting in the front row at my recital.'

'You have the right to know why Philip is what he is now, and why seeing you a few minutes ago was such a great shock to him. If you believe what I am about to tell you, with your help he will recover from that shock and regain a part of his life that has been lost to him for almost fifty years.'

'He has lost some of his life? I do not understand.'

'It is a long and complicated story but I will try to explain it as simply and briefly as I can. It all has to do with memory and loss of it.'

Winifred Smallwood spoke quietly for some ten minutes without interruption or question from Miriam Reinhardt.

'I hope I have convinced you. You may need time to think. I could say a great deal more and will, if you wish but now I am going to leave you alone with him. Please remember you are dealing with a man who appears normal but is deeply wounded in a way he knew nothing about until tonight.'

The alcove was a small globe of light in the still quiet darkness of the library. They held hands across the desk.

'Winifred has told me, Philip.'

'I don't know how to begin. I feel so confused. I feel as if, as if…as if I'm on a dark stage in a dark theatre and there's only one dim light and there are shadows moving about and at first I wonder who they are and then I see a face or hear a voice or feel one of them touch me and say my name as you did upstairs and I catch a glimpse of a face and *I know them,* Mireille, *I know who they are.* You know what started it? The music: the encore you played, the Satie Gnossienne. Suddenly I *knew* when I first heard it. It was Thérèse; she played it—in the house, in . . . La . . .'

'La Commanderie.'

'Yes! La Commanderie. Oh, god, Mireille, Thérèse: what have I done?'

He stared at her in desperation.

'Philip, I know now what happened to you. It was not your fault. It was the War.'

'Séverine said that. The War: I had to leave because of the War, leave them all, even my little son who you helped to be born. Do you remember that? And I swore I would come back. I swore it and I never did come back.'

'Philip you could not go back. You were lying unconscious for three years in hospital and when you woke, your memory of all those years had gone. You knew nothing of them anymore.'

'I wrote letters to them, many letters.'

'They never arrived. Something or someone stopped them.'

'I did things that I never should have done. I married again when I already had a wife, my Thérèse.'

'I know that your wife has died. I am very sorry, Philip.'

'I must go back. I must go back now and tell them all what happened. God, can they ever forgive me? Tell me about them. You must know about them and Justine and Jeannot and Jérôme and Serge and Henri: all of them. I want to know everything. Tell me, please.'

'Philip, I cannot do that. You must find out for yourself. You must go and find out for yourself. It is the only way.'

'I will go. You are right. It is the only way. Will you come with me?'

'No, Philip. I cannot do that. I fly to New York tomorrow.'

'Your brother, you had a brother. Did he . . .?'

'Yes, he lived. He owes his life to those brave people in the Velay who sheltered him, as I owe my life to Séverine and Thérèse and, Philip, to you. I stay with my brother in New York. He works for the United Nations.'

'Will I ever see you again, Mireille? Why do you call yourself Reinhardt, Miriam Reinhardt?'

'You remember? Séverine gave me the name Mireille because Miriam sounded too Jewish to be safe. My family name was always Reinhardt. My father changed it to Renard when he and my mother escaped to France. Renard sounds a little like Reinhardt so he said that we could remember what we used to be. Yes, I think we will see each other again—but after you have been back to La Commanderie and found out for yourself. Shall we join the others now?'

BIRNAM

The Warden looked rather relieved to see them return and swept Miriam Reinhardt away by himself. Winifred Smallwood put a glass in Lawless's hand.

'I discovered there was some single malt for those who knew where to look. I expect that you need something rather stronger than wine, although I must say you are looking better than I thought you might.'

'I have just been told straight that I must go back to France myself and sort everything out and not leave others to do it for me.'

'I was hoping something like that would happen.'

'I keep remembering something else every minute. There was a code name I had to repeat when I came back with a parcel of papers I was told to hand on to some one. Birnam: that was the name, Birnam. I put a report of my own in an envelope and wrote Birnam on it because I didn't want the others to know what was inside. The man in the dark suit: I just didn't trust him. I wondered why the name was Birnam, like the wood in Macbeth and I know now. Birnam, a forest or a wood, a small wood, Smallwood. You are Birnam, Winifred. Is there anything else you should tell me?'

'There is a very great deal I could tell you, Philip but I have no intention of doing so and not only because I am bound to keep silent. But to the name Birnam, I admit ownership.'

'So the man in the dark suit—whose name I never found out and Robinson and Johnson and who knows how many others with false names behind the scenes, maybe even that old doctor who examined me—they all answered to you.'

'One thing I will tell you and do not ask me anything else. I discovered that one of them was responsible for ensuring that none of the letters you wrote before your crash ever reached France. It was done out of sheer spite and he paid heavily for it. Enough of that: when are you going to France?'

'As soon as I can make arrangements. I shall write that I am coming.'

'I have a packet for you take. Promise not to open it until you arrive.'

'Mireille cannot come with me. Will you?'

'She said that you should do this on your own and that is what I think too. There is someone there who will explain why.'

'Who is it?'

'You will know when you get there. Now, the Warden has his eye on us. Find that single malt, refill the glasses and let us join the others.'

Winifred Smallwood waited all next day for Lawless to let her know when he was leaving for France but heard nothing, nor the next day. Sensing that something was wrong, she telephoned late in the afternoon.

'Philip, I'm still waiting to know when you leave. I have this package for you. Are you there?'

There was a long silence at the other end of the line. When finally he replied his voice was oddly dull and low.

'Philip, are you all right? Are you unwell?'

'No.'

'I'm coming round. Don't leave the house.'

'You look awful. You're still in your dinner jacket. Have you been sitting there for two days?'

'I don't know. I can't think. My head aches and I can't think.'

She searched in her bag for her diary, found it and looked up Dr Hemming's phone number. Eventually he answered. He sounded breathless.

'Dr Hemming, Winifred Smallwood. It's Philip Lawless. Something has happened. You must come at once. Take a taxi. This is the address.'

'I have an appointment . . .'

'Cancel it. Come at once.'

She put down the receiver and looked at Lawless.

'Where do you keep the whisky? No, where do you keep the tea? Never mind, I'll find it.'

Hemming pulled up a chair and sat down in front of Lawless. He took his wrist to feel his pulse.

'He's in shock, very cold. How long has he been like this?'

'It must be nearly two days. I've made some tea. He said his head was aching.'

'Plenty of sugar: make him drink it. What happened?'

She told him about Encaenia and the meeting with Reinhardt.

'I feared this might happen if he ever found out.'

'He looked rather nervous at the reception but he had a long talk with her and seemed not too upset later on: now this.'

'Delayed shock; I don't like this. I want to admit him. Telephone for a taxi, will you and get a few things together for him if you can find them.' He turned to Lawless.

'Professor, Philip, listen to me. Tell me, what do you see?'

'Birds, lots of birds, flocks of birds flying past.'

'Do they come near? Do any of them touch you?'

'Some, with their wings.'

Winifred Smallwood back came into the room carrying a small suitcase. 'I think the taxi is outside.'

'Help me with him. The driver can fetch his case. I think you had better come with us too.'

'You slept for over twelve hours. How are you feeling now?'

'My head still aches but I can see better.'

'And you know where you are?'

'Of course; this is your consulting room. I've been here many times.'

'Yesterday I asked you what you could see, and you said birds, flocks of birds. What did you mean?'

'I meant memories were coming back to me, so many of them and so quickly and all mixed up. Have you seen starlings flocking, how they swirl around and twist and swoop in thousands and clump so thickly you can hardly see through them, and dive to the ground and soar up again? They can look as dark as a thundercloud. I remember them from when I was a boy and they came so close I was terrified. That's what I felt. It was all I could see and I still see them in flashes, the memories—not now as I talk to you but I might.'

'You said that you were terrified when you saw them when you were a boy. What about now?'

'I don't know. I want to see them and I don't.'

'You mean the birds?'

'No, the memories.'

'Can we talk about them?'

'Not now, please.'

'I'll see you again tomorrow: perhaps then?'

'Perhaps.'

'Did he say anything to you, Lady Smallwood?'

'No, he was asleep all the time that I was there. I thought he looked rather peaceful. Have you given him something?'

'I would not use sedatives in such a case. He has become calmer over these past few days and yesterday he began to talk, not much, but it is a start.'

'May I ask what he said?'

'He spoke a little about a dog, a sheepdog. He said she saved his life.'

'Did he say anything else?'

'"Caramelle", the dog's name.'

'Not very much after almost two weeks.'

'The first step back to normality is the most important, Lady Smallwood. We must take one step, one memory at a time. He has survived the sort of crisis that a fever brings and his recovery will be very slow—to begin with, then he may surprise us.'

'Recovering his memory, you mean?'

'No, his memory is all there, already recovered. The suddenness of the recovery is what caused the shock. What I am trying to do is persuade him to confront his memories with all the agonies of responsibility and guilt and need to atone for what he thinks that he has done. If he can do that, he will be able to go back.'

'Has he told you that during the weeks before the recital he had been deeply disturbed by certain passages of music?'

'No; perhaps I can steer our conversation in that direction.'

'Yesterday all he wanted to talk about was a library that he was allowed to see in an old walled town in the Causses—not a part of France I am familiar with.'

'I know it and I knew the owner of the library. It was he who gave Lawless the text that he worked on and made his name.'

'Indeed. Then at the very end of our talk he mentioned his wife . . .'

'Thérèse?'

'Yes, Thérèse, and he said that they played duets on a Bechstein and she taught the Jewish girl whom they were hiding from the police.'

'The girl who is now the celebrated pianist Miriam Rheinhard, Dr Hemming.'

'His wife, Lady Smallwood, the woman whom he is ashamed of abandoning, and the girl, now the woman who unlocked his fettered memory: progress, no doubt about it, progress.'

'My dear Professor Lawless, if you want my answer I would say that you have been standing on the lip of a bottomless chasm, knowing you must jump across, but terrified to do so in case you fall or fail to find what you are looking for on the other side. Forgive the overcooked metaphor but I think you know what I mean. Now I think we may safely say you have made the leap.'

'Thanks to you, Dr Hemming.'

'All I did was listen. I think Lady Smallwood may have been more direct but to good purpose, I think you would agree.'

'I do. I cannot tell you how much I am in her debt.'

'If I may say so, I think to some extent she may feel the same towards you.'

'I fly to Paris and take the TGV to Lyon. It connects with the express to Montpellier. I should be there in the evening.'

'Hotel in Montpellier?'

'The Rabelais, as you suggested, Winifred.'

'Rather shabby but discreet. The food was excellent, the wine like disinfectant—unless you took Madame Soubeyran's fancy, as I expect you would have done. She won't be in charge now, of course but her daughter will be. The women always ran the Rabelais. You should find it interesting.'

'Trains don't go to Florac any more so I'll hire a car. There are some places on the way I want to see.'

'This is the packet I spoke about, Philip. Remember what I said: open it only when you get there.'

'Is it a surprise?'

'You will be the judge of that. Now, bonne route and tell me everything when you come back—if you do come back.'

CAUSSE MEJEAN

Some things had changed. The station at Florac was still there, but now converted into apartments by the look of it and the platform and track had gone. He was told the line along the valley past Cassagnas was now a path for walkers and cyclists. Some things had not changed. There was the fountain in the square in front of the Mairie and it was still dry. Lawless went into the café. It could have been the same bartender reading the paper, but of course it wasn't. He ordered a glass of red: still as good as it had been when he was waiting for Jérôme Janquet to come out of the Mairie while Séverine and Thérèse were with Dr Vaudet. There was no surgery in the narrow cobbled street leading up from the little bridge and Dr Vaudet was surely long dead. No need now to walk about with hunched shoulders, wondering if anyone might report a stranger to the Gendarmerie.

He went back to his car in the street with the avenue of trees and drove away across the river and turned north on the road to Mende. Six kilometres later he saw the sign for Saint Enimie on his left and turned to follow the road that ran close to the winding river as far as the bridge where on the other side one way led left to Montbrun and the other right to Castelbouc. He paused, tempted, and then turned left. Castelbouc and its memories would have to wait.

The car climbed slowly uphill through the bends, reaching level ground near where he and Serge had lain in wait for Lieutenant Grandjean's petrol lorry and drove on the last kilometre to the crossroad where he stopped and turned off the engine to let it cool down. The Causse lay before him. He got out and walked a little way along the track that led to the dolmen where they had hidden the petrol cans. Now, looking west he could see the long slope of the land where the Whitley had come down and careered through the snowdrifts before plunging over the lip of the gorge and down through the forest taking the dead crew with it. Except for him. Now where was the shepherd's shelter? He would look for it later. The sun was hot on his face and the bleached fronds of Angel's Hair at the side of the road barely stirred in the still air. He could hear bees at work, searching for the few flowers still in bloom. Nothing else seemed to be moving; no sheep in the green patch of a cloup, no cyclist on his way home for lunch, no yellow postal van bouncing down the rutted stony lane from some farmhouse or lonely cottage. He suddenly felt home again in the vast space and dryness and faintly sighing breeze. The strange, remote, twisted and eroded pillars of pale stone stood everywhere indifferent, but to him not unfriendly. He remembered the one with the fancied face of a mournful drunk and the other beyond it like a hooded Madonna. He breathed in the dry thyme-scented air and was back again in the picnic place in the shade of the ash trees, sitting with Thérèse and listening to a skylark and falling asleep because of the cider. But that had been in the Spring when there were daffodils and red Easter flowers everywhere and the Angel's Hair was green.

Long stretches of the road to St Chely had been resurfaced recently and it took him only ten minutes to reach the village. He left the car in the shade of an oak tree and walked, putting on sunglasses as he went. He hoped the café was still there and still open though it was now after lunchtime. The street was still cobbled but the setts were new and the surface even. Many of the houses had been renovated, their stone facades cleaned and re-pointed. Doors were newly painted a soft faded blue and pots of geranium and pink and white oleander stood next to nearly every doorstep. It was the same in the square. All the comfortable shabbiness he remembered had gone. Every house was clean and bright, doors and windows and shutters gleamed, bignonia and hibiscus competed with climbing roses to cover and colour the walls and balconies. The square was as clean as if newly swept and not a trace of horse muck was to be seen. Something else had changed. The smell of the place: the distinct tang of neglected septic tanks and old drains had been replaced by the scent of rose and oleander. Pretty and quaint as it undoubtedly now was, it was not the St Chely he so vividly remembered. But the Café de la Place was still there next to the smart-looking Mairie—and it *was open*. He felt his heart begin to beat faster.

Some of the old chairs had gone but not all; there was a lingering hint of gauloises and something approaching the old fuggy warmth and the zinc-topped bar had been preserved. It was being wiped clean by a wiry man in his sixties with a sharply intelligent face and close-cropped greying hair. He glanced up as Lawless approached.

'Monsieur?'

Lawless took off his sunglasses and the man gave him a searching look. On a cord round his neck, bright against the dark skin of his throat, hung a silver coin, a half-crown piece.

'Jeannot?'

'Yes, I am Jeannot.'

'Jeannot Bec, son of Jean-Pierre?

'Yes, what of it? Ah! My god. Sergeant! It is you?'

'Yes, it is. I have come back.' He held out his hand.

Jeannot Bec took it and pressed it firmly.

'You are much changed, Sergeant.'

'We all are, Jeannot. I see you kept the coin.'

'I remember the day, a very bad day for you.'

'It was a long time ago.'

'There was no word of you. Everyone thought you were dead.'

'I was dead, or as good as dead, but I am alive again now. And you are the boss here? Jérôme?'

'He died many years ago. Christianne—she is my wife—and I bought the café from Madame Janquet. And I have become Mayor after him.'

'Congratulations, Jeannot. You are an important man.'

'In this small commune, perhaps. Will you take something? And to eat? Christianne is not here but I will make omelette and salad for you, yes?'

'That is very kind. I will take a beer outside and look at your Mairie.'

After the first sip, Lawless realised that he was very thirsty and quickly swallowed the rest of the cold weak fizzy beer. He could hear sounds from within the café and decided to take a little stroll until his lunch was ready.

The door of the Mairie was closed, of course. He was sorry to see that a new notice-board had replaced the one on which the announcement of his and Thérèse's wedding had been been pinned. His eyes glanced automatically up to the war memorial stone above the doorway. He had to read it twice before he began to understand what was carved there.

SAINT CHELY LA BASTIDE
SOUVENIR A NOS MORTS POUR LA FRANCE
1914-1918

Twenty-one names with three Chevaliers, father and two sons and in the space below:

1939-1945

CHEVALIER FABRICE
CHEVALIER SÉVERINE
FONTAINE ROBERT
VABRETTE HENRI

Chevalier Séverine? *Chevalier Séverine*? He could not take his eyes away. Séverine, poor darling Séverine, what happened to you? He saw Henri's name too but he could think only of Séverine, beautiful proud Séverine, who kissed him fiercely those two times, who gave him a letter on that last night when he left them—the letter he had never read; where was it now?—and sometimes looked so ill and tired but so determined to fight. He felt the tears start to run down his face and let them fall. He had to wipe his eyes to read the plaque again. There was another year, another war and another name. He had to struggle to read the words

ALGÉRIE
1962
CHEVALIER LAWLESS ALEXANDRE SOUS-LTNANT

He read the name, his own son's name, again and again and then not knowing where he was going turned and stumbled out of the square and out of the village and away onto the Causse.

Jeannot found him two hours later staring into nothing. He took him by the arm and led him gently back to the village and put him to bed. He sat by the bedside until he was sure Lawless was asleep.

At supper he told his wife what had happened.

'He must have come in a car,' she said. 'Go find it, Jeannot and bring his things here. There will be a key in his pocket.'

When Lawless woke it was bright morning. He lay in bed trying not to think.

There was a knock on the door and a woman came in with a cup of coffee.

'Drink this, please. There is cognac in it.'

He shook his head but she insisted and waited until he had emptied the cup. The coffee was very sweet and half cognac.

'When you are ready, please come down and eat and talk with us. It is better if you are not alone.'

He did as she asked. There was more that he had to know.

He sat with them at a table in the café. Jeannot had put a 'Closed' sign on the door. He ate half of one of the croissants in the basket on the table and slowly drank more of the cognac-laced coffee. Then he was able to speak.

'I have a car. I must go to Thérèse. Will you come with me?'

Jeannot and Christianne looked at each other. They had decided the night before that he must not find out for himself.

'I am very sorry, Sergeant but Madame Chevalier died one year after the death of her son.'

'Oh God, not Thérèse as well. One year after, so long ago. I never knew. One year after Alexandre?'

'Yes, the doctor found that she had tuberculosis but we think she also had a broken heart. My mother was with her and Serge and the girl.'

'The girl: Mireille? I have seen Mireille again.'

'Not Mireille. Mireille had gone to Paris, to the Conservatoire. Mr Valentin was there with my mother. Madame Chevalier was not alone.'

'Where is she now?'

'In the cemetery, Sergeant. Henri Vabrette is there also and Mr Valentin.'

'Madame Séverine?'

'We do not know. The Germans took her to Ravensbruck. She was no longer there when the Russians liberated the camp in 1945.'

'So she was captured or betrayed, or what, Jeannot? Tell me.'

'If you wish. After you went away we, the group, made many raids. We blew up railway lines and trains and a bridge and cut down the electric and telephone wires and attacked convoys of lorries. We had weapons and explosives and radios sent from England. Madame Chevalier went with us every time. And always we escaped. When the Americans came and made the Germans retreat we attacked their men and lorries. We had your machine guns, Sergeant and Madame Chevalier fired one of them. Henri had the other one. The English sent us more ammunition in boxes by parachuting. And always we escaped: until the last time.'

'The last time?'

'Yes, the last time for Madame Chevalier and for Henri. We were told about a German column retreating along a road near Nîmes, a small road that the American bombers did not attack. We made an ambush but our information was bad. There were many more than we had been told and they were SS, a whole company and they had tanks. We attacked early in the morning just before dawn whenever we could. I remember it well. There was not yet much light which was good for us. We could see the first men but not the tanks behind. We began to shoot with the machineguns, one from each side of the road. I was with Madame Chevalier, feeding in the belts. We killed all the first men before they knew what was happening. The rest must have waited until the light was better, and while we were waiting some of them came behind the back of us through the woods. You remember they were SS, very hard trained soldiers, not like us. We did not know they were there. Then we heard the engines of the tanks and soon one came along the road. It stopped and turned the cannon towards where we were and fired. The shell exploded in the trees near us and we picked up the gun and ran to a different place. The tank fired again and some soldiers came up to be near it. Madame Chevalier began to fire at them and hit many and kept firing until all the ammunition was gone. I had my rifle and she had a pistol that she told me you had given her. We waited to see what would happen. I said we should escape into the woods and I think that she was going to say yes but then the Germans in the woods began to shoot at us.'

Jeannot stopped talking. Even in his present state of mind Lawless could see it was difficult for him to go on. Lawless knew what he must be feeling.

'She was hit by a bullet in her leg, not too badly but she could not get away. She told me to run into the woods and when I said no, she pointed the pistol at me and said go, shoot at them from the woods so I went. I am so sorry I left her, Sergeant. The Germans did not see me—I knew how to go quietly in the forest—and I heard her firing the pistol. I climbed up the hill to a place where I could see and shoot at the Germans. I saw two of them taking her down the hill and round a corner. I did not see her again. We lost many that day, Sergeant, Henri and many others and the guns, but she was our greatest loss.'

'Was your father there?'

'Yes and Serge Valentin: both escaped to where Jérôme was waiting with his car in the next valley. Jérôme could not fight in the forest because of his leg, you understand. Lieutenant Grandjean was wounded but we found him the next day when the Germans had gone and carried him to the road.'

'Lieutenant Grandjean, of the Gendarmerie?'

'He left the Gendarmerie to fight with us against the Germans. He was a very brave man. We took him to the American hospital but he died from the wounds.'

'You were all very brave men, Jeannot—and women.'

'*What else could one do for France?* Madame Chevalier said that to us always.'

'And Serge you say escaped but now he is dead too. Was he still living in St Chely when he died?'

'He went to live at La Commanderie with the ladies Chevalier. Some years after the War when only Madame Thérèse and the children were left, and we were sure you must be dead, Serge and Madame Thérèse were married here. Jérôme was still the mayor.'

'I am glad to hear Thérèse was not alone. Serge will have been very good to her. Tell me about my son, Jeannot.'

'He was a very handsome boy, Sergeant—may I call you that?' Christianne said. 'He grew up tall and handsome like you, and he had your colour of hair.'

Jeannot cut in. 'For his military service he trained as parachutist. He was posted to 3rd Paras. I was sergeant, already there and saw him sometimes in Algiers. He became Sous-Lieutenant with helicopters. In the last week of the war his machine was shot down in the mountains and all the crew were killed.'

'Too young, Jeannot; he was too young to die. He was the hope of the family.'

'Sergeant, he was the same age as you were when you first came here.'

'Madame Thérèse taught him to play the piano,' Christianne said, 'and Mireille told him he would go to the Conservatoire like her one day.'

'I thought Mireille had gone away; home, someone said.'

'Yes, but she came back to see everybody here and Madame Lamphier at Castelbouc in the vacation, many times. Madame Thérèse was so happy when she came. I know because I used to work for them at La Commanderie, with Jeannot. I listened outside when they all played the piano. They laughed and played and sang all the time. And dancing, they all loved to dance. We had picnics. Madame Thérèse knew all the best places and Madame Lamphier was very kind. She has such a lovely house.'

'I remember. We all went there in a trap pulled by a horse called, what was it?'

'Fleur,' Jeannot said. 'Madame Chevalier taught the children to ride on her.'

'Fleur, of course. You were there that day Jeannot, and your mother. Serge and I had bicycles, or was that another time? He was very good at fishing. How did he die?'

'You remember his chest was not good. It did not stop him from coming with us on the raids and working on the farm but in the end he died one year after Madame Thérèse, of tuberculosis like her, the doctor said. They are buried together in the cemetery. You can see the graves. The commune keeps the cemetery in good order.'

'Do you remember we buried my crew under the stones by the river, Jeannot? Henri told me to fire a salute. Are they still there? I would like to go: perhaps after I have been to the cemetery.'

'The English sent an official to St Chely and we told him there was little to see—you remember? I took him to the river and showed him what we had done. Jérôme showed him the names and date in the Mairie records and said the commune would wish to have a stone in the cemetery with all the names on it and some words to be agreed. Later an official letter came to the Mairie giving us permission. When we set up the stone an English officer came to the ceremony with a flag.'

There was a long silence after that and finally Lawless sighed and said,

'Jeannot, I came back to find my family again and ask them to forgive me for the terrible loss and pain that I caused them. I wanted to come back to live with them, see my son grow and my wife smile and listen to Mireille playing and meet all my old friends and become a Frenchman again as I once tried to be. I wanted to live here in La Commanderie for the rest of my life. But I have lost them all. I have no one left. My life is empty, ended. I have no family, no one, nothing.'

'Sergeant, you have friends. I am here, and Christianne. And there is Madame Lamphier. And you say you have seen Mireille. We have told you enough and given you too much sadness. You must go to see Madame Lamphier. She will tell you other things. She also has been waiting for you.'

'Philippe, my dear, can it be fifty years since we last embraced like this? In La Couvertoirade: do you remember? Not quite so innocently as this: do you remember? You look so sad, so desolate and lost. It would break the heart of any woman. You know; I see that you know. You have seen the plaque and the stones in the graveyard. Jeannot Bec has told you. That is enough.'

She pressed a cambric handkerchief into his hand for the tears but he seemed not to notice so she took it from him and dabbed his cheeks herself.

'They are all gone, Justine. I have no one. And I never knew. I should have known.'

'Philippe, sit down, here by me and look at me. Do you still like what you see? Tell me.'

He sniffed and took the handkerchief from her, managing a weak smile and nodding.

'A smile I think, and now he may come back to me and begin to talk. Will he?'

'Yes.'

'He whispers to me like a lover. What do you want to say, Philippe; what do you want to know?'

'I've lost them all, Justine; while I was in my own world, they suffered and I lost them, one by one. Even La Commanderie has gone, all changed: new owners with horses for hire and chambres d'hôtes for holidays. All that was left unchanged for me to see was the shepherd's shelter where Tressie and Caramelle found me. I lay down in there for I don't know how long, remembering and then I had to get out and run away because I couldn't bear the memories any more. And now I am lost and alone. I don't know what to do. Tell me what to do.'

'If you were lost, you would not be here and now that you are here you see that you are not alone. Loss? We have both suffered loss, Philippe, you and I and Winifred, in the Wars, or because of the Wars. What could any of us do? The War took you away from them and then took away even your memory of them. You could do nothing about that.'

'But I stayed alive, while they all died, one after the other, they all died. I feel so guilty for being still alive.'

'Philippe, listen to me. I have never in all my life felt guilt over anything that I have ever done. My mother told me it would spoil my looks. Guilt is the most deadly and destructive of feelings. You are clinging to your guilt and it will never let you go, never let you come back to life. In time in your mind it will kill those you loved and lost and you will come to hate them, blame them for creating your so precious guilt. You must forget again, Philippe, not Thérèse and Séverine and Alexandre and all the others: keep your love of them in your heart. But you must forget the guilt. Forget it or it will spoil your looks and I could not bear that. Ah, a much better smile. Go out onto the balcony and look at the river and the cliffs on the other side and think about what I have said. I will come to you in a few moments with wine for us both and I will show you how your guilt and feeling of loss can be washed away by telling you something you do not yet know.'

'I know this wine.'

'It's a Condrieu.'

'Winfred was given some of this wine by her brother.'

'Robert.'

'I did not know his name.'

'You did. He was your Commanding Officer.'

'Group Captain Smallwood, of course.'

'We were married, Philippe. He was my second husband.'

'Not Alexandre?'

'No, we never married. He said his man Sylvestre would never countenance it. Can you believe that? I approved: it meant that we remained lovers until he died.'

'How many lovers have you had, Justine?'

'That is not a question you should ask of any lady. Shame on you! All that you need to know is that you are included among them.'

'I humbly apologise and acknowledge the honour.'

'There now, a touch of the very young Sergeant.'

'Are you the last of the Chevaliers, Justine? I think you must be. I don't count.'

'Of course you do in one very essential way. I am not the last of the Chevaliers.'

'I don't understand.'

'Before you left England Winifred gave you a letter. Do you have it with you?'

Lawless took the envelope from his pocket.

'Read it, Philippe and you will understand.'

My very dear Philippe,

There is not much time and you must go. When you read this letter I will be in La Commanderie with Tressie and your little son, Alexandre. My own baby will be born there, perhaps this very night. I have kept this secret from you all, except for Serge. He knows and he knows that he is not the father. I have told him. You are the father, Philippe. I came to your bed the night before the marriage, not Tressie. I thought I was too old to have a child and that is why, although I loved you, I was glad that you fell in love with Tressie. But I was wrong. I could still conceive and Alexandre will have a brother or a sister and you are the father of both. No one but Tressie and Mireille and Madame Bec will know and they will never tell. Our child must be known as Tressie's child, the twin of Alexandre. We may never see each other again, Philippe. The War may take us both. But Alexandre and our child will be the next generation of Chevaliers. Love them well, Philippe. As I always loved you.

Séverine

Lawless let his hand still holding the letter fall to his side and looked at Justine.

He could see her only vaguely but he felt he must concentrate on her face because everything else had vanished, the river, the cliffs, the house, all had disappeared and only Justine's face and Séverine's words remained.

'Philippe?'

Her voice was very distant.

'Philippe, do you understand now?'

He held out the letter but she would not take it.

'You know what it says. Do I have a son? I thought my son was dead. I saw his name on the plaque in the village. Where is his brother?'

'His sister, Philippe: you have a daughter.'

'A daughter. Oh god, I have a daughter?'

'And so like you, Philippe: tall and slim, and with hair like her mother's and eyes the colour of yours. She is very beautiful.'

'Now I know what Jeannot was trying to tell me without actually saying it. I have a daughter; can you understand what that means?'

'I can see it in your face, Philippe.'

'Where is she, Justine. I must see her. She is all I have left, except for you. Tell me where she is, tell me now.'

'She never knew her real mother, but Tressie loved her as her own and she had Alexandre and Serge was there and Jeannot and Mireille of course. Then the terrible years came. First Alexandre, her twin as she always thought, then she lost her mother with a broken heart, and then Serge, who was like a father to her. And always she wondered when you would come home. Her great-uncle was good to her and Mireille, and I was here for her to come any time she wanted or needed. But she was left more and more alone and even though Jeannot worked so hard with her to keep the flock it could not last. Finally she came to see me and my Alexandre, and said she could not go on. She had to leave and make her life far away. I think she would have come to England to look for you but you would not have recognised her. You would have accepted her, I am sure, but you were married to someone not her mother. How could she have borne that?'

So where did she go? Tell me: where is she now?'

'Guadeloupe. She went to Guadeloupe to be somewhere completely different from the Causses. She took very little with her except for your Family Book, the Cavallier book with the pressed leaves in it and your wedding rings. She became a music teacher. She is still there, living in Basse-Terre.'

'You are sure?'

'Oh yes, she writes from time to time but never mentions coming back here.'

'Does she know about me?'

'Not yet. She still thinks you are dead.'

'What do you mean, "not yet"? Tell me what I should do.'

'Are you completely stupid, you so clever Oxford Professor? You go to Guadeloupe and find her. Bring her back home to Castelbouc. It will be hers one day, but until then she will live here with you and me.'

'Home. Here?'

'Yes, home. Here.'

'Tell me her name, Justine.'

'Séverine: Séverine Angeline Duschene Lawless Chevalier.'

ABOUT THE AUTHOR

David Bell is a geologist and Emeritus Fellow of University College Oxford. His research and service have taken him to many parts of the world, from the Solomon Islands to Virginia, from Ascension Island to Greenland. Though living in Oxford for over sixty years, he and his artist wife Betsy spent much of their time in their house in the south of France where they came to know and love the country and its people who endured times and events like those fictionalised in this story.

www.ingramcontent.com/pod-product-compliance
Lightning Source LLC
Chambersburg PA
CBHW020937310726
48980CB00007B/811/J

* 9 7 8 9 3 8 3 8 6 8 3 3 9 *

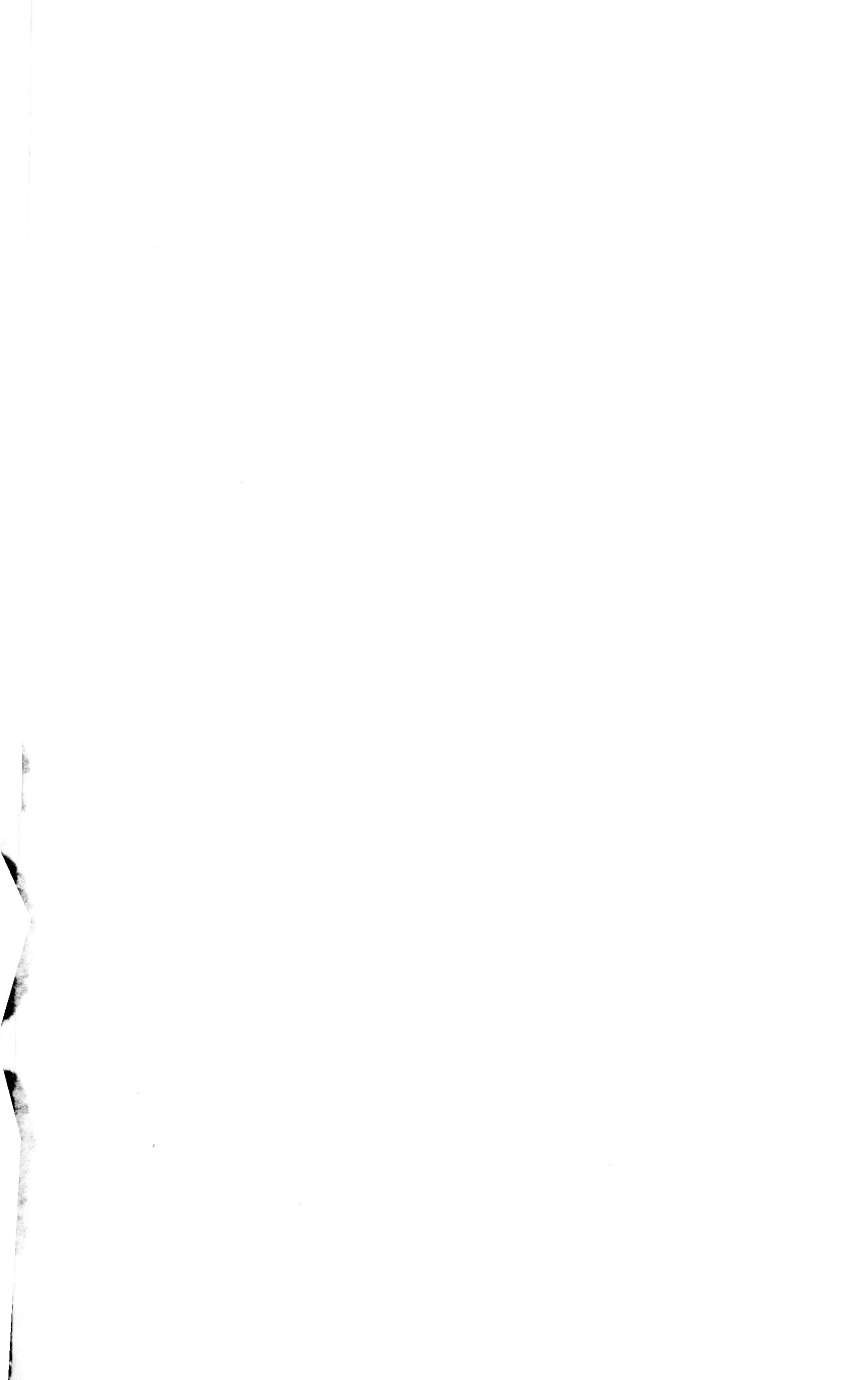